MYSTERY WRITERS OF AMERICA PRESENTS
VENGEANCE

EDITED BY AND WITH A BRAND NEW STORY FROM
LEE CHILD

CORVUS

First published in the United States by Mulholland Books, an imprint of Little, Brown and Company, a division of Hachette Book Group, Inc.

Published in hardback in Great Britain in 2012 by Corvus, an imprint of Atlantic Books Ltd.

Compilation Copyright © Mystery Writers of America, Inc., 2012
Introduction Copyright © Lee Child, 2012
Copyright notices for individual stories appear on page 387

10 9 8 7 6 5 4 3 2 1

A CIP catalogue record for this book is available from the British Library.

Hardback ISBN: 978 0 85789 901 9
Trade paperback ISBN: 978 0 85789 902 6
E-book ISBN: 978 0 85789 903 3
Printed in Great Britain by CPI Group (UK) Ltd, Croydon, CR0 4YY

Corvus
An imprint of Atlantic Books Ltd
Ormond House
26–27 Boswell Street
London
WC1N 3JZ

www.corvus-books.co.uk

CONTENTS

CONTENTS

INTRODUCTION

Editing this anthology was a lot of fun — not least because Mystery Writers of America's invaluable and irreplaceable publications guy, Barry Zeman, did all the hard work. All I had to do was pick ten invitees. And write a story. And then later on read the ten winning stories chosen by MWA's blind-submission process. Piece of cake. Apart from writing my own story, that is, which I always find hard, but that's why picking the invitees was so much fun — I love watching something difficult being done really well, by experts.

It was like playing fantasy baseball — who did I want on the field? And just as Major League Baseball has rich seams of talent to choose from, so does Mystery Writers of America. I could have filled ten anthologies. Or twenty. But I had to start somewhere — and it turned out that I already had, years ago, actually, when I taught a class at a mystery writers' conference in California. One of the after-hours activities was a group reading around a fireplace in the motel. A bit too kumbaya for me, frankly, but I went anyway, and the first story was by a young woman called Michelle Gagnon. It was superb, and it stayed with me through the intervening years. So I e-mailed her about using it for this anthology — more in hope than in expectation, because it was such a great story, I was sure it had been snapped up long ago. But no — it was still available. Never published, amazingly. It is now.

One down.

Then I had to have Brendan DuBois. He's a fine novelist but easily the best short-story writer of his generation. He just cranks them out, one after the other, like he's casting gold ingots. Very annoying. He said yes.

Two down.

And I had Twist Phelan on my radar. She's a real woman of mystery — sometimes lives on a yacht, sometimes lives in Switzerland, knows about oil and banks and money — and she had just won the International Thriller Writers' award for best short story. I thought, *I'll have a bit of that.* She said okay.

Three down.

Then there was the overtalented but undersung Jim Fusilli. He wrote two great New York novels that I really loved, and then four more just as good, and he's the rock music critic for the *Wall Street Journal.* We make lists together, like the top three bands most dependent on their drummers for their sound. (Led Zeppelin, the Who, and the Beatles, obviously.)

I asked; he said yes.

Four down.

And then, purely by chance, in the course of a conversation Karin Slaughter told me she'd just finished the nastiest story she'd ever written. Which had to be something, right? With Karin? I didn't ask. I just told her.

Five down.

Alafair Burke was next. I've followed her novels from the very beginning and loved them all. Then she went and wrote a terrific story for Michael Connelly's MWA anthology a few years ago. I thought, *Hey, she did it for him, she can do it for me.* I asked. She said yes.

Six down.

Then, because I'm a transatlantic person, I thought about a couple of great writers from the old country. First up: Dreda Say Mitchell. She's five novels into a terrific career, and I find her narrative voice completely fresh and utterly addictive. I asked; she said yes.

Seven down.

Then, Zoë Sharp. If I were a woman, I'd be Zoë. If Jack Reacher were a woman, he'd be Zoë's main character, Charlie Fox. A natural fit. I asked; she said yes.

Eight down.

Two spots left.

I thought: *Let's complete the lineup with a couple of heavy hitters.* I waited until both of my targets were drunk and happy at the Edgars, and I asked. Michael Connelly first. A busy guy, but a nice guy. He blinked. He said yes.

Nine down.

Then I turned to Dennis Lehane. Equally busy guy—he'd just had a kid. But equally nice too. He blinked. Twice. But he said yes.

Bingo.

So then it was about sharpening my editorial blue pencil and waiting for their stories to show up. They did, but I didn't need the pencil. I think there was a spelling mistake in there somewhere, but authors like these don't need help. So then it was about waiting for the MWA winning stories to arrive.

The way it works is that any paid-up MWA member can submit a story; the author's name is replaced with a code number, so the judges read each story blind. The selection panel evaluates them all and chooses the ten best. The panel for this anthology was Heather Graham, Tom Cook, David Walker, Joe Trigoboff, and Brendan DuBois (pulling double duty, which was good of him—he could have written another nine or ten stories, probably, in the time it took). I thank them all for their hard work, and for their excellent judgment—the ten they came up with are first-class, and when the numbers were matched to the names, it turned out we had an interesting bunch of people.

Ladies first: Anne Swardson submitted from Paris, where she's been living for fifteen years as a heavy-duty financial journalist. Tough gig, but hey, someone's got to do it. C. E. Lawrence is a multitalented New Yorker—writer, performer, poet, composer, and prize-winning playwright. Quite irritating. Janice Law is already an Edgar-nominated short-story writer (but the panel didn't know that—remember the code numbers). She's had stories published all over the place, so it's no surprise she made the top ten.

And the men: Rick McMahan is a special agent with the Department of Justice, so he walks the walk, and naturally he's also published here and there. Adam Meyer is an accomplished movie and TV writer and novelist and short-story writer who comes from New York but lives in DC. Michael Niemann is a German guy who lives in Oregon and is mostly a nonfiction writer specializing in African and global issues. Orest Stelmach is a thriller writer from the Northeast. He's fluent in four languages, which is four more than me on an average day. Darrell James lives in California and Arizona and is a multipublished and award-winning short-story writer, and also a debut novelist. Steve Liskow lives in Connecticut and is also a published novelist and short-story writer. And finally, Mike Cooper is a former financial guy from the Boston area whose stories have won a Shamus Award and been selected for *The Best American Mystery Stories* annual anthology.

INTRODUCTION

So, ten high-quality invitees and ten high-quality competition winners, plus me. We all got the same brief: Write about vengeance, revenge, getting even, maybe doing a bad thing for a good reason. Or a bad reason. It was a loose specification; a tighter one would have been ignored anyway. Writers are like that. Their imaginations run along unique and uncontrollable paths, as you will see. Or maybe as you've already seen. I know some people read anthologies back to front. If you're one of them, thanks for reading. If you're not, I hope you enjoy what follows.

Lee Child
New York

MYSTERY WRITERS OF AMERICA PRESENTS
VENGEANCE

THE FOURTEENTH JUROR

BY TWIST PHELAN

T he two detectives stood in the reception area of the judge's chambers on the fifth floor of the county courthouse. Ebanks made the introductions.

"We have an appointment to see the judge," he said.

The secretary smiled at them. She was a discreetly elegant woman with assisted blond hair and not too much pink lipstick.

"His Honor is expecting you," she said. "He shouldn't be too much longer. He's just finishing up a JNOV hearing."

Ebanks had to cough.

"May I get you something to drink?" the secretary asked.

Ebanks cleared his throat. "No, thank you," he said.

"Coffee would be good," Martinez said.

Ebanks was pinning his hopes on Martinez. The guy was no genius, but once he got an idea in his head, he was relentless. If Ebanks could get him pointed in the right direction on this case, the rookie's doggedness would pay off even after Ebanks retired next month.

Ebanks wasn't looking forward to turning in his shield. Some retired cops spent their days fishing or golfing or motor-homing to Arizona in the winter, but Ebanks didn't own a motor home or play golf. He did like to fish, but he wouldn't be getting up to the lake much. He'd be staying put in the house he'd grown up in. He and his wife lived there now.

The two cops sat down on a long sofa. An abstract painting hung on the wall facing them, its vivid reds and bright oranges warming the room. Martinez ran a hand along the plump leather arm of the sofa. "Nice."

Ebanks glanced around. Smooth parquetry floors gleamed with wax. The government-issue fluorescent overhead fixtures had been replaced with incandescent models. Magazines— current issues only—were lined up equidistant from the edges of the cherry coffee table. The lone plant, a ficus tree, had been trimmed into perfect symmetry, its leaves polished to a glossy green.

"Hmmm," he said. The rookie was observant, but he usually drew the wrong conclusions.

"How's Sheila?" Martinez said.

"Sonia," Ebanks said. He didn't really mind the mistake. After four years, hardly anyone on the force bothered to ask anymore. "Better," he lied.

Just then, the door behind the secretary's desk opened. A woman and a man wearing suits walked out. The woman smoldered with unhappiness. The man bore the dazed grin of a lottery winner.

The justice system at work, Ebanks thought.

———

THE JUDGE STOOD to greet them as they entered his chambers. His lean, intense face was incised with deep vertical grooves. His body was long and angular. Metal-rimmed glasses were perched on his nose and disapproval was apparent in the set of his mouth, like the preacher in the Pentecostal church Ebanks had attended as a kid.

"Sorry to keep you men waiting," the judge said. "JNOVs are never easy. But it's something that has to be done."

"JNOV?" Martinez said. "What's that anyway?"

The judge shook his head solemnly. "Of course—you're from the criminal side. I wish I could do more work over there, but I go only when they need me to fill in. *JNOV* stands for Latin words that mean 'judgment notwithstanding the verdict.' If a jury comes back with a decision that's contrary to the evidence, the judge has a responsibility to reverse it. The two people you saw leaving were a plaintiff's attorney, who just lost a two-million-dollar punitive-damage award, and a very relieved defense counsel."

Ebanks massaged the bridge of his nose. Sonia hadn't done well last night. He'd barely gotten two hours' sleep.

"Too bad crim court judges can't do that," Martinez said. "Some of these juries come back with the most half-ass—" He stopped himself, cheeks reddening.

The judge smoothly stepped in. "What you're saying is that jurors are often dazzled by attorney antics or irrelevant issues and so they don't focus on the evidence."

"Yeah," Martinez said gratefully.

"As long as the Constitution says 'jury of our peers,' that's who decides our cases," the judge said, "but my fundamental duty is to see that justice is done. That female lawyer you saw ran rings around the defendant's man; she bewitched the jury with her short skirts and PowerPoint closing argument. I can't let that kind of thing stand. It's my duty as a judge, in civil court at least. It's my responsibility."

Ebanks noted the confident righteousness in the judge's

baritone voice. He looked around the office. The room was large enough to hold not only the judge's desk and leather swivel chair but four guest chairs and a loveseat. The judge indicated they should take a seat in the guest chairs. He chose the leather swivel one.

There was a tray of dry fly-tying tools on the credenza, with hooks, thread, hackle pliers and guards, scissors, whip finishers, and a vise all lined up in a precise row alongside small containers of feathers and what looked to Ebanks like white goat body hair, usually used for wings. Ebanks preferred Swiss straw.

The photos on the wall behind the desk showed various images of the judge: proudly displaying a shoulders-wide trout; standing beside his partners—all wearing dark suits and rep ties—in the law firm he'd headed before ascending to the bench; and sitting stiffly with his wife in a room furnished in Modern Hunting Lodge (log timbers, antler chandelier, Black Watch plaid on the chairs).

The mountain range visible through the window in the last photo told Ebanks the house was in the new development on the north shore of the lake. The environmentalists had screamed, but high-priced lawyering had won the day. A small gated community of million-dollar homes had been built in the remote area. Ebanks had once had a place near the lake, a decades-old A-frame.

He used to fish the lake in a sweet little eighteen-footer. Sometimes Sonia went with him. She'd pack thick sandwiches and iced tea in the cooler, and she'd bring a book. Wearing her floppy sun hat, she was content to read while he dropped his line. He'd sold the A-frame, his boat, and most of his gear when Sonia couldn't go with him anymore. All he had left from those times was the nice Sage fly rod Sonia had given him one birthday.

Ebanks studied the photo of the judge at his lake house. He

noted the judge's blond wife, the modern painting over the fireplace, the polished wood floors.

Class, Martinez would say.

Ebanks knew there was something else. The decor of the judge's chambers matched the interior of his house. The shade of blond on the judge's wife was nearly identical to the color of his secretary's hair. The coffee table was cherry. The flowers in the vases were all trimmed to the same height and were the same shade as the red accent pillows.

His Honor was a man who made sure everything was in order. Ebanks understood that.

The judge regarded the two detectives, his gaze direct. "How can I help you gentlemen?"

"We need to ask you a few questions about the Dolan case," Martinez said.

———

UNDER THE SPEEDY Trial Act, a criminal defendant has the right to go to trial within seventy days of his indictment or his initial court appearance, whichever comes first. If the trial doesn't begin within that period, the charges are dismissed.

Overworked defense attorneys usually ask for, and are readily given, extensions. But occasionally the system logjams, with too many trials and not enough judges to hear them. When that happens, the presiding judge requests that the civil bench jurists assist their criminal colleagues. Civil proceedings are delayed while judges used to hearing securities-fraud claims and divorces preside over robbery and assault trials instead.

This judge had been drafted for such a criminal proceeding two weeks ago. Kenny Dolan was charged with second-degree murder for allegedly stabbing his wife during a domestic dispute. The case had gotten some pretrial coverage in the local press—Dolan was a catcher on the resident minor league team with a real chance of moving up to the big leagues.

The evidence of Dolan's guilt seemed insurmountable—his fingerprints on the knife, blood spatter on his shoes, his 911 call that was more a confession than a plea for help—but in the middle of the trial, it was revealed that one of the cops assigned to the investigation, an old bull named Borosovsky, had been convicted of planting evidence in another case. Despite a vigorous closing by the prosecutor and absolutely no indication of police misconduct in Dolan's case, the taint couldn't be eradicated in some jurors' minds. After four days of deliberations, the jury had hung, nine to three in favor of conviction.

"Speaking off the record, I believe Mr. Dolan was guilty." The judge made a face. "Never underestimate the power of celebrity, no matter how minor."

"Too bad you couldn't've done one of those JN-whatevers," Martinez said.

"I assure you, I would have entered the order in a heartbeat," the judge said.

"The way it turned out..." Ebanks said.

"Justice was done," the judge said briskly.

After the jury failed to reach a verdict, the judge had dismissed them and concluded the trial. During his posttrial press conference, the prosecutor vowed to retry Dolan. He'd wanted Dolan returned to jail pending the filing of new charges. But the baseball player's lawyer had argued that his client should be released on bond, and the judge had agreed. It all became moot two days later when Dolan was discovered dead at his lake house. The coroner hadn't released his final report yet, but the blogosphere had reported the furnace in Dolan's house had been leaking carbon monoxide.

Ebanks looked over at the tray of fly-tying paraphernalia. The judge noticed.

"Do you fish, Detective?"

"Not so much anymore," Ebanks said.

"How can you live without it? I get up to the lake every weekend. You should've seen the rainbow I caught the day after the Dolan trial—it was at least a foot long."

"Hmmm," Ebanks said. "So you tie your own flies?"

"I do." The judge held up his finger to display a Band-Aid. "Although it has its hazards."

"Like everything else," Ebanks said. He checked his watch. "You know, we're not focusing on Kenny Dolan right now."

"I don't understand," the judge said.

Ebanks nodded at Martinez. The rookie said, "One of the trial jurors was killed."

"Oh?" the judge said. "Which one?"

Martinez looked toward Ebanks again, and the older detective nodded once more.

Martinez consulted his notebook.

"Eric Shadid. He didn't even make it to the hospital. The car that hit him was going pretty fast. Witnesses said it aimed right for him, didn't brake, and *bam!*"

The judge furrowed his brow in concentration. "Mr. Shadid was the foreman, wasn't he?"

"Right," Martinez said.

"When did this happen?" the judge said. "Why didn't I hear about it?"

"A day after the trial ended," Ebanks said. "It didn't make the news."

"I would have missed it anyway. I'm always at the lake house after a trial." He grimaced. "This time it was a damn good thing

I got up there so fast. There was a burst pipe in the laundry room. I fixed it myself—a foot of half-inch pipe, some solder, a propane torch, and about two hours of labor." He turned to Martinez. "So you think this hit-and-run is related to the Dolan trial?"

"Maybe," Martinez said. "At first we just figured Shadid was in the wrong place at the wrong time."

"What changed your mind?"

Martinez looked embarrassed. "That magazine writer called."

"Writer?" the judge said.

"Leonard Lunney. He's one of those true-crime guys. Said he was writing about the Dolan trial. He got a copy of the jury list and started calling 'em to see if they'd talk. When he found out Shadid thought Dolan was innocent from the get-go and then Shadid's killed in that hit-and-run..."

"Journalists are rightly skeptical of coincidence," the judge said.

"Police too," Ebanks said.

"I've read some of Mr. Lunney's pieces in *Vanity Fair*," the judge said. "It's his job to spin the suspicious into the sensational."

"According to Lunney, the first vote was eleven to one to convict," Martinez said. "Shadid was the holdout. He ended up getting two other jurors to go along with him."

"I've seen some heated deliberations," the judge said. "That one was among the most acrimonious. I could hear the shouting in my chambers. The bailiff had to break up a scuffle at one point."

"You catch what the fight was about?" Martinez said.

"From what I heard, a juror in favor of conviction accused Mr. Shadid of being blinded by Dolan's status as an athlete." The judge spread his hands. "Of course you'll talk to the rest of the panel."

Ebanks frowned. "You're thinking maybe a juror who argued with Shadid wanted to kill him because Shadid thought Dolan was innocent?"

The judge looked at Ebanks over the top of his glasses. "Remember Jack Ruby? People have done worse in the name of justice, especially when they have some tangential involvement in the situation."

"The thing is, we checked into that," Martinez said. "All the jurors had alibis for when the car hit Shadid."

"So if a juror isn't a suspect, I'm not sure how I can help you," the judge said.

"We'd like to ask you about Mrs. Dolan's family," Martinez said. "Specifically, her brothers."

———

THE PROSECUTOR, AS usual, had made a point of extolling the victim's virtues at trial. Tina Lucchese Dolan was a loving wife who supported her husband's baseball career, cheerfully moving from town to town as he worked his way up from Class-A to Double-A to Triple-A ball. She sang at church and did volunteer work.

Tina's only blemish was her maiden name. The Luccheses were a second-tier New Jersey crime family. Dolan's lawyers, trying to create reasonable doubt, made some noise about Tina's death being payback for a sanitation-contract dispute, but that's all it was—noise. They didn't have any evidence to back up their claims, only innuendo, largely in the form of Tina's two brothers, who attended the trial every day. They sat in the first row behind the defense table and glared daggers at Kenny Dolan's back, tough guys stuffed like sausages into shiny suits. No one would sit next to them.

The judge blinked. "You think a *Lucchese* killed Mr. Shadid?"

"We talked to the Jersey police. The Luccheses really are pretty Old World when it comes to justice." Martinez leaned back in his chair and hooked his thumbs behind his belt. "Make that more like Old Testament. You should see their rap sheets."

"I'm not surprised," the judge said.

"Shadid didn't exactly keep his views to himself," Martinez said. "Right after the trial he told a blogger the police had planted evidence to frame Dolan. So when the prosecutor said he was going to retry Dolan, we think maybe the Luccheses killed Shadid."

A hung jury didn't mean a defendant walked. The prosecutor could try the defendant again, either immediately or after collecting more evidence, as long as the statute of limitations hadn't run out.

"But why now?" the judge said. "The trial's over. Mr. Shadid won't be a member of the new panel."

"To send a message to the next jury," Martinez said.

"You're saying the Luccheses killed Mr. Shadid to intimidate prospective jurors into voting for conviction at the second trial?" The judge steepled his fingers. "I don't know. Sounds a little far-fetched to me," he said.

"Fits the Luccheses' m.o.," Martinez said. "Besides, we're kinda running out of suspects. We've talked to Shadid's family, friends, business associates, enemies." He ticked them off on his fingers. "Everybody's got an alibi."

"What about Dolan?" the judge said.

"Dolan was already dead," Ebanks said.

"No," the judge said. "The Luccheses. If they were going to kill someone, I would have thought it'd be Dolan."

Police work was a lot like fishing. You stuck your best fly on your hook and waited for the hungry trout to come along and strike. The fish thinks he's the predator, but he's really the prey.

Sometimes an even bigger fish comes along and snags your catch right off the hook before you can reel it in.

"Funny you should say that," Ebanks said. "Because we just got the word that Dolan's death was no accident."

The judge looked surprised. Martinez looked confused.

At the press scrum on the courthouse steps, Dolan had expressed his faith in the justice system, refused to answer any questions, and announced he was heading for his lake house to chill. He then drove off in his black SUV.

When he didn't show for a meeting the next day, his lawyer was annoyed. Later that afternoon, when he couldn't reach Dolan by cell phone, the lawyer got worried. The next day, the lawyer called the cops. Dolan's body was found in his bed. He had died of asphyxiation.

"The furnace at the house didn't malfunction," Ebanks said. "Someone tampered with the heat exchanger and disabled the CO detectors. Dolan was murdered."

Now Martinez looked totally stunned. Ebanks shot him a look, and the rookie recovered his poker face.

After a trout bites, you have to set your hook. You can't allow any slack in your line, but you have to make sure not to pull too hard. Otherwise the fish can throw the hook.

"Let's talk some more about Tina's brothers," Ebanks said to the judge.

He asked a few questions, then let Martinez take over. The rookie led the judge through his prepared queries on how the Lucchese boys had behaved during the trial. Ebanks paid little attention to the questions or the answers. He spent the time reminiscing about past trips to the lake. Romance novels and cookbooks — that was what Sonia liked to read. He wondered where her sun hat was now.

After five minutes or so, Martinez closed his notebook.

The judge said, "Do you have any other suspects?"

Ebanks said, "We'll be working hard on that."

"I don't pretend to know your job..." The judge hesitated.

"It's okay," Ebanks said. "What's on your mind?"

"Well," the judge said. "Have you considered Mrs. Batista?"

"The pitcher's wife?" Martinez said. "Why would—"

Ebanks broke in. "What's your theory?"

———

CRIMINAL DEFENSE ATTORNEYS know it isn't enough to say their clients didn't do it. The jury always wants an alternative suspect for the crime, and if one suspect is good, two are better. In addition to offering the Luccheses' mob enemies, the Dolan defense team served up Nikki Batista, wife of Dolan's best friend on the team.

"The evidence will show Kenny and Nikki Batista were having an affair," Dolan's attorney announced in his opening. The "evidence" included several months of late-night phone calls and lunch meetings at out-of-the-way restaurants, but no hotel bills or photos of the tabloid variety. Claiming Dolan broke off the affair because he'd come to realize how much he loved his wife, the defense trotted out the "hell hath no fury/scorned woman" maxim and asserted that Mrs. Batista had no alibi for the time of the murder.

The prosecutor called a tearful Nikki to the stand to deny the affair, and to explain that the clandestine meetings and phone calls between Dolan and Nikki were to organize a surprise birthday party for Tina Dolan. As for the night of Tina's murder, Nikki said she'd driven up to the lake area to visit a friend, who turned out not be home. A PhotoCop shot dug up by the prosecution proved that she'd been doing fifteen over the limit while Tina was being killed.

"I didn't believe that birthday-party story," the judge said. "I think Dolan was having an affair with Nikki Batista. With his wife gone, Nikki expected to be the next Mrs. Dolan, but Dolan dumped her. Hell indeed hath no fury. Mrs. Batista knew Dolan was going to his lake house. She went there too, and rigged his death."

"There's only one problem with pointing the finger at Mrs. Batista," Ebanks said. "We did the background investigation for the prosecutor. Turns out she *was* having an affair, but not with Kenny Dolan. Apparently third basemen are more her type. They were in bed together fifty miles north. That explains the PhotoCop shot."

The judge slowly shook his head. "I must say, my brethren on the criminal bench have a challenging time sorting the sinners from the innocents."

Ebanks slapped the tops of his thighs. "Well, that's it, I guess. Sorry to have taken up so much of your time."

"I'm always happy to do whatever I can in pursuit of justice," the judge said. "Let me ask you this: What about the forensics? Tire tracks, paint transfer…" The judge permitted himself a smile. "My wife is a fan of those television shows," he said. "I suppose some of it has rubbed off."

Ebanks imagined the judge and his pretty blond wife in a large, tastefully decorated room, sitting in nice chairs like the ones he and Martinez were sitting in, watching TV. Sonia and he used to watch old movies every Friday night. He'd make popcorn and they'd curl up on the old plaid couch together. Sonia couldn't watch TV anymore. Fast-changing images triggered the seizures.

"Too bad we don't have a lab like the one on *CSI*," Martinez said. "But we need a lot more big-city crime before that happens. Right now, we have to process the crime scenes ourselves. If we want something tested for prints or DNA, we ship it off to the FBI."

. "We better get going," Ebanks said. He stood, and Martinez followed his lead. The judge pushed his long frame out of the swivel chair.

While his partner shook hands with the judge, Ebanks bent over to tie his shoe. In the wastebasket beside the tray of flies, a partially constructed Parachute Adams lay on top of a piece of Kleenex. Both the fly and the Kleenex were stained with what looked like blood.

Lucky break, Ebanks thought. He hadn't expected to find something literally soaked with DNA.

Martinez and the judge had walked over to the wall, where the judge was pointing to one of the photos. After making sure they weren't paying attention, Ebanks reached into the waste-basket and scooped up the bloody fly and the Kleenex. He slipped them into his pocket and straightened up.

The judge showed them into the reception area. The secretary was on the phone. She waved and smiled at them.

"Let's catch some lunch," Ebanks said, "but first I want to ask her something."

The secretary finished her call. "May I help you?" she said.

"About those JNOVs," Ebanks said. "Aren't they usually kinda rare?"

The secretary nodded. "They are, except for with this judge. You could almost say he's famous for it — some of the lawyers call him the 'thirteenth juror.' He takes his work very seriously. He always says if the jurors don't do justice, it's up to him."

"The thirteenth juror," Ebanks repeated. "Hmmm."

He and Martinez got into the elevator. As the mahogany-paneled box descended, Ebanks said, "Well, that was a bust. We didn't learn anything we didn't already know about Shadid."

"How'd you know about Dolan being a homicide?" Martinez said.

"I got a text when we were waiting for the judge," Ebanks said. "I thought you did too."

"Nope. But hey, no problemo." A few seconds later, Martinez said, "You know, that got me thinking about some of the stuff the judge said."

Ebanks kept his eyes on the numbers over the door. They lit up as the car passed the floors. "Such as?"

"Such as when you told him Dolan was murdered, he was pretty quick to finger Mrs. Batista, and when that didn't pan out, he tried to hand us the Luccheses."

Ebanks shrugged. "You heard him. He was just playing at *CSI* or *Law & Order.*"

"Maybe, but did you notice that his house is on that same lake as Dolan's?"

"So? I used to have a place near there too."

"Yeah, but the judge was at his house when Dolan was killed."

Ebanks folded his arms across his chest and made an effort to look thoughtful. "You know, you're right."

The elevator doors opened on the ground floor. The two detectives walked across the lobby. The rookie's thick eyebrows scrunched together whenever he was thinking something through. They were like that now.

"We had it backward," Martinez said. He pushed forcefully through the revolving door at the courthouse entrance, and Ebanks followed him. When they were out on the street, Martinez said, "We thought Shadid was murdered and what happened to Dolan was an accident."

"It does look like Shadid was just in the wrong place at the wrong time," Ebanks said.

"You mean, it was only a coincidence?"

"Hmm," Ebanks said. He nodded at the hot-dog cart on the corner. "Feel like a brat?"

"As long as they have mustard and kraut," Martinez said.

The two detectives walked down the sidewalk.

"You know, I think the judge is as Old World as the Luccheses," Martinez said. "All that JNOV stuff. What if he did let Dolan out on bail so he could, you know..."

Ebanks blew out a dismissive breath. "What the judge said about justice being done was just a joke."

"He strike you as the joker type? All I'm saying is, anyone who can fix a busted pipe would know how to rig a furnace."

Ebanks rolled his eyes. "You really think the judge killed Dolan?"

Martinez slowed to a stop in the middle of the sidewalk, forcing the other pedestrians to flow around him like water around a rock. He turned and stared back at the courthouse.

"Yeah, I do. After lunch, let's start at Dolan's place at the lake. I'd like to look around some more."

"Fine by me," Ebanks said. "But I think you're wasting your time."

"I don't," Martinez said.

The rookie's face expressed the joyful anticipation of a fisherman who'd just snagged a big fish...or of a big fish who'd just swallowed a hand-tied fly. Peace settled into Ebanks's soul, not unlike what he used to feel when he and Sonia were in his boat on the lake.

They ordered their brats, enjoying the thin warmth of the sun while the vendor assembled them. The scent of cut grass and freshly turned earth wafted on the breeze. Spring had finally arrived.

Ebanks had been a little worried that the judge might recognize him from Sonia's trial, although it had been four years ago. He remembered their day in court, even if the judge didn't. The jury came back after two hours with a seven-figure verdict against the trucking company whose driver had been amped on speed when he broadsided Sonia's car. The money would have paid for the experimental treatment the insurance company refused to cover. Ebanks still couldn't figure out what their lawyer, a chubby little bald guy in a bargain-basement suit, had done to offend the judge's sense of order and justice. Whatever it was, the JNOV killed their chance at the miracle cure. Now his wife was serving a life sentence in a prison of pain, and the judge was still spending every weekend at his lake house.

Ebanks chewed his hot dog and thought about the half-finished Parachute Adams in his pocket. He knew exactly where he'd leave it when they went back to Dolan's place. There'd be no stopping Martinez once he found it.

The only time he'd been back to the lake since Sonia's trial was the night the Dolan jury hung. Maybe after his retirement was official, he'd take his Sage rod up there and see if the trout were biting.

LOST AND FOUND

BY ZOË SHARP

He waits. No hardship there — he's waited half his life. But now, tonight, finally you provide him with that perfect moment.

The one he's been waiting for.

In the alley, in the dark, just the distant glitter of neon off wet concrete. And he's so scared he can hardly grip the knife. But anger drives him. Anger closes his shaking fingers around it, flesh on bone.

He tries not to know what the blade will do.

But he knows. He's seen it too many times. He remembers them only as a slur of violence, swirled with a lingering despair.

And he can't remember a time before you. A time when he was innocent, trusting. You taught him misery and guilt, and he's carried both through all seasons since. A burden with no respite.

Tonight, he hopes for respite.

Tonight, he hopes finally for peace.

There should be lights in the alley, but he's taken care of them. Something else you taught him — not to let anyone see.

It's fitting you should die here in the dark, amid the rats and the filth and the garbage. You are what they are — the detritus of life.

And he is what you made him.

He hopes you're proud.

But right now he just hopes you're ready. That he's ready. He's dreamed of this so often down the years between then and now that he feels suddenly unprepared, naked in the dark.

Shivering, he's a seven-year-old boy again, with all the majesty fresh ripped out of him, howling as he's punished for truth, punished for faith.

Punished for believing, when you told him you would take very special care of him indeed.

He's punished himself and those around him ever since. Lived a life stripped to base essentials, where "refinement" means cut with stuff that's only going to kill you slow.

Lost.

And now he's found you again, and he thinks, if he does this right, he may find himself again too.

He hears the footsteps, familiar even loaded by the drag and stagger of the years. He folds his hand tighter around the knife, takes in the sodden air, feels the pulse-beat in his fingertips.

Feels alive.

It's a privilege only one of you can share.

Attuned, he sees your figure sway into the open mouth of the alley, hesitating at the unexpected gloom. A stumble, a smothered curse, but he knows you won't play it safe. You never have. Going the longer way around will take time, and you're loath to be away from your latest pet project, whoever that might be.

He wonders if he will be in time to save them — not from what's been but from what's to come — even as he steps out of the recess, a wraith in the shadows, the knife unsheathed now and eager for the bite.

At the last moment you hear his lunge of breath and you begin to turn. Too slow.

He is on you, fast with the lust of it, strong with the manifestation of his own fear. His hand grasps your forehead, tilting your head back for the sacrifice. Is it instinct that tries to force your chin under, or do you know what's coming?

Too slow.

He can smell soap overlaying sweat and tobacco, the garlic of your last meal. Garlic that failed to keep this vampire at bay.

The knife, sharp as a butcher's blade, makes a first pass across your stringy throat. It slips so easily through the skin that for a moment he almost believes you are the demon of his childhood nightmares, to be slain by no mortal hand.

Then he remembers a laughing boast—that the first cut is for free.

The second cut, though, is all for himself.

He goes in deep, hacks blind through muscle, tube, and sinew, glances across bone. The blood that gushes outward now is hot, so hot he can almost hear it sizzle.

Your legs run out on you. Shock puts you down and sheer disbelief keeps you there. He steps back, hollowed out by the skill, watches your eyes as the realization finally sets in. *Your heart still pumps but you are dead, even if you don't know it yet.*

He expected a fierce joy. He feels only silence.

He turns his back, not waiting for your feeble struggles to subside, and walks away. At the mouth of the alley he drops the knife into a drain, and walks away.

The rain starts up again, like it's been waiting, like it's been holding its breath.

LOST AND FOUND

———

THE RAIN CLEANSES him. His feet take him past the gang tags, the articulation of alienation that forms the melody of his daily life, to the crumbling church. Not the same church, but another very like it. They have all become one to him — a place of undue reverence. A place where he was found and lost, and maybe found again.

A penance. And now a place of twisted sanctuary.

Approaching the altar, he makes jerky obeisance, slides into the second row. The wood is polished smooth by long passage of the tired and the hopeful. And the building smells of incense and velvet, wax dripped on silver, and the pages of old books lined with dusty words.

Still damp from the rain, he finds no warmth here.

Still restless from the act, he finds no comfort.

He wonders if he was expecting to.

You first came upon him sitting alone like this, all those years ago, scuffed and crying, pockets emptied and pride stolen. You comforted him then. He remembers a pathetic gratitude. *Salvation.*

The blood rises fast in him. His hands are clasped as if for prayer, the knuckles straining to release a plethora of fury and regret.

There was no release then. He had nowhere to take it other than the river, was so close to letting go when strangers wrestled him, a child demented, from the railing's edge. They were shocked at his vehemence, his determination.

They brought him back to you.

And you smiled as you told him suicide was the gravest sin. That he would go straight to the depths of hell, where he would be raped by every demon up to Lucifer himself.

So he chose to live rather than die, although it seemed to him that there was little to choose between one and the other.

———

LYING JUMBLED IN the alley, the truth of what's done finally descends on you, soft as snow.

You see the lights of passing cars, buttoned tight, oblivious. Flashes of colored sound made distant by the glass wall of your dysphonia. Out of reach. Out of touch.

You are nearly out of time.

But still you grip to the coattails of life with the stubborn savagery that is your nature. Logic tells you that you should already be dead, that somehow the blade has missed the vital vessels. You have gotten away with too much to believe you will not get away with this, if you want it badly enough.

After all, by will and nerve you have survived exposure, excoriation, excommunication.

Someone will come.

A stranger, a Samaritan. Someone who doesn't know you well enough to step over your body and move along through.

If he *doesn't come back to finish you first.*

Only a fatalist would believe this is some random act of violence, but not knowing *who* scratches at the back of your mind. There have been too many likely candidates to narrow it down.

You are troubled that he did not speak. You expected the bitter spill of self-righteous self-pity. Of blame.

See what you made me do, old man.

Killing you without triumph is pointless.

But the face…you don't remember the face. You are not good with the faces of men, although it's different with the boys. Unformed and mobile, fresh. You have never forgotten one of your boys.

Your special boys.

It tore your heart out to have them taken away from you. To be taken away from them. But they underestimated the number, and few came forward to be counted.

They called it shame.

You call it love.

Maybe that is the reason you are lying here, bleeding out into a rain-drummed puddle smeared with oil, in an alley, in the dark, alone.

Maybe he loves you too much to see you with anyone else.

———

HE IS ON his knees when the cops come for him. They shuffle into the church snapping the rain from their topcoats, muting radio traffic, hats awkward between their fingers. Like they've seen too much to believe in the solace of this place. Like they're embarrassed by their own lack of devotion.

For a moment panic clenches in him and he teeters on the cusp of relief and outright despair. He should have anticipated this.

He rises, crosses himself—a reflex of muscle memory—and turns to them with empty hands.

The cops don't need to speak. Their faces speak for them. It is not the first time they have come for him like this. Not here. He doesn't stop long enough to pull on a coat before they hustle him out, through the slanted rain to the black-and-white angled by the curb, lights still turning lazily.

The ride is short. The cops exchange muttered words in the front seat. He reads questions in their gaze reflected from glass and mirrors but has nothing to say. This is the place of his choosing, and they cannot understand the choice.

He stares out through the streaked side window at the passing night, at the tawdry glitz of hidden desperation.

The rain comes down with relentless fervor. Water begins to

pile up in the gutters, flash-flooding debris toward the storm drains. *If only sins were as easily swept clean away.*

The car slews to a halt beside two others just outside the crime tape. The lights zigzag in and out of sync with more urgency than the men around them.

Hope plucks at him.

The cops step out; one opens his door. They lift the tape to duck inside the perimeter, though there is nobody to keep at bay. Violence is too common here to draw a crowd in this rain.

A detective intercepts them with a doubtful glance, hunched into the weather. He has a day's tired stubble above his collar, and a tired suit beneath his overcoat.

"This him?"

One of the cops nods. "All yours."

"Let's go." The detective steps back with a spread arm, an open invitation tinged with mocking—for what he is, for what he represents.

"Wallet was still in the vic's hip pocket—how we knew he was one of yours," the detective says as they walk toward the alley. "But we would have made him sooner or later."

The detective waits for a response, for a simple curiosity that's not forthcoming.

"I do what needs to be done."

The detective shrugs. "Sure you do. For the sinners as much as the saints, huh?"

"That's always been the way of it."

"Sure." The detective's face bulges, bones pressing against his skin as if engorged. "This guy's a convicted pederast. He fucks boys—kids. The younger the better. And he was a priest when they sent him down. A goddamn priest."

"He'll be judged."

They reach the throat of the alley and the detective stops, as if to go farther will leave him open to contamination.

"Well, I'd say he's had his earthly judgment." And if the voice is ice, the eyes are fire. "All that's left for him is the fucking divine."

―――――

ADRIFT IN YOUR own circle of confusion, you catch only snatches of words you recognize but can no longer comprehend.

"...amazed he's lasted this long..."

"...nothing more we can do..."

"...had it coming..."

And you're colder than the sea, locked inside a faltering body and a breaking mind, locked into a tumult of regret and the terror of going to meet a vengeful Maker.

The medics rise, retreat, leaving the clutter of their futile effort strewn around you.

You want to cry for them not to leave you, not to let you die alone, but you lie muted by the blade, stilled by the approaching darkness. Darker than the alley, darker than the earth. The devil prowls the shadows, waiting without tolerance, watching with lascivious eyes. Soon he will engulf you, rip apart your body even as your last breath decays, and devour a soul already rotten.

Unless...

"...he's here..."

Your eyes flutter closed.

Thank God.

It takes effort to open them again, to see the priest approaching. The medics have moved back a respectful distance, clustering with the detective at the mouth of the alley, superfluous. The priest bends over you.

You prepare yourself for Penance, Anointing, Viaticum. He'll hear no spoken confession from your lips, but absolution assuming contrition surely must be granted.

You prepare yourself for a ritual worn with consoling familiarity. One you carried out often enough, back in a former life.

But as the priest bends low, you catch sight of his face, and this man's face you *do* remember, from behind the blade all the way back to his boyhood.

He was a special boy, all right.

Your first temptation on the path of sin.

And now your last.

The fear writhes in you, but he touches your forehead with a gentle finger and when he speaks, his voice is gentle too.

"God, the Father of mercies, through the death and resurrection of His Son, has reconciled the world to Himself and sent the Holy Spirit among us for the forgiveness of sins; through the ministry of the Church may God give you pardon and peace..."

Impatient, your mind runs on ahead:

...and I absolve you from your sins in the name of the Father, and of the Son, and of the Holy Spirit.

But the expectation is not fulfilled. The essential words do not follow.

Your eyes seek his, frantic, pleading. The devil growls at your shoulder, taking shape out of the umbra, exulting as he solidifies. Closer. You feel his talons pluck at your vision, begin to pull the fetid shroud across your eyes. You are sinking.

Quickly! Finish it!

The priest bends closer still, his voice a whisper in your closing ear.

"You found me, and I was lost. Now *you* are lost, because *I* found you..."

THE MOTHER

BY ALAFAIR BURKE

Diane Light closed the file folder and added it to the heap on her desk. At nearly a foot high, the pile began to wobble. She rested her forearm on top of the tower to hold it steady.

She resisted the urge to separate that last file from the rest. It was special. It deserved to be carried into court on its own.

"Jesus, I thought *I* was late." Diane heard harried footsteps rush past her office door, her coworker's generic voice fading as he moved farther down the hallway. "Stone's a stickler about time, you know."

She knew.

She stole a glance at her watch as she scooped the stack of files against her chest. Two minutes until Stone would be seated at his bench, tapping the face of his own watch, eager for the deputy district attorney to start calling cases.

Judge Stone was a stickler for promptness, but he was also a stickler for facts. She'd memorized the contents of Kiley's file, from start to finish.

———

Two hours in, Stone finally commented on the time. "Nice job this morning, Miss Light. You could teach your colleagues a thing or two about docket management."

Her previously foot-high pile was now down to two inches. Three more cases. Two more before Kiley's. And still an hour to go before Stone's hardwired lunch alarm would sound. The strategy was working.

She rushed through the next two cases. They were easy ones: Mothers complying with conditions. Social workers report progress and recommend continued monitoring and treatment. No request for immediate disposition, Your Honor.

Forty-five minutes to go, and only one more file. *The* file. Kiley's file. She called the case number and watched Kiley's father approach the opposition table with his court-appointed counsel. Kiley's assigned guardian ad litem stood between the two lawyers.

"Your Honor, you may recall this case. The State originally moved to terminate parental rights ten months ago, after police learned the child had been sold sexually by her parents. She was only twenty-two months old at the time." Twenty-two months sounded much younger than two years old. Somehow it sounded even more babylike than a year and a half.

"Objection." It came from the dad's attorney, Lisa Hobbins.

Hobbins pretended to care about her clients, but Diane knew for a fact that last Cinco de Mayo, after too many tequila shots at Veritable Quandary, Hobbins had puked her guts out in the gutter of First Avenue, crying about the scumbag parents she represents. "Miss Light is well aware that only the mother was convicted of those charges," Hobbins said now. "My client was estranged from his wife at the time the crimes occurred. He wanted to get clean. She didn't. He wouldn't have left Kiley with his wife if he'd known —"

"We dispute all of that, Your Honor. A grand jury indicted the father as well after finding probable cause for his involvement. The defendant was acquitted at trial after his wife testified about her sole responsibility, but the State's position is that his wife, a battered woman and not estranged from her husband at all, protected Mr. Chance —"

Judge Stone held up a hand to cut her off. "The State lost at trial, Miss Light. The jury must have rejected your theory."

"But this is a separate case, Your Honor. As an independent finder of fact, you can make a fresh assessment —"

"So where are we now?" He didn't try to mask the long glance at his watch.

"The mother has stipulated to a termination of parental rights, but Mr. Chance has not. The case has been continued seven times over the past ten months. At the third hearing, Judge Parker found grounds for termination but wanted assurances that Kiley would have a permanent home. The State objected to the condition and has continued to object since, but the case has been set over at each subsequent hearing pending further monitoring of the situation and while Kiley's foster mother, Janice Miller, decided whether to enter into a legal adoption."

Stone was rifling through the court's file, still trying to understand the procedural posture. She didn't want him thinking about continuances, hearings, and orders held at bay. She needed him to care about Kiley. That little girl was not just a number. She was not just the last case of the day. Maybe Diane should have called the case first. All that work. All that planning. And now she was blowing it.

"To cut to the chase, Your Honor"—she knew that was Stone's favorite phrase—"Kiley was not an easy child to place.

Adoptive parents are reluctant to take on children who have been through the kind of trauma Kiley experienced. In addition to having been subjected to repeated molestations, she was born drug affected. At the time of her parents' arrest, she was undernourished and suffering from PTSD. But after nearly a year as a foster parent to Kiley, Miss Miller was sufficiently comfortable with Kiley's physical and emotional progress. This was to be a hearing to finalize the termination of Mr. Chance's parental rights with a simultaneous adoption by Miss Miller."

"But?"

"But Miss Miller was struck and killed by a drunk driver two nights ago as she was jogging across Powell Boulevard." Judge Stone made a *tsk* sound. "The State is still seeking termination of parental rights. Although counsel notes that Mr. Chance was acquitted, it cannot be ignored that one of the men who was paying for sexual contact with the child was a former cellmate of Mr. Chance. At Mr. Chance's trial, that man testified that—"

Hobbins interjected on her client's behalf. "Your Honor, that man was a child rapist who testified in exchange for leniency. Given how child abusers are treated in prison, he would have said anything to get in the prosecutor's good graces."

The man's name was Trevor Williams. His status as a convicted felon was the primary reason the State's criminal case had come together. A neighbor in the Chances' apartment building called the police after she saw blood on a child's pair of pants in the communal laundry room. A fan of *CSI*, she went so far as to seize the evidence and seal it in a Ziploc bag. Police found not only blood but also seminal fluid. A search warrant executed at the Chances' home turned up a set of pajamas with a different man's fluids. Thanks to the state's DNA data bank for convicts, they linked the second sample to Williams.

Cutting a deal with that pedophile was the hardest bargain

Diane had ever struck. They might never identify the other man — or men — to whom Kiley was traded off, but they had Williams, and Williams was willing to give them both of the parents. It was the only way to protect the girl in the long run.

Judge Stone wasn't interested in the details of Williams's testimony, however. He raised an impatient palm again. "I'm not going to relitigate the criminal case here, ladies. You should both know that the standard is the best interests of the child."

And how the hell was it in Kiley's best interests to live with a man who sold her as a two-year-old to support his crack habit?

Diane knew her argument would only go downhill from there. The State had not yet secured a new foster placement for Kiley. She was staying in a group home, the youngest of all the children there.

Then it was Hobbins's turn. The conviction of Chance's wife and initiation of TPR hearings had been the wake-up call the father needed, she said. After some initial relapses, he had been clean for five months. He still denied all knowledge of his wife's crimes, but he had been willing to let Kiley go with Janice Miller because the woman had been there for his daughter when he had not. But now Miller was gone, and he was finally in a position to parent.

"Miss Hobbins, does your client live in a residence suitable for the child to be there now?"

Now?

"Yes, Your Honor. He has a private apartment with subsidization through Section Eight. It is a one-bedroom; Kiley would have the bedroom, and he would sleep in the living room. Were he granted custodial status, he would qualify for additional subsidization. He has a social worker through his drug rehabilitation program, and she would assist him in securing a two-bedroom. He is working part-time as a janitor at Portland State, but his sister has agreed to watch Kiley while he is at work."

Diane remembered the sister. She'd refused to take Kiley in because "my food stamps barely cover my own three kids, and you people don't pay foster parents for shit."

"And what does Kiley want?" The judge directed his question to the guardian ad litem.

"Your Honor, she's not even three years old," Diane said.

"I didn't ask if she wanted to run off and live with Santa Claus. I'm simply asking a question of our assigned guardian ad litem, since presumably she needs to justify her public-interest salary here today. Is that all right with you, Miss Light? Am I allowed to ask a question?"

The guardian ad litem's role was to advocate directly for Kiley, but in this case, Diane believed that the prosecution was doing precisely that.

Diane took a deep breath and forced herself to nod deferentially. She waited while the guardian ad litem rushed through the basics. In some ways, Kiley was lucky to have suffered the abuse at such at a young age. The psychiatrists said she was unlikely to retain any conscious long-term memory of the incidents.

She tested at below-average intelligence — most likely a consequence of her mother's prenatal drug use — but the experts attributed her delayed speech to the lack of environmental stimulation prior to her placement with Miss Miller. She had recently shown some willingness to vocalize but had become distracted and unresponsive in the two days since her move to the group home. She had seen her father six times during the last three months with the consent and supervision of her foster mom. According to the monitoring social worker, she demonstrated a "natural fondness" for him and "clearly recognized that he played some role in her life."

Kiley's father said, "I just want one more chance to be her

dad, Judge. I promise you on my life that I will not mess it up this time. Please, sir. *Please.*"

"Baby steps, Mr. Chance. We'll start with five-hour days with you, one hour supervised. She'll remain at the group home at night. We'll hear again from all parties in two weeks and make a decision then."

"Your Honor, that's four hours a day without supervision," Diane protested.

"I'm aware of basic math, Miss Light."

"But the best interests of the child—"

"—require some consistency for this little girl. The biological mother is in prison. The foster mother just died. She has one person left, and he stands here by all accounts a changed—and acquitted—man. You have nothing to offer but a group home filled with juvenile delinquents."

"I can offer myself, Your Honor. I'll take her if that's the only option. You can't put her back with this man."

"Good Lord, Miss Light. Get control of yourself. I recognize your indignation, and it's on the record. There's no need to be hyperbolic."

"It's not hyperbole, Your Honor. I've been on this case for ten months. I handled the criminal prosecution. I have shepherded the case through the family court process. I went to Miss Miller's home multiple times to talk to her about the adoption. He's seen Kiley—what, six times since this all happened? I've seen her on at least twenty occasions. Does he even know her favorite stuffed animal? It's a raccoon. Its name is Coo-Coo. It was one of the only times Kiley repeated after her speech therapists—she tried to say *raccoon,* and she said *coo-coo,* so that became the toy's name. I was there for that, not him. Kiley *knows* me. I know Kiley. I will take her."

The courtroom fell silent. Even Diane could not believe her

outburst. In all those hours studying the file, she had never once considered the possibility. But suddenly every piece fell into place. There was a reason she had been the major-crimes attorney assigned to the trial. There was a reason she had requested the transfer from criminal court to the family law unit. Maybe there was even a reason Janice Miller had been hit by a drunk driver.

Diane could do this. She could be a good mother to that girl. She and Kiley could be a family. The two of them, together.

Stone cleared his throat before speaking. "Well, that's very noble of you, Miss Light, but the best interests of the child value biological connections. Let's give Kiley a chance at a life with her father. I hope I'm not wrong about you, Mr. Chance."

"You're not, sir. I promise you, you're not. Thank you. Thank you so, so much."

Chance grabbed both of Hobbins's hands and shook them hard. Diane saw the defense attorney's eyes tear up and wanted to slap her.

———

THREE WEEKS LATER, Kiley officially moved in with her father full-time. Kiley's clothing and Coo-Coo were packed into a black Hefty bag at the group home. A social worker drove her and the bag to Chance's recently rented two-bedroom apartment, outfitted with a new twin bed for Kiley, and left her there.

———

DIANE STARTED HER car engine, searching for the comfort of the radio. All that silence made the minutes tick by too slowly. Where the hell was Jake?

The guy leaving the Wendy's was looking at her. He saw her notice him. He smiled.

She still wasn't used to that kind of smile from a man. She had spent her entire life as the type of girl men looked away from. Or if one looked, the glance would be followed by a nudge of his buddy, then a wisecrack and guilty giggle. *Dude, that's just wrong.*

At least they usually had the courtesy to keep their voices down. Well, not that one time, back in law school. She'd worn her knee-length purple sweater tunic to class. Even with the black leggings, it was a bold fashion choice. She'd thought she looked pretty good until she heard the male voices singing in the undergrad quad, "I love you, you love me..." Maybe she would have managed to forget the incident—the day abandoned somewhere in the recesses of her mind like that enormous sweater discarded in the bathroom garbage can—but someone had yelled, "Barney!" as she walked the stage at commencement. To this day, she couldn't see that big purple dinosaur without wanting to eat a pint of Häagen-Dazs.

Her cell phone buzzed on the console. A text message illuminated the screen. It was from Mark. *Will u pls change cable bill to ur name? Mindy tried 2 add Showtime. Mix-up b/c 2 accts under mine. Thx.*

Mark and Mindy. Just the sound of it was ridiculous. Diane had spent nearly thirty years with the man, and now her relationship with Mark was nothing but logistics hammered out through misspellings and abbreviations. She hit Delete.

Where the fuck was Jake?

Maybe pulling Jake into this had been too big a risk. At one point, they'd had something resembling a friendly relationship, albeit based on reciprocal compensation: He was her favorite informant; she was his benefactor in the drug unit. Relying on and rewarding the cooperation of criminals was one of the ugly realities of her job, but as drug dealers went, Jake wasn't so bad.

He sold only to adults and only in small quantities. Most important—for her purposes, at least—he always kept his ears and eyes open for information that he could trade for a get-out-of-jail-free card.

Jake was so well connected to Portland's white crack trade that she'd gone to him last January hoping he might recognize Kiley's parents. Maybe he was selling to them or had seen them in the usual spots looking to buy. Jake had never seen either one of the Chances, but Diane had mentally added a chit to his account, just for the time he spent studying their mug shots.

Jake the Snake had been popped fourteen times, but because of the chits, he had never taken a conviction.

That track record made him a good informant, but not a good ally. A senior deputy district attorney's head on a silver platter was some pretty hefty currency in Jake's trade, much more valuable to him than yet another IOU from her.

She wondered how the office would respond if she were tainted by the whiff of scandal. She'd been with the office for nearly eighteen years; she'd known colleagues who had DUIs, arrests for so-called domestic disturbances, even coke problems. Some had jobs waiting for them after the appropriate amount of rehab. Others got shipped off, their cases referred to the attorney general for investigation.

A year ago, she would have gotten the kid-glove treatment. She'd been a team player. Kept her head down. Put the office first, always.

And then Mark left her. The boy who'd taken her to the high school prom. The guy she'd shacked up with in college. The man she'd married the weekend after graduation. The asshole left her.

When he'd asked her to prom, she was already approaching two hundred pounds. She was nearly at three when he told her there was someone else.

Her weight was never really an issue for him. That's what she'd thought, at least. He was big too. They both liked to eat. They both said they were happy in their bodies and wished other people would accept them as they were. Instead, they had accepted each other. Now she wondered whether they'd loved each other only because no one else would.

Everything started to change about five years ago. They'd gotten married so young that they just assumed a baby would come along eventually. Before they knew it, their thirties were almost over. The doctors said her weight might be the reason she hadn't conceived.

She and Mark went on a diet together. They joined the gym. Success came faster to him than to her.

So did pregnancy.

Ironically, it wasn't until Mark broke the news that he was expecting a child with someone else — Mindy from spin class, naturally — that her own weight finally started to come off. It was as if that one conversation changed her physical makeup. Her metabolism, her glucose levels, her fat cells — all transformed. It was like waking up in someone else's body.

But by then, the body was too old. She was forty-four. On a government salary, she didn't have the money for in vitro, private adoption, or a surrogate. She'd always assumed she was lucky to have Mark, even when he'd looked like Jabba the Hutt. Now she couldn't believe the person she saw in her mirror every day. She was finally the kind of woman who was appealing to men, but to what end?

It wasn't just her body that changed. So did her determination. Before the weight loss, though she worked in an office filled with athletes and health nuts who viewed physical fitness as a measure of character, she had nevertheless excelled because she was like an uncaged tiger at trial. But the anger and indignation that had propelled her courtroom performances had somehow burned away with all those pounds. She found herself cutting corners. Winging opening statements. Last December, she'd snapped at a rape victim: *What do you think happens when you smoke meth with total strangers?* She rang in the new year by oversleeping on the final day of Kyle Chance's criminal trial, then delivering her closing argument in a groggy haze.

She'd barely had the energy to cry after the acquittal.

And so, after climbing the prosecutorial hierarchy for eighteen years, she'd asked for a transfer out of the major-crimes unit, the most coveted job in the office. She knew the rotation out of downtown and into the wasteland of family court was intended as punishment, a message to the rest of the attorneys that they requested changes at their own peril.

But now she realized the move had allowed her to stay in Kiley's life. Who else would have protected her?

She finally spotted Jake, who looked only in the direction of oncoming traffic on the one-way street before he dashed across Park Avenue. This was the kind of thing a mother noticed.

She rolled down her window halfway.

"Sorry, Light. No dice."

"You didn't find him?" According to the social worker, Chance worked janitorial duty at the campus until nine o'clock.

"I found him a'ight. Dude dipped." Jake's skin was white as Casper, but not his voice. She once tried getting him to drop the affect for his trial testimony, telling him he sounded like a twenty-first-century minstrel show. He responded by asking what religion had to do with it.

"Are you sure you talked to the right guy?" She hit her overhead light and showed him Chance's mug shot again. If only Jake had recognized this photo in January. If only he'd had some connection to Kyle and Rachel Chance. Testimony placing the couple together near the time of Kiley's abuse would have debunked their bogus story that the mother acted alone during a desperate binge brought on by their separation. "This picture's a year old. He's put on a little weight since then."

"I did my thing, you know? Acted like I was working the park blocks. Saw him coming. Sidled up to him. Asked if he was looking for rock. Dude just said no, thanks, and kept on walking."

"I'm not buying it, Jake."

"You're my girl, Light. Liked you better with that junk in your trunk, fo' sho', but you know I want to he'p you out. You think I'd cross you? I know better than to get DiLi mad."

She smiled, remembering the nickname he'd conjured up for her when J.Lo first hit the cultural lexicon, a decade earlier.

"I want to trust you, Jake, but I don't believe for a second that this guy turned down the opportunity to get high."

"Hey, whatchu want me to say?"

"That you just sold the man in this picture some dope."

"Then you send your man in there to frisk him down but he don't find no rock. That would make me a liar, and you know I only speak the truth. I bathe in the light of honesty, girl. I might sell folks to the law, but only if they did the crime, you know? Hey, don't get so upset, Light. I never seen you so down. It must be that diet. Get yourself some cheeseburgers and onion rings, you know what I'm saying?"

"You're *positive* it was the same guy?"

Jake looked back toward the park, but she could tell he was just buying himself time to answer. "If it makes you feel better, I could tell he was craving it. Real tempted, you know? Like pondering and shit. But—I don't know—maybe I made it seem too easy. I knew you wanted him, so I floated a half ball at a hundred. Price was too low; he probably figured I was po-po. Maybe try again in a few weeks? I'd do anything for DiLi."

A few weeks was too long. A man like Chance could break Kiley all over again in a few hours.

"No, that's all right. You want a ride back uptown?"

"Nah, I'm good. Might hang down here for a bit."

"Dumb question, Jake, but any chance I can persuade you to get into another line of work?"

"You cute, girl. And, seriously, you look good, Light. Maybe a little too *light*, if you get it. But good. Hang tough."

———

THE NEXT NIGHT, Chance showed up at home close to eleven o'clock. Diane watched Kiley hold his hand as they stepped from the bus onto McLoughlin Boulevard. From the university to the aunt's house to here should not have taken him the nearly two hours it had. Chance was definitely up to something. Not to mention, what kind of father let a three-year-old stay up that late?

She watched from her car as they walked together, hand in hand, to their apartment complex. She saw Kiley's bedroom light turn on. Five minutes later, it turned off. She waited another twenty minutes before stepping from her car out into the darkness.

The chill of the night was perfect. Her quilted black hat felt snug on her head. Her neoprene gloves provided just enough compression to make her fingers feel extra alive. She placed her hands in her coat pockets, felt the knife against her left hand, the brick-shaped wad of paper against her right.

He opened the door for her. Of course he did.

It was over fast. She knew it would be. He was a lifelong junkie with slow reflexes and no idea what was about to happen when he turned to get that glass of water she asked for. Blade into the carotid artery, the results of which she'd seen in so many autopsies. He never even touched her.

The hardest part was waking Kiley, but she had no choice. She lifted the girl from her bed. Was it her imagination or was the child lighter than the last time she'd held her at Janice Miller's house? Chance had probably been trading food stamps for drugs instead of feeding the poor thing.

She held Kiley close to her chest and grabbed the stuffed raccoon from the bed. "Shhh," she whispered. "It won't be long, baby girl."

She set Kiley on the worn linoleum of the bloody kitchen floor and then started walking backward toward the living room, waving the stuffed toy in front of her as she moved. "Come here, sweetie. Come play with your Coo-Coo. Yeah, good girl. You're such a good girl. Now you're safe. No more bad things in the kitchen, okay?" Kiley followed her. Diane gave her the stuffed animal.

She dialed 911 and let the receiver fall to the floor.

"Don't be afraid, Kiley. Someone will be here in just a few minutes. We're going to be all right." Diane tried not to cry as she looked one last time at Kiley, alone on the living room rug with nothing but a blood-smeared acrylic raccoon.

———

"THE FINAL CASE on the docket, Your Honor. Kiley Chance."

Stone nodded as Diane reminded him of the court's decision to reinstate custody of the child to her biological father, Kyle Chance.

"Mr. Chance's body was found in his apartment late Wednesday night." Stone emitted multiple *tsk* noises as she outlined the facts. Fatally stabbed. A wad of paper found at the scene. Not money, but a twenty-dollar bill folded around strips of newspaper cut to resemble bills. The police believe it was likely a drug deal gone bad. Chance tried to bilk the seller. Got a knife in the neck in return. The perpetrator at least had the decency to dial 911 before leaving.

The judge said, "I guess we'll have to chalk this up to a lesson about the fragility of recovery from addiction."

"Yes, Your Honor." As if she hadn't warned him.

"And what do you need from me today, Miss Light?"

"Nothing imminent. I thought you deserved the earliest possible update on the case status. The child is back in the group home where she resided prior to placement with her father, and the State is trying to secure a foster home for her."

"Sad stuff. All right, we're done here?"

She had expected Stone to at least ask about the chances of a foster placement before calling it a day.

"It won't be easy to find a home for this girl. The prenatal drug exposure, the sexual abuse, and now having apparently witnessed the murder of her father — she was covered in his blood — well, the deck is stacked against her."

I'm so sorry, Kiley. I'm so sorry for waking you. For putting you through that. For the blood. But I couldn't take a chance. According to dispatch, it was only six minutes before police arrived. Six minutes I hope you can't remember. Six minutes that were nothing compared to what your parents put you through.

"I thought there was an aunt or something?"

"The father's sister. Even she won't take her. Potential parents assume she's damaged goods."

"What about that offer you made, Miss Light? I don't suppose that door is still open?"

Stone laughed, mocking what he still considered her overly dramatic objection to his initial ruling. She joined him with an awkward giggle.

"Actually, Your Honor, I suppose I should put my money where my mouth is. Yes, I guess if it's acceptable to you, I am willing to take her home. Just temporarily. The child does know me, after all. Maybe something else will come through in a week or two. And if worst comes to worst, once she starts making progress with speech therapy, it will be easier to find another placement for her."

"Well, I'd say that's very generous of you, Miss Light. You're sure about this?"

"Sure, Your Honor. Why not?" Not one of the million little goose bumps she felt beneath her sleeves revealed itself in her voice.

———

THAT AFTERNOON, DIANE's cell pinged as she strapped on her seat belt. She pulled it from her purse and saw a new message on the screen. From Mark again. He couldn't call or even e-mail like a regular adult. He was like a teenager with the texting. *Mindy in Seattle so I'm mister mom this week. Any chance you're willing to meet Nicole? Know it's a lot to ask. Trying to find a way to be friends.*

Nicole. At least Mark and Mindy hadn't named their kid some stupid matching M-name.

She hit Delete and looked at herself in the rearview mirror. Behind her she saw last night's purchases: a child safety seat and the biggest, best stuffed raccoon she could find. Maybe they'd call him Coo-Coo Two.

She was careful as she backed out of the parking space. She was in a hurry but would need to be a more cautious driver now. She was picking up her daughter.

———

"WHAT COLOR IS this one?"

"Red!"

"How about this one?"

45

"Yellow!"

"And this?"

"Ahnje!"

"That's right. Orange. And all of these flowers are called *tulips*. Isn't that a funny name? *Tulips*."

Kiley smiled and pointed at Diane's mouth. "Two lips."

She and Kiley had been together nearly six months. The adoption wasn't quite finalized, but Diane had nevertheless succumbed to the calls from her old downtown colleagues to bring her daughter for a visit. It was a rare dry day in April, so after leaving the office, they'd gone over to enjoy the bloom of tulips on the Portland Park Blocks. The area's potpourri of college students and homeless people shared the lush green grass and an occasional park bench.

She reached into the brown sack in her purse. "What's this, Kiley?"

"Coo-kie."

Maybe someday her daughter would talk her ears numb, but for now, Diane cherished every word. In light of Kiley's progress, her speech and cognition therapists said she might even be ready to start kindergarten with her own age group.

Diane broke off an especially chocolaty piece of cookie for Kiley and kissed her on the forehead. "That's right. And you are my little cookie monster." She allowed herself a bite as well. She wasn't worried about the few extra pounds. It was normal to gain weight with a child around.

She heard her cell phone beep in her purse. She recognized the office extension on the display screen.

"Light."

"Hey, Diane. It's Sam Kincaid." Kincaid was the major-crimes attorney who'd inherited Diane's caseload last year. "I hope you don't mind my calling your cell, but I hear you and your sweetie were doing the rounds on your old stomping grounds."

"Yeah, we just headed out." Kincaid was a good lawyer but a little high maintenance for Diane's taste. They'd never been close.

"Shoot. I was hoping to catch you. Do you remember your case against Kyle and Rachel Chance? It was a rape one, compelling prostitution, bunch of other charges involving their two-year-old daughter?"

Twenty-two months.

Diane had told her friends she'd adopted a daughter but hadn't mentioned Kiley's connection to the earlier criminal trial.

"Not the kind of case you forget."

"I didn't think so. You flipped one of the men — Trevor Williams. He was the father's former cellmate?"

"Yeah, sure."

"You ever doubt him?"

"What do you mean?"

"Sorry. I mean, obviously, you wouldn't have put him on the stand if you doubted his testimony. I guess I'm just digging around here for more information about him. He's serving the seventy-two months he got as part of his deal with you and is trying to whittle it down by handing us his current cellmate. Williams says the guy confessed to a home invasion last year, but the cellmate doesn't match the vic's description. Looks like the story might be bogus."

"Well, it wasn't bogus in my case. Williams's DNA was found on Kiley Chance's clothing. That's why he's doing six years."

"Yeah, I saw that. But he would've been looking at nine, minimum, if it weren't for the plea. As I understand it, the mom said she was the one who made the agreement with Williams after seeing him at a bar and recognizing him from her visits to the prison. Wasn't Williams the only person to say that both the mom and dad knew what was going on?"

Rachel Chance had confessed but steadfastly refused to turn on her husband. If only Diane had found another witness. If only someone other than Williams could have placed the parents together during that time window—she would have had a second witness to contradict the Chances' fabricated story about separation.

"The mom's a piece of shit. So's the dad. And so is Williams. Maybe he's lying now, but he wasn't then."

"All right. I was all set to cut him loose. Wouldn't be the first time a jailhouse snitch lied to me. I'll take a closer look at the cellmate, just in case. Thanks for the info."

As she zipped her purse, Diane caught sight of a familiar face near Market Street. She was too far away to hear his words, but after eighteen years as a prosecutor, she could spot hand-to-hand drug transactions across a football field.

Once the customer had left, she waved in Jake's direction. Kiley turned to look, then held on to Diane's leg. Her sweet little brown eyebrows were furrowed.

"That's just a friend of your mommy." She'd have to ask Kiley's psychologist whether a lingering fear of men was to be expected.

Jake nodded, but then turned away to walk farther south. She supposed the presence of a deputy district attorney wasn't good for a drug dealer's business.

"You want some more cookie? Can you say *cookie?*"

Kiley was still clinging to her leg, but the worry in her eyes had transformed to panic. Her breath quickened, and Diane recognized all the signs of a serious meltdown.

"What's wrong, sweetie? Is Mommy's cookie monster all full? Is it nap time?"

Her daughter's gaze moved south, and her grasp tightened. "Jake."

"What did you say?"

Kiley's lower lip trembled, but her next words were unmistakable. She pointed to a spot between her legs. "Jake. Snake."

"How do you know—"

Snippets of images replayed in Diane's visual cortex. A pair of Kiley's soiled pants in a Ziploc bag, the source of the bodily fluids still unidentified. Jake's frantic banter when she'd approached him about the Chance case. His utter certainty when he'd finally said, "Sorry, DiLi, never seen either one of these ugly crackheads." Fourteen pops, no convictions. No convictions meant no blood sample for the DNA data bank.

She tasted bile and chocolate at the back of her throat. What else had she been wrong about?

She pictured Trevor Williams on the stand, promising to tell the whole truth. Rachel Chance's insistence of full responsibility: *I'm so ashamed, but I can't blame this on Kyle. I fell apart when he left me.* Kyle Chance hugging his lawyer when Stone allowed him back in Kiley's life. The lawyer for once appearing pleased to have helped a client.

As if Chance were standing before her, Diane remembered the clarity on his face when he'd opened the apartment door that night. She saw her daughter on that worn kitchen floor, gazing up with sleepy eyes, oblivious to her father's blood beginning to soak into the bottom of her flowered flannel pajamas.

The grass and the tulips shimmered in the sunlight and went out of focus, as though the laws of gravity had been set in abeyance and would not be restored anytime soon.

BLIND JUSTICE

BY JIM FUSILLI

Angie and Turnip were best friends for as long as either could remember, beginning when Angie came to Turnip's aid, grabbing Weber by his pale hair, bloodying his nose with a roundhouse right, then dribbling his skull on the sidewalk. Bobby Weber was in the first grade, Angie and Turnip in kindergarten at St. Francis of Assisi in downtown Narrows Gate.

That was twenty years ago, the winter of 1953, and since then nobody picked on Turnip twice.

Though they were unemployed, neither Angie nor Turnip lacked: Their widowed mothers, both of whom were born in the Apulia region of southern Italy, received pension checks from Jerusalem Steel as well as Social Security. They gave the boys what they wanted and then some, provided they spoke not of the source, figuring if anyone knew they received so much for doing nothing, the flow would be tapped. Whatever extra Angie and Turnip had, the neighborhood figured it came from those little jobs they did on the side.

Entering Muzzie's one afternoon, Angie and Turnip were surprised to find, lounging on a platform above the round bar, a woman wearing only a purple boa and shoes that seemed made of glass. Last time they were here, they had seafood with a marinara sauce so spicy Angie knew Big Muzz was hiding two-day-old scungilli.

"Muzz," said Turnip as he mounted the three-legged stool, "what happened to the scungilli?"

"There's the scungilli," Little Muzz said, nodding up at the stripper. He was checking pilsner glasses for cracks.

Propped on an elbow, the droopy blonde filed her nails.

Turnip held up a finger. "Yeah, but what's she do?" he asked the bartender.

A Ping-Pong ball shot from her *fica,* just missing his head.

"That," Little Muzz said.

"Who says?" Turnip asked.

Inching away, Angie already knew the answer.

"Who?" Little Muzz replied with a dark shrug. "Like you don't know who."

Big Muzz's voice rumbled from where the kitchen used to be. "Turnip," he bellowed. "Soldato wants you. Now."

Turnip frowned as he faced the red-velvet curtain.

"Muzz? Now? I ain't here for three months," he said. "What's 'now'?"

Little Muzz spoke soft. "Maybe he seen the car."

Turnip drove a '69 canary-yellow Super Yenko Camaro 427 with a V8, an M-22 four-speed manual transmission, and custom-made spoilers front and back. Zero to sixty in 3.7 seconds on the ramp to the turnpike. Now it was parked in the bus stop on the sunny side of Polk Street.

"Soldato wants me?" Turnip whispered. Without thinking, he tapped the .45 in his jacket pocket.

"Apparently," Angie replied, knowing full well the car had nothing to do with it. Big Muzz made a call. Which meant Soldato had an eye out for Turnip. For what, who knows?

———

TURNIP GOT HIS handle when some roly-poly ice cream man translated his surname to impress the other kids on line. That evening over dinner, he asked his father why the wiseass threw him a new hook. His father, who knew damned well *rapa* was Italian for "turnip," said, "Because you look like a fuckin' turnip, that big fat ass you got."

Later, Angie told Turnip his old man must've been thinking of a butternut squash or an eggplant, a turnip being more or less round. Either way, Turnip was displeased and he took to weight lifting to change his body shape. It worked, even if the name stuck, and now he looked like he didn't need Angie knocking the Webers of the world off his back.

At about the same time, Angie realized that he wasn't going to be much bigger than his old man, who went about five and a half feet in work boots. Also, he'd have to wear eyeglasses. But by then, he'd been discovered to have an IQ of 154 and was in a class for the advanced. Soon, it was common knowledge that Angie, the toughest kid in Narrows Gate, was also the smartest.

About fifteen years later, it dawned on Silvio Soldato that Angie and Turnip were a dangerous duo. *Very dangerous, these two,* he mused. Brains and brawn. Mind and muscle. Hmmm.

The problem in this case, he noted, was that usually when you had a Hercules and an Einstein, at the same time you had a moron and a weakling. Not so with these two. Turnip had a fresh head, especially with numbers and mechanics, and little Angie was *pazzo* times three—everybody in town knew he'd crammed those turnips down the ice cream man's throat when he was ten years old. Each time a guy turned up on the waterfront with his shins shattered or his ears pinned to his cheeks, Soldato made Angie for it, wondering how he always walked away clean.

Soldato wanted them broke up, now and forever, and for six weeks he thought about how to do it. Killing them both would look desperate, he reasoned, and killing one would send the other one seething toward revenge. He considered having the brakes go on the Camaro as Turnip and Angie headed down the viaduct, careening them to a fiery death at the Getty station. But then he started thinking maybe Turnip could figure some way out of the crash, twisting and maneuvering, tires squealing. Kid drives like he was born behind the wheel, that son of a bitch, him and his Camaro.

Then he decided, the lightbulb going bright.

Now Soldato was sitting in his booth at the Grotto, enjoying a late-afternoon meal of *zuppa di vongole* over linguine, and here comes Turnip. Alone and more or less right after Big Muzz said. A good sign, he thought as he watched Pinhead frisk him, concluding by giving his nuts a threatening tug.

Turnip shivered as he shook off the September chill.

"Mr. Rapa," Soldato began. "How's the Camaro? And Angie?"

———

"Two questions, and there was the entire plan," Turnip said. "The shit heap gave it up before I had my ass in the seat. What a fuckin' *babbo*."

"So he said that? Just like that?" Angie asked.

"Not in so many words, no. Different words."

"What words?"

"Ang, how the fuck do I know? I got the gist of it, all right?"

They decided to play it safe, leaving the Camaro in Turnip's garage. Angie had a beat-up burgundy Impala, one of about three thousand in Hudson County. He drove it north on Boulevard East while Turnip took the 22 bus up to Cliffside. Now they were in the Bagel Nosh in Fort Lee, figuring nobody was eyeing the joint.

"The one sentence," Angie insisted. "Repeat that one—"

"He said, 'I don't want to see him no more.' "

"Meaning what?"

"Well, I don't think he wants you to move, Ang," Turnip chuckled.

"And you don't take me out, he'll blow up the Camaro. What's wrong with this guy? Did you tell him they made a lot of Camaros?"

You had to be half a fag to drink Tab, but Turnip liked the taste. "In fact, Ang, they ain't made that many Super Yenkos."

Angie narrowed his eyes and sat back in the orange booth.

Silence hung heavy. Soon Turnip wondered if his friend could kill him with a plastic spoon covered with chicken liver.

"I'm saying, that's all."

Angie tapped his fingers, one after the next, and Turnip began to squirm.

"Ang," he said finally, palms up. "What the fuck…"

Angie adjusted his eyeglasses. The color began to return to his face.

"Let me guess your plan," Turnip said. "You let me guess?"

"Yeah. Go guess," he replied, dabbing at the corners of his mouth with his thumb and forefinger. He'd noticed the knockout behind the counter. A schnoz on her, but those dark curls and like an hourglass under the Bagel Nosh uniform. A streak of mischief too: He could tell she liked that he wouldn't return when they were done.

He had to ask if she had a friend. A friend with a car didn't mind driving Turnip down to Narrows Gate after.

"You want to find out where they got another '69 Camaro," Turnip said, sucking on a lemon slice.

Angie stood. "No. Jesus…"

Looking up, Turnip frowned. "What then?"

"When I come back, you tell me how Soldato's connected," he said. "Let me know if there's somebody maybe who wouldn't want to, you know, make a move, given his misstep."

———

THOUGH IT WAS a short ride under the Hudson from Little Italy, Narrows Gate no longer drew much attention from the Five Families. The Gigentis still had a slice via the creaking waterfront, but the shipyards had closed, the Great Atlantic and Pacific Tea Company moved, Venus Pencil too, and now the city's population, once as high as sixty thousand, was down to less than half that. And half of those left were *melanzane* who'd turned the projects into Little Harlem.

Seeing the Mob now thought the place an ass pimple, Soldato had moved in and set up his own operation, running a numbers racket that catered to the old-time Italians, the coloreds, and the *Irlandese*. Soon, come eight thirty at night and almost everybody left in Narrows Gate was throwing elbows, grabbing the bulldog edition of the *Daily News* for the total mutual handle at the track to see if the last three numbers matched their bet.

Given it's a thousand-to-one shot to hit on the nose, Soldato needed a rake to collect, taking in maybe two large a week in small change and paying out less than 7 percent. Most of that went to his army of bookies, all blue-haired grandmothers who knew everybody on the block who wanted in. Somebody gave him shit he'd send Pinhead to bruise her sensible. Grandma in

ShopRite with a fat lip and a shiner, and soon everybody's back in line, the thing almost running itself.

Angie knew the *donnaccia* with the Ping-Pong ball at Muzzie's was a sign that Soldato wanted to expand. But the Gigentis sent hookers through the Lincoln Tunnel for action all over the county: One Saturday 4:15 a.m., Angie and Turnip counted sixteen *zoccolas* waiting for a New York–bound bus outside a motel only a mile from Muzzie's platform.

Clear, Soldato asked nobody what he could do.

Angie got his meet at two thirty in the morning at Sal Rossi's on Houston Street with six feet of poured concrete named Bobo. Him and his giant melon coming out of the kitchen and Angie wondered if he'd made the right play.

Adjusting his sunglasses, Bobo passed on the handshake and said, "What?"

Angie was no pigeon. "It's about propriety," he said.

Bobo went, "Uh?"

"He put the *puttana* two blocks from a school. Muzzie's is the place. It used to be a nice restaurant. Long row of brownstones around the corner. Two, three generations in the same building."

"Muzzie's."

"Now you got mothers going by with their little kids, teenagers hanging around . . . It's not a class move and people are thinking it's you."

"Me?"

"The family." Jesus.

"Yeah, right, and . . ."

"And the cops come, and the newspapers," Angie said, "and soon they're closing down the York Motel and half the whorehouses on Tonnelle Avenue. In time, it blows over and he moves in on your territory."

Bobo thought. Then he said, "Who is this guy?"

"Soldato. Right now he's under the protection of nobody. But after he makes his move, he seeks an accommodation..."

"And you got a hard-on for this guy why?"

Angie sat back and lifted his palms. "Why?" he asked, feigning surprise. "Because he figured *this*. You and me. So he tells some guy he doesn't want to see me anymore."

"Maybe you hop a Greyhound or something."

"No good. Not for the long run."

Bobo agreed. Then he rubbed his chin. "You want in?"

"Hell no. It's yours and God bless you."

"But what?"

"One, Muzzie's goes back to scungilli and calamari."

"Two is...?"

"Nobody misses this guy."

Bobo couldn't decide on his own, Angie knew, but how the big guy left the table told him he was going to get his way.

———

HE WAITED UNTIL "Mala Femmina" ended on the jukebox and joined Turnip at Sal Rossi's horseshoe bar.

"So?" Turnip asked.

"It's done. You're off the hook. Drive in peace."

Turnip smiled his relief.

"So what happens?"

Angie said, "Stay out of the Grotto until I tell you."

They wandered onto Houston. Traffic to the FDR was backed up to Mulberry Street.

"Ang, I'm surprised at that guy, to tell you the truth."

"How so?" They turned up their leather collars in unison.

"If he gives you a hard time, I'm sitting there," Turnip said. "I can put two between the third and fourth buttons before he knows what hit him."

"Not likely," Angie said as they headed toward the garage on Elizabeth Street. "The guy at the bar with the wavy hair, black suit, resoled loafers? Playing with his onyx pinkie ring?"

Turnip frowned. "Three stools down? You're shitting me."

"Carrying double. On the right ankle and the ribs."

"How'd you—your back was to him. How'd you make him?"

"My guy's sunglasses," Angie said. "Plus your guy got up when the genius scratched his chin."

Turnip shook his head in wonder. "How you like that."

As they walked in silence toward the Camaro, Turnip pondered how much his friend could achieve if he had a speck of ambition.

———

PINHEAD WENT PAST the bar and poured himself a big cup of hot clam broth, dropping in a couple shots of Tabasco. Screaming at the widows gave him a scratchy throat, so he threw it down, thinking a Schlitz chaser.

"Yo, Pin," said Milney, the night bartender. He wiggled a crooked finger.

Pin said, "What?"

Milney leaned over. "The senior center on Fourth Street," he whispered. "Some bullshit in the lounge. Take a cab, but go."

Pin understood and he threw Sally B a fin.

Milney slipped it over the half a yard Turnip gave him a half hour ago.

Outside the Grotto, Pin flagged the first cab that rolled the corner. He didn't notice Angie behind the wheel.

Soon, they were on their way toward the Jersey City end of the viaduct, taking the cobblestone road behind the last horse stable in Narrows Gate.

"Angie, you got some set of *coglioni* on you, you know that?"

Pin said. "But I admire that. I do. Tells me we can do something, a guy like you."

Angie looked in the rearview, seeing if the barbed wire he'd used to tie Pin down was making a mess of the vinyl seat.

"Pin, there are five stages of receiving catastrophic news," he said. "You blew through anger—wisely, if you ask me—and you're bargaining now. Which means depression is next."

"Hey, Ang, smart is smart, but sometimes what's smart in books—"

"You don't hurry, there's no time for acceptance."

Fourteen minutes later, Pinhead went over the rusted rail atop the viaduct and landed two hundred and thirty feet below, smack on a chain-link fence outside the bus terminal, the cops trying to figure how the barbed wire got hooked so thorough around the weasel's neck and hands.

———

"SYMMETRY," SAID ANGIE as he entered Muzzie's, old Maxwell House coffee can in his hand. "I love it."

Muzzie and Little Muzzie came from the kitchen. The asbestos in their hair and on their faces reminded Turnip that soon they'd be coated in flour, making fresh linguine for the seafood and flaming-ass sauce.

Turnip sat next to his friend at the bar and pointed to the nothing where the platform had been. One of the Muzzolinis had spackled the holes.

"What happened to Miss Ping-Pong?" he asked.

Little Muzzie, who now feared Angie more than ever, shrugged. "I heard the Gigentis are opening some new clubs on Tonnelle Avenue."

"Could be," Angie said. "You of the mood to pour a little sambuca?"

Big Muzzie stepped up. "We're closed—"

"No problem," said Little Muzz, going quick to the round bar, yanking back the canvas cover, and coming up with a bottle. With Pinhead two weeks dead and Soldato missing, Little Muzz was looking to the future.

Turnip smelled the anise through the cap.

Two shot glasses, and Little Muzzie retreated as the friends set their elbows down to raise a toast.

"To what?" Turnip said.

"To Soldato," Angie replied, "and to being careful what you wish for."

Turnip didn't get it, but he sipped anyway, expecting a coffee bean to bump his lip. When he put down the little glass, he said, "So you're going to tell me?"

"Tell you..."

"What's in the coffee can?"

Turnip shook it and heard something rattle inside.

"You like to guess," Angie said. "Guess."

A minute later, Turnip said, "I could use a fuckin' clue, Ang."

"What did Soldato say?"

"He said he didn't want to see you no more."

"Which did not mean..."

Suddenly, Turnip recoiled.

"Bingo," said Angie.

"*Madonna mio,* Ang." Then he whispered, "You took his eyes?"

Figuring the Muzzies were peeping, Angie nodded slow.

Turnip blessed himself.

Angie said, "Nobody puts you on the spot, *il mio amico.*"

His head spinning, Turnip asked, "Ang, dead or alive?"

Angie dipped his little finger in the sambuca. "What do you think?"

THE CONSUMERS

BY DENNIS LEHANE

It wasn't that Alan didn't love Nicole. She was possibly the only person he did love, certainly the only one he trusted. And after he'd beaten her or called her all kinds of unforgivable things in one of his black rages, he'd drop to his knees to beg her forgiveness. He'd weep like a child abandoned in the Arctic, he'd swear he loved her the way knights loved maidens in old poems, the way people loved each other in war zones or during tsunamis—*crystallized* love, pure and passionate, boundless and a little out of control, but undeniable.

She believed this for a long time—it wasn't just the money that kept her in the marriage; the makeup sex was epic, and Alan was definitely easy on the eyes. But then one day—the day he knocked her out in the kitchen, actually—she realized she didn't care about his reasons anymore, she didn't care how much he loved her, she just wanted him dead.

His apology for laying her out in the kitchen was two round-trip tickets to Paris, for her and a friend. So she took the trip with Lana, her best friend, and told her that she'd decided to have her husband killed. Lana, who thought Alan was an even bigger asshole than Nicole did, said it shouldn't be too much of a problem.

"I know a guy," she said.

"You *know a guy?*" Nicole looked from the Pont Neuf to Lana. "A guy who kills people?"

Lana shrugged.

Turned out the guy had helped Lana's family a few years back. Lana's family owned supermarkets down south, and the guy had preserved the empire by dealing with a labor organizer named Gustavo Inerez. Gustavo left his house to pick up training pants for his three-year-old and never came back. The guy Lana's family had hired called himself Kineavy, no other name given.

Not long after Nicole and Lana returned to Boston, Lana arranged the meeting. Kineavy met Nicole at an outdoor restaurant on Long Wharf. They sat looking out at boats in the harbor on a soft summer day.

"I don't know how to do this," she said.

"You're not supposed to, Mrs. Walford. That's why you hire me."

"I meant I don't know how to hire somebody to do it."

Kineavy lit a cigarette, crossed one leg over his knee. "You hire somebody to clean your house?"

"Yes."

"It's like that — you're paying somebody to do what you don't want to do yourself. Still has to get done."

"But I'm not asking you to clean my house."

"Aren't you?"

Hard to tell if he was smiling a bit when he said it because he'd been dragging on his cigarette. He wore Maui Jim wraparounds with brown lenses, so she couldn't see his eyes, but he was clearly a good-looking guy, maybe forty, sandy hair, sharp cheekbones and jawline. He was about six feet tall, looked like he worked out, maybe jogged, but didn't devote his life to it.

"It feels so *odd*," she said. "Like, this can't be my life, can it? People don't *really* do these kinds of things, do they?"

"Yet," he said, "they do."

"How did you get into this line of work?"

"A woman kept asking me questions, and one day I snapped."

Now he did smile, but it was the kind of smile you gave people who searched for exact change in the express line at Whole Foods.

"How do I know you're not a cop?"

"You don't really." He exhaled a slim stream of smoke; he was one of those rare smokers who could still make it look elegant. The last time Nicole had smoked a cigarette, the World Trade Center had been standing, but now she had to resist the urge to buy a pack.

"Why do you do this for a living?"

"I don't do it for a living. It doesn't pay enough. But it rounds off the edges."

"Of what?"

"Poverty." He stubbed his cigarette out in the black plastic ashtray. "Why do you want your husband dead?"

"That's private."

"Not from me it's not." He removed his sunglasses and stared across the table. His eyes were the barely blue of new metal. "If you lie, I'll know it. And I'll walk."

"I'll find somebody else."

"Where?" he said. "Under the hit-man hyperlink on Craigslist?"

She looked out at the water for a moment because it was hard to say the words without a violent tremble overtaking her lower lip.

Then she looked back at him, jaw firm. "He beats me."

His eyes and face remained stone still, as if he'd been replaced with a photograph of himself. "Where? You look perfectly fine to me."

That was because Alan didn't hit her hard every time. Usually, he just held tight to her hair while he flicked his fingers off her chin and nose or twisted the flesh over her hip. In the last couple years, though, after the markets collapsed and Alan and men like him were blamed for it in some quarters, he'd often pop the cork on his depthless self-loathing and unleash on her. He'd buried a fist in her abdomen on three different occasions, lifted her off the floor by her throat, rammed the heel of his hand into her temple hard enough for her to hear the ring of a distant alarm clock for the rest of the day, and laid her out with a surprise punch to the back of the head. When she came to from that one, she was sprawled on the kitchen floor. He'd left a box of Kleenex and an ice pack by her head to show he was sorry.

Alan was always sorry. Whenever he hit her, it seemed to shock him. His pupils would dilate, his mouth would form an O, he'd look at his hand like he was surprised to find it attached to his wrist.

After, he'd fill the bedroom with roses, hire a car to take her to a spa for a day. Then, after this last time, he'd sent her and Lana to Paris.

She told this to Kineavy. Then she told him some more. "He punched me in the lower back once because I didn't move out of his path to the liquor cart fast enough. Right where the spine meets the ass? You ever try to sit when you're bruised there? He took a broomstick to the backs of my legs another time. But mostly he likes to punch me in the head, where all my hair is."

"You do have a lot of it," Kineavy said.

It was her most striking attribute, even more than her tits, which were 100 percent Nicole and had yet to sag; or her ass, which, truth be told, had sprouted some cellulite lately but still looked great for a woman closing in on thirty-six; or even her smile, which could turn the heads of an entire cocktail party if she entered the room wearing it.

Her hair trumped all of it. It was the dark of red wine and fell to her shoulders. When she pulled it back, she looked regal. When she straightened it, she looked dangerous. When she let it fall naturally, with its tousled waves and anarchic curls, she looked like a wet dream sent to douse a five-alarm fire.

She told Kineavy, "He hits me mostly on the head because the hair covers the bruises."

"And you can't just leave him?"

She shook her head and admitted something that shamed her. "Prenup."

"And you like living rich."

"Who doesn't?"

Nicole had grown up in the second-floor apartment of a three-decker on Sydney Street in Savin Hill, a neighborhood locals called Stab-'n'-Kill. Her parents were losers, always getting caught in the petty scams they tried to run on their soon-to-be-ex-employers and on the city and the welfare system and DSS and the Housing Department and just about anybody they suspected was dumber than they were. Problem was, you couldn't find dead fucking houseplants dumber than Jerry and Gerri Golden. Jerry ended up getting stomach cancer while in minimum-security lockup for check-kiting, and Gerri used his death to justify climbing into a bottle of Popov and staying there. Last time Nicole checked, she was still alive, if toothless and demented. But the last time Nicole checked had been about ten years ago.

Being poor, she'd decided long ago, wasn't necessarily a bad thing. Plenty of people had nothing and didn't let that eat their souls. But it wasn't for her.

"What does your husband do?" Kineavy asked.

"He's an investment banker."

"For which bank?"

"Since the crash? Bank Suffolk."

"Before the crash?"

"He was with Bear Stearns."

Finally, some movement in Kineavy's face, a flick in his eyes, a shift of his chin. He lit another cigarette and raised one eyebrow ever so slightly as the match found the tobacco. "And people call me a killer."

———

SHE THOUGHT ABOUT it later, how he was right. How there was this weird disconnect at the center of the culture around various acts of amorality. If you sold your body or pimped someone who did, stuck up liquor stores, or, God forbid, sold drugs, you were deemed unfit for society. People would try to run you out of the neighborhood. They would bar their children from playing with yours.

But if you subverted federal regulations to sell toxic assets to unsuspecting investors and wiped out hundreds of thousands, if not millions, of jobs and life savings, you were invited to Symphony Hall and luxury boxes at Fenway. Alan had convinced the entire state of Arkansas to invest in bundled sub-primes he knew would fail. When he'd told Nicole this, back in '07, she'd been outraged.

"So the derivatives you've been selling, they're bad?"

"A lot of them, yeah."

"And the CD, um, whatta you—"

"Collateralized debt obligations. CDOs, yeah. They pretty much suck too, at least a good sixty percent of them."

"But they're all insured."

"Well…" He'd looked around the restaurant. He shook his head slowly. "A lot of them are, sure, but the insurance companies overpromised and underfunded. Bill ever comes due, everyone's fucked."

"And the bill's going to come due?"

"With Arkansas, it sure looks like it. They bundled up with some pretty sorry shit."

"So why not just tell the state retirement board?"

He took a long pull from his glass of cab. "First, because they'd take my license. Second, and more important, that state retirement board, babe? They might just dump those stocks en masse, which would *ensure* that the stocks would collapse and make my gut feeling come true anyway. If I do nothing, though, things might — *might* — turn out all right. So we may as well roll the dice, which is what we've been doing the last twenty years anyway, and it's turned out okay. So, I mean, there you go."

He looked across the table at her while she processed all this, speechless, and he gave her the sad, helpless smile of a child who wasn't caught playing with matches until after the house caught fire.

"Damned if you do, damned if you don't," Alan said, and ordered another bottle of wine.

The retirees lost everything when the markets collapsed in 2008. *Everything,* Alan told her through sobs and whimpers of horror. "One day — fuck, yesterday — old guy worked his whole life as a fucking janitor or pushing paper at city hall, he looked at a statement said he'd accrued a quarter million to live off of for the final twenty years of his life. It's right before his eyes in bold print. But the next day—*today*—he looked and the number was zero. And there's not a thing he can do to get it back. Not one fucking thing."

He wept into his pillow that night, and Nicole left him.

She came back, though. What was she going to do? She'd dropped out of community college when she met Alan. The prospects she had now, at her age and level of work experience, were limited to selling French fries or selling blow jobs. Not much in between. And what would she be leaving behind? Trips, like the one to Paris, for starters. The main house in Dover; the city house twenty miles away in Back Bay; the New York apartment; the winter house in Boca; the full-time gardener, maid, and personal chef; the 750si; the DB9; the two-million-dollar renovation of the city house; the one-point-five-mil reno of the winter house; the country club dues—one country club so exclusive that its name was simply the Country Club—Jesus, the shopping trips; the new clothes every season.

So she returned to Alan a day after she left him, telling herself that her duty was not to honor a bunch of people she didn't know in Arkansas (or a bunch of people she didn't know in Massachusetts, New York, Connecticut, Maine, and, well, forty-five other states); her duty was to honor her husband and her marriage.

Honor became a harder and harder concept to apply to her husband—and her marriage—as 2008 turned into 2009, and then as 2009 turned into 2010.

Outside of losing his job because his firm went bankrupt, Alan was fine. He'd dumped most of his own stock in the first quarter of '08, and the profit he made paid for the renovation of the Boca place. It also allowed them to buy a house she'd always liked in Maui. They bought a couple of cars on the island so they wouldn't have to ship them back and forth, and they hired two gardeners and a guy to look after the place, which on one level might seem extravagant but on another was actually quite benevolent: three people were now employed in a bad economy because of Alan and Nicole Walford.

Alan cried a lot in early 2009. Knowing how many people had lost their homes, jobs, retirement savings, or all three ate at him. He lost weight, and his eyes grew very dull for a while, and even when he signed on with Bank Suffolk and hammered out a contract feathered with bonuses, he seemed sad. He told her nothing had changed; nobody had learned anything. No longer was investment philosophy based on the long-term quality of the investment. It was based on how many investments, toxic or otherwise, you could sell and what fees you could charge to do so. In 2010, banking fees at Alan's firm rose 23 percent. Advisory fees spiked 41 percent.

We're the bad guys, Nicole realized. We're going to hell. If there is a hell.

But what were they supposed to do? Or, more to the point, what was *she* supposed to do? Give it back? She wasn't the one shorting stock and selling toxic CDOs and CDSs. And even if she were, the government said it was okay. What Alan and his cohorts had done was, while extremely destructive, perfectly legal, at least until the prosecutors came banging on their door. And they wouldn't. As Alan liked to remind her, the last person to fuck with Wall Street had been the governor of New York, and look what happened to him.

Besides, she wasn't Alan. She was his wife.

Maybe she was doing a service to society by hiring Kineavy. Maybe, while she'd been telling herself she didn't want to leave the marriage because she didn't want to be poor, the truth was far kinder—maybe she'd hired Kineavy so he'd right a wrong that society couldn't or wouldn't right itself.

Seen in that light, maybe she was a hero.

———

IN ANOTHER MEETING, at another part of the waterfront, she gave Kineavy ten thousand dollars. Over the years, she'd been able to siphon off a little cash here, a little cash there, from funds Alan gave her for the annual Manhattan shopping sprees and the annual girls' weekends in Vegas and Monte Carlo. And now she passed some of it to Kineavy.

"The other ten when I get there."

"Of course." She looked out at the water. A gray day today, very still and humid, some of the skyline gone smudged in the haze. "When will that be?"

"Saturday." He looked over at her as he stuffed the cash in the inside pocket of his jacket. "None of your servants work then, right?"

She chuckled. "I don't have servants."

"No—what are they?"

"Employees."

"Okay. Any of your employees work Saturday?"

"No. Well, I mean, the chef, but he doesn't come in until, I think, two."

"And you usually go out Saturday, go shopping, hang with your girlfriends, stuff like that?"

"Not every Saturday, but it's not uncommon."

"Good. That's what you do this Saturday between ten and two."

"Between ten and two? What're you, the cable company?"

"That's exactly what you're going to tell Alan. On Thursday afternoon, your cable's gonna go out."

"Out?"

He popped his fingers at the air in front of his face. "Poof."

"Alan'll go crazy. The Sox play the Yankees this weekend; there's Wimbledon; some golf thing too, I think."

"Right. And the cable guy will be coming to fix it Saturday, between ten and two."

Kineavy stood and she had to look up at him from the bench. "You make sure your husband's there to answer the door."

———

AT NINE SATURDAY morning, Alan came into the kitchen from the gym. They'd had the gym built last year in the reconverted barn on the other side of the four-car garage. Alan had installed a sixty-inch Sony Bravia in there, and he'd watch movies that pumped him full of American pride as he ran on the treadmill — *Red Dawn, Rocky IV, Rambo III, The Blind Side*. Man, he loved *The Blind Slide,* walked around quoting it like it was the *Bhagavad Gita*. He was covered in sweat, dripping it all over the floor, as he pulled a bottle of OJ from the fridge, popped the cap with his thumb, and drank directly from the container.

"Cable guy come yet?"

Nicole took an elaborate look at the clock on the wall: 9:05. "Between ten and two, they said."

"Sometimes they come early." He swigged half the bottle.

"When do they come early?"

"Sometimes."

"Name one time."

He shrugged, leaned against the counter, drank some more orange juice.

Watching him suck down the orange juice, she was surprised to remember that she'd loved him this past week. Hated him too, of course, but there was still love there. He wasn't a terrible guy, Alan. He could be funny, and he once flew in her brother, Ben, to surprise her for her thirty-third birthday — Lord knows, he could always be depended on for the grand gesture. When he spent two weeks in Shanghai on business right after her third miscarriage, he sent her white roses every day he was gone. She spent the week in bed, and sometimes she'd place one of those white petals on the tip of her nose and close her eyes and pretend she'd have a child someday.

This past week, Alan had been surprisingly attentive, asking her if everything was okay, if there was anything she wanted, was she feeling under the weather, she seemed tense, anything he could do for her?

They'd fucked twice, once in the bed at the end of the day, but once on the kitchen counter — the same counter he was leaning against now — good and lusty and erotic, Alan talking dirty into her right ear. For a full ten minutes after he'd come, she'd sat on the counter and considered calling the whole thing off.

Now, only an hour (or four) away from ending her husband's life, her heart pounded up through the veins in her neck, the blood roared in her ear canals, and she thought there might still be time to call it off. She could just run upstairs and grab the number of Kineavy's burner cell and end this madness.

Alan burped. He held up a hand in apology. "Where you going again?"

She'd told him about a hundred times.

"There's an art fair in Sherborn."

Drops of sweat fell from his shorts and plopped onto the floor.

"Art fair? Bunch of lesbos selling shit they painted in their attics from the backs of Subarus?"

"Anyway," she said, "we won't be all day or anything."

He nodded. "Cable guy's coming when?"

She let out a slow breath, looked at the floor.

"I'm just asking. Christ."

She nodded at the floor, her arms folded. She unfolded them and looked up, gave him a tight smile. "Between ten and two."

He smiled. Alan had a movie-star-wattage smile. Sometimes, if he put his big almond eyes behind it, tilted his chin just so, she could feel her panties evaporate in a hushed puff of flame.

Maybe. Maybe...

"Don't be all day with the lesbians, that's all, okay? Money's like rust—shit doesn't sleep." He winked at her. "Know what I'm saying, sister?"

She nodded.

Alan took another slug of orange juice and some of it spilled into his chest hairs. He dropped the bottle on the counter, cap still off. He pinched her cheek on his way out of the room.

Nah. Fucking time for you to go, Alan.

———

KINEAVY HAD BEEN very clear about the timeline.

She was to stay in the house until 9:45 to make sure Alan didn't forget he was supposed to stick around for the cable guy, because Alan, for all his attention to detail when it came to money, could be absentminded to the edge of retardation when it came to almost anything else. She was to go out through the front door, leaving it unlocked behind her. Not open, mind you, just unlocked. At some point while she was out with Lana on a Bloody Mary binge at the bar down the street from the Sherborn Arts Fair, Alan would answer the front door and the cable guy would shoot him in the head.

Oh, Alan, she thought. *You aren't a bad guy. You just aren't a good one.*

She heard him coughing upstairs. He was probably sitting in the bathroom waiting for the shower to get hot, even though that took about four seconds in this McMansion. But Alan liked to turn the bathroom into a steam room. She'd come in after him, see his wipe marks all over the mirrors as her hair curled around her ears.

He coughed again, closer to the stairs now, and she thought, *Terrific. Your last gift to me will be a cold. My fucking luck, it'll turn into a sinus infection.*

He was hacking up a lung by the sounds of it, so she left the kitchen and crossed the family room, which would remain an ironic description unless she hired the von Trapps to fill it. And even then there'd be room for one of the smaller African nations and a circus.

He stood at the top of the stairs, naked, coughing blood out of his mouth and onto his chest. He had one hand over the hole in his throat and he kept blinking and coughing, blinking and coughing, like he was pretty sure if he could just swallow whatever was stuck in his throat, this too would pass.

Then he fell. He didn't make it all the way down the stairs — there were a lot of them — but he made it nearly halfway before his right foot got jammed between the balusters. Alan ended his life facedown and bare-assed, dangling like something about to be dipped.

Nicole realized she'd been screaming only when she stopped.

She heard herself say, "Oh, boy. Jesus. Oh, boy."

Alan's head had landed on the wood between the runner and the balustrade, and he'd begun to drip.

"Oh, boy. Wow."

"You got my money?"

To her credit she didn't whip around or let out a yelp. She turned slowly to face him. He stood a couple feet behind her in the family room. He looked every inch the suburban dad out on Saturday errands — light blue shirt untucked over wrinkled khaki cargo shorts, boat shoes on his feet.

"I do," she said. "It's in the kitchen. Do you want to come with me?"

"No, I'm good here."

She started to take a step and stopped. She jerked a thumb toward the kitchen. "May I?"

"What?" he said. "Yeah, sure."

She felt his eyes on her as she crossed the family room to the kitchen. She had no reason to think he had, in fact, turned to watch her go, but she felt it all the same. In the kitchen, her purse was where she'd left it, on one of the high bar stools, and she took the envelope from it, the envelope she'd been instructed to leave in the ivy at the base of the wall by the entrance gate on her way out. But she'd never gone out.

"You cook?" He stood in the doorway, in the portico they'd designed to look like porticos in Tuscan kitchens.

"Me? No. No." She brought him the envelope.

He took it from her with a courteous nod. "Thank you." He looked around the room. "This is a hell of a kitchen for someone who doesn't cook."

"Well, no, it's for the chef."

"Oh, the chef. Well, there you go then. Makes sense again. I always wanted one of those hanging-pot things. And those pots, what're they — copper?"

"Some of them, yeah."

He nodded and seemed impressed. He walked back into the family room and stuffed the envelope into the pocket of his cargo shorts. He took a seat by the hearth and smiled in such a way that she knew she was expected to take the seat across from him.

She did.

Directly behind him was an eight-foot-tall mirror in a marble frame that matched the marble of the hearth. She was reflected in it, along with the back of his head and the back of his chair. Her lower eyelids needed work. They were growing darker lately, deeper.

"What do you do for a living, Nicole?"

"I'm a homemaker."

"So you make things?"

"No." She chuckled.

"Why's that funny?"

Her smile died in the mirror. "It's not."

"Then why're you chuckling?"

"I didn't realize I was."

"You say you're a homemaker; it's a fair question to ask what you make."

"I make this house," she said softly, "a home."

"Ah, I get it," he said. He looked around the room for a moment and his face darkened. "No, I don't. That's one of those things that sounds good — I make the house a home — but is really bullshit. I mean, this doesn't feel like a home, it feels like a fucking monument to, I don't know, hoarding a bunch of useless shit. I saw your bedroom — well, one of them, one with the bed the size of Air Force One; that yours?"

She nodded. "That's the master, yeah."

"That's the master's? Okay."

"No, I said —"

"Anyway, I'm up there thinking you could hold NFL combines in that room. It's fucking huge. It ain't intimate, that's for sure. And homes, to me, always feel intimate. Houses, on the other hand — they can feel like anything."

He pulled a handful of coins out of his pocket for some reason, shook them in his palm.

She glanced at the clock. "Lana's expecting me."

He nodded. "So you don't have a job."

"No."

"And you don't produce anything."

"No."

"You consume."

"Huh?"

"You consume," he repeated. "Air, food, energy"—he looked up at the ceiling and over at the walls—"space."

She followed his gaze and when she looked back at him, the gun was out on his lap. It was black and smaller than she would have imagined and it had a very long suppressor attached to the muzzle, the kind hit men always used in movies like *Grosse Pointe Blank* or *The Professional*, the kind that went *pffft* when fired.

"I'm meeting Lana," she said again.

"I know." He shook the change in his hand once more and she looked closer, realized they weren't coins at all. Some kind of small metal things that reminded her of snowflakes.

"Lana knows who you are."

"She thinks she does, but she actually knew of another guy, the real Kineavy. See, they never met. Her father met him, but her father died—what—three years ago, after the stroke."

Her therapist had taught her breathing exercises for tense situations. She tried one now. She took long slow breaths and tried to visualize their colors, but the only color that came up was red.

He plucked one of the metal snowflakes from his palm and held it between the thumb and forefinger of his right hand. "So, Kineavy, I knew him well. He died too. About two years ago. Natural causes. And faux Kineavy—that's me—sees no point in meeting most clients a second time, which suits them fine. What do you do, Mrs. Walford? What do you do?"

She could feel her lower lip start to bubble and she sucked it into her mouth for a moment. "I do nothing."

"You do nothing," he agreed. "So why should I let you live?"

"Because—"

He flicked his wrist and the metal snowflake entered her throat. She could see it in the mirror. About a third of it—three metal points out of eight—stuck out of her flesh. The other five points were on the other side, in her throat. A floss-thin line of blood trickled out of the new seam in her body, but otherwise, she didn't look like someone who was dying. She looked okay.

He stood over her. "You knew what your husband was doing, right?"

"Yes." The word sounded funny, like a whistle, like a baby noise.

"But you didn't stop him."

I tried. That's why I hired you.

"You didn't stop him."

"No."

"You spent the money."

"Yes."

"You feel bad about it?"

And she had, she'd felt so terribly bad about it. Tears spilled from her eyes and dripped from the edges of her jaw. "Yes."

"You felt bad? You felt sad?"

"Yes."

He nodded. "Who gives a shit?"

And she watched in the mirror as he fired the bullet into her head.

Afterward, he walked around the house for a little bit. He checked out the cars in the garage, the lawn out back so endless you would have thought it was part of the Serengeti. There was a gym and a pool house and a guesthouse. A guesthouse for a seven-bedroom main house. He shook his head as he went back inside and passed through the dining room and the living room into the family room, where she sat in the chair and he lay on the stairs. All this space, and they'd never had kids. You would have thought they would've had kids.

To kill the silence, if for no other reason.

MOONSHINER'S LAMENT

BY RICK McMAHAN

Chapter 1

Goat McKnight's hands ached for a gun.

Walking up the mountain path, he yearned for one. The moonlight, where it penetrated the canopy of trees, bleached the open spaces in pools of white and created twisted shadows in the lee of crooked branches. Goat never feared the dark of night. Darkness held no sway over him. Not even while he trudged through the blackest jungles did fear of the dark edge into his heart.

Goat had never feared the law either, not even after he was caught with a load of moonshine. The judge had given him a choice. Prison or the army. Sometimes late at night, freezing on a jungle trail or facedown in a rice paddy under a hot sun as Charlie zinged rounds at him, Goat had thought he'd made the wrong choice. When he got back home, Goat had two options— go down in the mines or go back to hauling whiskey. The thought of the law catching him running untaxed whiskey didn't scare him, nor did it make him yearn for a gun.

A simple smell made Goat's hands ache for a gun. The thick and earthy scent rose up from the loamy creek Goat and Ralphie had waded across at the base of the hill. The primal smell brought back a rush of memories from the not-so-distant past spent hunting Vietcong. As the aroma filled his lungs, Goat found himself scanning the ground, his eyes searching for trip wires leading to bouncing Betties or scuffed earth that signaled an ambush. Oblivious, pulling the wagon, Ralphie babbled on the whole time.

When they were halfway up the path, a movement on the opposite hillside drew Goat's attention. As a figure slipped through a clear spot of moonlight, Goat saw the glint of a belt buckle and a shoulder and arm covered in a tan uniform just before the NVA soldier slipped back into the shadows.

Goat stopped.

He knew it was his imagination projecting the picture like a Friday-night drive-in movie. There were no NVA soldiers stalking the hills of eastern Kentucky. Still, he held his breath as he scanned the woods. He waited a whole minute, not taking a breath until his chest was tight, but the soldier never reappeared.

"Goat?" Ralphie called from up ahead in a low whisper. "Goat." This time louder.

Pushing the phantom soldier from his mind, Goat jogged up the trail. He nodded to his young cousin to keep moving. With the wagon wheels once again creaking, Ralphie continued his one-sided conversation. Goat wasn't sure what made more noise, the banging of the empty wagon or Ralphie.

"Groovy, I'm telling you," Ralphie was saying. Even though Goat had zoned out for a bit, he was sure Ralphie was still talking about what all teenage boys talked about. Girls. Ralphie had a crush on his new English teacher. Ralphie thought she was a hippie, even though Ralphie wouldn't know a hippie if one bit him in the ass. "She drives one of those little German buses painted up like a rainbow with a peace sign. I'm telling you, Miss Love's a hippie."

Goat glanced over his shoulder, searching the trail for the NVA soldier.

"And you know what they say about those hippies," Ralphie intoned. Goat wasn't sure what they said about hippies, but he was sure Ralphie was going to tell him.

"What do they say about them hippies?" a voice called down.

Goat grinned. From up ahead, a yellow glow leaked out around the edges of a tarp hung across the trail. Leave it to Luther to pull Ralphie's chain.

"Come on, Ralphie," Luther called, pushing aside the tarp so the glow from the lanterns and fire pit lit up the trail all the way to Goat and his cousin. "Tell me about them hippie gals like Carrie Love." From farther back in the stand of trees came low laughter.

Ralphie and the Radio Flyer were quiet.

Sliding past his cousin, Goat glanced at the younger man's face. Even in the dim glow of the lantern light, he saw that the kid was the same shade of red as the wagon.

Goat called, "Luther, at least the boy's got the good sense to have a crush on a young teacher. He's not prattling on about Old Mrs. Napier."

"No-Neck Napier." Ralphie gasped. "She has a mustache." There was more cackling from underneath the lean-to, and Luther told someone to shut up.

Luther held the tarp open so Ralphie could pull the Radio Flyer underneath and park it next to the other two. These weren't your kid's Radio Flyer wagons. No, sir. The original wheels had been replaced with thicker, bigger tires to handle more weight, and the wagon sides had been cut out and several-foot-high metal slats welded in so that boxes of full mason jars and plastic jugs could be stacked up. It made it a little easier getting the bootleg whiskey down the hill.

Once the wagon was in, Luther dropped the tarp. The tarp was meant to hide the lanterns' and fire's light. Not that anyone would venture up the mountain, but Luther's daddy was careful.

"No-Neck Napier," Luther said, punching Goat in the arm. "Like I'd ever." Luther was solidly built although shorter than Goat, which Goat thought served the man well down in the mines. Even in the lanterns' flickering light, the black coal flecks ingrained in his skin were visible. Just as the men stripping coal out of the dark holes they'd dug left an imprint in the mountain, the coal left its mark on the men. The coal dust permeated the clothes and soaked into the skin. And if it soaked in deep, it took a man's life.

Farther back in the grove sat the liquor still—all copper tubing and barrels holding the mash being heated by a fire tended by Luther's dad. Nearby, a pair of men sat on wooden milking stools. They were seventy if they were a day, and over time they'd become almost mirror images of each other, both white-headed, grizzled, and skinny in overalls and white dress shirts. One filled the mason jars from the still. The second screwed on the lids, wiped off the jars, and slid them into waiting cases. The sour smell of fermenting mash hung heavy in the air.

"Luther, what're you doing up here with us outlaws?" Goat asked.

"Just helping out." Nearby stacked knee-high were full cases of mason jars ready to go. Ralphie started hoisting the liquor up onto the red Radio Flyer, the glass jars rattling.

"You don't need to be up here. You have an honest job," Goat replied.

"Foolishness," Luther's dad said, stalking toward them, waving a piece of firewood. "Plumb foolishness."

"I took a stand," Luther replied.

"Ah." Luther's dad waved a hand. "Striking from a good job. Unions and such. Causing trouble, and a man won't be able to go back to that job."

"Me? I'm not stepping on Cassidy's toes."

Cassidy Lane was the closest thing Bell County had to organized crime. Though he owned gas stations all the way to Knoxville, everyone knew Cassidy's real money came from the bootlegging, gambling, and whoring he provided up on Kayjay Mountain. When preachers railed about a Sodom and Gomorrah in their midst, they were talking about Kayjay and Cassidy Lane.

"Ah, Cassidy just likes talking big," Luther's dad said, turning away from his son. In the glint of the light, Goat saw the smooth brown grip of a pistol poking out of the old man's back pocket.

Luther opened his mouth and closed it. Shaking his head, he turned away to help load the wagon. Goat figured the two had gone round and round as much about the father's making white lightning as they did about Luther's striking.

Deciding to stay out of the fight, Goat told Luther's daddy, "I'll have your money in two days, as soon as I run this load down to Jellico."

"Mama's wanting you to come to supper," Luther's daddy said.

Goat smiled. "I'll pay you then."

"You're ready," Luther said. Moving to the front of the wagon, Goat took over. Just like in the Pontiac parked below, when there was whiskey onboard, Goat drove.

"See you boys," Goat said. Putting his back into it, he swung the wagon in a tight circle with Ralphie pushing. As they headed down the trail, Goat glanced back in time to see Luther's silhouette raise a hand just before the tarp dropped, blacking out the lanterns' glow. With the wagon loaded, going downhill was a lot quieter. The wheels squeaked less, and the heavy load made Ralphie concentrate more on steadying the wagon and less on talking.

Halfway down the mountain, Ralphie finally spoke in a whisper. "I don't want to cross Cassidy Lane."

"We aren't," Goat answered. "And there won't be any trouble."

The words were still in the air when a distant gunshot cracked the night. Goat's first thought was that a pocket of sap in a log had popped in the flames at the still, but even as he thought this, the whole mountaintop erupted in a flurry of gunfire. The first gun was joined by the deep booming of shotguns and the long burps of a tommy gun on rock and roll, something straight from Nam. A mad minute. Dumping all of your ammo into a kill zone. Pure insanity firing until the wood stocks smoked and the barrels sizzled.

Goat turned the wagon and ran it off the path. Ralphie stood unmoving on the trail. Goat grabbed the teenager's shirt and yanked Ralphie over and down to the ground with him.

"A raid?" Ralphie gasped. Their faces were so close that Goat smelled the sweat beading on the young man's upper lip.

Goat shook his head. Neither the police nor the Revenuers did a raid like this. Sure they'd shoot you, but they wouldn't gun you down. The gunfire rose to a crescendo; then, as suddenly as it started, it stopped, leaving only the echoes bouncing back and forth in the hills.

Ralphie said, "We have to go back. We gotta help."

Goat shook his head. He knew the reality of killing. Up on the hill, armed men were doing the business of murder.

"We got..." The words died. Ralphie's Adam's apple bobbed up and down.

"They're dead," Goat said harshly. "They're all dead and we can't help a bit. What we gotta do is get off this mountain." Pulling Ralphie in his wake, Goat slipped back onto the trail.

In the heavy summer air, gun smoke drifted down the hill like a mist, the smell bringing an adrenaline dump and a rush of memories. Thumping helicopter blades beating the air as they dropped into an LZ. Orange muzzle flashes and the steady climb of an M16 on full auto during a firefight.

With Ralphie in tow, Goat moved quickly down the path, his eyes scanning for the irregular shape of a human. His ears strained to hear the snap of twigs or the racking of a gun. At the bottom of the hill, they paused to catch their breath.

The night was silent. Even the running water in the creek was holding its breath. No animals hooted or scurried.

Without speaking a word, Goat and Ralphie shared the same knowledge.

The four men they had just left were dead.

Chapter 2

Goat drove alone, the moonlight ticking through the trees, blackness and a milky slash alternating across the GTO's hood. White. Black. White. Black.

Goat and Ralphie had slipped down the hill to where the GTO was hidden. With the headlights off, they made their getaway by creeping down the winding road until they hit the main road, where Goat snapped on the lights and sped away. After making Ralphie promise not to tell a soul what had happened, Goat dropped his cousin off at the mouth of his holler.

Leaning down into the car, Ralphie asked, "Was it like that... over there?"

Goat knew what he meant. Vietnam. "Some. And sometimes worse."

Without a word, Ralphie closed the GTO's door and trudged into the darkness.

And Goat drove the night away. The slash of the moon's bone light and the ink of dark night played out across his windshield.

Black.

White.

The windshield awash in light.

Awash in darkness.

As the GTO's tires rolled along eating up the miles, the wheels in Goat's head ate up time. He thought of Luther, not as the man he'd seen just a few hours ago, but as the boy he'd met in a schoolyard wearing hand-me-down clothes and a serious look in his eyes. Goat thought of how Luther's daddy had helped him out, schooling him on making shine and teaching him how to handle a car with a full load. Goat's own father had died in the mine when a slate of coal broke free and crushed him, so Luther's dad helped fill a gap that Goat needed filled as a boy. Then there were the memories of the recent past in Southeast Asia; Goat knew the country had taken part of his soul. Driving, Goat let his mind ramble and bounce about as night gave way to morning.

At daybreak, he pulled into a filling station on a mountain road. As he pumped gas, the road rumbled like a freight train, and he shielded his eyes as a line of big coal trucks thundered down the road in convoy. The trucks were placarded for the Blue Diamond Mine. Luther's employer. Each truck had a driver and a passenger, and the passengers all had rifles poking out the truck windows. Bell County was one incident away from a full-blown coal war. Goat watched the trucks roll past, but his mind was elsewhere, had latched onto a memory. During the Tet offensive, Goat had found himself fighting alongside a unit of MPs. During one of the lulls, he had talked to the lieutenant, a Yankee from Boston named Cuddy, who said he was going to be an investigator. Goat didn't understand much about investigating, and John Cuddy had simplified it for him—you ask questions to find answers, but mainly you kick stuff around, hoping to stir things up.

Goat planned on stirring things up.

Chapter 3

Goat didn't want to go back. He had enough visions of dead men in his head, and he didn't want any more. Steeling himself, he went up the hill. The Radio Flyer was still half on the trail, half off in the weeds, just as he'd left it. Pausing, Goat put a hand on the cases of whiskey and used the tail of his shirt to wipe the sweat out of his eyes. Looking up the hill, he saw the green tarp hanging from a tree and flapping in the breeze. His mouth was dry, his throat constricted. Taking a deep breath, he left the Radio Flyer and slowly walked up the trail, keeping his eye on the edge of the swaying tarp.

Up close, he saw the tarp had been shredded by bullets. It was splashed with brown stains drying sticky, and flies congregated over the blood. The two old men with their well-worn white shirts lay next to their stools. One had fallen right and one had fallen left. One was facedown, and the other on his back with his arm thrown over his head. The still was riddled with bullet holes, and the stack of finished moonshine was toppled over, glass and cardboard scattered on the ground. The raw scent of fermenting mash, the smell of moonshine from smashed mason jars, was overpowered by the copper tang of spilled blood.

Luther and his daddy were farther away from the still. Luther was on his back, arms splayed, a single gunshot in his forehead.

Tears burned Goat's cheeks.

Luther's daddy was a few yards back down the hill, facedown, one arm stretched out toward his son.

Goat knelt in the open space between Luther's body and the old man's. Flies buzzed incessantly, but it was no match for the buzzing in his mind. A sob came from his chest, popping out of his mouth like an air bubble. He drove his fingers into the dirt and rocks and leaves, pushing his anger into the ground. Grinding his teeth. Following the sob came a long moan that turned into a primal scream. He shouted until his lungs hurt and he could no longer make a sound. His outburst scattered a flock of crows in the trees, their black ragged wings flapping as they dove and cawed through the valley.

Silence returned.

Goat pushed the rage back into the dark box in his chest. Calmly, he stood and surveyed the killing ground. Instead of seeing the sunlight streaming through the trees, Goat imagined the scene as it had been the night before. Darkness. Lanterns lighting the still operation.

Luther and his daddy were at the far edge of the light, almost into the trees. Luther heard the killers come. He went to check it out. His father followed. Goat remembered hearing the shot that at the time he'd mistaken for a popping in the fire. Now he saw it differently. That had been the first shot.

Maybe Luther's daddy had pulled his gun and that started the shooting. *No, wait,* Goat thought, looking at the bodies. The brown grip of the revolver stuck out of the old man's back pocket. Untouched. Turning his attention to Luther, Goat again saw his friend had been shot dead center in his forehead. An aimed shot. Aimed shots worked only at the start of an ambush, because once the firing got going, people bobbed and weaved, scrambled away. Luther was killed first. The leader of the killers shot Luther and that had been the signal to open fire. Then the mad minute of pure murder.

Goat moved forward to the crest of the wooded hill, his eyes scanning the ground. His gaze found a cluster of golden brass glistening. Squatting, he checked the pile of brass. There were six empty .357 Magnum casings. A revolver. Probably the leader's whose shot started the ambush. Goat stood and moved farther and found scattered, empty shotgun shells — 12-gauge double-aught buck. Man killers. More gold-glinting brass in the grass caught his attention, and he scooped one up, a .45 ACP. This brass was scattered everywhere. Goat knew he was right: One killer had used a Thompson submachine gun. Goat knew the sound of a tommy gun because he had carried one during the Tet street fighting.

He moved back down the hill and knelt beside Luther. Lightly, he rested a hand on his friend's cold chest. He continued on, stopping at Luther's daddy. This time, he pulled the revolver from the dead man's pocket. It was long-barreled Colt .38, the finish dulled and dinged.

"I'm going to kill 'em," Goat said out loud. Tucking the revolver into his belt, he repeated, "I'm going to kill every last one of them."

Chapter 4

"Goat, that's a pretty car," Clarence said. Goat was tilted back in the barber chair, hot lather on his face, Clarence's straight razor glinting three inches above. Poised.

"Thanks." His GTO sat at the curb right next to the striped

barber pole of Clarence's shop. The three wooden chairs lining the wall were held down by a trio of old men who spent their days spreading gossip. Goat needed information and he knew these old men knew more about what was going on than anyone else.

"That's not the one the revenuers took?" Clarence asked.

Goat waited until Clarence slid the razor across his chin, scraping as he went.

"Naw, that was a '61 New Yorker," Goat answered. He had loved that car. The New Yorker had lots of room in the trunk, and with double springs and shocks and a tuned-up engine, the car was fast enough for Goat to outrun any lawman in Kentucky and Tennessee, even hauling a full load of shine. Until the night he ran out of gas trying to outrun the law.

Clarence nodded, looking down at Goat over his half-glasses. "Yup, I remember now." Clarence damn well knew Goat had bought the car from Luther's daddy and hauled the man's shine. After all, Goat had delivered Clarence's stash of shine even before he could drive, pedaling his bike to the barbershop twice a week.

The newspaper in Goat's lap was folded open to the moonshine-murder story. It was two days since an anonymous call had led the state police to the massacre at the moonshine still. Goat thought the story was pretty much right, except for the police's claim that the killer had called in the murders. Goat figured the police were doing the same thing he'd been doing when he called in the murder: stirring things up. Just like he knew coming to the barbershop would cause a stir.

Goat stared out the window across the Pineville town square to the courthouse, where a dozen cop cars sat. The paper reported that the state police were bringing more troopers to Bell County to keep the peace. With striking miners and rumors of northern organizers trying to start up unions in Bell County, there were fears. After all, unions were just a step away from communism. With blown-up coal trucks and miners beaten on the strike lines, tensions were high, and now with the four men killed in the moonshine murders, the state police were trying to make sure things stayed cool in the summer heat. At least that's how the newspaperman had put it.

"A shame about them boys," Clarence said, trying for nonchalant. Goat waited as Clarence did his thing with two more swipes of the razor. He kept his eyes glued to the cop cars across the way, pretending not to be paying much attention to Clarence. "Weren't you and that one boy, Luther, friends?"

"Yup," he answered, feeling the barber's eyes on him. Goat watched as the side door to the courthouse opened and three men in uniforms came out. All three paused to shake out smokes.

"I knew his daddy was making moonshine, but I didn't know the boy was helping—did you?" Clarence asked. The trio of cops fired up their smokes and headed across the square.

Before Goat could answer Clarence, one of the men in the chairs behind him said, "Hell, everyone knew Luther was making deliveries for his daddy."

"I didn't," Clarence said.

"Oh, yeah," said the man Goat couldn't see. "Just a few jars. Like the milkman going door to door. I think everyone in my rooming house, including the teacher, was buying his liquor."

"I thought the boy was one of those agitators," another man said. Goat hated that he couldn't see who was talking behind him, but he didn't dare move with Clarence's straight razor working.

"Luther was no communist agitator," Clarence said. "He just wanted a good job."

"What are you talking about?" Goat asked, perplexed.

"Northerner socialists down here trying to get the miners unionized," the second old man explained. "Agitators."

"The mine owners want the unions stopped?" Goat asked.

There was a snort. "They want it nipped in the bud."

The three cops were on a direct course for the barbershop.

"Shame about them boys," Clarence repeated, taking the last of the shaving cream off Goat's face with a flourish of his razor.

"It is a shame," Goat said, pointedly nodding toward the approaching cops. "Think they'll find out who did it?"

There was another snort from one of the old men.

Clarence took a warm towel and patted Goat's face. "Everyone knows who had them boys killed." He looked to the approaching cops. "Even they know."

One of the men said, "Everyone knew that old man was making shine and not paying his due. If we knew, Cassidy knew."

Cassidy Lane.

The three cops stopped at the square as a farm truck rolled by. Two of them were state troopers in their gray uniforms and Smokey Bear hats. The last man, in a tan uniform, was Aaron Grubbs, chief deputy under the Bell County sheriff.

"You think Cassidy had them killed?" Goat asked.

"There any doubt?" Clarence asked just before the bell above the door jingled.

What Clarence didn't say but every man in the room knew was that Aaron Grubbs ran protection for Cassidy Lane. If Grubbs was involved in the investigation, there would never be any arrests in the murders on the mountain.

Raising his voice, the barber said, "Afternoon, Officers." He pulled the warm towel from Goat's face, threw it over his shoulder.

"How long a wait for a haircut?" the tall blond trooper said.

"We're all done here," Clarence said, spinning Goat's chair so he could see the haircut and shave in the mirror. Goat nodded before he stood.

"I told you Clarence would take care of you," Chief Deputy Grubbs said. Shifting his attention to Goat, he asked, "Is that your hot rod out front there?"

"Yes, sir," Goat answered, standing.

"One of those '65 Pontiacs?" Grubbs asked. His voice was thin and reedy. He rested his left hand on the butt of the big old Smith & Wesson holstered at his hip.

"It's a '66," Goat replied. The blond trooper removed his hat and took a seat in the barber's chair.

"Don't look like she's got much wear," Grubbs said. "But then I've not seen you around. Heard the judge sent you to Vietnam."

"He did," Goat replied as he paid the barber. "Now I'm back."

"Weren't you running shine for that old man that got himself killed?"

"No, sir," Goat lied, forcing a smile. "I'm making up for lost time, chasing girls and driving my hot rod."

"That a fact?" Grubbs said, like he didn't believe Goat.

"That's a fact," Goat replied, staring the older man dead in the eye.

Clarence produced a fresh sheet and wrapped it around the blond trooper with a flourish. The second trooper hooked his thumbs in his gun belt, watching the exchange.

"We found a load of whiskey abandoned halfway down that hill," Grubbs said. "Word going around is that you were driving for the old man."

"Is that a fact?" Goat asked, still smiling.

"That's a fact," Grubbs said. "Why would someone leave whiskey?"

"Don't know," Goat responded, letting an edge creep into his voice. "You should ask Cassidy Lane."

Chief Deputy Grubbs's eyes narrowed, and his lips set into a hard thin line.

"Is that a fact?" the standing trooper said with an amused look.

"That's a goddamn fact," Goat said as he strode past the lawmen toward the door.

Chapter 5

Goat was scared. He had definitely stirred things up at Clarence's barbershop, and now he was going to shove a stick in the hornet's nest. He knew it was insane, and he could think of only one person crazy enough to go along with his idea.

Goat idled the GTO to a stop. A road sign hung by a single nail from a pole. Copperhead Road. The road wasn't more than twin ruts leading up a lonesome holler. Along the way were a few abandoned houses, falling down, left to the weeds and animals. Goat powered the Pontiac all the way to the flat top of a ridge where a simple house with a rusty tin roof sat. All the windows in the house were open, and the Doors' "L.A. Woman" rattled the window frames.

Goat killed the engine and laid on the horn. Jim Morrison and the boys dropped away. The screen door banged open.

The first thing Goat saw was the .45 dangling loose in the man's hand.

"Goat McKnight, is that you, boy?" the man said.

"It's me, Johnny Lee," Goat said, stepping out of the car.

"Come on in the house." The man waved with the pistol.

John Lee Pettimore was shirtless and deeply tanned. He had on tie-dyed jeans; his hair was down over his shoulders.

"Were you expecting company?" Goat asked as he walked into the house, which smelled like fried bologna, incense, and pot.

"Naw," Johnny Lee said, tucking the pistol into his waistband, moving in front of Goat, and leading the way. "But you never know when Charlie will get through the wire."

No one had ever accused John Lee Pettimore of being stable. In fact, people who knew him said he was crazier than a shit-house rat, and that was before he went to Vietnam.

The entryway in the hall was hung with beaded curtains. And there were hand-painted canvases on the wall. One had a dove and a scroll that said PEACE AND LOVE. Another had a psychedelic-colored peace sign.

"What you been up to since you got back, Goat?" Johnny Lee asked as he went through the beaded curtain and headed toward the back of the house.

"Same as before," Goat answered as he followed. "Running shine."

"Gotta do what you're meant to do," Johnny Lee said, opening the door at the end of the hallway. Goat followed John Lee into the room.

"You're here about what happened up on the hill." It was a statement, not a question.

Goat didn't answer. He was taking in the room. There wasn't any furniture. All of the windows were boarded up, and the only light was from a lone bulb hanging from the ceiling. Crowded around were brown wooden boxes with stenciling, green crates, and even a stainless steel coffin. Some of the boxes had U.S. Department of Defense markings, and some had Chinese letters. The open coffin was packed tight with black M16s.

"We going to hunt?" Johnny Lee Pettimore asked with a cracked smile.

"I aim to make things right," Goat replied, picking up a green plastic case that said FRONT TOWARD ENEMY. A claymore mine. Looking up, he said, "Holy shit, Johnny Lee."

"Gotta be ready for when Charlie comes through the wire."

Then Goat started explaining what he wanted to do. The more Goat talked, the wider Johnny Lee's grin grew, until it was a skull's leer, which confirmed what Goat had already known. This was an insane idea.

Chapter 6

Talk about being in the lion's den. The car parked at the bottom of the hill wasn't the one Goat expected. It wasn't the well-washed sheriff's cruiser of Chief Deputy Aaron Grubbs, but rather a battered Oldsmobile with two rough-looking men inside watching the road. All Goat had to say was that he wanted to drink and play poker, and they waved him on up Kayjay Mountain to Cassidy Lane's three-story place, lit up like a road-house with bright neon lights. The parking lot was half full, Goat noted as he got out of his car, glancing back once to see Johnny Lee's shadow slither out of the trunk and then disappear into the darkness. The inside of the bar was like any place allowed to sell liquor — and Bell County wasn't one of them — filled with men spending their money on the booze or the gam-bling in the back or both. And for more money, the women serving the drinks would take the men to rooms upstairs.

Goat scanned the bar and found another rough-looking man sitting on a stool in the corner, not drinking, his eyes sizing up the patrons. Stopping directly in front of the man, Goat said,

"Tell Cassidy that Goat McKnight's here about those four dead men up at that still."

The man looked at Goat, studied his face, and, without saying a word, got up and left. A few moments later the guy returned. "Come with me," he said, and led him to the back of the bar, where they took two flights of stairs to a landing and a closed door. The man knocked.

"Come in," a deep voice said. The man opened the door for Goat.

Goat went into Cassidy Lane's den. Cassidy was a big man, both tall and wide, with a visage that reminded Goat of Ben Franklin's. His hair wasn't as long as Franklin's, but it did grow thick on only the sides and back of his head, and with a pair of half-glasses perched halfway down his nose, Cassidy did resemble old Ben. Cassidy was sitting on a couch looking at some papers, his legs crossed and bouncing lightly to Frank Sinatra playing on the record player behind him. He stared at Goat over his glasses.

"You come to kill me?" Cassidy finally asked in his baritone voice, almost a bearlike rumble.

Before Goat could answer, he heard the click of a hammer and felt a gun barrel pushing into the back of his head. "Careful how you answer," the man behind him said. The man's hand ran over Goat's body until he found the Colt, which he pulled free.

Cassidy kept his eyes trained on Goat. "You here to kill me?"

Hoping his voice wasn't cracking, Goat said, "If you murdered my friends, then I am going to kill you dead."

"That's a powerful statement for a man in your predicament," Cassidy said. Casually, he reached behind him and turned off the stereo; the record slid to a stop. Turning his attention to the man behind Goat, Cassidy said, "Give me the iron."

The man handed the Colt to Cassidy. Nodding toward the pistol in his hand, Cassidy said, "You don't have any play left.

98

Now, you listen—I had nothing to do with those four men's deaths."

"Why should I believe you?" Goat asked.

"I don't give a damn if you believe me or not," Cassidy said. "I'm telling you the facts. And you best worry if you're going to walk out of here or get carried out."

"One more buried up here won't make a difference," the man behind Goat said, emphasizing his words with a push of the muzzle into Goat's neck.

Goat nodded once. "I don't know if I believe you. But let me tell you one thing."

"What's that?"

"You kill me, and I promise you hell's coming." Goat opened his hand to show a small whistle in his palm.

"What the hell's that?" Goat's captor piped up from behind him.

"In Vietnam, the Cong used whistles since their radios were so poor. It got to be when you heard one of these, you knew Charlie was coming."

"What's that mean?" Cassidy asked cautiously.

"That means John Lee Pettimore is somewhere close." Goat heard the man behind him take a breath. Most people knew of crazy Johnny Lee. "If I don't blow this whistle, he'll be coming to kill every son of a bitch in here."

Cassidy looked at Goat for a moment.

The man behind Goat said, "He's bluffing."

Cassidy looked past Goat and the man behind him and said, "I don't think so." Slowly, he set the revolver on the coffee table. "He's not bluffing."

"No, he's not, son," Johnny Lee said. Goat glanced over his shoulder. Standing in the open doorway was John Lee Pettimore decked out in camos and black face paint, a large Bren machine gun weighing heavy in his hands.

"The plan was the whistle," Goat said.

"I don't like waiting," Johnny Lee said, grinning.

Goat picked up the Colt from the table, tucked it back into his waistband, and asked Cassidy Lane, "You kill my friends?"

"I had no reason to kill them men. Bad for business to draw attention."

"What about the old man not paying you to run liquor?"

"Him running shine didn't hurt me none," Cassidy replied. "I liked the old man, and he brought me a case of his shine once a month. We respected each other. We had no fight."

"People said he wasn't paying your tithe and you were mad."

Cassidy snorted.

"What?"

"Aaron," the man said with a sneer. "He tells folks that."

"Grubbs?" Goat asked. "Why would your man say that?"

"He doesn't work for me anymore," Cassidy said. "He's going legit, running security for a mine."

"Which mine?" Goat asked, things already clicking into place.

"The Blue Diamond," Cassidy said. Goat saw his own epiphany reflected in Cassidy Lane's face. "He's trying to lay these murders on me. I'm going to kill him."

"No, you're not," Goat said. "I am."

Chapter 7

The whole apartment on the third floor of the rooming house was lit up. Goat sat at the small kitchen table keeping company with a jelly glass of moonshine from a jar he'd found under the sink. The apartment was silent, but Goat thought echoes of the woman's crying lingered in the air. Goat and Johnny Lee had left Kayjay Mountain driving like hell for town. Once the pieces came together, Goat saw the whole thing plainly. Just like if you stir up sand and water and then wait long enough, the particles settle and you can see right through. The picture was clear.

The tan of the NVA soldier's uniform that night.

Luther calling Ralphie's teacher by her name — Carrie Love.

Luther telling his father he was taking a stand.

The old men at the barbershop talking about Luther delivering moonshine door to door.

Luther being shot in the middle of his forehead.

The six .357 Magnum rounds found on the hill. A cop's gun.

Bell County miners striking and the worry about northern agitators organizing unions. The mine owners wanting to nip things in the bud.

The North Vietnamese soldier Goat glimpsed on the mountain was actually the tan sheriff's uniform of Aaron Grubbs.

And the fact that Chief Deputy Aaron Grubbs was working for the Blue Diamond mine — Luther's mine.

Goat and Johnny Lee found Carrie Love in her apartment, and between sobs, she confirmed his suspicions. In other parts of the country, every time people had come to help the miners, the mine owners had busted them up, shipped them out, or killed them. Carrie was a teacher but she was an activist first. She'd been asked to come down and help organize the miners, but she was told she had to be careful. Only a few knew of Carrie Love's role. Luther was tasked with carrying messages between Carrie Love and the striking miners. Luther took and delivered messages with the jars of moonshine. Someone had leaked word that Luther was doing more than striking, and Carrie figured the mine owners thought Luther was pulling the strings, that he was the one calling the shots. No one suspected the hippie teacher was the mastermind.

Nip the union organizing in the bud.

Everyone knew Luther was helping his dad make moonshine, so it wouldn't take much for Aaron Grubbs to find the moonshine still. Then he and some hired thugs slipped up that mountain. Goat had spotted Grubbs's tan sheriff's uniform as they were making their way up to kill Luther and anyone else at the still.

The steps outside creaked. Carrie Love's apartment was on the third floor of the building, and it was the only apartment that was serviced by a rickety staircase running on the outside of the house.

The killers were here.

Goat took a swallow of the moonshine, the whiskey cool on the way down his throat but burning once it hit his stomach.

Damn, Luther's daddy did make good liquor, he thought.

Before sending Carrie Love away with John Lee Pettimore in the GTO, Goat had had her make a call to Chief Deputy Grubbs. She told him she knew he had killed Luther. She told him she was scared, and she would give him all the paperwork she had on the miners and the organizers. She offered to trade the information for safe passage out of Bell County. Grubbs promised he'd let her leave once he had the papers.

The doorknob turned slightly as a hand tested the lock.

Then the hand knocked.

"Carrie," Aaron Grubbs said.

Goat glanced at the green square propped against the door. Wires led back to the plastic square in his hand. He pushed back from the table and stood, making sure to be loud. The killers outside would think Carrie Love was coming to answer the door.

Goat stepped behind the refrigerator and pulled the revolver from his waistband. With his other hand, he readied the mine's trigger.

Goat called out, "Grubbs, I'm going to kill you." Outside there were confused voices. Goat pushed the mine's trigger. *Clack-clack.*

The claymore had a warning on it: FRONT TOWARD THE ENEMY. The warning was there for a reason.

The claymore was a shaped charge of C-4 packed with hundreds of steel ball bearings, and they blew out in a scythe-like arc of destruction.

The explosion shook the whole house.

The apartment's front door was blown out and clouds swirled inside. His ears ringing, Goat moved forward, kicking through the remnants of the front door. Outside, part of the landing was shredded. Below, in the alley, two bodies still clutching shotguns were splayed out on the roof of Aaron Grubbs's cruiser. Partway down the stairs was a body, the man's chest pulped by the claymore's ball bearings. A broken Thompson submachine gun was on the step below the dead man.

The blast had knocked Chief Deputy Aaron Grubbs down the stairs, where he knelt as if praying. His face bloody, his body listing to and fro like a bobbing ship.

Goat cocked the Colt.

Grubbs looked up and saw Goat. Tried to stagger to his feet, but stumbled and fell.

With the comforting weight of the Colt in his hand, Goat McKnight started down the stairs.

RIVER SECRET

BY ANNE SWARDSON

She took one tiny step toward me. Another—then hesitated. Her mother leaned down and murmured a few words in her ear. Reassured, the girl toddled forward more confidently and then, halfway to where I was playing, stopped again.

She wore a white wool coat that reached almost to her knees. A few strands of curly brown hair escaped from the fur around her hood, which had been carefully tied at the neck. By her sleek-haired mother, probably. Those dimpled hands were too little to tie anything.

Fortunately for me, they could hold a two-euro coin.

The child looked at her mother again. It was time to reel her in. I ended "Sous le Ciel de Paris" a verse early—kids never went for the melancholy material—and put the accordion down on its stand with a click. The girl turned her eyes back to me. I transitioned into 2/4 rhythm with the foot pedal on the bass drum. After picking up the trombone, I launched into the "Bayrische Polka," keeping the oompah with the drum, adding a cymbal stroke to each downbeat with my other foot, and bobbing forward each time the slide came out with a wailing *mwaa-mwaa*.

A big smile appeared on the little girl's face. She walked confidently to the beret lying upside down on the bricks in front of me and dropped in the coin. I grinned too and gave her another duck, almost a half bow, with a forward slide of the trombone. The girl looked amused, then beckoned her mother to come as she held out her hand for another coin.

"Maman!"

A few more spectators peeled off from the stream of Paris tourists who were coming down the steps of the Solférino footbridge over the Seine on their way to the tunnel leading to the Tuileries Garden. They joined the gaggle of Americans in tracksuits around me and my drums, horns, and stands, attracted by the polka lilt and by the exquisite little girl standing before me.

My location, at the entrance to the underground passage between the bridge and the stairs to the gardens, was the best in the business. When I blew a long note on the trumpet, the tones reverberated off the rounded tunnel ceiling. The cymbals were sharper, the drums crisper because of those acoustics. The river's flowing water gave a sense of space and openness. And with my back to the passage wall, I could spot the oncoming Italians in high-heeled sandals, the rotund British, and the tall Dutch wearing backpacks, and then adjust the musical selection accordingly.

Still, each day I needed something special to get an audience going, something to lure a real crowd around me. I needed that more than most, since I never sang, only played. The more people, the more likely I could pass the hat at the end of a set. It was always more lucrative than just waiting for the coins to drop in one by one.

If I was lucky, that moment had arrived.

But Maman wasn't about to chip in another coin. She was

distracted by a squat woman wearing a kerchief over her hair. In her grimy fingers, the woman held out a dull, gold-looking ring as she sidled closer to her target.

"Mais, madame, see voo play, madame, madame..." The woman didn't pronounce the words properly. Half her teeth were missing. Even though it was March, she was wearing sandals, without socks, along with a moth-eaten sweater and a long skirt with faded yellow flowers.

"Leave us alone, you disgusting thing! We're just trying to enjoy the music!" Maman held up a forbidding hand as the beggar took a step closer, waving the ring and giving a sidelong glance in the direction of the lady's Hermès handbag.

The mother tossed her head, cinched the tie of her cashmere coat, put one hand firmly around the clasp of her purse, and held out the other to her daughter. "Come, Marie-Christine. Let's go watch the boys sail the boats in the basin." The little girl ran to her, and without another look at me they were gone, up the steps and into the gardens. I tried to save the day by playing "Hello, Dolly," replete with plenty of slides and bass thumps, but it didn't help. The crowd melted away. There was silence.

Only the kerchiefed woman was left standing there. She looked at me like a whipped dog, her head down, barely meeting my eyes. I stared angrily. I didn't speak, because I never did. I didn't cross my arms or shake my finger at her, as I had sometimes done before. But she knew she had driven away my clientele, and she knew I was angry. It was one of our agreements. She was supposed to do her job, and I would do mine.

She twisted her hands in her skirt and sighed.

"I'm sorry, Baptiste. I thought I could help. Top us up a little."

Why I had decided to extend a hand to Tatiana I will never know. I had everything I wanted: a city license to play my one-man setup in a rainproof location that sucked in half the tourists in Paris; enough money to pay for my tiny studio in the Eighteenth Arrondissement and for the frozen dinners I bought each night at the Picard store. There was enough to send to my family in the south too, back when I used to do that. Back when I talked to them. Back when I talked. Before my memory told me I should speak no longer.

I nodded firmly toward the gardens and she knew what I meant: "Leave my customers alone. If people pay you for those stupid rings, they won't pay me for my music. And they certainly won't put money in my beret if they find their wallets missing."

She shuffled off slowly, cowering as she went. I turned back to my instruments, my anger passing. She needed the money more than I did, and every coin she pickpocketed in the park reduced the number I felt compelled to slip her at the end of the day.

Maybe I shared with Tatiana because no one else would. Gypsies are human rats, I'd heard the policemen say after they'd chased the beggars, pickpockets, and scamsters from the gardens. Send them back where they came from. Don't touch them; they're dirty. Even American tourists, the most gullible of all the nationalities that walked by me, eyed the rings the Gypsies proffered with suspicion, then turned their backs and patted their wallets.

So Tatiana got a few coins from me each day, coupled with a warning that if she ever stole from me, she'd never see another euro. She understood everything from my face, my gestures. I'd give her a shake of the head when I wanted her elsewhere, a tilt when a good potential mark walked by. I'd bring her the odd bit of *poulet rôti* from my previous night's dinner, a thin blanket when I had bought a new one.

What Tatiana mostly got from me was something no one else

gave her: an ear. As I packed up each night, she'd come by and tell me in broken French about her life: growing up in a camp outside Plovdiv, making her way with others of her kind in a series of ragtag caravans from Bulgaria, across Hungary, over the Austrian Alps, then here. Camping, stealing, camping. Along the way there had been a man, and a child or two. She didn't know where they were now.

———

I SAW THE little girl again not long after that. It was warmer, but she still wore the white coat. She was with her mother, and so was a handsome black-haired young man—younger than the woman. His arm was wrapped around the waist of his companion. His eyes were on the woman's face; his hand was atop the little girl's head, stroking her hair.

I wasted no time in pulling out the trombone and starting up the polka.

"Maman!"

The girl pointed to me and made an excited little jump. The Mother—what else could I call her?—reached for her purse, but the man pushed her hand away. Fishing in his pocket, he pulled out a pink ten-euro note and inserted it in the little girl's fist. He took her other hand in a firm grip, plastered a big smile on his face, and started walking with her across the paving stones toward my waiting beret. I kept up the beat. Tatiana, happily, was nowhere to be seen.

The child lost enthusiasm with each step. The farther she got from her mother, the more her feet dragged, the more she tried to turn back. Her face twisted into a pout. The beret was forgotten. The man kept the smile fixed in place and continued forward, pulling on her hand, trying to ignore her reluctance. The tourists were nudging one another and pointing.

The conflict ended when the girl stopped moving her feet entirely and collapsed on the ground, wailing. The man bent over her, ostentatiously trying to pick her up and get her pointed toward me, wrapping his arms around her and lifting. But she pulled away, dropped the ten-euro bill, and darted toward the Mother. When she got there, she buried her face in the cashmere coat. The woman made a gesture of resignation and picked up the sobbing girl, draping her over her shoulder as the man picked up the money and then rejoined them. They walked up the steps, side by side, the ten-euro note still in the man's hand. I had warned Tatiana away from the mother, but I wished she were nearby now so that I could nod my head toward that prey.

She came to my stand late that day as I was breaking down the equipment. Business had been good, she said. For me too. My pockets dragged with change, from yellow fifty-centime pieces to two-euro coins. I even had a few bills. As we sometimes did, we dragged my drum case and horn bags around the corner and sat on one of the concrete benches overlooking the Seine.

We often ended the day like that when the weather was good and the cops didn't chase us away. The setting sun shone pinkly on the cream-colored stone buildings across the river: the Beaux Arts rail-station structure of the Musée d'Orsay; next to it the squat headquarters of the Légion d'honneur. To the left, upriver, were the towers of Notre-Dame; to the right, the glass-paned cavernous roof of the Grand Palais, French flag flying atop.

The river itself was a sight to see. At this time of year, the Seine was fed by runoff from the mountains. A deep and viscous brown, the water was almost level with the cobbled walkway along the banks. The current slurped against the bridge's pilings and pushed against the prows of the Bateaux-Mouches as they slid up and down the waterway with their cargoes of tourists.

"Look at this," Tatiana said, lifting her skirt and taking her earnings out of a pocket sewn inside. "There was a guy waving a ten-euro bill around and when he put it in his pocket he left a corner hanging out. He never even saw me."

I clapped her on the back.

———

THE MOTHER, THE man—I'd named him Romeo—and the little girl came by on their way to the gardens often in the month that followed. They—at least the child and her mother—probably lived in the Seventh Arrondissement, on the other side of the footbridge, in one of those apartments with ten-foot ceilings. People in those apartments wore cashmere coats and dressed their little girls in clothing from Tartine et Chocolat, the fancy children's store on the boulevard Saint-Germain.

Romeo must have learned his lesson, because he never again tried to bring the girl to the beret. She let him hold her hand across the bridge, the Mother alongside. Then she always walked up to me alone. I'd play the polka and do my bobbing routine. It got to be a game: She'd smile at me and I'd respond with a couple of little dance steps and a trombone wail. More steps toward me and I'd twirl around. The girl would laugh and put a coin in. I felt like laughing myself, for the first time in years. Unlike my older fans, who seemed almost ashamed to be giving money to a beggar, albeit a musical one, the child looked straight into my face. Her expression, a kind of puckery smile with a flash of her blue eyes, made me imagine that she knew how much those coins meant to me.

On a gray day in April, I was just finishing a set with "La Vie en Rose" when I saw that the child was there, standing a bit in front of the usual bunch of tourists. Next to her was Romeo. No sign of the Mother. His hair was slicked back from his forehead in an expensive cut. My audience was with me; they had clapped to the theme from *Can-Can* and laughed when I swayed during the refrain of "I Love Paris." I'd lose them if I played the polka. Instead, I just winked at the child, and she smiled at me. She seemed unperturbed that her mother wasn't there. One hand held on to the hand of the man, who looked down at her as if he couldn't believe he'd won her over. Her other hand fiddled with a heart-shaped locket I'd never seen before and that I could tell was gold.

The girl gave me a bill this time, another ten-euro note from Romeo's wallet, and then they walked up the stairs and into the gardens. As they moved out of view, the man picked her up and whispered something in her ear.

The money flowed in that day. No sooner had one group left after a set than another would form around me, sometimes even before I'd started playing again. By late afternoon, I must have had forty people watching. I treated them to a jazz improv on the trombone, with only the cymbal tracking. I didn't try that often, but the crowd was with me.

Suddenly, sirens wailed from the gardens. A voice thundered from the public-address system; I couldn't make out the words. The *pah-paw* of police cars and fire trucks could be heard in the distance, then on the road above the tunnel. Two uniformed cops raced in from the bridge and rushed up the tunnel stairs, taking them two at a time as the tourists gawked. Just after the cops entered the tunnel, the great grilled gates, the ones that closed the park off from the bridge each evening, began sliding shut.

The tourists scattered in confusion. I could still hear noise from the gardens, but it was a muffled rumble. I was locked outside. This was not convenient: I'd have to drag my stuff along the quay and around the west side of the Tuileries to get to the Metro if I couldn't cross the park. Where was Tatiana? I had never before seen the gates close early. I began packing up.

There was a rat-a-tat, and one more set of racing footsteps sounded from the bridge. I turned and saw that they weren't being made by a late cop. The Mother, her face streaked with tears, coat hanging open, lipstick smeared, a cell phone in one hand, ran across the cobblestones in high heels and threw herself against the barred gate.

"My baby! My baby!" It was more a howl than a scream, a noise like no sound I had ever heard. "Let me in!" She hung on the bars as if without them she would melt to the ground.

Two uniformed policemen trotted down the stairs on the other side of the gate and came toward her. I could hear more shouts; someone was ordering that the gates be opened. The cops reached out through the grille and touched her hands. And I could hear some of the words they said to her:

"So terribly sorry."

"He says he only looked away for a second."

"We will find the villain who did this, madame."

———

MUSIC WAS THE only thing that ever filled me up inside. Even before the memories from my childhood came back and stopped my voice, even before the stairs and the tunnel and the broad river became my only horizons, nothing but music touched the hollow core inside me. That's why I learned so many instruments. Each one—not just my one-man-band ensemble, but the violin, the piano, the plaintive oboe—gave me a different facet of what others get from normal life. When I played, I felt complete.

But on this day, the day after the child, the day after the Mother stopped being a mother, I was just blowing air and whacking drums. The voice my instruments gave me was an ugly, blaring thing.

I had gone back to the bridge to work. What else was there to do? I played the most melancholy songs of my Edith Piaf repertoire. No polkas. I didn't even touch the trombone. It seemed unfair that the park was open as usual and that the beret filled up, even though I wasn't twirling, or bobbing, or smiling. How could those tourists be unaware that my music was crying, not singing? But I couldn't leave, couldn't go away from the last place I had seen her.

Around midday, a hard, thin man with steel-gray hair stepped up to where I was playing. He wore an impeccably pressed navy suit with a tiny square of yellow silk handkerchief poking from the jacket pocket. With him were a chubby sergeant in uniform and a thuggish lieutenant in a leather jacket. The small crowd around me dissipated as soon as they approached.

"I am Commander Bassin," the suited man said. "Are you acquainted with a Tatiana Plevneliev?" He pronounced the name as if his lips had never had to speak such horrible syllables before.

I had assumed the police would question me about the child. But why were they asking about Tatiana?

He got a nod of the head. It was tempting to deny our acquaintance, but the park cops had seen us together too many times.

"How does she make her living?"

I held out my hand, palm upward.

Bassin raised an eyebrow. The sergeant murmured something in his ear.

"They say you don't speak."

I shook my head.

"Are you physically incapable of speech or do you choose not to speak?"

I shrugged.

"I have to tell you, Monsieur...Baptiste, this is a very serious matter."

I put my arm to my side, palm out flat.

"Yes, it's about the child. Did you ever see her with Madame Plevneliev?"

Enthusiastic shake no. It was true. There was nothing in children's pockets to pick. Tatiana would have focused only on Romeo.

"When did you last see her?"

When was it? Had she come by yesterday morning? I shrugged and jerked my thumb over my shoulder in a a-while-ago gesture.

"Monsieur Baptiste, you must search your memory. We know she was in the park yesterday. We want to know if she came this way."

Bassin was standing motionless, looking straight at me as the sergeant took notes. I wondered what you wrote down if the person being interrogated didn't speak.

Raising both hands, I shook my head again. Yesterday was filled with the child. I had no recollection of anything else. All I could see in my mind's eye was the white-coated figure in the arms of the man as he carried her into the park.

"Have you ever seen the Gypsy with children?"

Children? My heart turned cold. I could see where he was heading, and it was very bad. No, I hadn't. I tried to shake my head as definitively as I could.

But I had a question. I clasped one hand in the other, one elbow high, the other low, then made a gesture straight back from my forehead as if slicking back my hair. Bassin looked puzzled for a second, then the sergeant whispered again.

"It's not something you need to know," Bassin told me. "But yes, Monsieur de Marigny says he saw her near the child." That wasn't quite what I was asking. But it sounded like the police had found Monsieur Romeo de Marigny to be a very helpful witness.

Bassin left without a look behind him, entourage trailing along.

It was another two days before a park cop told me what had happened. The child had been strangled, and her body had been found in one of the service closets dug into the high walls enclosing the Tuileries. Romeo had alerted the park police that she had vanished when his attention was briefly distracted by a Gypsy. The girl's gold locket was gone. And when the cops searched every Gypsy in the park, which was of course the first thing they did, they found the necklace. In the pocket that Tatiana had sewn on the inside of her skirt. Which Tatiana was wearing.

———

I DIDN'T VISIT her in prison, even though I was sure she was innocent. Gypsies lied, scammed, cheated, robbed, maybe even roughed people up a bit. I had known dozens during my years by the river. They didn't kill.

But even had I been able to tear myself off the tracks that marked my life — home, river, home — to make the one-hour trip to her holding center in Fontainebleau, there was nothing I could do. Tatiana had no more chance of escaping this charge than she had of growing new teeth. No antidiscrimination group would speak up for her, no well-meaning citizen would collect signatures on a petition for her, no politician would stand up in the parliament building across the river and rail against the false charges. When Tatiana told her questioners about finding the necklace on one of the park's pathways, even she probably knew that they wouldn't believe her.

I could imagine her in her pretrial appearances before the judges, looking nowhere but at the floor, twisting her skirt in her hands. Had they given her clean clothes to wear? Did she try to speak? Did her lawyer even make an effort? The front pages of the crumpled newspapers that the wind blew up on the embankment showed her photo more days than not: climbing into a police van, surrounded by hard-faced policewomen who seemed to be shoving a little too hard.

Until one day the front-page photo was of only her face, and what the article said was that she had died.

A brain aneurysm in the middle of the night. The authorities said she had gotten the best of care. The authorities said the case was now closed. I put the newspaper into the yellow recycling can on the other side of the tunnel and walked back to my stand and played something or other on my trumpet for the rest of the day.

It wasn't long after that that I saw the Mother — the Woman now, I guess. She was standing on the bridge, looking east toward Notre-Dame. She was alone, and silent, and thin. Spring had come and gone; it was July. The sun glittered on the river; it was one of those rare days when the water looked almost blue. The faint chatter of the tourists wafted down to me from the bridge. She paid no attention.

I picked up the trombone and began the "Bayrische Polka," looking straight up at her in the distance, ignoring the crowd of camera-pointing Chinese and sounding the notes as loud as I could. At first, it seemed as if the music didn't reach her. Then she slowly turned her head toward me and stared motionless for a long time. It was not until the last chorus that she lifted her hand and gave me a gentle wave.

Romeo turned up too, a week or so after that. I didn't see him at first. He was hanging back in the crowd a bit, as if he were trying to stay out of sight. As I played, I could feel, rather than see, him circling around the watching tourists, coming to rest behind a family of what must have been Americans. A smile was forming on his lips. They had two children, an elementary-school-age boy and a smaller girl. She had blond curly hair and looked like she might have been in kindergarten.

That was enough.

Right in the middle of "Les Rues de Paris," I put down the trumpet and rose from my stool. I walked through the ranks of astonished tourists, parting them with my hands and breaking through to the back of the crowd. I stood in front of him.

He tried to push by me, but I moved sideways and he stopped, the river on his other side.

I opened my mouth. Breathed in. Made a little cough; breathed again.

"M...M...Monsieur." My voice rasped. "I...I have some information that I think you need to hear about the little g-girl in the white coat."

If I had had any doubt, his expression dispelled it.

"I don't know what you mean." The tourists were staring at us as intently as if I were playing my trombone from the bell end. I said nothing. Stared at him. He shifted on his feet. "The suspect died in prison. The case is closed."

I lowered my voice.

"Monsieur, I think it would be better if you heard what I have to say. Better that I tell it to you than..."

"All right, what do you want?" No smile now. His arms were folded, his head cocked, but his body was rigid with tension.

"Return tonight, at midnight. I will be here."

———

HE CAME NOT across the bridge but from the quay, skulking past the long line of moored houseboats, one behind another, the tables and flowerpots on their decks ghostly in the moonlight. I stood with my back to my instruments.

"I've seen men like you before," I said. "I know what you did."

"Is it money you want?"

"I want to know the truth."

"Truth? I don't know what that is. I loved her. Maybe a little too much—is that what you're asking? I only wanted to touch her for a second. Nothing bad. But if she'd told her mother... Anyway, what will it take for you not to squeal?"

He put his hand into the pocket of the loose jacket he was wearing. As he looked down, I made my move, even before I saw that he was pulling out a knife, not money.

And if someday a body surfaces far downriver from where I still ply my trade, or if the police drag the river for some poor drowned child or missing teenager and turn up the corpse of a young man instead, I hope they notice that the victim is not just another casualty of the muddy waters.

I hope they see on the left side of his head, just above his ear, a deep, slanted wound made with a blow of such force that it sliced, rather than cracked, his skull. A blow struck with the force of love, and pain, and decades of pent-up silence.

I hope whoever finds him will know what went into that blow.

And every day now, the tourists who gather around to see me play and bow and bob can witness the other consequence of that force. My polka renditions are a little tinny, a little off-key. The music just doesn't sound the same now that the bell end of my trombone is bent so badly.

But the notes that come out are still haunting.

HOT SUGAR BLUES

BY STEVE LISKOW

Bish Underwood hasn't told the girl on the couch a single lie yet, which is a very good sign. Of course, she's only been here ten minutes.

Bish has just done three encores to top off a two-hour set in Trenton—our thirty-fifth concert in forty-one days—and he's left them twitching in the aisles. The LP, which came out two days after we left home, has been in *Billboard*'s top five ever since, the last three weeks at number one. Bish is in full wind-down-at-the-end-of-the-tour mode, and he's already ordered champagne and bourbon and fruit and ice and God knows what else from room service.

He's ready to celebrate, and the girl looks like she can probably help him. The whole suite—928, because it's his lucky number—is thick with sweat and hormones.

But she insists that business comes first.

No, not like that. Bishop Underwood has six platinum LPs under his belt, so he never has to pay for it. But this chick's a freelancer with the green light for an interview from *Rolling*

Stone, and that means they talk on the couch before they talk on the pillows.

I want to go to bed with someone too, and plenty of women have slipped by security and are patrolling the halls ready to help me do just that, but I'm Bishop's manager and he's never been good at editing his mouth, so I don't go away until this girl turns off her tape recorder and closes her notebook. What happens after that is *her* business.

"You were a folksinger first." She's done her homework. "Why did you switch to electric? Did Bob Dylan show you that was the way to go?"

"Sorta." Bish has his feet on the coffee table and is trying to entice her closer, but she's sitting at the far end of the couch, long legs in tight jeans, ending in scuffed sneakers mere inches from his right hand. Even dressed casual, she can put the groupies outside to shame. A blind man couldn't miss what she's got, and Bish is not blind, especially when it comes to women. He's still wearing the white shirt and leather pants from the show, the debauched-preacher look. And he plays the blues like nobody else can since Michael Bloomfield died in that car last year.

"See, Jack and me, we'd been playing the Village—that's Greenwich Village—and all the coffeehouses in the Northeast for about three years, but we were doing traditional stuff, Kingston Trio, Pete Seeger, the Limeliters, nothing original."

The girl doesn't look old enough to know any of them. Barely old enough to drink, but beautiful. She has skin the color of a sunburst Les Paul, but her delicate nose shows there's some white blood in her too, maybe a while back. All the groupies are doing the big-poufy-hair thing now, but she's cut hers short so it frames her face; eyes like lumps of coal on their way to becoming diamonds. She looks so natural and real that something in me wants to cry.

"Until Dylan," she says again. Her voice sounds a little too deep to be coming from her slight frame under that white silk blouse. She's hung her corduroy jacket in the closet and rolled up her sleeves like she's ready to play some serious poker and wants us to know she doesn't have to cheat.

"Yeah," Bish says. "He showed us we could write our own songs and still be legit. Authentic, you know?"

He tries to untie her shoelaces, but she pulls her feet away. Her flirty-playful eyes tell him to keep talking.

"So we wrote a few things of our own. The first ones were pretty bad, but we started to get a feel for it."

Actually, *I* got a feel for it. Bish sang lead, so people thought he wrote them. What the hell—my name was on them, so I could live with it.

That was until the pigs busted me with a nickel bag in Georgia. Drugs, Deep South, 1964, you do the math. They tossed me in a cell with half a dozen other guys, some of them inbred, most of them black, all of them drooling for a piece of the college kid. Bish wouldn't go my bail until I signed over the rights to the songs, and I knew that one way or another, I was going to get screwed. I still feel a little twinge when one of those songs pops up on an oldies station.

" 'Rainbow Girl,' " the girl says. Shonna Lee, her name is, just a hint of drawl she hasn't quite buried. "And 'Quicksilver Romance.' "

"You've studied up on me, haven't you, missy?" Next to hers, his drawl sounds fake. Well, we both grew up in New England and met at Columbia. But it's his bluesman image.

He's got hold of her foot now, getting the lace untied, and she's not struggling. He pulls her sneaker off and I hear a knock on the door.

The room-service guy rolls in a cart with enough stuff to feed a platoon: sweating silver bucket with a magnum of Moët, a fifth of Jim Beam Black, a cut-glass bowl overflowing with apples, cherries, lemons, oranges, strawberries, melon balls, and sliced pineapple on crushed ice. Plates, silverware, fancy pastries, sliced cheese, whipped cream, a big urn of coffee with one of those little burners under it to keep it warm. Enough napkins to clean up a serious food fight. I slip him a twenty and lock the door behind him again.

By the time I get back to the main event, Shonna Lee's sneakers are under the coffee table and Bish is massaging one little brown foot in his big white hands. She sags back against the cushions, her whole face softening like a kitten's and the notebook sliding out of her fingers, but the questions keep on coming.

"Why did you switch from folk to blues?" Her voice shakes just a tad when Bish finds that spot on the sole of her foot. For a second, he looks like he wants to suck her toes, one at a time, and I can't blame him. Even with her clothes on, she's the kind of girl who makes hit songs shoot out of your pencil.

"The blues is the truth," he tells her. "You can't go wrong with the truth."

It's the first flat-out lie he's told her, and I know that from here on, he's going to pick up speed. He's told the story before.

"In early '65, we heard the Blues Project play in the Village, and the crowd went crazy for what they were laying down. Old Muddy Waters and Howlin' Wolf, but reworked into rock. I'd always loved the stuff, but we didn't think anyone would buy it."

Shonna Lee moves a little closer and lets him run his hands up her calves.

I loved Bo Carter, Blind Blake, and Robert Johnson, and I'd been saying blues was our ticket for over a year by then, but Bish didn't want to know from nothing until Dylan had the

Butterfield Blues Band back him with electric instruments at Newport. Their LP came out and knocked everyone on their ass, and Bish finally heard what I'd been telling him.

Shonna Lee's eyes move over to me like she's heard the whole riff already.

Bish gives her a smile so sticky I expect her to wipe her face. "Then the Stones and the Animals and the Yardbirds started shipping it back to us. I knew there was a fast train coming in and we had to jump on board before it left the station without us."

I go to the cart and sink my teeth into an apple before I scream.

"I'd never played an electric guitar before, and it took Jack a while to persuade me to give it a try. See, I loved Muddy and Elmore James and the others, but I really felt like the acoustic country blues was in my blood."

My apple tastes like wax.

"My soul, more like."

His eyes are starting to glow and I wonder how much longer before he suggests they take this into the bedroom. We've been on the road off and on for twenty years now, and he's still the best there is, and she's one of the perks. In twenty more years, when he's turning into a lounge act or an oldies tour, she'll be able to tell her kids that she banged Bishop Underwood.

Damned if I know why that bothers me.

I break the seal on the bourbon and pour three fingers neat. I hardly taste it before I pour three more.

Then the girl's next to me, stacking melon and strawberries on a plate, squirting a little blob of whipped cream beside them. Two more buttons on her blouse are open now. Barefoot, she's still fairly tall and I'm still fairly not, so I get a good look before I straighten up and we look at each other eye to eye.

She pours two flutes of champagne and dumps a handful of ice into a glass and drowns that in the bourbon, clear up to the rim. Bish watches her walk back to him with everything on a tray, real slow, like honey dripping off a table. When I swallow, Jim Beam burns in my throat.

She and Bish clink flutes, then he drains his. Hers goes on the end table, and I'm not sure any of it even wet her lips.

"So you got a Les Paul," she says. "Any reason you chose that particular guitar?"

"Well, I was playing a Gibson acoustic, an old Humming-bird. It's in the other room, as a matter of fact. I still write songs on it."

Yeah, I catch myself thinking, *and muskrats really do ramble.*

"Maybe you can show me later," she says. This time, her voice doesn't seem to reach her eyes.

"I'd love to." He lets her slide a strawberry into his mouth and plays with it before he takes a swallow of the bourbon. "Anyway, I liked the neck on that Gibson, so I figured it'd be easier to move to an electric guitar if I was already used to the feel of it."

There was more to it than that, of course. I had a Martin D-45, loved it like my mother, beautiful sound, but by then I'd signed over my rights, so he was making the royalties and I was just the sideman, which meant that when "we" decided to go electric, it was my guitar that went. I don't even know what that beauty would be worth now, thirty years later. We've got enough money for me to buy a busload of them, but it wouldn't be the same.

"I tried a Gibson hollow-body first," he tells her. "But they feed back when you crank up the amplifier. Then I found a Les Paul."

Right. He heard Clapton playing one on that John Mayall LP and gave it a shot.

"What is it about that guitar you like so much?" The girl feeds him another strawberry. There's a look in her eyes, like before the night's over, she's going to ask him to cut his hair and wrestle a lion. She sees me raise my glass of bourbon again and shakes her head, just a little.

"Oh, the feel, the tone. I've had it so long, it's like an old friend; it just fits in under my rib cage and I feel like I'm not alone. And it's got that great sustain, you can hit a note and hold it forever, warm and soulful, like a woman crying on a rainy night."

That's one of my lines too. From "Pain of Loss." It went platinum in '74 and I got diddly for it. He's still collecting royalties, seven million dollars from that LP so far.

The girl refills his bourbon so surface tension is all that keeps it from spilling over her fingers. She sits back on the couch, but this time she tucks her feet under her.

"Tell me about 'Hot Sugar Blues.'"

Bish loses his rhythm for just a beat before he picks up the glass. "That song was the little pebble that started the avalanche. Sold two million copies and convinced the record company to let me cut a whole album of my own stuff."

Of our *own stuff, you bastard.*

"I've heard stories that you stole that song."

It gets so quiet I can hear water running in the pipes and the traffic nine floors below us.

"What you saying, missy?" His drawl is broad enough to paint a double yellow line down the middle of it. "I wrote the words, I wrote the music, I sang it."

Well, he sang it anyway. Shonna Lee looks like she's two verses ahead of him.

"Someone took you to court. Claimed he wrote that song and you cheated him out of the money."

"Yeah, yeah, yeah." Bish takes a long swallow of bourbon and I feel my hand put my own glass back on the cart. It's like I'm not even there in the room with them anymore.

"Everyone talks about that. But they don't remember the rest of it. We went to court and the judge threw out the case in ten minutes flat. Some old coot trying to make money off me. Well, we sent him packing."

"An old black musician," Shonna Lee says. "Mattix? Something like that?"

"Some broken-down drunk in Mississippi. Claimed he wrote the song and played it for me, and I took it up north and made the record without his permission. Tried to sue me, but I had the music in a safe-deposit box, dated before he'd had anything."

"Hot Sugar Blues" is the only hit he's had that I didn't write. We were in some little jerkwater town, still doing those Kingston Trio covers, and this guy followed us up on the bandstand and blew us off the stage. Deak Mattix. Best guitar player I ever heard, better than Charley Patton, Reverend Gary Davis, or Mississippi John Hurt, and he sang this song while Bish and I sat there with our chins down around our knees.

"See," I'd said to him, "this is why we ought to be doing the blues."

We bought the guy a few drinks, made him play the song again. Then a couple more drinks and play the song one more time. By then, Bish had watched his hands enough to figure out those weird changes. Actually, they weren't weird, he just had the guitar tuned to A-minor so the voicings were different. That night in our motel room, he wrote it down and mailed it to himself at our apartment in East Orange. When we got back, that's when he traded my Martin for his first Gibson electric.

The song came out three months later, and Deak Mattix sued. Well, try to find a jury in Mississippi in 1966 that's going to believe a black guy. Bish and I flew down there with exhibit A. The judge opened that sealed envelope, looked at the papers inside, and gave the poor bastard thirty seconds to get his ass out of the courtroom.

We flew back to New York the next morning.

"Deacon Mattix," Shonna Lee says. "He killed himself a few days later. His wife found him hanging from a beam in the basement."

"I heard that," Bish says.

"Left her and a couple of little kids."

I'd told Bish he should send the woman some money, but he said it would look like he really was guilty and trying to buy them off. As soon as I could scrape something together, I sent it to them with a letter saying how sorry I was. Never got an answer.

" 'Hot Sugar Blues,' " she says. "You ever eaten hot sugar, Mr. Underwood?"

The way he looks at her now, I want to kill him.

She raises her eyebrows. "You interested?"

Before he can say anything, she's back at the cart, digging through the sugar packets and the whipped cream and the strawberries.

"Pour the man more bourbon, will you, Jack?" she asks. "This always tastes better with a little chaser."

She finds her jacket in the closet while I refill Bishop's glass. When I hand it over, I can feel the heat pumping off him like a midnight freight. The girl comes back to the table holding a little envelope.

"What's that?" I ask.

"Some of my secret herbs and spices." She gives me a smile that would stun a snake. "Old family recipe, just for special occasions. This feels like a special occasion, doesn't it?"

She empties the envelope into her hand, mixes the contents

with the sugar in a highball glass, and puts it over that little flame that's been keeping the coffee hot.

"We need to melt the sugar," she says. "Just like the song, you know."

She adds a little bourbon and uses a strawberry to muddle everything together. When I can see it bubbling and steam rising, she breaks a cupcake in half, pours the mixture over it, and takes the plate over to Bishop. She gets down on her knees in front of him, and his smile glows like toxic waste.

"This is best if you take it all in one gulp, sugar. It's got a little bit of an after burn, but the bourbon makes it all better."

"What is this?" Bish asks.

"It's something my mama showed me. It'll keep you going for a good long stretch. If you get my meaning."

She offers him the cupcake on the plate. "One nice big bite. It's going to be hot, so you have to swallow it right down. Then chase it."

He takes the cake and looks at her. She winks like Delilah probably winked at Samson.

"Go for it, sugar. One time, just for me."

The cake disappears into his mouth, and she's already bringing up the glass and tilting it between his lips. He swallows and coughs a little before he sits back on the couch.

"Whoa," he croaks. "Hot."

"Yeah, it is, isn't it?" She squeezes his hand with the glass in it. "But it's going to be so good in a little while."

"That's what I'm thinking too, honey."

She stands up and looks at me, still over by the cart, most of the bourbon gone, and a lot of the fruit and champagne. She turns back to Bish.

"You like any of the young players out there now?" she asks. "Anyone coming up who can really play the blues?"

"There's a kid out of Texas." Bish taps his chest like he's got a big belch stuck in there. "Stevie Ray Vaughan. I saw him in Houston a couple of years ago. Heard that he's cutting an album now."

He tries to swallow again and she pours him another glass of Jim Beam.

"Funny," she says. "Blues is black music, but now only white guys seem to play it."

"Lots of black singers don't like blues now," I say. "They say it reminds them of slavery. And they think it's too country."

Bish rattles the ice in his glass. "Yeah. They're into rap now 'cause it's more modern. City music."

Shonna Lee offers him a cherry.

"Modern, my ass," he goes on. "It's a fad. A year from now, everyone will have figured out it's crap and it'll go away."

"I don't know if anything ever really goes away," she says. "I think maybe it all just goes underground until the time is right again."

"Sure." Bish chases the cherry and grimaces. "Like Santa Claus comes every year."

"Have you heard of a guy named Robert Cray? He's black." Shonna Lee watches Bish drink, and the bourbon seems to burn him all the way down like the melted sugar did.

"I've heard the name. Haven't heard him play, though. You like him?"

"He's not as hot as you, but he's got a sweet sound."

She looks at him like she's just decided not to trade in the station wagon for the fancy sports car after all. She threads her arm into the sleeve of her corduroy jacket and turns to me. I can feel her eyes from across the room.

"Jack." She sweeps her sneakers from under the coffee table and slides them onto her feet in one flowing motion. "It's getting awfully late. Would you care to walk me home?"

"What?" Bishop's voice rises, and it catches a little at the end. He's still holding the empty glass. "No way, honey, you're not leaving."

"Yes, sugar," she says. "I am. Thank you for the interview. I'll send you a copy when I get it written. And maybe I'll see you at breakfast."

I'm reaching for what's left of the bourbon, but she grabs my wrist.

"What the hell?" Bish slams his hand on the table, and I hear the highball glass crack.

"Oh, sugar, did you hurt yourself?" She moves over and grabs his hand. "You better take care of that cut."

She steers him into the bathroom, closes the door behind him, and smiles at me.

"I still need you to walk me home, Jack."

I'm too amazed to do more than nod. I put my arm around her waist and she leans her head against my shoulder while I walk her two doors down the hall to my own room. Her hair smells so good I almost drop the key trying to unlock my door.

The next few hours could be a dozen songs I'm never going to write, and she's still lying beside me when morning creeps through the curtains. I look at the clock while she's in the shower and wonder how I'm going to give her cab fare home without looking like the jerk of the universe. And if I'm still going to have a job when Bish sees me again.

Shonna Lee comes out of the bathroom in a cloud of steam and drops her towel on the bed like we've been together forever. She gives me a kiss and takes her time putting her clothes back on.

"We should go see Mr. Underwood, shouldn't we?"

"I'm not sure that's a good idea," I say.

"It's better if we're together." She opens the door and starts down the hall, leaving me to catch up.

There's no answer when I knock. I try the doorknob. It's not locked.

That cracked glass is still on the coffee table, the champagne is floating in the melted ice, and the fruit is getting a little brown around the edges. Bishop is nowhere in sight. I stick my head in the bedroom, but the bed hasn't been slept in.

Shonna Lee takes the few remaining bits of ice from the bucket and drops them into the cracked glass. She wraps a napkin around the bottle and pours just a tad of bourbon too, then she flicks the crack with the bourbon bottle, and the glass crumbles so liquid leaks onto the table. She puts the bottle on the table next to the glass and folds the napkin again before she looks at me, then at the bathroom door.

I don't hear the shower or any movement behind it. I knock a couple of times, but nobody answers. I try the knob.

Bish is lying on the floor, blood on the sink, blood on the toilet, blood around his mouth, blood soaking the white bath mat. His eyes are bulging and his face is blue.

I come back into the room and see the girl dipping one of the remaining strawberries in whipped cream. Her face looks like I don't have any surprises for her.

"What was in that envelope?" I ask.

"What envelope?" Her voice is smoother than the whipped cream and I feel a cold lump in my stomach.

"You flushed it down my toilet, didn't you?"

She looks at the champagne bottle leaning against the side of the bucket, then picks up another strawberry.

"I was with you all night, Jack. I'm your alibi."

"I had no reason to want him dead."

She raises her eyebrows and bites into that strawberry. I remember the night in jail when he made me give up my songs. And the day he sold my guitar. And all the rest of it.

"They'll think he was so drunk he swallowed the broken glass."

Along with the hot sugar she hid it in.

"Jesus," I say. "What an awful way to go."

"I imagine." She licks her fingers delicately. "Probably even worse than hanging."

For a second, I think I'm going to throw up. "What's your real name?"

"Shonna Lee."

We look each other in the eye. She reaches into her jacket pocket and pulls out another envelope.

"Shonna Lee Mattix."

My voice feels heavy as lead. "Why not me too?"

She hands me the envelope. It's addressed to the Mattix family in Tillerville, Mississippi, and I recognize my own handwriting.

She's right. Things never go away. They just go underground until their time comes around again.

"I'm your alibi too, aren't I?"

"Only if you tell them my full name." She slides the envelope back into her jacket and her eyes meet mine again. "And why would you do that?"

I pick up the phone and dial the front desk.

THE FINAL BALLOT

BY BRENDAN DuBOIS

Eventually the room emptied of the two state police detectives, the detective from the Manchester Police Department, the Secret Service agent, the emergency room physician, and the patient representative from the hospital, until only one man remained with her, standing in one corner of the small hospital room used to brief family members about what was going on with their loved ones. Beth Mooney sat in one of the light orange vinyl-covered easy chairs, hands clasped tight in her lap, as the man looked her over.

"Well," he said. "We do have a situation here, don't we?"

It took her two attempts to find her voice. "Who are you?"

He was a lean, strong-looking man, with a tanned face that seemed out of place here in New Hampshire in December, and his black hair was carefully close trimmed and flecked with white. If he looked one way, he could be in his thirties; if he looked another way, he could be in his fifties. It depended on how the light hit the fine networks of wrinkles about his eyes and mouth. Beth didn't know much about men's clothes, but she knew the dark suit he was wearing hadn't come off some discount-store rack or from Walmart. He strolled over and sat down across from her, in a couch whose light orange color matched the shade of her chair.

"I'm Henry Wolfe," he said, "and I'm on the senator's staff."

"What do you do for him?"

"I solve problems," he said. "Day after day, week after week, I solve problems."

"My daughter..." And then her voice broke. "Please don't call her a problem."

He quickly nodded. "Bad choice of words, Mrs. Mooney. My apologies. Let me rephrase. The senator is an extraordinarily busy man, with an extraordinarily busy schedule. From the moment he gets up to the moment he goes to bed, his life is scheduled in fifteen-minute intervals. My job is to make sure that schedule goes smoothly. Especially now, with the Iowa caucuses coming up and less than two months to go before the New Hampshire primary. In other words, I'm the senator's bitch."

Beth said, "His boy..."

"Currently in custody by the state police, pending an investigation by your state's attorney general's office."

"I want to see my daughter," Beth said. "Now."

Henry raised a hand. "Absolutely. But Mrs. Mooney, if I may, before we go see your daughter, we need to discuss certain facts and options. It's going to be hard and it's going to be unpleasant, but believe me, I know from experience that it's in the interest of both parties for us to have this discussion now."

Anger flared inside her, like a big ember popping out of her woodstove at home. "What's there to discuss? The senator's son...he...he...hurt my little girl."

She couldn't help it, the tears flowed, and she fumbled in her purse and took out a wad of tissue, which she dabbed at her eyes and nose. While doing this, she watched the man across from her. He was just sitting there, impassive, his face blank, like some lizard's or frog's, and Beth knew in a flash that she was outgunned. This man before her had traveled the world, knew how to order wine from a menu, wore the best clothes and had gone to the best schools, and was prominent in a campaign to elect a senator from Georgia as the next president of the United States.

She put the tissue back in her purse. And her? She was under no illusions. A dumpy woman from a small town outside Manchester who had barely graduated from high school and was now leasing a small beauty shop in a strip mall. Her idea of big living was going to the Mohegan Sun casino in Connecticut a few times a year and spending a week every February in Panama City, Florida.

And Henry was smooth, she saw. When she had stopped sobbing and dabbing at her eyes, he cleared his throat. "If I may, Mrs. Mooney...as I said, we have a situation. I'm here to help you make the decisions that are in the best interests of your daughter. Please, may I go on?"

She just nodded, knowing if she were to speak again, she would start bawling. Henry said, "The senator's son Clay...he's a troubled young man. He's been expelled twice before from other colleges. Dartmouth was his third school, and I know that's where he met your daughter. She's a very bright young girl, am I correct?"

Again, just the nod. How to explain to this man the gift and burden that was her only daughter, Janice? Born from a short-lived marriage to a long-haul truck driver named Tom — who eventually divorced her for a Las Vegas waitress and who got himself killed crossing the Continental Divide in a snowstorm, hauling frozen chickens — Janice had always done well in school. No detentions or notes from the principal about her

Janice, no. She had studied hard and had gone far, and when Janice came home from Dartmouth to the double-wide, Beth sometimes found it hard to understand just what exactly her girl was talking about with the computers and the internet and twitting or whatever they called it.

Henry said, "From what I gather, her injuries, while severe... are not permanent. And she will recover. Eventually. What I want to offer you is a way to ease that recovery along."

Beth said sharply, "Seeing that punk in prison — that'll help her recovery, I goddamn guarantee it."

He tilted his head slightly. "Are you sure, Mrs. Mooney?"

"Yes, I am."

"Really? Honestly? Or will having Clay in prison help *your* recovery, not your daughter's?"

"You're talking foolish now."

A slight shake of the head. "Perhaps. That's what happens when you spend so much time with the press, consultants, and campaign workers. You do tend to talk foolish. So let's get back to basics. From my experience, Mrs. Mooney, there are two avenues open to you. To us. The first is the one I'm sure has the most appeal for you. The attorney general's office, working with the state police, pursue a criminal indictment against Clay Thomson for a variety of offenses, from assault and battery to... any other charges that they can come up with."

Beth crossed her legs. "Sounds good to me."

"I understand. So what will happen afterward?"

Beth tried to smile. "The little bastard goes to trial. Gets convicted. Goes to jail. Also sounds good to me."

Something chirped in the room. Henry pulled a slim black object from his coat, looked at it, pressed a button, and returned it to his pocket. "That may occur. But plenty of other things will happen, Mrs. Mooney, and I can guarantee that."

"Like what?"

"Like a media frenzy you've never, ever experienced before. I have, and I wouldn't wish it on my worst enemies, personal or political. Your phone rings constantly, from all the major networks, the cable channels, the newspapers, and the wire services. Reporters and camera crews stake out your home and your hair salon. Your entire life is probed, dissected, and published. Your daughter's life is also probed, dissected, and published. All in the name of the public's right to know. If your daughter is active sexually, that will be known. Her school grades, her medical history, information about old boyfriends will all be publicized. If you've ever had a criminal complaint—drunk driving, shoplifting, even a speeding ticket—that will also be known around the world."

Beth bit her lower lip. "It might just be worth it, to see that little bastard in an orange jumpsuit."

"No doubt you feel that way now, Mrs. Mooney," the man said. "But that will be just the start of it. You see, in a close-fought campaign like this one...the opponents of the senator will see you and your daughter as their new best friends, and they'll try anything and everything to keep this story alive, day after day, week after week, so the senator will stumble in the Iowa caucuses and lose the New Hampshire primary and then the White House."

Her hand found another tissue. Henry went on, talking slow and polite, like he was telling her the specials from the deli counter at the local Stop & Shop. "And that's the senator's enemies making your life miserable. The senator's supporters...they would be much, much worse."

Beth said with surprise, "His supporters? Why would they be worse?"

Henry spoke again, sounding like a bored schoolteacher

talking to an equally bored student. "For more than a year, many of them have been volunteering and donating time and money to the senator. They truly believe—as do I—that he is the best man to be our next president, the man who can bring justice back to this country and to our dealings with the world. But if you and your daughter were to pursue a criminal case concerning the senator's son... there will be threats and accusations against the two of you. Some will say that it was a setup. That you are allied with political groups that are against the senator. That you resent the senator, or your daughter has a grudge against the senator and his family. You'll be harassed at home, at work, and places in between. People on the internet will publish your home address and telephone number, as well as pictures of you, your house, and your hair salon. And it would go on for months... perhaps years."

"But that's not fair!"

Henry said, "That's the state of politics today, I'm afraid."

Beth pushed the tissue against her lips, keening softly. This night wasn't supposed to be like this. It was Tuesday night. Grilled hamburger and rice for dinner. Followed by *Jeopardy!*, the *Real Housewives,* and to bed. This wasn't supposed to be a night with an apologetic phone call from the Manchester police followed by a frantic drive to the hospital, and facing all of this...

She took the tissue away. "All right. You said there's two streets—"

"Avenues," he corrected.

"Avenues," she repeated, face warm, "available to us. What's the second one?"

He said, "One that I, if I were in your place, would find much more attractive. The senator's son is a very troubled young man. I admit it; the senator admits it. And the senator is devastated at what happened to your daughter. You're looking for justice, and the senator understands that. What we propose is this: If you and your daughter ask the proper authorities not to file formal and public charges against the senator's son, we will immediately place Clay in a secure mental-health facility, where he will no longer pose a danger to anyone."

"He gets away, then," Beth said sharply. "And your senator boss doesn't have to answer embarrassing questions."

"The senator isn't afraid of questions, Mrs. Mooney. And his son, no, he doesn't get away with anything. He gets the treatment he needs, in a secure place that is quite similar to a prison facility, with locked rooms, few privileges, and lots of discipline and treatment. And while the senator's son is treated, your daughter will be treated as well. Whatever insurance you have won't be billed. The senator will take care of it all, for as long as your daughter needs it. The very best in care...for life, if necessary, though I believe she'll make a full recovery in time. All future educational expenses as well. And since you, Mrs. Mooney, would no doubt have to take time off to be with your daughter, the senator is prepared to offer a generous monthly stipend to assist you."

"To keep my goddamn mouth shut, you mean."

Henry's face was impassive. "The senator wants to do right by you and your daughter. But by doing this, the senator would expect some...consideration from both of you. I'm sure you recognize, Mrs. Mooney, the delicacy of the situation."

"All I want is justice for my girl," she said.

"And I'm here to make sure justice is done. Among other things."

She sat and thought, and then pushed the wad of soaked tissue back into her purse.

"I want to see my girl, Janice," Beth said. "It's going to be up to her."

———

HER DAUGHTER WAS now in a two-patient room, with the curtain drawn to separate her from a young blond girl, who apparently had a broken foot and who was watching the wall-mounted television while chewing gum and texting on her cell phone at the same time. Beth sat down and looked at her Janice, feeling flashes of cold and heat race through her. Tubes ran out of both of Janice's slim wrists, and there was an oxygen tube beneath her nose. Her face was bruised; her left eye was nearly swollen shut; and her lower lip was split. She looked better than she had when Beth first saw her in the ER; now she was in a hospital gown and her face had been washed.

Henry walked in and said, "I'll leave you be for a while," and then he strolled out.

She clutched Janice's hand, and Janice squeezed back. Beth said, keeping her voice soft and low, "Honey, can I talk to you for a minute?"

And Beth told her what the man from the senator's staff had said and offered, and when she was done, Beth thought her little girl had fallen asleep. But no, she was thinking, with that mind that was so sharp and bright. She whispered back, "Mom...take the deal...okay? I'm so tired..."

"Janice, are you sure?"

Her voice, barely a whisper. "Mom, I'm really tired..."

———

HENRY CAME IN after a half an hour and Beth said, "We'll do it. The second...whatever it was. Choice. Option."

"Avenue," he said. "Mrs. Mooney, trust me, you won't regret it. Give me a few minutes and I'll have the necessary agreements prepared. All right?"

Beth turned to her girl, who was sleeping. "You know...what I'm really thinking...I wish I could spend the night here with my little girl. But I know the hospital won't allow it."

"Is that what you want, Mrs. Mooney? To spend the night here, in this room?"

Beth said, "Yes...of course. But there's no space."

Henry said, "Give me a few moments."

He slipped out.

Beth heard voices raised, phones ringing, more voices. Less than ten minutes later, two young, burly hospital attendants came in, and the girl with the broken foot yelped about why she was being moved, what the hell was going on, where was her boyfriend as her personal items were placed in a white plastic bag, and then she and her bed were wheeled out. An empty bed was wheeled in; a grim-faced nurse made it up; and the curtain was pulled back, making the room bigger and wider.

And Henry had returned and watched it all while typing on his electronic device. When the room was settled, he said, "Is that satisfactory, Mrs. Mooney?"

"How...how in hell did you do that?"

Henry said, "Problems. I'm paid quite well to solve them."

———

LATER IN THE evening, in a private conference room down the hall from Janice's hospital room, Beth signed a bunch of papers that she had a hard time puzzling through, but Henry said signing them was just a formality. When she was done, he nodded and smiled for the first time that evening.

"Very good, Mrs. Mooney. You won't regret it. I promise. Here—"

He slid over a business card, which she picked up. On the back was a handwritten phone number. "My private, direct line. You have any questions, any problems, anything at all, give me a call. All right?"

"Thank you, thank you very much," she said.

"And here," he said, putting a white envelope on the conference table. "An initial...stipend for your worries."

Beth looked inside the envelope and saw a number of bills, all with Ben Franklin's face on them. She quickly closed the envelope and shoved it into her purse. She said, "I'd like to ask you a question, if that's all right."

"Mrs. Mooney, the senator and I are in your debt. Go ahead."

"Why do you do this? I mean, I'm sure you get paid a lot. But what's in it for you?"

The question seemed to catch him by surprise. "I guess you deserve an answer...for the troubles you've been through. I'll tell you something, though I'll deny ever having said this. What I want, and what I've worked for my entire life, is to put a man in the White House, to know that I did it, and, in return for my work, to be chief of staff for him. But that's always up in the air until the final ballot. That's something I've learned the hard way over the years."

"Chief of staff...is that an important job?"

He abruptly stopped talking, as if afraid he had said too much. He put on his coat. "Mrs. Mooney, if you don't mind, I need to catch a flight to Atlanta tonight...is there anything else I can do for you?"

Beth was suddenly exhausted, like she had spent twelve hours on her feet at the hair salon. "No, I'm going to be with my girl. Thanks for making it so I can spend the night next to her."

The second smile of the evening. "My pleasure."

———

THE NEXT FEW days went by in a daze of working at the salon, being at the hospital, and then being at the rehabilitation facility when Janice was transferred. There, Beth was pleased to see her little girl—all right, young woman!—recovering well. The bruises faded some, and she could walk up and down the hallway without leaning on someone or having to stop to catch her breath.

Beth should have been encouraged, but so many things were bothering her. Janice was always one to talk her mother's ears off about the latest political scandal, the latest celebrity wedding, and the latest news on whatever online or off-line technology she was involved with at that moment, but now, she just stayed in her bed and watched television or read paperback books. Beth had once offered to bring Janice's laptop in, but with some curt words, Janice said she was no longer interested.

Beth was confused and scared, but still, it was good to see her daughter get better, week after week. And as promised, a weekly check made out to her arrived, and she caught up on all her bills and even managed to start a savings account, a first. But truth be told, she always felt a bit self-conscious depositing the checks, like she was doing something bad. Yet Janice was slowly improving, and Janice didn't say anything more about the senator's son, so Beth let everything be and kept hoping for the future.

And so it would have remained, if it weren't for the night of the Iowa caucuses.

———

IT HAD BEEN a long day, first at the rehab center in the morning and then at the hair salon in the afternoon. Beth had accidentally double-booked two of her clients, so she had to work later than expected. Dinner was a quick takeout from McDonald's and after she got home, she went through the mail—another stipend check and an electricity bill from PSNH—then washed up and went straight into her bedroom.

There she switched on the TV, and instead of her usual *Law & Order,* there was a special report about the Iowa caucuses being held that night. In the dark bedroom, covers pulled up around her neck, she watched the panel for the news discuss the Iowa results, and something chilled her feet when she learned that the senator from Georgia had squeaked out a victory. He was now the front-runner, but as some of the commentators stated, he was still on shaky ground. A win in three weeks in New Hampshire could make him unstoppable.

The view of the camera switched to the senator making his victory speech at an auditorium in Iowa. His face was happy and lit up as he stood in front of a large blue curtain and waved to the cheering crowd, the supporters holding signs high. And there was the senator's man Henry Wolfe standing to one side, applauding hard, smiling as well, sometimes ducking his head to say something to somebody on the stage.

She picked up the remote to change the channel, and her hand froze. Just like that. A young man was there as well, cheering and laughing and looking very, very happy indeed.

The senator's son.

In Iowa. In public. On the stage!

He didn't seem to have a care or worry in the world, looked fine indeed as he applauded and cheered his winning father —

Beth stumbled out of bed, raced to the bathroom, and made it to the toilet before vomiting up her small fries and Quarter Pounder with Cheese. She washed her face with cold water, wiped it down with a towel, refused to look at herself in the mirror, and went back out to the bedroom.

The senator was speaking, but Beth muted the television, stared at the screen. His son Clay... out. Free. Not punished at all.

While her daughter, Janice, was still in rehab, still trying to form words and sentences, still refusing to use her computer.

Beth went to her bureau, roughly pulled out the top drawer, went through a few things, and came back out with Henry Wolfe's business card with the handwritten phone number on the reverse. Hands shaking, she sat cross-legged on her bed and dialed the number.

It started ringing. And kept ringing. With the phone up to her ear, she watched the television, and it was like being trapped in one of those horror movies where you saw something bad happening and couldn't do anything to save yourself, for what she saw was...

Henry Wolfe onstage, listening to his boss speak, and then pausing. Reaching inside his coat pocket. Pulling out his phone or minicomputer or whatever they called it.

From little New Hampshire to busy Iowa, she was calling him, was calling him to find out what in hell the senator's son was doing up there onstage. What about the promise, the pledge, that justice would be served?

She stared at the television, willing herself not to blink, for she didn't want to miss a thing.

Henry Wolfe stared down at his handheld device. Frowned. Pressed a button, returned it to his coat.

And her call went to voice mail.

Later on during the night, she called the number six more times, and six times, it went straight to voice mail.

———

AFTER A RESTLESS night, she woke with her blankets and sheets wrapped around her, moist from her night sweats, her phone ringing and ringing and ringing. She reached across to the night-stand, almost knocked the phone off the stand, and then got it and murmured a sleepy hello.

The voice belonged to Henry Wolfe, who started out sharply:

"Mrs. Mooney, I don't have much time, so don't waste it, all right?"

"What?" she asked.

He said brusquely, "I know you called me seven times last night, and I have a good idea what you're calling about. And I'm telling you don't waste your time. You have a signed nondisclosure agreement with a very attractive compensation package and a very unattractive clause that will open you up to financial and legal ruin if you say one word about the senator and his son."

She sat up in bed. "But he's free! That bastard Clay, I saw him last night! The one who hurt my daughter! You promised me that he'd be sent away!"

Henry said, "And he was sent away."

"For three weeks? Is that all?"

"His doctors judged that he had recovered well, and—"

"Doctors you paid for, I'm sure!"

Henry said, "This conversation isn't productive, Mrs. Mooney, so I think I'll—"

"Is that what you people call justice? Throwing some money around, making promises, and walking away? You promised me justice for my girl!"

By then, she was talking to herself.

———

THE NEXT DAY she met with Floyd Tucker, an overweight and fussy lawyer who had helped her sort through the paperwork when she had divorced Joe. He sighed a lot as they sat in his tiny, book-lined office. He flipped through the pages of the agreement she had signed for the senator, sighed some more, and finally looked up. "Beth, you shouldn't have signed this without running it by me first."

"I didn't have the time," she said.

"This agreement"—he held up the papers—"there's a good compensation package, no doubt about it, but the restrictions... Hell, Beth, if you even hint at breathing what's gone on with the senator's son and your daughter, you open yourself up to lawsuits, financial seizures, and penalties totaling tens of millions of dollars. Do you understand that?"

"I do now," she said, staring at the polished desk. "But I didn't have the time."

"Beth, you should have called me," he said.

She reached over, plucked the documents from his hand.

"I didn't have the time," she whispered.

———

A DAY LATER, she was at her town's small library. Past the rows of books and the magazine racks, there were three computers, set up in a row. She sat down and stared at the screen, which showed a picture of the library and said that this picture and the words on it were something called a home page. She put her hands over the keyboard and then pulled them away, as if she were afraid she would make something blow up if she pushed the wrong key.

Beth leaned back in the wooden chair. What to do? She felt queasy, empty, nervous, like the first time she had approached a paying customer with a pair of sharp scissors in her hands.

"Mrs. Mooney?" a young girl's voice said. She turned in her seat, saw Holly Temple, a sweet girl whose hair Beth cut and styled. She said, "Do you need any help?"

Beth said, "I'm afraid I don't know how to use this, Holly. I'm looking for some information, and I don't know how to begin."

Holly pulled over a chair and sat down next to her. "Well, it's pretty easy. I'm surprised that Janice couldn't help you."

Her voice caught. "Me too."

———

SHE WAS DRIVING to the rehab center to visit Janice, who had had what the doctors and nurses delicately called a setback. Physically she was improving day by day; emotionally, she was withdrawing, becoming more silent, less responsive. Beth found that she had to drive with only one hand, as she had to use the other to keep wiping her eyes with a wad of tissue.

At a stoplight, scores of supporters for the senator were gathered at the intersection, holding blue-and-white campaign signs on wooden sticks that they raised as they chanted. They waved at cars going by, gave thumbs-up to passing cars that honked in support. Two young men were staring right at her as they chanted. The light changed to green and she drove by, and she couldn't help herself — she gave them the middle finger.

———

THAT NIGHT, FOR hour after hour, she dialed and redialed Henry Wolfe's number. Eventually, at two a.m., he answered, and she got right to the point.

"Mr. Wolfe, next Tuesday is the New Hampshire primary. The day after tomorrow, I plan to drive to Concord and visit the offices of the Associated Press. There, I'm going to show them the documents that I signed and tell them what the senator's son did to my little girl."

Voice sharp, he said, "Do that, you silly bitch, and you'll be destroyed. Ruined. Wiped out."

"And come next Tuesday, so will your candidate. I may be silly, but I'm not stupid. I know if he wins the primary with a good margin, he'll be your party's nominee. And after that, he'll be the favorite to be president. So destroying him in exchange for losing my shop and my double-wide and the one thousand two hundred dollars I have in my savings account…that sounds like a pretty fair deal to me."

She could hear him breathing over the phone line. "What do you want?"

Beth said, "The first time we met, you said the senator's life was scheduled in fifteen-minute chunks of time, and that your job was to make sure that time went smoothly. So here's the deal. Sometime over the next two days, I want five minutes with him. And with you. Alone."

Henry said, "Impossible."

"Then make it possible," she said curtly. "After all, you're paid to solve problems."

This time, she hung up on him.

———

Two hours later, her phone rang. She picked it up and a tired voice said, "A deal. The Center of New Hampshire hotel. Two this afternoon. Room six ten."

"Sounds good to me," she said.

"Look, you need to know that—"

Taking more pleasure in it this time, she hung up on him again. And went back to sleep.

———

Later that day, Beth drove to Manchester—the state's largest city—and instead of going into the pricey parking garage, she found a free spot about four blocks away. She trudged along the snowy sidewalk and walked into the hotel, past guests and people streaming in and out. In one corner of the lobby, there were bright lights from a television news crew filming an interview with somebody who must be famous.

She took the elevator to the sixth floor, got off, and within a minute, she found room 610. A quick knock on the door and it opened up within seconds, a frowning and worn-looking Henry Wolfe on the other side. He was dressed as well as ever, but his eyes were sunken and red-rimmed. Beth had a brief flash of sympathy for him before remembering all that had gone before, and then she didn't feel sympathetic at all.

He started to speak and she brushed by him and into the room. *Wow,* she thought. This wasn't a room. It was a palace, bigger than the interior of her double-wide trailer. Couches, chairs, big-screen television, kitchen, bar, and doors that led into other rooms. Flowers and baskets of fruit and snack trays and piles of newspapers.

She turned to Henry. "Is this what they mean by a suite?"

"Yes," he said. "Look, Mrs. Mooney, before the senator comes in, I really need to know that—"

"A suite," Beth said, shaking her head in awe. "I've heard of hotel suites, but to think I'd ever actually be inside of one, well, I never figured."

"I'm sure," Henry snapped. "Mrs. Mooney, we don't have much time before the meeting and I must insist—"

She made a point of looking around again. "All of those nice senior citizens, the retirees who send your senator a dollar bill or a five-dollar bill or whatever they can scrape together to help elect him president, do you think they know that their money is paying for this suite? And all those who donated time and money because they believed in the senator's idea of justice, what do you think they'd say if they knew what his son did to my daughter?"

"Mrs. Mooney—" he began again, and then another door within the suite opened up, and the senator walked in, tall, smiling, wearing a fine gray suit and a cheerful look. The room he was emerging from, she saw, was filled with well-dressed men and women, most with cell phones against their ears or in their hands, and then the door was shut behind him.

The senator strode over, and Beth felt her heart flip for a moment. It was one thing to see him on the cover of a magazine or a newspaper, or on the nightly news, but here he was, right in front of her. *My God,* she thought. *What am I doing?* This man coming at her could very well be the next president of the United States, the most powerful and famous man on the planet. And she was a single mom and a hairdresser. For a moment she felt like turning around and running out the door.

Then she remembered Janice. And she calmed down.

"Mrs. Mooney," the senator said, holding out a tanned hand with a large, fancy watch around his wrist. "So glad to meet you. I just wish it were under better circumstances."

"Me too," she said, giving his hand a quick shake. "And, Senator, I know you're very, very busy. In fact, I can't imagine how busy you are, so I will make this quick."

The senator looked to Henry, who looked to her and said, "We appreciate that, Mrs. Mooney."

Beth took a breath. "So here we go. I'm sure you know your son's actions, what happened to my daughter, and the agreement that was reached between me and Mr. Wolfe."

The senator said, "If there's something that needs to be adjusted in the agreement, I'm sure that—"

"Senator," Beth said forcefully, "I don't want an adjustment. I don't want an agreement. In fact, you can stop all the payments. What I want is justice for my little girl."

The senator's eyes narrowed and darkened. Now she could see the toughness that was inside this man who wanted to be president.

"Do go on," he said flatly.

She said, "You can stop the payments. Stop everything. But I intend to go public with what your son did to my daughter today, this afternoon, unless my one demand is met."

Both men waited, neither one saying a word. So she went on.

"By the end of the day today, I want you to announce the firing of Henry Wolfe," she said. "And I want your pledge that he will never be in your employ ever again, either directly or indirectly."

The senator didn't make a sound, but Beth heard a grunt from Henry, like he had just been punched in the gut. She went on. "That is it. Nonnegotiable."

"Why?" the senator asked. "Why should I fire Henry?"

"To keep me from going to the newspapers," she said. "And because he promised justice for my girl. And she still doesn't have it."

She could sense the tension in the air, something disturbing, as she noted both men looking at each other, inquiring, appraising, gauging what was going on. The senator checked his watch. "Well, our time is up, Mrs. Mooney, and—"

Henry spoke desperately. "Tom, please—"

"Henry," the senator said calmly, touching his upper arm. "We have a lot of things to talk about, don't we?"

Henry continued, "For God's sake, Tom, the primary is in just a few days and—"

The two of them went through another door, and Beth was left alone. She looked around the huge, empty suite, went to a fruit basket, picked up two oranges, and left.

———

THE NIGHT OF the New Hampshire primary, she rented a DVD—*Calendar Girls*—and watched the movie until she fell asleep on the couch. She had no idea who had won and didn't rightly care.

———

Two months later, Beth was in her hair salon checking the morning receipts when the door opened and Henry Wolfe walked in. He wasn't dressed fancy, and his face was pale and had stubble on it. When she looked in his eyes, she was glad there was a counter between them.

"Looking for a trim?" she asked cheerfully.

"You...I..."

"Or a shave?" she added.

He stopped in front of her and she caught his scent. It was of unwashed clothes and stale smoke and despair. "You...do you know what you've done?"

"I don't know," she said, flipping the page on her appointment book. "But I'm sure you'll tell me."

"The senator...he barely won the New Hampshire primary. There was a shit storm of bad publicity when he announced my firing, talk of a campaign in crisis, a senator who couldn't choose the right staff, of chaos in his inner circle. And then he lost the next primary, and since then, he's been fighting for his political life. There's even speculation about a brokered convention. What should have been a clear road to the White House has become a horror show. All thanks to you."

"Gee," she said. "I don't think so."

"But that's what you wanted, isn't it?" he demanded. "To get back at the senator. To hurt his chances of becoming president. All because his son didn't get punished the way you wanted. You knew that firing me, his most trusted fixer and adviser, days before the New Hampshire primary would cripple him."

The phone rang, but she ignored it. The door opened and her newest employee walked in, nodded to Beth, and then got a broom and started sweeping near one of the chairs.

Beth said, "You just don't get it, do you?"

He gave a sharp laugh, and in a mocking tone, he said, "I'm sure you'll tell me."

She picked up a pen. "I didn't know much about you when we first met. So after I saw the senator's son up onstage in Iowa, and after you blew me off on the phone, I did some research. I goggled you."

"You did what?"

"I goggled you."

He shook his head. "Stupid woman, it's *Google*. Not *goggle*."

Beth smiled. "Well, whatever the hell it is, I had a friend at the library do research for me. And I found out that you've tried four times to get a man elected president, and each time, you've lost. You have a reputation as a political loser. But this time, you were the closest you've ever been. Years and years of political failure, and you were now so very close to having your dream come true, to be chief of staff. The most powerful man in Washington, right after the president. Four, maybe eight years in the White House as chief of staff, and then millions of dollars doing consulting and lobbying work. It looked like your losing streak was finally about to break. And then the senator's son started dating my daughter."

She paused, looking at his drawn face. "I could give a shit about your senator. Or any other politician. But you promised me justice, and you didn't deliver. So I gave you a taste of what it's like to be betrayed after so many promises. And I was the one to cast the final goddamn ballot."

Beth was surprised to see him wipe at his eyes. It looked like he was weeping.

"Was it worth it, then?" he asked, his voice just above a whisper. "To destroy me like this, to hurt the senator, maybe even prevent him from getting to the White House?"

She looked over at the corner of the store, where her daughter, Janice, was quietly and dutifully sweeping up the floor, her hands holding a broom, the same hands that still hadn't gone back to her computer.

"Yes," she said calmly. "It was worth it."

AFRICA ALWAYS NEEDS GUNS

BY MICHAEL NIEMANN

S ome days everything works out. Valentin Vermeulen hadn't had one of those days in a while. He brushed a damp strand of blond hair from his broad forehead, a forehead inherited from generations of Flemish farmers. Like these ancestors, he waited for his luck to change.

There was a slim chance it might. If, that is, the Antonov An-8 cargo plane was sufficiently late.

He looked over the shoulders of the Bangladeshi air traffic controller. The radar scope's scan beam raced in a circle, like the hands of a clock on fast-forward. No blips. The plane was about an hour and a half behind schedule.

The reality of his assignment stared back at him through the dirty windows of what passed for the control tower of the Bunia airport. The humid bush, a single asphalt runway, white UN helicopters parked on makeshift helipads, white armored personnel carriers at strategic positions, soldiers in blue helmets milling about, a peacekeeping operation at the edge of the world.

The usual Congolese hangers-on—were they Hema or Lendu? He never could tell the difference—sat in the shady spots, hoping for a small job, cash, or food. A quiet day in a very unquiet part of the world.

Vermeulen pulled a Gitane Papier Maïs from its blue pack and lit it. He was used to air-conditioned offices in New York, to pulling together evidence from files and interview transcripts. Sure, there were trips to the field—Kosovo, Bosnia, even Cambodia once—but he always had his office in New York. Until he'd stepped on some important toes during the Iraq oil-for-food investigation. Next thing he knew, the UN Office of Internal Oversight Services sent him to the eastern Congo.

An ancient air conditioner rattled in its slot above the door, blowing humid air into the room. It wasn't any cooler than the air outside. He wiped the perspiration from his forehead and took off his jacket. It had dark spots under the arms. The Bangladeshis didn't seem to mind the climate. Their uniforms looked crisp.

"There is the Antonov now, sir," the air traffic controller said with the lilt of South Asians. He pointed to a blip on the radar. The timing was just about right.

"How far is it?"

"About ten miles, sir."

"How long until it lands?"

"Fifteen minutes, give or take. Maybe more. Depends on the approach Petrovic takes."

"Is he usually late?"

"Sometimes Petrovic is on time, sometimes he isn't. This is Africa."

A loud voice crackled over the radio.

"Central Lakes Air Niner Quebec Charlie Echo Juliet requests permission to land."

The voice had a strong Slavic accent.

"Niner Quebec, this is Bunia air control, Bangladeshi Air Force controller Ghosh. Permission granted for runway ten. Visual flight rules in effect. Westerly winds, about three knots."

"Ghosh, you dumb Paki. When're you gonna get a decent radar to guide me in?"

"When you fly a decent aircraft, you lazy Chetnik."

Ghosh smiled and scribbled something into a logbook.

"Can I intercept the plane right after it lands?" Vermeulen asked.

"No, sir. No vehicles allowed on the tarmac during taxiing."

"Where will he stop?"

"At the cargo area over there, sir." Ghosh pointed in the general direction.

Vermeulen grabbed his jacket.

"Thank you, Lieutenant."

Good thing he remembered their insignia.

————

PETROVIC'S STOMACH BULGED over jeans made for a man twenty years younger. The Hawaiian shirt revealed dark chest hair decorated with a gold chain. His bullet-shaped head was shaved except for a bushy mustache—he was a bruiser who'd gone to seed.

He stood by the cargo door of the Antonov and supervised a Nepali engineering platoon. Three soldiers pushed a pallet along a track to the rear gate, where a fourth put the pallet on a forklift and took it to a storage tent.

Vermeulen found the corporal in charge inside the storage tent. The man checked his ID, shrugged, and gestured to the two pallets already unloaded.

They were wrapped in plastic netting. The freight bill attached to each listed the number of boxes and their contents. Vermeulen checked each bill and counted the items on that pallet. They added up.

He pulled at the netting of the nearer pallet. It didn't budge.

"You want it off?" the corporal asked.

"Yes, I need to check the contents."

The corporal took a box cutter from his pocket.

"Get the fuck away from my cargo," a voice shouted from the entrance.

Vermeulen and the corporal turned. Petrovic had jumped to the ground and hurried to the tent.

"You better get the goddamn freight manifest signed before you open anything."

"What's the matter with you, Ranko?" the corporal said, brows raised. "You never gave a rat's ass about paperwork before."

"It's my cargo until the paper's signed," the pilot said. His eyes—the color of dishwater—were cold and menacing, and he had the stare of a street fighter. It reminded Vermeulen of all the bullies he had encountered from grade school on. He took an instant dislike to the pilot.

"Who the fuck are you?" Petrovic asked.

"Valentin Vermeulen, OIOS investigator." He pulled out his ID. "I don't need a signature. I can investigate anything I like."

The pilot stepped closer. At six feet six, Vermeulen towered over Petrovic, but the latter's bulk made him a formidable obstacle.

"You ain't getting near that cargo until the paperwork is signed."

"Okay, then let's get it signed," Vermeulen said. He turned to the corporal. "Just sign his manifest."

"I'm not allowed. The master sergeant does that, but he isn't here right now."

"So I won't be able to inspect the cargo until he returns?"

The corporal nodded.

"When will that be?"

The corporal hemmed and hawed. "I'm not sure. Probably not today."

Vermeulen shook his head. This wasn't going to be his day after all. He saw the sneer on Petrovic's face and turned to leave the tent. The corporal followed him.

Outside, he watched the forklift hoist a large aluminum container — wider and deeper than the pallets — from the plane.

"What is that?" Vermeulen asked the corporal.

"A refrigerated unit, sir."

"What's in it?" he asked, realizing too late that it was a dumb question.

"Perishable food for the troops. Meat, frozen vegetables, and the like."

Vermeulen nodded. What was that old saying? An army travels on its stomach. That was also true for UN peacekeepers. The UN could not feed a whole brigade from local resources. Hell, the locals barely had enough to feed themselves.

Petrovic climbed back into the plane. The white Toyota pickup assigned to Vermeulen waited outside the fence that enclosed the cargo area. He turned to it. Another wasted day on a lousy mission. Time for a drink.

"To the hotel, monsieur?"

Walia Lukungu's arm hung out of the window. He was one of the locals who'd been fortunate enough to snag a job with the UN. His driving skills, though, were questionable. Vermeulen had the feeling of sitting in a Formula One race car every time they went anywhere.

He was just about to nod when one of the soldiers inside the plane called to the corporal. The corporal answered, then shrugged.

"Anything the matter?" Vermeulen shouted from the open pickup door.

"No, sir. It's just that those chaps in Kampala have trouble counting past three. Now there's one refrigerated unit more than the cargo manifest says, but one was missing last week. It happens all the time." The corporal shook his head. "That's the trouble with contractors."

It took a moment before the significance of the corporal's comment sank in. Once it did, Vermeulen felt a familiar adrenaline rush. A clue. He ran back to the tent. The container hovered on the tines of the forklift. Its front consisted of a grille that covered the compressor and fan, and the large door was sealed with a plastic cable tie and bore some sort of label.

"I must check that extra unit. Now."

The corporal shook his head.

"You heard Petrovic. We can't open anything until the cargo is signed for."

"I don't care. I'll take responsibility for opening it."

Vermeulen signaled the forklift driver to place the unit on the ground. He pulled his pocketknife out and bent down to cut the plastic tie. A strong hand grabbed his shoulder and yanked him back from the container. Petrovic.

"Keep your fucking hands off that unit," he hissed, taking a boxer's stance.

"I won't and you can't stop me."

Vermeulen turned back to the unit. Before his knife reached the plastic tie, he felt a gun barrel against his head.

"Drop the knife and turn around slowly."

Vermeulen turned to face Petrovic, who kept pointing

the gun at him. The corporal and the other soldiers stood and gaped.

"Listen, asshole. You can't check the cargo until it's signed for. So why don't you go to your hotel, get some rest, find a whore, whatever, until that formality has been taken care of."

The sight of the pistol took the wind out of Vermeulen's sails. But he decided to play tough.

"What are you going to do? Shoot me?"

Petrovic's eyes narrowed.

"I will," he said. His tone left no doubt that he meant it. "'Courageous Pilot Prevents Pilfering of UN Supplies.' It'll play well in New York. And don't count on these guys helping you. They don't want any trouble. They want to go home."

Vermeulen swallowed. He had overplayed his hand. Without a weapon, he could do nothing. In a vain attempt to maintain his dignity he picked up his knife, straightened his jacket, and turned to the Toyota.

"Take me to Colonel Zaman, Walia."

———

THE CEILING FAN spun lazily. Small eddies in the smoke rising from his Gitane were the only indicators that the hot air moved at all. Stripped to his shorts, Vermeulen lay on the bed in his hotel room. His third bottle of Primus rested on his stomach. At least the beer was cold, even though it tasted like piss. He lifted the bottle to check the name of the brewery. *Brewed under license of Heineken.* Damn! You'd figure a former Belgian colony would at least have a decent Belgian beer, like De Koninck or Celis. Hell, he'd even settle for a bottle of Duvel.

He drew hard on his cigarette. The coarse tobacco crackled and sparked.

Colonel Zaman, commanding officer of this UN outpost, had been unavailable. His deputy, a timid paper pusher in a major's uniform, was afraid to make a decision. He rattled off the usual excuses: Can't order Nepali soldiers without talking to their superiors. Better wait until their master sergeant signs the manifest. Yes, the pilot was out of line, but he was right about his cargo. No harm done. The weapons, if they were there—the major made no effort to hide his skepticism—would still be there in the morning. Extra guards would make sure of that.

What was Vermeulen doing here? Chasing gunrunners? That seemed so futile. There'd be plenty whether or not he nailed that son of a bitch Petrovic and whoever worked with him. But would it come to that? Judging from his past experience, no.

He could easily write his report now. Inconclusive evidence, no witnesses, peacekeepers absolved—the usual bureaucratic-speak that declared victory even as it left everything unchanged. It would make everyone happy.

This job stank, Vermeulen knew that. More than once, he'd been ready to call it quits. But each case was a new opportunity, a chance that, this time, justice would be done. That's why he couldn't write the report yet. But his reservoir of hope was slowly running dry.

He lit another cigarette and watched the smoke curl upward until it reached the faint turbulences below the fan.

A door slammed down the corridor. The UN had chosen Bunia as the headquarters for the Ituri Brigade, so a bevy of aid organizations had descended here as well. Those with more money occupied several rooms the Hotel Bunia reserved for its important visitors. He'd seen a few at breakfast, B-list Hollywood personalities wearing brand-new safari clothing and big smiles.

More steps in the corridor. They slowed as they reached his door. He raised his head. A slight scraping on the floor. A quick retreat.

He jumped up, almost spilling the beer. A note was stuck under the door. He pulled the door open. The corridor was empty.

The note contained a single sentence: *Come to the Club Idéal at 9 tonight.*

He checked his watch. Eight thirty.

————

THE DRUMMER HAD played this beat a million times. Half asleep, he rested against the wall. His hands seemed to have a life of their own. The two guitar players were a little more animated, stepping out, swinging their guitars as they kept the soukous melody flowing at the right speed. Not that it mattered. Nobody was paying attention to the music. Two couples moved on the tiny dance floor, but to Vermeulen it seemed more like foreplay than dancing. Sure enough, one of the couples disappeared behind a ragged curtain, the girl squealing in pretend delight.

He found an empty table. The reek of sweat, cigarettes, and beer that had assaulted his nose began to fade into the background.

A man with a limp had waited for him outside the hotel and hustled him into a beat-up old Citroën 2CV. The man said, "Club Idéal," over and over until Vermeulen figured the ride would be no riskier than walking alone at night. Like all OIOS investigators, he was unarmed.

A girl in a blond wig, maybe seventeen, if that, wiggled her hips as she came to his table. Her breasts were barely concealed beneath a ragged tank top.

"Je suis Lily. Tu veux quelque chose?"

Lily's blond wig stood in startling contrast to her ebony skin.

He stared at her. Although there was no real resemblance, Lily reminded him of his own daughter. Gaby had run away at age fifteen after he divorced his wife. The police didn't care much. Runaways were common in Antwerp. So he searched for her himself. Staking out her friends, asking questions until he found her, in a hole not much different from the Club Idéal.

Lily's smile faded a little under his stare. She suddenly seemed self-conscious. He caught himself.

"Yes, a beer, please."

"Primus or Nile Special?"

Tired of Primus, he chose Nile Special.

The girl came back with the bottle and sat down at his table.

"You want company?"

He took a swig from the bottle and examined her again. *You should be doing homework,* he thought, *or working at a decent job.* His own daughter had finally turned a corner, gotten clean, and made it to the university. But the price had been estrangement. They hadn't spoken in five years. All he knew was that she worked for an import-export company.

Lily lingered a little and bent forward, hoping to change his mind by giving him a glimpse of her breasts. He shrugged and smiled apologetically. She got up, wiggled her hips under the impossibly short skirt, and rejoined the other girls by the bar.

None of the men in the bar was in uniform, but he knew most of them were UN soldiers or contractors. What else was new? Wherever there were soldiers, there were whores.

He finished his beer and noticed the beginnings of a pleasant buzz. One more and he'd be in the right spot. But he held back and lit a Gitane instead. Who knew what this meeting would bring?

A big woman waddled to his table. Of indeterminate age, she wore a brightly colored muumuu and an equally colorful cloth wrapped around her hair. She sat down. Close up, her round face showed the ravages of living at the margins in a poor country.

"My girls, you do not like them?"

He really didn't feel like defending his celibacy to the madam of the brothel. "Your girls all seem a little too young for their jobs."

She waved her right hand with a worldly flair. "Age, what is it? Polite men don't ask."

"I thought that applied only to women over thirty."

Her face lit up with a smile. "A gentleman in Mama Tusani's club! What a surprise. Let me buy you another beer."

She motioned to the counter. Lily brought another bottle and a glass with a milky fluid for Mama Tusani. She didn't leave.

Vermeulen clinked his bottle to her glass and took a swig.

"Nice place you got here," he said.

It was a blatant lie. She knew it but smiled anyway, swaying to the rhythm of the music. When the song ended, she leaned over.

"Please, go with Lily to the back."

He lifted his hands, angry. Mama Tusani took his hands and continued smiling for anyone watching.

"Please, it is important," she said in a tone quite unlike her smile.

He finally understood and got up.

The girl pulled him toward the curtain, giggling, clinging to him, rubbing his chest. He couldn't make himself play the part. To the rest of the crowd, he must have looked like a sixteen-year-old being dragged to his first sexual encounter.

They moved past ill-fitting doors through which unrestrained — and obviously faked — sounds of various stages of ecstasy could be heard. She pushed open the last one and pulled Vermeulen into a cubbyhole. The smell of sex and cheap perfume was overpowering. A filthy bed—reflected in a cracked mirror on the ceiling—took up most of the room. The couple next door was hard at work.

She sat on the bed and smiled. The door opened again and Mama Tusani slipped in. She whispered something to Lily, who began moaning loud enough to compete with the couple next door.

"You are here to stop the gun smugglers, no?" Mama Tusani whispered.

Vermeulen stared at her, speechless for a moment.

"How do you know?" he asked.

"Mama Tusani knows everything. When the men come here, they drink and talk. My girls tell me what they hear."

"Yes, I'm investigating the role of UN troops in illegal arms transfers."

"The plane that came today, it carried guns."

"Are you sure?"

"Yes, the pilot was here earlier. Every time, he comes here right from the plane. He brags to Lily. Says he can fool UN asshole in his sleep."

Lily nodded and smiled at him as she continued moaning.

"Why are you telling me?"

Mama Tusani looked at him. He felt her gauging his character. "My girls, they have a bad past. It's the war that made them so. They have no home to go back to."

"You seem to be doing all right."

Her face hardened.

"You think I like this life? I had a hotel once. The war destroyed everything. Yes, I run a whorehouse. But I keep the girls safe. And they earn some money."

Vermeulen felt a pang of shame.

"The guns make the war go on," she continued. "We want no more war. We want our lives back."

She stared into his eyes with a force that made him squirm. "The pilot, he's a bad man," she said. "He should not walk on this earth. Now go and do your job."

She turned toward the door. Lily simulated the sounds of the final stages of orgasm. At the door, Mama Tusani stopped.

"Go out the rear. The driver will take you back to the hotel."

———

VERMEULEN DIRECTED THE driver to the airport instead. The guard gave him an inquisitive look, but Vermeulen forestalled any questions by flashing his OIOS ID. The guard was appropriately awed—he even saluted.

Once they were inside the airport, it took Vermeulen a while to get his bearings. Twice, he pointed the driver in the wrong direction. The man, of course, knew the way and got them to the cargo area.

He got out of the car. A solitary lamp on a post cast a milky light. Contrary to the major's assertion, there were no guards. A simple padlock kept unauthorized people out.

He circled the fence, looking for a good spot to climb over. He grabbed the wire mesh with both hands and tried hoisting himself up but realized he was fooling himself. The fence was seven or eight feet high. The days when he could tackle anything that height were long gone.

Back at the padlocked gate, he thought about Mama Tusani's words. She was the first person in a long time who actually wanted him to do his job. Everyone else wished he and his investigations would just go away. Even those who had no stake in whatever swindle he was digging up feared that his reports would cast them in a bad light and upset the routines they had grown to like. Everybody had an interest in keeping the status quo.

He examined the padlock again. It was solid. The fence posts didn't move when he pushed against them. The latch was fastened to the post with large screws. He tugged on it. It didn't budge. A metal rod might be strong enough to force the latch open. He thought of a tire iron and turned toward the Citroën.

The driver tried to be helpful, but the trunk was empty, no spare tire and definitely no tire iron.

Vermeulen rifled through the contents of his pants pockets and found his penlight, his lighter, and his pocketknife. The small blade doubled as an emergency screwdriver.

He tried the first screw. It was fastened tightly. He twisted the knife with both hands. The handle dug into his palm. The screw budged a half a turn. He stopped and repositioned the knife. After five minutes, he had removed the first screw. Sweat streamed down his forehead.

The driver observed him for a while but then must have decided that breaking and entering were not his cup of tea. He and the car disappeared.

By the time there were two screws remaining, the knife had scraped his right palm raw. In anger, he kicked the gate. It creaked, and the latch rattled. He aimed carefully and put all the force he could muster into the next kick. The gate sprung open with the sound of screws being wrenched from wood.

The inside of the tent was dark. By the narrow beam of his penlight he made out five pallets in the rear. The refrigerated units stood closer to the front, their compressors humming. A tangle of power cords connected them to the outlets mounted on a pole to the left of the entrance.

The extra refrigerated container—he remembered the code number—sat closest to the entrance. Its door was still sealed with a plastic cable tie. Without hesitation, he cut the tie and opened the door.

A wave of putrid stench enveloped him immediately. The beer in his stomach gurgled uneasily, sending a wave of nausea upward. He pulled a handkerchief from his pocket and held it over his mouth and nose. His penlight revealed the source of the reek. The bags of once frozen food had swollen to resemble grotesque pillows. Many had burst. Mold blooms as large as pizzas covered the interior of the container.

It all fit together. This container was extra, and last week one had been missing. The plane had stopped somewhere, dropped off the container, and then picked it up a week later. Without electricity, the food'd be rotten, all right—a perfect cover for smuggling weapons.

The sound of a truck arriving stopped him. Doors slammed. Angry voices. They had discovered the open gate. He stuck the penlight in his pocket and slipped toward the rear of the tent.

Not a moment too soon. The door of the tent opened and the bright beams of flashlights danced across the tent fabric. He ducked behind a pallet.

"Hijo de puta," somebody swore.

"Fuck! Somebody opened the container!" Vermeulen recognized the pilot's voice. "Raúl, check if anyone is still here. The rest of you, get the guns out now. We gotta move fast."

A flashlight lit up the rear of the tent. Raúl came closer. Vermeulen's mind ran through his options. There were none. These men had guns; he had a little knife. No contest.

Raúl stopped on the other side of the pallet. His flashlight bounced across the dark reaches of the tent. Raúl stepped to the left. Vermeulen crawled to the right, keeping the pallet between them.

He was now in plain view of the men at the entrance, but they were busy tossing the rotten food on the ground.

Raúl walked toward the last pallet.

"*¡Nadie!*" he shouted to the front.

Vermeulen felt exposed. He crawled to the pallet on the left and knelt in the dark space between it and the side of the tent. The beam of Raúl's flashlight swung around. The beam stopped, lighting the space he had just left. Vermeulen's heart skipped. There, glinting in the beam, lay his penlight. It must have dropped from his pocket.

"*¡Mira!*" Raúl shouted and held the penlight in the beam of his torch. Vermeulen crawled behind the pallet Raúl had just left.

The men in front had started stacking the guns in a pile. They were in a hurry.

Another voice told Raúl to hurry up, they didn't have all night.

Raúl shrugged, pocketed the penlight, and joined the men up front.

Time was running out. Vermeulen had to stop them before his evidence disappeared. He knelt down and cut a long slit into the tent fabric. His escape prepared, he took his lighter and lit the plastic netting around the nearest pallet. The flame licked up quickly. The other pallets caught fire just as fast. He crawled out of the tent and held his lighter to the tent fabric. The nylon fabric burst into flames.

Voices shouted inside. In no time, flames erupted through the top of the tent. The soldiers raced to safety in a mad scramble. The tent had turned into a torch, lighting up the airport like a bonfire.

———

COLONEL ZAMAN STOOD up when Vermeulen was led into his office the next morning. His appearance evoked memories of the

Raj—a uniform that looked as if it had been ironed after he'd dressed; a dark mustache, neatly twirled at the ends; slicked-back dark hair with a few white strands that framed the pale olive narrow face; keen eyes and a sharp nose. He seemed distraught.

"Mr. Vermeulen? What can I do for you? We have to make this quick. I have to deal with the aftermath of a fire."

His clenched jaws told the whole story—endless investigations, reviews of procedures, new training protocols, a complete nightmare.

"I know. I was there. The objects of my investigation were in that tent."

The colonel shook his head.

His day has just gotten worse, Vermeulen thought.

"You were at the airport in the middle of the night? Why?" the colonel asked.

"I just wanted to make sure the cargo area was secured, as your deputy had assured me it would be. It wasn't."

"Did you see the fire?"

"Yes, I saw the flames when I arrived. I saw the pilot and several Spanish-speaking soldiers."

"Spanish-speaking, you say? Did you see any insignia?"

Vermeulen shook his head. The colonel made some notes on a pad.

"Did they find guns in the tent?" Vermeulen asked.

"Yes, AK-47s and MP-5s. All burned, of course. It took a while to get the fire extinguished."

"Have you ordered anyone arrested?"

"Arrested? Why? The cause of the fire is unknown."

"What about the people by the tent?"

"Lots of people were there, trying to douse the fire."

"I just told you who started it."

"But you don't know that. You only got there after the fire had started."

The truth began to sink in slowly. And when it finally hit, Vermeulen had to press his lips together to keep from screaming. Setting the fire had ruined his investigation. He knew who the culprits were but couldn't finger them unless he admitted to setting the fire. Which would mean the end of his job.

"You should at least arrest Petrovic," he said, sounding deflated.

"The pilot?" Colonel Zaman raised his left eyebrow. "Why?"

"Because the guns came on his plane. I need to question him." The colonel shook his head. Vermeulen knew what would come next.

"We don't know that. Besides, he's a civilian contractor. I can't arrest him on your say-so."

"My mission," Vermeulen said, trying to conjure gravitas out of thin air, "authorizes me to interview anyone attached to the UN operation here. That includes Petrovic."

The colonel sighed.

"You may interview him if you can find him, but I can't arrest him; I trust you understand that. Now, if you'll excuse me."

———

IN DAYLIGHT, MAMA Tusani's club was even less appealing. The bar still reeked of stale beer and tobacco smoke, but the shabby interior was no longer hidden by the darkness. An ancient tape player looped through a scratchy collection of American hip-hop. Some girls were hanging around the bar, but one o'clock in the afternoon was clearly not the main business hour.

Vermeulen had gone to the club after leaving Colonel Zaman's office. It was an obvious choice. He'd met men like Petrovic before. Despite their swagger, or maybe because of it, they were essentially stupid. Of course Petrovic would be at the club. One last screw before flying back to Kampala.

Mama Tusani stood behind the bar. She nodded and held up two fingers.

"Be careful, he's got a gun," she whispered.

He marched past the ragged curtain and ripped open the second door. Lily lay on the bed, her arms tied to the bed frame, her eyes wide with fear. Petrovic lay on top of her, pressing down hard.

Images of Gaby in that hellhole in Antwerp ran through Vermeulen's mind. His heart pounded and he had to stop himself from pulling Petrovic off the girl.

Petrovic smiled when he saw him.

"Vermeulen. What a surprise. Want to join the party? Lily here has many talents."

Petrovic's smile turned Vermeulen's blood to ice. The gangsters who held Gaby had smiled like that. The crooks he investigated smiled like that. Certain they were untouchable. Too often, they were right. But not this time.

"Get dressed, Petrovic, you're coming with me," he hissed through clenched teeth. His heart pounded.

"I'm not going anywhere," Petrovic said. He rolled to his side languidly. "Hey, Lily, let's show this guy a good fuck."

Petrovic's clothes lay piled at the foot end of the bed. Vermeulen bent down, rifled through them, and found the gun, a Beretta. He flicked off the safety and pointed the pistol at Petrovic. "Get dressed, Petrovic. Now!"

"Hey, careful with that," Petrovic said with a bored expression. "It doesn't suit you. I bet you never even fired one."

"You're wrong there. We shot all kinds of vermin on our farm. Now get up and get dressed."

Petrovic crawled to the edge of the bed and started putting on his underwear. "Tell me this is a joke. You haven't got anything on me."

"Oh, I've got plenty. I have all your departure and arrival times. You were late because you made unscheduled stops to pick up guns. I also know you stored them in refrigerated units because every time you brought an extra one, it had rotten food in it. I've put all the pieces together."

Petrovic pulled on his jeans, a sneer on his face. "That won't do you any good. You'll never make it stick. What court will hear your charges? I'll just walk away from this and fly somewhere else. No big deal. Africa always needs guns."

A rage Vermeulen hadn't known before erupted. It ruptured the dam that held back a sea of frustration accumulated over a decade. No need to think anymore. The flood swept away any hesitation. He saw everything—the room, Petrovic, Lily—with unearthly clarity. There was only one thing he could do.

"You're wrong again," he snarled, and stepped toward the bed.

Petrovic realized something had changed.

"What are you talking about?" he asked, his voice suddenly uncertain.

Vermeulen grabbed Petrovic by the shirt, pressed the Beretta's muzzle against his temple, and pulled the trigger. The side of Petrovic's head exploded. Lily screamed. A sick spatter of blood and tissue marbled the wall. Petrovic went limp. Vermeulen let the body slide onto the bed.

Briefly deafened by the gunshot, he took a handkerchief from his pocket and cleaned the gun. Then he opened Petrovic's right hand, placed the Beretta in it, stuck the index finger through the trigger guard, and closed the hand again.

Mama Tusani waited in the hallway.

He opened his mouth, grasping for an explanation. She put her finger on his lips.

"I'll take care of Lily. Go out the rear. The driver will take you back to the hotel."

He nodded and strode to the back door. A strange lightness took hold of his body. Tomorrow, he'd call his daughter.

THE UNREMARKABLE HEART

BY KARIN SLAUGHTER

June Connor knew that she was going to die today.

The thought seemed like the sort of pathetic declaration that a ninth-grader would use to begin a short-story assignment—one that would have immediately elicited a groan and failing grade from June—but it was true. Today was the day that she was going to die.

The doctors, who had been so wrong about so many things, were right about this at least: She would know when it was time. This morning when June woke, she was conscious of not just the pain, the smell of her spent body, the odor of sweat and various fluids that had saturated the bed during the night, but of the fact that it was time to go. The knowledge came to her as an accepted truth. The sun would rise. The Earth would turn. She would die today.

June had at first been startled by the revelation, then had lain in bed considering the implications. No more pain. No more sickness. No more headaches, seizures, fatigue, confusion, anger.

No more Richard.

No more guilt.

Until now, the notion of her death had been abstract, an impending doom. Each day brought it closer, but closer was never too close. Always around the corner. Always the next week. Always sometime in the future. And now it was here, a taxi at the foot of the driveway. Meter ticking. Waiting to whisk her away.

Her legs twitched as if she could walk again. She became antsy, keenly aware of her pending departure. Now she was a businesswoman standing at an airport gate, ticket in hand, waiting to board the plane. Baggage packed. Luggage checked. Not a trip she wanted to make, but let's just get it over with. Call my row. Let me onto the plane. Let me put back my seat, rest my eyes, and wait for the captain to take over, the plane to lift, the trail of condensation against the blue sky the only indication that I have departed.

How long had it been since the first doctor, the first test, predicted this day? Five and a half months, she calculated. Not much time, but in the end, perhaps too much to bear. She was an educator, a high school principal with almost a thousand kids in her charge. She had work, responsibilities. She hadn't the time or inclination for a drawn-out death.

June could still remember going back to work that day, flipping through her calendar—standardized testing the following month, then the master schedule, which no one but June understood. Then the winding down of the school year. Grades due. Contracts signed. Rooms cleaned. The school was to be repainted this year. Tiles replaced in the cafeteria. New chairs for the band room. Lockers needed to be rekeyed.

"All right," she had said, alone in her office, staring at the full days marked on the calendar. "All right."

Maybe she could fit it all in. If she could last four months, maybe she could get it all done.

So June had not taken her dream vacation to Europe. She had not gone skydiving or climbed a mountain. She continued to work at a job she had grown to despise as if what she did made a difference. Suspending students. Lecturing teachers. Firing a slovenly gym coach she'd been collecting a file on for the last three years.

Clumps of hair fell onto her desk. Her teeth loosened. Her nose bled. One day, for no obvious reason, her arm broke. She had been holding a cup of coffee, and the heat from the liquid pooling on the carpet in front of her open-toed sandal was the first indication that something was wrong.

"I've burned my foot," she had said, wondering at the dropped jaws of the secretaries in the front office.

What had forced her on? What had made her capable of putting on panty hose and pantsuits every morning, driving to school, parking in her spot, doing that hated job for four more months when no one on earth would have questioned her early retirement?

Willpower, she supposed. Sheer determination to finish her final year and collect her full pension, her benefits, after giving thirty years of her life to a system that barely tolerated her presence.

And pride. After all this time, she embraced the opportunity to show her suffering on the outside. She wanted them to see her face every day, to watch the slow decline, to note the subtle changes that marked her impending death. Her last pound of flesh. Her last attempt to show them that they were not the only ones who'd sustained damage. Jesus on the Cross had made a less determined departure.

There was no best friend to tell. No family members left to whom she could confide her fears. June announced it in a school-wide e-mail. Her hand had been steady as she moused over to the icon showing a pencil hovering over a piece of yellow paper. Compose. Send to all. No salutation. No tears. No quibbling. She was fifty-eight years old and would not live to see fifty-nine, but a sentence of death did not give her license to lose her dignity.

You should all know that I have inoperable stage-four lung cancer.

The first thing people asked was, Are you a smoker? Leave it to June to get the sort of disease that had a qualifier, that made strangers judge you for bringing on your own illness. And even when June told them no, she had never smoked, never tried a cigarette or even thought about it, there was a glassy look in their eyes. Disbelief. Pity. Of course she'd brought this on herself. Of course she was lying. Delusional. Stubborn. Crazy.

It was all so eerily similar to what had come before that by the end of the day, June found herself laughing so long and so hard that she coughed blood onto her blouse. And then the horrified looks had replaced the pity, and she was back in those dark days when her only comfort was the thought that the sun would rise and set, the years would go by, and, eventually, she would die, her shame taken with her to the grave.

Irony, June thought now. An incongruity between what might be expected and what actually occurs.

The lung cancer had quickly metastasized. First to her liver, which gave her an alarming yellowish pallor, then to her bones, so brittle that she was reminded of angel hair pasta before you put it into a pot of boiling water. And now her brain, the last thing that she could truly call her own. All cancerous. All riddled with tumors, cells multiplying faster than the palliative radiation and chemotherapy could keep up with.

The doctor, an impossibly young man with a smattering of acne on his chin, had said, "The metastasis are quite pronounced."

"Metasta*ses*," June had corrected, thinking she could not even have the luxury of dying without having to correct the English of someone who should clearly know better. "Five months." He'd scribbled something in her chart before he closed it. "Six if you're lucky."

Oh, how lucky June was to have this extra time.

The tumors in her brain weren't impinging on anything useful. Not yet, at least, so it would seem not ever. This morning, she imagined them as similar to the shape of a lima bean, with tiny, round bottoms that fit puzzle-piece-like into curving gray matter. Her speech was often slurred, but the gift of brain metastases was that oftentimes she could not hear her own voice. Memory was an issue, though maybe not. She could be paranoid. That was a common side effect of the myriad medications she ingested.

Short-term-memory loss. Palsy. Dry mouth. Leaky bowels.

Her breathing was borderline suffocation, the shallow gulps bringing wheezing death rattles from her chest. She could no longer sit up unaided. Her skin was cold, the constant temperature of a refrigerator's vegetable crisper, and, in keeping with the metaphor, its texture, once smooth and even, was now entirely wilted.

In the early days of her diagnosis, she'd had many questions about her impending death but could find no one to answer them. There were plenty of tracts in the doctor's office on keeping a good attitude, eating macrobiotic diets, and making your way back to Jesus, but June could find nothing that spoke frankly of the actual act of death itself. There must have been information online, but if June wanted to read endless paragraphs of poor-me navel-gazing, she could walk down to the reading lab and start grading creative-writing assignments. Besides, she could not overcome her long-held belief that the internet was designed to render human beings functionally retarded.

Years ago, when June had had gallbladder surgery, she had talked to other patients to find out what to expect. How long was the recovery? Was it worth it? Did it take care of the problem?

There was no one to talk with this time. You could not ask someone, What was it like when you died?

"It's different for everyone," a nurse had said, and June, still enough life to feel the injustice of her situation, said, "That's bullshit."

Bullshit, she had said. *Bullshit,* to a perfect stranger.

Five years ago, the air conditioner at the house had finally given up the ghost, and the repairman, a former student of June's who seemed disproportionately fascinated with the minutiae of his job, had described in great detail where the fatal flaw had occurred. Condensation had rusted the coil. The Freon had leaked, depriving the system of coolant. The hose to the outside unit had frozen. Inside the house, the temperature had continued to rise rather than fall, the poor thermostat not understanding why cooling was not being accomplished. Meanwhile, the fan had continued on, whirring and whirring until the motor burned out.

Cause and effect.

And yet, while June could easily find a semiliterate HVAC repairman to explain to her the process by which her air conditioner had died on the hottest day of the summer, there was no medical expert who could reveal to June the minutiae of death.

Finally, on one of the last days that she was able to leave the house unaided, June had discovered a book in the dusty back shelves of a used-book store. She had almost overlooked it, thinking that she had found some New Age tripe written by a pajama-clad cultist. The cover was white with the outline of a triangle inside a solid circle. The title was an idiotic wordplay she could have done without—*How Do You Die?*—but she found comfort inside the pages, which was more than any living being had offered her.

The following text will serve as a guide to the physical act of dying, Dr. Ezekiel Bonner wrote. *Though every human being is different, the body dies in only one way.*

"Well," June had mumbled to herself. There, finally, was the truth.

None of us are special. None of us are unique. We may think we are individuals, but in the end, we are really nothing at all.

June had taken the book home, prepared a pot of tea, and read with a pen in her hand so that she could make notations in the margins. At points, she had laughed aloud at the descriptions offered by Dr. Bonner, because the physical act of the body shutting down was not unlike that of her dying air conditioner. No oxygen, no blood flow, the heart burning out. The brain was the last to go, which pleased June until she realized that there would be a period in which her body was dead but her brain was still alive. She would be conscious, able to understand what was going on around her, yet unable to do or say anything about it.

This gave her night terrors like she'd never had before. Not believing in the afterlife was finally getting its own back.

How long would that moment of brain clarity last? Minutes? Seconds? Milliseconds? What would it feel like to be suspended between life and death? Was it a tightwire that she would have to walk, hands out, feet stepping lightly across a thin cord? Or was it a chasm into which she would fall?

June had never been one to surrender to self-pity, at least not for any length of time. She considered instead the day ahead of her. She had always loved making lists, checking off each chore with a growing sense of accomplishment. Richard would come soon. She could already hear him downstairs making coffee. His slippers would shuffle on the stairs. Boards would squeak in the hallway. The hinges would groan as the door was pushed open. Tentatively, he would poke his head into the room, the curiosity in his eyes magnified by the thick lenses of his glasses.

Her eyes were always open. The morphine wore off in the early-morning hours. The pain was like thousands of needles that pricked her skin, then drilled deeper and deeper into the bone as the seconds ticked by. She lay in bed waiting for Richard, waiting for the shot. She would stare at him as he stood at the door, his hesitancy a third person in the room. He would not look at her face but at her chest, waiting for the strained rise and fall.

And somehow, she would force air into her constricted lungs. Richard would exhale as June inhaled. He would come into the room and tell her good morning. The shot would come first, the sting of the needle barely registering as the morphine was injected into her bloodstream. He would change the catheter. He would wet a rag in the bathroom sink and wipe the drool from her mouth as she waited for the drug to take away the gnawing edge of pain. He would ignore the smells, the stench of dying. In his droning monotone, he would tell her his plans for the day: fix the gutter, sweep the driveway, paint the trim in the hall. Then his attention would turn to her day: Are you hungry this morning? Would you like to go outside for a while? Would you like to watch television? Shall I read you the paper?

And today, as always, he did these things, asked these questions, and June checked each item off her mental list, shaking her head to the offer of food, to the trip outside. She asked for the local paper to be read, wanting him here, unreasonably, after wanting him away for so long.

Richard snapped open the newspaper, cleared his throat, and began reading. "'A severe weather pattern is expected to hit the county around three this afternoon.'"

His voice settled into a low hum, and June was consumed with the guilty knowledge of what the day would really hold. It was a secret that reminded her of the early days of their marriage. They had both been children of loveless unions, parents who hated each other yet could not survive in the world outside the miserable one they had created. In their young fervor, June and Richard had promised each other they would never be like their parents. They would always be truthful. No matter how difficult, there would be nothing unsaid between them.

How had that facade cracked? Was it June who had first lied? The obfuscations had come in dribs and drabs. An ugly shirt he loved that she claimed had been ruined in the wash. A "forgotten" dinner with friends that she did not want to attend. Once, June had accidentally dropped a whole chicken on the floor and still put it in the pot for supper. She had watched him eat that night, his jaw working like a turning gear, and felt some satisfaction in knowing what she had done.

Had Richard done that to her as well? Had there been a time at the dinner table when he had stared at her while relishing the knowledge of his crimes? Had there been a night when he made love to her in this bed, his eyes closed in seeming ecstasy, as he thought not of June but of others?

"'The school board has decided to renew the contract with Davis Janitorial for the maintenance of both the elementary and middle schools,'" Richard continued.

Early on in this process, June had felt much derision for the simple stories told by the *Harris Tribune* to the twelve thousand residents of the small town. Lately, the articles had taken on the importance of real news — The Renewed Maintenance Contract! The New Bench Erected in the Downtown Park! — and June found herself thinking of all those foolish stories people told about near-death experiences. There was always a tunnel, a light up ahead they chose to walk toward or away from. June saw now that there was, in fact, a tunnel — a narrowing of life, making a story as simple as what the elementary school was serving for lunch that week take on infinite importance.

"What's that?" Richard was staring at her, expectant. "What did you say?"

She shook her head. Had she actually spoken? She could not remember the last time she'd participated in a real conversation beyond her grunts for *yes* or *no*. June was capable of speech, but words caught in her throat. Questions caught — things she needed to ask him. Always, she said to herself, *Tomorrow. I'll ask him tomorrow.* The Scarlett O'Hara of dying high school administrators. But there would be no tomorrow now. She would have to ask him today or die without knowing.

" 'Harris Motors has asked for a side setback variance in order to expand their used-car showroom. Those wishing to speak either for or against the proposal can — '"

His shirt was buttoned to the top, the collar tight around his neck. It was an affectation he'd picked up in prison. The pursed lips, the hard stare — those were all his own, conjured during the lead-up to the trial, when June had realized with a shocking sense of familiarity that for all their attempts, they had become the one thing they'd set out not to be: two people trapped in a loveless marriage, a cold union. Lying to each other to make the day go by quickly, only to get up the next morning and find a whole new day of potential lies and omissions spread out before them.

She remembered glancing around the prison visiting room, seeing the other inmates with the stiff collars of their blue shirts buttoned snug around their necks, and thinking, *You've finally found a way to fit in.*

Because Richard had never really fit in. Early on, it was one of the things she loved about him. Friends joked about his lack of masculine pursuits. He was a voracious reader, couldn't stand sports, and tended to take contrary political views in order to play devil's advocate. Not the ideal party guest but, to June, the perfect man. The perfect partner. The perfect husband.

Before her cancer diagnosis, she had never visited Richard in prison, not once in the twenty-one years since he had been sent away. June was not afraid of losing the hate she felt for him. That was as firmly rooted in her chest as the cancer that was growing inside of her. What scared her most was the fear of weakness, that she would break down in his presence. She didn't need a Dr. Bonner to tell her that love and hate existed on the same plane. She didn't need him to tell her that her bond with Richard Connor was at once the best and the worst thing that had ever happened to her.

So it was that the day she drove to the prison, not the day that she was diagnosed with end-stage lung cancer, was the worst day of June Connor's life. Her hands shook. Tears rolled down her cheeks. Standing outside the door to the visitors' area, she let the fear take hold and imagined all the horrible things that could make her weak before him.

The feel of his lips when he kissed her neck. The times she had come home from school, exhausted and angry, and he had cupped her chin with his hand or pressed his lips to her forehead and made everything better. The passionate nights, when he would lie behind her, his hand working her into a frenzy. Even after decades of living apart, after loving him and hating him in equal measure, she found the thought of his body beside her still brought an unwelcome lust.

He never closed drawers or cabinet doors all the way. He never put his keys in the same place when he got home from work, so every morning he was late for school because he couldn't find them. He belched and farted and occasionally spat on the sidewalk. He took his socks off by the bed every night and left them there for June to pick up. There was not an item of laundry he knew how to fold. He had a sort of domestic blindness that prevented him from seeing the furniture that needed to be dusted, the carpets that needed to be vacuumed, the dishes that needed to be washed.

He had betrayed her. He had betrayed everything in their lives.

This latter bit was the only reason June was able to walk through the visitors' door, force herself through the pat-down and metal detector, the intrusive rifling of her purse. The smell of prison was a slap in the face, as was the realization that five thousand grown men were living, shitting, breathing the same air in this miserable place.

What was she worried about—her nose wrinkling, her hand going to her mouth—that she'd get lung cancer?

And then Richard had shown up, a shuffling old man, but still much the same. Stooped shoulders, because he was tall but never proud of it. Gray hair. Gray skin. He'd cut himself shaving that morning. Toilet tissue was stuck to the side of his neck. His thick, black-framed glasses reminded her of the ones he'd worn when they'd first met outside the school library, all those years ago. He was in two of her classes. He was from a small town. He wanted to teach English. He wanted to make kids feel excited about learning. He wanted to take June to the movies that night and talk about it some more. He wanted to hold her hand and tell her about the future they would have together.

There was nothing of that excited eagerness in the old man who'd sat across from her at a metal table.

"I am dying," she'd said.

And he had only nodded, his lips pursed in that self-satisfied way that said he knew everything about June before she even said it.

June had bristled, but inside, she understood that Richard had always known everything about her. Perhaps not the dropped chicken or the ugly shirt she'd gladly sent to the town dump, but he could see into her soul. He knew that her biggest fear was dying alone. He knew what she needed to hear in order to make this transaction go smoothly. He knew, above all, how to turn these things around so that she believed his lies, no matter how paltry the proof, no matter how illogical the reasoning.

"I'm a good man," he'd kept telling her. Before the trial. After the trial. In letters. On the telephone. "You know that, June. Despite it all, I am a good man."

As if it mattered anymore. As if she had a choice.

The secret that horrified her most was that deep down, part of her wanted to believe that he was still good. That he cared about her, even though the hatred in his eyes was so clear that she often had to look away. She could snatch the truth from the jaws of a tenth-grader at twenty paces, but her own husband, the man with whom she'd shared a bed, created a child, built a life, remained an enigma.

June turned her head away now, stared out the window. The curtains needed to be washed. They slouched around the window like a sullen child. Her hands still remembered the feel of the stiff material as she had sewn the pleats, and her mind conjured the image of the fabric store where she had bought the damask. Grace had been eight or nine then. She was running around the store, in and out of the bolts, screaming, so June had finally given up, quickly buying a fabric she wasn't particularly fond of just to get the annoying child out of the store.

And then came the horrible realization that the annoying child would be in the car with her, would come home with her and continue screaming the entire way. Outside the store, June had sat in the blazing-hot car and recalled stories of mothers who'd accidentally left their kids unattended in their cars. The children's brains boiled. They died horrible, agonizing deaths.

June had closed her eyes in the car, summoned back the cool interior of the fabric store. She saw herself browsing slowly down the aisles, touching bolts of fabric, ignoring the prices as she selected yards of damask and silk. No child screaming. No clock ticking. Nowhere to go. Nothing to do but please herself.

And then her eyes popped open as Grace's foot slammed into the back of the seat. June could barely get the key in the ignition. More shaking as she pressed the buttons on the console, sending cold air swirling into the car, her heart stopping midbeat as she realized with shame that it was not the idea of killing her child that brought her such horror, but the thought of the fallout. What the tragedy would leave behind. Grieving mother. Such a sad story. A cautionary tale. And then, whispered but still clear, *How could she...*

Every mother must have felt this way at one time or another. June was not alone in that moment of hatred, that sensation of longing for an unattached life that swept over her as Grace kicked the back of her seat all the way home.

I could just walk away, June had thought. Or had she said the actual words? Had she actually told Grace that she could happily live without her?

She might have said the words, but, as with Richard, those moments of sheer hatred came from longer, more intense moments of love. The first time June had held little Grace in her arms. The first time she'd shown her how to thread a needle, make cookies, decorate a cupcake. Grace's first day of kindergarten. Her first gold star. Her first bad report card.

Grace.

June came back to herself in her dank bedroom, the sensation almost of falling back into her body. She felt a flutter in her chest, a tapping at her heart; the Grim Reaper's bony knuckles knocking at the door. She looked past the dingy curtains. The windows were dirty. The outside world was tainted with grime. Maybe she should let Richard take her outside. She could sit in the garden. She could listen to the birds sing, the squirrels chatter. The last day. The last ray of sunlight on her face. The last sensation of the sheets brushing against her legs. The last comb through her hair. The last breath through her lungs. Her last glimpse of Richard, the house they had bought together, the place where they had raised and lost their child. The prison cell he had left her in as he went off to live in one of his own.

"'A house on Taylor Drive was broken into late Thursday evening. The residents were not at home. Stolen were a gold necklace, a television set, and cash that was kept in the kitchen drawer...'"

She had loved sewing, and before her life had turned upside down the second time, before the detectives and lawyers intruded, before the jury handed down the judgment, June had thought of sewing as a metaphor for her existence. June was a wife, a mother. She stitched together the seam between her husband and child. She was the force that brought them together. The force that held them in place.

Or was she?

All these years, June had thought she was the needle, piercing two separate pieces, making disparate halves whole, but suddenly, on this last day of her life, she realized she was just the thread. Not even the good part of the thread, but the knot at the end—not leading the way, but anchoring, holding on, watching helplessly as someone else, some*thing* else, sewed together the patterns of their lives.

Why was she stuck with these thoughts? She wanted to remember the good times with Grace: vacations, school trips, book reports they had worked on together, talks they had had late at night. June had told Grace all the things mothers tell their daughters: Sit with your legs together. Always be aware of your surroundings. Sex should be saved for someone special. Don't ever let a man make you think you are anything but good and true. There were so many mistakes that June's own mother had made. June had parented against her mother, vowing not to make the same mistakes. And she hadn't. By God, she hadn't.

She had made new ones.

We didn't raise him to be this way, mothers would tell her during parent-teacher conferences, and June would think, *Of course you did. What did you think would happen to a boy who was given everything and made to work for nothing?*

She had secretly blamed them—or perhaps not too secretly. More often than not, there was a complaint filed with the school board by a parent who found her too smug. Too judgmental. June had not realized just how smug until she saw her own smirk reflected back to her at the beginning of a conference about Grace. The teacher's eyes were hard and disapproving. June had choked back the words *We didn't raise her this way* and bile had come into her throat.

What had they raised Grace to be? A princess, if Richard was asked. A perfect princess who loved her father.

But how much had he really loved her?

That was the question she needed answered. That was *literally*—and she used the word correctly here—the last thing that would be on her mind.

Richard sensed the change in her posture. He stared at her over the paper. "What is it?"

June's brain told her mouth to move. She felt the sensation—the parting of the lips, the skin stuck together at the corners—but no words would form.

"Do you want some water?"

She nodded because that was all she could do. Richard left the room. She tilted her head back, looked at the closed closet door. There were love letters on the top shelf. The shoe box was old, dusty. After June died, Richard would go through her things. He would find the letters. Would he think her an idiot for keeping them? Would he think that she had pined for him while he was gone?

She *had* pined. She had ached. She had cried and moaned, not for him, but for the *idea* of him. For the idea of the two of them together.

June turned her head away. The pillowcase felt rough against her face. Her hair clung to wet skin. She closed her eyes and thought of Grace's silky mane of hair. So black that it was almost blue. Her alarmingly deep green eyes that could penetrate right into your soul.

"We're almost out of bendy straws," Richard said, holding the glass low so that she could sip from the straw. "I'll have to go to the store later."

She swallowed, feeling as if a rock were moving down her throat.

"Does it matter to you if I go before or after lunch?"

June managed a shake of her head. Breathing, normally an effort, was becoming more difficult. She could hear a different tenor in the whistle of air wheezing through her lips. Her body was growing numb, but not from the morphine. Her feet felt as if they were sliding out of a pair of thick woolen socks.

Richard placed the glass on her bedside table. Water trickled from the straw, and he wiped it up before sitting back down with the paper.

She should've written a book for wives who wanted their husbands to help more around the house. *Here's my secret, ladies: twenty-one years in a maximum-security prison!* Richard cooked and cleaned. He did the laundry. Some days, he would bring in the warm piles of sheets fresh from the dryer and watch television with June while he folded the fitted sheets into perfect squares.

June closed her eyes again. She had loved folding Grace's clothes. The tiny shirts. The little skirts with flowers and rows of lace. And then Grace had gotten older, and the frilly pink blouses had been relegated to the back of the closet. What had it been like that first day Grace came down to breakfast wearing all black? June wanted to ask Richard, because he had been there too, with his nose tucked into the newspaper. As she remembered, he had merely glanced at June and rolled his eyes.

Meanwhile, her heart had been in her throat. The administrator in June was cataloging Grace the same way she cataloged the black-clad rebels she saw in her office at school: *drug addict, whore, probably pregnant within a year.* She was already thinking about the paperwork she'd have to fill out when she called the young woman into her office and politely forced her to withdraw from classes.

June had always dismissed these children as damaged, half-way between juvenile delinquents and adult perpetrators. Let the justice system deal with them sooner rather than later. She washed them out of her school the same way she washed dirt from her hands. Secretly, she thought of them as legacy children—not the sort you'd find at Harvard or Yale, but the kind of kids who walked in the footsteps of older drug-addled siblings, imprisoned fathers, alcoholic mothers.

It was different when the errant child, the bad seed, sprang from your own loins. Every child had tantrums. That was how they learned to find their limits. Every child made mistakes. That was how they learned to be better people. How many excuses had popped into June's mind each time Grace was late for curfew or brought home a bad report card? How many times did June overlook Grace's lies and excuses?

June's grandmother was a woman given to axioms about apples and trees. When a child was caught lying or committing a crime, she would always say, "Blood will out."

Is that what happened to Grace? Had June's bad blood finally caught up with her? It was certainly catching up with June now. She thought of the glob of red phlegm that she'd spat into the kitchen sink six months ago. She had ignored the episode, then the next and the next, until the pain of breathing was so great that she finally made herself go to the doctor.

So much of June's life was marked in her memory by blood. A bloody nose at the age of seven courtesy of her cousin Beau, who'd pushed her too hard down the slide. Standing with her mother at the bathroom sink, age thirteen, learning how to wash out her underpants. The dark stain soaked into the cloth seat of the car when she'd had her first miscarriage. The clotting in the toilet every month that told her she'd failed, yet again, to make a child.

Then, miraculously, the birth. Grace, bloody and screaming. Later, there were bumped elbows and skinned knees. And then the final act, blood mingling with water, spilling over the side of the bathtub, turning the rug and tiles crimson. The faucet was still running, a slow trickle like syrup out of the jar. Grace was naked, soaking in cold, red water. Her arms were splayed out in mock crucifixion, her wrists sliced open, exposing sinew and flesh.

Richard had found her. June was downstairs in her sewing room when she heard him knocking on Grace's bedroom door to say good night. Grace was upset because her debate team had lost their bid for the regional finals. Debate club was the last bastion of Grace's old life, the only indication that the black-clad child hunched at the dinner table still belonged to them.

Richard was one of the debate-team coaches, had been with the team since Grace had joined, back in middle school. It was the perfect pursuit for two people who loved to argue. He'd been depressed about the loss, too, and covered badly with a fake bravado as he knocked, first softly, then firmly, on her door.

"All right, Gracie-gray. No more feeling sorry for ourselves. We'll get through this." More loud knocking, then the floor creaking as he walked toward the bathroom. Again, the knocking, the calling out. Richard mumbled to himself, tried the bathroom door. June heard the hinges groan open, then heard Richard screaming.

The sound was at once inhuman and brutally human, a noise that comes only from a mortal wounding. June had been so shocked by the sound that her hand had slipped, the needle digging deep into the meat of her thumb. She hadn't registered the pain until days later when she was picking out the dress Grace would be buried in. The bruise was dark, almost black, as if the tip of June's thumb had been marked with an ink pen.

The razor Grace used was a straight-edge blade, a relic from the shaving kit that had belonged to June's father. June had forgotten all about it until she saw it lying on the floor just below her daughter's lifeless hand. Grace didn't leave a suicide note. There were no hidden diaries or journals blaming anyone or explaining why she had chosen this way out.

The police wanted to know if Grace had been depressed lately. Had she ever done drugs? Was she withdrawn? Secretive? There seemed to be a checklist for calling a case a suicide, and the detectives asked only the questions that helped them tick off the boxes. June recognized the complacency in their stance, the tiredness in their eyes. She often saw it in the mirror when she got home from school. Another troubled teenager. Another problem to be dealt with. They wanted to stamp the case solved and file it away so that they could move on to the next one.

Washing dirt off their hands.

June didn't want to move on. She couldn't move on. She hounded her daughter's best friend, Danielle, until Martha, the girl's mother, firmly told June to leave her alone. June would not be so easily deterred. She called Grace's other friends into her office, demanded they tell her every detail about her daughter's life. She turned into a tyrant, firing off warning shots at anyone who dared resist.

She studied her daughter's death the way she had studied for her degrees, so that by the end of it all, June could've written a dissertation on Grace's suicide. She knew the left wrist was cut first, that there were two hesitation marks before the blade had gone in. She knew that the cut to the right wrist was more shallow, that the blade had nicked the ulnar nerve, causing some fingers of the hand to curl. She knew from the autopsy report that her daughter's right femur still showed the dark line of a healed fracture where she'd fallen off the monkey bars ten years before. Her liver was of normal size and texture. The formation of her sagittal sutures was consistent with the stated age of fifteen. There were 250 ccs of urine in her bladder, and her stomach contents were consistent with the ingestion of popcorn, which June could still smell wafting from the kitchen when she ran upstairs to find her daughter.

The lungs, kidneys, spleen, and pancreas were all as expected. Bones were measured, cataloged. The brain was weighed. All appeared normal. All were in the predictable margins. The heart, according to the doctor who performed the autopsy, was unremarkable.

How could that be? June had wondered. How could a precious fifteen-year-old girl, a baby June had carried in her womb and delivered to the world with such promise, have an unremarkable heart?

"What's that?" Richard asked, peering at her over the newspaper. When she shook her head, he said, "You're mumbling a lot lately."

She couldn't tell from his expression whether he was annoyed or concerned. Did he know that today was the day? Was he ready to get it over with?

Richard had always been an impatient man. Twenty-one years in an eight-by-ten cell had drilled some of that out of him. He'd learned to still his tapping hands, quiet the constant shuffling of his feet. He could sit in silence for hours now, staring at the wall as June slept. She knew he was listening to the pained draw of breath, the in-and-out of her life. Sometimes she thought maybe he was enjoying it, the audible proof of her suffering. Was that a smile on his lips as he wiped her nose? Was that a flash of teeth as he gently soaped and washed her underarms and nether regions?

Weeks ago, when she could still sit up and feed herself, when words came without gasping, raspy coughs, she had asked him to end her life. The injectable morphine prescribed by the doctor seemed to be an invitation to an easy way out, but Richard had recoiled at the thought. "I may be a lot of things," he had said, indignant, "but I am not a murderer."

There had been a fight of sorts, but not from anything June had said. Richard had read her mind as easily as he could read a book.

He'd as good as killed her two decades ago. Why was his conscience stopping him now?

"You can still be such a bitch," he'd said, throwing down a towel he'd been folding. She didn't see him for hours, and when he came upstairs with a tray of soup, they pretended that it hadn't happened. He folded the rest of the towels, his lips pressed into a thin line, and June, in and out of consciousness, had watched his face change as if she were looking at it through a colored kaleidoscope: angry red triangles blending into dark black squares.

He was an old man now, her husband, the man she had never bothered to divorce because the act would be one more reason for her name to appear beside his in the newspaper. Richard was sixty-three years old. He had no pension. No insurance. No chance of gainful employment. The state called it compassionate probation, though June guessed the administrators felt lucky to get an old man with an old man's medical needs off their books. For Richard's part, June was his only salvation, the only way he could live out the rest of his life in relative comfort.

And she would not die alone, unattended in a cold hospital room, the beep of a machine the only indication that someone should call the funeral home.

So the man who had robbed her of her good reputation, her lifelong friendships, her comfort in her old age would be the man who witnessed her painful death. And then he would reap the reward of the last thing, the only thing, they could not take away: the benefits of her tenure with the public school system.

June chuckled to herself. Two birds with one stone. The Harris County Board of Education would remit a check once a month payable to Richard Connor in the name of June Connor. They would be reminded once a month of what they had done to June, and once a month, Richard would be reminded of what he had done to her.

Not just to her—to the school. To the community. To Grace. To poor Danielle Parson, who, last June had heard, was prostituting herself in order to feed her heroin addiction.

June heard a loud knocking sound, and it took a few seconds for her to realize the noise was conjured from memory, something only she could hear. It was Martha Parson banging on the front door. She'd pounded so hard that the side of her hand was bruised. June had later seen it on television; Martha held the same hand to her chest, fist still clenched, as she talked about the monster in their midst.

Grace had been dead less than a month, and the police were back, but this time they were there to arrest Richard.

Whenever June heard a child make a damning statement against an adult, her default position was always disbelief. She could not be blamed for doing this at the time. This was not so many years removed from the McMartin preschool trials. False allegations of child abuse and satanic sexual rituals were still spreading through schools like water through sand. Kern

County. Fells Acres. Escola Base. The Bronx Five. It was a wonder parents didn't wrap their children in cellophane before sending them into the world.

More girls stepped up for their moments in the spotlight: Allison Molitar, Denise Rimes, Candy Davidson. With each girl, the charges became more unbelievable. Blow jobs in the faculty lounge. Fingerings in the library. He'd let them watch adult movies. He'd given them alcohol and taken suggestive photographs of them.

June immediately pegged them as liars, these former friends of Grace. She thought with disgust about the fact that she'd had these girls in her home, had driven them to the mall and the movie theater and had shared meals with them around her dinner table. June had searched the house, the car, Richard's office at home and school. There were no photographs. The only alcohol in the house was a bottle of wine that had sat in the back of the refrigerator since June's birthday. The cork had been shoved down into the open bottle. She'd pried it out, and the smell of vinegar had turned her stomach.

If June Connor knew about anything, it was teenage girls. Half her school day was spent settling she-said arguments, where rumors and innuendo had been used by one girl to tear down another. She knew the hateful, spiteful things they were capable of. They lied as a way of life. They created drama only to embrace the fallout. They were suggestible. They were easily influenced. They were spiteful, horrible human beings.

She said as much to the detectives, to the media, to the women who stopped her at the grocery store. Anyone who met June Connor during that time got the same story from her: *I know these girls, and they are all lying for attention.*

For his part, Richard was outraged. Teaching was his life. His reputation was sterling; he was one of those teachers students loved because he challenged them on every level every single day. He had devoted himself to education, to helping kids achieve something other than mediocrity. The previous year, four of his kids had gone on to full scholarships at Ivy League schools. Twice he had been voted teacher of the year for the district. Every summer, former students dropped by his classroom to thank him for making them work harder than they had ever worked in their lives. Doctors, lawyers, politicians—they had all at some point been in one of Richard's English classes, and he had done nothing but help them prepare for their exemplary lives.

That first week was a blur; talking to lawyers, going to a bail bondsman in a part of town June had not known existed. There was an entirely different language to this type of life, a Latin that defied their various English degrees: *ex officio, locus delicti, cui bono.* They stayed awake all night reading law books, studying cases, finding precedents that, when presented to the lawyer, were dispelled within seconds of their meeting. And still, they went back to the books every night, studying, preparing, defending.

There is no bond tighter than a bond of mutual persecution. It was June and Richard against everyone else. It was June and Richard who knew the truth. It was June and Richard who would fight this insanity together. Who were these girls? How dare these girls? To hell with these girls.

June had often lectured Grace about responsibility. Like most children, Grace was a great subverter. Her stories always managed to shift blame, ever so subtly, onto others. If there was a fight, then Grace was only defending herself. If she was late with an assignment, it was because the teacher's instructions had not been clear. If she got caught sneaking out in the middle of the night, it was because her friends had threatened her, cajoled her into being part of the group.

"Which is more possible," June had asked, "that every single person in the world is conspiring to make you seem a fool, or that you are only fooling yourself?"

But this was different. June was vindicated. One by one, the girls dropped away, their charges dismissed for lack of evidence. The parents made excuses: The girls were not lying, but the public scrutiny was too much. The limelight not what they had expected. All of them refused to testify—all but one. Danielle Parson, Grace's best friend. Richard's original accuser.

The prosecutor, having tremendously lost face when the bulk of his case fell apart, would have sought the death penalty if possible. Instead, he threw every charge at Richard that had even the remotest possibility of sticking. Sodomy, sexual assault, statutory rape, contributing to the delinquency of a minor, providing alcohol to a minor, and, because the debate team had traveled to a neighboring state for a regional tournament, child abduction and transporting a minor for the purposes of sexual concourse. This last one was a federal charge. At the judge's discretion, Richard could be sentenced to life in prison without the possibility of parole.

"It's come-to-Jesus time," their lawyer had said, a phrase June had never heard in her life until that moment. "You can fight this and still go to jail, or you can take a deal, serve your time, and get on with your life."

There were other factors. Money from a second mortgage they had taken on the house would get them through jury selection. Obviously, Richard wasn't allowed back at work or within three hundred yards of any of the girls. The board had told June they were thinking of "transferring her valuable skills" to a school that routinely ended up in the news for campus shootings and stabbings. Then there were the signs left in their front yard, the burning bag of shit on their front porch. Nasty phone calls. Deep scratches in the paint of their cars.

"It's like Salem," June had muttered, and Richard agreed, making a comment that burning at the stake was preferable to being slowly drawn and quartered in front of a crowd of hysterical parents.

June decided then and there to dig in her heels. They would fight this. They would live in a homeless shelter if that's what it took to clear Richard's name. She would not let them win. She would not let this lying, cheating whore who had been her daughter's best friend take another life.

She was certain then that Danielle had had something to do with Grace's death. Had she taunted her? Had Danielle hounded Grace until Grace felt that picking up that straight razor and opening up her skin was the only way to save herself?

Leading up to the trial, June was consumed with such hatred for Danielle Parson that she could not look at a blond, slight, simpering teenager without wanting to slap her. Danielle had always been mouthy, always wanted to push the limits. Her mother let her dress like a whore. She skipped class. She wore too much mascara. She was a hateful, hateful child.

More obscure Latin: from *depositio cornuum*, "taking off the horns," came *deposition*.

The twenty-one years since Richard's conviction had given June plenty of time to reflect on what happened next. They were sitting at a table in the prosecutor's conference room. Richard and June were on one side of the table—he because he was the accused, and June because she would have it no other way—while Danielle, Martha, and Stan Parson sat opposite. The lawyers were in between, lined up like dominoes ready to knock one another over with objections and motions to strike.

June relished the prospect of confronting the girl face-to-face. She'd prepared herself in the mirror that morning, using her best teacher gaze, the one that caused students to stop in their tracks and immediately apologize even when they weren't quite sure why.

Cut the bullshit, June wanted to say. *Tell the truth.*

There was no such confrontation. Danielle would not look anyone in the eye. She kept her hands folded in her lap, shoulders drawn into a narrow V. She had that fragility some girls don't lose even when they cross into womanhood. She was the type who would never have to take out the trash or change a tire or worry about paying her bills because one flutter of her eyelashes would bring men running to her aid.

June hadn't seen Danielle since Grace's funeral, when the girl had sobbed so uncontrollably that her father had to physically carry her out of the church. Recalling this scene, June experienced a revelation: Danielle was acting out of grief. Grace had been her best friend for almost a decade, and now she was gone. Danielle wasn't hurt, at least not in the physical sense. She was mad that Grace was gone, furious at the parents who couldn't prevent her death. There was no telling what reasons had clogged her mind. She obviously blamed Richard for Grace's death. She was lost and confused. Children needed to know that the world was a place where things made sense. Danielle was still a child, after all. She was a scared little girl who didn't know that before you could get out of a hole, you had to stop digging.

In that crowded conference room, a tiny bit of June's heart had opened up. She understood fury and confusion. She understood lashing out. She also finally understood that the loss of Grace had left a gaping hole in the girl's chest.

"Listen to me," June had said, her voice more moderate than it had been in weeks. "It's all right. Just tell the truth, and everything will be fine."

Danielle had finally looked up, and June saw in her red-rimmed eyes that she was not angry. She was not vindictive. She was not cruel. She was afraid. She was trapped. The slumped shoulders were not from self-pity, but from self-loathing.

"It's my fault Grace died." Danielle's words were a whisper, almost too soft to be heard. The court reporter asked her to repeat herself as the girl's lawyers clamored to ignore the declaration.

"She saw us," Danielle said, not to the room, or to the lawyers, but to June.

And then, with no prodding from the prosecutor, she went on to describe how Richard had seduced her. The longing glances in the rearview mirror as he drove the girls to and from school. The stolen kisses on her cheek, and sometimes her lips. The flattery. The compliments. The accidental touches — brushing his hand across her breast, pressing his leg against hers.

The first time it happened, they were at school. He had taken her into the faculty lounge, deserted after the last bell, and told her to sit down on the couch. As Danielle described the scene, June moved around the familiar lounge: the humming refrigerator, the scarred laminate tables, the uncomfortable plastic chairs, the green vinyl couch that hissed out a stream of air every time you moved.

Danielle had never been alone with Richard. Not like this. Not with the air so thick she couldn't breathe. Not with every muscle in her body telling her to run away. June did not hear the girl's words so much as experience them. The hand on the back of her neck. The hissing of the couch as she was shoved face-down into the vinyl. The agonizing rip as he forced himself from behind. The skin shredded by his callused hand when he reached around to touch her.

Why hadn't she told anyone?

The lawyer asked this question, but June did not need to hear the girl's answer.

If June Connor knew about anything, it was teenage girls. She knew how they thought, what they did to punish themselves when something bad happened, even if that bad thing was beyond their control. Danielle was afraid. Mr. Connor was her teacher. He was Grace's father. He was friends with her dad. Danielle didn't want to lose her best friend. She didn't want to upset June. She just wanted to pretend it hadn't happened, hope it would never happen again.

But she couldn't forget about it. She turned it over again and again in her mind and started blaming herself, because wasn't it her fault for being alone with him? Wasn't it her fault for not pulling away when he brushed up against her? Wasn't it her fault for letting their legs touch, for laughing at his jokes, for being quiet when he told her to be?

Slowly, in her little-girl voice, Danielle described the subsequent encounters, each time shifting the blame onto herself.

"I was late with an assignment."

"I was going to miss my curfew."

"He said it would be the last time."

And on and on and on, and finally it really was the very last time because Grace had walked into Richard's office at home. She'd come to find out if her dad wanted some popcorn. She'd found instead her dad raping her best friend.

"That's why..." Danielle gasped, looking up at June. "That's the night..."

June didn't have to be told. Even if she had wanted to, there was no way she could clear that night from her mind. June had been working in her sewing room. Danielle and Grace were upstairs eating popcorn, lamenting their lost chance at the regional championship. Richard was in his office. Martha Parson called, looking for her daughter. Richard offered to drive her home but the girl chose to walk. Why hadn't June thought it strange that a fifteen-year-old girl would rather walk six blocks in the cold than get a lift from her best friend's father?

"It's my fault," Danielle managed between sobs. "Grace saw us, and..." Her eyes were nearly swollen shut from crying. Her shoulders folded in so tight that she looked as if she were being sucked backward down a tube.

There was a long row of windows behind Danielle and her parents. June could see Richard's reflection in the glass. His face was impassive. There was a glint of white from his glasses. She glanced down and saw that his hands were in his lap.

She glanced down and saw that he was enjoying the story.

By the time the deposition was over, June's jaw was so tight that she could not open her mouth to speak. Her spine was hard as steel. Her hands were clenched into fists.

She did not say a word. Not when the girl described a birthmark on Richard's back, a scar just below his knee, a mole at the base of his penis. Not when she talked about the obsessive way he'd stroked her hair. The way he had held her from behind and used his hand on her. The way he had seduced this fifteen-year-old child in the same way he had seduced June.

And June had thought of her words, long ago, to Grace: "Which is more possible," she had asked, "that every single person in the world is conspiring to make you seem a fool, or that you are only fooling yourself?"

June had left the prosecutor's conference room without a word to anyone. She drove straight to the school's administration offices, where they gladly granted her request for a temporary leave of absence. She went to the dollar store and bought a packet of underwear, a toothbrush, and a comb. She checked in to a hotel and did not go home until the newspaper headlines told her that Richard would not be there.

He had left the heat on eighty, he who had fastidiously turned off hall lights and cranked down the thermostat on even the coldest days. The seat was up on every toilet. All the bowls were full of excrement. Dirty dishes spilled over in the sink. Trash was piled in the corner of the kitchen. The stripped mattress held the faint odor of urine.

"Fuck you too," June had mumbled as she burned his clothes in the backyard barbecue.

The school board couldn't fire her for being married to an imprisoned sex offender. Instead, she was moved to the worst part of town, a job for which she was routinely called to testify in court cases of students who'd been accused of armed robbery, rape, drug trafficking, and any number of horrors. Her social life was nonexistent. There were no friends left for the woman who had defended a pedophile. There were no shoulders to cry on for the principal who had called the students raped by her husband a pack of lying whores.

Over the years, June had considered giving an interview, writing a book, telling the world what it was like to be in that room listening to Danielle Parson and knowing that her husband had as good as killed them both. Each time June sat down to write the story, the words backed up like bile in her throat. What could she say in defense of herself? She had never publicly admitted her husband's guilt. June Connor, a woman who relished the English language, could find no words to explain herself.

She had shared a bed with Richard for eighteen years. She had borne him a child. They had lost their child. They had loved together. They had grieved together. And all the while, he was a monster.

What kind of woman didn't see that? What kind of principal did not notice that her own husband was brutally sodomizing her daughter's fifteen-year-old best friend?

Pride. Sheer determination. She would not explain herself.

She did not owe anyone a damn explanation. So she kept it all bottled up inside of her, the truth an angry, metastasizing tumor.

"Another story about the weather," Richard said, rustling pages as he folded the paper. "Umbrellas are suggested."

Her heart fluttered again, doing an odd triple beat. The tightness in her chest turned like a vise.

"What is it?" Richard reached for the mask hanging on the oxygen tank.

June waved him away, her vision blurring on her hand so that it seemed like a streak of light followed the movement. She moved her hand again, fascinated by the effect.

"June?"

Her fingers were numbing, the bones of her hand slowly degloved. She felt her breath catch, and panic filled her—not because the time was here, but because she still had not asked him the question.

"What is it?" He sat on the edge of the bed, his leg touching hers. "June?" His voice was raised. "Should I call an ambulance?"

She looked at his hands. His square fingers. His thick wrists. There were age spots now. She could see the blue veins under his skin.

The first time June held Richard's hand, her stomach had tickled, her heart had jumped, and she'd finally understood Austen and Brontë and every silly sonnet she'd ever studied.

Love is not love which alters when it alteration finds.

This was the feeling she wanted to take with her—not the horror of the last twenty years. Not the sight of her daughter lying dead. Not the questions about how much Grace knew, how much she had suffered. Not the thought of Danielle Parson, the pretty young girl who could make it through the day only with the help of heroin.

June wanted the feeling from the first time she had held her child. She wanted the bliss from her wedding day, the first time Richard had made love to her. There were happy times in this home. There were birthdays and surprise parties and Thanksgivings and wonderful Christmases. There was warmth and love. There was Grace.

"Grace," Richard said, as if he could read her mind. Or perhaps June had said the word, so sweet on her lips. The smell of her shampoo. The way her tiny clothes felt in June's hand. Her socks were impossibly small. June had pressed them to her mouth one day, kissing them, thinking of kissing her daughter's feet.

Richard cleared his throat. His tone was low. "You want the truth."

June tried to shake her head, but her muscles were gone, her brain disconnecting from the stem, nerve impulses wandering down vacant paths. It was here. It was so close. She was not going to find religion this late in the game, but she wanted lightness to be the last thing in her heart, not the darkness his words promised to bring.

"It's true," he told her, as if she didn't know this already. "It's true what Danielle said."

June forced out a groan of air. Valentine's Day cards. Birthday balloons. Mother's Day breakfasts. Crayon drawings hanging on the refrigerator. Skinned knees that needed to be kissed. Monsters that were chased away by a hug and a gentle stroke of hair.

"Grace saw us."

June tried to shake her head. She didn't need to hear it from his mouth. She didn't need to take his confession to her grave. Let her have this one thing. Let her have at least a moment of peace.

He leaned in closer. She could feel the heat from his mouth. "Can you hear me, wife?"

She had no more air. Her lungs froze. Her heart lurched to a stop.

"Can you hear me?" he repeated.

June's eyes would not close. This was the last minute, second, millisecond. She was not breathing. Her heart was still. Her brain whirred and whirred, seconds from burning itself out.

Richard's voice came to her down the long tunnel. "Grace didn't kill herself because she caught me fucking Danielle." His tongue caught between his teeth. There was a smile on his lips. "She did it because she was jealous."

IT AIN'T RIGHT

BY MICHELLE GAGNON

I t ain't right, is all I'm saying."

Joe just kept walking the way he always did, shovel over his shoulder, cigarette clinging to his bottom lip.

"You hear me?"

He stopped and turned, lifting his head inch by inch until his eyes found my hips then my breasts then my eyes. A dust devil whirled away behind him, making the bottom branches of the tree dance like girls on May Day, up and down. He stared at me long and hard, and I felt the last heat of the day seeping into my skin and down through my bones, reaching inside to meet the cold that burrowed into my stomach early that morning.

"She's dead, ain't she?" With his free hand, Joe scratched his belly where the bottom of his T-shirt had pulled away.

"Just 'cause she's dead don't mean she should be put down like this."

He looked past me toward where the road met the hill and dove behind it, wheat tips glowing pink in the twilight. "What else we gonna do with her?"

We stared each other down while the shadows crept in and heat eased into darkness like air escaping a balloon. Night surrounded Joe's head, digging under his cheekbones and into his eye sockets, carving out the face that had been so handsome years earlier that I swore he could've been in pictures.

I turned and shuffled back to the house, kicking up pebbles and dust with my sandals, crossing my arms against the cold that radiated out like there was a snowball growing inside me.

He was gone a long time. The six o'clock news came and went, then *Wheel of Fortune* and *Jeopardy!,* and me checking the clock every five minutes, getting up from time to time to peer through our fading curtains. It was always so quiet at night, I swear the TV was the only thing keeping my head screwed on my shoulders.

Law & Order was on when he finally came in, bolted both locks, and went to the sink without so much as a word. Joe washed his hands for a long time. I stared at the screen, trying to figure out why some girl was crying over someone who from the look of things she hadn't much liked anyway. He plunked down beside me and made the same sigh as his beer when he popped it open.

"So it's done, then," I said.

"Yep."

And that was the last we spoke of it. But once that cold burrowed inside me, it seemed dead set on staying. It got so I couldn't watch Joe standing in a towel with the mirror steamed up, shaving in that slow, careful way he did everything without wanting to sock him over the head with something. I kept washing his clothes and making his dinner, but when he entered me I stared up at the ceiling and endured his gasps and cries without a word, both of us pretending there wasn't another person lying there with us, when both of us knew there was.

Winter made it better somehow, made it so I couldn't imagine her trying to claw through the roots and soil to the air. I knew she was done then, that she wouldn't be able to come after us, at least not till spring. I figured maybe we'd move, head to the city like we always said we would when we were young and such things still might just happen one day. I had almost put it out of my mind, even managed a smile for Joe when he showed up with a new scarf and mittens in my favorite periwinkle, when lights pulled into our driveway. The police didn't say much, just probed our eyes while they asked, *Ever hear what went on over there? Any word on who she was seeing?* Joe did most of the talking, smiling a little too large, taking so long to answer you could practically hear him sounding it out in his mind before the words left his lips. I thought, *Always so handsome in those uniforms, so shiny.* Then I caught myself twisting the dish towel around and around my hand.

"She's the type," I heard myself saying.

"What type, ma'am?" One of them was eyeing me now, the older one with the small mustache.

"Loose—you know. She'd head off with any Tom passing by—since the day she was born, dead set on getting outta here. I heard her say once she wanted to go to Vegas, see the lights."

"Vegas, huh." The two of them looked at each other and nodded, slapped shut their notebooks, and waved their way out the door. Joe leaned back on the couch again and started flipping through channel after channel: knives slicing meat, kids swinging on ropes, women cleaning their kitchens. He went through all five hundred twice and I saw he wasn't stopping anytime soon, so I got my new mittens on and went outside for more of that quiet I was always complaining about.

It was cold and crisp and the moon shone flat on the field with a strange dead light, all gray and unnatural. I started down the road without really thinking, 'cause if I had been I would've said to myself, *Sadie, the cops just been here and this ain't no way to behave,* but something about the moon and the quiet erased those thoughts and suddenly I was there. It looked the same as all the other fields. *This is why they put up markers,* I thought, tapping my feet to keep out the cold. *Otherwise no one knows where you last set foot on earth.* I tasted the salt before I knew I was crying and was suddenly on my knees tearing at the snow, periwinkle blue pounding at the crust then throwing handfuls of cold past my legs. *It should be red,* I thought, *I'll dig down until I see some red...*

And then Joe's hands were on my shoulders, and he was carrying me in those arms that looked too thin to hold anything heavier than a shovel, and I woke up in my bed, sun warming the curtains and the smell of coffee sneaking under the door.

After a knock-knock, Joe came in holding my favorite mug, steam licking his face, and he kind of smiled at me. He put the mug on the table and smoothed my hair back and said, "I know you didn't mean to do it. I made you, and I'm sorry."

We were fifteen again, and he was the only boy in the world for me, movie-star handsome standing on the side of the quarry, beads of water glowing on his skin before he dove in and came up laughing.

We were twenty, and married, and I was pregnant and he had a decent job, and we were moving to the city soon as we saved enough money.

We were thirty, still happy even though none of the babies had worked out, and his job was the same, and I had trouble breathing in summertime.

We were forty, and even though we had each done a terrible thing, he still bought me mittens and lied to the police and brought me coffee in the morning. And I thought to myself, *This is a good man.* And I said, "Let's move to the city." And we never spoke of it again.

SILENT JUSTICE

BY C. E. LAWRENCE

B less me, Father, for I have sinned."

Father Aleksander Milichuk pressed his fingertips hard against the sides of his forehead in an attempt to stop the throbbing in his right temple. Another Monday morning, another migraine on the way. He really needed to back off on the Sunday-night drinking at McSorley's. He wasn't as young as he used to be, as his mother was so fond of reminding him. Maybe she was right; he was nearing forty, and these days just a couple of drinks could bring on a wicked headache. He took a deep breath and cleared his throat.

"How long has it been since your last confession?"

"Three weeks." The voice on the other side of the confessional was a breathy tenor, the voice of a young person.

"Is it a venial sin or a—"

"A mortal sin, Father."

Something in the man's tone made him lean forward.

"And what was this sin, my son?"

The answer came in a low voice, barely audible.

"Murder, Father."

Father Milichuk sat up very straight on his narrow bench, his mind snapping into sharp focus. He was no longer aware of the throbbing in his head. Panicked, he tried to think of a response, but his tongue was dry as paper and stuck to the roof of his mouth. There was a rustling sound from the other side of the confessional, as though the man were removing something from a plastic bag. Crazy, improbable thoughts darted through the priest's head. *What if he brought a gun with him?* His knees shook as fear flooded his veins. *Say something!* He tried to remember if he had ever heard this voice before.

"Aren't you going to give me penance, Father?" The man's tone was patient, weary.

The priest was very good at identifying voices and was certain he had never heard this man's voice before.

"Uh, yes, of course," he sputtered finally. "Say twelve Hail Marys—" He stopped, stunned by the feeble inadequacy of his response.

The man on the other side of the booth chuckled sadly. "That's all?"

"H-have you confessed your sin to the police?"

"I'm confessing it to you."

"Yes, I know, but—"

"I don't want to go to prison."

"Who did you—kill?"

"It doesn't matter. I took a life; that's all I'm required to tell you. Give me absolution, Father. Please."

"It's just that—"

"Please." It was half entreaty, half threat.

The priest looked at the lattice of shadow cast by the metal grille between them, crisscrossed like miniature prison bars.

"All right," he said. "But—"

"Deus meus, ex toto corde paenitet," the man began, *"me omnium meorum peccatorum, eaque detestor, quia peccando..."*

He finished his flawless Latin recitation with a final "Amen."

"Now will you give me absolution?"

Father Milichuk could see no way out of it. Crossing himself, he began to recite the familiar litany.

"May our Lord Jesus Christ absolve you —"

"In Latin, Father — please."

The priest crossed himself again. His head throbbed, and his palms were sweating.

"Dominus noster Jesus Christus te absolvat..." The words seemed to stick in his throat. He coughed and managed to complete the prayer, crossing himself one final time. But he failed to find the usual comfort in the gesture; it felt futile, desultory.

"Thank you, Father." The man sounded genuinely grateful. Whatever else he was, the priest thought, he was a true Catholic who believed in the power of absolution.

"Say twelve Hail Marys," he began, "and —"

"I will, Father — thank you. God bless you."

"God be with you, my son."

Before the priest could say another word, he heard the door hinges creak open, then the sound of rapidly receding footsteps on the stone floor of the church. Father Milichuk peered out through a hole in the carved design of the door, but the lighting was dim and all he could make out was the figure of a man dressed in dark clothing walking quickly away. Medium height, medium build; he could be anyone.

One thing the priest was certain of was that the mysterious supplicant was a Roman Catholic, not Greek. His perfect Latin was spoken in the Roman way, and he had said "I have sinned" rather than "I am a sinner," which was the Greek manner. But why had he come here? St. George was a Ukrainian Greek

Catholic church; surely this man had a Roman Catholic church he attended regularly. The answer came to Aleksander Milichuk suddenly: The man had chosen a place where he wouldn't be known. His own priest was bound to recognize his voice and would perhaps pressure him to turn himself in. Here, he was guaranteed anonymity.

The priest sighed and leaned back in the cramped cubicle, which smelled of stale sweat and candle wax. He put a hand to his temple in an attempt to control the throbbing. What did it matter who the man was or where he was from? Aleks wasn't a detective, and it wasn't his job to hunt the man down. He felt the full weight of the sinner's guilt upon his own shoulders. Perhaps that was what God intended—maybe he was doing his priestly duty now more than ever before, but the thought made him feel only more anxious.

The rest of the day passed in a haze of meaningless activity. There were parishioners to call, schedules to arrange, events to discuss—choir practice, the Wednesday-night church supper, vendors for the annual Ukrainian festival. He wished he could drown himself in the barrage of mundane details, but all he could think of was the terrible secret he would be forced to carry to his grave. He considered the idea that the man was lying, but rejected that hopeful notion. Either he was telling the truth or he was the best actor in the world.

Aleks gazed idly out the window, but even the sight of the white blossoms on the mimosa trees failed to cheer him up. He sat at his desk staring blankly, his head buzzing with apprehension. Normally he would now start writing his sermon for next week's service, but he was unable to concentrate.

His secretary, the ever-intrusive Mrs. Kovalenko, noticed his mood.

"Are you feeling all right, Father?" she asked, one hand on her plump hip, the other clutching a freshly filled teapot. Mrs. Kovalenko was a great believer in the healing power of tea, and she had the persuasive ability of a used-car salesman combined with a Mafia enforcer. If she wanted to serve you tea, there was little you could do about it. He had briefly considered firing her for the sake of his bladder, but Mrs. Kovalenko was not the kind of woman you fired, so he had resigned himself to frequent visits to the bathroom.

"I'm fine," he replied, but his heart wasn't in it, and she continued to stand there studying him. "I just have a headache," he added when she didn't move.

She shook her dyed blond curls and clicked her tongue, then she brightened. "A good cup of tea is what you need," she proclaimed. "Straighten you right out."

"That would be nice," he replied; at least it might throw her off the scent for a while. She had nagged him about his drinking in the past, but he had cut down recently—partly because of the headaches. She busied herself gathering the honey and cream, bustling about the office happily humming a Ukrainian folk song. He knew she didn't speak a word of the language, but she liked to impress people with her knowledge of the culture, and had picked up a few songs and phrases here and there.

"I just bought this tea last week," she said as she poured him a steaming cup from the ornate ceramic pot, decorated with chubby, beaming angels. She had found it at the weekly yard sale on Avenue A and had presented it to him with great pride. Father Milichuk gazed at an especially porcine angel and sighed. He hated angels. The angel leered at him with a self-satisfied smirk; he yearned to smash the pot and erase the grin from its fat little face.

He made a point of telling Mrs. Kovalenko how delicious the tea was. "What's it called?" he said, taking a sip and smacking his lips.

"It's Russian caravan!" she declared, clapping her hands with delight. "From the new tea store around the corner. I'm so glad you like it."

In truth, it tasted like turpentine. But nothing tasted good right now, not even the butter cookies from the Polish bakery he usually adored. Still, to make Mrs. Kovalenko happy (and less suspicious), he choked down several cookies with his tea. They tasted like dust.

And yet when evening came, he left the church reluctantly. It would be even worse at home, when he had no happily bustling secretary, only his aged and morose mother. His father used to joke that his mother cooked like a Ukrainian but had the disposition of a Russian, dour and depressive, with occasional flights of high-spirited gaiety. She could be giddy as a schoolgirl, but her physical complaints could fill a medical dictionary. If it wasn't the lumbago in her back, it was the arthritis in her knees. She also enjoyed regaling Aleks with the health problems of her friends at the senior center. Illness was her chief conversational topic, and her eyes would brim with tears of delight as she reported the latest grim pronouncements her friends had received from various medical professionals.

"Do you know that Mrs. Danek's doctor told her that her heart valve could just pop like a grape? Like a *grape*, Sasha!" she would say, her eyes wide with amazement. She addressed him by his nickname but always called her friends by their last names, in the formal manner, which she thought indicated superior breeding.

He left St. George as the last rays of the sun slid across the windows of McSorley's Old Ale House, across the street. He resisted the urge to head straight for the bar—he would go there later, after his mother was in bed. He turned east and walked the half a block to his apartment, trudging up to the third floor on narrow, creaky stairs worn by decades of feet. The hall always smelled of boiled cabbage; the Polish couple on the second floor seemed to cook little else.

He unlocked the door quietly, in case his mother was napping. He often found her asleep in the big green chair, their fat orange cat purring in her lap. He opened the door to the smell of homemade soup and the sound of snoring. After his father died, four years ago, Aleks invited his mother to come live with him—not that he had much choice. It was expected that a good Ukrainian son would look after his mother. After all, he wasn't married and needed a woman's touch around the place, as her friends declared over coffee and cheese blintzes.

He hung his hat and coat on the rack and crept into the living room, where his mother lay in her usual position, mouth open, her snores rattling the windowpanes. Their orange cat was perched on top of the back of the chair and regarded Aleks through half-closed eyes. A white lace antimacassar had slipped from the top of the chair onto his mother's head. It sat at a rakish angle, like a lace yarmulke, the edges fluttering delicately with each racking snore. He stood watching her for a moment, then tiptoed to his room. He wanted to be alone with his thoughts.

It wasn't long before he heard a soft tapping at his bedroom door. Aleks opened it to find his mother smiling up at him. She was a tiny woman, barely five feet tall, but sturdy and stout, with the broad, rosy-cheeked face of a Slavic peasant. She wore her thick gray hair in a long braid, and her blue eyes were clear and sharp. In spite of her obsession with illness, Aleks felt she would outlive everyone around her.

"Hello, *myla*," he said, using the Ukrainian term of endearment. His mother liked that. "How are you tonight? It looked like you were having a nice nap."

She sighed dramatically. "I'm feeling badly today, Aleksander."

The heat rose to his face, and he fought to control his irritation. "You mean you're feeling *bad* today. If you were feeling *badly* you would be having trouble with your sense of touch."

She waved him away impatiently. "Don't carp at your sick old mother, Sasha. Lord knows I have enough to worry about with Mrs. Petrenko's boils acting up. I shall have to get up early tomorrow to make her my special poultice. She is counting on me; the doctors can do nothing for her, you know."

Aleksander Milichuk had no idea if anyone counted on his mother for anything, and he murmured a vague response. Perhaps the ladies at the senior center were enjoying her ministrations whether her remedies actually worked or not. Sometimes it was just pleasant to have someone who cared enough to go out of her way for you. That was one reason he kept Mrs. Kovalenko on as his secretary. She was an incorrigible gossip and a busybody, but she fussed and clucked over him in a manner that both irritated and pleased him.

Dinner tonight consisted of homemade split-pea soup, brown bread, and cheese. His mother was a superb cook and enjoyed cooking for her "little Sasha," just as she had for his father. Aleks knew that the standard Ukrainian diet was not the healthiest in the world, but there was little hope of training his mother in new cuisine techniques at this point in her life. He sometimes thought his father's overindulgence in his wife's excellent cheese and potato pierogi had contributed to his fatal heart attack—but in his darker moments, Aleks felt that his father had died of a broken heart.

As if reading his mind, his mother said, "I dreamed about her last night, Sasha." He gazed down at his soup, which was so thick that the croutons didn't so much float as perch on top of the viscous mass of dark green liquid.

"She came to me as I slept, Sasha—she looked just as she did that last day of her life."

He continued to stare at his soup. Ten years had passed since his sister, Sofia, had been killed by a hit-and-run driver, and yet the rage shivered within him like a wind that would not be stilled. His father had never been the same afterward. When the police failed to make an arrest or even come up with a viable suspect, he began to wither like an unwatered houseplant, until finally his heart gave out. Aleks coped with the loss by drinking too much, and his mother... well, she had her physical ailments to keep her company.

Ignoring his silence, she rattled on, as if helpless to stop. "When she comes to me like that, I know something is going to happen. Mark my words, Sasha, something will happen—something big."

"Yes, Mama," he said. He was too troubled by the events of the day to pay much attention to his mother's words. The last thing he needed was to think about his sister; it only made him angry. He refused a second bowl of soup and rose from the table. The cat lurked nearby, hoping for scraps of cheese.

"Are you going out tonight, Sasha?" his mother asked, slipping the cat a piece of cheese under the table.

"Just for a while," he replied, putting on his coat. "I told Lee Campbell I'd meet him at McSorley's for a drink."

"That handsome policeman friend of yours?" she asked, all smiles.

"He works for the police department, but he's a psychologist, not a cop."

"As you say, Sasha—but he is good-looking, you have to admit."

"Yes, Mama. Thanks for the soup—it was delicious."

"Don't be too late, Sasha. You're looking a little peaked."

"I won't—don't worry."

"And you won't have too many, will you, Sasha?"

"You know I've cut back lately, Mama."

"Promise?"

"I promise."

He kissed her and slipped out, locking the door behind him. Outside, the evening was crisp and sharp, the late days of April hugging the streets in a feathery embrace. It was the time of year when trees blossomed overnight and flower beds came alive with riotous bursts of yellow.

Inside the bar, Lee Campbell was sitting at a window table with four beers in front of him. Beer at McSorley's came two at a time, in heavy glass mugs wielded by stocky, red-cheeked waiters— fresh off the boat, if they were young, and former policemen if they were older. Their waiter was a retired cop Aleks had seen numerous times here, a burly man with the heavy shoulders and head of a mastiff. He nodded at the priest, which made Aleks unaccountably nervous.

Aleks slid into a seat across from his friend, resting his elbows on the ancient, scarred oak table. McSorley's Old Ale House was the oldest pub in continuous operation in the city, dating back to 1854. It hadn't changed much since then: the floors were still covered with sawdust, and the potbellied woodstove in the front room still huffed out heat during the cold winter months. Decades of dust lay on strands of abandoned spiderwebs hanging from ancient knickknacks over the bar. There was hardly an inch of bare space on the walls, which were crammed with photos, paintings, and mementos.

"Sorry I'm late," Aleks said, reaching for the icy mug of ale that Lee pushed across the table.

"I got us one of each," Campbell said, nodding at the twin mugs, one dark and one amber. Only a single beverage was available at McSorley's: ale. You could order it dark or amber, but either way you got two mugs of it.

"Thanks," Aleks said, drinking deeply. "The next one's on me."

"It's a deal," Lee said. "I have a head start on you already."

The two men had met at St. Vincent's in the dark days following 9/11. Aleks had had a series of anxiety attacks, something he'd never experienced before, and by the time he showed up at the hospital for psychiatric treatment, he needed very much to talk to anyone who would listen. Because of his position, he was used to giving comfort and advice to others but was not very good at taking it himself.

In the weeks after the attack, a lot of people needed help, so he wasn't alone. Psychiatric wards all over the city were seeing a record influx of patients. Lee Campbell was another patient at the St. Vincent's clinic, and they struck up a friendship. Campbell's position as New York City's only full-time criminal profiler was unique, and Aleks was drawn to the tall, charismatic Scot. After all, they each dealt with matters of morality, good and evil, though perhaps from different viewpoints. They had other things in common: Both loved music, had played rugby in college, and, to top it off, lived on the same block of East Seventh Street. And, as they liked to joke, both had difficult and devoted mothers.

But what really united them was shared tragedy. Each had lost his younger sister in a misfortune with loose ends, the loss like an open wound that would never heal. The driver of the car that killed Sofia had never been caught, but Lee's heartbreak was even worse, Aleks thought. His sister, Laura, had disappeared without a trace some years after the accident that took Sofia's life. When Aleks thought about this, he took some small comfort in the fact that at least he knew what had happened to his sister. Lee Campbell's tragedy had caused him to go from being a therapist to being a forensic psychologist, while Aleks had given up a promising career as an academic, turning from philosophy to the priesthood.

He looked forward to their monthly Monday-night meetings at the pub, where they talked about everything from Beethoven to Jakob Böhme, the seventeenth-century German mystic. Aleks had written his Columbia honors thesis on Böhme, and when he found Lee Campbell had read the German's work, it cemented their friendship.

And, Aleks thought as he gazed at those deep blue eyes, it didn't hurt that Campbell was a hell of a good-looking man. His mother was right about that, at least. Aleks had renounced ways of the flesh when he took his vows, but he had a weakness for Lee's kind of looks: curly black hair, blue eyes, and ruddy cheeks. He sighed deeply as he drained his first beer and started on the second.

"Are you all right?" Campbell asked.

"Why do you ask?" Aleks said. *Was it that obvious?*

"You look preoccupied. And it's unusual for you to show up late."

The priest gazed into the glass of amber ale and cleared his throat, a nervous habit. "I just, uh—I had a few last-minute things at the church, you know."

"Okay. I don't want to pry or anything."

"I had to take confession from someone, and—let's order another round, shall we?"

He flung a hand into the air, and the waiter gave a tiny nod of his massive head. Moments later, four more beers were thrust roughly in front of them, a few drops sloshing onto the table. The serving style at McSorley's was abrupt, bordering on surly. You would never find the androgynous, fey waiters here you saw elsewhere in the East Village. There were no metrosexuals working at McSorley's Old Ale House.

Father Milichuk took a long swig and wiped his mouth. The beer was good, bitter and cold and comforting. The room was already starting to haze nicely around the edges. He gazed at the words carved into the cabinet behind the bar: *Be good or be gone.*

"So," he said, setting the mug down on the table with a plunk, "how are things?"

Campbell smiled. "On one hand, I can sympathize with Sherlock Holmes when he claimed to be bored because there were no interesting criminals in London. On the other hand, it's creepy to actually wish for something bad to happen."

"But isn't something bad always happening?"

"Sure, but in most cases it's routine stuff the cops can handle without my help. It's only the really weird crimes where I get called in."

Father Milichuk drained his third mug and started on the next one.

"You're thirsty," Lee commented, raising an eyebrow.

"I guess I am." Aleks felt his secret gnawing at him, carving a hole in his soul. He felt an overpowering urge to share it with someone. "I don't suppose—" he began.

"What?"

"Can I ask you something?"

"Sure."

"When you were a therapist, if someone told you he had committed a crime, did you have to keep it confidential?"

"No. If I thought my patient was a threat to himself or others, I was ethically bound to report that to the police."

"Oh."

"Why do you ask?"

"No reason; I was just wondering."

He knew his answer was unconvincing and realized that perhaps he wanted it to be. His friend peered closely at him.

"What's bothering you, Aleks?"

"Well, we've talked about how our jobs are similar, and I—I was just wondering about that particular point."

"You mean the seal of the confessional?"

"Uh, yes."

Lee Campbell leaned his long body back in his chair and shook his head. "You're a terrible liar, Aleks. I knew the minute you walked in something was wrong. You don't have to tell me what it is—in fact, from what you've just said, I'm thinking you can't. But if there's anything I can do, let me know, okay?"

Aleks nodded, staring miserably at the empty glasses in front of him. He wanted more than anything to tell his friend everything about the mysterious supplicant and his cryptic confession. And yet he couldn't; he was bound by his sacred vows.

"I wish I could talk to you about this."

"It's okay," said Lee.

"It's making me question . . . well, everything."

"Your profession? Are you questioning that?"

Aleks took another long swallow and traced his finger in one of the deep hollows carved into the wooden table. "I don't know."

"You made a hard choice when you became a priest."

Aleks ran a finger over the lip of his mug. "Sofia's death changed everything. You must understand that better than anyone."

"Yes, but I haven't made the sacrifices you have."

Aleks gazed out the window and saw it was raining. He watched the thin, hard droplets slice through the soft pink blossoms on the mimosa trees. "I've never told anyone this before, but a few days after it happened, I was lying in bed one night, and I had a vision."

"In your sleep?"

"No, I was wide awake."

"What happened?"

"Sofia came to me. She was standing at the foot of my bed, and she glowed, as though she were made of light beams. And I felt a sense of utter peace and joy come over me like I had never felt before."

"Wow. Did she say anything?"

"No. She just smiled at me. And I knew that she was an angel, and that she was there because God had sent her to comfort me. Suddenly I saw the meaning of Sofia's death: I was being called by God to comfort those in need, people who had experienced the kind of anguish I had. I knew that if I answered the call, this sense of complete peace might be mine again someday."

"So you became a priest?"

"The next day I applied to seminary school, and I was accepted."

"And Sofia? Have you seen her again?"

"No. But sometimes I have a sense that she's nearby."

Lee raised a hand to signal the waiter for another round. Aleks took a deep breath. It was now or never.

"I, uh, don't suppose I could ask you a hypothetical question?"

"What is it?"

Is even that acceptable? Aleks wondered. If he told his friend the story of the mysterious confession as a hypothetical, would that violate the seal of the confessional?

He had never been faced with a dilemma like this before.

"You won't mention this conversation to anyone, will you?"

"Not if you don't want me to."

Aleks looked around the pub to see if anyone was listening in.

Luckily, Monday evening was the thinnest time at the popular watering hole. There were a few people in the back room, but only two other tables in the front room were occupied, one by a young couple too interested in each other to be eavesdropping. Sitting at the other table were half a dozen corporate types who looked as if they had been boozing ever since leaving work. Their jackets were slung on the backs of their chairs, their shirtsleeves rolled up, and their shiny faces were flushed from alcohol. Bursts of boisterous laughter erupted from their table from time to time.

He leaned in and spoke in a low voice.

"If one of your patients confessed to committing a terrible crime, would you report it to the police?"

"What kind of crime?"

Aleks looked down at his hands, which were trembling.

"Murder."

Lee Campbell sat back, obviously nonplussed. It was clear he knew that the question was not hypothetical for Aleks. Lee shook his head.

"If I had taken a vow to respect the seal of the confessional, no, I wouldn't."

"Even if it meant a murderer would go free?"

"Yes."

Aleks stared out the window; it was raining harder. He watched the pink mimosa blossoms fall under the cascading droplets, fluttering softly before surrendering to the pavement.

Lee Campbell leaned forward, resting his elbows on the ancient oak table.

"Is there any chance—in this hypothetical scenario—that this person is making up the entire thing just to screw with the priest's head?"

"I'm afraid not."

The waiter shot an inquiring look in their direction, and Aleks nodded, though he knew all the amber ale in the world couldn't fill the gnawing hole in his heart. He stared out the window at the soggy puddle of pink petals on the sidewalk, and knew it was going to be a very long night.

———

AT HOME IN bed later, he watched car headlights flickering across the walls of his room, unable to sleep, tormented by the unwelcome knowledge locked inside his heart. Finally he arose and thumbed through his volume of the collected works of Jakob Böhme. His eyes fell on a passage from *Threefold Life of Man:* Man, Böhme said, "cannot see the whole of God's One," and "it follows that a part of it is hidden from him." In order to reach God, Böhme claimed, man had to go through hell itself.

These ideas, which had been little more than an intellectual puzzle to him when he was a philosophy student, now struck him as deeply personal. He felt as if Böhme were talking directly to him and that the key to solving his dilemma lay in Böhme's words, if only he could dig deep enough to uncover the wisdom there. Perched on the side of his bed, he turned the pages, searching desperately for something to help him. One quote in particular gave him some cause for hope: "What now seems hard to you, you will later learn to love the most."

Finally exhausted, he fell into a fitful sleep sometime before dawn. His dreams swarmed with disquieting images of masked murderers stalking their victims inside the stern marble interiors of churches, their steps echoing against the unforgiving floors. He followed them down endless corridors, but they always remained ahead of him, just out of sight. Finally he turned down one hallway to see his sister standing there gazing at him. She was glowing, as in his vision years before, but her large brown eyes were searching, beseeching him—to do what?

He awoke in a sweat, the book still in his lap, unable to shake the feeling that she wanted something from him. His eyes fell on the passage on the open page: "The anguished work of the creature in this time is an opening and a generation of divine power by which God's power becomes moving and working." He sensed the words had a deeper meaning for him, but he didn't know what they were.

Later that morning, after a quick breakfast, Father Milichuk dragged himself to St. George and took his usual place in the confessional. His hours were rigid: He was at his post every weekday morning from ten o'clock until noon. He had a wicked hangover, and that combined with his lack of sleep had put him in a foggy state of surreal, dreamlike consciousness.

It felt even more like a dream when the door to the adjoining booth creaked open. He slid open the wooden cover of the metal grate between the two sides in order to listen and was stunned by what he heard.

"Bless me, Father, for I have sinned."

It was the same voice Aleks had heard the day before. More weary, perhaps, and more wary—but the same. There was no mistaking it.

He tried to speak, but no words came out. Finally, he croaked out a response. "B-bless you, my son."

Jagged rays of light sliced through his field of vision, interrupting his sight—the familiar aura telling him another migraine was on the way. He pressed a hand to his forehead; he could feel the blood vessel in his head throbbing through his fingertips.

"What do you have to confess?" Aleks longed to peer through the metal grate separating them so he could see the man's face, but he could hardly bear to keep his eyes open. Pain sliced through his head, and he stifled a groan.

"I have committed another mortal sin."

"What is it, my son?"

"I have killed again."

Father Milichuk's intestines turned to ice. Cold sweat spurted onto his forehead, and he fought to control the buzzing in his ears.

To his horror, the man continued. "Not only that, Father, but I enjoy it. I like killing. Even now I'm thinking of the next time I can go kill again."

"My s-son," he said, hearing his voice shake, "you need help. Please—*please* tell the authorities what you have done."

The man laughed softly. "That's not likely to happen, Father. I'm not going to tell anyone else what I've done, and certainly not the police."

"Then why are you telling *me?*" Milichuk cried, his voice ragged.

"I enjoy talking about it. And my secret is safe with you." There was a pause, and then he said, "It is safe with you, isn't it?"

When Father Milichuk spoke, it was the voice of a dead man.

"Yes. It's safe with me."

"Good," the man said. "I would hate to be the cause of your breaking your solemn vows to God." His tone was mild, but Aleks sensed the threat lurking beneath it.

The man went on to tell him the details of his crime. He preyed on prostitutes, he said, the unfortunate women who prowled Tenth Avenue near the entrance to the Lincoln Tunnel. Some were runaways whose families had no idea where they were; some were transvestites; and others were strung out on drugs, trying to earn enough money for their next fix. The man owned a nice car, and it was no problem getting them inside.

Once there, the women were his prisoners; he could do what he liked with them. When he described just what that was, Father Milichuk's stomach lurched and churned. The throbbing in his head crescendoed, and he vomited.

"Oh dear," the man said as the sour smell rose to engulf them. "I'm sorry. I'd better go so you can get cleaned up. I'll come back again soon — maybe even tomorrow."

Before Aleks could respond, he heard the door latch click open and then the sound of retreating footsteps.

But this time something inside him rebelled. He whipped out his handkerchief and wiped his mouth, then stuffed the hankie back into his pocket. With trembling hands, he ripped off his soiled cassock. Dropping it to the ground, he threw open the door to the confessional and charged out into the church.

He dashed down the aisle just as the man reached the front of the church. Not noticing his pursuer, the man pulled open the heavy front door. Daylight streamed into the foyer, and he was briefly silhouetted in a blinding halo of sunlight. Shielding his eyes as pain shot through his cranium, Father Milichuk staggered after him, following him out into the street, where the man headed west, toward Third Avenue.

To his relief, the man didn't look behind him as he rounded the corner to join the parade of people on the avenue. Aleks put his head down and shoved his hands into his pockets, losing himself in the crowd, just another pedestrian in New York. All the while he kept an eye on his quarry, following half a block behind as he headed for the Astor Place subway station. As before, the man was dressed in dark clothing — a straight black raincoat over gray slacks. His head was bare, with curly brown hair and a tiny bald spot in the back. Aleks focused on the bald spot, following it through the thick weave of bodies. As Aleks walked, Jakob Böhme's words echoed through his aching head. *God's power... moving and working...*

He followed his quarry past the Cooper Union Building to Astor Place, where people were lined up in front of the pumpkin-colored Mud Coffee truck, waiting for their caffeine fixes. The man took the stairs down to the uptown-subway track. Aleks hung back, head lowered, blending in with the crowd, keeping an eye on that bald spot. The jagged interruption in his vision narrowed his line of sight, and he held on to the railing as he stumbled down the steps, heart pounding.

Joining the swarm of people on the platform, he could see the man in the black raincoat ahead of him, peering down the track in the direction the uptown train would be coming from. Aleks slowed his pace, then strolled toward him in a deliberately casual manner. He stopped in front of a map of the subway and pretended to study it, glancing up from time to time to see if the man had moved. But he still stood in his spot, waiting patiently for the local train. Aleks stared at the map, the colored grid of the subway lines dancing in front of his eyes as he fought to focus, trying to control the blinding pain in his head.

There was a faint rumble from the tunnel, and a shaft of yellow light spilled across the tiled wall of the track. The train was arriving.

The crowd surged forward, a great mindless beast driven by force of instinct and habit. The priest saw his chance. After quickly slipping into the mosaic of bodies, he pushed through to the front until he was just behind the yellow warning line. Glancing out of the corner of his eye, he saw he was only two people away from the man with the bald spot. The rumble of the train was louder now, the wall awash with the headlights of the oncoming train.

It was now or never. *God's power... moving and working...*

Aleks weaved quickly between the people separating him and his prey until he stood directly behind the man with the bald spot. He was slightly taller than the priest, and smelled of Old Spice. Aleks leaned forward and whispered into his ear.

"Thy will be done."

Before the man could turn around, Aleks gave him a quick, hard shove in the small of his back. He watched as the man lurched forward, his hands clawing uselessly at the air, watched as he fell onto the tracks. The train was upon him before anyone could react.

There was a roar in the priest's head, and the sound of a woman screaming. The crowd recoiled, and a man yelled, "Someone call nine-one-one!" A young student standing next to him covered his eyes, and his girlfriend began to cry.

In the pandemonium that followed, nobody was in charge. Aleks fully expected to be apprehended, but no one seemed to know exactly what had happened. Everyone looked dazed, except for a man in a business suit who whipped out his cell phone and dashed up the steps two at a time. The priest followed him, gripping the railing to steady himself. To his surprise, no one came after him. He staggered out onto the street and sucked up a lungful of fresh air.

Out on Astor Place, there was a disquieting atmosphere of normalcy. Taxis shot up Lafayette Street, careening around the curve in the road where it turned into Fourth Avenue. The orange Mud Coffee truck still sat at the curb, dispersing the aroma of French roast into the surrounding air. With a final glance behind him, Aleks walked quickly toward the Cooper Union building, then cut through the small park in the back.

His cell phone rang. Panic tightened his throat; he thought wildly that the police had found him. To his relief, the caller ID read *Lee Campbell.* He pressed the Talk button with trembling fingers.

"Hello?"

"I'm just calling to see if you're okay."

Aleks hesitated. Above him, a moody gray cloud slid across the sky, obscuring the sun. A pigeon pecked at a few scraps of bread on the pavement, then cocked its head and gazed up at him with its bright orange eye.

"I'm fine," he said. "Thanks for asking."

His friend seemed unconvinced. "Look, I have some time later today if you want to get together."

"I have something I have to do, but maybe I'll call you later."

"Please do, all right?"

"Sure, thanks," Aleks said, and snapped the phone closed.

He headed east, toward the river. It was a quick ten-minute walk to Most Holy Redeemer Catholic Church on Third Street. He had been there several times, though not for some years now. He did not know the current pastor or any of his staff.

The front door was open, and his footsteps clicked a stark echo as he strode down the aisle to the back of the church. The air smelled of incense and lilies, and he was reminded that Easter was only a few weeks away.

He stepped into the confessional and closed the door behind him. Welcoming the dim lighting, he leaned back in the narrow cubicle. He could hear the sound of gentle snoring, then the rustling of the priest's garments as the man awoke.

Father Milichuk leaned forward, his face nearly touching the grate between them. He took a deep breath, relief coursing through his veins like holy water.

"Bless me, Father, for I have sinned."

EVEN A BLIND MAN

BY DARRELL JAMES

The Greyhound arrived in Atlanta, midafternoon, swinging into the terminal on Forsythe Street to let off passengers. A hiss of air brakes, a mechanical unfolding of accordion doors—it marked the end of the journey for Earl Lilly. Three days in the seat from LA, his dog, Melon, curled up at his feet.

He'd come on a mission, the way he thought of it. A copy of his granddaughter's last letter stuffed into his breast pocket. What had happened to her? And why the sudden cry for help? He had crossed the country to find out.

Earl waited until all the other passengers had disembarked, then called to his dog. "Up!" was all he had to say. And Melon— a cocker-terrier mix—came wearily to his feet and nosed his way out from between the seats.

The bus driver was waiting impatiently, one hand on the lever, wanting to close the doors against the August swelter. He eyed Earl in the rearview mirror.

Earl took his good-natured time. He strung his camera

around his neck and centered it just so, adjusted his dark glasses on his nose for comfort, gathered his carry-on bag, smoothed the front of his poplin jacket, and moved up the aisle toward the exit. He was making something of a show of it. And why not? He was seventy years old and a black man back in the South.

Melon followed, brushing at Earl's pants cuff.

As they reached the exit, Earl turned to the driver, keeping his gaze off and distantly focused. He pushed his dark glasses higher on his nose, giving the man his best Ray Charles sway-and-grin. "Thank you so much for the ride," he said.

The driver studied him with a puzzled look on his face. "You don't mind my asking…if you're blind, how do you use the camera to take pictures?"

"I let the dog take 'em," Earl said in a polite tone. Then he turned, leaving the driver to ponder that image, and stepped down off the bus. "Jump!" he said. And Melon made his leap of faith to the ground.

See, it was the dog that was blind, not Earl.

Earl led the way through the wash of hot diesel exhaust, across the bus paddock, to the street, where a row of taxicabs sat parked at the curb. The first two cars in the queue were manned by Middle Eastern drivers. They stood outside the vehicles, chatting near the sign that read TAXIS ONLY. They seemed wholly indifferent to his approach, indifferent to the possibility of a fare. At a third taxi, a black woman had already prepared the passenger door for arrival.

Now she was calling to Earl's dog, "Here, boy! Bring your daddy right on in. Let Loretta give you fine gentlemen a ride."

Earl crossed past the two Middle Easterners, who found need to voice objection now. Loretta flipped them off and waved Earl and his dog on over.

The idea that Earl was blind and that Melon was his service dog was a ruse they played routinely. It got them onto public transportation together and into the bars along Vermont Street back in LA. And so far, it had won them a few courtesies here in the South. Few seemed to question it. The dark glasses also served to shade Earl's aging eyes from the light. They were both getting old, he and Melon. They depended on each other for their respective advantages.

Earl folded himself into the backseat, saying, "Up," for Melon to join him. The dog found his place on the seat, and they both settled in for the ride.

"You know where Cabbagetown is?" he said as his lady driver slid in behind the wheel.

"Sho' do," Loretta said, cranking the engine. "I know where e'thing is. North to Buckhead, east to Conyers. You ain't really blind, is you?"

"How could you tell?"

She was looking at Earl in the mirror. "I seen blind folks; they's always hesitant. You seem to know where you goin'. Dog's somethin' else, though. Playing along like a regular little con man."

"He's the one that's blind," Earl said.

"You say! I saw the way he come jumpin' off the bus. Must trust his master somethin' fierce."

"We've been together for a while," Earl said.

They had come off Forsythe Street onto Memorial Drive heading east. It had been forty years since Earl had last been in Atlanta, the place of his birth. The city didn't seem much different really from what he remembered. Maybe a few more glass-and-chrome buildings was all. It still had the same shady streets, the same sleepy feel to it. LA, by comparison, never seemed to stop.

"What's your name, big man?" Loretta asked, nosing the cab through traffic.

"Earl…Earl Lilly…but most people call me Little Earl."

"Cause you so tiny and all," Loretta said, metering out the sarcasm.

"Yeah, 'cause of that," Earl said.

"So, what brings you two good-looking dudes to Hotlanta? Come to howl at the moon?"

"I think we're both a little too old to be howling at anything, except in pain. Actually, I'm here to find someone," Earl said. He fished a photograph from inside his jacket and passed it across the seat to her. "You ever seen this young lady?"

Loretta looked briefly at the photo, keeping an eye on the traffic ahead. "She a beautiful young woman. One of yours?"

"She's my granddaughter," Earl said. "I'm sure you get around; you ever run across her, by chance?"

"She look a little familiar. But then, I see a lot these young girls on the streets. They's all just faces after a time. Know what I mean?"

"I guess I do," Earl said.

"Still, I should remember this one. Pretty an' all." Loretta took a last look at the photo and passed it back. "What she do?"

Earl had little to go on, just the name of a gentlemen's club where his granddaughter worked and a return address on her letters, presumably where she lived. "She tells me she's going to school during the day. Wanting to become a physical therapist. And dancin' nights to pay her way. A place called Bo Peep's Corral. You ever hear of it?"

"Peep's? Yeah, I know somethin' about the place," Loretta said. Her response was heavy with disdain. "Might not look it now, but I used to dance there myself. Was a good-paying job, but I got fed up with the owner. Always trying to get me to do things I didn't want to do. If you know what I mean."

"Still the same owner?"

"Ray Tarvis," Loretta said, a nod to Earl in the mirror. "Redneck asshole from the word *go*. She dancin' there, huh?"

"That's what she tells me."

"Your grandbaby got a name?"

"India," Earl said.

"That her real name?"

"What she tells me."

"You don't know?"

"Actually, I didn't even know I had a granddaughter until a few months back. I've never met her mother—my daughter. I went off to prison a month before she was born. After I got out, my wife and I just never reconnected. Somehow, little India ran my address down and started to write to me. Says her mother is probably dead or eaten up by the streets."

"This town can do that," Loretta said, grim eyes looking back at him in the mirror. "Either you claim it or it claims you."

Earl considered the woman driver in the seat ahead of him. It appeared the town had claimed her. She may have, in fact, been pretty once. But she looked nothing short of used up these days. She was possibly only thirty-eight, thirty-nine, but could pass for fifty. She was painfully thin. Deep lines were etched in her forehead. Her eyes were darkly cratered.

"So, you were sayin'?" Loretta said.

"Well, I was getting letters from her almost every day. Exchanging pictures and the like. Then about four weeks ago they just stopped coming. Then I got one last letter asking for my help."

"Help in what?"

"That's just it. She didn't say."

"An' you jumped on a bus and rode all the way out—what? three, four days?—just to see what she want? You gotta be grandpappy of the year, sugar. Have to hand it to you."

"Well, I haven't had anyone in my life for a good long time. 'Cept Melon."

Melon lifted his head at the sound of his name. Earl gave the dog a stroke for reassurance.

"I was enjoying her letters," Earl continued. "Made me feel connected a little. See, my life hasn't been what you would call exemplary. You get to a certain age, you start adding up your markers. I added mine and found I didn't have all that many. I don't know how much time I've got left. Me or my dog."

"I guess I see what you sayin'."

"I'm guessing she needs money. I've got a little tucked away from my photography," he said, lifting the camera for her to see in the mirror. "I figure maybe she wants help with her tuition and all."

"You take pictures?"

"Photos of life on the streets. Things that just happen. Some of my work hangs in a gallery in Beverly Hills. It's all on consignment, but now and then one of them brings a price."

"Well, I hope financial support is all your grandbaby is asking for. 'Cause that joint, Bo Peep's, is no place for a fine little African princess like your granddaughter. You find her, you tell her to get her ass over to Starbucks or someplace. Or" — Loretta caught his eye in the mirror to make sure he was paying attention — "she end up like me. This here's Cabbagetown, you got an address?"

They had rolled into an aging area of the city known for the cotton mill that once turned out bags for the agricultural industry; Loretta told him all about it as she drove. There were remnants of shotgun houses along the streets — little box huts that looked like they might have housed dwarfs or something. They were intermingled with modern apartment buildings. The mill had been converted to lofts. "We becoming yuppies," Loretta said. "That number again?"

"Six-six-two," Earl said, consulting the envelope from his granddaughter's last letter.

"Here you go," Loretta said pulling the taxi to the curb.

Earl ran his eyes along the series of stores on the street; 662 was a glass-fronted building sitting right ahead of them. "That's a postal service."

"Yeah, it is," Loretta said.

They sat with the engine idling. Earl double-checked the address on the envelope and compared it to the numbers along the street. He'd come all this way to find a PO box.

"You want to try the club where she works?"

"She says she works nights. I'll have to wait until this evening," Earl said. "You know of a hotel? Something cheap for the night?"

"I think we can find you something," Loretta said.

Loretta routed them back a dozen blocks to the Savoy Hotel. It was a dingy old three-story, stuck between a liquor store and a dry cleaner's. Earl paid her across the seat back, then pulled Melon to the opposite side so he could slide out first. When he was on the sidewalk with his carry-on, he called, "Out!" and Melon obeyed, leaping blindly to the sound of Earl's voice.

"Can you wait till I see if they got a room?" Earl said to her, her window rolled down to see him off.

"Just tell 'em Loretta sent you. They'll have somethin', sugar. Say I pick you up around eight tonight. We go check out Bo Peep's together."

"You sure?" Earl asked.

"Yeah, you got Loretta's curiosity up. Have to see how this mystery turns out."

Earl nodded, and Loretta pulled away, leaving him and his dog alone on the sidewalk.

Earl took a moment to survey his surroundings. They were on

the dark side of town, as he thought of it, not far from where he had once lived. It was mostly cut-rate, by-the-week rooming, filled with the city's black aging and infirm. There were a few independent shops, their storefronts covered in gang graffiti, their windows secured behind iron bars. A pair of homeless men sat on the sidewalk leaning against the wall of the Savoy, their backs against the bricks. All this beneath the gleaming glass skyline that was today's modern Atlanta.

"I told you it'd be different. And not different. Didn't I say so?" Earl asked his dog.

Melon nosed against his pants cuff with a whimper, and the two made their way inside.

At the desk, Earl was greeted, more or less, by a kid with spiked hair. He told the kid Loretta had sent him.

The kid didn't seem all that impressed and didn't ask about the dog neither. But he handed him a card to fill out—his name, address, and phone number. "One night, thirty dollars."

Earl paid in cash.

"Number four, upstairs. Second door on the right." The kid slid a key onto the counter. He hadn't looked at Earl once during the entire exchange.

Earl took the key and made his way to the stairs, bag in hand. Melon followed, keeping Earl's pants cuff against his face. "Step-step..." Earl said.

They reached their room. Earl let them inside.

The space smelled of mildew and urine. The bedcovers were stained a permanent yellow. "Jump," Earl said. And, with unquestioning trust, Melon leaped onto the bed he couldn't see.

"My man," Earl said, feeding his dog a treat from his coat pocket.

Earl removed his dark glasses and laid them on the dresser. The last letter from his granddaughter had been unsettling. It had been more than just a call for financial assistance, as Earl had implied to his lady cabdriver. It had been a desperate cry for help. There was something troubling going on in her life, something he couldn't ignore.

Her letters had started coming earlier that year. First one was a polite introduction; he wrote back, and they'd grown into a pen-pal friendship as they learned of each other's lives.

India had been consistently optimistic in her letters, looking forward to a degree from a real college. A better life. Maybe outside Atlanta, she'd hinted. Leaving the idea hanging at the end of an ellipsis, waiting for his response.

Yeah, maybe he could help her find a job, he'd written. LA being "exciting" and all for a young woman.

The last letter had been nothing like the previous correspondence. It was one word. *Help!* Nothing more. It was in an awkward blocky print, almost as if a child or someone of limited education had written it.

Earl took his camera from around his neck and crossed with it to the window. Beyond the tattered curtains, the buildings cast their late-afternoon shadows across Mitchell Street. He focused, framing the shot to capture the disparity between the richest-of-rich and the poorest-of-poor. Maybe he'd do a series of photos on the theme. He clicked off four shots in rapid succession.

He'd been told on occasion that his work looked like crime scene photos. The style had come to be known as urban evidentiary, a term the good-looking Beverly Hills gallery owner had coined to give Earl's work a brand. Earl didn't know what it meant exactly. But he had to admit, most of his work had a haunting, disturbing quality. Maybe something of his past, his own life, was wrapped up in it.

Earl let the curtains fall shut. He was tired and had a dark sense of foreboding about his granddaughter. Melon was already lying quiet on the bed, maybe absorbing his dark mood from his master.

Earl crossed back to the bed and set his camera on the night-stand. He stretched out on top of the covers next to Melon and closed his eyes.

It was a little after four. He would nap until dark, then set out to find the girl.

Just as she'd promised, Loretta was waiting at the curb when Earl and his dog came out of the hotel. It was a little after eight.

She drove them north into midtown, telling Earl a little about the place they were headed. "Bo Peep's Corral, mostly just top-less lap dancin' and all. But they's a VIP room where you can get just about anything you want, you got enough money. You best watch yourself, though. This place," she warned, "no place for a black man. This is still the South, sugar. And Peep's is filled with rednecks."

"I'll keep it in mind," Earl said. "I just want to see if she's there and know she's all right."

"Just the same," Loretta said.

They arrived at the gentlemen's club, which was in the trend-ier part of the city. A beefy young bouncer in a tuxedo that was tight across his chest stood, arms folded, at the entrance.

"Maybe I better wait," Loretta said.

"I'm not planning on any personal services. I won't be long."

"You want to leave your little buddy with me?"

"No," Earl said. "I almost lost him in a fire once. Now he goes where I go."

Earl slipped his dark glasses on and adjusted the camera around his neck. He withdrew a retractable white cane from his belt for good measure and extended it, then stepped out. "Jump!" he called. And Melon followed.

At the entrance, the bouncer stopped him with a hand on his chest. He lifted Earl's camera and looked at it; studied the dog at Earl's side a minute. "Okay," the bouncer said, and let them pass.

The place was dark and smoke filled. Heavy-metal music blared from loudspeakers. A tall brunette, undressed down to her G-string and high heels, was on the runway, grinding her pelvis provocatively against a brass pole mounted center stage. Young women paraded past in scanty attire. Waitresses—Bo Peeps, one and all—moved about the room in exaggeratedly short blue-and-white-gingham skirts and belly-tied blouses. Young white boys lined the runway, mesmerized by the woman above them on the stage. Others sat brooding at tables in the dark, beyond the lights.

Earl was the only black man in the place, he noticed. He tapped his way with the cane to the back. Melon followed at his cuff until Earl found a seat, then he curled up beneath his chair.

"What can I get you?" a waitress said, appearing almost magically and before Earl's butt had even adjusted to the hard chair. She was bent toward him, her tail jacked high by her spiked heels, showing lots of cleavage. A routine.

"Glass of water," he said, staying with his own routine, eyes off and distantly focused.

"There's a two-drink minimum. I'll have to get you two and charge them like they're beers," she said.

Earl nodded.

The waitress went off to get his order.

Earl sat, eyes skyward, pretending to use his ears to draw life from the sound-filled room. From time to time he would sneak glances at the faces of the young dancers who passed. There were two black girls among the exotic mix of women. One was just mounting the stage as the music shifted to a sultry beat, replacing the brunette who gathered up the tossed dollar bills on her hands and knees before slinking off, liquid-hipped, toward the back. The other black girl was just starting a lap dance for a table full of young professionals in suits and ties. The group cheered her on as she lavished attention on one of their comrades. Neither of these two women was his granddaughter, and neither was half as pretty.

Earl considered the possibility that there were other young women offstage, in the dressing rooms or someplace. And from where he was sitting, he could see through parted curtains into the VIP room. It was currently unoccupied. It occurred to him that maybe it was India's night off. But it was a Friday and more likely that all of the staff would be on duty. He waited. The waitress brought him his two glasses of water and Earl gave her a twenty without looking up.

Earl sipped his water.

"You want a dance?" a young blond woman asked, appearing over his shoulder. She was dressed in a sheer camisole and white lace panties. Earl waved her off without looking directly at her.

He sipped some more water and watched the room for signs of India.

Only minutes had passed when Earl noticed a man at the corner of the bar looking at him with interest. He was barrel-chested, balding, midsixties maybe, with a mass of dark chest hair showing through the open front of his Hawaiian shirt. Earl had the impression the man had been observing him for some time.

He pretended not to see. He sipped his water, eyes turned skyward.

But now the man was sliding off his stool and coming Earl's way. This was Ray Tarvis, the owner. Earl was sure of it.

The man pulled a chair close to his.

Tarvis said nothing at first. Then he nudged Earl to get his attention. "Hey!" he said.

"Who's there?" Earl asked.

"I'm the owner of this place," Tarvis said. "I noticed you're not interested in my girls dancing for you. You're not here to drink. I'm wondering to myself just what the hell a blind man gets from spending twenty bucks for water."

"I like the music!" Earl said, swaying his head in time to the beat.

"Yeah, well, you can get music a number of places, pop. But I don't allow cameras in my club."

"Don't intend to take no pictures," Earl said. "How could I?"

"Then what are you doing with it?"

"Was a present from my sister. A little joke among us. I like the way it feels."

"Uh-huh. Well, we don't allow dogs neither. I think you best go."

"You mean you don't allow Negroes."

"If you weren't fucking blind you'd see I keep a number of young black girls in my employ. I'm trying to be nice."

"Nice would be allowing me to stay," Earl said, not backing down.

"All right!" Tarvis said; his patience had run out. He rose to his feet, dragging Earl up by the elbow. "You can take your water with you. Just get out!"

Melon suddenly came out from under Earl's chair, baring his teeth and issuing a deep, sustained growl at the voice that had become threatening.

"It's okay, boy," Earl said. "We've worn out our welcome, as usual."

Earl extended his cane and moved off toward the exit, tapping his way between the rows of tables and chairs. Melon fell into formation at his cuff and together they left the club.

Tarvis followed them all the way through the door. He stopped just outside the entrance, next to the bouncer, and watched until Earl and his dog were inside the taxi and its door was closed. Then he smacked his bouncer upside the head and turned and went back in.

Loretta was slumped far down in her seat behind the wheel. "He gone?" she asked.

"He went inside," Earl said.

Loretta straightened. "Man told me if he ever saw me near his club again he'd kill me, no questions asked, and I believe him."

"He reminds me why I didn't come back to this town," Earl said.

"Why I should be gettin' out myself. No luck finding little India, huh?"

"I didn't see her."

Loretta turned worried eyes on him in the mirror. "Friday night, there's only one other place she could be."

"Where's that?"

"The Atlanta boys' club," she said.

"Boys' club?" Earl repeated.

Loretta threw a quick glance at the bouncer near the entrance, then turned to look at Earl directly across the seat. "I didn't want to tell you this till I was sure . . . but I been worried she might not be here."

"Why do you say that? And why do you —"

"Care?" Loretta said, finishing his thought for him.

Earl studied Loretta's eyes, the woman inside them. She was harboring pain, he could see it now. "It was you," he said. "You were the one who sent the last letter, not my granddaughter. But how would you know . . ."

Loretta lowered her gaze.

"You're..."

"Don't matter who I am!" she snapped, her eyes coming back to challenge his.

Earl examined the woman he'd only just met but now believed to be his daughter. He saw her in a somewhat different light than he had before. More determined than pathetic. More feral than beaten. "Where's India?" he said.

"They's a house out in Walton County, a cabin twenty miles from here, tucked way back in the trees. I was hoping we'd find India at Bo Peep's, and everythin'd be all right. But now my worst fear is she's out there with them."

"Them who?"

"The boys. They got this little club, see. An appreciation-of-little-black-girls club. Five of them, including Ray Tarvis. But they ain't throwing no charity benefit out there, huh-uh! They're mean and cruel and like to take their aggressions out on sweet young black females." She avoided looking at him.

"How do you know all this?"

Loretta brought her eyes to his now. There were tears streaming down her cheeks. "Kept me out there for nearly a year once."

Earl felt his heart cave in. The anguish in her eyes was born of deeply guarded pain. Melon stirred on the seat next to him.

"Why didn't you just go to the police?"

Loretta's eyes were pleading now. "Daddy, they *is* the po-leece!"

Earl stared at the daughter he'd never known. He recalled that his estranged wife's grandmother was named Loretta. He couldn't take his eyes off her, off the pained, crippled expression on her face. "Can you take me to this boys' club?" he said.

"I was so hopin' you'd say that. I had no one else to call; I got no one. And I wouldn't get two steps inside 'fore Tarvis would put a bullet in me and drop me in the bottoms someplace."

"I understand," Earl said. "The world can be a hard place. Just take me to her."

Loretta wiped at her tears and turned back to the wheel. In minutes, they were on the freeway headed east.

There was nothing left to say between them. Earl sat quiet in the back, Melon dozing next to him. Loretta kept her eyes on the road.

By the time they reached the outskirts of civilization, the moon had risen full above them. Loretta exited the interstate and followed back roads into the piney hillscape. Soon, she pulled off onto the gravel shoulder and brought her taxi to a stop.

"I don't see anything," Earl said.

"It's through those trees. I'd like to go, but they see me, they'll deal with both of us the same way, no questions."

"Get the car off the road, out of sight," Earl said.

Loretta produced a handgun. "You want to take this along."

"No, I'll handle it my way."

"There'll be a guard out front."

"Don't worry," he said.

Earl opened the door and stepped out with his cane and dark glasses in hand, his camera still strung around his neck. "Jump!" he called to Melon. And together, they set off through the trees — blind dog and seeing-eye master — to face whatever fate held for them.

"You stay close now," Earl said to Melon, putting his dark glasses on.

Melon gave him a whimper in return.

In minutes they arrived at a cabin set deep in the woods. There was a single light over the porch. A muscled young white boy in blue jeans and a tank top stood guard outside the door.

Earl came out of the trees, tapping with his cane, Melon at his cuff.

"The hell you doing, old man? You lost?"

"Come looking for Masta Tarvis," Earl said, laying it on thick.

"Yeah, well, you got the wrong place. This here's private property, so just turn your black ass around and head on back the way you came."

Earl never stopped walking. He continued tapping his way forward, ignoring the threatening glare, until he was face-to-face with the man.

The young guy was a good head shorter than him, Earl now realized, and probably half his weight. But Earl was also a good fifty years older. He couldn't let this boy get the first strike.

"Nigger, you deaf as well as blind—"

In one swift move, Earl came up with a right and drove a huge fist into the young man's face. It caught him square on the nose and dropped him like a loose sack of grain onto the porch decking. The force of the blow also drove pain up Earl's arm and into his shoulder, and for a second he thought he might cry out.

He rubbed at his shoulder until the pain subsided. "Stay," he said to Melon. Then he dragged the boy off the porch, letting his head bang on its way down the steps. He found a section of the telephone line leading up the side of the house and used a switchblade he found in the kid's boot to cut a long section of it free. He wired the kid's feet and hands and cut a slice of his shirt away and used it to gag him. Then he dragged the still-limp body into the trees and dumped it there. All the while, Melon remained on the porch.

Earl returned to him and let them both quietly inside.

The cabin was dark but for a wedge of light that spilled from a room at the end of a long hallway. He could hear men's voices, bawdy laughter and crude talk, over the wash of southern rock. He crossed down the hallway, the switchblade closed but cupped in his right hand. Melon followed.

Through the open doorway, Earl saw what he had feared the most. His granddaughter was on the bed naked and spread, tied to the bedposts. Four men were ganged around and over her. All were in their late fifties to early sixties; flabby white bodies, hairy backs and legs. They spouted crude epithets as they worked, prodding and jabbing with implements to coax some life into their crippled prey.

This was the Atlanta boys' club, minus one — Ray Tarvis — and they were preparing for another round.

Earl stepped into the room and tapped his cane hard on the floor twice. It brought four faces swiveling toward him.

"Jesus Christ!"

"What the fuck?"

"Who the hell are you?"

The protests came in unison.

Earl didn't respond. He raised his camera and clicked off a series of auto-shots in quick succession, capturing the men, their naked bodies, the implements in their hands, and the girl tied spread-eagle on the bed.

"Now, wait a minute," one of them said, stepping away from the bed, a bottle of Southern Comfort in his grip. The other men came to join him, the gang of them standing there, genitals dangling.

Earl snapped another shot.

There was a stunned moment in which no one moved. Earl was broader and at least a foot taller than any man in the room. But there were four of them. He no longer felt the need to keep his eyes distant. He slipped his glasses off and leveled a steely gaze their way.

Just then, Melon began to bark. Another man had entered the room behind Earl. "The fuck you doing here?"

It was Ray Tarvis, come to join his club mates for the festivities.

Earl put his glasses back on and stepped to one side, his shoulders in line with his flanking opponents'.

"Who the hell is this asshole? What's he doing with the camera?" the man with the bottle wanted to know.

"He's fucking blind!" Tarvis said. "He ain't seen a thing!"

"He sees enough to take pictures!"

Tarvis studied Earl more closely now, trying to peer beyond the lenses of his dark glasses.

Earl tipped the glasses forward on his nose and looked across them, let the man see the truth of the matter for himself.

"You're going out in a fucking box!"

Tarvis started forward, then —

Chick!

— the sound of the switchblade clicking open stopped him in his tracks. The other men had closed a step. They also halted.

"I see you all understand the language of the streets," Earl said. "I took it off your boy."

Earl pointed the knife alternately at Tarvis and at the gang of men.

Tarvis grabbed a heavy ashtray from a nearby dresser and hurled it in Earl's direction. It whizzed past Earl's head, missing by inches. Tarvis followed with a charge. "Give me the goddamned camera!" Tarvis cried, rushing Earl, head down like a bull.

Earl let the cane drop and caught the man about the neck with one big arm. The momentum of his charge rocked Earl back a step, but he used his size to quell the force. He wrenched Tarvis's head upward so he could see the bed, the girl, the savage damage that the men had inflicted. He still had the knife pointed toward the men.

"Take a good fucking look!" Earl said.

There was nothing but hate in the man's eyes. "Fuck you!" Tarvis said. "And fuck the little whore!"

Earl brought the blade around in a swift arc and buried it deep in Tarvis's stomach, just below the rib cage.

There was an expression of startled disbelief on Tarvis's face. Earl let it linger there a moment. Then he shoved the knife up hard beneath the ribs and held on until the light in Tarvis's eyes flickered and died.

Earl let him drop to the floor. Melon let out a chuff.

The others had remained fixed in place, unsure of Earl's prowess, perhaps, or just insecure in their naked vulnerability. But now they started forward as a group.

Loretta suddenly burst into the room. She had her gun out. Her eyes were wild with fear.

It halted their advance.

"Cut the girl loose!" Earl said to them.

A couple of the men moved to carry out his orders; the other two glared at him as if trying to say *We will remember you and there will come a time.*

Loretta handed the gun to Earl and rushed to her daughter's aid. The girl-child lolled, made dopey by the weight of Rohypnol or some other rape drug. But her eyes were aware and shifting between Earl and her mother.

Loretta dragged her to her feet, gathered her clothing, and dressed her as best she could.

When they were at the door and ready, Earl popped the small memory card from his camera and held it for the men to see. "You try to fuck with me or my family ever again, not only will this go to the media, but I'll come looking for each of you myself."

There was little of what could have passed for shame on the four white faces. Earl considered for one brief moment the idea of opening up on them with the gun. But the priority for now was to get his daughter and granddaughter to safety. "Are we clear on all this?" he asked, fixing his eyes on each of the men in turn.

"What about him?" one man asked, motioning to Tarvis lying on the floor in a pool of his own blood.

"I understand you're all members of Atlanta's finest," Earl said. "I'm sure you got ideas how to make a body disappear, make a crime as though it never happened."

Earl could see by their eyes they were already considering the possibilities. He backed his way to the doorway with Melon at his cuff. And with his daughter and granddaughter, he fled off into the moonlit Georgia night.

———

AT THE GREYHOUND bus terminal at four in the morning, Earl bought two one-way tickets to Los Angeles. His granddaughter was still docile and quiet, but she was starting to come around.

Loretta had managed to clean her up and get her properly dressed for the trip. And India herself had managed a smile.

"Take good care of our little girl," Loretta said. "See she get a good education."

"You sure you don't want to come with us?" Earl asked.

"It's too late for me," she said, pride overriding the sadness in her eyes. "Will you be all right?"

"I'll let you know. But I don't think the mystery of what happened to Ray Tarvis will ever be solved. A Jimmy Hoffa kinda thing. Still, I wish the rest of the bastard boys' club could receive some evens."

Earl studied his daughter, feeling a certain sense of guilt-layered pride. She was a survivor, at the very least. And though he couldn't change the past, he could give her some justice for the pain and humiliation both she and India had suffered.

Earl took Loretta's hand and folded the memory card from his camera into it. "What's this?" Loretta asked, looking down.

"It's a bit of justice," Earl said. "Put it in an envelope and send it anonymously to the *Atlanta Journal*."

Loretta brought her eyes back to his. "It'll stir up a hornets' nest that could come back on you."

"It doesn't matter," Earl said. "I'm an old man with an old dog and just as blind as I need to be. I'll take what comes."

Loretta gave him a strong hug and wished him and her daughter well. Then she turned toward her taxicab parked at the stand.

Earl put his arm around his granddaughter. And together they watched Loretta gather a waiting fare from the curb and drive away.

"Been some kind of visit, eh, Melon?" Earl said to the dog at his feet. "And we got a new member of the family to share our house with."

Melon chuffed and nuzzled India's ankle to show his approval.

"What about you?" Earl said to his granddaughter. "You ready for a new life?"

India gave what passed for a smile and boarded the bus ahead of him.

The driver was waiting to close the door against the heat.

Earl pulled his dark glasses from his inside pocket and slipped them on. He adjusted the camera around his neck, extended his cane, smoothed the front of his poplin jacket.

He was making a show of it. And why not?

Even a blind man could see he was seventy years old and a black man back in the South.

THE GENERAL

BY JANICE LAW

E ven after he went into a comfortable, if still bitter, exile in the north, the General hired only men from his own country. He trusted the loyalty of those who had been comrades and subordinates and the poverty of the others. Of the two, he regarded poverty as the surer thing, but the General was never without a sidearm, and the inner recesses of his handsome house—a glossy, glamorized version of the old stucco mansions of his homeland—held a small arsenal. He had enemies, some persistent, who had fled north a few years ahead of him. That political power was fleeting was a basic tenet of the universe.

Power of other sorts—the power of money, influence, personality—had proved more durable. Overseeing his silent, well-trained indoor staff and the ever-changing retinue of gardeners, pool attendants, and chauffeurs, the General felt as close as he was ever going to be to his old life of unquestioned authority. Dismissing a gardener for an ill-raked path or sacking a cook for a soup too cold or too hot satisfied impulses that he'd feared he was leaving behind when he boarded the plane, late and secretly, on the night the government fell.

But the north, with its labyrinth of immigration laws, had given him new levers to control his employees, and the General used them all, partly to avoid familiarity and partly for pleasure, because the General had loved only two things: power and his young son, Alejandro, a slim, dark boy of eight who reminded the General strongly of his late wife. Not that there was anything effeminate about the child, who played noisy soccer games at St. Ignatius and who could set the kitchen staff laughing the moment he returned from school, but from his earliest years, Alejandro had been thoughtful, and what he was thinking was not always transparent to his father.

Like his mother, the boy kept his own counsel, and he could be as quiet as he was noisy, spending hours reading in his room or playing one of his squeaking video games or frolicking in the far reaches of the garden and learning ungrammatical Spanish from the gardeners. He looked like his mother too, being rather pale, with eyes neither brown nor green, but a speckled amalgamation of the two. He had her nose, already quite large and angular; her full mouth; her thick, glossy black hair.

Watching him run joyously about on the playing field, the General had moments when some angle of jaw or cheek or hairline brought Maria back with a sharp, unwelcome ache. Aware of her own innocence, she had been as fearless as the boy, and she had paid for her carelessness when a motorcycle roared up to her limousine and the pillion rider loosed a burst of fire. The assailants had expected the General to be in the car, and though he'd escaped, he had known that his days were numbered.

Eventually, he fled north, where he had contacts, protection, assistance of useful kinds, and money. He hadn't gone into either the army or politics to remain poor. Now he lived in luxurious retirement; in exile, true, and with greatly diminished powers, but with vastly enhanced safety and comfort. Alejandro would grow up to be a citizen of this new and often enigmatic country, where power of many sorts would be available to him. The General had no doubt of that.

So he was as content as a man of his past and temperament could be. He raged sometimes — though never at Alejandro. The General was known to strike his kitchen staff and even his young and pretty mistress, who lived in an apartment a mile away from his home, but he did nothing worse. The past was gone and buried, and all that he had done and seen and ordered — for the good of his country and his party — was put to rest.

With wealth, a gated acreage, state-of-the-art alarms, and armed guards, the General could be confident that his life would run smoothly. It was therefore surprising that he allowed one irritant: Manuel, the gaunt, silent head gardener whom it had pleased the General to hire after precipitously firing the last one for burning the perfect turf with a carelessly placed glass tabletop.

Manuel was, naturally, one of the General's countrymen, an old, dark, sad Indian without papers. The General preferred illegals, whom he could pay next to nothing. But although his salary was minimal, the elderly gardener was permitted to live in the shed at the back of the yard.

Why the General arranged this is unclear, since he was cautious to the point of paranoia. Yet to save a few dollars on Manuel's salary, dollars that the General could well have afforded, having left the capital with a suitcase full of gold bars, he allowed a stranger, and a mysterious one at that, to live within his gates and beyond his immediate oversight.

There was no physical danger, of course. The General's two bodyguards, Hector and Jesus, were always vigilant. One or the other was perpetually on duty, and at some point, it would surely please the General to throw the old man into the street. Yet from a strict security standpoint, Manuel's residence in the garden, even briefly, was unwise.

If asked about this, the General would have said that Manuel was a wonderful gardener who would get the place into shape. The orchids, the lilies, the flowering cacti, the bananas, the bamboo, all the various ornamentals and tropicals thrived under his care. Every time the General went into his garden, he was reminded of his patio back in the capital and of evenings sitting with friends under the palms.

But, as with so many aspects of the General's life, the situation with Manuel was complex. Even in retirement, the General had considerable business dealings and still retained influence back home. He was absent a good deal, and Alejandro, who was lonely, had taken a great liking to Manuel and a great interest in the operation of the garden.

At home, the General would have put a stop to that at once. The son of the General was not training to be a gardener. But here, things were subtly different. The boy missed his adored mother and none of the housekeepers or cooks had won his heart to the degree the old gardener had. When the General was away, the boy spent hours down in the garden shed talking to Manuel and learning the mysteries of propagation and pruning.

One evening the General asked Alejandro what he and Manuel found to talk about, the old man being, as the General knew, quite illiterate.

"We talk about the plants," said the boy.

"Nothing else?"

"This and that. He comes from the highlands."

The General pricked up his ears at that, and it came into his mind to fire Manuel instantly.

"He says," Alejandro added, "that you were a great man at home, and one day I'll understand the sort of man you are." The boy gave a smile of such trust and sweetness that the General was disarmed. There were, after all, some good people in the highlands, faithful, sensible souls. Even there.

Just the same, he began to take a greater interest in Manuel and in what Alejandro was learning in the garden. He had the boy show him which plants he had pruned and how the small orchids—propagated, as even the General could see, with delicate skill—were progressing. Sometimes in the evening when Alejandro was in bed, the General would wander through his garden, smoking a thin cigar, thinking of this and that, of days in the capital when his power was supreme, and of earlier days in the mountains when his word, his every impulse, was law.

Often as he strolled along the immaculate paths, the General found his way past the plots holding chilies and cilantro, yams, jicamas, beans, tomatoes, and corn to the little potting shed. There was a pipe for water, and some fastidious former owner had installed a small toilet. Manuel or one of his predecessors had acquired a hot plate and a barbecue, and on some nights the General smelled bracing, peppery concoctions or, more rarely, the scent of meat or chicken bathed in herbs.

It was on these nights that the General thought of the back-country, so terrible and beautiful, and of what he had done and ordered there. Sometimes, the smells were so intense, so delicious—as if they were the scent of memory rather than the cookery of an impoverished gardener over a few charcoal briquettes—that the General imagined a single mouthful of such food would restore him to his old headquarters deep in the past.

I'm getting old, thought the General one evening. He felt that it would be wise to fire Manuel that night, that very moment, and yet he did not. In fact, he found himself drawn more and more to the night garden and to the shed, which always seemed dark to him, though he knew for a fact that it was wired for power, and he sometimes saw a faint light emanating from it when he looked out his bedroom window at night. He told himself that he could have the power cable disconnected, just as he could fire Manuel. There were always gardeners in need of work.

One day, Alejandro had an orchid to show him, a minuscule cluster of green leaves. It was a hybrid, the boy said. A new one. If it turned out to be as beautiful as he hoped, it would be named for his mother.

The General looked at his smiling face and said, "What a splendid idea."

Nonetheless, when Alejandro went off to school, the General felt grumpy and out of sorts. Who was this gardener to remind him of Maria? He stepped onto the terrace and studied his lush foliage. The original garden had been too tidy and suburban for his taste. Now, without its ever looking sloppy or unkempt, the garden reminded the General of his native thickets and jungles. Though the birds' songs were different, there were moments when he felt at home, when he felt returned, almost. He traced the beginning of those moments to when Manuel had taken up residence in the garden.

It would have seemed a simple matter for the General to question the old man directly, but this he did not do. First, he was confident that the man would lie, on principle, if not out of fear, and second, it was surely beneath his own dignity to investigate one of his servants. If he had real questions, he would let Hector and Jesus handle the business; they would soon discover anything he needed to know about Manuel. Anything.

The awareness that this might be done consoled the General.

In his mind, having the power to do something ran a close second to actually doing it. Besides, Alejandro was often alone, and the General preferred for him to have a companion within the compound instead of running wild among the neighborhood boys with their motorized scooters and skateboards and their delight in surfing rough water.

Already the boy's English was full of slang and his Spanish corrupted. There could be no harm in the old gardener, and the General thought himself well enough protected by asking the occasional question.

"Manuel must be very patient," the General said one day. "He teaches you a great deal."

"He had a son once," Alejandro said. "A boy like me."

"And where is his son? Back home or here?"

Alejandro shook his head. "He did not grow up. He is dead."

"Ah," said the General. That explained much. Alejandro looked reflective, even melancholy, and the General thought it well to add, "So many children die back home. The peasants are ignorant of even the simplest care."

Alejandro did not answer this observation, and some delicacy kept the General from pressing him.

Another time, he asked Alejandro where Manuel came from.

"The highlands," Alejandro said. "He picked coffee and then he made gardens for the plantation owner."

"Do you know what village that might be?" The General kept his voice low. There were lots of coffee plantations, and he did not fear the answer. It would be too much of a coincidence. Still, even the idea was unwelcome.

Alejandro shrugged—a nasty habit he had picked up from the boys next door.

"Answer your father." Unintentionally, the General spoke so sharply that Alejandro flinched.

"I don't know."

"I was just curious," the General said, to pass over the moment.

"I can ask him," Alejandro said.

"It is not important," said the General, though now he greatly desired to know, to know that it was not Santa Lucia de Piedras. But he did not want to disturb Alejandro. There were surely other ways to find out.

One day, quite spontaneously, Alejandro said, "I think Manuel is very sad."

Sorrow was always a danger, and the General thought again of firing the old man. "Perhaps he would be happier in another job."

"I hope he never leaves us," his son said quickly. Oh, the boy was careless like that, just like his mother. *The innocent are careless,* the General thought, *trusting.* He felt a moment of fear — and then of anger. His son would have to learn caution. It would serve him right if he fired Manuel, but, weakened by his love for the boy, the General said, "I would be very sad if I lost you. The death of his son is why Manuel is sad."

"I think that is true. He can never forget what happened," said Alejandro, but his face told the General nothing.

"The child was ill, wasn't he? There was no one to blame."

"I don't know," said Alejandro. "Mother —" He started to speak, then stopped. The General looked at him sharply.

"Mother didn't die of illness."

"Evil men murdered your mother," the General said. "She was too trusting. She went out in the car when I had warned her —" He broke off, moved in spite of himself. Though there had been threats, she had never understood the hatred against him. Of necessity, he had kept her innocent of his life, and that innocence had killed her. To prevent Alejandro from meeting the same fate, the General had fled to the north, even though his prime impulse had been to seek revenge.

"A lot of people were killed at home," observed Alejandro.

Well, what had the General expected? There were stories in the Yankee papers, perhaps even in Alejandro's school lessons, for the General suspected that even St. Ignatius, chosen for its tradition and rigidity, was infected with new and liberal ideas. "Most of them deserved to die," he said. "The men who murdered your mother—death would have been too good for them."

"They got away, didn't they?"

"Things fell apart. We had many enemies. It was me they wanted to kill, because I defended our country."

He spoke passionately, and as if to console him—for the boy had a tender heart—Alejandro said, "I know. I know you were a great man at home. When I am older, I will study your career. You will be in history books."

The General was pleased; then it struck him that this was a strange phrase for a boy to use, even a bookish boy. He remembered again that Manuel had told the boy that his father had been a great man at home and that one day Alejandro would understand the sort of man he was. *Not if I can help it,* thought the General.

Still, he did nothing about the old man's residence in the garden, which bloomed ever more luxuriantly. *I am getting old,* thought the General, *I am succumbing to nostalgia.* He sat out on his terrace smoking and listening to the night sounds and imagining himself back in the capital. Or, and these were moments he both loved and feared, he sat in the darkness with only the torches lit and envisioned the highlands with the moon rising over the jungle trees of Santa Lucia de Piedras, and he saw himself turning toward the interrogation rooms. He'd always liked to work at night. Certain things do not belong with daylight.

Possibly, neither did Manuel. The General avoided the garden during the heat of the day, and even at night, when, courting a confrontation, he walked around the vegetable patch and passed the shed, the old man remained as invisible as if he were a figment of the General's imagination — or of Alejandro's.

But the latter idea was disturbing, for why should Alejandro have any knowledge of the villages of the hinterlands, villages he had never seen? Why should he imagine an old man who offered him the promise of seeing the General as he was? No, this was a warning, and the General had just resolved to fire Manuel and make the shed uninhabitable when Alejandro raced inside, crying that his friend had taken ill, that he must have a doctor.

"He is probably just drunk," said the General, and saw the shock in his son's eyes. Then there was nothing for it but to go down to the garden and see for himself.

Alejandro ran ahead, his anxiety for Manuel all too apparent. Perhaps the gardener really was sick; perhaps he could be sent to the hospital, or even home. The General gave a tight smile at that and entered the shed. The afternoon light came in over the potting bench, stacked with clean terra-cotta pots and shining trowels and containers of soil, sand, and peat moss.

The old man, very thin, very gray, was lying on a small cot in the shadows. The General saw at once that this was serious. "Get out of here," he told Alejandro. "It may be contagious." Then he took out his cell phone and dialed for an ambulance. "We will get you a doctor," he told the old man in Spanish.

One hand, brown, cracked, and callused, moved on the covers, a gesture of gratitude — or indifference.

"Should we notify someone?"

Again the gesture.

"At home?" In his interest and anxiety, the General leaned closer and whispered, "Where is your village?"

271

There was a long silence; the dark eyes, dilated by pain, studied his face. The General had almost given up when, in a whisper, his eyes closing, Manuel said, "Santa Lucia de P..."

The General took in a breath and stood up, but the old man had lost consciousness and did not seem to notice his agitation. In a few minutes, emergency medical personnel arrived with their screaming ambulance and carried Manuel out of the garden. When Alejandro pleaded to go with him—young as he was, he understood the necessity of insurance—the General realized that he would have to become involved.

The doctors kept Manuel in the hospital for a week, gave him intravenous fluids and antibiotics, took X-rays and ran expensive blood tests. They cured a variety of small illnesses common to the General's countrymen, but they could not touch the cancer that was taking his life. At the end of a week, the old man came back—ghostly pale and thin, scarcely capable of walking—and returned to his bed in the shed.

"We will have to send him home," said the General. "To his own family. A little money too," he added, to soothe Alejandro. "They will be able to take care of him better there."

"He has no one," said Alejandro. "His son is dead."

"He will have relatives; everyone has relatives."

But Alejandro shook his head, and knowing Manuel came from that ghost village, Santa Lucia de Piedras, the General did not argue. He wanted to close the discussion; even more, he wanted the gardener gone, and he walked into the garden. When he opened the shed door, he saw at a glance that the old man was dying. *What is one more casualty of Santa Lucia de Piedras?* the General thought, and considered calling a cab. He could have Manuel at the airport before Alejandro returned. But there were no papers; and after employing Manuel all this time, the General might have trouble with the *migra*. No, unless he took drastic action, he was stuck with the old man until he died. This knowledge spoiled the garden.

The General began to avoid the terrace in the evenings, and he closed the broad wooden shutters of the windows overlooking the rampant tropical foliage. Alejandro remained faithful. He visited Manuel twice a day, before he went to school and as soon as he returned home on the bus from St. Ignatius. He was forever begging the cook for special broths and bits of meat and even for the bottles of wine that appeared to be Manuel's preferred painkiller. All this the General saw with dread—and with anger, too, at being reminded of Santa Lucia de Piedras after so many years and in such a manner.

Now it seemed to the General that he had been right from the start, that Manuel's skill in the garden had returned him to his days of power and command, back to nights in the interrogation rooms, back even further, to a day of sun and blood and the smell of gunpowder and diesel fuel, back to Santa Lucia de Piedras, to what was now beyond explanation. The gardener had no right to awaken these ghosts, and when Alejandro reported that Manuel was feeling a little better and talking about some work in the garden, the General decided to act.

He waited until the boy went to school, but though he checked the garden periodically from his window, he saw no sign of the old man. Perhaps Alejandro had been wrong. Perhaps Manuel was worse; perhaps he was already dead. It was late afternoon before the General saw a thin, white-clad figure with a straw hat moving through the trees.

Manuel was using his machete as a cane, leaning heavily on it and sometimes grasping at branches to stay erect.

The old fool, thought the General. *He thinks he can show me that he can still work. He'll be asking for his pay next. If he's well enough to work, he's well enough to be on the first bus south. Whatever it costs will be worthwhile.*

In a rush of anger, the General went out onto the terrace and crossed the lawn toward the pool. Manuel's high cheeks were flushed, and his dilated and unfocused eyes were fathomless. He staggered a little when he saw the General, then straightened up and stared directly at him. In Manuel's shadowed eyes, the General was surprised to read rage and desperation without the slightest trace of fear. *We have both come a long way from Santa Lucia de Piedras,* the General thought, and he smelled blood on the hot afternoon breeze.

"How fortunate that you are out of bed," the General said. "I won't be needing you in the garden anymore. For Alejandro's sake, I will make arrangements to send you home."

"I will never leave you, General," Manuel said. His voice was low and hoarse, the voice of the rebels and criminals of Santa Lucia de Piedras, the General thought. He had done his duty. They had no right to haunt him.

"If you give me trouble, you will wind up in the gutter," the General said. He raised his voice so angrily that he did not hear the familiar wheeze and grunt of the school bus stopping.

"Give me back my son," said Manuel.

"You have no son."

"He was ten years old, a mere boy, no bigger than Alejandro."

"I know nothing of him." But the General remembered the bodies in the plaza, men and women and other, smaller corpses — they had spared no living thing, not even the chickens and donkeys. And what did a few peasants more or less matter? The hills were full of bandits and rebels.

"I was gone on the day of the massacre," said Manuel. "I came home to find them all dead."

"It was war," said the General. "It was an accident of war."

Now Manuel gave a thin, ghastly smile. "You drink blood," he said.

"That's enough." The General slipped his hand into his pocket for the stubby handgun that never left his side.

Manuel took a step toward him. He was so unsteady that he lurched against one of the ornamental planters beside the pool. "Give me back my son," he cried in a voice fit to wake the dead. "Before I die, give me my son."

He took another step, and it seemed to the General that the old man was covered in blood, that he had risen from the wet red ground of Santa Lucia de Piedras or from the filth of the interrogation room, that he was advancing irresistibly. The General raised his pistol, and, though he heard a cry at the very periphery of his awareness, he fired.

Manuel's hat was flung off; his white shirt blossomed red, and he collapsed at the edge of the pool, his blood spoiling the pure aquamarine of the water. He looked past the General and struggled to say one last thing, his throat already rattling: "You see now what your father is."

And the General knew, even before he turned around, that Manuel spoke to Alejandro.

A FINE MIST OF BLOOD

BY MICHAEL CONNELLY

The DNA hits came in the mail, in yellow envelopes from the regional crime lab's genetics unit. Fingerprint matches were less formal; notification usually came by e-mail. Case-to-case data hits were rare birds and were handled in yet a different manner—direct contact between the synthesizer and the submitting investigator.

Harry Bosch had a day off and was in the waiting area outside the school principal's office when he got the call. More like a half a day off. His plan was to head downtown to the PAB after dealing with the summons from the school's high command.

The buzzing of his phone brought an immediate response from the woman behind the gateway desk.

"There's no cell phones in here," she said.

"I'm not a student," Bosch said, stating the obvious as he pulled the offending instrument from his pocket.

"Doesn't matter. There's no cell phones in here."

"I'll take it outside."

"I won't come out to find you. If you miss your appointment

then you'll have to reschedule, and your daughter's situation won't be resolved."

"I'll risk it. I'll just be in the hallway, okay?"

He pushed through the door into the hallway as he connected to the call. The hallway was quiet, as it was the middle of the fourth period. The ID on the screen had said simply *LAPD data* but that had been enough to give Bosch a stirring of excitement.

The call was from a tech named Malek Pran. Bosch had never dealt with him and had to ask him to repeat his name twice. Pran was from Data Evaluation and Theory—known internally as the DEATH squad—which was part of a new effort by the Open-Unsolved Unit to clear cases through what was called data synthesizing.

For the past three years the DEATH squad had been digitizing archived murder books—the hard-copy investigative records—of unsolved cases, creating a massive database of easily accessible and comparable information on unsolved crimes. Suspects, witnesses, weapons, locations, word constructions—anything that an investigator thought important enough to note in an investigative record was now digitized and could be compared with other cases.

The project had actually been initiated simply to create space. The city's records archives were bursting at the seams with acres of files and file boxes. Shifting it all to digital would make room in the cramped department.

Pran said he had a case-to-case hit. A witness listed in a cold case Bosch had submitted for synthesizing had come up in another case, also a homicide, as a witness once again. Her name was Diane Gables. Bosch's case was from 1999 and the second case was from 2007, which was too recent to fall under the purview of the Open-Unsolved Unit.

"Who submitted the 2007 case?"

"Uh, it was out of Hollywood Division. Detective Jerry Edgar made the submission."

Bosch almost smiled in the hallway. He went a distance back with Jerry Edgar.

"Have you talked to Edgar yet about the hit?" Bosch asked.

"No. I started with you. Do you want his contact info?"

"I already have it. What's the vic's name on that case?"

"Raymond Randolph, DOB six, six, sixty-one—that's a lot of sixes. DOD July second, 2007."

"Okay, I'll get the rest from Edgar. You did good, Pran. This gives me something I can work with."

Bosch disconnected and went back into the principal's office. He had not missed his appointment. He checked his watch. He'd give it fifteen minutes, and then he'd have to start moving on the case. His daughter would have to go without her confiscated cell phone until he could get another appointment with the principal.

———

BEFORE CONTACTING JERRY Edgar at Hollywood Division, Bosch pulled up the files—both hard and digital—on his own case. It involved the murder of a precious-metals swindler named Roy Alan McIntyre. He had sold gold futures by phone and internet. It was the oldest story in the book: There was no gold, or not enough of it. It was a Ponzi scheme through and through and like all of them, it finally collapsed upon itself. The victims lost tens of millions. McIntyre was arrested as the mastermind, but the evidence was tenuous. A good lawyer came to his defense and was able to convince the media that McIntyre was a victim himself, a dupe for organized-crime elements that had pulled the strings on the scheme. The DA started floating a deal that would put McIntyre on probation—provided he cooperated and returned all the money he still had access to. But word leaked about the impending deal, and hundreds of the scam's victims organized to oppose it. Before the whole thing went to court, McIntyre was murdered in the garage under the West-wood condominium tower where he lived. Shot once between the eyes, his body found on the concrete next to the open door of his car.

The crime scene was clean; not even a shell casing from the nine-millimeter bullet that had killed him was recovered. The investigators had no physical evidence and a list of possible suspects that numbered in the hundreds. The killing looked like a hit. It could have been McIntyre's unsavory backers in the gold scam or it could have been any of the investors who'd gotten ripped off. The only bright spot was that there was a witness. She was Diane Gables, a twenty-nine-year-old stockbroker who happened to be driving by McIntyre's condo on her way home from work. She'd reported seeing a man wearing a ski mask and carrying a gun at his side run from the garage and jump into the passenger seat of a black SUV waiting in front. Panicked by the sight of the gun, she didn't get an exact make or model of the SUV or its license-plate number. She'd pulled to the side of the road rather than following the vehicle as it sped off.

Bosch had not interviewed Gables when he had reevaluated the case in the Open-Unsolved Unit. He had simply reviewed the file and submitted it to the DEATH squad. Now, of course, he would be talking to her.

He picked the phone up and dialed a number from memory. Jerry Edgar was at his desk.

"It's me—Bosch. Looks like we're going to be working together again."

"Sounds good to me, Harry. What've you got?"

———

DIANE GABLES'S CURRENT address, obtained through the DMV, was in Studio City. Edgar drove while Bosch looked through the file on the 2007 case. It involved the murder of a man who had been awaiting trial for raping a seventeen-year-old girl who had knocked on his door to sell him candy bars as part of a fundraiser for a school trip to Washington, DC.

As Bosch read through the murder book, he remembered the case. It had been in the news because the circumstances suggested it had been a crime of vigilante justice by someone who was not willing to wait for Raymond Randolph to go on trial. Randolph was intending to mount a defense that would acknowledge that he'd had sexual intercourse with the girl but state that it was consensual. He planned to claim that the victim offered him sex in exchange for his buying her whole carton of candy bars.

The forty-six-year-old Randolph was found in the single-car garage behind his bungalow on Orange Grove, south of Sunset. He had been on his knees when he was shot twice in the back of the head.

The crime scene was clean, but it was a hot day in July and a neighbor who had her windows open because of a broken air conditioner heard the two shots, followed by the high-revving and rapid departure of a vehicle in the street. She called 911, which brought a near-immediate response from the police at Hollywood Station three blocks away and also served to peg the time of the murder almost to the minute.

Jerry Edgar was the lead investigator on the case. While obvious suspicion focused on the family and friends of the rape victim, Edgar cast a wide net—Bosch took some pride in seeing that—and in doing so came across Diane Gables. Two blocks from the Randolph home was an intersection controlled by a traffic signal and equipped with a camera that photographed vehicles that ran the red light. The camera took a double photo — one shot of the vehicle's license plate, and one shot of the person behind the wheel. This was done so that when the traffic citation was sent to the vehicle's owner, he or she could determine who'd been behind the wheel when the infraction occurred.

Diane Gables was photographed in her Lexus driving through the red light in the same minute as the 911 call reporting the gunshots was made. The photograph and registration was obtained from the DMV the day after the murder and Gables, now thirty-seven, was interviewed by Edgar and his partner, Detective Manuel Soto. She was then dismissed as both a possible suspect and a witness.

"So, how well do you remember this interview?" Bosch asked.

"I remember it because she was a real looker," Edgar said. "You always remember the lookers."

"According to the book, you interviewed her and dropped her. How come? Why so fast?"

"She and her story checked out. Keep going. It's in there."

Bosch found the interview summary and scanned it. Gables had told Edgar and Soto that she had been cruising through the neighborhood after filling out a crime report at the nearby Hollywood Station on Wilcox. Her Lexus had been damaged by a hit-and-run driver the night before while parked on the street outside a restaurant on Franklin. In order to apply for insurance coverage on the repairs, she had to file a police report. After stopping at the station, she was running late for work and went through the light on what she was thought was a yellow signal. The camera said otherwise.

"So she had filed the report?" Bosch asked.

"She had indeed. She checked out. And that's what makes me think we're dealing with just a coincidence here, Harry."

Bosch nodded but continued to grind it down inside. He didn't like coincidences. He didn't believe in them.

"You checked her work too?"

"Soto did. Confirmed her position and that she was indeed late to work on the day of the killing. She had called ahead and said she was running late because she had been at the police station. She called her boss."

"What about the restaurant? I don't see it in here."

"Then I probably didn't have that information."

"So you never checked it."

"You mean did I check to see if she ate there the night before the murder? No, Harry, I didn't and that's a bullshit question. She was—"

"It's just that if she was setting up a cover story, she could've crunched her own car and—"

"Come on, Harry. You're kidding me, right?"

"I don't know. We're still going to talk to her."

"I know that, Harry. I've known that since you called. You're going to have to see for yourself. Just like always. So just tell me how you want to go in, rattlesnake or cobra?"

Bosch considered for a moment, remembering the code they'd used back when they were partners. A rattlesnake interview was when you shook your tail and hissed. It was confrontational and useful for getting immediate reactions. Going cobra was the quiet approach. You'd slowly move in, get close, and then strike.

"Let's go cobra."

"You got it."

———

DIANE GABLES WASN'T home. They had timed their arrival for 5:30 p.m., figuring that with the stock market closing at 1:00 p.m., Gables would easily have finished work for the day.

"What do you want to do?" Edgar said as they stood at the door.

"Go back to the car. Wait awhile."

Back in the car, they talked about old cases and detective bureau pranks. Edgar revealed that it had been he who had cut ads for penile-enhancement surgery out of the sports pages and slipped them into an officious lieutenant's jacket pocket while it had been hanging on a rack in his office. The lieutenant had subsequently mounted an investigation focused squarely on Bosch.

"Now you tell me," Bosch said. "Pounds tried to bust me to burglary for that one."

Edgar was a clapper. He backed his laughter with his own applause but cut the display short when Bosch pointed through the windshield.

"There she is."

A late-model Range Rover pulled into the driveway.

Bosch and Edgar got out and crossed the front lawn to meet Gables as she took the stone path from the driveway to her front door. Bosch saw her recognize Edgar, even after five years, and saw her eyes immediately start scanning, going from the front door of her house to the street and the houses of her neighbors. Her head didn't move, only her eyes, and Bosch recognized it as a tell. Fight or flight. It might have been a natural reaction for a woman with two strange men approaching her, but Bosch didn't think that was the situation. He had seen the recognition in her eyes when she looked at Edgar. A pulse of electricity began moving in his blood.

"Ms. Gables," Edgar said. "Jerry Edgar. You remember me?"

As planned, Edgar was taking the lead before passing it off to Bosch.

Gables paused on the path. She was carrying a stylish red leather briefcase. She acted as though she were trying to place Edgar's face, and then she smiled.

"Of course, Detective. How are you?"

"I'm fine. You must have a very good memory."

"Well, it's not every day that you meet a real live detective. Is this coincidence or..."

"Not a coincidence. I'm with Detective Bosch here and we would like to ask you a few questions about the Randolph case, if you don't mind."

"It was so long ago."

"Five years," Bosch said, asserting himself now. "But it's still an open case."

She registered the information and then nodded.

"Well, it's been a long day. I start at six in the morning, when the market opens. Could we—"

Bosch cut her off. "I start at six too, but not because of the stock market."

He wasn't backing down.

"Then fine, you're welcome to come in," she said. "But I don't know what help I can be after so long. I didn't really think I was much help five years ago. I didn't see anything. Didn't hear anything. I just happened to be in the neighborhood after I was at the police station."

"We're investigating the case again," Bosch said. "And we need to talk to everybody we talked to five years ago."

"Well, like I said, come on in."

She unlocked the front door and entered first, greeted by the beeping of an alarm warning. She quickly punched a four-digit combination into an alarm-control box on the wall. Bosch and Edgar stepped in behind her and she ushered them into the living room.

"Why don't you gentlemen have a seat? I'm going to put my things down and be right back out. Would either of you like something to drink?"

"I'll take a bottle of water if you got it," Edgar said.

"I'm fine," Bosch said.

"You know what?" Edgar said quickly. "I'm fine too."

Gables glanced at Bosch and seemed to register that he was the power in the room. She said she'd be right back.

After she was gone Bosch looked around the room. It was a basic living room setup with a couch and two chairs surrounding a glass-topped coffee table. One wall was made up entirely of built-in bookshelves, all filled with what looked by their titles to be crime novels. He noticed there were no personal displays. No framed photographs anywhere.

They remained standing until Gables came back and pointed them to the couch. She took a chair directly across the table from them.

"Now, what can I tell you? Frankly, I forgot the whole incident."

"But you remembered Detective Edgar. I could tell."

"Yes, but seeing him out of context, I knew I recognized him but I could not remember from where."

According to the DMV, Gables was now forty-one years old. And Edgar had been right: She was a looker, attractive in a professional sort of way. A short, no-nonsense cut to her brown hair. Slim, athletic build. She sat straight and looked straight at one or the other of them, no longer scanning because she was inside her comfort zone. Still, there were tells: Bosch knew through his training in interview techniques that normal eye contact between individuals lasted an average of three seconds, yet each time Gables looked at Bosch, she held his eyes a good ten seconds. That was a sign of stress.

"I was rereading the reports," Bosch said. "They included your explanation for being in the area—you were at the police station filling out a report."

"That's right."

"It didn't say, though, where your car was when it got damaged the night before."

"I had been at a restaurant on Franklin. I told them that. And when I came out after, the back taillight was smashed and the paint scraped."

"You didn't call the police then?"

"No, I didn't. No one was there. It was a hit-and-run; they didn't even leave a note on the car. They just took off and I thought I was out of luck."

"What was the name of the restaurant?"

"I can't remember—oh, it was Birds. I love the roasted chicken."

Bosch nodded. He knew the place and the roasted chicken.

"So what made you come back to Hollywood the next day and file the report on the hit-and-run?"

"I called my insurance company first thing in the morning and they said I needed it if I wanted to file a claim to cover the damages."

Bosch was covering ground that was already in the reports. He was looking for variations, changes. Stories told five years apart often had inconsistencies and contradictions. But Gables wasn't changing the narrative at all.

"When you drove by Orange Grove, you heard no shots or anything like that?"

"No, nothing. I had my windows up."

"And you were driving fast."

"Yes, I was going to be late for work."

"Now, when Detective Edgar came to see you, was that unsettling?"

"Unsettling? Well, yes, I guess so, until I realized what he was there for, and of course I knew I had nothing to do with it."

"Was it the first time you'd ever encountered a detective or the police like that? You know, on a murder case."

"Yes, it was very unusual. To say the least. Not a normal part of my life."

She shook her shoulders as if to intimate a shiver, imply that police and murder investigations were foreign to her. Bosch stared at her for a long moment. She had either forgotten about seeing the armed man with a ski mask coming out of the garage where Roy Alan McIntyre was murdered, or she was lying.

Bosch thought the latter. He thought that Diane Gables was a killer.

"How do you pick them?" he asked.

She turned directly toward him, her eyes locking on his.

"Pick what?"

Bosch paused, squeezing the most out of her stare and the moment.

"The stocks you recommend to people," he said.

She broke her eyes away and looked at Edgar.

"Due diligence," she said. "Careful analysis and prognostication. Then, I have to say, I throw in my hunches. You gentlemen use hunches, don't you?"

"Every day," Bosch said.

———

THEY WERE SILENT for a while as they drove away. Bosch thought about the carefully worded answers Gables had given. He was feeling stronger about his hunch every minute.

"What do you think?" Edgar finally asked.

"I think it's her."

"How can you say that? She didn't make a single false move in there."

"Yes, she did. Her eyes gave her away."

"Oh, come on, Harry. You're saying you know she's a stone-cold killer because you can read it in her eyes?"

"Pretty much. She also lied. She didn't mention the case in 1999 because she thought we didn't know about it. She didn't want us going down that path, so she lied and said you were the only detective she'd ever met."

"At best, that's a lie by omission. Weak, Harry."

"A lie is a lie. Nothing weak about it. She was hiding it from us and there's only one reason to do that. I want to get inside her house. She's gotta have a place where she studies and plans these things."

"So you think she's a pro? A gun for hire?"

"Maybe; I don't know. Maybe she reads the paper and picks her targets, people she thinks need killing. Maybe she's on some kind of vigilante trip. Dark justice and all of that."

"A regular angel of vengeance. Sounds like a comic book, man."

"If we get inside that place, we'll know."

Edgar drove silently while he composed a response. Bosch knew what was coming before he said it.

"Harry, I'm just not seeing it. I respect your hunch, man, I have seen that come through more than once. But there ain't enough here. And if I don't see it, then there's no judge that's going to give you a warrant to go back in there."

Bosch took his time answering. He was grinding things down, coming up with a plan.

"Maybe, maybe not," he finally said.

———

TWO DAYS LATER at 9:00 a.m., Bosch pulled up to Diane Gables's house. The Range Rover was not in the driveway. He got out and went to the front door. After two loud knocks went unanswered he walked around the house to the back door.

He knocked again. When there was no reply, he removed a set of lock picks that he kept behind his badge in his leather wallet and went to work on the dead bolt. It took him six minutes to open the door. He was greeted by the beeping of the burglar alarm. He located the box on the wall to the left of the back door and punched in the four numbers he had seen Gables enter at the front door two evenings before. The beeping stopped. Bosch was in. He left the door open and started looking around the house.

It was a post–World War II ranch house. Bosch had been in a thousand of them over the years and all the investigations. After a quick survey of the entire house he started his search in a bedroom that had been converted to a home office. There was a desk and a row of file cabinets along the wall where a bed would have been. There was a line of windows over the cabinets.

There was also a metal locker with a padlock on it. Bosch opened the venetian blinds over the file cabinets, and light came into the room. He moved to the metal locker and started there, pulling his picks out once again.

He knelt on the floor so he could see the lock closely. It turned out to be a three-pin breeze, taking less than a minute for him to open. A moment after the hasp snapped free he heard a voice come from behind him.

"Detective, don't move."

Bosch froze for a moment. He recognized the voice. Diane Gables. She had known he would come back. He slowly started to raise his hands, holding his fingers close together so he could hide the picks between them.

"Easy," Gables commanded. "If you attempt to reach for your weapon I will put two bullets into your skull. Do you understand?"

"Yes. Can I stand up? My knees aren't what they once were."

"Slowly. Your hands always in my sight line."

"Absolutely."

Bosch started to get up slowly, turning toward her at the same time. She was pointing a handgun with a suppressor attached to the barrel.

"Easy," he said. "Just take it easy here."

"No, you take it easy. I could shoot you where you stand and be within my rights."

Bosch shook his head.

"No, that's not true. You know I'm a cop."

"Yeah, a rogue cop. What did you think you were going to find here?"

"Evidence."

"Of what?"

"Randolph and McIntyre. Maybe others. You killed them."

"And, what, you thought I'd just keep the evidence around? Hide it in a locker in my home?"

"Something like that. Can I sit down?"

"The chair behind the desk. Keep your hands where I can see them."

Bosch slowly sat down. She was still standing in the doorway. He now had 60 percent of his body shielded by the desk. He had his back to the file cabinets. The light was coming in from behind and above him. He noticed she had now lowered the muzzle to point at his chest. This was good, though from this range he doubted the Kevlar would completely stop a bullet from a nine-millimeter, even with the suppressor slowing it down. He kept his hands up and close to his face.

"So now what?" he asked.

"So now you tell me what you think you've got on me."

Bosch shook his head as if to say *Not much.* "You lied. The other day. You didn't mention the McIntyre case. You didn't want us linking the cases through you. The trouble is we already had."

"And that's it? Are you kidding me?"

"That's it. Till now."

He nodded at her weapon. It seemed to confirm all hunches.

"So, without a real case and the search warrant to go with it, of course you decided to break in here to see what you could find."

"Not exactly."

"We have a problem, Detective Bosch."

"No, you have the problem. You're a killer and I'm onto you. Put the weapon down. You're under arrest."

She laughed and waggled the gun in her hand.

"You forget one thing. I have the gun."

"But you won't use it. You don't kill people like me. You kill the abusers, the predators."

"I could make an exception. You've broken the law by breaking in here. There are no gray areas. Who knows, maybe you came to *plant* evidence here, not find it. Maybe you *are* like them."

Bosch started lowering his hands to the desktop.

"Be careful, Detective."

"I'm tired of holding them up. And I know you're not going to shoot me. It's not part of your program."

"I told you, programs change."

"How do you pick them?"

She stared at him a long time, then finally answered.

"They pick themselves. They deserve what they get."

"No judge, no jury. Just you."

"Don't tell me you haven't wished you could do the same thing."

"Sure, on occasion. But there are rules. We don't live by them, then where does it all go?"

"Right here, I guess. What am I going to do about you?"

"Nothing. You kill me and you know it's over. You'll be like one of them—the abusers and the predators. Put the gun down."

She took two steps into the room. The muzzle came up toward his face. Bosch saw that deadly black eye rising in slow motion.

"You're wearing a vest, aren't you?"

He nodded.

"I could see it in your eyes. The fear comes up when the gun comes up."

Bosch shook his head.

"I'm not afraid. You won't shoot me."

"I still see fear."

"Not for me. It's for you. How many have there been?"

She paused, maybe to decide what to tell him, or maybe just to decide what to do. Or maybe she was stuck on his answer about the fear.

"More than you'll ever know. More than anybody will ever know. Look, I'm sorry, you know?"

"About what?"

"About there being only one real way out of this. For me."

The muzzle steadied, its aim at his eyes.

"Before you pull that trigger, can I show you something?"

"It won't matter."

"I think it will. It's in my inside jacket pocket."

She frowned, then made a signal with the gun.

"Show me your wrists. Where's your watch?"

Bosch raised his hands and his jacket sleeves came down, showing his watch on his right wrist. He was left-handed.

"Okay, take out whatever it is you need to show me with your right hand. Slowly, Detective, slowly."

"You got it."

Bosch reached in and with great deliberation pulled out the folded document. He handed it across the desk to her.

"Just put it down and then lean away."

He followed her instructions. She waited for him to move back and then picked up the document. With one hand she unfolded it and took a glance, taking her eyes off Bosch for no more than a millisecond.

"I'm not going to be able to read it. What is it?"

"It's a no-knock search warrant. I have broken no law by being here. I'm not one of them."

She stared at him for a silent thirty seconds and then finally smirked.

"You have to be kidding me. What judge would sign such a search warrant? You had zero probable cause."

"I had your lies and your proximity to two murders. And I had Judge Oscar Ortiz—you remember him?"

"Who is he?"

"Back in 1999 he had the McIntyre case. But you took it away from him when you executed McIntyre. Getting him to sign this search warrant wasn't hard once I reminded him about the case."

Anger worked into her face. The muzzle started to come up again.

"All I have to say is one word," Bosch said. "A one-syllable word."

"And what?"

"And you're dead."

She froze, and slowly her eyes rose from Bosch's face to the windows over the file cabinets.

"You opened the blinds," she said.

"Yes."

Bosch studied the two red laser dots that had played on her face since she had entered the room, one high on her forehead, the other on her chin. Bosch knew that the lasers did not account for bullet drop, but the SWAT sharpshooters on the roof of the house across the street did. The chin dot was the heart shot.

Gables seemed frozen, unable to choose whether to live or die.

"There's a lot you could tell us," he said. "We could learn from you. Why don't you just put the gun down and we can get started."

He slowly started to lean forward, raising his left hand to take the gun.

"I don't think so," she said.

She brought the muzzle up but he didn't say the word. He didn't think she'd shoot.

There were three sounds in immediate succession: The breaking of glass as the bullet passed through the window. A sound like an ice cream cone dropping on the sidewalk as the bullet passed through her chest. And then the *thock* of the slug hitting the door frame behind her.

A fine mist of blood started to fill the room.

Gables took a step backward and looked down at her chest as her arms dropped to her sides. The gun made a dull sound when it hit the carpet.

She glanced up at Bosch with a confused look. In a strained voice she asked her last question.

"What was the word?"

She then dropped to the floor.

Staying below the level of the file cabinets, Bosch left the desk and came around to her on the floor. He slid the gun out of reach and looked down at her eyes. He knew there was nothing he could do. The bullet had exploded her heart.

"You bastards!" he yelled. "I didn't say it! I didn't say the word!"

Gables closed her eyes and Bosch thought she was gone.

"We're clear!" he said. "Suspect is ten-seven. Repeat, suspect is ten-seven. Weapons, stand down."

He started to get up but saw that Gables had opened her eyes.

"Nine," she whispered, blood coming up on her lips.

Bosch leaned down to her.

"What?"

"I killed nine."

She nodded and then closed her eyes again. He knew that this time she was gone, but he nodded anyway.

LEVERAGE

BY MIKE COOPER

I was counting on that pension." Joe Beeker looked up from his hands, knuckled together in his lap. "I need the money."

"We all need money," said the lawyer. He was younger than Joe, but so was everyone nowadays. He clacked at the silver laptop sitting open on his desk. "Doesn't mean they have to give it to you. The bankruptcy wiped out their obligations."

"I worked there thirty-seven years." And Joe knew he was marked from those decades: scarred fingers; flash burns on his arms; a small, weathered scar right under one eye. "On the line, mostly, and maintenance. Overtime every single week. You could look up my pay stubs."

"I'm sorry."

The office was small and undecorated, its window open to the parking lot off Mill Street. Humid summer air coming through the window oppressed the room rather than cooling it.

"I'll lose the house," said Joe softly.

"You'll get Social Security." The lawyer was trying to be helpful, Joe knew that. The youngster's tie was still snug at his throat, even if he'd rolled his cuffs back in the heat. He studied the computer screen for a moment. "And it looks like you've been at the same address for nearly four decades. Surely the mortgage is paid off by now?"

"We bought in 1972. Right after I got out of the service, with a VA loan. Marjo loved that house."

"And property taxes are certainly low around here."

"I had to take another mortgage." Joe looked away from the lawyer's disappointed sigh. "When Marjo got the cancer."

"Oh." The lawyer's sigh turned into a cough. "Insurance?"

"It wasn't enough." Joe shook his head. "I'm not complaining. She needed the nurse at home all those months. And the hospice. That's okay."

"I don't see anything in the file."

"She..." Joe felt his voice trail away. "Three weeks ago."

"I'm sorry," the lawyer said again. The fourth time since Joe had sat down.

"At least she didn't have to see me laid off. That would have killed her—" Joe stopped abruptly. "Never mind."

"Do your children...?"

"We never had any." Another old wound.

"Oh." The lawyer fussed a moment, then changed the subject. "The company's new owners are rehiring, I'm told."

"New owners?" For the first time, Joe couldn't keep his anger stopped up. "New owners? It's the same bastards, far as I can tell. They bought the company cheap, busted every single contract, sold off the inventory—and now they're starting up again. Yeah, they're rehiring. That's right. You know what they're paying? Six-fifty-three an hour. That's only one dollar more than I *started* at in 1974!"

"It's not quite that simple—"

"And you know what? I might have to take it, if I don't get the pension. I might have to take that fucking slop-hauler's wage, even though it's one-fourth what I was making a month ago, because I need to eat. I'm going to lose the house, probably get a boarding room over in Railton, listen to the bikers gunning their engines all night. But I need to fucking eat."

"I understand how you feel."

"No, you don't." But Joe's anger drained away. "That's okay."

"At least you can get unemployment during the layoff, if you're not applying for early SSA."

"They owe me the pension."

"Not anymore."

"And it's not even—you know how much I'm due? Thirty-seven years, paying in every single week? All I'm supposed to get is eighteen thousand dollars a year. Barely fifteen hundred a month. These *new owners*"—Joe heard his voice coarsen—"eighteen grand, they probably lose that at the cleaners. Loose change in their pants."

"Everything they did was completely legal."

"Legal." Joe slumped back in his chair.

"Believe me, if there was any possibility for a claim, I'd have filed already. Class action, in every jurisdiction Valiant has so much as driven his Lamborghini through." The lawyer seemed to have some anger of his own stored away. "But they've got two-thousand-dollar-an-hour attorneys out of Washington negotiating these deals and writing the agreements. It's bulletproof like plate armor. We can't touch them."

"Okay, it's legal." Joe looked out the window, at the late-afternoon sun and, far in the distance, a low line of clouds. "But it's not *right*."

———

TWO WEEKS LATER, midmorning. Dim inside the community room with the lights off, but dog-day heat shimmered outside the windows. An air conditioner rattled and dripped, not doing much.

A dozen men and two women sat on metal folding chairs, filling a third of the room. The Rotary was coming in later, and their dusty flag stood in one corner. No one could hear the projected video very well, not over the air conditioner, and the facilitator had closed her eyes, fanning her face with the same copy of "Writing a Killer Résumé!" that was on everyone's lap.

"I still don't understand how they did it," Stokey said in a low voice to Joe. They'd taken seats in the rear. Long-forgotten memories: grade-school desks, ducking the teacher's eye, daydreaming.

"Leverage," he whispered back. "The lawyer walked me through it three times." No one in the room had any interest at all in the career-counseling service, but they had to show up to keep the unemployment checks coming.

"It worked because Fulmont had borrowed all the money, six or seven years ago," Joe said. Fulmont was the plant's owner, the third generation to run Fulmont Specialty Metals. "For the modernization—ISO 9000, all that? But when the economy tanked, it looked like we were about to go out of business, and Valiant's hedge fund bought up the debt."

"How can you buy debt?"

"Like Rico laying off his markers? Fulmont doesn't owe to First City National anymore, he owes to Valiant."

"Oh." Stokey squinted. "I guess."

"So then Valiant called the debt, drove us into bankruptcy, and the bankruptcy court let him cancel every single obligation the company had. Suppliers, customers, subcontractors—they all got totally screwed, and we lost our pensions. Everything went into Valiant's pocket."

Tinny music came from the video. On the screen, young,

well-dressed men and women strode through high-tech offices, smiling and making decisions and managing big projects.

"And then he opened the plant up again, only now everyone's getting paid minimum wage." Joe glanced at Stokey. He hadn't shaved either. "You could do better pumping gas at the interstate plaza."

"They ain't hiring."

"I know." Joe felt his shoulders sag. "I asked out there too."

"Valiant stole every penny that could be squeezed out of Fulmont," said Stokey. "No different than he took dynamite and a thermal drill down to the bank after hours. Except instead of trying to stop him, the judges and the courts and the sheriff, they were all right there helping him do it."

"Pretty much."

"That's how I see it. That's how you see it. That's how everyone in this fucking room sees it." Stokey was getting worked up. Joe noticed the facilitator's eyes had opened. "What country are we living in here? Russia? France? Who wrote these damn laws anyway?"

"The best politicians money can buy. You know that." Joe put a hand on Stokey's arm. "Forget it. Watch the movie."

Stokey subsided, grumbling, and they sat through the rest of the session. People got up wearily when it was done, chairs scraping on the worn floor.

"Next week we're doing social networking," said the facilitator, shutting down her computer. "We'll get you all going on Facebook."

Outside, the sun and heat was a hammer blow.

"Where you going now?" asked Stokey. He'd taken a Marlboro box out of his shirt pocket and was gravely considering the remaining cigarettes. Seven bucks a pack. Joe knew he was figuring how long he could stretch them out.

"Down the river, by the bluff. Thought I might shoot a deer."

"They ain't in season."

"There's no season on being hungry."

Stokey nodded. "Put some venison up for the winter."

"That's the idea."

They separated, going to their trucks, and Stokey drove off first. Joe sat for a few minutes, despite the heat, gazing at nothing in particular.

———

THE DROUGHT FINALLY broke, like it always did, and the weather turned beautiful again. Mid-September, the high school's first home game, and some of the nights were already cool.

On one of those nights, Joe ran into Stokey in the gravel parking lot out behind Community Baptist. Quarter to nine, mostly dark, right before the church food pantry closed up. Joe was walking out, carrying his paper sack of canned beans and margarine and Vienna wieners. Stokey hesitated, then started to turn away.

"It's all right," said Joe.

"I was just—you know."

"I've been coming every week. No shame in it."

"Yeah." But there was, of course. Stokey wasn't the only one to show up after dusk, at closing, hoping to avoid running into anyone he knew. Joe had nodded to two women inside, and none of them had spoken.

"Annie said we had to come." Stokey sighed. "I didn't want to. Didn't let her last week. But she insisted. So I said I'd do it."

"She trust you?" Joe tried to lighten it up, but Stokey just shook his head.

"It ain't right, taking handouts. It's not her job to be begging food."

"It's not begging."

"Same as."

They stood for a few minutes while Stokey finished a cigarette. Traffic noise drifted over from Route 87, across the soybean fields. The moon had risen, almost light enough to read by. Joe pulled a folded envelope from his shirt pocket. "Got this today," he said, running his finger along the torn edge. "From the bank."

"Uh-oh."

"Yeah." He looked at Stokey. "Foreclosure. I must have called six times since August, trying to talk them into a workout, but no go. They're taking the house."

"When?"

"Don't know."

"Harrell and his wife, they're still in their place. Haven't paid a dime since March. Sheriff's even been out, and Harrell just says he's working on it, shows another letter, and they let it go."

"Working on what?" Joe didn't know Harrell well, but once he'd seen him walking through the neighborhood at dawn, checking trash bags. "Buying Hot Lotto tickets?"

"It's a game. The bank, they don't really want to foreclose, because then they're stuck with it. People ain't exactly lining up to buy houses around here, you notice that? You could string them out for months, just like Harrell."

Joe *had* thought about it, but he shook his head. "That wouldn't be right."

Stokey grimaced. "What's not right is the whole fucking system. Everything's rigged for the fat boys."

The screen door at the back of the church banged, and a shadowed figure came out, carrying two sacks. A family allotment. Joe thought he recognized the woman, but she went by without greeting them, got in her car, and drove away.

"I'm leaving," Joe said.

"What?" Stokey looked up.

"Marjo's gone, my job is gone, the house is going. I got nothing to do here."

"Yeah, but—" Stokey didn't seem to know what to say. "Where?"

"Connecticut."

"*Connecticut?* What the hell for?"

"I'm going to..." Joe stopped. When he said it out loud, it sounded stupid.

"What?"

"Valiant lives there. His office is in New York City, but he lives in some little town in Connecticut. I want to talk to him."

"*Talk* to him?"

"Ask him why he did it. Ask him to make things right."

Stokey made a choking noise. He put his hands up, then dropped them. "Why the *fuck* would Valiant talk to you? Why would he even see you?"

"I'll make an appointment." Joe straightened up. "Look, he's another human being, right? We're all walking the earth. Maybe he just needs to see things clear."

"That's just plain—Valiant's *not* walking the earth, not the same one as you and me. He'll probably have you arrested. You can spend your golden years at Fort Madison."

"I don't think so." Joe shifted the sack of food he'd never put down. "But it doesn't matter. I've got nothing to do here. Seems worth a shot."

They fell silent. Stokey's energy faded. A light wind rustled the bean fields.

"You got to get in there," Joe said finally. "They're closing up, and Annie's waiting on you."

"Yeah." Stokey started to move off. "Hey, when are you leaving?"

"Tomorrow."

"Tomorrow? When are you coming *back?*"

"When it's done." Joe felt — not happy, but somehow . . . eager. "When it's done."

———

MANHATTAN WASN'T SO bad.

Joe had been there before, but not since he was in the service — for some reason he'd been shipped home via Germany, even though the West Coast was a lot closer to Vietnam. New York in the early seventies had been spiraling into chaos, bankruptcy, and gang violence, and that's how Joe remembered it. But the modern city was all clean streets and shiny buildings. He didn't recognize Times Square at all.

Valiant's firm had its offices on Park Avenue, the fortieth floor of a glass skyscraper called the Great Prosperity Building. Chinese characters on the largest logo in the atrium suggested the building was no longer owned by Americans.

"Mr. Valiant is out of the office this week," said the receptionist.

"How about next week?"

"Fully booked, I'm afraid."

The woman sat at her desk facing the elevator bank, but two husky young men stood by, one on either side, both staring at Joe. The carpet felt deep and plush beneath his feet.

He figured the bouncers were just guys who worked there, not real security. Their hands looked soft, and they didn't have that wary, hooded gaze Joe remembered from the MPs. But they'd been out in the foyer already when Joe stepped off the elevator.

He'd had to sign in at the main desk in the lobby, downstairs, and show a driver's license; he'd received a printed pass. The guard there must have called up. Somehow Joe didn't look right.

"Why don't you call him and check?" Joe said.

"I'm sorry, Mr. Valiant's schedule is very busy."

Back on the street, Joe stood on the small plaza, under a tree just starting to blaze orange. Early afternoon and people seemed to be on extended lunch breaks, sitting in the sun, tapping at smartphones, eating paper-wrapped takeout.

After a minute he walked back to his truck, drove around the block, and entered the garage underneath the Great Prosperity Building.

On the A level, closest to both the surface and the elevator, Joe coasted slowly, counting. Two Ferraris, five high-end Audis, BMWs, Mercedeses, several Range Rovers...and a single Lamborghini Gallardo, the distinctive rear end unmistakable.

The lawyer had mentioned the model Valiant owned. Before leaving town, three days earlier, Joe had looked through old *Car and Driver* issues at the library until he'd found it.

"I didn't even park," he told the attendant at the exit, "I got a phone call, have to go right back out."

"Ten minutes." The attendant was black, with an accent from somewhere far away. He pointed to the sign at the booth. "Five dollars."

Joe started to protest, then shrugged and dug out his wallet. No reason to attract more attention.

This time there were no good parking spaces on the street. Good thing he'd had the tank filled that morning in New Jersey, at a gas station near the highway motel he'd stayed at. Joe started driving around the block again, taking his time. Sooner or later a spot would open up, one with a nice view of the garage exit. He had all afternoon.

Valiant would have to leave the building eventually.

———

THE RESTAURANT SEEMED far too crowded, barely room to walk between the tables and people standing two deep at the short bar. Despite some kind of fancy cloth on the walls and a carpeted floor, it was noisy, with constant clatter, chattering, and glassware clinking.

"I'm meeting someone here at eight thirty," Joe said, glancing at his watch. He'd put on his old jacket and tie, good enough to pass under the dim lamps that barely illuminated a podium at the door.

"Certainly," said the maître d'. "Care for a drink at the bar?"

"That would be perfect."

Valiant was already at a small table, a woman probably twenty years younger sitting across from him. Joe had followed the Lamborghini straight here when Valiant left for the day, but Valiant used valet parking, and Joe had to take twenty minutes to find a spot on his own. He didn't want to leave any more obvious a trail than necessary.

"Seltzer," he told the barman after jostling his way to the front.

"Fourteen dollars."

He made the drink last. People drifted in and out. Finally, after a quarter hour, Valiant's companion stood and made her way to the restroom, in an alcove at the end of the bar.

When she came back out, Joe had maneuvered himself to stand where she had to brush past him.

"Excuse me?" he said, as politely as he could.

"Yes?" Up close she looked even more like someone accustomed to brushing off strange men in bars — flawlessly beautiful, dark eyes, precisely cut hair.

"I'm sorry. I don't know if I should even tell you this, but..."

"What?" She was on the verge of pushing through and ignoring him.

"While you were in there? I happened to see your fella — he's the handsome man in the blue shirt, right? He, well, he put something in your wineglass."

That got her attention. "Say that again."

"I'm waiting for my date, she's coming down with one of her friends, so, you know, I'm just killing time. And I noticed, after you stood up—pardon me, miss, but I noticed *you* and I hope you're not offended by that. But after you left, your man, he took something out of his pocket and reached across the table and held it over your drink. Like he was dropping something in."

A long pause. The woman stared hard at Joe, then even harder at Valiant, who hadn't noticed her returning yet.

"Are you sure?" she said.

"I'm afraid so. But surely, if he's a good friend of yours—"

"I met him this weekend at a party." She made up her mind. "Thank you."

"Oh, no. Really, I'm sorry."

"Yes." And she walked straight out of the restaurant.

Joe finished his seltzer, placed the glass on the bar, and went into the dining area.

"Mr. Valiant?" He pulled out the woman's chair and sat down. "Mind if I join you for a moment?"

"Wha—"

"Don't worry, your companion won't be here for a few minutes."

"Who are *you?*"

"Joe Beeker." Joe held out his hand, not expecting Valiant to take it. "I used to work at Fulmont Metal."

Valiant looked around. Up close, he had presence—fit, strong, clear-eyed, with a haircut and clothes that even Joe could tell cost vast amounts of money. Someone accustomed to watching other people get out of his way.

"You're interrupting a private dinner," he said. "Leave now, or the police will haul you away."

"Yeah?" Joe said. "Do you *really* want to do that? Because I won't go quietly. I'll be hollering about how badly you treated us, stealing the company, stripping the pensions, cheating the suppliers. I'll bet there are forty cell phones with cameras in here. You'll be all over the internet in half an hour—and I'll walk, since I haven't actually done anything wrong." He paused. "Unlike you."

A smile flashed. "You're trying to threaten me?"

"Me? I just turned sixty-two. I'm a tired old man. I'm not threatening anybody."

Valiant shrugged. "What do you want?"

"Just to talk for a couple minutes." Joe looked closely at Valiant's eyes. "Mostly, I'm wondering, do you understand what you did to us?"

"I—"

"Deep down? Because I don't think a regular person would have gone there. I think you just don't realize the suffering you caused in order to make an extra few million bucks for yourself."

"Just business." Valiant looked toward the bar, frowning a bit, then drank from his wineglass. "You wouldn't understand."

"Oh, I—"

"Everything we did was perfectly legal. By the book."

"I keep hearing that."

"Your boss had run the company into the ground. What you don't get is, we saved the place. If we hadn't come along to fix it, the entire operation would have gone under, and *nobody* would be working anymore."

"Fulmont was doing fine until you called the debt."

"That was entirely within our rights."

"That was ruthless and unnecessary—except to give you an opening to loot the place." A waiter appeared, looking confused.

"Excuse me, sir, are you joining the party? And the lady...?"

"We're fine," Valiant said.

"Ah, shall I bring out the first course?"

"I'll let you know when."

"Very good." He slipped away, still frowning.

"You can't fix everything," said Joe. "Not completely. I know that. But at an absolute minimum, you need to give the pension back."

"Oh, go to hell." Valiant's patience had begun to wear.

"It's only six million dollars. Last year you boasted about earning, what, nine billion? You can afford it."

"It was all legal. There's no obligation."

"Legal." Joe sighed. "What you did—it was wrong."

He didn't get anywhere. Valiant sat obstinate for another minute, disregarding him. When the waiter came back again, with the maître d' for support, Joe stood up.

"Thanks for the time, Mr. Valiant," he said.

"If I ever see you again, you're going to jail."

"Beeker," said Joe. "With three *e*'s. You need some time to think it over, that's okay. Let's say, by Wednesday? A public announcement. I'll be waiting."

"Fuck you."

Joe nodded. "Wednesday," he said again, and left.

———

NOTHING HAPPENED, EXCEPT that Valiant hired some body-guards. They were at his house—Joe followed the Gallardo one evening, an hour's drive out of the city and into horse country, to see a blacked-out SUV waiting at the gate. In the morning the bodyguards arrived early at the office, and when Valiant went out for lunch, Joe saw at least one musclehead nearby the entire time.

On the other hand, they didn't actually drive with him. The sports car was a two-seater, hardly built for six-foot linebackers carrying automatic weapons. Joe thought about this, and he followed Valiant to and from his house for a few more days.

At a distance—a great distance. He wasn't going to be accused of stalking.

Thursday afternoon, Joe stopped waiting for Valiant's announcement and started thinking about plan B. He had to borrow a phone book from the desk guy at the motel—the room didn't have one, and pay phones seemed to have disappeared from the city. He'd never find this particular kind of shop back home, but Manhattan didn't disappoint: three choices in Midtown alone, and more in the boroughs.

New Yorkers seemed to like spying on one another.

———

"THE LENS IS easy," said the clerk. He gestured at a glass case alongside the counter, its shelves crammed with glinting electronics. "You need wireless?"

"I don't think so." Joe remembered the combat radio he'd humped through Vietnam, twenty-three pounds of steel and plastic knobs. The equipment here would fit inside a pencil. "I can wear the recorder on my belt or something, connect it under my shirt."

"Sure. Pin-wire mike too—put it separate, different buttonhole or something, makes it harder to catch."

"You sure it can record everything someone says to me? Video too?"

"So long as you're facing them. The exact orientation doesn't matter much. A lens like this"—he held up a tiny crystal bead, two thin leads trailing away—"has a seventy-degree field of view. Looks a bit like a fishbowl on playback, but you'll see everything."

"Good." Joe pulled out his wallet.

As the clerk settled the components into a plastic bag, he said, "I ought to tell you, the courts don't accept this sort of thing."

"Excuse me?"

"If you're planning to catch someone, go undercover? It's not admissible. I'm just saying."

"Oh, that's not what this is about." Joe took the bag. "We're way beyond a court of law."

———

On Friday he started late, checking out of the Rest-a-Way at noon and eating a full lunch at a diner off 280. By three o'clock he was in Connecticut, the truck parked in Old Ridgefork's municipal lot. The town was small and charming, with pottery shops and coffee boutiques on the renovated main street. Joe walked a few blocks north, to the edge of the town center, and sat on a park bench near a stoplight where Bluff Street crossed Main.

Late sunlight slanted across trees and Victorians. Children's shouts drifted from a playground a block away. Traffic was light but steady, a stream of cars headed mostly east. Old Ridgefork sat on one of the commuter arteries into Fairfield County, as Joe had determined from careful study of a state map.

Valiant had driven this way all three times Joe had tailed him home.

He sat for ninety-five minutes, and then he saw the Gallardo coming through town, a few blocks away.

Joe stood and began to walk along the sidewalk to the street corner, his back to Valiant. He could hear the car—the sort of whiny rumble that came from overpriced, overpowered Italian engines—and paced himself accordingly. When the Lamborghini was still a block behind him, Joe hit the pedestrian-crosswalk button, and the light turned red just in time to halt Valiant at the intersection.

Two feet away.

Joe turned, leaned over, and put his hand through the open passenger window to unclick the lock latch. In one smooth motion, he opened the door, slid in, and slammed it shut behind him.

"Hey, Prince," he said. "Light's green, you can go."

Valiant recovered, snarled, and twisted in his seat, reaching across in a lunge that was half punch, half grab. Joe pulled out his .45 and pointed it at Valiant's face.

"Settle down or I'll shoot you," Joe said.

Valiant froze.

"My service weapon." Joe held the Model 1911 comfortably, with his elbow against the door, keeping as far from Valiant as possible. "I wasn't supposed to take it, but no one was paying attention on those MAC flights forty years ago. New ammunition, of course."

"You're over the line."

"Yeah, I'm afraid so." Joe considered the handgun. "I suppose I really could go to prison for this."

"You will!"

"Maybe." Joe looked back at Valiant. "See, that's the difference between you and me—I own up to my responsibilities."

"What do you want from me?"

"I told you—the light's green. Start driving."

Valiant glared another moment, then put the car into gear and started up the road.

"Turn up here," said Joe. "Yes, there, on Valley Road. No need to bother anyone behind us."

They followed the winding road up a hill, soon leaving the scattering of houses that marked the edge of Old Ridgefork proper. Fall foliage had just started to turn, and the trees glowed in the setting sun. As they ascended, Joe could see a lake sparkling in the distance. "Slow down," he said. "Around this bend...yup, there it is. Pull in."

They stopped at a roadside historic marker—a faded metal sign standing on a wide verge so cars could pull over. The road was deserted. Valiant killed the engine at Joe's direction, and in the quiet they could hear birds and crickets.

"You rich assholes," said Joe. "Playing Wall Street games. Hundreds of us, you ruined our lives, and that was just at Fulmont. I figure you have thousands and thousands to answer for, all the deals you've done."

"I told you, we followed every single law, every single regulation." Valiant didn't look at the pistol.

"That's kind of not the point, which you still don't seem to understand."

"We kept that business alive."

"By screwing every single guy who worked there."

"At least they're working."

"Is that why you did it?"

"What?"

"To put us all on minimum wage? Take away our retirement? Force us to work until we die?"

Valiant breathed hard. "Why are you doing this?"

"I just want to understand."

"Understand?"

"You."

Cool forest air drifted through the open window, bringing a

smell of earth and fallen leaves. Far away, the sound of traffic on the state road was barely audible.

"Was it just money?" Joe said. "I really want to know. You can't possibly need another million dollars."

Valiant said nothing for a long moment.

"Well?" Joe moved his pistol slightly, bringing it back into the conversation.

"You just want me to explain myself?" Valiant seemed uncertain. "That's all?"

"If I wanted revenge, I'd have shot you already." Joe shrugged. "I thought about it. But what's the point?"

"So put the gun away!"

"Don't get any ideas," Joe said. "Self-defense cuts both ways."

Not actually true, but Valiant nodded.

A minute later he was talking, talking, talking.

"You worked at Fulmont a long time, didn't you? The rolling line, right? Not just pressing buttons, turning cranks. You think I don't know anything about the industry, but you're wrong. I study every detail before I make a deal. *Everything*. So I know about your job. It takes skill. Years, maybe, to get good at it."

Joe raised an eyebrow.

"That's the reason Fulmont's not in Mexico," said Valiant. "Or Indonesia, or Poland. Skills. You guys know what you're doing, and that can't be yanked up and dumped in some cheap, overpopulated free-trade zone."

"Thanks."

"Not my point. Look, you were good at your job, I bet. Spend years learning a craft, there's satisfaction in performing it. Real satisfaction. Doing a job and doing it well—that's what makes people happy."

Joe stared at him. "So why—"

"Because what *I* do is, I make deals."

"That's not the same thing."

Valiant shook his head. "I find value to unlock, synergies to realize. Ways to bring people together, so everyone comes out ahead. And I'm *good* at it, just like you're good at the milling press."

"Good at destroying lives?"

"Good at two-plus-two-equals-five. Seeing possibilities where no one else does and bringing them to life."

Not a single car had passed by. The sun was descending into a bank of purple.

"But you walk away with seven figures," said Joe. "And I have to eat day-old bread and government cheese."

Valiant frowned. "That's not my fault. That's how the world works. You make strap steel. I create billions of dollars of value. Billions! Of course I get paid more."

They fell silent. Valiant looked away. Time passed.

"I should tell you," Joe said finally. "You're on tape."

"Huh?" Valiant swung back.

Joe kept the gun steady but used his left hand to pull the camera lens from concealment in his shirt placket. He held it up, thin wires dangling.

"All recorded, picture and sound both."

"So what?" Valiant grimaced. "Take it to some prosecutor, he'll just laugh. I keep telling you, there's nothing illegal going on here!"

"I know." Joe let the lens fall. "I was thinking I'd put it on the internet. YouTube? Get some attention on what you've done. What you *are*."

After a moment, Valiant's face cleared. "Go ahead," he said. "Sure, post it. My lawyers can get a takedown notice in an hour. And even if they don't, who cares?"

"The rest of the world cares."

"I don't think so." Somehow he'd recovered every last sniff of self-confidence.

"You *want* yourself seen like this?"

"Sure." Valiant laughed. "All you'll be doing, really, is proving that I know how to find a bargain—and capitalize on it."

"That's..." Joe's voice trailed away.

"It's like free advertising. Asshole."

They sat silent, eyeing each other.

"So," Valiant said. "Now what?"

Joe wondered how he'd ended up here. He looked out the windshield, unable to hold Valiant's smirking gaze.

The setting sun pierced the cloud bank, and golden light dappled the trees below them. Joe sighed.

"I'm not sure." The 1911 was heavy in his hand.

"Well, I don't care. Do what you want."

Joe turned back. "Okay," he said.

He raised the pistol and shot Valiant in the heart.

———

"THE FBI TALKED to me," said Stokey. "And the state police. Even the DA—and I voted for him last year."

"Me too." Joe closed the iron firebox, adjusted its damper, and checked the thermometer poking out from the smokehouse planking. "Down in the courthouse. They took over the whole second floor, it felt like."

Hardwood smoke drifted from blackened vents. They were in Stokey's backyard, where he'd built the little smokehouse twenty years before.

"I told them you went up there." Stokey shifted uncomfortably. It was the first time he'd brought up the subject directly. "To see Valiant. You told me you were going."

"You did the right thing," Joe said. "I did tell you that, and I went to New York. Of course you had to tell them the truth."

"They're convinced you did it." Stokey looked at Joe square. "That you killed Valiant."

"Lots of guys wanted to."

The October morning was cool and overcast. Joe had shot a deer the day before—in season, permit and everything—and what hadn't been frozen, he and Stokey were turning into sausage and jerky.

"Did you?" Having finally asked, Stokey wasn't letting it go.

"They don't seem to have any evidence," said Joe. "Whoever did it, he probably walked away all bloody, but if he burned the clothing and got rid of the gun, there's no connection."

"But eyewitnesses—"

"Saw a man in a dark jacket and a hat. Worthless."

The wood smoke was sharp and clean. A couple dogs from the neighborhood had shown up and were now sitting out by the road, watching with keen attention.

Stokey gave up. "You taking your old job back?"

Joe studied the smoke rising, drifting slowly into the gray sky. "I don't think so," he said. "That wouldn't be right."

THE HOTLINE

BY DREDA SAY MITCHELL

Rukshana Malik wasn't angry when she was passed over for promotion at the London bank where she worked. It was true that Sarah, the successful candidate, wasn't as well qualified. It was also true that she was a bit younger, but Rukshana didn't want to draw any conclusions from that. After the selection process was over, her manager had given her a debriefing in which he explained that it had been a very close thing and that Rukshana still had a very bright future with the company—after all, she was only twenty-nine. He also suggested that the next time a position came up, she should go to him so he could prep her with some interview practice. Rukshana liked Jeff; he was a great boss. So she was disappointed and a bit puzzled, but she wasn't angry.

Her family was, though. They suspected that the reason she hadn't been given the promotion was that she was a Muslim who wore a headscarf. Her sister, Farah, asked, "This girl who got the job, what does she look like?"

"Well, she's young and blond..."

"And very good-looking, I imagine?"

"I suppose."

"Oh, wake up, Rocky." Farah waved her hands in the air. She was wearing her pale blue soft leather gloves with the fancy fringe at the end and the three white buttons on the tops, one of her newest fashion accessories.

"It's not like that; they have strict policies on race, religion, gender, and the rest of it."

Her sister sighed and shook her head with pity. Sometimes it was easy for her to forget that Rukshana was the older of the two, and an outsider could be forgiven for not realizing they were related at all. Farah wore her faith lightly, dressed in Western clothes, and was a party girl with dark brown eyes that flashed and sparkled like her gold jewelry.

The following week, Rukshana was called away from her desk to see a guy from Personnel. As soon as he told her that she was a highly valued member of the staff and a key member of the team, she knew what was coming, and sure enough she was right. He went on, "Unfortunately, in today's harsh financial climate, tough decisions have to be taken . . ."

Rukshana was let go, but she still wasn't angry. She was handed a letter that included a nice payoff and a glowing reference, and all her coworkers said that they were sorry to see her leave. But she was nonetheless let go. She was in tears as she cleared her desk and didn't see an angry Jeff appear from his office.

"Is this true, what I've heard?" he asked.

"Yes."

"This is outrageous. I'm going up to Personnel, they're not getting away this." He started walking toward the elevator.

She grabbed his arm and dragged him back. "Please, don't. It's all right, honestly."

"I don't care."

He stormed off, and she didn't see him again before she left. Farah was equally angry when Rukshana told her what had happened. "You should sue the bastards."

"For what?"

"Like Marlon Brando said in *The Wild One,* 'Whaddya got?' There's race, religion, gender—sue them for all three. Make them pay. Drag their arses through the courts, embarrass them in public, chuck dirt at them, and make them wish they'd never heard your name."

"It's not worth it."

Farah was genuinely baffled. "What's the matter with you, Rocky? Why aren't you angry? I'd be fizzing if people treated me like that."

"I'm just not angry."

And it was true—she wasn't. She was upset, scared, shocked, and confused. London could be a tough city at the best of times, and when you had no job and bills to pay, it was a very frightening place indeed. But she still wasn't angry.

That evening she got a call from Kelly, her best friend at the bank. "Rukshana, I can't believe they've done this to you. You've got to get them back."

Not another person telling her to sue . . .

"You can't take an employer to court for letting you go. That's not how it works."

"I'm not talking about the bank. I'm talking about Jeff and that bitch Sarah."

Confused, Rukshana answered, "It's got nothing to do with Jeff and even less to do with Sarah."

There was a long silence before Kelly said, "Oh, of course, maybe you don't know . . ."

"What don't I know?"

"About Jeff and Sarah. About them having a bit of slap-and-tickle."

Rukshana was horrified. "They're not having an affair. He's married with kids; he's got a photo of them on his desk, he's always going on about his family."

"Oh, Rukshana, puh-leeze—you can't be that naive. They're carrying on, everyone at the bank knows that."

"I didn't know that."

Kelly hesitated. "Well, people didn't like to tell you gossip, what with you being a Muslim and everything—they thought you wouldn't like it."

Rukshana was disgusted. She loved gossip. Kelly went on to tell Rukshana what everyone knew. "It's been going on for months. They think it's a big secret, but of course everyone knows. That's why he fixed it for her to get the job, to keep her sweet. Then he advised Personnel to get rid of you, so in case you sued them about missing the promotion, they could say you were just bitter because you'd been fired. That's what everyone's saying happened."

"That's what everyone's saying?"

"That's what everyone's saying. He was on your interview panel, wasn't he? He goes up to Personnel every five minutes, doesn't he? Every lunchtime at noon, Jeff and Sarah meet up. He goes out and waits a couple of streets away, and then five minutes later she follows and they get a cab to some Holiday Inn, where they do their dirty business. Then at two o'clock on the dot, he comes back, and five minutes later, she arrives on her own so no one will guess that they're at it. I mean, can you imagine? It'd take a lot more than a promotion to persuade me to shag that fat ugly bastard. Talk about lie back and think of England. Rukshana? You've gone very quiet. Are you still there?"

Rukshana was still there. She was just very, very angry.

———

RUKSHANA DIDN'T DO anything the following day because she was still too angry; she wanted a clear head when she decided what to do next. Twenty-four hours later she was still too angry but had decided to ring a couple of lawyers anyway to see if she had a case against the bank. They were a bit skeptical but thought she might be able to do something on discrimination grounds. They were less sure about Kelly's preferred option, that Rukshana sue Jeff for being a lying, cheating, disloyal, fat ugly bastard who'd taken her job away. Rukshana was glad the lawyers didn't advise that. She didn't want to sue anyone; that wasn't what she was after.

She couldn't relax. The only person in the house during the day was her granddad. He was in his eighties. He got a little confused sometimes, but on other occasions he was very sharp. Whatever—she didn't feel like chatting. She tried doing a little housework to calm down. That didn't help, but she did it anyway. In Farah's room, she picked up the clothes her sister had scattered around after she'd come in from a party the previous night. Rukshana held a miniskirt against her hips; it really was immodestly short. A few months ago, their cousin had come from Pakistan to visit and had shared a room with Farah; what a culture shock it must have been for her. Their cousin refused to leave the house without wearing a burka, so when she went out, she was covered in black, only her eyes visible to the outside world. When she returned to Pakistan, she'd left one of her burkas behind, and it was still sitting on a shelf, possibly meant to serve as a reproach to her wayward cousin. Rukshana picked it up.

From the bedroom window, she could see the towers of the City, London's financial district, looming over the rooftops;

down below those towers was the bank where Jeff and Sarah were having a good laugh at her expense. She looked at the clothes in her hands and then out over the city, and she bit her lip.

Rukshana knew what she was considering was a serious criminal offense and that she'd go to prison for several years if she was caught. She'd have to get everything right and not make any mistakes. There were a lot of things that could go wrong, and there was her family to think about. Then she thought about Jeff appearing from his office and telling her how outrageous her sacking was and how he wasn't putting up with it. She gripped the clothes tightly in her hand. Every single day she spent staring out the barred windows of a prison cell would be worth it. Jeff was going to pay. She smiled and whispered to herself:

"It's on."

————

IT WAS A Thursday. Rukshana had everything prepared and all the timing worked out. She was wearing one of her sister's short skirts, a low-cut top, and ballet shoes on her feet. In her shoulder bag were silver high heels, a pair of fashionably outsize Jackie O. sunglasses, and her cousin's burka. Out in the hall was the family bike that she'd oiled and left ready. And she'd picked the day very carefully.

Her grandfather was a cricket fanatic. He was already in his armchair with various fruit juices and nibbles in easy reach, getting ready for the first day of the England-Pakistan match being played in London. Every ball would be shown on the TV, along with the replays and analyses. Rukshana knew her grandfather; he wouldn't be moving from that spot all day. He might briefly go upstairs for a call of nature, but even that wasn't certain. Where cricket was concerned, he had very firm bladder control.

And there was a house rule—no one disturbed Granddad when the cricket was on. Knocks on the door went unanswered, the phone was left to ring, and any attempt to start a conversation was ignored.

When the first ball of the match was bowled, Rukshana looked up at the clock on the wall. It was half past eleven. She had thirty minutes to complete the first part of her plan.

"I'm just going upstairs to read a book."

She was met with silence. Out in the hall she put on her cousin's burka and wheeled the bike out onto the street. Very, very gently, she pulled the front door shut. She mounted the bike and began pedaling, the burka wrapped around her, only her eyes visible. She rode to the end of her street and turned onto the main road that led to the City.

On a typical day in London, you could see almost anyone dressed almost any way, but even so, a woman cycling in a burka was unusual. Truant schoolkids laughed as she flew by. Some drivers did double takes when they saw her, which were quickly followed by contemptuous stares directed not at her but at her burka. Rukshana almost wobbled on her bike, she was so shaken by the response to her clothing. She'd heard women in her family talk about how they were sometimes insulted and verbally abused on the street when they wore their burkas, but Rukshana hadn't thought it was as bad as this. And—perhaps it was inevitable—one guy leaned out of the window of his van and yelled "Terrorist!" when she stopped at a traffic light. She threw off her shock. She began to feel mad and bad. She felt like an outlaw.

It took her twenty minutes to arrive at her destination, a quiet side street two blocks away from the bank where she'd worked. She parked the bike, locked it up, and checked the street. There was no one looking. She pulled the burka off over her head and put it in her bag before swapping her slippers for the high heels. She put on sunglasses. She used a mirror to apply some makeup and arrange her long raven-black hair so that it waved and flowed around her face. She smiled at her image. She looked fantastic, nothing like her normal headscarf-wearing self. She couldn't help thinking that she could give her sister a run for her money in the looks department.

Unsteadily at first, but with growing confidence, she clip-clopped down the street on her heels and then turned onto the main road. With her new look, she might as well have been in a different country. The same sort of male drivers who had given her dirty looks when she'd been on her bike were now slowing down to admire her bronzed legs. When a man leaned out of a van's window and shouted, "Oi, oi! Do you fancy a portion, sweetheart?" Rukshana avoided eye contact and kept walking. She wondered if it was the same man who'd shouted "Terrorist!" at her fifteen minutes earlier.

She walked the two blocks. On the left was the bank, and on the right was a small park where the staff sometimes went to eat their lunches. Rukshana took a seat on a bench that gave her a view of the entrance to the bank. She crossed her long bare legs and looked at her watch. It was 11:55 a.m. She'd made it. A bicycle courier walked past her wheeling his bike; he clocked her legs, and she heard him whisper "Asian babe" as he went by. She smiled and looked at her watch. It was noon. She looked over to the entrance and sure enough, just as Kelly had foretold, Jeff emerged from the bank and walked down the steps. He adjusted his tie and ran his fingers through his hair a few times before trotting off and turning down a side street.

Five minutes after that, Sarah too came out of the bank. She turned and walked down the same side street Jeff had. Rukshana shook her head and whispered, "Bastards." Then she stood up, adjusted her hair again, and walked across the road. There were hundreds and hundreds of employees in this building, so she was sure she would get away with it. On the steps of the bank, she took a deep breath and said to herself, "This is it," before walking into the lobby.

In front of her was a security gate that you needed a swipe card to pass through. To the left of it sat Mark, a security guard, a big barrel of a man in a peaked cap. She fished around in her shoulder bag and took out her now-invalidated employee swipe card along with another one that she used for her local library. She wriggled her shoulders like her sister and giggled at Mark; he smiled back. When she got to the gate, she used her library card to try to get through. A red light flashed and the machine honked at her. She tried again. Another red light and another honk. She looked at Mark helplessly and waved her swipe card at him. Like a middle-aged knight, he got out of his chair and came over to help.

The bank had strict procedures about access. Mark's role was to examine her card and see whether there was a problem and, if necessary, refer her to the security office. But Rukshana knew Mark well. His view was that strict procedures didn't apply to ditzy, sexy women with long legs. And today, Rukshana was a very ditzy, very sexy woman with very long legs. Mark towered over her.

"Is there a problem, miss?"

"Oh, yes, Mark," she breathed. "My card is always letting me down."

Mark slipped his own security card into the machine, and there was a green light, a ping, and the gate swung open. She squeezed his arm.

"Oh, Mark, you're such a sweetie..."

Mark saluted and Rukshana walked through with the almost

physical sensation of his eyes drilling into her backside. She walked to the elevator and went up to the fifth floor, taking out her sister's blue leather gloves and putting them on. When the doors slid open, she was face-to-face with Renata, a colleague who knew Rukshana as well as Rukshana knew her. Rukshana stiffened; everyone who might have recognized her, with or without her headscarf, should have been out at lunch. Renata smiled at her.

"Do you really need those sunglasses in here, dear?" For a few seconds Rukshana thought it was all over. Renata held the elevator door open for her and said, "If you don't get out, you're going back down." Rukshana got out, fingered the sunglasses, and stammered, "G-got to look cool..."

Renata got in the elevator, smiled, and said, "You look very cool, darling. You'd better watch out or you'll have that sleazy lecher Jeff after you."

The elevator doors closed. Rukshana hurried down the corridor to Jeff's office and peered in the window. It was empty. With her gloved hands she pulled the handle and went inside. She sat at his computer. On the screen was a website featuring romantic breaks for two in Paris: *The city of love...a weekend of amour... for that special person in your life...*

Rukshana had the feeling it wasn't Jeff's wife who would be going. She took a list out of her handbag and began typing in the web addresses of radical Islamic websites, one after another, so that a casual observer of Jeff's computer history might think Jeff spent all his time looking up death-to-the-infidel!, death-to-the-great-Satan!, death-to—well, death-to-pretty-much-everyone-really! websites. Then she changed his screen saver from a sugary snapshot of Jeff's wife and kids to a photo of a radical Islamic cleric.

She decided to skip the elevator and took the stairs down to the lobby. Mark didn't wait for her to try her card this time; he jumped up smartly and opened the gate for her, assuming her card still wasn't working. She gave him a long, sultry look with the promise of the East in it—a look her sister had perfected—and with that she was back out on the street.

She walked the two blocks to her bike and changed into her burka and ballet shoes. She checked her watch. It was 12:40 p.m. She had to move. She pedaled furiously away from the glass and glitz of London's financial district to a poorer quarter of town and parked her bike in the yard of a disused workshop. Over her loomed a minaret. She walked a couple of streets until she was standing in the shadow of the tower.

Al-Nutjobs Mosque. That wasn't its real name, of course. It was called Al-Nutjobs by the British newspapers; they claimed that every Muslim extremist in London was a regular there, but the members of the Muslim community weren't so sure. Their view was that most of the people who hung out at Al-Nutjobs were undercover newspaper reporters, police spies, and operatives from various Western intelligence agencies. Whatever the case, Rukshana knew the street was plastered with CCTVs and other forms of surveillance and that all the local public phones were bugged. She had to be very, very careful.

She walked up to the pay phone opposite the mosque. She checked that her gloves were on and then went inside. She picked up the phone, put some coins in, and called the special police antiterrorist hotline. When she got through, she faked an Indian accent, the sort that had been thought very amusing on British comedy shows in the 1970s but that in these more liberal times wasn't considered funny anymore.

"Please, please, this afternoon, bombs, bombs! *Bombs!*"

Rukshana explained in her accent that she'd overheard a campaign being planned in Al-Nutjobs, and the ringleader was an undercover white convert who worked at — and she gave them all Jeff's details. As the operator desperately tried to keep her on the line, Rukshana shouted, "Please, please, this afternoon, bombs, bombs! *Bombs!*"

She hung up and walked smartly down the street. Rukshana collected her bike from the disused workshop and checked her watch. It was 1:15 p.m. Time was short. As she jumped on the bike to pedal back to the bank, a siren wailed through the air. Shit — she hadn't expected the cops to move that quickly. A police car screamed down the street heading toward the mosque. Rukshana didn't look back as she cycled to the bank. Once there, she parked her bike in the same spot as before, took off her burka, and slipped into her heels.

Her old bench opposite the bank was still available, and she sat down and checked her watch. It was 1:55 p.m. She was just in time. At 2:00 p.m. precisely, just as Kelly had said he would, Jeff appeared and walked back into the bank. Five minutes later, Sarah arrived, looking a little red-faced and with her clothes askew, and followed him in. Now Rukshana just had to wait.

If you reported any ordinary crime, the police would assess the evidence and decide what, if anything, to do. If you reported a terrorist bombing from a pay phone outside Al-Nutjobs, the police couldn't wait. They couldn't investigate the threat to see if it was serious; they couldn't weigh things up. They had to act fast and worry about it later.

At 2:15 p.m., the police acted. In the distance Rukshana heard sirens, and then more sirens as other police vehicles joined the chorus, and then they all came around the corner, brakes squealing, lights flashing, careering down the street. A police van mounted the pavement and juddered to a halt; it was followed by police cars and motorbikes. The doors to the van flew open and a half a dozen cops in black-and-white-checkered baseball caps, submachine guns slung over their shoulders, jumped out. Pistols were pulled from holsters; safety catches were disabled. The police raced up the stairs and into the bank. Other vehicles arrived, and soon there were so many flashing blue lights, you might have thought you were at a carnival.

Five minutes later, Rukshana rose to her feet to enjoy the view. Jeff was dragged down the steps, being frog-marched by two burly cops. He was thrown to the ground and spread-eagled; one cop kept a pistol to his head while the other cop pressed his knee into Jeff's back and handcuffed him. Down the steps came another officer holding Jeff's computer. Then the doors to the bank flew open as two policemen tried to stop Sarah from running after Jeff. She screamed, "Leave him alone, he hasn't done anything, what's the matter with you?"

Rukshana winced as Sarah punched one of the policemen in the face, after which Sarah was bundled to the ground, long legs akimbo, and thrown into the back of a van. Then the two suspects were driven away.

Rukshana sat back down. An old teacher of hers had once quoted a French saying: Revenge was a dish you ate cold. Perhaps that was true. But it certainly filled up the belly.

———

"OH, RUKSHANA, YOU should have been there!" Kelly rang that evening to tell Rukshana about the day's events. "The cops turned up and nicked Jeff. And they took Sarah away too, it was so funny."

Rukshana put on her best sympathy voice. "Poor Jeff..."

Kelly couldn't believe it. "Poor Jeff? After what he did to you?"

The following evening Kelly updated Rukshana. "It was all a hoax! The police released Jeff in the small hours without charge. Now we've had a team of detectives in all day trying to find the hoaxer. They're drawing up a list of suspects. It'll be pretty heavy for the guy who did it. The police don't take too kindly to that sort of thing—the cops say it'll mean jail time for the culprit. That won't help Jeff, of course, now that it's all out about him and Sarah. The bank's really embarrassed. Word is that when it's all calmed down, they're going to sack him. And Sarah."

"Poor Jeff."

"Poor Jeff? You have more reason to hate him than anyone…" There was a long pause before Kelly added, "I don't want to worry you, Rukshana, but I think you might be on the list of suspects, what with being let go." There was another long pause and then Kelly asked, "It wasn't you, was it?"

"Of course not."

"That's what I told the police! A nice inoffensive Muslim girl like Rukshana—no way was it her. The thing is, though…I'm not sure they believed me."

———

IT WAS THE following Tuesday, the last day of the cricket match between England and Pakistan. The commentators agreed it was going to be a thrilling finish, and Rukshana's grandfather was in position in his armchair for it. Rukshana was jumpy. Every time she heard a noise outside, she got up and looked through the window. Then at about noon it happened. A silver sedan pulled up outside her house and a man got out and walked up the garden path. There was a knock on the door.

Rukshana's grandfather snapped, "Ignore it."

Instead Rukshana ignored him and went to the door. She opened it to a man with a flashy suit, sunglasses, and slicked-back blond hair. He'd obviously modeled himself on a character from an American cop show. He showed her some ID.

"Rukshana Malik?"

"Yes."

"Detective Constable John Martin, Metropolitan Police. I'm investigating a very serious crime and I'd like to ask you some questions."

She looked into his eyes. He knew. And what's more, he knew that she knew that he knew—but could he prove it? Rukshana had been ultra careful. She'd made sure she was unrecognizable in the burka and in her sister's clothes. She'd burned all the evidence and left the bike on the High Street, where some kids had promptly stolen it. She'd worn gloves. She had a story worked out and she was sticking to it. She knew what to do; she watched the same American cop shows as DC John Martin.

"You'd better come in."

John Martin said good afternoon to her grandfather and was ignored for his trouble. Rukshana whispered, "He's watching the cricket, he doesn't like to be disturbed."

"I see."

They sat down on a sofa. John Martin went through the preliminaries, explaining why he was there and giving Rukshana the chance to avoid wasting everyone's time.

"Is there anything you'd like to tell me about the events of last Thursday?"

"I'm sorry, I don't know what you mean."

John Martin sighed. He knew. But could he prove it?

"Could you tell me where you were last Thursday?"

"I was here all day with my granddad."

John Martin looked over at the cricket fanatic. "Could you confirm that, sir?"

Martin was ignored. Rukshana explained, "He'll confirm it when the cricket's over."

John Martin was disgusted. "I'm sorry, I'm not waiting seven hours for the cricket to finish."

Rukshana shrugged her shoulders. "I'm sorry."

John Martin moved on. "You must have been very disappointed to be passed over for promotion at the bank?"

"Not really, no."

John Martin feigned surprise. "Not really?"

"I'm a person of faith, Detective Constable. Do you know what that means?"

John Martin looked blank. Islamic theology obviously wasn't his strong suit. Rukshana went on. "I accept everything as part of the divine plan. So, no, I wasn't disappointed."

"Very commendable, I'm sure. But you must have been a little upset when you were let go? Angry?"

She smiled at him. "That's for atheists, I'm afraid."

John Martin had the feeling he was being put down, but he pressed on. "Were you aware that the successful candidate was having intimate relations with your manager?"

"Jeff and Sarah? I certainly was not. I had no idea. People don't pass gossip on to me. It's because I'm a Muslim, you see."

John Martin pursed his lips and produced a photo from a file. He handed it to Rukshana. "Do you know who that is?"

It was a CCTV still photo from the lobby of the bank. It showed Rukshana at the security gate in her heels, short skirt, low-cut top, and sunglasses. Rukshana passed it back.

"No, sorry."

John Martin passed it back to her. "Have another look. Rack your brains."

Rukshana studied it again before handing it over.

"Still no."

John Martin moved in for the kill. "It's you, isn't it?"

Rukshana feigned outrage and tugged at her headscarf. "Certainly not. I'm a good Muslim. That girl looks like a prostitute. Totally inappropriate clothes for any decent Muslim woman."

John Martin passed her another photo, asked her if she recognized the subject. This one was a CCTV still of Rukshana in her burka outside Al-Nutjobs. But Rukshana had hit her stride. "I doubt her own mother would recognize her. If it was a woman, of course; perhaps it was a man in disguise? We don't wear burkas in this house."

John Martin played her the tape of the phone call to the anti-terrorist hotline. When it was finished he said, "That was you, wasn't it?"

"It sounds more like a white comedian making fun of Asians. There's too much of that sort of racism in our society. I don't know why the police don't crack down on it."

And so it went on. For an hour, John Martin probed and Rukshana parried. But Rukshana could see the detective was getting frustrated. He knew, okay, but he couldn't prove it. Eventually, John Martin accepted a cup of tea and a couple of Samosas that he found "very tasty." Then, with obvious reluctance, he returned to the attack.

"Our inquiries have revealed — oh, I say, good shot!"

John Martin was looking over Rukshana's shoulder at the cricket. A young Pakistani batsman had just hit the ball clean into the cheering crowd. Granddad turned around and said to him, "What about that kid, eh? What a prospect!"

John Martin returned to his questioning, but he began going around in circles. He admitted the photos could have been of anyone. He also confessed there was no fingerprint evidence and that the tape didn't really prove anything. He admitted — off the record — that the police had quite a list of people who didn't much like her ex-boss Jeff, so they had a lot of others to interview. In fact, some of his fellow officers suspected Jeff's wife was the real culprit, and, frankly, they didn't blame her. The wife was certainly a more promising suspect than a nice Muslim girl like Rukshana.

"Okay, Miss Malik, I think we're about finished for now."

But as he got up to go, he noticed something on the mantelpiece. He walked over and picked up the large pair of sunglasses that Rukshana had worn the previous Thursday when she'd framed Jeff. They were sitting where she'd left them when she'd gotten back. John Martin looked at the shades and then fished out the CCTV still of Rukshana in the bank lobby and studied it. They were obviously the same distinctive pair. Rukshana felt her stomach tense. She'd been so careful, and now this…

But before John Martin had a chance to ask Rukshana for an explanation, her granddad snapped, "What are you doing with my sunglasses?"

"Your sunglasses?"

"Yes. They're medicinal, I use them to cut out the glare from the TV."

Granddad got up, took the sunglasses from the cop's hand, and put them on. He looked quite natty in them. John Martin was not convinced.

"You use them to cut out the glare from the TV?"

"That's right."

"So why weren't you wearing them when I came in?"

"I was. But I take them off when we have visitors. I don't want to look like a prat, do I?"

"I'm sorry, sir, but…"

Granddad angrily turned on the unfortunate police officer. "Are you calling me a liar? And by the way, the girl is right — she was here all day last Thursday and I was here all day watching cricket in my sunglasses and I'd like to see you prove otherwise. Now, why don't you clear off and catch some real criminals?"

———

WHEN JOHN MARTIN was gone, Rukshana sat down in the front room by her grandfather.

"So you were listening then?"

"I can listen and watch cricket at the same time. I'm not stupid. And that was a very foolish thing you did. You could have gone to prison."

"I know. And thanks, Granddad. For backing me up."

Her granddad nodded and then said, "If you'd wanted revenge on someone, you should have spoken to me. I know all about that. When I was a child, a British prime minister came to our village and was a little bit rude and arrogant." Rukshana's granddad forgot the cricket for a moment and became lost in thought. Then he added, "Now, that was a revenge story…"

BLOOD AND SUNSHINE

BY ADAM MEYER

Most people don't believe in pure evil, and neither did I until I met five-year-old Dylan Brewster.

Before I ever laid eyes on Dylan, I saw his nanny. She was barely older than I was, clearly much too young and pretty to be anyone's mother. Her lush blond hair was pulled back in a ponytail, her toned arms pushing a heavy stroller. A few-months-old baby in a pink onesie was strapped inside.

"Can I help you?" I asked, trying for a mix of helpful yet suave. Not easy when your hands are covered with finger paint and you're wearing a yellow T-shirt that says SUNSHINE SUMMER CAMP.

"Is this the Dolphin room?" she asked, turning back as if she'd lost something, or someone. About halfway down the hall I saw him: a small, dark-haired boy with his head stuck in one of the cubbies that lined the hall. "Dylan! Come over here, please."

He did, and there's no denying he was awfully cute. Long, straight hair cut in a neat line over his forehead, and a nose that looked like a button in a snowman's face. He wore plaid sneakers so small I could've swallowed one whole.

"Hi, Dylan," I said, kneeling down to look him in the eye. "I'm—" But he marched past me and into the classroom where the rest of the Dolphins were busy playing. This was midmorning during my third week of camp, but it was the first time Dylan had come.

"Sorry we are late," the nanny said, and there was a precision in her words that hinted at a faint accent. "We had some trouble getting out today."

"Trouble?"

The nanny glanced down at the baby in the pink jumper, then at Dylan. "Sometimes he acts a little"—she wriggled her fingers, searching for the word—"a little crazy."

"That's okay. I act a little crazy myself sometimes."

At first I wasn't sure she got the joke, but then she smiled. "I'm Britta."

Before I could get my name out, Rebecca bellowed it from behind me. "Eddie! Where on earth have you—oh." The frown on her face dissolved as soon as she saw Britta. "You must be Dylan's caretaker."

Britta nodded and Rebecca put on one of her biggest, phoniest smiles. She was in charge of the group and I was her assistant. She was pretty old—early thirties, at least—and a full-time kindergarten teacher, which seemed to require that she speak to virtually everyone as if they had the intelligence of a five-year-old. Especially me.

"Eddie, why don't you go in and get the morning snack ready. Would that be all right?"

I glanced at the wall clock—it was half an hour before our usual snack time—but I didn't argue. She clearly wanted to get rid of me, and maybe even embarrass me in front of Britta.

"Yes, ma'am," I said, saluting Rebecca. She didn't look amused, but Britta did, and that was even better. I washed my hands, then slipped back into the room and saw the dozen boys and girls in our Dolphin group hard at play. Some had clustered in the toy kitchen, and others finger-painted at the child-size tables. The last few kids were in the corner stacking wooden blocks into what looked like a fort.

Dylan stood to one side, watching the block builders. I crouched beside him, lining up plastic cups for apple juice.

"We're glad to have you here at camp with us," I said. "Have you had a good summer so far?"

"I went on a trip."

"Oh, yeah? Where'd you go?"

His eyes narrowed, his gaze still on the kids with the blocks. "Ug-land."

At first I wasn't sure what he meant. And then I got it: England. "Was it fun?"

He shrugged. "It's *far*."

"It sure is."

I was from Queens and had never been farther than Newark. It burned me that kids like Dylan got to take trips overseas they didn't appreciate while I worked all summer just to cover the cost of college textbooks. But that was how it was. Upper West Side kids like Dylan had nannies and European vacations and summer camp, and kids in Astoria didn't.

"You want to help me pour the juice?" I asked.

"I wanna build a galley," Dylan said.

I wasn't sure what a galley was, but I let that go and unscrewed the top of the juice bottle. "Sure, go build whatever you want. I'm sure the other kids will let you play with them."

"I wanna do it myself."

I sharpened my tone. "Dylan, we all have to play together here. But if you ask nicely—"

Clearly Dylan had no intention of asking, nicely or otherwise. He was already headed right for the play area, and by the time I'd put down the apple juice and gotten over to him, it was too late. He had stomped right through there, blocks tumbling down and flying every which way.

Amber—one of the block builders—threw up her hands, showing off the Band-Aids stuck to each of her elbows. It was lucky the falling blocks had missed her because she always seemed to be getting hurt. "He knocked down our house."

"That's not very nice," I said, pointing a finger at Dylan.

At first, he looked defiant, and then his face crumpled and tears appeared. "They said I couldn't play with them."

"Now, that's not true," I said. "You just went right over and—"

"Enough," Rebecca said from behind me. I turned around. She looked sharply at me and then put on a smile, her mood changing as abruptly as Dylan's. "It's cleanup time, everyone."

The kids grumbled, but then Rebecca held up a bag of sugar cookies, and that got them motivated. "Maybe you should finish pouring the juice now," she said to me, using the same tone she had with the kids. I grabbed the juice bottle and glanced over at the doorway.

Britta was there. Her big blue eyes were aimed at me, and I smiled, but she missed it and focused on Dylan, who watched the other kids clean up while he stood by, doing nothing. Britta turned from him, her expression hard to read. It was only when she wheeled the stroller away that I recognized the emotion.

It was relief.

———

THE SUNSHINE SUMMER Camp was housed on the top two floors of a private elementary school on Central Park West and Seventy-Fourth Street. We had everything an urban camp for little rich kids needed: a rooftop swimming pool, an indoor playground, and classrooms chock-full of educational toys and games. A far cry from the Boys' Club camps where I'd spent the summers of my early years, and a relatively easy way to make some cash before I headed back to Binghamton in the fall.

Or at least it had been, until Dylan showed up.

My next run-in with him happened during afternoon nap time. All the kids gathered their blankets from their cubbies and spread them out through the classroom while I stood watch. Rebecca had gone to lunch.

The kids were supposed to lie down without talking or moving, which of course isn't easy when you're five. Unlike Rebecca, I tried to be understanding when they began to stir. First Amber raised her Band-Aided elbow and said, "I'm thirsty." Then Michael, who would wear only green socks, complained that Royce had kicked him. No surprise there. Royce never stopped moving, even when he was flat on a blanket half asleep.

After settling everyone down, I put on a CD, *Peter and the Wolf.* As the gentle music filled the room, the children seemed to relax. I did too. I pulled out my cell phone to check my e-mail — a no-no with Rebecca around, but she wasn't there — and I saw a movement from the corner of my eye. Dylan was upright, gathering a stack of blocks from the shelf beside him.

The other children watched, wide-eyed. Royce leaped up, eager to get in on the action. "Can I play too?"

"Nobody's playing," I said, storming over to Dylan's blanket.

But he didn't seem to hear me. He continued to pile up the blocks, one after the other, making a tower as high as the table beside him. Then he added a long block and balanced it across the top, the tower threatening to topple.

I snatched away this last block and glared. "Put these back."

"I don't want to." There was no anger, just a simple declaration.

"If you don't, you're going to have a time-out."

This was a punishment the kids dreaded as much as losing pool time. But Dylan was unfazed. He reached out to the shelf and found another block the same length as the one I had just taken away. He added it to the top of his column of blocks to form what looked like an upside-down L.

"See, it's a galley."

I had no idea what he was talking about and I didn't much care. Besides, I felt the eyes of all the other kids on me. If I didn't establish authority over Dylan, and fast, they'd think I was a pushover.

"You need to listen to me," I said firmly. "No playing during nap time."

He looked up with eyes as dark as charcoal. "But my galley isn't done."

"Trust me, it is," I said.

Music swelled from the boom box, the soaring violins that represented the wolf's arrival. Dylan smiled then, as though he knew something I didn't, and it made me so angry I started to pull my hand back. I wasn't really going to hit him, of course, it was just my anger getting the best of me. And then I heard the door open.

When Rebecca walked in, my hands were back at my sides, and Dylan looked at her. "Eddie and I made a galley."

"That's very nice," she said, but the look on her face was stern. "But Eddie knows there's no playing during nap time."

"Of course I know that, but—"

Rebecca gave me a sharp look that said she didn't care what I had to say and shook her head. Disappointed. Dylan had made a fool out of me once more, and I didn't much like it. But then, it was my own fault. I promised myself that I wouldn't let him take advantage of me again.

———

DYLAN WAS ON his best behavior for the rest of that week, at least until the encounter with the ice vendor. It was a Friday, and the promise of the weekend was bright—I'd finally have some time with my old high school friends and away from camp. I stood on the hot Manhattan sidewalk, the sun crisping my skin. There were kids all around, being herded by their mothers and nannies.

A middle-aged street vendor was selling Italian ices in paper cups. I waited in line behind some of the campers and then ordered a pineapple ice. I'd just taken my first lick when I heard a familiar voice. Britta. She was calling after Dylan, who'd stormed toward the ices cart. She was a dozen feet behind him, struggling to push the stroller over a large sidewalk crack.

"Tell the man what you like," she said, wheeling up to the cart.

"Chocolate," Dylan said.

"No chocolate," the vendor said in what was barely English. "You want grape?"

Dylan closed his hands into fists. "No, I want chocolate."

The vendor looked at Britta with concern. He didn't want to be the cause of a full-fledged tantrum in the middle of Seventy-Fourth Street. "No chocolate."

I glanced at Britta, who looked like she was about to have a meltdown of her own, and then at Dylan. "I've got pineapple. It's pretty tasty. You want to try some?"

"I don't know," he said.

"Go ahead. I think you'll like it."

I held out my soggy paper cup. Dylan took it and lapped up a mouthful of pineapple ice.

"It's good," he said, surprised. "I want one of these." Instantly, the vendor began to scoop pineapple ice into a cup. Britta gave me a look of pure gratitude.

"Thank you."

"Of course. Anything to help."

"How has he been doing?" she asked quietly, adjusting the bonnet around the doughy face of Dylan's baby sister. Dylan was a few steps away.

I shrugged, playing coy. "Pretty good, mostly. What's he like at home?"

She shook her head sharply, which I took to mean *Don't ask*. I wanted to know more, but just then Dylan inserted himself between us, still sucking on my pineapple ice. He looked sharply at Britta.

"He won't let me make my galley."

I smiled. "Yup, I'm Mr. Mean, all right." I tousled Dylan's hair and leaned in closer to Britta. She smelled of baby powder and suntan lotion and looked as beautiful as any girl I'd ever seen. "What's this galley he keeps talking about?"

She turned away, and I couldn't tell if she didn't know or if she felt this wasn't the moment to tell me. I wanted to press her further, but I didn't have the chance. Something cold and sticky began to dribble onto my leg, and I saw that Dylan had turned over the paper cup and was pouring pineapple ice on me.

"Goddamn it, what the..." Glancing at Britta, I let the anger sputter out, smiling instead. "Lost your grip, huh, little guy?"

Dylan said nothing, just let the paper cup fall to the ground. He reached out to the vendor to take his own cup of ice and began to lick it with relish.

"I'm so sorry," Britta said. "Let me buy you another one."

"No need," I said, and I was about to say *Why don't you make it up to me by going out with me sometime,* but then the baby started to squawk. I noticed that Dylan was beside her, one hand around his ice, the other inside her stroller. He must've pinched her or hit her and made her cry.

You little bastard, I thought, but I kept that smile right on my lips, still sticky from pineapple ice.

"Let's go," Britta said, spinning the stroller away from me. As I watched them head down the sidewalk, Dylan looked back, only once, a faint smile on his lips.

———

EARLY THE NEXT week, a heat wave settled over the city. Temperatures soared into the high nineties, and the humidity was off the charts. The kids moved sluggishly through our barely cool classroom, and even Royce hardly stirred during nap time. No one showed any signs of energy all day until it was time to go up to the pool.

The aboveground pool sat on the rooftop and was filled with just enough water to reach most kids' chins. There was an area on the far side of the roof for those who didn't like to swim, with a sprinkler and a sandbox. Rebecca and I switched off which of us went in the pool, and that day was my turn.

She sat on a wooden picnic bench beside a mound of towels, wiping sweat from her face. I couldn't help but smile. Although the water only came up to my belly button, it was deliciously cool.

"Look at me," squealed Amber, whose soggy Band-Aids hung from her elbows. "I'm going underwater."

She ducked her face at the surface, went just deep enough to splash her nose and some of her round cheeks.

"That's great," I said. "Do you want to maybe try putting your *whole* head under?"

"No." Amber giggled. "That's too scary."

"You want to see scary?" I asked, ducking underwater and

sticking my elbow up like a shark fin. Amber splashed away, giggling. When I rose, Dylan tugged at my leg.

"You want to see me swim?" he asked.

Dylan was like a little duck, one of the few kids who could swim. Dutifully, I watched him churn across the pool as I tossed a beach ball back and forth with Amber and a couple of the other kids.

After a few minutes I got tired of Dylan's swimming and turned away. "You're not watching," Dylan whined, and Amber threw the ball at me again but missed.

The ball drifted toward Dylan. He grabbed it and hurled it over the side of the pool, onto the roof.

Amber leaned out. "Hey, someone get the ball!" But everyone else was on the far side of the roof, out of earshot, including Rebecca.

"I'll get it," I said, going right for the ladder since I was closest. I didn't even think about it, really. It wasn't a big deal. I'd have my hands on the ball in five seconds and be right back in the pool. What could possibly happen?

My feet had barely touched the hot rubber that covered the roof when I heard a shriek from behind me. At the sandbox, Rebecca had whirled and spotted me outside the pool. Anger crossed her face.

"Who's watching the kids?" she shrieked.

I was halfway up the ladder when I saw Dylan holding Amber's head underwater, her hair floating like kelp. I broke the surface with a crash, landing inches from the two kids. Dylan let go of Amber instantly and swam away.

I picked her up, wiped tendrils of hair out of her face, and made sure she was breathing okay. I felt Dylan brush by my legs, circling like a piranha.

"Shhh, it's okay," I told Amber, leaning her against my shoulder.

But she just cried, rubbing her eyes with her hands. The wet Band-Aids had fallen off her elbows.

"You are in very serious trouble," Rebecca said, and Dylan and I both looked up at once. I didn't know if she meant me or him.

———

APPARENTLY SHE'D MEANT me. "That's goddamn unacceptable, leaving those kids in the pool alone." I'd never heard Rebecca curse before. Of course at the moment, our kids had gone off with another group, so we were alone by the pool. "Somebody could've drowned in there."

"Yeah, like Amber," I said. "But only because Dylan was holding her underwater."

"Don't be ridiculous. The kids were horsing around, that's all. Which would've been fine if someone were supervising." She shook her head at me. "This is it, your last free pass. Don't screw up again."

I nodded and went to the bench where I'd stashed my clothes. As I started to slip on my sneakers, I noticed that one of the laces was gone. I looked around inside the sneaker and under it, but I couldn't find the lace. Was this some trick the kids were playing on me? But I didn't have time to dwell on it. I had only fifteen minutes until afternoon snack.

———

I STAYED IN the city after work that day and saw a movie, a comedy. I was glad to get some laughs, but my good mood didn't last. Soon I was standing on the sweltering subway platform, my anger starting to resurface. Then I noticed a familiar figure at the edge of the platform. Britta.

"How's the nanny business?" I asked.

She smiled when she saw me, and my bad mood disappeared again in an instant. "Pretty good."

"Seems like a tough job. Dealing with Dylan, I mean."

She opened her mouth to answer, then closed it. After a moment, she said, "He's... how do you say it? Hands full?"

"Hands full is right," I said, and we both laughed. "How long have you worked for his family?"

"Three months. My friend worked there before me. She told me not to take the job, but..." She shrugged. "I need the money."

"Tell me about it." I looked down at the end of the platform, then back at her. I wanted to find out more about Britta, who she was and where she came from, but I couldn't stop thinking about Dylan. I was still haunted by that image of him holding Amber's head underwater. "Have you ever wondered if he might be... dangerous?"

I thought about a case we'd studied in criminal justice during spring semester, involving two seven-year-old boys who had murdered a toddler. We discussed whether they should be punished as severely as teenagers, or even as adults, despite their age. Their attorney had argued they were too young to know what they had done and should be released, but the court disagreed. The boys were sentenced to juvenile detention until the age of twenty-one, which some of my classmates thought was extreme.

Not me. I believed they were stone-cold killers. They wouldn't stop. As soon as they got out, they'd just do it again.

"Dangerous? No, not little Dylan." Britta shook her head emphatically, but there was uncertainty in her eyes.

A train rumbled at the edge of the tunnel, its headlights blasting through the dark. I turned to Britta.

"So I was thinking... do you want to get together sometime? For coffee? We could even talk about something besides Dylan."

She smiled, beaming at me. "Yes. I would certainly like that."

———

AFTER THE POOL episode, Dylan was on his best behavior for the next two days, and I started to think that maybe I was wrong about him. Maybe he wasn't such a bad kid, and I had just overreacted.

And then there was the incident with the Star Wars figures.

Kids weren't supposed to bring their own toys to camp, but I didn't see it as any big deal. He'd brought them out of his cubby during afternoon playtime, and since Rebecca hadn't noticed, I didn't say anything.

"This is me," he said, holding out an Anakin Skywalker figure. "And this is you."

Apparently I was Darth Vader.

When I reached for the figure, Dylan pulled it away. "Huh-uh," he said with a fake babyish voice. "It's mine."

He sat at one of the tables and moved the figures across an imaginary starscape. Ignoring him, I let myself get drawn into the kitchen area by Amber, who served me an imaginary breakfast of pancakes and ice cream. "Delicious," I said, spooning it up.

And then I heard Dylan call my name. "Eddie! Eddie!"

I looked over but all I saw was Royce jabbing his paintbrush furiously at the easel, creating a splotchy mess, and Michael painting a picture of a dog the exact same shade of green as his socks.

"Eddie!" I heard for the third time, and when I finally saw him, I was shocked.

Dylan had built his favorite shape, the tall tower with a single long block on top, only this time he had added something else to it. My missing shoelace. Dylan had tied one end of it along that top block and the other end of the lace hung down, forming a makeshift noose around the Darth Vader action figure.

"You're on my galley," he said, smiling.

And I thought: *gallows. He's been saying* gallows. He must have learned about them on his family vacation to England, during a visit to some medieval castle or other. Now instead of a fort or a spaceship or anything a normal kid would create, the little son of a bitch was making a gallows, just so he could threaten me.

I charged across the room, my arm pulled back, and Dylan flinched as though he thought I might hit him. I didn't. Instead, I swatted the blocks aside, watched them scatter across the floor. A couple of the pieces flew toward the easel and landed at Royce's feet. He stared at me in utter shock. Rebecca whirled and stared at me. But I ignored her and looked right at Dylan.

"You knocked down my galley," he said, his lower lip starting to quiver.

"Yeah, well, fuck you and your goddamn galley."

I was about to say more when Rebecca stomped over, kicking aside one of the fallen blocks. "Eddie, get your stuff and go." That was all she said, that I was fired.

When I got down to the lobby, I went into the bathroom and splashed cold water on my face and then ducked into a stall, where I tried to throw up. But I couldn't. I was angry and confused. I went through it all, trying to imagine what I should have done differently, but I knew that things had had to end like this. Dylan had made sure of it.

I sat in the stall for an hour, maybe more, and tried to calm myself down. Dylan was dangerous. He was sick, truly sick. At least I wouldn't have to see him again, but what about Britta? What if he tried to hurt her to get back at me? Or one of the kids I really cared about, like Amber?

I couldn't allow that. I wouldn't.

I slipped out of the bathroom, but instead of going for the exit, I ducked into the shadows of the sprawling lobby. Behind me, the basement door had been propped open and I stepped inside the stairwell and peered out from there. I heard the murmur of restless adults waiting for the elevators to come down. Through the faint noise, I soon heard the voices of eager campers, including some of mine: Amber and Michael, Royce and Cory.

I stepped out from the shadows and saw Britta leaning wearily on the baby stroller and talking to Rebecca. I wanted to wait for Rebecca to go away so that I could explain to Britta what had really happened with Dylan. I felt sure that she would understand.

In the stroller, Dylan's sister opened her mouth in a wide O and began to wail. Britta fumbled around in the stroller, opening and closing zippers, muttering. Finally, she found a bottle and stuffed it in the baby's mouth.

"Let's go," Dylan said, tugging at Britta's hand. "I want an ice."

"Just one minute," she said, turning back to Rebecca.

Dylan began to push his sister's stroller in circles around the lobby. Britta watched casually, listening to Rebecca, nodding. I wondered what kind of lies my former boss was telling her. Would Britta even want to go out with me after what she'd heard?

Dylan wheeled closer to me. It was almost as if he knew I was there. But no, he must not have, because he jumped when I put a hand on his shoulder.

"You think you're so smart, don't you, you little shit."

Dylan was as solemn and obedient as if he were standing in a church pew.

"I am smart," he said.

"Not as smart as me."

I hadn't thought about what I would do next, not really. It

just happened. I grabbed the stroller from Dylan and started walking, looking down at the baby cocooned inside, sucking on her bottle, swinging her tiny fists, Dylan must have looked like that once too, I thought, so helpless and small. No one ever would've suspected what he would someday become.

"Where we going?" Dylan asked in surprise as I wheeled the stroller through the basement door.

"You're going away, my little friend," I said, and then the baby dropped her bottle. It rolled into the corner of the stairwell and she started to scream, but only for a moment. I had no choice but to act, so I did. I pushed. The whole thing took maybe three or four seconds and then the baby was quiet, the sound of Dylan's tears filling the void.

I don't know what happened next. I was already gone, out the service door, then walking calmly down the sidewalk. But I imagine that Britta and Rebecca ran over, and so did everyone else who was there, and they all covered their mouths in horror. I see the baby lying at the bottom of the basement stairs, covered in blood, head cracked open like a coconut. Dylan must've stared down at her in disbelief as Britta shook him by the front of his shirt and said, *Why did you do this?*

No, it was him.

It was who? Rebecca would have asked.

Eddie did it. Eddie, not me! He pushed her, he hates me, he did it!

But as everyone knew, I had left camp at least an hour earlier. The police interviewed me several times, but they weren't suspicious. Dylan was the guilty party. Of course, no charges were filed, since Dylan was only five and no one could—or wanted to—prove that he had purposely pushed the baby down the stairs. It was probably just an accident. Some blamed the janitor who'd left the basement door propped open, while others blamed Britta for not watching the kids more closely.

I went back to college that fall and I met a girl, one even prettier than Britta, and joined a fraternity. I had a lot of friends and a good life and whenever I thought about Dylan, I felt a little sadness mixed with relief.

Dylan's story got lots of coverage in the papers. I read that he was hospitalized for a while and faced a barrage of psychiatric tests and behavioral evaluations. They must have prescribed him tons of pills. Someone who saw Dylan on the street three or four years later told me he was like a walking zombie, so drugged up that he wasn't capable of hurting anyone. Not even himself.

I also heard that no matter how many times Dylan was asked, he wouldn't admit to pushing his sister down the stairs. That's too bad, because, as I'm sure someone must have told him, confession is good for the soul.

IN PERSONA CHRISTI

BY OREST STELMACH

Two days before the killers came for Maria, a gang of teenagers rampaged across church property. I was washing the liners under my prosthetic arm when I heard them. Their whistles and shouts came from everywhere, as though they had the rectory surrounded. It was just past dusk, too dark to see clearly out the window. All I could detect were amorphous black images, vaguely human, flitting in and out of my field of vision.

Manuel, Maria's thirteen-year-old son, was the first to come downstairs. As always, he spoke with facial expressions and physical gestures, as opposed to using his tongue. He hadn't said a word to me since he and his mother had moved into the rectory, two months ago. Given his father had recently been hanged to death over the course of an hour while a block of ice melted beneath his feet, I wasn't surprised. He stood now at the base of the stairs, his deceased father's gold watch around his wrist, lips quivering and eyes bulging, begging me to tell him his mother and he weren't in danger again.

A Catholic priest must be a father. He is a spiritual provider and protector in the image of God, in the person of Christ. The role of father is my favorite part of being a priest, the one that comes most naturally to me and gives me the most joy.

I walked up to Manuel and put my arm around him. I spoke to him in Spanish. "Don't worry, son," I said, as though he were my own child. "There's nothing to fear. I'll take care of you."

When I opened the front door, the clucking and crowing stopped immediately. The sight of a six-foot-three, two-hundred-twenty-pound, one-armed and one-legged priest limping on his prosthetic limb as an empty sleeve dangled at his side sent the boys scurrying. All I could hear was the sound of feet pounding the asphalt as they escaped into old Dillon Stadium, across the street.

"You boys go on now," I said. "And don't come back. This is a church, you know."

The screen door was against my back. When I turned and swung it open, the springs let out a long, eerie squeak. It was followed by the sound of a teenage male voice from the direction of the stadium.

"You need me to hear your confession, Father?"

After a few howls and laughs, more footsteps followed and the voices faded. I went back inside and explained to Manuel that the hooligans were just a bunch of bored kids. He calmed down and returned to his room to finish his homework. His mother, Maria, taught violin at the local university during the day and studied English at home at night. She was in her room listening to language tapes on her headphones and had missed the entire event.

After reattaching my prosthetic arm, I called the police and reported the incident, just to establish a record in case the next time the kids decided to break into the church and steal an icon or a chalice. It took ten minutes for a police cruiser to arrive. That didn't surprise me.

Once Bermuda usurped Hartford as the insurance capital of the world, the companies moved out and the drug gangs moved in. Now Hartford is just a waypoint between Boston and New York City, and you need a different kind of insurance to walk around at night. With the Kings of Solomon in the South End, 77 Love in the North End, and city and state budget crises, the police are spread thin. There are precious few resources to dedicate to the eastern fringe of the city near the defunct Colt's gun factory and Dillon Stadium, where the old Hartford Knights used to play semipro football back in the day. The oldest Catholic church in Hartford, however, still stands on a tiny wooded lot, serving a small but devoted parish whose members live in the projects nearby.

After I told them what happened, the patrolmen stared at me as though I were a self-indulgent moron. They exuded the arrogance of the armed and immortal. One of them looked like Mr. Clean, with a shaved head and a physique that could double as a battering ram. His partner was long and wiry, with an untrustworthy-looking pencil mustache that he might have lifted from an uncooperative nightclub owner.

Their eyes told me I was wasting their time. There were serious crimes being committed in other parts of town.

A priest must be a mediator. Just as Moses revealed the law to Israel, the priest brings the human family together through eternal redemption. In this case, though, I needed to redeem myself for appearing to be a pain in the ass in the cops' eyes.

"I didn't mean for you to come out," I said. "I didn't dial nine-one-one. I told the dispatcher not to send anyone if you were busy."

They continued glaring at me, as though motives mattered little in their world. "Hot June night, Father," Mr. Clean said.

"Probably kids from Franklin Avenue, Father," Pencil Mustache said. "They break into the stadium to party. They never hurt no one. But we'll drive around and take a look for you."

"Yeah, Father," Mr. Clean said. "We'll take a look."

The police car radio squawked. They jumped inside, answered the call, and peeled out of the driveway, lights flashing and siren blaring. They took off toward the center of town, away from the stadium. Understandably, there was no time to drive around, no time to take a look.

Maria was at the base of the stairs with her arms wrapped around Manuel when I went back inside.

"Why were the police here, Father Nathan?' she said. "Are they here to deport us? Are we being sent back to Mexico?"

"No, no one is sending you back to Mexico. Would you make us some tea, Maria? I can't stop thinking about that *tres leches* cake you made. Is there another piece left in the fridge?"

Twenty-two years ago, Maria's mother was my teacher at the Consultoria Española y Lingüística in Santa Volopta, Mexico, where I studied Spanish and worked with Mother Teresa of Calcutta's Missionaries of Charity. Maria was nine years old at the time.

Santa Volopta lies within the Golden Triangle of the Chihuahua state, the most violent territory in the world outside of actual war zones. Not all the violence is a result of the drug trade. Over the past ten years, 937 women have been murdered, their bodies tossed in random dumps and ditches. Although no arrests have ever been made, high-level policemen and prominent citizens are suspected.

At age eighteen, Maria married a lawyer in Volopta. When he

became the municipal prosecutor, he launched an investigation into the murders of the daughters of Volopta; it led to his own assassination. Maria's mother called me immediately after his body was found, put her daughter and grandson on a plane, and sent them to live with me in Connecticut. She didn't trust the municipal or federal governments. She was certain her son-in-law's murderers, the drug czars, and the high-level officials responsible for the killings of the daughters of Volopta were one and the same. In Maria's mother's mind, her daughter and grandson were as good as dead if they stayed in Mexico.

From the moment Maria and Manuel arrived, my goal was to provide a spiritual and physical home for them while they integrated themselves into the community and began new lives. The gossipers in the parish, of course, didn't want to see it that way. It was far more entertaining to contemplate a priest violating his vow of celibacy with the beauty living beneath his roof.

As soon as Maria started appearing in church, attendance and contributions at Mass increased. A dozen men, single and married alike, received a thunderbolt of devout inspiration and started showing up daily. When I turned from the altar to bestow a blessing during morning Mass, I would catch one or more of them trying to steal a glance at her from a side pew. She possessed an elegance that could make men sob in anguish because they would never touch her. Her hair fell past her shoulders in silken strands that shone under the ceiling lights like onyx.

She tended to gaze at the ground, either because she didn't want to encourage any suitors or because she was desperate to disappear. This habit lent her an air of innocence. When she looked up, there was a gentleness and purity in her oval face and chestnut eyes that took one's breath away.

It didn't take long for the comments to start.

"There they are," a widow said. "The Thorn Birds."

"His third leg still work?" a former altar boy said.

"If it didn't, it does now," his friend replied.

I am forty-five years old. I've been a priest for seventeen of those years, and over time, it has been my observation that ethical and moral standards are deteriorating, nowhere more so than in the Catholic Church. And no one has disappointed the faithful more than the Catholic priest. As a result, people have become cynical. It's just a profession, they say; there is no special calling. For some folks, it's unimaginable that a heterosexual man such as I would not lust for a woman such as Maria, would not lie in bed wrestling with temptation every night.

And yet, I must insist: I do no such thing. I do not think of her in the way that other men do. I do not want to touch her. I do not want to possess her. I pray only for her and her son's health and salvation. Seeing them alive and healthy at Mass fulfills me in every way. Such is the joy of priesthood: contentment beyond the scope of sexual fulfillment. In the twenty-one years since a priest gave me a prayer book and changed the course of my life forever, I've said the Lord's Prayer three million, six hundred, and sixty-six times. That is how much prayer it has taken me to reach such a state of contentment.

I was not always this way. There was a time in my youth when I would have broken doors down to get to Maria, and no one would have tried to stop me. I was once the golden boy, a star collegiate baseball player with a bazooka for a right arm, a flame-throwing pitcher drafted in the third round by the New York Yankees. I had all the girls I wanted, and then the only one I ever needed died in a car accident when I was behind the wheel.

The day before the killers came for Maria, the same gang of kids tried to break into the church. They attempted, unsuccessfully, to jimmy open the padlock to the front door with a tire iron, and they ran away when I limped over from the rectory. I wished I could have caught one of them and had a discussion with him, helped him channel his energies into something more useful, such as the boys' baseball team I coached in the Rotary league. It consisted of misfits and orphans, the shunned and unwanted. But this gang of kids was too fast for a one-legged priest.

"Hey, Father," the same boy said from his hiding place in the stadium across the street. "You need me to hear your confession, Father?"

It was just past 9:00 p.m. when I got back to the house, sweat rolling down my cheeks from one minute of exertion. That's all it took on a sultry June night. Manuel was waiting for me at the bottom of the stairs, like the first time. After reassuring him there was nothing to fear, I dialed 911. I didn't want to bother the cops, but I had no choice. The kids had tried to enter the church. The church belonged to everyone, but its safekeeping was my responsibility.

This time it didn't take the cops ten minutes to get there. It took them twenty.

"Doesn't look serious, Father," Mr. Clean said as we studied the old wooden door to the church.

"See the dent here?" I said, pointing to a welt in the church's door. "That's where they pushed off with the tire iron."

Pencil Mustache tilted his head at me. "Just kids, Father. You actually saw them, though. Like, with your own eyes. Right, Father?"

"Yes, Officer. I saw them. I may have only one arm and one leg, but I still have vision in both eyes."

Sirens sounded in the distance. The radios attached to their belts squawked. One of them answered the call, barked a clipped response into the microphone, and nodded at his partner. "We'll write it up, Father," Mr. Clean said.

"Yeah. And we'll drive around and take a look for you," Pencil Mustache added.

"Yeah, Father. We'll take a look."

They rushed back into their cruiser and peeled out of the driveway, lights flashing and siren wailing. They took off toward the center of town, away from the stadium. Understandably, once again, there was no time to drive around, no time to take a look.

The day the killers came for Maria, I was driving back home from the hospital when I spotted Manuel huddled with two older teens along the far side of the stadium. The teens were more than a foot taller than Manuel. They wore inscrutable expressions, knapsacks, and black bandannas wrapped around their foreheads like headbands. I had to swerve away from a telephone pole at the last second to avoid a head-on collision when I remembered I was driving a car.

When Manuel got home, I went to his room and asked him if he felt like a game of catch. He didn't answer exactly. Instead, he shrugged, grabbed his glove, and shuffled out the door with his head hanging.

Since losing my right arm, I have become more proficient at throwing with my left, though my pitching wouldn't remind pro scouts of Goose Gossage's anymore. My prosthesis is a trans-humeral one, commonly known as an AE because it replaces the arm above the elbow. Both the hand and the arm are myoelectric, meaning a battery-powered device converts the electric signals of my muscles above the arm into movements of the prosthesis. It offers the strongest grip of any type of prosthetic; that's the upside. The downside is the time lag between my muscles signaling a movement and my replacement parts reacting. Consequently, some of Manuel's throws sailed past me even though they were within my reach. Although I saw the ball coming, I was a second slow when I tried to catch it.

After half an hour, we were both drenched and went back inside. There is no air-conditioning in the rectory and it doesn't cool down until midnight, at which point the attic fan finally begins to help. The kitchen seemed hotter than the yard. I poured each of us a tall glass of lemonade from the pitcher that Maria had fixed that morning and asked Manuel to sit down for a moment.

A Catholic priest must be a teacher. He helps his parishioners understand the Church and deal with conflicts and adversity. I am less comfortable with my role as Manuel's teacher because a great teacher should fully comprehend his student's life. Maria's mother told me that Manuel had been hiding in a closet and witnessed his father's murder. Since I can't truly comprehend what the boy has been through, I'm uncertain if I can establish an authentic bond with him.

He guzzled half the glass and gasped for air when he was done. Sweat trickled down his cheeks. His lungs heaved gently. I took a big swig of lemonade myself to celebrate seeing him diverted from his recent realities.

"When I was driving home, I saw you walking from school with those two boys," I said.

He choked on air.

"It's okay, it's okay," I said. "I just want you to understand two things. Those bandannas they were wearing around their heads? That's the fashion accessory of choice for members of the Aztec Rulers. You know who the Aztec Rulers are?"

Manuel shook his head, but his eyes flickered in a way that told me he was lying.

"They're an international gang that specializes in drugs and illegal-weapons distribution. You hear what I'm saying, right? Drugs and illegal weapons."

He acknowledged me with a slight nod.

"Good. I'm telling you this just to make sure you understand that they may or may not be who they appear to be. But whether or not they're Aztecs, they are welcome here. Everyone is welcome here. Especially friends of yours. Okay?"

He finished his lemonade. As he stood there with the glass tipped to his mouth, I thought there was something different about him, but I couldn't tell if it was his physical appearance, his carriage, or just my imagination.

That evening I listened to confessions after Mass, as was customary on Friday nights during the summer. I heard seven in a row, and then I waited fifteen minutes to make sure there weren't any stragglers, engrossing myself in a series of obscure prayers for wayward souls written by Saint Ignatius of Constantinople. I was drifting on a parallel plane of consciousness, meditating on missing and lost parishioners, when the kneeling bench creaked on the other side of the confessional screen.

At first, the person didn't say anything. English and Spanish are spoken in equal measure in my parish, so I usually have to guess which language to use to break the silence in cases like this. Now, however, there was no guesswork involved. They say a priest's chastity increases his sensory strength. I'm not sure that's true, but I smelled Maria's rose perfume as soon as she arrived. The hint of lily, vanilla, and white musk gave her away.

"In the name of the Father, and of the Son, and of the Holy Spirit," I said in Spanish.

She repeated the Trinitarian formula. "Forgive me, Father, for I have sinned." Her voice cracked with emotion.

I let a few seconds pass. "Yes?"

She could barely get the words out. "It's been four weeks since my last confession. But my last confession was a lie."

I let a few more seconds go by. "Why was it a lie?"

"Because I was unfaithful to my husband. I was unfaithful to my husband...with one of the men that had him killed."

As she sobbed, I dreamed of stepping out of the confessional, lifting her in my arms, and comforting her like a man. This pleasant vision flitted in and out of my mind in a nanosecond and was usurped by the reality that a priest must be a judge. He has jurisdiction over the penitent, and the power to forgive sins.

The role of judge is my least favorite. As a priest, I relish the opportunity to help the penitent heal, but as a man, I've never fully forgiven myself for one particular sin, so I am insecure about sitting in judgment of others.

After absolving Maria of her sins, I waited a few more minutes to let Maria say her penance before turning off the lights and locking the church. I saw her walking to the rectory ahead of me, and as she passed under the streetlamp at the corner of the church lot, the light illuminated her figure. I couldn't help but notice her hips gently sashaying in the fabric of her capri pants. And once again I insisted to myself that I did not think of her in the way that other men did. I did not want to touch her. I did not want to possess her. I did not love her more for having the strength to confess to her transgression.

When I got to the rectory, I locked myself in my room and prayed for her and her son's health and salvation, and for the strength to keep my vows. As I prayed, it occurred to me that if Maria knew who was responsible for her husband's death, she and her son might be in constant mortal danger.

By 11:00 p.m., the lights were off in Maria's and Manuel's rooms. The prosthesis on my leg is a transfemoral one, commonly known as an AK, because the leg was replaced above the knee. It also uses a myoelectric, battery-powered device that works with a time lag. I have to put on additional socks intermittently because the fit fluctuates during the day. I was taking off the last pair in preparation for my nightly stretching routine when I heard a car door close.

My bedroom sits atop the living room at the front of the rectory. I peeked through the curtain and saw a Lincoln Town Car parked across the street. I assumed it was a livery car—no one actually *buys* a Lincoln Town Car—and looked around to see if some well-heeled party animal was taking a leak along the fence after a night of drinking at Black-Eyed Holly's up the street. I didn't see any such person.

Instead, a man got out of the driver's side. He was short and squat and dressed in a suit. He was looking toward the church when a second man appeared in my line of sight, coming from beneath my window, presumably from the steps to the rectory. He was tall and lean and also dressed in a suit, with a fedora on his head. The tall man went to the car, where the short man whispered something to him. Beneath the light of the streetlamp in front of the house I could see their dark complexions. It occurred to me that while no one bought a Lincoln Town Car, people did rent them. At airports. When they were in town on business.

The men reached inside their suit coats, pulled out guns, and headed down the walkway toward the door to the rectory.

I scrambled to my feet, grabbed the phone, and dialed 911.

I cupped my hand over the phone and kept my voice at a whisper. "This is Father Nathan, from St. Valentine's Church on Huyshope Avenue."

"Yes, Father." It was the same dispatcher as before. Muted voices barked in the background. "What is the nature of your emergency?"

"Two men with guns. They're here. They've come for Maria and Manuel. The woman and the boy who are staying with me."

A siren sounded on her end. "Please hold, Father."

An unbearable number of seconds followed. I held my breath to try to hear what was going on outside, but the sound of my heartbeat filled my eardrums.

When the dispatcher finally picked up again, a combination of sirens, screaming, and static echoed from her end. "I'm sorry, Father. Are these the kids that have been bothering you all week?"

"No. They're not kids. They're two men with guns. They came in a Lincoln Town Car. They're assassins. The woman who's staying here—her husband was a prosecutor who was murdered in Mexico. They're here for her. For her and her son."

"Please calm down, Father. These men, are they in the house?"

"No. Not yet."

"Officers will respond as soon as possible. Please keep the doors locked—" A knock on the front door.

I hung up the phone and limped down the stairs, cursing the creaks in my prosthetic leg. When I got to the foyer, I faced the door and held my breath.

Three more short knocks followed. It was a smart move, I thought. A church was a shelter for all. A priest's first instinct was to open his door to anyone who needed assistance. Why break into a house when you can wangle an invitation?

It took the cops ten minutes to arrive the first time, twenty minutes the second time. It seemed, based on the background noise during the call with the dispatcher, that the natives were restless this evening. The odds the cops would arrive faster than the previous two times were zero.

I didn't own a gun. The closest thing I had to a weapon was a butcher's knife. But the idea of using it, the thought of sinking a blade into another human being's flesh, was unimaginable under any circumstances.

Sweat streamed down my back and created an itch beneath my cassock but I didn't dare scratch it. A minute passed. Still, I didn't dare move, for fear of making any kind of noise. Perhaps I'd misread the situation. Perhaps they weren't killers. Perhaps I could will them away with my thoughts.

Something clattered outside the living room.

I forced my feet to move, crept around the corner into the living room, and hid behind a curtain. A night-light cast a semicircle of light beside a red-velvet couch. Above the sofa, the window rattled gently. They were checking to see if a window was open. Why break a window if you can slide it open?

They were killers. They were here for Maria and Manuel.

These words should have motivated me. They should have summoned an adrenaline flow and spurred me to action. But they didn't. Instead, I stood solemnly in place, resigned to my fate.

It simply wasn't in me. Twenty-three years ago, a stranger had groped my girlfriend's breasts as we filed out of a rock concert at the Civic Center. When we got outside, I broke his jaw with a single punch. Unbeknownst to me, he followed us to a bar in his monster truck, and when we parked, he drove his vehicle through the passenger door. Matilda died and I lost two limbs, all because I raised my hand to another man. I couldn't do it again. Two decades of meditation and three million, six hundred, and sixty-six repetitions of the Lord's Prayer had absorbed all my rage.

The glass broke inward with a muted crack. I remained behind the curtain, feet frozen in place, my vision wet and blurry. One of the men reached inside with a gloved hand, wiggled a shard of glass free, and removed it. After he repeated the process several times, a third of the window was gone. In sixty seconds, they would slip into the house.

"Kill the cripple and the boy," one of the men whispered, "but not the woman. She's dessert."

Images of the killers raping Maria and then strangling her with their bare hands flashed before me. I slipped out from behind the curtain and headed straight for the kitchen closet. Swinging the door open just a smidge so the rusty hinges wouldn't squeak, I thrust my good hand inside in search of my Hillerich & Bradsby bat. No luck. I felt the broom and mop handles but no stick.

Another crack in the adjoining room told me the window was half gone. I had thirty seconds, if that. I lowered my reach and got the fire extinguisher. Better than nothing, but not what I wanted. I raised my hands six inches and grasped again. Pay dirt. The cold, hard wood felt good as soon as it hit my hand.

I pulled the bat out of the closet. It was a vintage 1967 Roberto Clemente model, 36 inches long and weighing 36.4 ounces, a gift from my high school coach in Rockville after I hit thirty-four home runs in thirty games my junior year.

I slipped into a nook between the living room and the staircase. The killers could not get upstairs without passing me, and they wouldn't see me until it was too late. I'd drop the first man with a tomahawk swing and pulverize the second one's skull with an uppercut blast. I hadn't crushed a baseball in decades. There was nothing like the sensation of hitting the ball square on its sweet spot, the thud of the wood generating maximum force, the satisfaction of slamming one out of the park.

Abraham waged war. Abraham was a warrior.

Joshua laid siege to Jericho. Joshua was a warrior.

A priest must be a warrior.

I must be a warrior.

I couldn't see the window from my hiding place, so I had to rely on sound and shadow. I heard a scratching noise, followed by a gentle thud. One of them was inside. The short one, I suspected. The second man made almost no noise. He had the first one to help him. The living room was small, and there was only one way to go.

The night-light cast ghoulish shadows on the wall. The ghouls moved.

They were upon me faster than I expected. I raised the bat with both hands high in the air. As soon as I saw the first man— the short one— I swung downward with all my strength. My left hand led, but the right arm seemed slow to react—of course it was; the prosthetic lagged—and then it just stopped. In midair. My left arm fought to bring the bat down but it wouldn't move.

My prosthetic arm was locked. It had malfunctioned.

The killer saw me. He jumped back. The taller man with the fedora came into view. The three of us stood there for a couple of seconds, frozen in mutual disbelief. A priest, posing like an ax murderer for a wax museum, and two assassins, silencers attached to the barrels of their guns.

The short one laughed. It was the deep, resonant laugh of a lifetime scoundrel and smoker, coarse enough to sand wood without touching it. The tall one chuckled like the calculating kind of person for whom genuine laughter was too frivolous. They raised their guns in tandem and pointed them at me, grins etched on their faces.

Gunshots exploded. The floor shook. Pain racked my eardrums.

I opened my eyes. I hadn't even realized I'd closed them.

The killers lay on the ground, the left sides of their chests riddled with multiple bullet holes.

Manuel appeared in the stairwell, arms outstretched, clutching a gun with both hands. When he spoke for the first time, his voice had a youthful pitch, but his delivery was shockingly composed.

"Leave my mother alone," he said.

When I saw Manuel's arms stretched out, I realized how his appearance had changed and figured out what I'd failed to detect when we'd shared a glass of lemonade in the afternoon. His wrist was bare. His father's gold watch was gone. He'd met the Aztecs to trade his father's watch for a gun.

By the time Maria arrived, hysterical, I'd removed my prosthetic arm from the socket and the gun from Manuel's hands. I'd taken an EMT course and knew how to check for a pulse. I found none in either man. Manuel had shot each of them through the heart. They were dead.

The rage I'd managed to build receded quickly. A sense of calm fell over me, as though I'd gone on a trip I'd detested and now I was back home.

If the police saw that Manuel shot two men, he and his mother could be deported to Mexico. After all, he'd shot them with an illegal weapon, and he wasn't an American citizen. In Mexico, they would die. In America, they would live.

A priest I knew from seminary lived in upstate New York. He was a friend and kindred spirit. We would create new names and birth certificates. Manuel and Maria would start new lives. No one would know their past. Manuel's father's killers would never find them.

I took the gun and wiped it down with the end of my cassock to make sure Manuel's fingerprints weren't on it. Then I fired two shots with my left hand into the wall behind the place where the killers had stood.

Maria screamed at me, "What are you doing?"

"Gunpowder and cordite leave burn marks," I said. "Especially when fired at close range. If the burn marks are on my fingers, no one will bother checking Manuel's hands. Why would they? It was my gun. I bought it from persons unknown."

A siren sounded in the distance. Its blare grew gradually louder.

A Catholic priest must be a father. He is a spiritual provider and protector in the image of God, in the person of Christ: *in persona Christi*. The role of father is my favorite part of being a priest, the one that comes most naturally to me and gives me the most joy.

I stepped closer and put my arm around Maria and Manuel. "Don't worry," I said, as though they were both my children. "There's nothing to fear. I'll take care of you."

THE HOLLYWOOD I REMEMBER

BY LEE CHILD

The Hollywood I remember was a cold, hard, desperate place. The sun shone and people got ahead. Who those people were, I have no idea. Real names had been abandoned long ago. Awkward syllables from the shtetls and guttural sounds from the bogs and every name that ended in a vowel had been traded for shiny replacements that could have come from an automobile catalog. I knew a guy who called himself LaSalle, like the Buick. I knew a Fairlane, like the Ford. I even knew a Coupe de Ville. In fact I knew two Coupe de Villes, but I think the second guy had his tongue in his cheek. In any case, you were always conscious that the guy you were talking to was a cipher. You had no idea what he had been and what he had done before.

Everyone was new and reinvented.

That worked both ways, of course.

It was a place where a week's work could get you what anyone else in the country made in a year. That was true all over town, under the lights or behind them, legitimate or not. But some got more than others. You were either a master or a servant. Like a distorted hourglass: Up above, a small glass bubble with a few grains of sand. Down below, a big glass bubble with lots of sand. The bottleneck between was tight. The folks on the top could buy anything they wanted, and the folks on the bottom would do whatever it took, no questions asked. Everyone was for sale. Everyone had a price. The city government, the cops, regular folks, all of them. It was a cold, hard, desperate place.

Everyone knew nothing would last. Smart guys put their early paychecks into solid things, which is what I did. My first night's work became the down payment on the house I've now owned for more than forty years. The rest of the money came with a mortgage from a week-old bank. And mortgages needed to be paid, so I had to keep on working. But work was not hard to find for a man with my skills and for a man happy to do the kind of things I was asked to do. Which involved girls, exclusively. Hollywood hookers were the best in the world, and there were plenty of them. Actresses trapped on the wrong side of the bottleneck still had to eat, and the buses and trains brought more every day. Competition was fierce.

They were amazingly beautiful. Usually they were better-looking than the actual movie stars. They had to be. Sleeping with an actual movie star was about the only thing money couldn't buy, so look-alikes and substitutes did good business. They were the biggest game in town. They lasted a year or two. If they couldn't take it, they were allowed to quit early. There was no coercion. There didn't need to be. Those buses and trains kept on rolling in.

But there were rules.

Blackmail was forbidden, obviously. So was loose talk. The cops and the gossip columnists could be bought off, but why spend money unnecessarily? Better to silence the source. Better to make an example and buy a month or two of peace and quiet. Which is where I came in. My first was a superhuman beauty from Idaho. She was dumb enough to believe a promise some guy made. She was dumb enough to make trouble when it wasn't kept. We debated disfigurement for her. Cut off her lips and her ears, maybe her nose, maybe pull every other tooth. We figured that would send a message. But then we figured no LA cop would stand for that, no matter what we paid, so I offed her pure and simple, and that's how I got the down payment for my house. It was quite an experience. She was tall, and she was literally stunning. I got short of breath and weak at the knees. The back part of my brain told me I should be dragging her to my cave, not slitting her throat. But I got through it.

The next seven paid off my mortgage, and the two after that bought me a Cadillac. It was the eleventh that brought me trouble. Just one of those unlucky things. She was a fighter, and she had blood pressure issues, apparently. I had to stab her in the chest to quiet her down, and the blade hit bone and nicked something bad, and a geyser of blood came out and spattered all over my suit coat. Like a garden hose. A great gout of it, like a drowned man coughing up seawater on the sand, convulsive. Afterward I wrapped the knife in the stained coat and carried it home wearing only shirtsleeves, which must have attracted attention from someone.

Because as a result, I had cops on me from dawn the next morning. But I played it cool. I did nothing for a day, and then I made a big show of helping my new neighbor finish the inside of his new garage. Which was a provocation, in a way, because my new neighbor was a dope peddler who drove up and down to Mexico regular as clockwork. The cops were watching him too. But they suffered an embarrassment when we moved his car to the curb so we could work on the garage unencumbered. The car was stolen right from under their noses. That delayed the serious questions for a couple of days.

Then some new hotshot LAPD detective figured that I had carried the knife and the bloody coat to my neighbor's garage in my tool bag and that I had then buried it in the floor. But the guy failed to get a warrant, because judges like money and hookers too, and so the whole thing festered for a month and then went quiet, until a new hotshot came on the scene. This new guy figured I was too lazy to dig dirt. He figured I had nailed the coat into the walls. He wanted a warrant fast, because he figured the rats would be eating the coat. It was that kind of a neighborhood. But he didn't get a warrant either, neither fast nor slow, and the case went cold, and it stayed cold for forty years.

During which time two things happened. The LAPD built up a cold-case unit, and some cop came along who seemed to be that eleventh hooker's son. Which was an unfortunate confluence of events for me. The alleged son was a dour terrier of a guy with plenty of ability, and he worked that dusty old file like crazy. He was on the fence, fifty-fifty as to whether the floor or the wall was the final resting place for my coat, and my coat was the holy grail for this guy, because laboratory techniques had advanced by then. He figured he could compare his own DNA to whatever could be recovered from the coat. My dope-peddling neighbor had been shot to death years before, and his house had changed hands many times. None of the new owners had ever permitted a search because they knew what was good for them, but then the sub-primes all went belly-up and the place was foreclosed, and the hotshot son figured he could bypass the whole warrant process by simply requesting permission from whatever bank now held the paper, but the bank itself was bust and no one knew who controlled its assets, so I got another reprieve, except right about then I got diagnosed with tumors in my lungs.

I had no insurance, obviously, working in that particular industry, so my house was sold to finance my stay in the hospital, which continues to this day, and from my bed I heard that the buyer of my house had also gotten hold of my neighbor's place and was planning to raze them both and then build a mansion. Which got the hotshot son all excited, naturally, because finally the wrecking ball would do the work of the warrants no one had been able to get. The guy visited me often. Every time he would ask me, how was I feeling? Then he would ask me, wall or floor? Which showed his limitations, to be honest. Obviously the coat and the knife had exited the scene in the dope dealer's stolen car. I had put them in the secret compartment in the fender and left the key in the ignition when I parked the car on the curb. They were long gone. I was fireproof.

Which brought me no satisfaction at all, because of the terrible pain I was in. I had heard of guys in my situation floating comfortably on IV drips full of morphine and Valium and ketamine, but I wasn't getting that stuff. I asked for it, obviously, but the damn doctor bobbed and weaved and said it wasn't appropriate in my case. And then the hotshot son would come in and ask how I was feeling, with a little grin on his face, and I'm ashamed to say it took me some time to catch on. Everyone was for sale. Everyone had a price. The city government, the cops, regular folks, all of them. Including doctors. I have no idea what the son was giving the guy, favors or money or both, but I know what the guy wasn't giving me in return. The Hollywood I remember was a cold, hard, desperate place, and it still is.

ABOUT THE AUTHORS

Alafair Burke is the author of seven novels, including the best-selling thriller *Long Gone* and two mystery series, one featuring NYPD detective Ellie Hatcher and one featuring Portland deputy district attorney Samantha Kincaid. A former prosecutor, she now teaches criminal law and procedure at Hofstra Law School and lives in New York City. She welcomes e-mails from readers at alafair@alafairburke.com.

Lee Child was born in 1954 in Coventry, England, but spent his formative years in the nearby city of Birmingham. He went to law school in Sheffield, England, and after part-time work in the theater, he joined Granada Television in Manchester for what turned out to be an eighteen-year career as a presentation director during British TV's "golden age." But after being let go in 1995 as a result of corporate restructuring, he decided to see an opportunity where others might see a crisis, so he bought six dollars' worth of paper and pencils and sat down to write a book, *Killing Floor,* the first in the Jack Reacher series. It was an immediate success and launched the series, which has grown in sales and impact with every new installment. Lee spends his spare time reading, listening to music, and watching the Yankees and Aston Villa and Marseille soccer. He is married with a grown-up daughter. He is tall and slim, despite an appalling diet and a refusal to exercise.

ABOUT THE AUTHORS

Michael Connelly's latest novels are *The Fifth Witness,* featuring Mickey Haller, and *The Drop,* with LAPD detective Harry Bosch. His books have been translated into thirty-five languages and have won the Edgar Award, Anthony Award, Macavity Award, *Los Angeles Times* Best Mystery/Thriller Award, Shamus Award, Dilys Award, Nero Award, Barry Award, Audie Award, Ridley Award, Maltese Falcon Award (Japan), .38-Caliber Award (France), Grand Prix Award (France), Premio Bancarella Award (Italy), and the Pepe Carvalho Award (Spain). Michael was the president of the Mystery Writers of America organization in 2003 and 2004 and edited both the MWA anthology *The Blue Religion* and the Edgar Allan Poe anthology *In the Shadow of the Master.* He lives with his family in Florida.

Mike Cooper is the pen name of a former financial executive. Under a different name, his short stories have received wide recognition, including a Shamus Award and inclusion in *The Best American Mystery Stories.* His new novel, *Clawback,* has just been published by Viking. Mike lives outside Boston with his family. Visit his website at www.mikecooper books.com.

Brendan DuBois of New Hampshire is the award-winning author of twelve novels and more than a hundred short stories. His latest novel, *Deadly Cove,* was published in July 2011 by St. Martin's Press. His short fiction has appeared in numerous magazines and anthologies, including *Playboy, Ellery Queen's Mystery Magazine, Alfred Hitchcock's Mystery Magazine,* the *Magazine of Fantasy and Science Fiction,* and *The Best American Mystery Stories of the Century,* edited by Tony Hillerman and Otto Penzler. His short stories have twice won him the Shamus Award from the Private Eye Writers of America and have also earned him three Edgar Allan Poe Award nominations from the Mystery Writers of America. Visit his website at www.BrendanDuBois.com.

Jim Fusilli is the author of six novels; his latest, *Narrows Gate,* is a gangster epic set in the first half of the twentieth century in the

Italian-American community of a gritty waterfront city in the shadow of Manhattan. A resident of New York City, Jim is also the rock and pop critic of the *Wall Street Journal.* His book *Pet Sounds,* described as "an experiment in music journalism," is his tribute to Brian Wilson and the Beach Boys' classic album.

Michelle Gagnon is the author of *The Tunnels, Boneyard, The Gatekeeper,* and *Kidnap & Ransom.* Her bestselling thrillers have been published in North America, France, Spain, Argentina, Denmark, Norway, Sweden, Finland, and Australia. In 2012, she will release two young-adult novels: *Don't Turn Around,* under the HarperCollins Teen imprint, and *Strangelets,* with Soho Crime. She lives in San Francisco, California.

Darrell James is a fiction writer with residences in both Pasadena and Tucson. His short stories have appeared in numerous mystery magazines and book anthologies and have garnered a number of awards and honors, including finalist for the 2009 Derringer Awards. His first novel, *Nazareth Child,* was published in September 2011 by Midnight Ink/Llewellyn Worldwide Publishing. His personal odyssey to publication appears in the *Writer's Digest* book *How I Got Published,* along with essays by J. A. Jance, David Morrell, Clive Cussler, and many other notable authors.

Janice Law is a novelist who frequently commits short mystery stories. Her first novel, "The Big Payoff," was nominated for an Edgar, and her stories have been reprinted in *The Best American Mystery Stories, The World's Finest Mystery and Crime Stories, Alfred Hitchcock's Fifty Years of Crime and Suspense, Riptide, Still Waters,* and the fabulist anthology *ParaSpheres.*

C. E. Lawrence is the byline of a New York-based suspense writer, performer, composer, poet, and prize-winning playwright whose previous books have been praised as "lively" (*Publishers Weekly*); "constantly absorbing" (starred *Kirkus Review*); and "superbly crafted prose"

(*Boston Herald*). *Silent Screams, Silent Victim,* and *Silent Kills* are the first three books in her Lee Campbell thriller series. Her other work is published under the name of Carole Bugge. Her first Sherlock Holmes novel, *The Star of India,* has recently been released in England by Titan Publishing. Visit her website at celawrence.com.

Dennis Lehane grew up in the Dorchester section of Boston. Since his first novel, *A Drink Before the War,* won the Shamus Award, he has published, with William Morrow, eight more novels that have been translated into more than thirty languages and become international bestsellers: *Darkness, Take My Hand; Sacred; Gone Baby Gone; Prayers for Rain; Mystic River; Shutter Island; The Given Day;* and *Moonlight Mile. Mystic River, Shutter Island,* and *Gone Baby Gone* have been made into award-winning films. Dennis Lehane and his wife divide their time between St. Petersburg, Florida, and Boston. Visit his website at www.dennislehanebooks.com.

Steve Liskow is a member of both Mystery Writers of America and Sisters in Crime and serves on panels for both groups. His stories have appeared in *Alfred Hitchcock Mystery Magazine* and several anthologies, and his novels include *Who Wrote the Book of Death?, The Whammer Jammers,* and the newly released *Cherry Bomb.* A former English teacher, he often conducts writing workshops throughout central Connecticut, where he lives with his wife, Barbara, and two rescued cats. Visit his website at www.steveliskow.com.

Rick McMahan is a special agent for the Bureau of Alcohol, Tobacco, Firearms and Explosives. The year 2012 marks his twentieth in law enforcement. Rick's work takes him to counties across central and southeastern Kentucky, including Bell County, the area featured in "Moonshiner's Lament." His mystery stories have appeared in various publications, including the Mystery Writers of America anthology *Death Do Us Part.* He also has a story in the International Association of Crime Writers' forthcoming collection of crime fiction from around the world.

Adam Meyer is the author of the suspense novel *The Last Domino*. His short fiction has appeared in *The Year's Best Horror Stories, 100 Wicked Little Witch Stories,* and other anthologies. He also wrote and directed the independent feature film *Two Fireflies* and has written television series for Fox, the Discovery Channel, and the History Channel. A native New Yorker, he now lives in Washington, DC. Visit his website at www.adsasylum.com.

Dreda Say Mitchell is a novelist, broadcaster, journalist, and freelance education consultant who describes herself as a "complete busybody." She is the author of five novels. Her debut novel, *Running Hot,* was awarded Britain's 2005 CWA's John Creasey Dagger for best first crime novel. She has appeared on BBC television's *Newsnight* and *The Review Show* and has presented BBC Radio 4's *Open Book.* She was the 2011 chair of the Harrogate Crime Writing Festival. Her commitment and passion for raising the life chances of working-class children through education has been called inspirational and life-changing. Visit her website at www.dredasaymitchell.com.

Michael Niemann has traveled widely through Europe and southern Africa. He has published the short story "Kosi Bay" in *Mysterical-E* and a number of nonfiction items on global and African affairs. A native German, he now lives in southern Oregon and is busy finishing up a novel featuring Valentin Vermeulen. Visit www.michael-niemann.com.

A Stanford graduate and former (vengeful) plaintiff's trial lawyer, **Twist Phelan** writes the critically acclaimed legal-themed Pinnacle Peak mystery series published by Poisoned Pen Press. Her short stories appear in anthologies and mystery magazines and have won or been nominated for the Thriller, Ellis, and Derringer awards. Twist's current project is a suspense novel set in Santa Fe featuring a corporate spy. Visit her website at www.twistphelan.com.

ABOUT THE AUTHORS

Zoë Sharp opted out of mainstream education at the age of twelve. She created her highly acclaimed ex–Special Forces–turned–bodyguard series heroine Charlie Fox after receiving death-threat letters in the course of her work as a freelance photojournalist. Sharp lives on the edge of the English Lake District, where she and her husband, a nonfiction writer, built their own house. She blogs regularly on her website, www .zoesharp.com, and on the award-nominated www.murderati.com.

Karin Slaughter has written eleven books that have sold twenty-five million copies in thirty languages. A *New York Times* bestselling author, Karin's books have debuted at number one in the United Kingdom, Germany, and the Netherlands. She lives in Atlanta, where she is working on her next novel.

Orest Stelmach is the author of the thriller *The Boy from Reactor 4,* the first in the Tesla trilogy, and the historical mystery *Lady in the Dunes,* the first in a series set in 1950 Provincetown featuring Father Sean Kale. A Connecticut native, he went to kindergarten speaking only Ukrainian. He still tries to use as few words as possible. Orest and his wife divide their time between Connecticut and Cape Cod. Visit him at www.oreststelmach.com.

Anne Swardson is an editor-at-large with Bloomberg News in Paris and a former European economic correspondent for the *Washington Post.* "River Secret" is her first published work of fiction. She is also the author of a mystery novel. Like "River Secret," it is set in Paris, where Anne has lived with her husband and two children for fifteen years.

ABOUT THE MYSTERY WRITERS OF AMERICA

The Mystery Writers of America, the premier organization for established and aspiring mystery writers, is dedicated to promoting higher regard for crime writing and recognition and respect for those who write within the genre.

COPYRIGHTS

peroxide-blonde hair and a huge bust, the girl looked a bit like the up-and-coming actress Barbara Windsor. Sue was aware of this and had taken to emulating the starlet's gyrating walk and style of dress. Joan shook her head against the sight of Sue's tight sheath dress, her bust thrust out in front as she wandered closer. Unlike Yvonne, she didn't look decent. She looked like a floozie and Joan had no idea what her son saw in her.

'Bob left early for the yard,' Sue said. 'He said something about a meeting. Do you know what it's about?'

'You know better than to ask me that,' Joan snapped as she dipped her scrubbing brush into the water. 'I'm cleaning my step and it's about time you had a go at yours.'

'Why bother? The kids are in and out every five minutes and will only muck it up again.'

Joan's eyes flicked along the alley. 'Where are they?'

'I gave them their pocket money so they've gone straight to the sweet shop to spend it.'

No sooner had Sue spoken than the two lads came careering into the alley, skinny legs pumping, six-year-old Robby in pursuit of his younger brother.

'Mum! Mum!' Paul yelled. 'Robby's trying to nick my sweets.'

'No I'm not,' Robby protested, skidding to a halt beside Joan.

'He is, Gran,' four-year-old Paul insisted, making

sure that, though she was kneeling, his grandmother was between them. 'He's got his own sweets, but he's after my gobstopper.'

'Look, it's up to your mother to sort this out, not me,' Joan protested. 'Go away and leave me in peace. I've got work to do.'

'Yes, come here, boys. After all, you can't come between your grandmother and her housework,' Sue said sarcastically.

Joan looked daggers at her daughter-in-law, but she ignored her, dragging the boys inside and slamming the door. Joan shrugged, unconcerned. When the boys had been born her daughter-in-law had expected her to baby-sit, but she'd soon nipped that in the bud. She'd told Sue that she had no intention of looking after her kids whilst she went out gallivanting – she'd done her stint, had six kids, and wasn't prepared to start all over again.

Joan wrung out the cloth, her mouth grim. Sue resented it, didn't like her, but Joan didn't care. The feeling was reciprocated, but the two women held their animosity in check for Bob's sake. On the surface the marriage appeared fine, but Joan doubted her son was happy. With Sue for a wife and his house a tip, how could he be?

Chapter Three

Back at number three, Sue was grim-faced. Who the bloody hell did her mother-in-law think she was? All right, Sue's own step might be dirty, but there was more to life than flaming housework. When she had met Bob, she had loved the kudos of courting a local villain. She fancied being married to a bloke who had a few bob rather than having to work in a rotten factory, but once they'd tied the knot, things hadn't turned out quite as she'd expected. She had dreamed of being an actress, even a film star, stupidly hoping that being married to a Draper would open doors.

So much for that dream. The Drapers didn't have any links to showbusiness. Bob had been so keen to have her on his arm that he'd lied, and now she was stuck in the alley, surrounded by his family. She hated it, especially being close to her sanctimonious mother-in-law, *and* that uppity cow next door. Yvonne was another one who was housework mad,

35

and not only that, she was a crawler, always up Joan's arse. Not that she envied Yvonne her husband. Danny might be a good-looking bloke, but she wouldn't trust him as far as she could throw him.

Sue thought about her own husband, and though Bob wasn't as handsome as Danny, she'd choose him any day. He was placid, amiable, and despite her disappointment, theirs was a happy marriage, with infrequent rows.

'Mum! Mum, tell Robby,' Paul cried.

'For Gawd's sake, leave your brother alone,' Sue yelled, glaring at her elder son. Robby was a handful and though he'd been at school for only a year, he was already in trouble for being a bully. As was tradition, she'd called her firstborn Robert after his father but although they were similar in looks, their natures were the exact opposite.

'I only want a suck on his gobstopper,' Robby wheedled.

Sue sighed in exasperation. 'Go on, Paul. Give him a suck.'

'No, he won't give it back.'

'Yes, he will – won't you, Robby?'

'Yeah.'

With reluctance, Paul handed the sticky, wet sweet over to his brother, watching in horror as Robby shoved it in his mouth, one cheek bulging like a hamster as he headed for the stairs.

'Mum!' Paul protested.

'Robby, you little sod! Come back here!'

'See, Mum, I told you,' whined Paul, his grey eyes filling with tears.

Paul was a gentle, quiet child, and secretly he was Sue's favourite. When it came to Robby she felt helpless, unable to control her wilful elder son, and usually left any discipline to his father.

'Look, don't cry, Paul,' she placated. 'It ain't the end of the world. I'll buy you another one.'

'Now.'

'No, not now, but we'll pop to the shop later.'

Paul hung his head, his fair, coarse hair sticking up like a brush. Sue swept him into her arms, then, sitting down, she plonked him on her lap. 'Who's my good boy then? I just wish your brother was more like you.'

They sat like that for a while, Sue ignoring the state of the room as she cuddled her son. Her brown sofa was piled with the ironing she'd intended to tackle last night, but then hadn't bothered. The lino on the floor was dirty, the rug by the hearth grimy, yet none of it concerned Sue.

There were footsteps on the stairs, and then Robby appeared, grinning cheekily as he held out the tiny remnants of the gobstopper. 'Here you are, Paul. You can have it back now.'

Paul jumped down, but as he approached his brother, Robby ran round him to take his place on Sue's lap. 'Nah, nah,' he mocked, shoving the sweet back in his mouth.

Sue pushed Robby off, and as he landed with a thump on the lino she reared to her feet. 'You little bugger! Wait till I tell your father. He'll give you a bloody good hiding.'

'Don't care,' said Robby, his chin tilted upwards, eyes defiant.

Paul was crying now and Sue could feel the start of a headache coming on. 'Don't cry, darling,' she placated. 'Look, I tell you what, how about we go next door? You can play with your cousin.'

Paul nodded, mollified at the thought of seeing Oliver, who, though much older than he at nine, was his favourite playmate. 'I don't want Robby to come.'

'I can't leave him on his own, love,' she said.

Robby scrambled to his feet and Sue's voice was hard as she threatened, 'You'd better behave yourself, Robby, and don't upset Oliver. You know Auntie Norma won't put up with any of your shenanigans.'

'He's a sissy.'

'No he isn't, he's just quiet, that's all. In fact, it wouldn't hurt you to take a leaf out of his book.'

Robby scowled, but followed them next door, dragging his feet as they left the house. Sue glanced to her right, saw that her mother-in-law had returned inside, and hoped she'd stay there. She wouldn't put it past the woman to come round later to check up on her and as she hadn't done a scrap of housework, that was the last thing she wanted.

Sue grimaced, but then shrugged. So what? If her mother-in-law didn't like the state of the place, she could just bugger off again.

Sue's husband, Bob, was at the yard, resentful of the fact that he didn't have a car. He could have cadged a lift from his father, or eldest brother, Danny, but it was his job to open up today and he'd had to leave well before them.

There was no denying that they were making good money, but by the time it was shared out between six families, it wasn't a fortune. It was all right for Danny. With no children, he could afford a car, and with a thrifty wife like Yvonne, he had a good few bob to spare.

If only Sue was more like Danny's wife. Instead she was a spendthrift, buying stupid fripperies that he was sure they could do without. The mantelshelf was lined with animal ornaments, usually covered in dust. Every windowsill was the same. Dog ornaments, cat ornaments, some so garish and cheap they looked like prizes from a fairground.

After his mother's obsession with housework he had at first found Sue's attitude refreshing. He'd enjoyed being able to relax in his own home without worrying if he so much as moved a cushion. Now, though, it was wearing thin, especially when it was hard to find a chair to sit on that wasn't piled high with rubbish.

Bob shook his head. No, he was being stupid. He didn't want Sue to be like his mother, or Yvonne, who looked like a cold fish to him. Sue was a cracker, a real goer who liked nothing better than a bit of slap and tickle. He worried sometimes when he saw her looking at Danny, and now he ran a hand through his wispy, brown hair. He hated it, wishing it was thick and dark like Danny's. He envied his brother his height too. Though he had a similar, beefy build, he was a good four inches shorter. He was sure that Sue fancied Danny, and no wonder, but he made sure he kept her happy in bed, well satisfied, something that took a bit of doing at times. Yes, she was a goer all right, but if Danny so much as looked at her the wrong way . . .

An early customer broke Bob out of his reveries, and then a couple more turned up before he saw his father's car pulling into the yard. As Dan Draper climbed out, Bob frowned, noticing that his father was showing his age. His large build still looked intimidating, but there was a slight stoop to his shoulders and a beer belly hung over his trousers. Blimey, when did he get old? He knew his father wanted to retire and was salting cash away by taking the biggest cut, but unless they drew in more money, his retirement would be a long way off.

'Morning, Robert. Are the others here?'

'No, you're the first to show,' Bob replied, wishing

his father wouldn't call him by his full name, but knowing better than to complain.

'Shit. This meeting was Danny's idea so he'd better show his face soon. There's racing at Sandown and I want to be away by one o'clock.'

Bob hid a smile. So, the number-one son was in his father's bad books. Good. 'What has Danny got in mind?'

A black Jaguar screeched into the yard, cutting off his father's answer. Danny climbed out of the car, his face dark with annoyance as he walked towards them. 'I told Yvonne I had to get up this morning, but the silly cow forgot to wake me.'

'Another late night, was it?' Bob asked, hoping to stir trouble.

Danny ignored him, saying only, 'I'm sorry I'm late, Dad.'

Dan wrapped an arm around his son's shoulder. 'Never mind. You're here now, and I'd like to go over the finer details of this plan before the others arrive.'

They moved away and Bob followed, but he was halted in his tracks when his father said, 'Look after the business for now. We'll shut up shop as soon as the other boys arrive.'

Bob stayed behind, inwardly seething. It was always the same. Danny and his father were thick as thieves, whilst the rest of them were left out of the loop until they were good and ready to allow

41

them in. Bob chewed on his lower lip, wondering why his father was blind to Danny's faults. All right, they were all villains, but Danny was more than that. He was a nasty piece of work and a womaniser, but so far had been clever enough to keep his antics from their father.

As Bob walked behind the counter he was wondering if he should put his father in the picture, but then shivered. No, if Danny found out he'd opened his mouth, he'd go ballistic. And you didn't upset Danny, even if he was your brother, not if you wanted to stay in one piece.

Dan sat behind an old desk that was littered with paperwork, receipts, and an ashtray overflowing with dog-ends. 'Your mother would have a fit if she saw the state of this office. Mind you, it's just as well that she stays out of the way or we'd never find a thing. Make the tea, son, and then tell me more about this plan of yours.'

Danny junior switched on the kettle, then eagerly launched straight into his plan. 'There's more money to be made if we diversify into hard porn, a lot more.'

'Yeah, you told me, but have you thought about the risks? If we muscle in on that side of the business we'd be treading on Garston territory, for one thing.'

'We can deal with Jack Garston.'

'I ain't so sure. If the money's as big as you say, he ain't gonna take a competitor lightly. He's got a fair bit of muscle behind him too. So far we only peddle soft porn and we can deal with the small fry in the same game, but Garston's mob . . . well . . .'

'You said it, Dad, small fry. That's all we are too. Yeah, we're making money, but it's peanuts compared to what we could rake in.' The kettle began to whistle and Danny turned to make two mugs of tea, handing one to his father.

Dan pursed his lips. He didn't like being called small fry and had to admit he wanted to be up amongst the big boys. He had a reputation as a decent safe breaker and had pulled off a few big jobs in the past, but this porn game was new to him. They had started it up a couple of years ago, still using the yard as a front, and as it was doing well he couldn't see the sense of rocking the boat.

'I'm not sure, son. For a start, what about distribution?'

'I've already put out feelers and there's a demand – a big one.'

'I'm not sure the girls we use now would be willing to take it up a notch, let alone the blokes. Just what sort of photographs and films have you got in mind?'

'All sorts. They want everything. Bondage, three-somes, queers. A couple of outlets asked for kids and they're willing to pay big money too.'

43

Unable to believe his ears, Dan's voice rose in anger. 'Do what? Kids! I ain't getting into that.'

'It pays the most.'

'I don't give a fuck what it pays! Christ, son, we're talking about children here! Ain't you got any morals?'

'Dad, we deal in porn so it's a bit late to talk about morals. If the demand's there, we should capitalise on it.'

'No!' Dan yelled, slamming his mug down, regardless that tea slopped onto the desk. 'Our girls and their partners are willing participants, and that's fine with me. They do their act, get paid, but you won't be able to say the same about children. They'd have to be forced! Have you even thought about that?'

The office door opened and Bob poked his head inside. 'What's going on? What's all the shouting about?'

'Get out!' Dan bellowed.

Bob swiftly disappeared, and Danny turned to his father. 'Calm down, Dad.'

Dan sprung to his feet, leaning over his desk and so angry that spittle flew out of his mouth as he yelled, 'Calm down! We're talking about child pornography and you expect me to calm down!'

Danny's manner became placatory. 'Look, Garston provides what the punters want, and that includes kids. It was just a suggestion, that's all, and I must admit I hadn't thought it through. If you don't like the idea we can just forget it.'

'Of course I don't like the fucking idea! In fact, the meeting's off.'

'Hold on, Dad. Don't cut off your nose to spite your face. There's still a lot of money to be made from the other stuff.'

Dan fought his anger as he sat down again, but failed. All right, he was no angel, but he had standards, a code that he lived by. When the boys had suggested getting into this game, he'd been against it, but they had talked him round. He had to admit that the thought of easy money had been a big factor in his decision – that and the fact that he was getting too old for safe breaking, his hands and ears not as good as they used to be. He glared at his son. Christ, using children! Danny said he hadn't given it a lot of thought, but that was no excuse. The boy was his firstborn, he'd been proud of him, yet now it was as if he was seeing his son for the first time – and he didn't like what he saw. Maybe Danny had seen too much – maybe that was it, Dan thought, searching for excuses. Danny had a talent for photography and was involved in the technical side of making the films, but surely that wasn't responsible for turning him into a sick bastard who could suggest using innocent kids? He had to get out of there, to breathe fresh air. Pushing himself up, he growled, 'Wait for the boys. I'll be back later.'

'But, Dad . . .'

Dan didn't stay to hear the rest of Danny's words.

He stormed out of the office, brushing past Bob as he headed for his car. He needed to think, to clear his head. He started the engine and drove off, not caring where he was heading.

'What's up with Dad?' Bob asked as he went into the office.

Danny was behind the desk now, lounging back on the chair, feet up and hands linked behind his head. 'He didn't like one of my suggestions.'

'What suggestion was that?'

'He vetoed it, so there's no point in talking about it.'

'I'd still like to know.'

'Tough. Now bugger off. I need to think.'

Just because Danny was the eldest, he thought he could give out orders, but Bob wasn't ready to give up yet. It gave him some satisfaction to know that Danny had fallen out with their father – a rare occurrence – yet he was still curious to know why. 'Was it to do with this new idea of yours?'

'I don't want to talk about it. Ain't that a customer?'

Bob's lips tightened. He was only fifteen months younger than Danny and was sick of being treated like an underling. All right, he didn't have his brother's brains or looks but he wasn't an idiot. The trade counter bell rang again but he ignored it.

'Is Dad coming back for the meeting?'

'Yeah, I expect so.'

'Why don't you run your idea by me? If I like it, maybe between the two of us we can talk him round.'

'He'll do his nut if I suggest it again.'

'Maybe, but this is a family business and we're all entitled to a vote.' Bob watched as Danny's eyes narrowed speculatively, and hid a smirk. He would never go against his father, but Danny didn't know that. This might turn out to be the ideal opportunity to score a few brownie points with the old man.

'All right,' Danny said, 'see to that customer and then I'll fill you in.'

Chapter Four

Norma Draper tutted with impatience when there was a knock on the door of number four, where she lived with her husband, Maurice. Norma fixed a smile on her face as Sue walked in with her two sons.

'Hello, Sue, I'm surprised to see you so early. Maurice hasn't left for the yard yet,' she added, hoping that her sister-in-law would take the hint and come back later.

'Yeah, but the meeting starts at eleven so no doubt he'll be off soon. Do you know what it's about?'

'I've no idea.'

'Old face-ache said the same, *and* she had the cheek to pick me up about my doorstep.'

Norma smiled, knowing that 'face-ache' referred to their mother-in-law. She had to agree with Sue. Since the day she'd met Maurice, Joan Draper had made it obvious she disapproved of their relationship. All right, she was eight years older than

48

Maurice, but she hadn't meant to get pregnant, despite what the woman thought. In fact, Norma was deeply ashamed and had hated giving birth to Oliver six months after their marriage. Not only that, she had lost contact with her parents in the process. They had been appalled by her pregnancy and also disapproved of the Drapers – a family they'd decided were as common as muck.

She looked at Sue and said sympathetically, 'Don't let Joan upset you.'

'Where's Oliver, Auntie Norma?'

'He's in the back yard feeding his rabbit,' she told Paul.

'I'm going out there to see him,' Robby said.

Norma liked Sue's youngest lad, Paul, but couldn't feel the same about Robby and tensed nervously as the two boys made for the yard. She was worried that Robby would upset Oliver and wanted to follow them, but as Maurice came downstairs she looked at him worriedly. His eyes were still thick with conjunctivitis, his face wan. Maurice wasn't robust, unlike his brothers, and she worried constantly about his health. If anyone had a cold, Maurice would catch it, then nine times out of ten it went to his chest. If stressed, he suffered with bouts of asthma, the attacks leaving him weak and exhausted. Over time she had learned how to deal with them, and thankfully how to calm him down.

'Are you off to this meeting now?' she asked.

'Yes, I'd better get a move on.'

Sue plonked herself on the sofa, her tight dress riding up to reveal shapely legs. Maurice grinned as he said, 'Hello, Sue.'

'Watcha, Maurice. Do you know what this meeting's about?'

'No, sorry, I don't.'

His smile was warm and Norma felt a surge of jealousy. Unlike her, Sue was pretty, vivacious, big-busted and feminine. Norma glanced at her own reflection in the mirror over the fireplace, disliking what she saw. She was plain, her features too large, with only her long, wavy, auburn hair saving her face from masculinity. She hated her body too, and wished that she had Sue's curves, but when Maurice came to her side, she dragged her eyes away from her reflection.

He dropped a kiss on her cheek, asking, 'Where's Oliver?'

'In the yard with Paul and Robby.'

'I'll pop out there to say goodbye.'

'He dotes on that boy,' Sue said as soon as Maurice was out of sight.

'Yes, I know. He's a marvellous father.'

Maurice soon appeared again. 'I'd best get a move on. See you later, ladies.'

Sue giggled. '"Ladies". Well, ain't that nice?' she said as the door closed behind Maurice. 'Mind you, he must know what the meeting's about.'

'Probably, but you should know better than to ask.'

'Yeah, that's what old face-ache said. I don't know why they have to be so secretive. We ain't stupid. We know they do jobs and we'd hardly go shouting our mouths off. It's been a long time since the last one, though – do you think they're planning another robbery?'

'I don't know,' Norma replied. She didn't want to get into this conversation, hating any mention of the family's less respectable sideline. Her parents thought the Drapers were common, but that was the least of it. If they'd known she was marrying into a family of thieves they'd have had heart attacks. Oh, why wouldn't Maurice listen to her? He was clever, mathematically astute and handled the business accounts. If they left the alley, and his awful family, he could get a decent job. She wanted a better life for her son, a respectable life where she could hold her head up high. Instead she was stuck here amongst this den of thieves. Maybe it wouldn't have been as bad if she could have made friends outside of the alley, but as soon as it became known that she was a Draper, she was avoided like the plague. Norma had dreaded Oliver going off to school, and her fears had been well founded when the other mothers made sure that their children gave him a wide berth. At first Oliver had seemed unaware of it, but had started to ask questions when he found it hard to make friends, ones she found difficult to fob off. It had helped when Ivy's elder boy started at the same school a couple of years later. Oliver had taken Ernie under his wing, but it still angered Norma that she and her son were tarred with the same brush as the rest of the Drapers.

'Any chance of a cuppa?' Sue asked. 'I'm spitting feathers.'

'Yes, of course,' Norma replied, but as she went through to the kitchen her son came stumbling through the back door.

'Mum! Oh, Mum,' he sobbed. 'He ... he killed my rabbit.'

Norma pulled her son into her arms, holding him tightly. She didn't have to ask who the culprit was, only saying, 'What did he do, love?'

'He said Shaker could fly and launched him like an aeroplane. Shaker hit the wall and now he ... he's dead.'

Norma's voice rose. 'Sue! Sue, get in here!'

'Gawd blimey, what's the matter?' Sue asked, wide-eyed as she tottered on high heels into the room.

Teeth grinding with anger, Norma spat, 'Your son has killed Oliver's rabbit.'

'No, Robby wouldn't do that.'

'Huh, I didn't say which son, but I see you've jumped straight to Robby's defence.'

Paul came running in the back door, face alight

with excitement. 'He's woken up, Oliver! Shaker's woken up.'

Oliver pulled himself from his mother's grasp and ran outside. Norma followed to see Robby hunkered down beside the rabbit, his eyes wide and innocent as he looked at them.

'He's all right, Ollie,' Robby said.

'Oliver!' Norma automatically corrected as she too crouched down. She hated the diminutive use of her son's name and refused to let anyone use it. Shaker was indeed alive, but lay on his side, trembling as she stroked him.

'You shouldn't have thrown him like that,' Oliver accused as he pushed Robby aside.

'I didn't mean to hurt him. I thought he could fly.'

'Don't tell lies, you nasty little boy,' Norma snapped.

'Hold on, Norma, there's no need to talk to Robby like that. He's only six,' Sue protested.

'I told him, Mummy,' cried Paul. 'I told him that rabbits can't fly.'

Norma looked up at Sue. 'See, out of the mouth of babes – and your Paul's only four.'

Shaker became alert, up on all fours now, his nose twitching. 'Look at that,' said Sue. 'He's all right now so I don't know what all the fuss is about.'

Norma struggled to hold her temper. Robby looked like butter wouldn't melt in his mouth, but she knew what he was capable of and wasn't fooled. The boy might be only six years old, but he had a nasty, malicious streak, and Sue must be blind if she couldn't see it.

'Put Shaker in his pen, Oliver,' she said, 'and you, Robby, I would prefer it if you come inside where we can keep an eye on you.'

'Can I stay out here, Auntie Norma?' Paul asked.

'Of course you can.'

'I want to stay in the yard too,' Robby whined.

'He didn't mean any harm, Norma. It won't be fair to drag him inside.'

Norma's lips tightened. She hated Sue's weakness, the way she pandered to the boy. 'Every time you bring Robby to see us there's a problem. Until he learns to behave himself, he must remain where I can see him. In fact, I would rather you kept him away from my son.'

'Sod you then,' Sue snapped. 'Come on, Robby, you too, Paul. We're going home and we won't bother to come round here again.'

'But, Mummy,' cried Paul, 'I want to play with Oliver.'

'Tough! Now come on,' Sue demanded, grabbing their hands before marching off.

Norma walked inside just in time to hear her front door slam. She was used to Sue's volatile temper. They had fallen out over Robby before, but her sister-in-law had a short memory. No doubt she'd be around again in no time, but Norma just wished that she'd leave Robby behind. If the Drapers weren't so feared, Oliver could find friends outside of the alley, but as it was there was only Sue or Ivy's boys to play with. She wasn't keen on Bob's cousin, Ivy, the woman always trying to cause trouble, but she preferred her older son, Ernie, as a playmate for Oliver.

It was only a few minutes later when Oliver came in, his bony knees grubby, and a piece of hay from the rabbit's hutch stuck in his floppy fringe. Norma's eyes softened as she gently removed it. Like his father, Oliver was thin, with light brown hair, but thankfully he was a robust child. At nine years old he was Dan and Joan's first grandchild, but Joan had little time for the boy. Dan had tried to prevent her from naming him Oliver, saying it was no name for a Draper, but she had stood her ground. After all, she wasn't common like her in-laws. She came from a better family, her father an electrical store manager and their home in Wandsworth far superior to this.

Norma hung her head, thinking back to when she had met Maurice. She'd been lonely, had craved love, but she was so plain that she expected to remain a spinster. When Maurice came along he was the first man to show her any attention, but, afraid of losing him, she had stupidly let him go too far. The question arose again, one that plagued her. If she hadn't been pregnant, would she have married Maurice?

'Can I have a glass of orange juice, please, Mummy?'

'Of course you can, darling.'

As she poured Oliver's drink, Norma knew it was stupid to keep questioning her decision, especially when, in truth, she knew the answer. Yes, she would still have married Maurice, preferring marriage to the life of a spinster. Her two brothers had both married well, and she was the last one left at home, destined to a life of caring for her parents as they aged.

As Norma handed Oliver the juice, she smiled at her son, loving him dearly. He had become her one consolation, and though she couldn't love her husband, she liked him, liked him a lot. But, oh, if only he wasn't a Draper!

When Maurice reached the yard, he rubbed his eyes, then picked at the corners, his finger coming away covered in yellow pus. He'd have to get another prescription from the doc, but hated going to his surgery. He wasn't strong but drew comfort from knowing that his role in the family business was an important one. He kept the books, making sure that no fault could be found in the accounts, the taxes paid on time and in full. The other books, the ones that covered their sideline, were kept well away from prying eyes, but he had them on hand just in case they were needed at the meeting.

'Morning, Bob,' Maurice greeted. 'I've just said goodbye to your lovely wife.'

'What's that supposed to mean?'

'Sue called round to see Norma and was still there when I left.'

'Oh, right,' Bob said, then gestured with his thumb towards the office. 'Danny's been here a while and Chris turned up ten minutes ago.'

'What about Dad? I can't see his car.'

'He went off with the hump.'

'Really, and who ruffled his feathers?'

'He had a bit of a falling-out with Danny.'

'Did he now? What about?'

'Search me,' Bob said, looking pleased as he added, 'but they were having a right old ding-dong.'

Maurice could sense that Bob was being evasive, sure that he knew more than he was letting on. Bob was always a bit funny when it came to Danny – the rivalry plain to see – but he was wasting his time if he wanted to take Danny's place. Next to their father, Danny was the top man, the position unlikely to change. There was only one person their father favoured above Danny, and that was Petula.

'Hello, Maurice,' said Chris as he came out of the office. 'The meeting might be off.'

'Yeah, Bob told me that Dad went off with the hump. Is it worth hanging around?'

'Search me. Danny ain't saying much, only that they had a difference of opinion.'

Maurice studied his youngest brother. Chris was looking snazzy. He had run the gauntlet of fashion, changing from a teddy boy to a mod, and lately had taken to wearing Italian suits. He was a good-looking bloke, a sort of soft replica of their father, and though he didn't have an aggressive personality, he could look after himself. Chris was his favourite of all the brothers, and before he had married Sue they had knocked about together, either going down the pub, or to the local snooker hall.

'How's your love life? Are you still seeing that girl from Chelsea?'

'No, she was getting a bit too keen and hinting about engagement rings.'

'So, you're footloose and fancy-free again. Do you fancy a game of snooker tonight?'

'No can do. I've got a date tonight. I took Pet to buy a record this morning and a nice-looking bird behind the counter caught my eye.'

Maurice raised his brows, but then he shouldn't be surprised. Chris was good at pulling birds, one following another in quick succession. 'What's she like?'

'Tasty, but she's blonde and I prefer them dark.'

'What's the matter with blondes?' Bob protested. 'My Sue's a cracker.'

'Yeah, she is,' Chris agreed, 'but I still like brunettes, and ain't your Sue's hair out of a bottle?'

Bob was saved from answering when their father drove into the yard. He climbed out of his car and, judging by the look on his face, he was still in a foul mood.

'Is everyone here?' he snapped.

'We're still waiting for George,' Bob told him.

'Shit! Well, we'll have to start without him. Lock up, Bob, and then join us in the office.'

Maurice frowned. With their father in this mood he couldn't see it being a very productive meeting. Curious to know what Danny had come up with, he silently followed his father through to the office, Bob and Chris behind him.

Danny hastily took his feet off the table and stood up. 'The meeting still on then, Dad?'

'Yeah, it's on, but you're skating on thin ice.'

Maurice frowned again. It was obvious that Danny had already discussed his plans with their father, but, judging by his tone, the old man didn't approve of them.

They all grabbed chairs and, once seated, Dan said, 'Maurice, did you bring the books?'

'Yes, Dad.'

'How are we doing?'

Maurice opened to the current page, pushing the book across to his father. 'As you can see we've made the same amount this quarter as we did the last. Profits are still good, but I think we've reached saturation point and they're unlikely to increase.'

'Oh yeah,' Dan snapped, 'very convenient. Have you spoken to Danny ahead of this meeting?'

'No. What makes you ask that?'

'It's a bit funny that just when we need to increase profits, your brother has come up with an idea.'

'Well, he didn't discuss it with me,' Maurice said, 'but he's certainly timed it right. What have you got in mind, Danny?'

Danny rose to his feet. 'If we want to make money, big money, we need to diversify. I've discussed this with Dad, but there's one aspect of it that he doesn't like and I expected to drop. However, I had a word with Bob and he's as keen on the idea as me.'

'He's what?' Dan exploded. 'Is this true, Bob?'

'Nah, no way,' Bob protested. 'Danny told me what he's got in mind, but I think he's off his head. I'm with you, Dad. I've got kids and the thought of it turns my stomach. What he's got in mind is disgusting, sick, and I can't believe he even suggested it.'

'Why, you . . .' Danny growled, advancing towards Bob, '. . . you two-faced bastard. I'll fucking kill you!'

'That's enough!'

Their father's order was enough to halt Danny in his tracks, but his fists were clenched as he yelled, 'He said he was for it!'

Bob was pale, his voice wheedling, 'No, Danny. I'm sorry, but when you told me what you've got in mind I was a bit stunned. I can't remember what I said, but maybe you got hold of the wrong end of the stick.'

'Leave it out. I didn't come over on a fucking

banana boat so don't take me for a mug. I don't know what your game is, but you agreed all right.'

'Look, what's this all about?' Maurice asked, his eyes flicking between his brothers.

It was Danny who answered. 'When I discussed my idea with Bob, he said we should have a vote on it.'

'That's right, I did,' said Bob, 'but it doesn't mean I like the idea. I just said it's only fair that everyone gets a chance to hear it.'

'Shut up, the pair of you,' Dan yelled. 'Bob, I'm glad to hear that, unlike Danny, you seem to have decent morals, but there'll be no vote on the shit that your brother has come up with.'

When Maurice saw Bob's smug smile, he was sure that his brother had somehow manoeuvred this to discredit Danny, enabling him to get into their father's good books. He also saw Danny step forward, about to round on Bob again, his face livid. To defuse the situation Maurice quickly asked, 'Just what is this idea?'

It was their father who answered. 'Danny wants us to go into hard porn, but I'll leave him to tell you about the bit that I can't stomach and will never allow.'

'All right, Danny, let's hear it,' Maurice said.

Chapter Five

In number five, George Draper was growing impatient. He'd overslept, not getting up until after ten that morning, and if Linda didn't pull herself together soon he'd have to leave without any grub. Bloody hell, this pregnancy was a nightmare. Linda threw up continuously and looked awful, her face the colour of dough. Morning sickness. Huh! Hers sometimes lasted all day, and if this was what it was like to have a pregnant wife, he'd make sure it was the last time.

He glanced at the clock and his expression turned grim when he saw it was after half-past ten. If he didn't get a move on he'd be late for the meeting and the old man would do his nut.

Linda staggered in through the back door, wiping her hand across her mouth. 'I hate using that outside toilet. When are we going to get a bathroom?'

'For Christ's sake, stop whinging,' George snapped, fists clenched as he fought the urge to smack her in the mouth. Realising that he should have put more value on his freedom, he was already disillusioned with marriage. It had been the thought of having nooky on hand whenever he wanted it that had decided him to propose, and not only that, Linda had been a tasty piece, one he'd been proud to have on his arm.

Marriage had been great at first, sex on demand, but the novelty soon wore off, especially when the stupid mare told him she was pregnant. She was letting herself go too, her face always bare of make-up. Her long, ash-blonde hair still cascaded down her back, but these days it looked like rats' tails.

'I'm gonna be late,' he snapped. 'For fuck's sake, pull yourself together and make me a bacon sandwich. I'll eat it on the way to the yard.'

'Yes, all right, and I'm sorry, George. I won't complain again,' Linda wheedled, but then she raised a hand to her mouth. 'Oh God, I'm going to be sick again.'

George held his temper, just, and as she staggered outside again he yelled, 'You useless cow. Forget my breakfast – I'm off.'

With that, George left the house. His stomach rumbled as he hurried down the alley, his expression dark with fury. When he turned into Aspen Street a bloke was coming out of his house, and though he looked quickly away, George was ready for a fight.

'Who do you think you're looking at? Got a problem, have yer?'

'Nah, mate,' the man said, holding his hands up as though in surrender.

The bloke's obvious fear mollified George, and anyway, with his father waiting he didn't have time to hang about. With a last scowl at the bloke he hurried past, intent now on reaching the yard.

Linda leaned over the toilet, retching, but only bringing up bile now. Oh, she hated this morning sickness. She had hoped that her pregnancy would soften George, but so far all it had done was arouse his anger, making her more afraid of him than ever.

When they'd first met, his dark brown hair, gorgeous blue eyes and a smile to die for had bowled her over, and she had willingly gone out with him. Of course she had heard of George's family, their reputation, but in truth she'd been bored with life and excited at the hint of danger. Her previous boyfriends had been ordinary, staid and, compared to George, as dull as dishwater. She'd been blinded by him, fell madly in love, and at first there'd been no sign of the violence that lay beneath his charming persona.

Linda wiped a hand across her mouth, recalling how during their courtship the other side of George had come to light. He would get into numerous fights, usually a result of another bloke showing interest. God, what a fool she'd been. Instead of seeing what was under her nose, she'd been flattered by his jealousy – proud of his prowess – proud too to be part of a family that was both feared and respected in the area. When they had married, everything had been wonderful at first, but after only two months, George had changed. His violence turned on her, but it was her own fault, she knew that, finding out the hard way not to question him when he came home late without explanation.

Linda heaved again, her head swimming. She felt awful, and longed for her mother's arms. Tears threatened and she gulped, deciding that as soon as she felt better, she'd go to see her parents. George wouldn't like it. If he found out, she'd probably get another smack, but it had been weeks since she had last seen her mum and she missed her so much.

At last, feeling marginally better, Linda made her way inside. She still felt nauseous, unsure if she could make it to her mother's house, but maybe she could pop next door to have a word with Ivy. She'd had two children, so might know something that could settle this dreadful morning sickness.

Of course Sue and Norma had children too, but Linda knew that Ivy would be the most sympathetic. When she had first moved into Drapers Alley, it was Ivy who made her welcome, and nowadays they often had a gossip over a cup of tea. So far she hadn't told Ivy how violent George was becoming, but with only thin walls between them, she felt sure that the woman already knew. Maybe she should bring the subject up, confide in her. Ivy was vitriolic in her dislike of most of the brothers, with the exception of Chris, but so far they had never discussed George.

Linda went upstairs where she took off her night-clothes before stepping into a skirt. With nothing else clean, she pulled a creased blouse out of the ironing basket, but the garments had piled up, several spilling over the side and onto the floor. Her stomach flipped again, and ignoring the mess, she fled downstairs, one hand over her mouth as she headed again for the outside toilet.

When George reached the yard he was surprised to find it locked. All right, he was a bit late, but surely the old man could have waited. With a tut of impatience he pulled out his keys.

There was the sound of raised voices as George went inside, but as he stepped into the office, all went quiet for a moment before his father's voice rang out.

'Where the bloody hell have you been?'

'Sorry, Dad. Linda's got morning sickness and I couldn't leave her.'

'Morning sickness? That's no excuse. Your mother had that and it's nothing to worry about.'

George wasn't going to admit that he'd overslept,

so creasing his face into an expression of worry he said, 'Linda was really rough, Dad.'

'Yeah, well, there's no need to get upset. It'll soon pass and she'll be fine.'

George nodded. 'Have I missed much?'

'You've just missed your brother telling the others that he wants to peddle child porn.'

'Oh, right. Is there a lot of money in it, Danny?'

'Yeah, a mint, but it's been vetoed.'

'Why's that?'

A chair went back, crashing onto the floor as Dan reared to his feet. 'Why's that?' he screeched, face red and eyes bulging. 'For fuck's sake, ain't it obvious?'

Despite this display of temper, George scratched his head, unable to understand what was upsetting his father. His eyes swept over Bob, Maurice and Chris, noticing for the first time that they looked none too happy. 'Can someone tell me what's going on?'

It was Chris who answered. 'Danny wants us to go into hard porn. We're fine with that. Adult movies are acceptable, but not ones using kids.'

Out of the corner of his eye, George saw his father sit down again and finally cottoned on that he had better tread carefully. Danny might be for the idea, but it seemed the others were against. 'Yeah, well, I suppose I can see why. It'll be bad enough if the Vice Squad catches us making hardcore films with adults, but if they find kids we could be in the shit – big time.' George's eyes shot to his father, seeking approval, but instead saw him shaking his head with disgust.

'You're as bad as Danny,' he growled. 'We've agreed to the other stuff, but now I ain't so sure.'

Confused, George looked to Danny, and it was he who spoke.

'Dad, listen, as I said there's a mint to be made if we up the ante. Maurice has pointed out that we've reached saturation point with the soft stuff so an increase in profits is unlikely. Yes, we're doing all right, but if you want your early retirement we need to give the other stuff a try.'

'Oh, so it's for my benefit, is it?' asked Dan, his voice dripping with sarcasm.

'We'll all benefit, Dad. We could make a fortune.'

Dan's eyes swept over the others before settling on Maurice. 'Well, you're the brains of the family so what do you think?'

'I've got a few more questions to ask before I make a decision.'

Dan nodded. 'What about you, Bob?'

'Well, as long as we keep away from child porn, I'm for it.'

There was a low growl from Danny, but then Chris said, 'If everything we do is consensual, then I think we should give it a go.'

Dan's lips pursed. 'And you're willing to risk treading on Garston's toes?'

Again there was silence as each brother pondered, but then Danny said, 'If the worst comes to the worst we can always hire a bit more muscle. Do you want me to have a word with some of the boys at the gym, Dad?'

'No, leave it for now. We won't need it until Garston gets wind of what we're up to, and that's likely to be when we start distribution.'

'So it's on then?'

Dan exhaled loudly. 'Maurice still has questions, but yeah, if he's happy with your answers, I suppose so.' He then stood up. 'I'll leave you to go over the finer points. I'm off to the races.'

He didn't say goodbye and, still confused, George looked to Danny, his brother hissing, 'We'll talk later.'

George nodded, and as Danny sat in the chair vacated by their father, he too took a seat, listening to the questions that Maurice raised.

'Have you spoken to the girls and their partners, Danny?'

'No, not yet, but if they don't fancy upping the stakes, we can still use them for soft porn, finding others to take on the hard stuff.'

'They won't be cheap.'

'I've factored that in.'

'And the filming? We use Eddy Woodman now, but he might not fancy the added risks.'

'It's not a problem. I've learned all I need from Eddy, and I've decided to keep this strictly in the family by handling the filming myself. With this kind of operation, the fewer people who know about it *and* where we're based, the better. Bob has proved himself good at editing, so he can take that on. Chris is great with sales so we can continue getting orders and sorting out distribution. George can make up the sets and Maurice can handle the lighting.'

'Will Ivy's old man still do the deliveries?'

'Yeah, but I'll send George out with him just in case there's any trouble.'

'Dad's right,' Maurice mused. 'Garston ain't gonna take this lightly, and he ain't the only one.'

'Fuck them,' Danny snapped. 'There's a market out there, a good one, with room for another crew. All right, we might come across a bit of trouble, but with the money we'll make it's worth the risk. Anyway, as I told Dad, there's plenty of muscle for hire if we want it.'

'That's gonna cost a pretty penny,' Maurice complained.

'Only until we sort Garston out. In fact, if it becomes necessary, I know someone who'll take the bastard out permanently.'

'It may come to that. He's a nasty piece of work and has been known to use shooters.'

Danny shrugged. 'So what? Garston doesn't frighten me and he shouldn't put the shits up you either. Bloody hell, Maurice, we're the Drapers. We're feared – maybe not as much as Garston, but we can soon put that right.'

'Yeah, Danny,' said George. 'In fact, if Garston tries anything I'll take the fucker out myself.'

'That's more like it,' Danny said, smiling with approval. 'There speaks a Draper.'

George was gratified by Danny's remark. He knew he wasn't the brightest of the bunch, but other than Danny, he was the toughest. Maurice was a weakling, and though Bob and Chris could handle themselves in a fight, they didn't have the killer instinct. He'd been around them during punch-ups, and it was usually left to him to put the final boot in, something he had no qualms about doing. His neck stretched, pride in his stance. If anyone wanted to mess with the Drapers they'd have to take the consequences, and that included Jack fucking Garston.

'All right, Danny,' Maurice said. 'I'm in. Does that still go for the rest of you?'

George grinned as one by one his brothers nodded. It had been too quiet lately. The business had been chugging along nicely so it had been a while since he'd had a chance to use his fists. Now, though, things were looking up.

One by one they left, until just he and Danny remained in the office.

There was still something puzzling George. 'I still don't get it, Danny. Why did they veto child porn?

Was I right about the Vice Squad? Is that why they turned you down?'

'No, you silly sod. They don't like the idea of using kids.'

'But you said there's a lot of money in it.'

'Yeah, there is. Never mind. I'll bide my time. Dad's going soft, getting past it, and the sooner he retires the better.' Danny's smile was assured. 'When he does, who do you think will be running the show?'

George scratched his head, but then the answer dawned on him. 'You, Danny, you'll be the boss.'

'Yeah, that's right – with you as my right-hand man.'

'What about Bob? Surely he's next in line to you.'

'No, I don't trust the two-faced bastard. When I run the show there'll be changes – big ones – and I'll need you to back me up.'

'What sort of changes, Danny?'

'For one, what I say goes. There'll be no more bloody votes, and if anyone doesn't like it, they'll be out.'

'You won't be able to do that. The others won't stand for it.'

'Can you really see Bob, Maurice or Chris going up against me?'

'Well, I dunno. Chris might.'

'Not if I've got you on my side, George. He wouldn't fucking dare – none of them would. Now are you with me or not?'

George floundered. There was too much to process and his brain couldn't take it in. Yeah, Dad was sure to retire soon with Danny next in line, but surely it would still be a family business? 'I don't see how you'll be able to make these changes, Danny.'

'I'll make them, you can be sure of that. Be warned, though. If you ain't for me, you're against me.' His eyes narrowed menacingly. 'Do you really fancy taking me on?'

'No, Danny, I'm with you,' George said. He might not be the brainbox of the family, but he knew better than to go up against Danny.

'Good, now come on, let's get out of here. One more thing, George, keep this conversation to yourself. As I said, we've got to bide our time until Dad retires, but when he does . . .' Danny tailed off.

'Don't worry, I know when to keep my mouth shut,' said George as he followed Danny outside. 'I'm off to have a pint. What about you?'

'No, I've got things to do.'

'Oh, right, do you want me to come with you?'

'Sorry, mate, but what I've got in mind only takes two.'

Confused, George said, 'But if I come with you, there'd only be the pair of us.'

Danny chuckled. 'You daft bugger. Yeah, what I've got in mind takes two, but one of them is female.'

'Oh . . . oh, right, I get it.' But as Danny locked the gates, George added, 'What about Yvonne?'

With a wink, Danny said, 'What the eye doesn't see, as the saying goes.'

'You jammy bastard,' George grinned.

He watched as his brother walked away, struck by a thought. If Danny could have a bit on the side, then so could he. Yeah, why not? The next time Linda was too ill, or when her belly was too swollen for a bit of nooky, he'd go on the pull.

Chapter Six

Ivy Rawlings, formerly Draper, scowled as she looked around her living room. This was number six, the last house in the row, and she hated the interior. Money was tight and her battered furniture was second-hand, the surface of her sideboard badly scratched. Unlike her Uncle Dan and Aunt Joan, Ivy had few luxuries and resented it. She *did* have a bathroom, so felt superior to George and Linda, who lived next door in number five, but Ivy had waited over three years to get it. No doubt George, being a precious son who'd been married less than a year, would get preferential treatment, with an extension built soon.

Her lip curled and she took her anger out on Steve, her husband. 'I hear they're having a meeting at the yard. Why aren't you there?'

'I wasn't invited. Anyway, it's my day off.'

'Day off! Leave it out. The yard closes at one o'clock so it's only half a day. You're a mug to put up with it,' Ivy said, shaking her head at her husband's stupidity. 'Do you know what the meeting's about?'

'No.'

Ivy bristled. Getting anything out of Steve was like trying to get blood out of a stone, but she wasn't ready to give up yet. 'Are they planning a job?'

'Leave it out. Your uncle hasn't touched a safe in years.'

'They're up to something. I can feel it in me water. Come on, you must know what's going on.'

'I don't, and even if I did, I know when to keep my mouth shut.'

'Don't give me that. You don't like my relatives, so why the loyalty?'

'It ain't loyalty, you silly cow. It's more like self-preservation.'

'Bloody hell, Steve, you can tell me. I ain't about to blab.'

'Blab about what? For Gawd's sake, Ivy, I've been working for your uncle for less than a year so I'm as much in the dark as you are. I prefer it that way too. I'm happy just working in the yard and doing deliveries.'

'Yeah, but compared to the boys you get paid peanuts. It ain't right, Steve. You do twice as many shifts as them. In fact, they hardly show their faces at the yard, so what do they get up to?'

'I dunno, but I ain't complaining.'

Ivy saw the shifty look in her husband's eyes and wasn't fooled. He knew something, she was sure of it. He'd been a totter when she met him and it had taken her years to persuade Uncle Dan to give him a job in the family firm. Steve should thank her, but instead of telling her what they were up to he'd become as secretive as the rest of the male members of the family. She knew that at only five feet tall Steve was the butt of their jokes and, like her, he was no oil painting. He was thickset, and his lack of neck made his head appear to sit on his wide shoulders. On top of that, his legs were slightly bowed, due to malnutrition as a child. He had nice eyes, though, deep green and fringed by long, dark lashes.

The sound of a ball banging repeatedly against the wall made Ivy's chin jut. She rushed to the back door, throwing it open. The culprit was Ernie, her elder son, seven years old and football mad.

'Pack it in!' she yelled. 'If you want to play with that ball, go to the park.'

'Can I go too, Mummy?' five-year-old Harry pleaded.

'Yeah, bugger off, the pair of you. And you, Ernie, make sure you hold your brother's hand when you cross the road.'

They scuttled off and Ivy heaved a sigh of relief, glad of the peace. But no sooner had the boys disappeared than there was a knock on the door. 'Christ, what now?' she complained.

Steve opened it. 'Watcha, Linda, come on in.'

'Hello, love, you look a bit rough,' Ivy observed.

'I'm sorry to bother you, Ivy, but do you know of anything that can ease this morning sickness?'

Before Ivy could answer Steve said, 'I'm just popping down to your Aunt Joan's.'

'What for?'

'Dan wants me to fix a catch on one of their windows.'

'Oh, so now you're his handyman too. Huh, so much for your day off. I wanted you down at the allotment. You ain't touched it for ages and it's running wild with weeds.'

'Don't start. Fixing the catch won't take a minute.'

'Oh, just bugger off,' Ivy said, glad to see the back of him. No sooner had the door closed than she turned to Linda, her bad mood lifting at the thought of a good old gossip with the only person who seemed to like her in the alley. 'Sit down, love. I'll make us a nice cup of tea.'

'Thanks, Ivy, but I doubt I'll be able to keep it down.'

'You poor cow. I was the same with my first pregnancy. There ain't much you can do about it, but don't worry, it usually only lasts for the first three months. How about a couple of dry biscuits? That usually helps a bit.'

'I'll try anything. I was hoping to pop round to my mum's, but if this sickness doesn't pass I won't get to the end of the alley before throwing up again.'

Ivy bustled into the kitchen and found a few cream crackers, which she put on a plate. With a pot of tea made she poured two cups, placing the lot on a plastic tray to carry back into the small living room.

'Here, get that down you,' she urged. 'How is it going with George? Is he still unhappy about the baby?'

Linda sighed as she picked up a cracker, taking a tentative nibble before laying it down again. 'Things are no better and this morning sickness doesn't help. I was so bad this morning that he had to leave without any breakfast.'

'Oh dear, poor George,' Ivy drawled, her voice dripping with sarcasm. 'He ain't a cripple and could have made himself a couple of bits of toast.'

'George never does anything in the kitchen. He says cooking and cleaning are woman's work.'

'Most men are the same, but if I'm feeling rough, Steve will muck in. He'll even have a go at cooking something simple. Anyway, changing the subject, do you know what this meeting at the yard's about?'

'No, in fact I didn't know there was a meeting. George never discusses the business with me.'

'If you ask me, there's something in the wind. I reckon they're planning a job. It's been ages since they've done one.'

Linda blanched. 'A job! What do you mean?'

'Surely you're not *that* naïve. You must know what sort of family you've married into.'

'Well, I heard rumours, but George told me that nowadays they're just builders' merchants.'

'Really? So you think the business makes enough to pay the wages for six households, do you?'

Linda's brow creased. 'I . . . I hadn't given it a lot of thought, but it's a big yard, so yes.'

'It might be big, but you can't tell me it takes seven men to run it. My Steve does most of the shifts and I'd give my right arm to know where the others disappear to every day. I've tried asking Steve, but he won't tell me anything. Why don't you see what you can get out of George?'

'Oh, no, I couldn't do that! George would go mad if I start asking questions.'

Ivy didn't envy Linda her husband. She'd heard the rows next door, and suspected that George wasn't slow in giving Linda a slap or two. 'Yeah, I've heard him doing his nut.'

'George was lovely when we first got married, but lately, he . . . he's given me a few clouts. I'm scared for my baby, Ivy, and I don't know what to do.'

'Sort him out. Nip it in the bud.'

'I wish I could, but I don't know how.'

'It's simple. If George tries to hit you again, pick up the nearest heavy object, such as a frying pan, and bash him over the head with it.'

'Oh, no, Ivy, I couldn't do that. I'm not strong like you.'

'You don't need strength to bash him with a frying

pan. Men who hit women are bullies. The only way to deal with George is to give him a dose of his own medicine. Once he knows you'll fight back, he'll soon back off.'

'Do you really think so?'

'Take my word for it, love. Now come on, cheer up. Things will look up once you've sorted George out, and you'll soon be over this morning sickness.'

For the first time Linda smiled. She picked up the cracker again, and finished it in no time, washing it down with a gulp of tea. 'My goodness, I've managed to keep it down,' she said.

'That's the ticket. You should be able to pay your mum a visit now.'

With a little colour in her cheeks at last, Linda rose to her feet. 'Thanks, Ivy. I think I'll go and tidy myself up and then I'll do just that. It feels like ages since I've seen my mum and I really miss her. My dad too.'

Linda wasn't the only one, Ivy thought, as she showed the girl out. She missed her parents too. Her father had been Uncle Dan's younger brother, but he'd been killed during the war. She and her mother had been grief-stricken, but Uncle Dan had taken them under his wing, continuing to support them until her mother died. Oh, yes, nice Uncle Dan, kind Uncle Dan – or so everyone thought. Ivy knew better.

At twenty-three years old she had married Steve,

pretending to be grateful when Uncle Dan had secured them the tenancy of this house. Her eyes darkened with hate. She wasn't grateful, why should she be? Not when she suspected the truth. Of course she couldn't prove it, but her resentment had festered until it became an obsession. Oh, she'd make him pay – somehow – someday, she'd find a way. Until then she had to be content with stirring things up, causing mischief for the family at every opportunity.

With a thin smile Ivy consoled herself with the thought that she had a bit of information now. George had been hitting Linda, something that would upset her aunt and put the cat amongst the pigeons. She hated the way her aunt wanted for nothing – the way Uncle Dan called her 'Queen'. Her own mother should have been equally well off, but instead had suffered the humiliation of Uncle Dan's so-called largesse.

Ivy made for number one, looking forward to wiping the smile off her aunt's face.

With a Woodbine between his lips, one eye shut as the smoke curled upwards, Steve Rawlings endeavoured to ease paint-encrusted screws out of the window frame. Joan was bustling about as usual – the woman never stood still. He could hear the thump, thump of Petula's record player, but at least the music was a bit muted since Joan had told the girl to close her bedroom door.

He'd been glad to get away from Ivy's questions, worried that one day she'd wear him down and he'd blurt out the truth. Like Ivy, he didn't have a lot of time for the Draper boys – well, except Chris, who was always friendly – and he was shit scared of Danny and George.

Ivy had talked him into joining the family business, wearing him down with her nagging. They might be better off, but in truth he hated working for Dan Draper. He'd started at the yard and it hadn't been a bad job, until after only a few months he'd been roped into the other stuff.

He'd been happier as a totter, his own man, riding the streets with his horse and cart, picking up scrap from households all over the borough. He may not have made a lot of money, but he'd never been frightened – not the gut-wrenching churning in his stomach he now felt every time he took out a delivery of the shit that the Drapers turned out. He dreaded getting stopped by the police, dreaded a vehicle search, knowing that if and when it happened, he'd have to take the fall. There was no way he'd dare implicate the Drapers – not if he wanted to stay alive.

His lips tightened. Of course, Ivy had no idea that the Drapers produced porn. The daft cow still thought they made their money from the yard, with a bit of thieving thrown in. Ivy still had her suspicions, of course, but there was no way he could tell her the truth, not when Dan had made it clear what would happen if he did. With a sigh he continued working on the catch, but then scowled when Ivy knocked on the door before sticking her head inside.

'Hello, Auntie Joan. Can I come in?' she called.

'I suppose so, but I'm up to my eyes at the moment,' Joan replied from the kitchen, her tone making it obvious she resented the interruption.

Ivy ignored the rebuff and Joan came fully into the room, wiping her hands on her apron as she said, 'I'm cleaning out my cupboards. Everything's upside down.'

'I won't stay long. I just popped down to see how Steve's getting on.'

'I'm nearly finished,' Steve said, annoyed to think that Ivy was checking on him, but when she spoke again he realised the truth of her visit.

'I hear there's a meeting at the yard, Auntie Joan,' Ivy said. 'Do you know what it's about?'

'No,' Joan said shortly, adding as an afterthought, 'why don't you ask your husband?'

'He doesn't know either, do you, Steve?'

'No, I don't,' he said, wishing his wife would leave. His muscles tensed with nerves, hoping she wasn't up to mischief as usual. His hopes died when she spoke again.

'I've just had Linda round to see me, Auntie Joan. The poor girl looks dreadful. She's got morning sickness, but worse, your George has taken to giving her a clout or two.'

Joan paled. 'Did she tell you that?'

'Yes. I think the girl needed someone to confide in, but even if she hadn't, I ain't deaf and can hear a lot through the walls.'

Steve twisted the last replacement screw into place, wanting only to be away from this conversation. Ivy was stirring again – something she took great pleasure in doing – yet he was at a loss to know why. Like him, she had no love for the Drapers, so why the bloody hell had she accepted a house in the alley?

'Right, the job's done and I'm off,' he said loudly.

Neither woman acknowledged him as he scurried out. One of these days Ivy would go too far and he dreaded the consequences. Dan Draper would never take it out on his niece and instead would get Danny or George to take it out on him. He had seen some of their handiwork and the thought made his guts churn.

Joan hardly heard the door as it closed behind Steve. She kept her gaze fixed on Ivy and fought to hide her dislike of Dan's niece, but knew she was failing as usual. There was no family resemblance, and Joan wondered how Dan's brother had produced such an ugly offspring – one with an ugly personality to match. The young woman seemed to enjoy causing her discomfort, taking every opportunity to make trouble.

Even as a child, Ivy had been sly. She could understand Dan helping both mother and child out when his brother had been killed during the war, but was at a loss to understand why he continued to help Ivy when she became an adult. The last house in the row should have been earmarked for Chris, a home for him when he decided to marry, but instead Dan had tipped up money to someone at the council for Ivy to move in with her husband. Not only that, he had gone on to give Ivy's husband a job in the firm.

'I reckon you should give George a talking-to, Auntie Joan. It ain't right that he's hitting that poor girl.'

Joan, doubting the truth of Ivy's story, ground her teeth together. 'I think you must have got the wrong end of the stick. George wouldn't hit his wife.'

'Ask Linda herself if you don't believe me.'

'Oh, I will, you can be sure of that,' Joan snapped. 'Now if you don't mind, I've got work to do.'

'All right, I'm off,' Ivy said, a false look of concern on her face before she turned to leave. 'I hope I haven't upset you, Auntie Joan, but I thought you should know what George has been up to.'

Joan made no comment, but as the door closed behind Ivy, she raised a shaky hand to rub it across her forehead, still unable to believe that George was hitting his wife. She knew that Dan had once been a criminal, and that as they grew up he had roped the boys in, yet he was also a gentleman, bringing the boys up to respect women. Dan might rule her, but he had never laid a finger on her and certainly wouldn't stand for the lads laying into their wives.

Dan had protected them all, yet in the past her nerves had been shattered by the police raids. Dan had laughed at her worrying, telling her they were too clever to get caught, but the only way she had been able to cope was to bury her fears behind a barrier of indifference, all her energies focused on her home. Of course, nowadays they were respectable, running a family business, and thank goodness she no longer had anything to worry about. At least she hoped so, but still she sensed that something was going on, and fear fluttered like a tiny bird against her ribcage.

Joan scuttled to the kitchen. Was Ivy telling the truth? Was George really hitting his wife? With gritted teeth she tackled the cupboards again, trying to force her worries to one side as she vigorously attacked a stain that had dared to appear on one of the doors.

At last, with her emotional barriers in place again, Joan calmed down. She would do what she always did when there were signs of trouble within the family. She'd leave it for Dan to sort out.

*　　*　　*

Petula switched off her gramophone, returning the record to its sleeve. She moved to the mirror, gazing with displeasure at her reflection. Unlike lots of girls in her class at school, she had hardly any bust, her figure still gangly and boyish. She had hoped that when her periods started a figure would follow, but no such luck.

With a swift look over her shoulder, Petula picked up her satchel, groping under her school books until she found the hidden tube of lipstick. If her dad knew she had it, he'd go mad, but with him out, and Mum busy as usual, she risked smearing some on her lips.

Petula's head cocked to one side. Yes, she looked marginally better, but longed to be glamorous, with a bust like Bob's wife, Sue. Her expression saddened. In truth, her figure and build was more like Yvonne's, a woman that she didn't want to emulate. Yvonne was too skinny, and though she dressed well, her clothes were plain. Sue, on the other hand, wore full skirts and close-fitting jumpers, or tight dresses that clung to her waist and ended just below her knees. Her make-up was bold, skilfully applied, and with this thought Petula wiped off the lipstick before lightly running downstairs.

'Mum, I'm just popping along to see Sue.'

There was only a grunt in reply, but Pet was used to this – used to her mother's distant manner and lack of affection. She also knew that her mother disapproved of Sue and thought she was a tart, but Pet liked her.

In no time she was outside, giving Sue's letter box a rap before poking her head inside. 'Hello, can I come in?'

'Of course you can,' Sue said, but unusually there wasn't a smile on her face.

'Is something wrong?'

'Nah, not really, it's just that I've had a falling-out with Norma. Honestly, I don't know who she thinks she is, but she's getting as uppity as Yvonne.'

'What did you fall out about?'

'She was really nasty to my Robby. The poor kid thought rabbits could fly and launched Shaker. All right, it was a daft thing to do, but he didn't mean to hurt the bloody thing.'

Petula hid her thoughts. Robby was her least favourite nephew, the boy already a bully who picked on his brother and cousins mercilessly. There had been many occasions when she had seen the kids playing outside, and it was always Robby who was the troublemaker, with one of the others usually running home crying. Ivy's boys had taken to staying out of Robby's way, and she didn't blame them, but now, acting the role of peacemaker, Pet said, 'Never mind. You know how protective Norma is of Oliver. I'm sure she'll come round.'

'I don't bloody care if she doesn't. Oh, sod it, forget Norma. How are you doing, love?'

'I'm fine, but I wanted to ask if you'd show me how to put make-up on.'

'Leave it out, Pet. Your dad would go mad.'

'He doesn't need to know.'

'You'll never be allowed to wear it.'

'Not now, maybe, but I'll be fifteen in December and leaving school. It would be nice to know how to apply make-up for when I start looking for a job.' Pet held her breath, hoping that Sue would agree. There were girls at school who already wore powder and lipstick when they went out, and she'd been invited to join three of them at the local youth club that evening. She wanted to go, but couldn't face the embarrassment of being met by one of her brothers. Oh, why couldn't her dad see that she was old enough to walk herself home?

'With the way you speak, I expect you'll be going for an office job, but even when you leave school, I can't see your dad letting you wear make-up.'

'I didn't try hard enough to pass my eleven plus, so I doubt I'll get an office job. I hated it when Dad sent me for elocution lessons too, but now realise they might help. I'm thinking of applying for a job in an upmarket shop, you see, perhaps in Knights-bridge.'

'Good idea, but you'll have to look the part too and a bit of slap would make all the difference. Mind you, I still think your dad won't stand for it.'

'I'm sick of being overprotected, Sue. I'm not a

90

child now and I'm determined to have it out with him.'

'Well, rather you than me, but all right, I'll show you how to apply make-up. The kids have gone out to play so we've got the place to ourselves for a while. Just make sure you keep it to yourself, and you'll have to wash it off before you leave.' With her head cocked to one side, Sue studied Pet's face. 'With your looks, I reckon you could be a model. I always wanted to be an actress, and you could even try that.'

'Oh, no, I'd be too shy to go on stage. I didn't know you wanted to be an actress. What stopped you?'

'Marriage and kids. Oh, don't get me wrong, I love Bob, but having kids has ruined my figure.'

'No, surely not? I'd love to have a figure like yours.'

'Leave it out, Pet. My boobs have drooped something rotten.'

Sue got out her make-up bag and Pet smiled with delight, amazed at the array of cosmetics. There was panstick, face powder, eye shadows and lipsticks.

'Right, let's get on with it,' said Sue.

To begin, Pet was shown how to apply foundation, followed by powder and blusher. When it came to eye make-up, Pet found it harder than she'd expected. She spat on the block of mascara before coating the small brush, but when she tried to apply it to her lashes, the brush went into her eye. 'Ouch!' she cried, her eyes streaming.

'Don't rub it!' Sue cried. 'Dab it. Oh, blimey, too late – now you look like a bleedin' clown. Wash it off, love. We'll have to start again.'

Now that the stinging had eased, Petula had to laugh. It was true, with black mascara ringing her eyes, she did look funny. She rose to her feet, still giggling as she went to the bathroom, but the make-up was hard to get off, her eyes now stinging with soap.

At last, with the last vestiges of mascara removed, Petula was rubbing her face dry when she heard voices. She hung the towel on the rack, leaving the bathroom to find that Bob was home.

'Hello, Pet,' he said, but then frowned. 'Your eyes look red. Have you been crying?'

Pet felt a blush stain her cheeks and stuttered, 'No . . . no, of course not.'

'Are you sure you're all right?'

'Yes, I'm fine,' and grasping for a change of subject, she blurted, 'You're home early. I thought there was a meeting at the yard.'

'It was a short one.'

'What was it about?' she asked.

'It was nothing,' Bob said dismissively.

'You all had to be there, so it must have been something.'

'We're just thinking of expanding, that's all.'

Petula had no interest in the business, but her tactics had worked. Sue had now shoved the make-up back into the large satin bag, and thankfully Bob hadn't put two and two together. She loved all of her brothers, but they were overprotective, just like her father, and still treated her like a child. If any of the locals so much as gave her a funny look, they would rush to sort them out, so much so that over the years she had learned to keep her mouth shut. She thought that this would help her find friends, but it only made things worse and she was more avoided than ever.

The door flew open and Paul ran in, with Robby close behind. 'Dad,' he cried, throwing his arms around his father's leg, 'Robby kicked me.'

'Did he now?' said Bob, his eyes hardening as he looked at his elder son.

'Yes, and that's not all he's done,' Sue complained. 'He's been bloody murder all morning. First he nicked Paul's gobstopper and then when we went round to see Norma, he nearly killed Oliver's rabbit.'

'How did he do that?'

When Sue told him, Bob's face flushed with anger. 'You're old enough to know better, you little sod,' he said, raising his hand.

Petula said a hasty goodbye. Robby was going to be punished, and she didn't want to be around to witness the scene, even though he deserved it. 'I'll see you later,' she called, but had barely closed the door when she heard Robby's yelp of pain. With a wry expression she returned to number one, sure that the boy's backside would be sore for the rest of the day.

Petula found her mother still cleaning. The day stretched ahead, but worse was the thought of missing the dance at the youth club. Oh, she wanted to go, she really did, but not with one of her brothers turning up to escort her home. Her lips thinned, determined once again to have it out with her father when he came home.

Chapter Seven

Maurice walked home from the yard with Bob, the two of them discussing Danny's proposition. He was regretting his decision to go along with the plans, worried about the repercussions of treading on Garston's territory. As a child he had suffered from one illness after another, his school attendance patchy between bouts of asthma or conjunctivitis. When he'd been well enough to attend school, his brothers had protected him when there was any sign of trouble in the playground, encircling him and taking on anyone who wanted a fight.

He loved mathematics and had dreamed of becoming an accountant, but with so much time off school he had failed his exams. Things hadn't changed when he became an adult. His brothers still enjoyed a good fight but Maurice kept out of it, preferring to stay at home with his nose in books. He'd taken on the accounts for the family business and had once attended night school to gain qualifications, but his ambitions had been thwarted again when illness caused him to miss too many classes. Maurice pursed his lips. At least his role in the family business gave him a measure of respect with his brothers.

Maurice had stopped off at the newsagent's, and now paused before going into his house, hoping his wife was in a good mood. He was tired of Norma's nagging to leave Drapers Alley, unable to make her understand that without proper qualifications he would be hard-pressed to find a well-paid job. At the moment they enjoyed every comfort, and though the house was small, the council rent was low, enabling him to add regularly to their savings. One day he hoped to buy his own property, and to that end he had no intention of leaving the family firm. He just wished Norma would stop her constant carping. He knew she didn't get on with his mother, the old girl disgusted that Norma was already pregnant when they married. Yes, his mother was a prude, but if Norma tried harder, he was sure they could get on.

Maurice quietly opened the door. Unlike his brothers, he hadn't enjoyed much success with women and Norma had been only the second girl he'd taken out. At twenty, he'd still been a virgin, shocked and gratified when his fumbling attempts with Norma had been allowed to go all the way. Of course he hadn't been prepared, so Oliver had followed six months after their marriage, much to his mother's disgust. All right, Norma was older than he, but he didn't regret marrying her, and when he was up to it, they still had a good sex life – something he would rarely have enjoyed if he'd stayed single.

'Hello,' he said, walking to the kitchen, but one look at Norma's face made him wish he'd stayed out. 'What's up?'

'It's that bloody child next door. He threw Oliver's rabbit against the wall and it's a wonder he didn't kill it.'

'I suppose you mean Robby.'

'Of course I mean Robby. The boy's a menace, but Sue didn't even punish him.'

'Do you want me to have a word with Bob?'

Both then heard the sound of yelps through the thin adjoining wall and at last Norma smiled. 'Judging by that racket, I don't think it'll be necessary. If I'm not mistaken it sounds like the boy's getting a lathering.'

'Well, there you go then. Now, where's Oliver?'

'He's in the yard, no doubt checking on Shaker again. It really upset him, Maurice, and I'm just about sick of Robby's behaviour. Every time he shows his face there's trouble, but it got up Sue's nose when I told him off.'

'You can't blame her for that, love. It's up to her to sort Robby out – not you.'

Norma's eyes glinted with anger. 'So, you're taking

Sue's side as usual. Pretty Sue – sexy Sue. She's only got to bat her eyelashes and you go all aquiver.'

Experience had taught Maurice that there was only one way to deal with Norma when jealousy reared its head. He moved forward, pulling her into his arms. For a moment she was stiff, but as his lips kissed her neck, he felt the familiar tremble. 'There's only one woman who makes me go aquiver, love, and that's you,' he whispered. 'How about we pop upstairs?'

'Oh, Maurice, we can't. Oliver's only in the yard.'

'I'll just have to wait until tonight then,' he murmured, still nibbling at her neck. Norma might not be a beauty, but she didn't have a bad figure and he loved her long, auburn hair. A tent was forming in his trousers and, pressed against him, Norma could feel it, he was sure. 'See, it's you who turns me on,' he said huskily.

'Oh, get off me,' she complained, but Maurice could feel that the angry tension had left her body. Norma pushed him away, yet a small smile was now visible as she added, 'But as you say, there's always tonight. Now leave me in peace to get on with my housework.'

Maurice released her, and left the kitchen to take a seat in the living room. Taking up his newspaper, he scanned the pages. His imagination had been captured by a story that had appeared towards the end of April and he was hoping to read more about it. An American rocket had successfully reached the far side of the moon, but the mission to take television pictures of the lunar surface during the landing had been a washout when the internal power of the spacecraft failed. There was nothing further on the story and he felt a twinge of disappointment. The earlier rocket, launched in January, had missed the moon entirely, so surely actually reaching the moon's surface deserved a bit more coverage? What was the matter with journalists? Didn't they realise that one day this could lead to men actually walking on the moon? He shook his head in wonderment at the thought, his imagination fired up as he pondered what they'd find there.

'Hello, Dad.'

Maurice looked up from the newspaper. 'Hello, son. Is your rabbit all right?'

'Yes, but he seems a bit nervous.'

'After hitting a wall, I think that's to be expected.'

'I don't like Robby.'

As always when he looked at his son, Maurice felt a surge of pride. From the moment the boy had come into the world, he'd watched him like a hawk, fearing he'd pass his weaknesses to his son. Thankfully his fears proved unfounded. Oliver was sturdy, intelligent and a source of joy to both of his parents.

'Robby's your cousin – he's family. Though he's

a bit of a hooligan at the moment, I'm sure he'll grow out of it.'

Oliver didn't look convinced and, in truth, Maurice was doubtful too. Bob may have punished the boy, but nothing seemed to work. He knew his brother thought Oliver a sissy, a boy who wouldn't stand up for himself, but for Maurice it was a blessing. He wanted his son to grow up using his brains rather than his fists. He wanted him to make something of himself, and unlike him, to gain qualifications – something unheard of in the Draper family.

Maurice was glad that Oliver wasn't like Bob's elder son. Robby didn't take after Bob; in fact he was more like George, who had also enjoyed torturing animals as a child. Thankfully he had grown out of it, but a love of violence remained, and he got into a fight at every opportunity. The trouble was, George didn't know when to stop and Maurice feared that one day he'd kill someone. Oh, not with a weapon like Jack Garston. George didn't need that – not when he was capable of doing it with his fists and boots.

Unaware that his brother was thinking about him, George wasn't happy when he walked into a local pub for a lunchtime drink, and it showed, several customers looking at him warily. He'd agreed that he'd back Danny when the time came, but was now wondering if he'd been a bit hasty. It didn't pay to get into their father's bad books, but now that Danny had done just that, anything could happen. Bloody hell, when he retired the old man might even be so annoyed that he'd go over Danny's head, handing the running of the business over to Bob.

Danny had said he'd put his plans into action as soon as he took over, and would get rid of any brother who opposed them. Now, though, George was having doubts. The old man was no fool, and would probably put something in place to make sure it couldn't happen. Their father was a hard man, who always had to be in control. He ruled them with a rod of iron, yet he was fair, and George was sure that he'd take steps to ensure that the business remained a family concern when he stepped down. He might choose one of his sons to run the firm, but he would make sure that they all had equal shares.

Shit, George thought, his face blanching. All that could change if the old man found out about Danny's plans, *and* that he'd been daft enough to back them! Bloody hell, if that happened, they could both be out!

George ran a hand through his hair, grimacing. All this thinking was making his head hurt again. He scowled as he ordered a pint of beer and, obviously aware of his mood, the barman waived payment, sliding the glass nervously across the bar.

George drank deeply, afterwards wiping the back of his hand across his mouth as his eyes roamed the bar. Cigarette smoke hung in the air like fog, and on one table a game of dominoes was in progress. Not one person would give him eye contact and George's tension eased. Yeah, they knew who he was – knew he was a Draper and feared him, something he loved.

At the far end of the room he saw a couple of blokes playing darts so, hoping to put his thoughts about Danny and the business to one side, he walked up to the players. 'I'll give you a game.'

'You'll have to wait,' one of the men said. 'We ain't finished this match yet.'

George's eyes narrowed. He didn't recognise the bloke, but the other's face was familiar. It was Bernie Jackson and his fear was plain to see as he spoke to his mate.

'No, Vince, it's all right,' Bernie said. 'If George wants a game, that's fine. We'll start again.'

'You heard the man,' George snapped, and without further ado he walked up to the scoreboard, erasing the chalked running totals with a cloth.

'Oi! Fuck off! I said we ain't finished our game yet.'

George spun round to see Bernie Jackson grabbing his mate's arm, his voice a hiss of caution. 'Leave it, Vince. Don't you know who he is?'

'I don't give a shit if he's the Pope. He ain't got the right to muscle in on our game.'

This was all the excuse George needed for a fight and a surge of excitement blazed in his eyes. In two strides he was in Vince's face, fists pummelling his nose. Blood spurted everywhere and George loved it, the sight of it – the smell of it. He moved in again, fists raised.

'That's enough, George!'

George spun round to see the publican, Charlie Parkinson. The man was an ex-heavyweight boxer, well past his prime now, but George felt a measure of respect for the man. He was also a friend of his father's, and as George's eyes briefly flicked towards his prey again, he saw that Vince was trembling with fear.

'Huh, he ain't worth the bother. He's just a piece of shit.'

Charlie beckoned Bernie Jackson over, his voice quiet but firm. 'Get your mate out of here, and tell him to keep his mouth shut. Nobody touched him. He just walked into a door. Is that clear?'

'Yeah, as a bell,' Bernie said, then turning to George with a sheepish expression, 'Sorry, mate.'

George just nodded, ignoring Bernie as he urged Vince out of the pub. He snatched up his pint again, peeved that the fight had ended before he'd had time to vent his feelings. The pressure was still there – the feeling that his head was going to burst.

'How's your dad, George? I ain't seen him in a while.'

'He's fine. At Sandown races today and no doubt picking out a few nags to have a bet on.'

'And your mum?'

'She's good too.'

Charlie moved off to serve another customer whilst George leaned on the bar, staring into his pint. It was strange really, but after a fight he always felt randy, and though he'd only landed a few punches, he decided to go home. Linda was sure to be all right now, ready for him to give her a seeing-to. He may have missed out on turning that bastard into mincemeat, but a bit of sex was another way to let off steam.

He swallowed the pint then slammed the glass down as he called, 'See yer, Charlie.'

'Yeah, see you,' Charlie called back, and had George looked over his shoulder as he left the pub, he would have seen the look of relief on the land-lord's face.

Linda's mother smiled with delight as she opened the door. 'Hello, ducks.'

'Hello, Mum, how are you feeling?'

'I'm all right,' Enid Simpson replied. 'The warmer weather makes all the difference.'

Linda followed her mother to the kitchen, the lie evident as her mother hobbled in obvious pain to the nearest chair.

'Is your hip playing you up again?'

Enid dismissed the question. 'Sod my hip. How are you? Have you still got morning sickness?'

'Yeah, but I'm not feeling too bad at the moment.'

'You look tired, love. How is George treating you?'

Linda would have loved to blurt it all out – to tell her mother that she was frightened of her husband – that she feared his fists. Instead she lowered her eyes, knowing that there was no way she could worry her mother. Arthritis riddled Enid's body, her face lined with the daily grind of pain, but she never complained and Linda loved her deeply. She forced a smile. 'George treats me like a princess,' she lied, 'and he's dead chuffed about the baby.'

'Are you telling me the truth, Linda? When you come to see us you're always on your own and your dad was saying the same thing only the other day. We'd visit you, but to be honest, on the one occasion we called, George didn't seem pleased to see us.'

Linda fought for an excuse. 'George is busy, Mum. He works long hours and when he comes home he's worn out. You caught him at a bad time, that's all.'

'He must get some time off. It's Sunday tomorrow. Why don't you both come to us for dinner? Or we could come to you.'

Linda tensed, her thoughts racing. 'It's not a good time at the moment, Mum,' she lied. 'George is doing things around the house and we're all upside down. It's not that he doesn't want to visit you, it's just that he's too busy. He's the same with his mother. They live in the same street but he rarely bothers to pop in to see her.'

Enid acknowledged this with a nod of her head. 'Yeah, when I come to think of it, your father was the same. When my mother was alive I had to practically drag him to see her, and I could see that the whole time he was itching to leave.'

'Would you like me to make a cup of tea, Mum?' Linda asked, anxious to change the subject.

'That'd be nice, love. Your father should be home soon. He'll be pleased to see you.'

Linda was relieved when the conversation turned to the baby, her mother obviously delighted at the prospect of being a grandmother.

'I hope it's a boy,' she said.

'I don't mind what I have, as long as it's all right.'

'Is George's mum pleased about the baby?'

'Well, yes, I think so, but she hasn't said much. In fact, I hardly see her. Dan calls her Queen, and though it's a daft title, she does seem sort of distant and unapproachable.'

'What about your sisters-in-law? How do you get on with them?'

'I don't see much of them either. Yvonne seems a bit stuck-up, and so does Norma. Sue's all right, but to be honest, I prefer Ivy.'

'Ivy! Is she the niece? The one who looks as strong as an ox, with a face to match?'

'Oh, Mum, don't be cruel. I know she isn't much to look at, and the rest of the family don't seem to think much of her, but I think she's kind.'

'Yeah, sorry, love, it just sort of slipped out and as the saying goes, you can't judge a book by its cover. Anyway, back to your mother-in-law, and I'm sure she's nice too. You just need to get to know her, though I must admit she hardly said a word at your wedding. Still, unlike me, this isn't her first grandchild so I don't suppose she's as excited. I just wish my fingers would let me do some knitting, but I can't grip the needles. I made everything for you when you were a baby, and you should have seen the lovely shawl I crocheted . . .'

Enid rambled on, but Linda had heard it all before so hardly listened. As an only child she'd been spoiled, and hadn't appreciated how much love her parents showered on her until she'd left home at twenty to marry George. Before then she had found their love cloying, their expectations of her future restrictive. They had always shown great interest in her boyfriends, wanting her to marry one with prospects and insisting that she invited them home for inspection. Linda smiled ruefully. One boy, a bank clerk, particularly found favour, but he was weak, boring, and she'd resented the way her parents tried to push her into his arms. She had rebelled, breaking up with him to go out with George. Her parents had been horrified, but she wouldn't listen.

George was so different – rough, handsome, and exciting. He hadn't been soft like her other boyfriends, and when he held her in his arms his strength had made her shiver with delight. She had fallen in love with him – still loved him – but now, along with love, there was this awful fear.

'Hello, sweetheart.'

Linda spun round, her eyes lighting up. She ran across the room, throwing herself into her father's arms. She loved her mum, but it was her father who always showed affection, her mother more reticent.

'And how's my girl?' Ron Simpson asked.

'I'm fine, Dad.'

He was a small man, only an inch taller than his wife, their bodies equally thin. His light brown hair was thinning too, but his brown eyes twinkled as he stepped back to look his daughter up and down. 'I can't see any sign of a bump yet.'

'Give it a chance, Dad. I'm only three months gone.'

'Only six to go then,' he said. 'I hope you give me a grandson.'

'You're as bad as Mum,' Linda told him. 'What happens if it's a girl? Are you going to reject a grand-daughter?'

'No chance,' he said.

'Did you get it, Ron?' Enid asked.

'Yes, I did. It's in the hall.'

'I hope you got the right one.'

'Of course I did, woman.'

Enid struggled to her feet, beckoning Linda to follow her. 'We were hoping you'd be down to see us today, and it's just as well. There isn't much room in the hall so you'll need to take it home with you.'

Puzzled now, Linda walked behind her mother, her eyes rounding like saucers when she saw the shiny new carriage pram. The navy-blue, highly polished exterior gleamed, as did the chrome wheels.

'Oh, Mum,' she gasped.

'Now don't get all emotional. It isn't good for the baby,' Enid warned.

'But it must have cost the earth!'

'We want the best for our first grandchild, and other than you, who else have we got to spend our money on?'

'Yourselves,' Linda protested. 'You could have had a holiday with the money you spent on this pram.'

'I can't travel far, love, you know that. Now come on, don't cry. We thought you'd be thrilled to bits.'

'Oh, I am, Mum, I really am,' Linda choked as she dashed the tears from her eyes, 'but you paid out a lot of money for the wedding – and now this!'

'Huh, Dan Draper hardly let us put our hands into our pockets. All we paid for was your wedding dress and the flowers. Your father wasn't happy about it, I can tell you, but Dan Draper had to act the big man.'

'What's up? Don't you like it, sweetheart?' Ron Simpson asked as he joined them in the small hall.

'Of course I do. It's lovely,' Linda cried, her emotions all over the place. Her father's job as a bus conductor didn't pay a fortune and she knew the cost of this gift would have been overwhelming.

'That's all right then,' he said with a wink and a loving smile, 'but haven't you just made a pot of tea? One that's growing cold?'

'Oh, Dad . . .'

They returned to the kitchen where Linda got her feelings under control as she poured the tea. George might return that afternoon so she'd have to go soon, but was suddenly swamped with dread at the thought of leaving her parents' house. Here she was loved and felt safe. All the doubts about her marriage that she'd tried to quell forced themselves to the front of her mind. She was afraid to go home! Oh God, please let George be in a good mood.

Chapter Eight

When George left the pub at two thirty, he arrived home aroused and ready to take Linda upstairs. His brows creased. Where the hell was she?

'Linda!' he yelled.

There was no reply. Swiftly he ran upstairs to the bedroom, but finding it empty his mellow mood began to melt. It didn't take him long to look around the rest of the small house, then he strode next door to rap loudly on Ivy's knocker.

'Is Linda here?' he snapped.

'No, but she was around earlier,' Steve told him.

'Who is it?' Ivy shouted from inside.

'It's George. He's looking for Linda.'

There was a small pause before Ivy's voice rang out again: 'Try your mum's.'

George didn't bother to say goodbye, just turning on his heels to head for number one. He didn't bother to knock and walked in to find his mother on her knees washing the skirting boards.

'Have you seen Linda?' he asked.

Joan pushed herself up, giving him a look that George couldn't fathom. 'I haven't seen the girl, but from what Ivy tells me, your wife isn't too well. Not only that—'

'She's got a bit of morning sickness, that's all,' George interrupted.

As Petula came running downstairs, George asked, 'Have *you* seen Linda?'

'No, sorry.'

George saw Linda walking past the window and swiftly threw open the front door.

'Oi, you! Where have you been?' he shouted.

Linda halted in her tracks, her knuckles white as she gripped the handle of a huge carriage pram.

George moved forward, his eyes narrowed. 'What the bloody hell have you got there?'

Still Linda didn't speak and to George's annoyance his sister joined them.

'Oh, isn't it lovely?' Petula said when she saw the pram.

At last Linda spoke, her voice quivering. 'It . . . it's a present from my mum and dad.'

George's fists clenched. So, she'd been to see her parents, sneaking off without telling him. He couldn't stand Ron and Enid Simpson, the pair of them interfering old busybodies who had made it obvious from the start that they didn't think him good enough for their precious daughter. He'd been determined that once they married he'd make them pay, keeping Linda away from them as much as possible. Now, though, the cow had gone behind his back to pay them a visit.

He eyed the pram, seething. They must think he couldn't provide for Linda, or the coming child. To George it was like a slap in the face, his voice a growl as he said, 'That bloody thing will take up half the house. It's got to go.'

'Oh, no, don't say that,' Linda cried. 'We can keep it in the yard.'

'I said it's got to go!'

'Don't be silly, George,' said Pet. 'I know it's big, but you'll need a pram.'

'Who asked you?' George snapped and turning to Linda again he pointed towards their house. 'Home – now!'

He saw the frightened look that Linda shot towards Petula, but at least she obeyed him, pushing the pram to number five.

As soon as they went indoors, with Linda struggling to manoeuvre the pram through the house to the back yard, George's temper was let loose. He ran ahead of her into the kitchen, opening a drawer to grab the carving knife.

'I told you we don't want the fucking thing,' he yelled as, knife raised, he grabbed the pram, pushing Linda to one side as he sliced at the upholstery, the blade cutting through the material like butter.

Linda's scream was shrill, but George ignored her, the plush grey interior now in ribbons as he continued to slash again and again with the knife.

Pet stood on the pavement, watching George and Linda as they went inside number five. Linda had looked petrified, but surely George wouldn't hurt his wife? Involuntarily she began to walk towards their house, almost at the door when she heard the scream.

For a fraction of a second Pet froze, but then without thought she dashed inside, her eyes widening with horror. 'George! George, stop it! What are you doing? Stop it!'

He turned, the knife raised, and Pet blanched at the manic look on his face. Linda was white-faced too, rooted to the spot, but Pet knew they had to get out of there. She ran forward to grab Linda's arm.

'Come on,' she urged, dragging her outside.

In a few steps they were at Maurice's house. Pet thrust the door open, pushing Linda inside. 'Maurice! Maurice! George has lost it.'

'Yeah, I heard the racket.'

Linda swayed and it was Norma who took over, leading her to a chair. She then ran to fetch a glass of water, urging, 'Here, drink this.'

'What set George off?' Maurice asked as he watched his wife attending to Linda.

'Linda's parents have given her a lovely pram, but for some reason it upset George. I went into their place to find him shredding the inside of it with a knife. We've got to stop him, Maurice.'

Maurice shook his head, his breathing beginning to sound laboured. 'When George is in one of his moods, it's best to leave him to it.'

'But the pram!'

'It's too late to stop him now.'

'Are you all right, Maurice?' Norma asked. 'You're not having another asthma attack, are you?'

Petula had run to the nearest door, but now realised that Maurice would be the last one to intervene. Her father and Danny were out, and that only left Bob, but he wouldn't want to interfere either.

'Pet, take Linda down to your mother's,' Norma ordered. 'George wouldn't dare kick off there.'

Pet could see that Maurice was now gasping for air, but Linda looked awful too, her face deadly white.

'All right, we'll go,' Pet agreed, 'but I'll have to make sure we're in the clear first.'

'Listen, love, I don't want you hurt,' Maurice gasped, 'so be careful.'

Pet gingerly opened the door, stuck her head outside and then beckoned Linda. 'Come on, there's no sign of George.'

Linda looked terrified but rose to her feet. Taking her hand, both of them ran to number one.

Only moments later there was a knock on Maurice's door and he gasped with fear, but it was Bob who walked in.

'I've just seen Pet and Linda dashing past. What's going on?' he asked.

'George is kicking off,' Norma told him. 'Pet brought Linda in here but I told her to take the girl to her own house.'

'Is Pet all right?'

'Yes, but she's frightened of George and I don't blame her.'

'What set him off?'

Norma told him, ending with, 'Your brother's a bloody menace. Linda looked terrified . . . Pet too, and look at Maurice.'

'Not another asthma attack! Come on, Maurice, there's no need to get in a state. You know George. He'll be all right once he's gone off the boil.'

Maurice could only nod, whilst Norma bristled with anger. 'I've had just about enough for one day so he'd better not come knocking on our door. Oh, yes, Bob. Talking of menaces, I suppose Sue told you what Robby did to Oliver's rabbit?'

'Yes, she did, and I've given the boy a thrashing.'

'I'm glad to hear it, but as I've said before, Robby's getting out of hand.'

'Look, I know he's a little sod, but he's had a good hiding. If that doesn't do the trick, I'll come down even harder.'

'It'll need both of you to sort the boy out, but *she* lets him get away with murder.'

'Yeah, I know Sue can be a bit soft. I'll have a word – tell her that Robby needs a firmer hand.'

'Good, I'm glad to hear it,' Norma said, at last looking mollified.

'Norma, can I have a drink, please?' Maurice managed to gasp.

'Yes, all right.'

'Make one for Bob too,' Maurice wheezed, hoping that Bob wouldn't turn it down. He wanted him to stay for a while – wanted him there in case George turned up.

Joan looked up from her task as Petula and Linda almost fell into her living room.

'What's going on?' she snapped.

'It's George. He's gone mad. We ran to Maurice first, but he got upset so Norma told us to come here.'

'Gone mad! What are you talking about?'

'Linda's parents have given them a pram, but George is wrecking it.'

'Is he? Why's he doing that?'

'I don't know, Mum.'

Linda's face was wan, her body shaking. Joan asked sharply, 'Did my son hit you?'

'No . . . not this time.'

'Does that mean he's hit you in the past?'

'Yes,' she whispered, tears spurting and running down her cheeks.

Joan was ashamed of her son, sickened. Linda was pregnant and if George wasn't stopped she could lose the baby. It could be some time before Dan returned from the races, but she had to get Linda out of sight in case George came looking for her.

'It might be best if you stay out of the way for a while. You look exhausted, so why don't you go up to my room, have a lie-down? And don't worry, Dan will sort George out when he comes home.'

Linda's eyes flicked nervously to the window. 'Yes, all right,' she agreed.

Joan waited until she was out of sight before turning to Petula. 'Run next door, see if Danny's home, and if he is, tell him I want to see him. Just make sure that you stay out of George's way.'

Petula nodded, and as the girl ran outside, Joan hoped her eldest son was there. If George hadn't calmed down when he came looking for Linda, she doubted she'd be able to handle him.

Petula's mind was racing. George's behaviour had shocked her. She knew he had a temper, but had never actually witnessed his violence. When George lived at home his anger had been verbal, soon snuffed out by her father. Now, though, she was seeing another side of him, and it was one she feared. Was this how other people saw him?

Was this how he behaved outside of the alley? If so it could be another reason why they were shunned.

As a child Pet could remember the police turning up at the house, but her father and brothers had always explained it away by telling her that they had made a mistake. None of the family had ever been arrested, so she believed them, at least whilst she was at junior school. Doubts set in when she went to secondary school where some girls avoided her, making their reasons clear. When she'd asked questions, Maurice had been the only one who'd been a little more forthcoming, telling her that all the gossip concerned shady deals in the past. Nowadays, he had said, the family ran a respectable business and she had nothing to worry about.

Yet stories still reached her ears – whispers of her family being involved in fights and intimidation. She loved her father, her brothers, and didn't want to believe the gossip, but friendships had been hard to form. Over time there were three girls she considered friends, yet even so she was always the odd one out – the one who didn't enjoy the same freedom as them.

Yvonne's door was unlocked, like the others in the alley, but Pet rapped the letter box before going inside. 'Yvonne, is Danny home?'

'No, he isn't.' Yvonne looked at Pet's anxious face. 'What's wrong?'

'It's George. I'm surprised you haven't heard the racket.'

'I've been turning out the back bedroom so I didn't hear a thing. What's he been up to?'

Pet told her, then added, 'I think Mum's nervous that George will come looking for Linda.'

'I'll come back with you.'

Pet paled as they stepped outside to see George marching towards them. She gripped Yvonne's arm, her heart thumping with fear.

'Is Linda with Mum?' he snapped.

'Er . . . yes, but she isn't feeling well and went to lie down. She's asleep now, but when she wakes up, I'm sure she'll come home.'

'She'd better,' George warned, 'and you can tell her that from me.' With that he brushed past them, ignoring number one to march out of the alley.

'Thank God for that,' Yvonne said.

Pet told her mother what had happened, seeing her own relief reflected on her mother's face.

Joan sank onto a chair, shaking her head as she said, 'It ain't right, Yvonne. I shouldn't be nervous of my own son. Dan will have to sort him out. Ivy told me that he's been hitting Linda, but I didn't believe her. I've heard it from the horse's mouth now, though.'

'Dad has always told the boys that men who hit women are the lowest of the low. When he finds out about George, he'll go mad,' Pet warned.

She saw the women exchange looks, and then her mother said, 'You shouldn't be hearing this, Petula. Go to your room.'

'I'm not a child!'

'You're not an adult either. Now do as I say.'

Pet flung herself out, marched upstairs, and only just resisted the urge to slam her bedroom door. She sat on the edge of her bed, but only a moment later the door opened, Linda coming into the room.

'Oh, Petula,' she cried, moving to sit beside her. 'I . . . I want my mum.'

As Linda sobbed, Petula wrapped an arm around her and, despite what her mother had said, it was she who felt like the adult as she held this frightened young woman in her arms.

Chapter Nine

It was six o'clock and Dan wasn't in the best of moods as he made his way home. Not one of the horses he'd placed a bet on had come in, and he was considerably out of pocket. He had hoped to forget about Danny at Sandown, but he continued to intrude on his thoughts. He still couldn't believe that his son had suggested using kids. He was shocked to the core, and it hadn't helped when George seemed to go along with the idea.

Dan thought he knew his sons inside out – thought he had the business sorted and the future sewn up. When he retired, he'd planned for Danny to take over, but now he'd seen a side of his son that he didn't like and would have to have a rethink.

One by one Dan brought the boys to the front of his mind, starting with the youngest. Chris was a good boy with a keen brain. He had potential, and was able to hold his own in a fight, yet he didn't look for trouble. Yes, a good boy, but too young and, as yet, unsettled.

Next came George, and now Dan scowled. As a father, he knew he should love his sons equally, but with George he found that impossible. From the day the boy had been born Dan had sensed something bad in him. Not only did George lack intelligence, he also had a love of violence, wanting to provoke fights at every opportunity. He'd been forced to come down harder on George than any of the others – but maybe he'd calm down now that he was married and about to be a father. Dan nodded; marriage would be a stabilising influence. George was taking care of his wife, obviously worried about the morning sickness, and it was good to see that he had a softer side. There was still the problem of his intelligence, though, and worse, his lack of morals, making George totally unsuitable to run the business.

Dismissing George from his mind, Dan focused on Maurice. This son was definitely the brains of the family. He was capable of running things on the financial side, but he was weak, often ill, and hopeless when there were any signs of trouble from competitors. There had to be strong leadership and therefore he'd have to dismiss Maurice.

Bob seemed the obvious choice. He was the second eldest and next in line to Danny, but Dan had to dismiss him as successor too. Bob had none of the business acumen needed to run things. He could take orders, yet was incapable of giving them. Like Maurice, he'd be unable to keep the rest of his brothers in line.

Dan's problem was still unresolved as he drove into his garage, and his foul mood worsened when Joan pounced on him as soon as he walked in the door.

'Thank God you're home,' she cried. 'I've been dreading George showing his face before you got here.'

'What are you on about, woman?'

'Linda's upstairs and too frightened to go home. I don't blame the girl, not after what George has been up to . . .'

Dan's face darkened as Joan continued, her hands wringing with nerves. When she finally stopped gabbling, he snapped, 'Why didn't Danny sort him out?'

'I sent Petula to get him but he wasn't in.'

'And Chris?'

'I don't know where he is.'

'What about Bob and Maurice?'

'They didn't show their faces. When George kicked off, Pet dragged Linda into Maurice's house, but Norma sent them here. That's not all. Ivy came to see me this morning and she seemed to gain great pleasure from telling me that George has been hitting Linda. I didn't believe her, but Linda told me it's true.'

'He's what?' Dan thundered. He had no idea why George had shredded the interior of a brand-new pram, but that was nothing compared to laying into his pregnant wife. By God, he wasn't going to stand for that! 'Where's Petula?'

'I sent her upstairs to look in on Linda. The poor girl cried herself to sleep in Pet's arms.'

'Hello, Dad,' said Pet, her expression grim as she came into the room. 'Linda's still asleep, Mum, but I doubt she'll want to go home when she wakes up.'

'She'll have nothing to worry about once I've had a word with George,' Dan assured his wife and daughter.

'Oh, Dad, she was scared stiff. So was I. George was like a madman. He was using a knife on the pram and I was terrified he'd turn it on us.'

At his daughter's words, Dan's anger reached boiling point. He had always protected Pet, making sure that the alley was a safe haven, not just for her, but for all the family. Over the years he and the boys had made it plain that the alley was their domain, using fear and fists if necessary. It had worked and now, apart from Betty Fuller, only the police dared to enter without permission.

Dan's fists clenched. Pet had now been exposed to violence – not from an outsider, but from her own brother. Dan knew George had a temper, and struggled to keep it under control, but now his violence had overspilled into the alley. So much for

125

marriage having a stabilising effect. Instead, with George no longer under his roof, the reverse had happened.

Through clenched teeth he hissed, 'I'll see if he's turned up yet.'

'Dan, your dinner's ready,' Joan called.

'Sod me fucking dinner,' he growled, slamming out of the house and striding to George's door. He found it locked, and hammered the wood with his fists, yelling, 'Open this bloody door!'

'He ain't in, Dad.'

Panting, Dan looked round to see Maurice, then another door opened and Bob appeared. Dan's lips curled in disgust as his sons walked to his side. 'Your sister was terrified and your mother's been going out of her mind with worry. Why didn't you two sort George out?'

Maurice said, 'Leave it out, Dad. You know what George is like when he loses it.'

'You pair of useless tarts! Rather than step in, you left Pet and your mother to face George.'

'No, Dad,' Bob protested, 'I'd have done something if he started on them, but he didn't. He left the alley, and between us we've been keeping an eye out in case he showed up again.'

Dan glared at Maurice. 'According to your mother, Pet brought Linda here, yet Norma couldn't get rid of them fast enough.'

'You can't blame Norma for that. She could see

I was having trouble breathing, and not only that, there's our kid to think about. You know as well as I do what George is capable of when he loses his rag. Do you really think I could have stopped him?'

Dad eyed his son, noting his narrow chest and arms that were a fraction of George's size. 'No, I don't suppose you could have done much,' he admitted. Maurice was a weakling, but there was no excuse for Bob. 'What about you, Bob? Where were you when all this was going on?'

'I was gonna do something, but George buggered off before I got the chance.'

Dan could see the shifty look in his son's eyes and wasn't fooled. If there was a fight Bob would wade in, but only if he had backup, and he always made sure that Danny or George had the front row. 'You could have gone to see if your mother needed any help.'

'When George went off I assumed she was all right.'

'How can she be all right when she's got a maniac for a son? Did the pair of you know that George has been hitting his wife?'

'What!' Bob spluttered. 'No, it's the first I've heard of it.'

'What about you, Maurice? You live next door and must have twigged something.'

'I've heard George yelling, but that's all. I can't believe he'd hit Linda. Are you sure you've got it right, Dad?'

'Yes, I'm sure,' Dan growled. 'Ivy told your mother before all this kicked off and now it's been confirmed by Linda.' He raised a hand to rake his fingers through his hair. Ivy should have come to him instead of upsetting Joan, and the girl knew that. He had hoped that by bringing her to Drapers Alley he could assuage his guilt – that he'd finally be able to let go of the past. But no, it still plagued him. 'Keep an eye out for George,' he told his sons, 'while I go and have a word with Ivy.'

Ivy opened the door to her Uncle Dan and stood to one side to let him in. She had watched the shenanigans in the alley with pleasure, only disappointed when George had stormed off and hadn't come back. Steve had wanted to see if her Auntie Joan was all right, but she had prevented him from going to number one, telling her daft husband that it was for George's brothers to sort out.

Uncle Dan looked upset, and that pleased her. 'You missed out on all the fun, Uncle Dan.'

'Fun! I'd hardly call it that,' he said, his expression hardening. 'I've told you this before, but you haven't listened. You know how bad your aunt's nerves are and that I don't want her worried. Instead of telling her about George, why didn't you come to me?'

'You weren't around and I was more concerned about Linda and the state she was in,' Ivy lied. She then took the opportunity to bait her uncle. 'You should give Auntie Joan a bit more credit. She's stronger than you realise, in fact much stronger than my mother ever was. I know you keep Auntie Joan in the dark about certain things. Did you do the same with my mother?'

He paled, but recovered quickly. 'Of course not. I never had reason to keep anything from your mother.'

'Really?' she drawled. 'Well, my mistake then.' Ivy smiled thinly; sure she could see guilt written all over her uncle's features. Oh, he had kept a big thing from her mother, she was sure of it, and once again she was determined that one day she'd make him pay.

'Yes, well, despite what you think, your aunt isn't strong. As I've said before, I don't want her worried. In future, bring any concerns you have to me.'

Ivy bit her bottom lip, annoyed at her uncle's sharp tone. Her mother hadn't had the privilege of being free from worry, and despite Dan's so-called help, life had still been a struggle. They lived in poverty, while her uncle rose in power, opening a business to make even more money. She wanted to face him with it, but knew it would be a waste of time. He would deny it and she had no proof.

Taking a deep breath to stay calm she said, 'I hope you're going to sort George out.'

'Oh, I will. You can be sure of that.'

When her uncle left, Ivy closed the door. She wanted to see him unhappy – in fact she wanted to see all of the Drapers in misery – just as her mother had been before she died.

Dan marched back to number one, his guts churning. Sometimes he felt that Ivy knew something, but surely it wasn't possible? She'd been just a kid when his brother had been called up.

'Was he in?' Joan asked as he walked inside.

Dan saw Pet sitting at the table and just shook his head. Ivy's snide remarks had added fuel to the flames of his anger. He just wanted George to show his face so he could vent his feelings and as he began to pace the room his eyes returned again and again to the window as he kept a lookout for his son.

'Dan, you've got to calm down,' Joan said, moving to stand in front of him.

'Calm down! I'll fucking kill him,' he yelled, shoving his wife to one side.

As she staggered back, Joan's hip hit the side of the table and she yelped with pain but Dan was unaware of it as he continued to pace. He was also unaware that his daughter had fled upstairs.

Joan moved to stand in front of him again, laying a hand on his arm. 'Dan!' she begged. 'Dan, listen to me. Petula has seen enough for one day without you kicking off too. She saw you shove me and it frightened her. Now she's run upstairs.'

He stared down at his diminutive wife, her voice

130

penetrating his anger. 'Sorry, Queen. I didn't mean to push you so hard.'

'Yeah, I know that, but I dread to think what will happen if you confront George while you're in this mood.'

Dan knew that Joan was right. Pet had seen enough, yet when George turned up he'd have to sort him out and he doubted he'd be able to control his temper. Thoughts churning, Dan finally came up with a solution. 'Pet, come down here,' he called.

When Pet came downstairs, Dan saw that Linda was behind her. His temper almost overspilled again when he saw how frail his daughter-in-law looked and he had to fight to hide his feeling when he spoke to her. 'How are you, love?'

'I . . . I feel a bit better,' she said.

'Come and sit down, all of you,' Joan urged, and after going into the kitchen, she returned with plates of sausages, onion and mash. Dan was given his first, followed by Linda, Joan saying, 'You've got to eat, love. You're having a baby and need to keep your strength up.'

Dan saw how Linda's eyes flicked nervously to the door. He sat down, leaned across the table and laid his hand over hers. 'Don't worry. Leave George to me. I'll make sure he never touches you again.'

She looked back at him, her face devoid of colour. 'I . . . I'm not going back. I'd rather go to my mum's.'

'Oh, Linda, there's no need for that,' Joan said.

Linda's eyes filled with tears, her voice a wail. 'I want my mum.'

'All right, don't cry,' Dan placated. 'Eat your dinner and then I'll run you to your mother's house.'

'George won't be happy if he comes back to find her gone,' Joan warned as she gave Petula her dinner.

'I don't give a shit how George feels. Anyway, it's best that Linda is out of the way until I sort him out.'

He then turned to Pet, seeing that she was picking at her food too. Forcing a soft tone, Dan put his idea into action. 'Pet, didn't you say you wanted to go to the youth club tonight?'

'Yes, but it doesn't matter now.'

'Don't be daft. When you've finished your dinner, get yourself ready. I can drop you off at the club when I take Linda to her mother's.'

'No, it's all right, I don't want to go.'

'Why not?'

'I don't feel like it, and anyway, the other girls will laugh at me when one of my brothers turns up to escort me home.'

As planned, Dan said, 'All right, you can walk yourself home, but make sure you're in by ten fifteen.'

Pet's eyes widened. Dan knew he shouldn't lie to her, but like Linda, he wanted her well out of earshot when he confronted George. They wouldn't pick Pet up, but just to be on the safe side, she'd be followed home. If Chris showed his face, he'd assign that task to him.

Still Pet hesitated, but Dan urged, 'Come on, eat up, and then get your glad rags on.'

With a nod, Pet ate a little of her dinner. She then pushed her plate to one side before heading for her bedroom whilst Dan turned his attention back to Linda. With her face pale, hands shaking as she half-heartedly forked up a bit of mashed potato, she looked not much older than Pet. His son had a lot to answer for, and if he lost Linda it would be no more than he deserved. Her frailty so touched him that Dan wanted nothing more than to wring George's neck.

Only moments later the door was flung open. Linda gasped in fear, but it was Chris who walked in.

'Where the hell have you been?' Dan snapped.

'I went to Oxford Street to have a look around the shops, and then I had a drink with a mate.'

'You were needed here!'

'Why? What's going on?'

'George needs sorting out,' Dan said, and went on to tell Chris all that had happened.

'Bloody hell,' Chris gasped as his eyes flew to Linda. 'Are you all right?'

'No she bloody well isn't,' Dan growled.

Chris took a seat, picking up his cutlery as his mother laid a plate of food in front of him. 'Where's George now?'

'I dunno, but I'm taking Linda to her mother's. I'll be dropping Pet off at the youth club too.' Dan lowered his voice. 'I want you there when she comes out at around ten, but keep out of sight. I've told her that she can walk home on her own, so just trail her to make sure she's all right.'

'I can't. I've got a date tonight.'

'You'll do as I say.'

'Shit, Dad, can't you ask one of the others to meet Pet?'

'Oi, watch your language. There's ladies present.'

'Sorry, Mum – sorry, Linda.'

'Your father's one to talk. He hasn't stopped swearing since he walked in the door.'

Annoyed at the comment, Dan shot Joan a look, but she ignored him, turning on her heels to walk back into the kitchen. He frowned, wondering what had come over his wife, but then Chris spoke again.

'Dad, this is a first date – I'll look a right mug if I insist on dropping her home before ten.'

Dan pursed his lips, then after a small pause he said, 'Yeah, all right. I'll get Maurice or Bob to meet Pet, but stay in until I get back. George might turn up and I don't want your mother facing him on her own.'

Chris nodded, biting into a sausage with relish. 'I've arranged to meet Julie at eight. You're sure to be back before that.'

'Yeah, I will, and God help your brother when he decides to show his face.'

Chapter Ten

Pet stepped into her bedroom and closed the door. She felt that she was seeing her family for the first time, that a veil had been lifted from her eyes. Her brother George had terrified her, but she'd seen the madness in her father's eyes too. He had shoved her mother and she'd gone careering into the table, but he hadn't even noticed. If he'd been like that with her mother, she dreaded her father's reaction when George turned up. George deserved a telling-off – and more – but just how far would her father go?

What neither of her parents realised was that Linda had no intention of ever going back to George. Linda had confided in her before falling asleep on her bed, saying that she was now so frightened of George that she not only feared for herself, she feared for her unborn baby. Pet chewed her lower lip and wondered what to do. If she told her parents it would cause more friction, so maybe for the time being she should keep it to herself.

Pet moved to her wardrobe and took out a flared skirt and white blouse. The skirt looked all right, but the blouse, with its Peter Pan collar, looked prissy to her. At first she'd been surprised when her father suggested the dance, and even more so when he said she could walk home alone, but had soon realised why. He wanted her out of the way – making her even more frightened of what he'd do to George.

In any other circumstances she'd have been thrilled that for the first time she wasn't being escorted home like a kid, but her mood was low and she didn't feel a bit like dancing. Still, she decided, it would be better to go to the youth club than to be around when George faced the music.

Pet dressed, then studied her face in the mirror. She knew there wasn't a chance in hell that she'd be able to get out of the house wearing make-up, so she took a handbag that Sue had passed on to her and stuffed the lipstick inside, adding a block of mascara and blue eye shadow, which she had bought with her pocket money but never used. Until now, she thought, hoping she'd be able to apply the mascara without sticking the brush in her eye this time. Shoes were a problem. She only had pumps, whereas her friends would be wearing heels and she'd look childish beside them. With a sigh Pet brushed her hair, wishing she could style it like Sue's, but once again, her father would have a fit.

'You look nice,' Chris said approvingly as Pet went back downstairs.

'Yeah, you're as pretty as a picture,' Dan agreed.

Pet could see the tension in her father's face and wasn't fooled. He was hiding his anger – putting on a front – not just for her, but for Linda too. But it had worked. Linda was now calm and her face dry of tears.

'I'm ready, Dad,' she said as though wanting to be away before George appeared. She rose to her feet and, after saying a swift goodbye, they left the house, Linda looking fearfully behind her as they headed for the lockup.

'There's no need to be nervous,' Dan said, taking hold of her arm. 'George won't touch you again.'

Linda didn't reply and was visibly relieved when she had climbed into the back of the car. Pet sat next to her father, wondering if Linda would tell him that she wasn't coming back, but the girl said nothing during the journey.

They were soon at the youth club. Pet turned in her seat to look at Linda. 'Bye, and take care,' she said, feeling that her words were inadequate.

'Bye, Pet, and thanks,' Linda replied.

'Have a good time, but don't forget I want you home by ten fifteen.'

'Yes, Dad, I know.'

Pet climbed out of the car and shut the door behind her, waving to Linda as her father drove off.

She then went into the youth club with her head down and made straight for the cloakroom, relieved to get there before anyone saw her without make-up. The room was empty and, standing at the mirror, Pet applied eye shadow and mascara, pleased that she managed it without a problem. She finished with lipstick, and then, with a final pat to her hair, approached the hall.

Music was playing and quite a few girls dancing, but no boys. Some were standing watching the girls, whilst others were around the pool table at the far end of the room. Pet stood on the threshold of the dance floor, but then Wendy Baker spotted her and hurried to her side.

'Pet, I didn't expect you to come. You look nice – it's unusual to see you wearing make-up. Crumbs, your eyes look fabulous.'

'Thanks. You look nice too,' she replied, eyeing with envy Wendy's blue, full-skirted dress and the matching short bolero. Her mood began to lift, but as someone put on a recording of 'Moon River' by Andy Williams, Wendy frowned.

'Blimey, we can't dance to that. I can't see any of the boys asking us for a smooch.'

Wendy was wrong, Pet thought, as a tall, good-looking bloke ambled towards them. She didn't recognise him from school, and if anything he looked a bit too old for the club. His eyes were grey, his hair blond, and he was dressed in the motorcycle fashion of jeans with a black T-shirt. Wendy began to preen and simper, obviously certain that the young man was going to ask her to dance, but then both girls' eyes widened when he touched Pet's arm.

'Fancy a dance?' he asked.

Pet shot a glance at Wendy before she answered and saw that she looked annoyed. 'Er, no . . . no thanks.'

'Come on, I don't bite,' he urged.

Wendy spoke then, her words clipped. 'Go on, Pet, dance with him. I'm going back to join my *friends*.'

Pet was about to protest, but Wendy had marched off, whilst the young man put his arm around Pet's waist, drawing her into his arms. She went rigid, but then, as he began to move slowly, swaying to the music, she found herself responding.

'I heard your friend call you Pet. What's that short for?'

'It's just Pet,' she lied, unwilling to admit that she had the daft name of Petula. She glanced around the floor, embarrassed to see that they were the only ones dancing.

'My name's Tony. I haven't seen you before. Do you live around here?'

'I live about fifteen minutes' walk away.'

'That's not too bad,' he murmured, drawing her closer whilst crooning the words of the song softly in her ear.

This was the first time Pet had been held in a boy's arms and as he pulled her body imperceptibly closer to his, strange feelings assailed her. Embarrassed, she pulled back.

'I told you, I don't bite,' Tony said, but allowed the distance between them. 'I see you're a friend of Wendy's. Are you still at school too?'

'Yes, but I'll be leaving shortly.'

'You're just a kid.'

'I most certainly am not,' Pet protested.

'I love the way you speak,' he murmured, as he pulled her closer again.

They continued to dance, Tony saying no more until the record came to an end, when he released her. 'See you later,' he said abruptly, before walking off to join three other young men who were propping up the wall.

For a moment Pet stood in the middle of the dance floor, floundering and unsure of what to do, but then hurried to Wendy's side.

Wendy didn't speak, but Jane did. 'I see you've met our local heartthrob. But you want to be careful: Tony Thorn has got a bit of a reputation.'

'I only danced with him,' Pet said and, hoping to placate Wendy, she added, 'Anyway, he's not my type.'

'Huh, who do you think you're kidding?' Wendy snapped, and then turning to Jane she added, 'And as for reputations, his is nothing compared to Pet's family.'

'I've told you before, my family run a legitimate business now,' Pet protested.

'So you say, but it's not what we've heard.'

'Now then, Wendy,' said Jane, 'don't be nasty. Just because Tony danced with Pet, there's no need for sour grapes. We know he usually dances with you, but you know what he's like and I expect he saw Pet as fresh meat.'

Pet frowned, not sure that she liked being referred to as meat, but she couldn't resist a peek at Tony over her shoulder. He was lounging against the wall, but as their eyes met, he winked. The beat of music filled the hall and Pet flushed as Tony began to cross the floor in their direction. She quickly looked away, tense, but it was Wendy he spoke to.

'Come on, Wendy,' he invited.

With a triumphant grin, Wendy hit the dance floor, skirt swirling as she jived with Tony. For a moment they were the only two dancing, but then another couple joined them. Pet recognised the girl as one from her school, but not the boy, and though he looked a bit strange, he was a brilliant dancer.

'Who's that boy dancing with Josephine?' Pet shouted above the noise of the music.

'That's Ian, Tony's younger brother,' Susan answered.

'Younger brother? How old is Tony then?'

'He's eighteen.'

'Eighteen! Isn't he a bit old for the club?'

'Yes, but Ian's slow, retarded. He loves music and dance, so Tony always brings him.'

'That's nice.'

'Don't let that fool you,' Jane said. 'If you want my advice, you'll keep away from Tony Thorn.'

'Why?'

'He's just bad news, that's all.'

Jane's answer left Pet confused, but then she urged both Pet and Susan onto the dance floor. The girls were skilled dancers and Pet did her best to copy their moves, yet despite this she couldn't resist the occasional glance towards Tony and Wendy. Would he ask her to dance again? God, he was gorgeous and she hoped so.

Linda had hardly spoken during the journey, and when Dan dropped her off at her parents' house she had flown inside as though in fear of her life. Maybe he should have stopped to have a word with the girl's father, but instead, ashamed of his son and unable to defend him, he had driven off.

After parking his car, Dan went straight to Bob's house. 'Any sign of George?' he asked.

'No, he ain't shown his face,' Bob said as he stepped outside, pulling the door partially closed behind him.

'He'd better turn up soon, while Pet's out of the way. I want you there when she comes out of the club, but keep out of sight. Just trail her to make sure she arrives home safely.'

'Blimey, Dad, do I have to? Can't you ask Chris to do it?'

'He's busy.'

'What about Maurice?'

Dan's temper was close to the surface, and it didn't take much to set him off. 'I'm telling you to meet her, so just do it!'

Paling, Bob nodded in agreement, both then turning at the sound of footsteps. George had entered the alley, obviously unaware of his father's mood as he ambled towards them.

'Leave this to me,' Dan growled, hardly aware of Bob shooting inside and firmly closing his door.

'All right, Dad?' George asked.

'All right! Of course I'm not all right!'

'Why? What's up?'

Dan surged forward. He grabbed George, and despite his son's bulk, almost frogmarched him to number five.

'Here, what's going on?'

'Get inside,' Dan ordered.

George fumbled for his keys, and as he unlocked the door, Dan shoved him violently from behind, into the house.

'Bloody hell, Dad. Leave it out,' George cried as he staggered inside, only just able to remain on his feet.

Dan ignored his son's protests. He slammed the door behind them and glared at his son. 'You fucking worthless piece of shit.'

'Why? What have I done?'

Dan grew hot as he felt the blood pumping through his veins, barely able to control himself now as he screamed, 'Done! You've got the nerve to ask me what you've done! For one, you scared the life out of your sister *and* your mother, but worse, you fucking scumbag, you laid into your pregnant wife!'

'I didn't touch her,' George protested. 'I wrecked the pram, that's all.'

'Sod the pram . . . Linda told your mother that you've been hitting her.'

George shrugged. 'Yeah, well, I might give her a slap or two now and then, but it's nothing to make a fuss about, and no more than she deserves.'

At this, Dan's anger unleashed. His fists connected with his son's face again and again, putting all the force he could muster behind each blow. Dan heard George's grunts of pain but, intent on giving his son the lesson he deserved, he ignored them.

Dan didn't know when George began to return the punches, only aware as he staggered backwards that blood was pouring from his nose. 'You bastard!' he yelled, surging forward again, enraged that his son had dared to hit him.

As George continued to fight back, Dan began to tire, painfully aware that his son's strength was greater than his. The next few blows that George landed had Dan grunting in pain and each punch he tried to return became weaker than the last. For a moment he paused, gasping as he bent over, but then George's fist connected with his chin in a ferocious uppercut. Dan reeled backwards, hitting the floor with a thump that knocked the last of the breath out of his body.

Dazed, Dan looked up, trying to focus on his son as he lifted one arm, panting, 'Enough!'

It didn't stop George. Madness blazed in his eyes as he lifted a foot, the boot aimed at his father's kidneys. Pain tore through Dan's body, excruciating pain, but then he felt another kick, the sickening crunch as George's boot connected with his skull. Dan grunted, but then knew no more as he sank into a pit of darkness.

Chapter Eleven

Trancelike, George looked down on his father, but as a red mist cleared his eyes, he vigorously shook his head. Like a dog shaking off water, sweat sprayed around him, his mind foggy. What had happened? 'Dad! Dad!' he cried, dropping to his knees by his father's side.

There was nothing – not even a groan. George frantically tried to find a pulse, without success, and jumped to his feet in horror. No! No! His father couldn't be dead!

George became aware of blood dripping from his nose and raised his hand to wipe it away, his thoughts clearing. Yes, that was it. He had come home to find his father waiting for him, the old man furious because he'd hit Linda, so furious that he'd laid into him like a madman. He could remember his father's attack, the pain as each blow landed, then pressure mounting again in his head until he felt that his brain was going to explode. After that there was nothing – a black void.

Had he done this? Had he killed his own father? 'Dad!' he cried, once again dropping to his knees to shake his father's shoulder. 'Wake up! Come on – wake up!'

There was no response and George heard an unholy wail, hardly aware that it was issuing from his own mouth. 'It wasn't my fault, Dad! You shouldn't have gone for me like that! I only gave Linda a slap or two – that's all!' He leaned forward, his ear to his father's mouth. On hearing nothing, terror gripped his stomach like a vice.

George didn't know when his mind suddenly shifted but as though unable to face the horror of what he'd done, he now found himself calm as he reached out for someone else to blame. Linda! Linda and her big mouth! He jumped to his feet, running from the house, leaving the door wide open behind him as his boots pounded the pavement.

It was nearly ten o'clock and Pet's hopes were dashed. Tony hadn't asked her to dance again. He'd taken Wendy to the floor several times, but hadn't even glanced her way. It was her clothes, Pet was sure of it. Beside Wendy she looked prissy and plain, like a kid, whereas Wendy looked older than her years and very self-assured. None of the other boys had asked her to dance either, all of them avoiding not just her but, by association, her friends too.

She felt she had ruined their evening, and whilst Wendy was dancing with Tony she said, 'I . . . I'm sorry. It's my fault that you haven't been asked to dance. People are frightened of my family, but there's no need, and I wish they knew how wrong they are. I've spoiled things for you and shouldn't have come.'

'Yeah, well, don't worry about it,' Jane said. 'Anyway, the blokes are always like this.'

Pet doubted it was true, but as usual she couldn't help jumping to her family's defence. 'I know my father and brothers have got a reputation, but I don't know why. They're builders' merchants, that's all.'

She saw the swift glance that passed between Jane and Susan, but neither said anything.

Moments later Wendy left the floor, grinning as she joined them. 'That was the last dance and as usual, Tony made sure he had it with me.'

Pet hid her feelings, only saying, 'I'd best make a move or I'll be late home.'

The four girls left the hall together, but Pet would have to turn in the opposite direction to the others for her walk home. She glanced around, pleased that her father had kept his word and hadn't sent one of her brothers to meet her.

She said good night to her friends. Wendy was looking smug as Tony emerged with his brother, smiling in her direction.

'It's still early and Tony lives only over the road. Once he's dropped his brother off, I'm sure he'll be back to say a proper good night,' Wendy whispered, adding with a wink, 'if you know what I mean.'

Pet forced a smile as she said goodbye again. 'See you at school on Monday.'

'Yes, see you,' the girls echoed.

Pet gave a small wave as she walked away, but now her smile dropped. She had no chance with someone like Tony, but couldn't help dreaming, wondering what it would be like if she were the one he kissed good night.

She walked slowly. Had George turned up? Had her father sorted him out? God, she hoped so – hoped that peace had returned to the alley.

'Hello, Pet.'

With a start, Pet spun round, her eyes widening at the sight of Tony smiling down at her. 'Er . . . hello.'

'Do you mind if I walk you home?'

'No . . . no, of course not,' she stammered, glad that the darkness was hiding her blushes.

He tucked her arm in his, and as they passed under a streetlamp, she looked up at his face, her heart skipping a beat. He was so good-looking! She was so nervous, and desperately tried to think of something to say, but words failed her. Come on, she cajoled herself, say something. At last she stammered, 'Er . . . one of the girls told me that you're eighteen. What sort of work do you do?'

'Oh, a bit of this and a bit of that.'

Pet frowned. 'That sounds rather enigmatic.'

Tony laughed. 'Rather enigmatic! Now that's classy. As I said before, I love the way you speak. I've always had a soft spot for a posh twang.'

'Posh! I'm not posh.'

'Don't kid a kidder. I can't wait to see where you live.'

Pet almost stopped in her tracks. Goodness, she couldn't let Tony take her all the way home. Her father would go mad if he saw her with a boy – let alone her brothers. Her mind raced. She'd let him walk her part of the way, but then insist that he turn back. All she needed now was an excuse. 'My father insisted that I take elocution lessons, but I can assure you that we aren't posh. In fact, I'm afraid he's rather strict so it might be better if we part company on Lavender Hill.'

Tony smiled. 'Yeah, all right, I get the picture.'

They continued to walk, the conversation now turning to music. Pet was enthusiastic in her praise of Elvis Presley, thrilled to find that Tony was a fan too.

They discussed his records and with something in common, Pet found that her nerves had eased.

They had just turned onto Lavender Hill when Tony pulled into a recessed shop doorway, one that was deep and in total darkness.

'What . . . ?' Pet protested, but as Tony pulled her

into his arms, bending to kiss her neck, a wave of delicious feelings made her gasp. Only moments later, his lips found hers, but as his tongue snaked in her mouth, she didn't know how to react. Was she supposed to do it back? God, she felt so gauche, out of her depth. She tentatively tried, finding it strange, yet sort of nice too. The kiss seemed to go on for ever, but then Tony began to run his hands over her body, one touching her breast.

Instantly Pet tried to pull away, but Tony held her fast.

'No, no, let me go,' she protested.

'Come on,' he said huskily. 'You know you want it.'

'I said let me go!'

Tony abruptly released her, his tone scathing. 'I should have stuck with Wendy. At least she ain't a tease.'

Pet's eyes widened in the darkness. Was Tony inferring that Wendy let him go all the way? She drew herself upright, unaware of how haughty she sounded as she said, 'Unlike Wendy, I am *not* that type of girl. She may not be a tease, but she must be a tart.'

Tony chuckled. 'Oh, Pet,' he gasped, 'it's like I said. You've got class. Look, I'm sorry, but you can't blame a bloke for trying it on. Have I spoiled my chances or can I see you again?'

'I'll think about it,' she said, yet knowing full well that she'd jump at the chance of a date with Tony, despite his fumbling.

'Fair enough,' he said, as they moved out of the doorway. 'Now can I walk you a bit further, or are we close to where you live?'

'It isn't far so you'd best turn back. I live in Drapers Alley.'

'Bloody hell! Don't tell me that you're related to the Drapers!'

'Well, yes. Dan Draper is my father.'

'Jesus,' he groaned, 'of all the girls to choose from, I had to pick Dan Draper's daughter. Look, forget I asked you out. In fact, forget you ever saw me,' and on that abrupt note he hurried off without a backward glance.

'Tony . . . wait,' Pet called, but he didn't come back.

She saw him turn into a side street, out of sight now, and desolately she began to walk home again. She liked Tony a lot, but had seen the fear in his eyes when he realised who her father was.

Pet felt sick, at last facing her nightmare: the fact that all the gossip, the talk of her family being criminals, could be true. And not only that, judging by Tony's reaction, if they were criminals, they could be dangerous ones. No, no, it had all been in the past – it had to be . . .

As Pet drew near to Drapers Alley, all these thoughts were stripped from her mind when she saw an ambulance parked outside. Someone was being carried out of the alley! George! My God, what had her father done?

She ran – saw the family surrounding a stretcher and that her mother was sobbing.

'Mum! Mum! What happened?'

It was Bob who stepped in front of Pet, obscuring her view. 'Pet, go inside. You don't want to see this.'

'Oh God! What has Dad done to George?'

'It isn't George on the stretcher – it's Dad.'

'What? No, no!' she cried, pushing him aside, but her father was being loaded into the ambulance and it was too late for her to see anything. Her mother climbed inside, followed by Maurice, and then the doors closed. In seconds the ambulance sped away, lights flashing and the bell piercing the night air.

'Pet, I'm taking Dad's car,' Bob said. 'Yvonne and I are going to the hospital. You go to my place. Wait with Sue, and when Danny and Chris turn up tell them where we are.'

'I'm coming with you.'

'No, it's best you stay here.'

Pet's shoulders stiffened. 'He's my dad too and I've got a right to be there. Yvonne should be the one to stay behind. She can wait for Danny and Chris.'

'Mum will need Yvonne, love. You know that.'

Pet's stomach lurched. 'Why does Mum need Yvonne? Oh, Bob, don't tell me that Dad's dead?'

'No, he's still alive, but he's in a very bad way.'

'Then I'm coming with you,' Pet said firmly.

Yvonne spoke then. 'Pet's right, Bob, she should be there,' and turning to Sue she said brusquely, 'Keep an eye out. When Danny and Chris turn up, tell them what's happened.'

Sue looked momentarily annoyed, but then nodded. 'Yeah, all right.' She then took Norma's arm. 'Come on, girl, let's get you inside.'

Norma looked awful, her voice high. 'What if George turns up again?'

'Keep out of his way. Leave Danny or Chris to deal with him,' Bob said as he urged Pet and Yvonne forward.

Pet broke as she climbed into the car. 'Oh, Yvonne, I can't believe this is happening.'

'Don't cry, love. Your father's tough. He'll pull through, you'll see. Now come on, dry those tears. Your mother will need you to be strong.'

Strong? thought Pet. How can I be strong when my father might be dying?

Pet lost all track of time, and had no idea how long they had been sitting in the waiting room. Her mother was quiet, saying nothing, but Maurice was breathing heavily and Pet feared he was going to have a full-blown asthma attack.

As though aware of her eyes on him, he said, 'Don't worry, I'm all right. What about you? How are you doing?'

'I'm just worried sick about Dad.'

The door flew open and Chris came running into the waiting room, his face drawn with anxiety. 'What's going on? How's Dad?'

'We don't know,' Bob told him.

'We've been waiting for nearly an hour. It's about time someone came to tell us how he's doing,' Maurice complained.

Yvonne stood up. 'I'll see if I can find anyone.'

'Are you all right, Mum?' Chris asked as Yvonne left the room.

When his mother didn't reply, Chris sat down and placed his arm around her shoulder, but she shrugged him off. He shook his head, standing up again to move close to Bob, and though his voice was a hiss, Pet heard every word. 'What the hell happened? And where's Danny?'

'I'm not sure what happened, but going by Dad's injuries, I'd say that George kicked him in the head. As for where Danny is, your guess is as good as mine.'

'Kicked him in the head!' Pet cried. 'You didn't tell me that.'

Chris looked annoyed. 'What the hell is Pet doing here?'

'I told her not to come, but she wouldn't have it,' Bob said.

'You're the adult. You should have put your foot down.'

'Stop it!' Pet cried. 'Stop talking about me as if I'm not here.'

'All right, that's enough! Can't you see that you're upsetting Mum?' Maurice said.

They all looked at their mother, but she didn't look up, her hands wringing in her lap. 'You all right, Mum?' Chris asked again and when she didn't reply, he hissed, venomously, 'When George shows his face I'll fucking kill him.'

Yvonne came back, shaking her head as she said, 'The nurses can't tell me anything. We've got to wait for the doctor.'

'What's taking him so bloody long?' Maurice complained.

'I think they're still working on your father.'

'Bloody hell,' Bob murmured.

Time slowly passed, and their conversation was sporadic. Despite her fears, Pet found her eyes drooping, but when the door swung open at midnight, she sat up with a start. But it wasn't a doctor who walked in, it was Danny.

'What the hell's going on? How's Dad?'

'We're still waiting for news,' Maurice told him. 'The doc . . .'

Danny was gone before Maurice finished the sentence; his brothers hurrying after him.

'I expect Danny is going to see if he can find anything out, but like me, I doubt he'll have much luck,' Yvonne said. 'Can I get you anything, Mum? Would you like something to drink?'

Joan just shook her head, but at least there had been a reaction.

'What about you, Pet?' Yvonne offered.

'No, no, thanks. Oh, Yvonne, why is it taking so long?'

'I don't know, love, but we're sure to hear something soon.'

Danny came back into the room, trailing his brothers behind him. 'Fucking nurses,' he spat. 'They won't tell me anything.'

'Danny, please,' Yvonne begged. 'There's no point in losing your rag. The nurses do their best.'

'I want to know what happened, from the beginning,' Danny demanded. 'All I got was a garbled report from Sue about George attacking Dad.'

'That's about it,' Bob told him. 'I saw George running off and when I went round to his place I found Dad unconscious on the floor. He was in a state, so I called an ambulance.'

'There must be more to it than that.'

'George has been hitting Linda, and Dad was livid. He went round to sort him out, but don't ask me what happened after that because I wasn't there.'

Pet listened to this exchange, her stomach churning. George had attacked their father and beaten him. A sob escaped her throat.

Danny looked at her, his expression darkening. 'What the hell are you doing here?'

Pet just shook her head, too choked to reply.

'Chris, take her home.'

'No, Danny,' Pet begged. 'Please, I can't go home, I can't . . . not until I've found out how Dad is.'

Before Danny could say anything, the door opened.

'Mrs Draper?' a doctor asked as he walked into the room.

Joan stood up, her eyes suddenly clear. 'How is he?' she asked.

'Mr Draper is stable now, but he will have to remain in hospital until we can assess the extent of his injuries. He's obviously been badly beaten, and the police will have to be informed.'

'No,' Danny snapped. 'He wasn't beaten – he fell down the stairs.'

The doctor's bushy eyebrows rose. 'I find that unlikely.'

'My father will tell you the same thing.'

An expression crossed the doctor's face, one that Pet couldn't fathom, but then Danny spoke again.

'Can we see him?'

'Just for a few minutes and only two of you, please.'

Danny stepped forward and Joan leaned on his arm as they left the room. 'That's nice, ain't it?' Bob complained. 'Why Danny? Why not one of us?'

'He's the eldest,' Yvonne said.

Bob grunted but said nothing further, and they were back after only five minutes.

Pet, seeing how grey her mother looked, blurted out, 'How is he? How's Dad?'

It was Danny who answered. 'Dad's conscious, but he ain't right. When he tried to talk, he just sort of gibbered.'

'Oh, Danny, surely his brain hasn't been damaged?' Yvonne gasped.

As Joan's legs began to wobble, Chris hurried forward to take her other arm.

Pet's head was reeling. Did her father have brain damage? Was the knowledge of that what she had seen on the doctor's face?

Danny looked grim as he answered Yvonne. 'I don't know and the doctor said it's too early to tell. Dad needs more tests.'

'Mum's near collapse; we should get her home,' Chris said.

'No, no, I can't leave,' Joan protested.

'Mum, you heard the doctor,' Danny said. 'Dad's stable now, but as we can't see him again tonight, there's no point in staying. Now come on, you look exhausted and you won't be fit to see him in the morning unless you get a bit of kip.'

Joan allowed Chris and Danny to lead her from the room, Pet and the others following. Danny helped his mother into the front seat of his car, leaving Yvonne to climb into the back.

'Bob, drive Dad's car home,' Danny ordered. 'Take Maurice and Chris with you, then come round to my place.'

'Bloody hell, it's well after midnight. Can't it wait?' Bob complained.

'No it can't.'

'Danny, we're all worn out,' Maurice protested.

'Just do as you're told,' Danny growled.

Pet paused in the act of getting in beside Yvonne. Danny sounded harsh, but his tone was at odds with the expression on his face. If anything, he looked pleased. No, she had to be imagining it. Yet as he climbed into the car, she was sure he was smiling. Why? With all that had happened, how could Danny smile?

Chapter Twelve

Danny sat on the sofa, his trump card in his pocket. He was tired, but fought it off. There were things to sort out – and the sooner the better.

'Norma was none too pleased about me coming round here at this time of night. I got a right earful,' Maurice complained, 'but Ivy came up trumps. It was good of her to have that hot chocolate waiting for us and it went down a treat.'

'I got an earful too. Sue waited up but I couldn't tell her much and now she's gone to bed with the hump. I'm gonna get nothing but grief in the morning.'

'Who wears the trousers in your houses? My Yvonne does as she's told and I can't believe I'm hearing this.'

Both Bob and Maurice lowered their heads, whilst Danny said to Chris, 'If ever you decide to get married, make sure you rule the roost from day one. If you don't, you'll end up like this pair of dozy gits.'

'I can't believe you lot,' Chris said, shaking his

head in disgust. 'George nearly killed Dad, and here you are talking about your bloody wives.'

'Yeah, Chris is right,' said Danny. 'We need to get down to business. First, we don't want the police involved, so as I told the doc, Dad fell down the stairs. Second, we need to find George.'

'Too right we do,' Chris growled. 'He can't be allowed to get away with half killing Dad. When I get my hands on him – he's dead. Instead of sitting here, we should be out looking for him.'

Maurice yawned widely. 'Chris, from what Danny and the doctor told us, Dad's in a bad way. I feel the same as you about George, but it's after one in the morning and I can hardly keep my eyes open. It'd be a waste of time looking for him now. He's had plenty of time to get away and will be well out of the borough.'

'Maurice is right,' Danny said. 'George could be anywhere by now.'

'We can at least put the word out that we're looking for him,' Chris argued.

'We'll do that first thing in the morning. Maurice can run Mum to the hospital while the rest of us start the search.'

'No way,' Bob protested. 'I'll take Mum to the hospital. I want to see how Dad's doing.'

'Yeah, me too,' Chris agreed.

Danny wasn't going to stand for this. He was in charge now and the others had better get used to it. 'I said Maurice is taking her, and that's that. They won't let all of us in, so we'll go to the hospital after we've had a scout around for George.'

'Who gave you the right to tell us what to do?' Bob snapped. 'Dad is the head of this family, not you.'

'Now listen, and this goes for all of you. I saw Dad, and believe me it's going to take a long time before he's fit to run things again. In the meantime, I'll be taking over and you'll take your orders from me.'

Bob jumped up, his face red. 'No way! Until Dad tells us different, we've all got an equal say.'

Danny smiled thinly as he pulled out the document. 'Dad had this drawn up some time ago. This ain't his will – I admit I ain't privy to that – but for the time being this piece of paper is all I need. As you'll see, it states that if Dad is in any way incapacitated and unable to run the business, as the eldest son, I'm to take over.'

'How come we didn't know about it?' Bob asked.

Danny shrugged. 'You know Dad. He always does things on a need-to-know basis.'

'I bet you put the idea into his head.'

'Dad knows the score. In our game there are always risks and he saw the sense of my suggestion.'

'It ain't fucking right. In fact, if you ask me, Dad was livid about your idea of using children in films and I ain't so sure he'd want you running things now.'

'We had a chat and sorted it out. He agreed that as long as we stick to consensual sex, he's for it.'

'And we're supposed to believe that! When did you have this so-called chat?'

'Are you calling me a liar?'

'Come on, both of you, calm down,' Maurice urged as he scanned the document. 'Bob, if this is what Dad wants, then so be it. He obviously thinks that Danny is the one to hold the business together, and anyway, it's only until he's on his feet again.'

'Sod this,' Chris spat. 'I'm bushed. If we ain't doing anything until the morning, I'm going to bed. As for you running the business, Danny, it's fine with me.'

Danny hid his satisfaction. George didn't know it, but by putting the old man out of action, he'd done him a big favour. He'd now be able to put *all* his plans into action without any resistance. In the meantime, he issued his instructions again. 'Maurice, as I said, first thing in the morning I want you to run Mum to the hospital. Take Yvonne and Pet with you.'

'Norma and Sue might want to go.'

'Tough. Anyway, as I said before, they won't allow many visitors until Dad's out of intensive care.'

'How come Yvonne's going then?' Bob complained.

Danny, sick of Bob's constant carping, exhaled loudly. 'Mum's fond of Yvonne and she'll want her there.'

Bob was about to protest again, but Maurice broke

in, 'Danny's right, Bob, and anyway, with it being Sunday, Norma and Sue will have the kids to sort out.'

Danny stifled a yawn. He felt unusually tired, his eyes bleary with fatigue. 'Right, that's it for now. I'll see you in the morning.'

They all trooped out, and after closing the door behind them, Danny locked up. He went straight upstairs, undressed, but as he climbed in beside Yvonne, she stirred, saying, 'It was ages before you turned up at the hospital tonight. Where were you?'

'Doing a bit of business.'

'Is there someone else, Danny? Are you playing away again?'

'Of course not, you dozy mare.'

'I'm sure I could smell perfume on your shirt this morning.'

'For fuck's sake, Yvonne, leave it out. I don't need this. My dad's lying in a hospital bed, in a bad way, and I've got to take over the running of the business. There ain't another woman, so just shut up and let me get some kip.'

Danny heard Yvonne huff, but ignored it. He turned over, his back towards her, and closed his eyes, thoughts drifting. Yes, he had a tart on the side, but that's all she was, a tart. Yvonne was all right in bed, but she didn't like anything a bit different or kinky, whereas Rita had no such qualms. Still, he'd have to be a bit more careful,

165

and the daft cow would have to stop smothering herself in cheap perfume.

Danny plumped up his pillow, his thoughts now turning to George. He'd always known that his brother was a mental case, yet even so, he'd never expected him to turn on the old man. If they found him, he'd have to be punished, but surely even George would have the sense to keep his head down.

George never reached Linda's parents' house. Instead he was slumped on a bench on Clapham Common. He didn't know when his brain had shifted again, but as he pounded the pavement, intent on sorting his wife out, the awful truth had returned to hit him. He had killed his father!

Hours had passed, and only the light from a distant lamp pierced the gloom. George had no idea what to do. He shivered. It was as though his life was over. He couldn't return to Drapers Alley. Ever! Yet it was all he knew. He would have to go away – far away from his brother's reach. He didn't care about Maurice or Bob, and he could even handle Chris if he had to. It was Danny he feared. Danny would kill him! Yet where could he go? Where would he be safe? Maybe he should turn himself in – maybe he should tell the police that he'd killed his father. They'd lock him up and in a cell he'd be out of Danny's reach. George groaned in despair. No, he couldn't

166

do that. He'd get life for murder, and the thought of being locked in a cell for ever was unbearable.

For a moment he considered leaving the country, but as his addled brain turned, George realised it wasn't possible. He didn't have any money, or a passport. But there was money in Drapers Alley – plenty of it. Maybe he could find a way to get into his mother's house without detection. Yet dare he risk it?

Still he sat on the bench, his thoughts turning to Linda again. He'd made the biggest mistake in his life when he'd married her. It was her big mouth that had caused this and he felt like wringing her neck. No, don't be stupid, he told himself. He was in enough trouble. Fuck her! He never wanted to see her again and, as far as he was concerned, she and her unborn brat could rot in hell.

Finally, at three in the morning, realising he had no choice, George rose to his feet. To get away he had to have money, and if he had any chance of taking the hoard, he'd have to do it now.

George trudged home, but the closer he got to Drapers Alley, the more nervous he became. What if Danny was laying in wait?

As he entered the alley, George kept close to the wall, peering at the houses for signs of life. All were in darkness. George had one thing in his favour. When he'd married Linda and moved into number five, he had kept the key to his father's house and it remained on his fob.

Treading as softly as he could, he edged along the wall to number one, just about to put the key into the lock when he froze. His father was dead! Shit, what if he was laid out in the living room? In a cold sweat now, he remained rooted to the spot, but then a glimmer of reason returned. No, his dad wouldn't be laid out yet – it was too soon.

Carefully turning the key, George held his breath as he opened the door. The living room was empty, in darkness, and he crossed the room with his arms outstretched. He made it without bumping into anything and now headed for the bathroom. George still couldn't see a thing and had no other choice but to turn on the light so, pulling the door almost closed, he flicked the switch. For a moment he paused, his ears pricked, but hearing nothing he moved to the window. It was set back in the wall, with a plant on the windowsill that George carefully removed. He had always been in awe of how clever his dad was, and now as he fumbled under the sill for the hidden catch he recalled his amazement when he'd first been shown this secret hiding place.

His dad's idea had been ingenious, but now as George lifted the windowsill to pull out the long, metal box that fitted perfectly in the wall cavity, a sob escaped his lips. His dad was dead! He'd killed him! *Oh, Dad, I'm sorry. I didn't mean to do it. Oh, Dad, I'm never gonna see you again.* Grief hit George with such force that his legs caved beneath him. He slumped on the floor, the metal box cradled in his arms as he rocked back and forth.

George was immersed in an agony of grief, his back to the bathroom door and unaware that it had opened fully. Nor was he aware of anyone approaching him from behind until a hand grabbed his hair, pulling his head back. 'Wh . . . what . . .'

These were the last words George uttered as a knife sliced his throat, the cut deep. He opened his mouth, but could only gurgle as his blood spurted, splattering the walls. His head was pushed forward again, his chin now down as the rest of his life force drained onto his mother's immaculately polished lino.

Only minutes later, George's killer removed his body, dumping it in a place that wasn't far away, but one where it was unlikely to be discovered. Later, it would be hidden, but there wasn't time now. The effort of carrying George had almost drained his killer, but there was still the bathroom to clean up and time was short.

His killer hadn't anticipated that George's blood would spurt so far and it would take longer than expected to clean up, but every trace had to be removed. It seemed to take for ever, but finally it was done, and now there was only one thing left to do. The killer took the money, leaving the metal box wide open on the bathroom floor.

Chapter Thirteen

Joan was the first one up on Sunday morning. She hadn't expected to sleep, but surprisingly she'd gone off as soon as her head hit the pillow. Now, though, groggy but awake, her first thought was for her husband and all she wanted was to get to the hospital. Oh, Dan, Joan inwardly cried, please be all right. Please get better.

Chris emerged as she came out of her bedroom, his face grey. 'You look awful, Chris. Didn't you get any sleep?'

'Yeah, I slept. What about you? Are you all right?'

Joan forced a smile. Chris was a lovely lad, thoughtful and caring. He had always been her favourite, but ashamed of preferring one child over the others, she hid her feelings. 'I'm anxious to get back to the hospital.'

'Yeah, me too, but we should grab a bite to eat first. I'll give Pet a nudge while you make a pot of tea.'

Joan went downstairs and in the kitchen she placed the kettle on the gas before hurrying to the bathroom. On the threshold, she paused, her eyes on a metal box on the floor. Where had that come from? Something else looked odd, out of place, and at first she couldn't comprehend what it was, but then saw that her plant was on the floor too. Joan looked at the window and frowned. The sill looked odd, raised, and crossing the room she investigated what looked like a concealed compartment.

'Chris? Chris, come down here!'

In moments Chris was beside her. 'What's this?' she asked, 'and where did that metal box come from?'

For a second Chris didn't react, but then, his voice high, he said, 'Bloody hell, I'd best get Danny.'

'Wait,' Joan called, but Chris ignored her as he ran out.

Joan stared down into the cavity, her eyes then returning to the metal box. In minutes Chris was back, Danny behind him, his hair dishevelled.

'Mum, go back to the kitchen. Leave this to us,' Danny ordered.

'I've worked out where the box came from, but what was in it?'

'It was nothing, Mum. Just paperwork to do with the business, that's all.'

'But . . . but why was it hidden under the sill? And who took the papers?'

'Mum, please, we don't know, but there's nothing

to worry about, honest. Look, why don't you get yourself ready and Maurice will run you to the hospital?'

Danny's eyes were veiled and Joan could sense that he was hiding something, but in truth, she didn't want to know. It was bound to be something illegal, something her husband and sons were mixed up in, and as usual she buried her head in the sand. All she wanted was to find out how Dan was so, leaving them to it, she hurried to get dressed.

'That was quick thinking,' Chris hissed as soon as his mother was out of sight. 'Papers, that was a good one.'

'It's gone, Chris. All the money. Dad's savings, our savings, the business capital, gone!'

'Yeah, I can see that.'

'Was there any sign of a break-in?'

'No, I don't think so.'

'That's a bit odd. Didn't you hear anything?'

'Not a sound.'

'Are you sure?'

'Yeah, I'm sure. What are you trying to imply, Danny? Are you accusing me?'

'No, but why are you so touchy?'

'What do you expect? There was no sign of a forced entry so you must think it's an inside job.'

'No, Chris, I think George did it and I should have seen this coming. I should have realised that

George would need money to do a runner. We're well and truly in the shit now,' Danny moaned as he closed the box and returned it to its hiding place. 'Come on, the others will need to hear about this. You go to Bob's whilst I tell Maurice.'

'What's going on?' Pet asked as she came downstairs.

'Nothing for you to worry about,' Danny told her. 'Just get yourself ready and go with Mum to the hospital.'

'But—'

Danny and Chris both ignored their sister as they left the house, one going to number three and one to number four. Both looked grim as they knocked on the doors, and with Maurice the first to answer, Danny stepped inside.

'There was no need to knock me up. I'm getting ready,' Maurice said.

'Where's Norma?'

'She's still in bed.'

'Good. Now listen . . .'

As Danny told Maurice what had happened, he saw his brother's eyes widen in shock.

'What? It's all gone?'

'That's what I said. The bastard took the lot.'

'Blimey, I'm glad my savings are in a bank.'

'Mine were in the box.'

'Danny, I told you that money in the bank would have made a bit of interest.'

'Yeah, I know, but I never got round to it.'

'We had to hide the business capital, and now that it's gone we're in the shit. Bloody hell, Danny, we've got to get it back. We've got to find George.'

'Don't you think I know that? Oh, we'll find him, and when we do . . .' Danny left the sentence unfinished as he paced the small room. 'Look, for now we'll carry on as planned. You take Mum, Yvonne and Pet to the hospital while the rest of us have a scout round.'

Norma came downstairs, preventing further conversation.

Danny left, but as soon as he walked into his own house, Yvonne said, 'What did Chris want?'

'Someone broke in last night and nicked Dad's papers,' Danny lied.

'Papers? What papers?'

'Stuff to do with the business.'

Yvonne frowned. 'Why would anyone want them?'

'I don't know, and I ain't got time to worry about it now. Mum will want to get to the hospital so you'd best get a move on.'

Yvonne cocked her head to one side, her gaze intent. 'Danny, what's really going on?'

'Nothing! Now shut up about it and do as I said, get yourself ready.'

Yvonne did as she was told whilst Danny's thoughts raced. With their funds gone, they would need to make money, and fast. Hard porn was the answer, but how were they supposed to get it up and running without capital? If they didn't find George, he'd have to find a way. With six families to support, Danny knew he had no choice.

By ten o'clock, only two women remained in Drapers Alley. The events of last night had caused Sue and Norma to put their differences to one side, and with the kids playing outside, they sat gossiping at Norma's table.

'Have you seen Ivy this morning?' Sue asked.

'Yes, I saw her pass by earlier.'

'I was surprised that she waited up last night, and that she made them a chocolate drink. She's never had time for any of us, so why the switch?'

'Dan's her uncle so she's bound to be worried,' Norma said.

It was true that Ivy didn't have any time for them, but she didn't blame her. She was sickened by the Drapers too. As far as she was concerned, Maurice was the only decent one amongst them. She'd had enough and intended to push even harder to make him see sense. They had to get away from his family, from the alley, and the business. How he could allow Oliver to grow up in this environment was beyond her, but she wasn't going to allow her son to become tainted by this rotten family.

'Bob's gone off with the others to look for George. I wouldn't like to be in his shoes if they find him.'

'More violence – and what will it solve? Nothing. They should leave George to the police.'

'Leave it out, love. The Drapers take care of their own business and always have. They won't want the rozzers involved.'

'And what if Dan dies? That means that George has got away with murder.'

'Norma, don't say that! Bob told me that Dan was stable when they left the hospital last night.'

'Yes, but he's in intensive care and that means it's serious.'

'Oh, Norma, I hope Dan makes it. Bob would fall apart if anything happened to his dad. He's going to the hospital later and I wish I was going with him. He'll need me if the worst happens.'

'I doubt you'll be allowed to go. It seems Yvonne is the only daughter-in-law with that privilege.'

'Yeah, stuck-up cow.' Sue paused before saying, 'It's Petula I feel sorry for. She worships her dad and he spoils her rotten. She'll be in bits if anything happens to him.'

Norma wondered how Pet was coping. She was a nice girl, the only one of the Drapers she had any time for. Now, though, the girl had seen what her family was capable of, and her cosseted little world must be shattered. She doubted Pet would get much comfort from her mother. Joan was a cold fish, and from what she had seen last night, too wrapped up in her own world to worry about her daughter. 'Yes,

I feel sorry for Pet too. Now then, do you want another cup of tea?'

'I won't say no,' Sue replied. 'I've got a stack of ironing to do, but sod it, I'm not in the mood for housework.'

Norma smiled faintly. Sue was never in the mood for housework. Norma went through to the kitchen to make a fresh pot of tea, deciding her own cleaning could wait too. What did the house matter? She hated it, drawing no pleasure from her surroundings, and only kept it nice for Oliver's sake. Once again she was determined to leave Drapers Alley, and if Maurice wouldn't see sense, she'd leave without him, taking Oliver with her. Norma paused, biting her bottom lip. Yes, brave thoughts, but just where could they go? There was her parents' house, of course, but would they take her back? Yes, probably. They'd welcome her home, and as before, use her as a servant, someone to take care of them, but would they accept Oliver?

By eleven o'clock, her stomach awash with tea, Sue said, 'I wonder what time they'll all be back.'

'I don't know, and I expect they'll go again this evening.'

'Yeah, well, my place looks like a bomb's hit it so I'd best give it a quick tidy-up.'

Norma opened the street door, relieved to see that Oliver was happily playing football with his cousins, Robby for once behaving himself.

177

Sue stepped outside. 'Look,' she said, 'there's Ivy.'

Norma frowned. Ivy was coming into the alley from the other end so she wouldn't be passing their doors, but even from this distance she looked harassed. 'I wonder where she's been?'

'I dunno, but she looks a right mess,' Sue giggled.

'Hello, Ivy,' Norma said as the woman drew closer. 'What on earth have you been up to?'

'I've been down to our allotment.'

'I thought you left that to Steve?'

'Yeah, well, this is his only day off so I thought I'd give him a break. The allotment's been going to seed, and anyway, I don't mind a bit of hard work. Now if you don't mind, I need to clean myself up.'

On that note Ivy went inside and Sue's eyes rounded. 'Blimey, rather her than me.'

'Yes, well, unlike you, Ivy is built like an ox.'

'She's bigger than Steve, that's for sure. He's such a funny-looking bloke and I don't know what she sees in him.'

'With Ivy's looks, beggars can't be choosers. Anyway, see you later, Sue.'

'Yeah, see you,' Sue said, gyrating to her door.

Norma pursed her lips, feeling the usual surge of envy. Sue was so dainty, so sexy, but then Norma stiffened her shoulders. All right, she may not be as pretty as Sue, but after seeing Ivy, she at least felt feminine.

With a last glance along the alley, Norma went

inside, and though she tried to tackle her house-work, she couldn't get last night's events from her mind. George had almost beaten his father to death. How could a son do that to his own father? Bad blood, that was the problem, Norma decided, with Maurice the exception. She picked up a duster, running it over her sideboard, but then Oliver came charging in, a hand held over his eye. 'What happened?'

'Robby kicked the ball into my face.'

Norma took her son through to the kitchen where she bathed his eye, her jaws clenched in anger. Robby was a menace, another one with bad blood, an inher-ited love of violence. She just *wouldn't* have Oliver tainted. When Maurice came home she'd insist, once and for all, that they left Drapers Alley.

Ivy's lips were set as she walked into her house. There was no sign of Steve and the kids, but she could guess where they were. They'd be at the park, watching a local football match. Ivy scowled. She'd seen the way Sue and Norma had looked at her – disdain from Norma, and amusement from Sue. She hated them. Who were they to judge her? What did they know of her life? It was all right for pretty, petite Sue, and though Norma wasn't exactly an oil painting, she didn't draw pitying looks.

Ivy threw off her clothes, hastening to clean the dirt from her body, yet even when clean, she knew she'd still be ugly. From childhood she had suffered either pity or nastiness, and at school she'd been the butt of many cruel jokes. When she looked at her cousins, especially Petula, she couldn't understand why she was so different. Her parents had been good-looking; in fact her mother had been prettier than Auntie Joan, so why had she been born to look like an outcast amongst the Drapers? It wasn't fair, it really wasn't, and because of her looks she had known more humiliation than kindness since the day she was born.

Only her mother had loved her and Ivy still hadn't come to terms with her death. She had watched her suffer, longed to do something, anything to ease her pain, and without support from her so-called family, she had felt so alone. Auntie Joan hadn't come once, and though Uncle Dan had called occasionally, she could sense he had been itching to get away.

She had been heartbroken when her mother died, and when Steve came along she had grabbed at the chance for a little comfort, allowing him liberties from day one. Making love had helped her to drown out her sorrows. Marriage and kids followed, and though the boys were little buggers at times, she loved them dearly. All she wanted for them was a better life, and had watched their developing features with anxiety. Thankfully, they hadn't inherited her looks. Though they weren't exactly handsome, their features were even and both had Steve's lovely eyes.

Ivy thought about George and felt some satisfaction, a feeling at last of superiority. Yes, her boys might be naughty at times, but look what Auntie Joan had bred: a son who had beaten his father, and from what she had seen before he'd been carried off in an ambulance, Uncle Dan was in a terrible state. Good, Ivy thought. She hoped her uncle was in pain, pain that was worse than her mother had suffered. After all, it was no more than he deserved.

After cleaning herself up, Ivy heard voices in the alley, so quickly threw on fresh clothes and went outside. Sue and Norma were going into number one, which meant her Auntie Joan was back from the hospital. She ran to join them, her voice solicitous as she walked inside.

'Auntie Joan, what's the news on Uncle Dan? How's he doing?'

It was Maurice who answered. 'He's a bit better, but he's not out of the woods yet.'

'He looks dreadful,' Pet said, her eyes beginning to fill with tears, 'and he can't talk.'

'Come on now, buck up,' Yvonne said. 'The doctor said he's out of danger, and though it may take a while for him to recover, at least he's on the mend.'

As Joan flopped onto a chair, Maurice said, 'I think we all should leave now. Mum's just about had enough and needs to rest.'

Ivy's blood grew hot. They were at it again, pushing her out; well, she wouldn't rise to the bait. 'Auntie

Joan, is there anything I can do to help?' she said, whilst hoping the bloody woman would say no.

'No, it's all right, and as Maurice said, I would rather you all went home. My head is pounding and with everyone in here I feel like a sardine in a can.'

Ivy caught the look that Sue threw at Norma and guessed they were none too pleased to be chased out either.

'Yes, come on, let's leave Mum in peace,' Maurice said, taking his wife's arm to lead her outside. 'I'll be back later to run you to the hospital again, Mum.'

Ivy had no choice but to follow them. Her lips were set in a grim line, but she brightened up again when in her own home. It had happened at last, she was seeing the Drapers brought low. It sounded like her Uncle Dan was in a terrible state and she felt a surge of satisfaction.

Joan was glad when everyone left. She was unable to settle, almost out of her mind with worry. She'd do some housework, anything to fill her mind, and she'd start with the bathroom.

With a bucket of nice hot water, Joan was soon on her knees, scrubbing the bathroom linoleum. When she got to one corner she frowned to see that it had begun to lift, so rising to her feet she went to look for some glue.

With the tube in hand Joan went back to the bathroom, but as she raised the linoleum further to apply the glue, her eyes widened. The concrete floor and back of the linoleum were coated in something sticky. When she realised what it was Joan's hand went to her mouth in horror. Blood! But where had it come from?

'What are you doing, Mum?'

'Oh, Chris, you made me jump. Look, I've found blood on the floor.'

Chris bent to have a look, saying dismissively, 'It won't be blood, Mum, it must be something else. Look, leave it to me. I'll clean it up.'

'But—'

'No buts, Mum. You look worn out and shouldn't be doing housework. Now go on, make us both a cup of tea and I'll have this cleaned up in no time.'

Joan wanted to protest, but something in Chris's manner stilled her. Despite what he said, she was sure it was blood and couldn't understand where it had come from. Why had Chris denied it? Oh God, had Chris caught the robber in the act? Had there been a fight? But no, if that was the case surely Chris would have said something, and not only that, if he had caught the robber, Dan's papers wouldn't be missing. Joan's head began to buzz. Oh, she couldn't think straight. Dan was in hospital and that was enough to worry about. She didn't want to think about anything else – she didn't want to know what had happened, not when she was fearful of the answers.

Chapter Fourteen

Pet had noticed a change at school – more whispers, but also a difference in some of the other girls' behaviour. Instead of being nervous around her, there were some who openly made comments and asked questions. She was facing one now.

'How's your dad, Petula? Still rough, is he?' asked Kate, a girl who had previously shunned her.

'Yes, he's still in hospital.'

'And what about your brother George? We heard that he's gone missing. Has he turned up?'

'No, not yet.'

'My dad said that with your father in hospital and George missing, things are looking up. Your other brothers haven't got so much backup now.'

'What do you mean? Backup for what?'

'Leave it out. You know just what I mean.' And, turning away, she grabbed another girl's arm, both giggling as they walked across the playground.

Petula frowned, but then seeing Wendy walking

in the gate, she hurried over to her. She hated coming to school, wanting to be at her father's side until he got better, but her mother wouldn't let her take any time off.

'What's up, Pet?' asked Wendy.

'Oh, nothing, I just wish I could leave school after the summer term instead of waiting until the end of the year.'

'Yeah, me too. My mum's already put a word in for me at work and they said there's a job waiting for me.'

'Really! Where does your mum work?'

'In the sugar factory.'

Pet didn't envy Wendy. She didn't want to work in a factory, and still held on to her dream of working in an upmarket shop. But with her father so ill, any thoughts of getting a job when she left school had been pushed to one side. She remembered when she had gone to Sue for make-up lessons, thinking her mad to suggest that she could be a model, whereas Wendy definitely had the looks.

'I think you could be a model, Wendy.'

'Are you taking the mickey?'

'No, of course not.'

'Yeah, well, it's nice of you to say so. How's your dad?'

'He's still in a bad way.' Indicating Kate, she added, 'She asked me the same question, but it was funny, almost as if she enjoyed the fact that he's ill.'

'What do you expect? There are a lot of people around here who probably think the same.'

Pet wanted to protest, to defend her family, but once again she was assailed by doubts. Her father and brothers were supposed to be running a legitimate business but there was still gossip, and uppermost in her mind was the way Tony Thorn had acted when he found out that she was a Draper. Were they still criminals? Had she been a blind fool in allowing her father and brothers to fob her off? Her lips set into a thin line. Well, no more, she decided, determined to find out the truth.

'There they are,' Wendy said.

Pet turned to see Jane and Susan walking arm and arm through the gates, smiling when they saw them, but with the bell ringing there was no chance to chat as they made their way inside the building.

Despite putting the word out in Battersea and boroughs beyond, George hadn't been sighted. Over a month passed without finding him, and they had all but given up hope.

By mid-June a routine was in place in the alley. Maurice was the one who drove his mother to the hospital every day and, though Sue and Norma complained, it was always Yvonne who accompanied her.

Because she was at school during the day, Pet went with her mother in the evenings, usually accompanied by one of her brothers. With her father so ill, George still missing and her brothers so busy, she hadn't had a chance to question them about their activities so far, but she was keeping her eyes and ears open, hoping to snatch some information.

One Monday evening only Maurice was with them, and as Pet sat by the bed she couldn't understand why her father wasn't getting any better. He had changed so much. Instead of the strong man he had once been, in just this short time, he appeared shrunken, beaten and aged.

'What did you say, Dad?'

He tried to speak again, but there was only a stream of babble. Spittle began to run down his chin and Pet watched as her mother gently wiped it away.

'The doctor said you can come home next week, Dan.'

'What?' Pet said. 'Mum, why didn't you tell me? When did he say that? How can Dad come home when he still can't talk? Surely there's more they can do?'

There was another stream of babble as Dan tried to speak, one arm waving in frustration. Pet's eyes met those of her mother and she paled at her words.

'That's enough, Pet! Your father may not be able to speak, but he ain't deaf. Maurice,' she continued, 'take Pet outside. She's upsetting your father.'

'But—'

'Come on, Pet. You can see Dad's had enough now. Say goodbye and we'll wait in the car for Mum.'

Tears brimming, Pet bent over her father, kissing him on the forehead. 'Sorry, Dad, I didn't mean to upset you.'

'Just go,' Joan snapped.

Reluctantly Pet left the ward. 'Maurice, why didn't Mum tell me that Dad's coming home?'

'She only found out this afternoon, but you know now, so why all the fuss?'

'Because I sense that you're all hiding something from me and this is the last straw. Please, Maurice, I'm not a child. Tell me what's going on.'

Maurice stopped walking and turned to face her. 'Look, we didn't want to upset you and we hoped that Dad would recover, if only his speech.'

'But why isn't he getting any better?'

Maurice exhaled loudly, then said, 'All right, the others might not like it, but I'll give it to you straight. At first we were told that the kick to Dad's head had caused a swelling around the brain. We hoped that when it went down, he'd recover his speech. It looked hopeful, but then Dad had a stroke.'

'A stroke! Is that why his arm is so weak that he can't hold a pen?'

Maurice nodded. 'Yes, it affected one side of his body.'

'I can't believe you kept this from me!'

'As I said, we were hoping that he'd improve.

Come on, love, don't cry. After the beating it was touch and go for a while, and we nearly lost Dad. He may have had a stroke, but at least he's still alive.'

'Does . . . does this mean he'll never be able to speak again?'

'We don't know, Pet. I suppose there's always a chance.'

'He won't get any worse, will he?'

'As long as he doesn't have another stroke, I doubt it, and who knows, once he's home in familiar surroundings, he may improve.'

Pet clung to that hope.

Joan gripped Dan's hand, inwardly fighting her tears. Since the day she had met him, Dan had always protected her, shielded her, and she had leaned on his strength. Diminutive beside him, he had called her his Queen, and she loved him for it. Now, though, it felt as if the tables had turned and it was she who would have to be the carer, the protector. Somehow she had to keep him free from worry, free from stress. If she could do that, then maybe he'd get better.

As the eldest son, Danny would have to step in permanently. He would need to continue running the business, and she would have to ensure that if there were any problems, they didn't reach Dan's ears. It wouldn't be easy. The boys always came to their father if there were any problems. But no more!

She'd have a word with Danny, in fact with all of them. Their father had to have complete peace, and she'd see that he got just that.

As her determination to protect Dan rose, Joan was surprised at the well of strength she felt. Dan squeezed her hand and she said earnestly, meeting his eyes, 'It's all right, love. I'll look after you, I promise.'

He shook his head and as a stream of incomprehensible words issued from his mouth, Joan frowned; sure that she had caught one of them. Danny! Had he said 'Danny'? 'It's all right, love. Danny is taking care of everything. The business, the boys, the lot.'

Once again Dan tried to speak, his eyes wild as the bell rang to signal the end of visiting time.

'I've got to go now, Dan, but don't worry, everything is fine. As I said, Danny is taking care of everything. He's a good lad, and a chip off the old block.'

Dan became increasingly agitated and a nurse approached the bed, saying, 'You really must leave now, Mrs Draper. Your husband looks upset and I think he needs to rest.'

Joan tried to kiss Dan goodbye, but his good arm flapped as though pushing her away. She stood helplessly as the nurse took over.

'Come on now, Mr Draper,' the nurse said brusquely as she tidied the bed. 'Say goodbye to your wife and isn't it lovely that you're going home next week?'

Dan slumped, spent, and at last Joan was able to give him a swift kiss goodbye. 'I'll see you tomorrow, love.'

He didn't respond, his head turned away from her now. Joan left the ward, wondering what she had said to agitate him.

When Joan climbed into the car beside Maurice, Pet said, 'I'm sorry, Mum. I didn't mean to upset Dad.'

'Yes, well, he was still in a state when I left. When he comes home he's going to need complete quiet. I hope you realise that, my girl.'

'Yes, I know. Maurice told me about the stroke and when Dad comes home, I'll help you to look after him.'

'There's no need. I can cope, but just watch what you say in front of him.' Joan was surprised that Maurice had told Pet. It hadn't been her idea to keep the girl in the dark, but as usual, her brothers had wanted their little sister protected. Well, she'd have to grow up now, and though Joan didn't want any help with Dan's care, it was about time Pet learned how to do a bit of housework.

Joan settled in her seat as Maurice drove them home. Dan had seemed upset when Pet had asked a string of questions in front of him, but she was sure there was more to it than that. He had become worse when Pet left, and now Joan realised it was the mention of Danny that had started him off.

Yet surely that should have relieved him of any worry, not cause him to nearly have a fit.

'Maurice, did your father have a falling-out with Danny?'

'Er, no, Mum, not that I'm aware of. Why do you ask?'

'I'm probably imagining things, but he seemed to get out of his pram when I mentioned Danny's name.'

'He's probably just worried about the business.'

'Yeah, maybe,' Joan said, but somehow she thought there was more to it than that. She was then struck by a thought. Yes, that must be it. She'd have a word with Danny as soon as they arrived home.

Danny was turning over the things he needed to say. He'd called a meeting for nine o'clock that evening, and rather than return to the yard, he'd told Yvonne to disappear as soon as the boys came round. He didn't intend to discuss business in front of her, so she could bugger off next door to sit with his mother.

When there was a knock on the door, he was surprised to see his mother on the step. 'Hello, Mum. How's Dad?' he asked as she stepped inside.

'About the same, but something's worrying him. He became very agitated when I mentioned you and I've been thinking about it on the way home. I reckon it's because you haven't been to see him lately.

Your brothers all go, but when was the last time you went to the hospital?'

'I ain't been for over a week, but I've been busy. I've got the business to run, and since George took our capital, there's a lot to sort out.'

'What are you talking about? What capital? And when did George take it?'

Danny ran a hand over his face. 'Oh, shit, that just slipped out. Look, we didn't want you to know this, but I suppose I'll have to tell you now. That box you found on the bathroom floor, well, it had money in it: Dad's savings and capital for the business. George sneaked back and took the lot.'

He saw the blood drain from his mother's face. 'Mum, are you all right?'

There was a pause but then she said, 'I'm fine. It was just a shock, that's all. I don't know why you had to keep it from me in the first place. Mind you, I dread to think what your father will say when he finds out.' Her hand went to her mouth. 'Oh, listen to me, I'm not thinking straight. It would be best if we keep it from your father for now. The shock would be too much for him and might bring on another stroke.'

'Until he's on his feet and can talk again, we won't tell him, Mum.'

'Danny, I hate to say this, but he might never recover his speech, or be able to walk again. Now I know that you're busy, but you must find time to visit him.'

193

Danny hung his head, fighting for an excuse. Whenever he went to visit him, the old man got upset, and nowadays he avoided the hospital like the plague. Though his father couldn't talk coherently, Danny could guess what he was trying to say. He was out of favour and there was no way the old man would want him running things. It was just as well he couldn't talk, or it might be Maurice or Bob handling the business. If he went to see the old man when the others were there, they might twig and that was the last thing he wanted.

He met his mother's eyes now, the lie easy. 'I'm sorry, Mum, it's, well . . . it does my head in to see Dad like that.'

'I know it's hard, but go to see him, and when he comes home, I don't want him pressured. Have a word with the boys – tell them that if they have any problems they must bring them to you.'

'Yeah, all right.'

'If your father has complete peace, you never know, he might get better. In the meantime, I don't want him involved in running the business, so when you go to see him, don't mention it. Well, other than to say that everything is fine.'

Danny could see the change in his mother, the icy determination in her eyes. She no longer looked distant and remote. In fact, she looked like she was suddenly made of steel.

'Don't worry, Mum. We all want Dad to get better

and know we shouldn't worry him. I can look after the business for as long as it takes.'

'You're a good lad, and as I told your father, you're a chip off the old block.'

Yvonne had remained quiet during this exchange, but when Bob knocked on the door she rose to her feet. 'The boys want to talk business, so if it's all right with you, Mum, I'll come round to your place for a while.'

'I suppose so.'

When they had both left, Bob said, 'What did Mum want?'

'She wants to make sure that we don't pester Dad. When he comes home he's got to have peace and quiet so there's to be no business talk in front of him.'

When the others turned up, Danny repeated what their mother had said, and then it was on to business. 'I wanted to keep the hard porn strictly in the family, but with George taking our capital, it's impossible. I've come up with another idea and had a word with Eddy Woodman. He doesn't want to get involved in the making of hard porn, but he's agreed to let us use his equipment until we can buy our own.'

'That won't be for some time,' Maurice said. 'A decent camera won't be cheap, not to mention the gear for developing and splicing.'

'What about the girls, and the blokes, are they willing to take it up a notch?' asked Bob.

'Only one pair; the others don't want to know. I had a word with Lillie Ellington and she can supply what we need, but it's gonna cost a good few bob.'

'Why go through that old hag? Why can't you get a few girls off the street? There's plenty around Soho.'

'Use your head, Bob. We don't want anyone finding out about our setup or where it is. When Garston gets wind of what we're up to he's gonna put feelers out, and tarts like that won't keep their mouths shut. They'd soon blab to save their skins.'

'Lillie's crew would be the same.'

'No they won't. Lillie has her lot well under control. They know what would happen to them if they open their mouths.'

'I hope you're right,' Maurice said doubtfully, 'but I still think it's too risky.'

'Look, we've got to take a few risks if we want to make money. As I said before, we can soon hire some muscle if Garston gets wind of us.'

'Yeah, and that's gonna cost too,' Maurice complained.

'For the time being, we'll just have to tighten our belts a bit more. The most important thing is to get up and running, the sooner the better. In fact, I want to schedule our first shoot for Friday.'

'That soon?'

'Yes, Maurice, that soon,' Danny said. 'Me and Chris have been out and about and we've got advance orders.'

'What's on the agenda for tomorrow?' Chris asked.

'We've still got the usual stuff to make so I'll need you at Wimbledon. Maurice will be needed here to run Mum to the hospital, and Bob, I want you at the yard. There's a delivery of bricks and we can't leave that little weasel Steve to handle it on his own.'

'Why me?'

'For fuck's sake, just do it, Bob. It'll only be for a couple of hours and then you can join us at Wimbledon.'

Danny exhaled loudly, fed up with Bob's constant carping. He hadn't forgotten that Bob had tried to put him in the shit with the old man, but he'd get his revenge. What his brothers didn't know was that when the money came rolling in again, he intended to stash some away until he had the capital he needed. With the old man out of the way, he could go ahead with his plans to film kiddie porn. There was loads of money to be made, but he was going to keep his brothers out of the loop and ensure that all the profits were his. He'd already put a few feelers out, making discreet enquiries about getting hold of kids, and it had proved to be easier than expected.

Joan's mind was racing and she hardly listened as Yvonne chattered. She had been so intent on Dan that she had put the blood on the bathroom floor out of her mind, but after speaking to Danny and finding out that George had come back to take the money, her stomach was churning.

Had Chris caught George stealing it? Had he gone for him? Was it George's blood? No, no, of course it wasn't. Chris would never hurt his own brother. He was a good, kind lad, the best of the bunch. She was being silly and had to forget these daft suspicions.

'Are you all right? I don't think you've heard a word I've said.'

'What? Oh, sorry, Yvonne, I was miles away.'

'I said I'll help you when Dan comes home, but before then you'll have to think about where he's going to sleep.'

'Sleep! What do you mean?'

'Mum, he's going to be in a wheelchair. He won't be able to manage the stairs.'

Joan gave herself a mental shake. Dan was her main concern – his care when he came home. 'Yes, you're right, Yvonne. He'll have to sleep down here. I'll get a day bed, but it means getting rid of the sofa.'

'What a shame. And what about a commode? I know the toilet's downstairs, but it might be a job to wheel him through the kitchen to the bathroom.'

For the rest of the evening, Joan concentrated solely on Dan's homecoming, but when Chris came in, she just looked at him and her stomach did a somersault.

'Why are you looking at me like that, Mum?'

'Like what?'

'Like I've done something wrong.'

'Don't be silly, you're imagining things.' Yet even as she said these words, Joan knew she wasn't telling the truth. She did think that Chris had done something wrong, very wrong. Since the day that George had attacked his father, Chris hadn't been the same. There was something in his eyes that hadn't been there before, something deep, something haunted. Joan shuddered. The thought that her favourite son had done something to his brother, along with the fact that George had nearly killed his own father, was unbearable. She couldn't deal with it, she just couldn't, and as usual when unable to face things, she buried her head in the sand.

Chapter Fifteen

The following morning, Danny parked in the drive, and as he and Chris climbed out of the car, his eyes took in their surroundings. The spot in Wimbledon had been chosen for its location: down a narrow lane, it was well out of the way. There were no neighours to question the comings and goings, and they had put Pete Saunders in the cottage. He was an ex-con with a past, reclusive, grateful to work the small-holding, to grow vegetables, and to live rent free in return for his silence. He was the perfect foil should anyone decide to call, playing his part perfectly and acting like an eccentric old git if anyone asked questions. Not that many people had called over the years, but there were the meter readers, the occasional religious touts, and when there were local elections, the party candidates. So far the ploy had worked perfectly and Danny hoped it would continue to do so.

As they walked into the large barn, the high rafters hung with lighting, Danny interrupted the babble of voices. 'Right, let's get started,' he snapped, but he was pleased to see that the girls and their partners were ready. Bored with filming the soft stuff, and looking forward to making the real money-spinners, Danny just wanted to get it over with. He moved to inspect the set.

'We're nearly ready,' Eddy Woodman said as he tested the lighting with his meter.

A harem scene had been attempted with lots of soft draping, the bed covered with red satin sheets. Bright, embroidered silk cushions had been scattered along the headboard, but Danny shook his head, saying in disgust, 'You fucking morons. Since when did sheiks sleep in beds?'

'You and Chris are a bit late so we'd thought we'd get things moving,' Eddy protested, 'and it looks all right to me.'

Danny was about to explode again when Chris spoke.

'We're supposed to be in a desert, not a suburban bedroom, but it won't take long to put right. Give me a hand, Eddy. We'll take the mattress off the bed and put it on the floor. Set up a canvas backdrop and hang a few lamps around.'

'I'm supposed to be the cameraman, not the bloody labourer,' Eddy moaned. 'George used to do the humping.'

'Well, he ain't here, so just get on with it,' Danny snapped.

After one look at Danny's face, Eddy hurried to do his bidding, the task soon completed.

'It looks nice,' Andrea said as she preened in her mauve, chiffon costume.

With her midriff exposed and long shapely legs visible through the gauze trousers, Danny had to admit she looked tasty. Her long, dark, straight hair tumbled down her back, but the effect was spoiled by her chewing vigorously on gum.

'Have you looked at your part?' Danny asked.

'Yeah, it's a piece of cake. I'm dragged in, protesting, and when the sheik pulls off my veil I act scared. Then when he starts on me, I struggle for a little while before giving in. I then start to enjoy it and we get down to business.'

Danny exhaled loudly. 'Yeah, well, just make sure you ain't chewing that bloody gum.'

Andrea giggled and once again Danny was struck by how innocent she looked. Innocent – that was a bloody laugh. The girl was a tart, but she usually played her parts well. His eyes flicked to the so-called sheik, a bloke they used regularly. Tall, muscular and covered in tan-coloured panstick, he looked the part, and his costume wasn't bad either. He had played many roles but, like Andrea, he wanted to be on the stage. The soft-porn roles were just a way of making money whilst he waited for his big break.

At first Danny had loved the filming, finding

himself aroused every time he watched the action, and though they pretended otherwise, he knew his brothers had felt the same. Of course, unlike him, they went home to their wives, whereas he would call round to his latest girlfriend to indulge his fantasies. Some of the girls they used were on offer, but Danny wouldn't touch them with a bargepole. He'd never fancied going in after they'd been with someone else, and he wasn't about to start now, despite the inviting smile he got from Rusty, a redhead who made it obvious she fancied him.

'Right, let's get started,' he ordered.

Eddy checked the lighting again before moving behind the camera, saying to Danny as though it was an afterthought, 'How's your dad?'

'About the same, but he's coming home soon so things can get back to normal. Bob will be able to do the editing full time again, and Chris will here to handle the sets.'

With a few more tweaks to the scenery they were ready, and Danny stood behind Eddy as the camera began to roll. Andrea was dragged in by two blokes dressed up to look like eunuchs, her eyes wide with fear, her acting perfect as she got into the role. For once it went without a hitch, and Danny found his thoughts drifting, bored with seeing sex acted out.

He thought back to what his mother had said: that if the old man had peace and quiet, lack of stress, he might make a recovery. If that was the case, his father would be in charge again, but Danny loved being in control and didn't want to give it up.

By ten o'clock that evening, most of the residents of Drapers Alley were at home. In number six, the kids were in bed, and with only the gentle ticking of the mantel clock, all was quiet. Steve put down his newspaper, and then ran a hand over his face.

'Why haven't you been to visit your uncle?' he asked Ivy.

She shrugged. 'I haven't had the chance, and anyway, I haven't been asked. Maurice drives Joan and Yvonne up there every day, but I ain't been invited, and in the evenings it's the same. The boys and Pet go, but not one of them has given me a thought.'

'You could go on the bus.'

'Why should I get a bus when the others are all driven in style? Anyway, I ain't the only one who hasn't seen him. Sue and Norma haven't been either.'

'I still think it looks bad.'

'And I think it's bad that you've had to take a cut in your pay. After all, you're the one who does all the work at the yard and the others have hardly shown their faces lately. You should speak up for yourself. Tell Danny you want the same pay *and* a day off every week.'

'With Dan in hospital, the boys are busy. Things will get back to normal once he's home.'

'Don't count on it. Uncle Dan had a stroke so it's doubtful he'll ever be fit to run things again. Anyway, when the boys ain't at the hospital, they still ain't at the yard so I'd love to know where they go and what they get up to.'

'Search me,' Steve said, hoping that Ivy would stop quizzing him. He knew what the boys were up to – knew that when they weren't filming in Wimbledon, they were touting for business. Mind you, he was sure something else was in the wind, but so far he'd been kept in the dark. Despite Ivy telling him to complain, he knew better than to open his mouth. Dan might be ill and incapable of running the business, but his eldest son was even less approachable. Danny was throwing his weight about, snapping orders, with all of them expected to jump at his commands.

Steve's expression was wry. It could be worse. At least Danny had taken over and, though prone to violence, he was a pussycat compared to George. Steve wasn't sorry that George had disappeared off the face of the earth, and he had his own theory about that. He reckoned that George had jumped ship and gone abroad, well out of his brothers' reach.

'Steve, how do you feel about moving away from Drapers Alley?'

Steve's face stretched in disbelief. It was Ivy who had wanted to live here in the first place, but he'd move out again like a shot. 'Yeah, it would suit me, but what makes you think the council would rehouse us?'

'I don't know if they will, but it wouldn't do any harm to give them a try.'

'What's brought this on, Ivy?'

'Oh, I dunno. It's just that we don't fit in. I may have been born a Draper, but we're treated like outcasts. Linda was the only one who bothered with me, but now she's living with her parents again and I'm stuck on my own, day in, day out. Yvonne and Norma are snobs, and though Sue's as common as muck, she doesn't give me the time of day.'

Steve wanted to tell Ivy why – to tell her that it was her own fault – but if it meant getting out of Drapers Alley, he'd continue to keep his thoughts to himself. The truth was that instead of trying to make friends with any of them, Ivy made mischief, playing one off against the other. It had worked at first, but they had soon got wind of what she was up to and now they avoided her like the plague.

He shifted in his seat, smiling at the thought of leaving the alley. He could go back to totting, but in fact he'd do anything to earn a bob or two, anything but work for the Drapers. No more fear of getting stopped by the police – of them finding the bloody films he was delivering. He could be his own boss again!

'Get on to the council first thing in the morning, love,' he said, standing up to give his wife a swift hug.

'Yeah, I will, and I might even ask if we can be housed outside of the borough.'

'Suits me, love,' he said, winking before adding, 'and how about an early night?'

'All right, you're on.'

Steve smiled. Ivy may not be an oil painting, but beggars couldn't be choosers, and, with his loins stirring, he eagerly followed her upstairs.

Next door, Maurice was getting his usual earful from Norma, his voice tired as he answered, 'I've told you business is slow, and until things pick up you'll have to make do with what I can give you.'

'Make do! Do you think I can conjure shoes for Oliver out of thin air? Yes, I can cut down on food, bulk up with vegetables, but I can't force Oliver's feet into shoes that are now a size too small. You should be thankful that Oliver takes care of his shoes, unlike Sue's boys, so they last a good while. However, he can't help it when he grows out of them.'

'With what they cost, they should last. Anyway, can't you get him some cheap plimsolls for now? I used to wear them as a kid and they didn't do me any harm.'

'Are you mad?' Norma shrieked. 'They're only fit for PE, and I am *not* sending Oliver to school wearing plimsolls. You'll have to give me extra house-keeping this week and that's that!'

'Enough, Norma!' Maurice snapped. 'I'm sick to death of your demands! When you're not nagging me to leave Drapers Alley, you're on about money. You'll get what I give you and I don't want to hear another word about it!'

Maurice had to hide a smile when he saw the shock on his wife's face. Her mouth opened and closed, for once floundering for words. He rarely lost his temper, rarely stood up to her, in fact for a quiet life he seemed to spend most of his time placating Norma. It felt good to take a leaf out of Danny's book, but this thought was wiped out when Norma found her voice again.

She rose to her feet, her face red with anger. 'How dare you speak to me like that? I'm not asking for money for myself, I'm asking for money to buy *our* son a decent pair of shoes. I don't know what's come over you lately, but I won't be spoken to like a common fishwife.'

Maurice quickly broke in. It was all right for Danny to talk about controlling their wives, but if he didn't calm Norma down she'd go on and on until he couldn't stand it any more. 'All right, I apologise. I shouldn't have snapped at you like that. It's just that with Dad in hospital and the loss of trade at the yard, I'm feeling a bit stressed.'

Norma stood glaring at him, arms folded across her chest, but then exhaled loudly. 'All right, Maurice, I know you're under a lot of strain at the moment so I'll let it pass, but there is still the question of new shoes for Oliver.'

'I'll see what I can do,' he said, hoping that it would be sufficient to placate her for now. If only she'd be content with plimolls or a cheap pair of shoes, but no, Oliver always had to have the best. That had been fine in the past, and no doubt there'd be more money available soon, but for now they really did have to tighten the purse strings. His brothers' wives seemed to have accepted that, so why couldn't she?

Maurice found his chest wheezing as he took a breath. 'I really am bushed, Norma. If you don't mind, I think I'll go to bed.'

'I'll just tidy up, then I'll join you,' she said, her voice clipped.

Maurice wearily went upstairs, but as he undressed and climbed into bed, his chest was whistling, his breathing so laboured that he had to prop himself up on several pillows. He closed his eyes, finding that, as usual, his thoughts turned to his father. It was such a relief that the old man had survived George's beating, but it looked doubtful that he'd recover from the stroke. It meant that Danny would continue to be in charge, and now Maurice's chest heaved as he fought for air. He didn't trust Danny lately and was worried about where he was taking the business. Yes, they'd agreed to hard porn, and there was no doubt that they needed to make more money, but he couldn't dismiss his fears. Garston and other competitors weren't going to take the intrusion into their territory lightly and they were sure to retaliate. Under their father's leadership, they'd had little to worry about, with Drapers Alley a safe haven. Now, though, with taking on the hard stuff, all that could come to an end, and Maurice feared the future. His chest tightened and in panic he fought for air, sweat beading his forehead. For the first time he understood why Norma wanted to leave, and was horrified by the thought of Oliver in danger.

'Maurice, you look awful. Here, drink this.'

He turned his head, grateful for Norma's ministrations. Yes, she was a nag. Yes, she drove him mad sometimes, but when he was feeling like this, unable to breathe, his heart beating wildly in his chest, Norma always tended to him. Taking a cloth dipped in cool water, Norma bathed his forehead, whispering reassurances until at last he was able to fill his lungs with air.

'You poor darling. Are you feeling better now?'

'Yes, thanks, love.'

He watched now as Norma undressed and when she climbed into bed, she snuggled close. All right, he may not be the boss, unable to control his wife like Danny, but none of this mattered now as Maurice closed his eyes and drifted off to sleep.

* * *

Sue and Bob were still up, snuggled on the sofa as they listened to the radio. The room was untidy, a pile of ironing still untouched, but Bob hardly noticed as Sue ran a hand along his thigh.

'Was your dad any better this evening? Did he manage to say anything?'

'No, and as usual he seemed agitated. Mum thinks he wants to see Danny, but he didn't turn up.'

'Pet came to see me after school. She knows that your father had a stroke.'

'Yeah, Maurice told her, and Danny wasn't too pleased about it.'

'She isn't a child now, Bob.'

'She's still only fourteen.'

'Oh, for God's sake, Pet leaves school soon and it's about time you all let her grow up. She hates being treated like a child.'

Bob ran a hand over his face, changing the subject as he blurted out, 'Sue, I can't stand it that Danny's in charge. It ain't right, and I reckon we should all have an equal say in the running of the business.'

'It's only a builders' merchants. Surely it doesn't take much to run it.'

Bob swallowed. Blimey, he'd have to watch his mouth. 'Yeah, well, we should still have an equal say.'

'Never mind,' Sue consoled. 'Things could change. When your dad's home in familiar surroundings, he may get better.'

Sue continued to stroke his thigh and, glad of the distraction, Bob twisted in his seat. 'If you don't stop doing that I'll have to take you to bed. I wouldn't say no to a bit of slap and tickle.'

'I thought you'd never ask,' Sue said, smiling teasingly as she quickly stood up. 'Come on then, big boy, let's see what you're made of.'

Bob made a grab for her, and Sue squealed, giggling as he chased her upstairs.

Through the thin walls, Yvonne heard Sue's squeal and felt a surge of jealousy. For the first time in ages, Danny had come home early, but instead of the fun and games that she could hear next door, she felt only the pain of rejection. Danny had hardly spoken to her, and not long after ten he had gone to bed, saying he was tired and needed an early night. She had followed him upstairs, but he'd fallen asleep as soon as his head touched the pillow, whilst she had lain beside him, frustrated. It had been over a month since he had touched her, held her, or even kissed her, and now she was in despair. There was another woman, Yvonne was sure of it, and knew from past experience that he wouldn't make love to her until his affair ran its course. Was this one serious? Would he leave her?

Unable to sleep she had got up again, and after making herself a cup of cocoa, she sat alone in the living room. An hour passed, and still wide awake,

Yvonne rose to her feet to look out of the window. She pulled back the curtain, but as usual there was little to see, just the factory wall and the entrance to the alley. A shape appeared, and as it passed the bollard, she saw it was Chris. Yvonne frowned. It was late and she wondered where he had been, but then she shrugged. Unlike Danny, Chris was a single man, and a nice-looking one at that. Secretly, he was Yvonne's favourite brother-in-law. Chris was always polite, always thoughtful and, unlike Danny, she felt that when he finally settled down he'd be faithful. She stepped back from the window, knocking the small side table and sending her empty cup crashing to the floor. Swiftly Yvonne bent to clear up the mess, startled when she heard a voice.

'What are you doing? Why aren't you in bed?'

Yvonne looked up to see her husband framed in the doorway. 'I . . . I couldn't sleep so I came down to make myself a drink. I'm sorry I woke you.'

Instead of berating her, Danny said softly, 'Leave that until the morning. Come on – come to bed.'

Yvonne left the broken china where it was to follow Danny upstairs. She threw off her dressing gown, surprised when she got into bed to feel Danny's arms snaking around her. She turned her head, and in the soft glow from the bedside light, she saw his slow smile. Yvonne knew that look and felt a thrill of anticipation. Danny made love to her, slowly at first, but then with increasing passion.

Yvonne revelled in the feelings that he aroused, ones that were mixed with relief. Her fears dissolved. Danny may have been seeing another woman, but as always, he had come back to her.

Chris, the last member of the family to arrive home, carefully unlocked the door, trying to make as little noise as possible as he went upstairs. He didn't want to wake his mother, not when she was under so much strain lately. She had always been distant, remote, but he was seeing another side of her now. She was so focused and protective that it was like seeing a mother guarding her child, instead of a wife with her husband. Chris's lips tightened. She had never been protective of him. Instead, as a child, it had been his father he had to run to when he was upset or in trouble. He had longed to feel his mother's love, longed to be held in her arms, but when he had gone to her, she had pushed him away. Chris had never forgotten it and her rejection still haunted him. With older brothers he had hidden his feelings, knowing that if he cried they would have called him a sissy. Instead he had tried to toughen up, and when he was old enough his father had initiated him into the family business.

Chris felt a surge of pain. It broke his heart to see his father now – the man he had looked up to and admired, reduced to a babbling wreck. George had done that to him. George had all but destroyed their father.

His guts tightened and his heart rate rose as he moved past his mother's room. He wanted to fling open her bedroom door, to confide in her, but she would never understand. It was impossible. He had to keep his secret, not just from his mother, but from his whole family.

'Hello. You're late,' Pet said, stepping out of her bedroom. 'I can't sleep and I'm going downstairs to make a drink.'

Chris fought to pull himself together. 'Shush, you'll wake Mum.'

'Can we talk?'

'Yeah, all right,' Chris said as the two of them went quietly downstairs, and it was only when they were both sitting at the table that he spoke again. 'I'm surprised you're still awake. What do you want to talk about?'

'This family. Dad's ill in hospital and I know that he had a stroke. Until now, I've pushed everything else to the back of my mind, but he's coming home soon and I can't stop thinking about it.'

'Thinking about what?'

'The fact that Dad, and all of you, are criminals.'

'Don't be daft, that's all in the past.'

'Don't bother denying it, Chris.'

For the first time Chris saw the change in his sister. She looked harder, her eyes less innocent. He'd been so wrapped up in his father's recovery and the changes to the business, that he'd hardly noticed or given a thought to his little sister. 'What makes you think we're criminals?'

'It started with George and the way he treated his wife. I saw the violence, and Dad's reaction was just as bad. Then when I went to the dance at the youth club I met a chap, but as soon as he found out that I'm a Draper, he ran off, obviously scared out of his wits.'

'It's just as well. You're too young to be going out on dates.'

'Stop it! You're treating me like a child again. Tell me the truth, Chris. Just what is this family involved in? What made that chap run off like that?'

Chris lowered his eyes. For years they had kept Pet in ignorance, fobbing her off by telling her that they now ran a legit business, but she was growing up and blokes were starting to sniff around. With the family's reputation he wasn't surprised that one had bolted as soon as he found out that Pet was a Draper. Bugger it. He'd have to give her some sort of explanation, but it could hardly be the truth. 'Look, we ain't really criminals. Until recently we did a bit of money lending, and for a backhander we offered local business protection. That's all, Pet. If businesses didn't stump up, or anyone welshed on a loan, we sometimes had to be a bit heavy with them and it gave us a bit of a reputation.'

'Heavy. What does that mean? Did you beat them up, is that it?'

'Well, not exactly beat them up, but if they weren't wary of us, they'd have tried to get out of paying their dues.'

'Don't take me for a fool, Chris. What you're telling me is bad enough, but if it was true, I'm sure I would have heard about it. What are you really up to?'

Chris abruptly stood up. He had done his best, but he hadn't fooled Pet. He'd have to have a word with Danny. Maybe his brother could come up with something to fob her off, but he'd have to get to him in the morning before Pet did. In the meantime, he didn't want to face any more questions. 'Look, I've told you the truth, but if you don't believe me, ask Danny.'

'Oh, I will, but what about Mum? Did she know what you were up to?'

'Of course not. Dad ain't proud of what we did, but at the time the yard wasn't making enough to support six families so it's something we got into to make a few extra bob. Dad doesn't want Mum to know about it, so keep your mouth shut. Now it's late and I'm going to bed. With school in the morning, I suggest you do the same.'

'Yes, I'll go to bed, but you needn't think I've swallowed your lies. I'm not giving up until I hear the truth.'

Chris felt his temper flare. 'And what good would that do? If you find out the so-called truth, do you think it will make any difference? Do you think it will make your life any better? Believe me, it won't. You'd be better off remaining in ignorance.'

On that note, Chris turned on his heels, this time forgetting to tread quietly as he went upstairs. In his room, he threw off his clothes before flinging himself onto his bed. He'd made a mistake telling Pet that they were loan sharks, but he shouldn't have lost his temper. Maybe he should have told her that they were thieves, robbers, because even that would be preferable to her finding out what they really did. If she ever discovered their secret – his secret – he dreaded to think what her reaction would be. Despite saying she wasn't a child now, Pet was still innocent, untouched, and finding out that they were involved in the seedy world of porn could destroy her.

Chapter Sixteen

Chris had managed to talk to Danny before Pet was up the next morning, and now his brother was scowling. 'She's just a kid. Tell her to mind her own bleedin' business.'

'I don't think that'd work. Pet's growing up, and she's seen too much lately. She won't be fobbed off with the story I came up with.'

'I'm not surprised. Did you really expect her to believe that we offered protection and loans?'

'It was all I could come up with at the time.'

'Leave Pet to me. I'll have a word with her, but unlike you, I'll make sure she keeps her nose out of our affairs. Despite what you say, she's still just a kid, and a girl at that. What we men do to put bread on the table is none of her business and I'll make sure she understands that.'

Chris doubted that Pet would stand for it, but he kept his thoughts to himself. Danny had made it clear that he was running the show now, and that meant sorting out any problems within the family too. That was fine with Chris. He knew that he was considered to be Mr Nice Guy, and he wanted it to stay that way.

'Yeah, right, I'll leave Pet to you. Are we making another film today?'

'Yeah, I think we'll do a hospital theme. It seems apt, and a lot of men fantasise about nurses.'

'Ain't we done that before?'

'Yeah, but it was a while ago. To be honest, I'm running out of ideas. If you ask me, we've covered just about everything.'

'I don't suppose it would hurt to use all the themes again. We just have to rotate the girls and their partners and make a few adjustments to the storylines. What have you got in mind for the first hard-porn film?'

'It's got to be good, different; something that will top anything Garson has come up with. I was thinking of three in a bed.'

'Ain't that a bit old hat?'

'Not the threesome I've got in mind.'

Chris was about to ask more when Danny held a finger to his lips. 'Shush, Yvonne is on her way down. She's usually up at the crack of dawn, but I think I wore her out last night, if you know what I mean.' He gave a lewd wink.

'Morning, Yvonne,' Chris said, eyeing his sister-in-law as she walked into the room. She was wearing a long, pink candlewick dressing gown and looked thin, yet soft with her hair tousled and cheeks flushed.

'Hello, Chris. Goodness, look at the time. Why didn't you wake me, Danny?'

'It's only seven thirty and I was just about to, but then again, I was considering coming back to bed for another bit of slap and tickle.'

'Danny!' she exclaimed, the blush turning from pink to red before she almost ran into the kitchen, calling over her shoulder, 'I'll get your breakfast going.'

'I'm off,' Chris said. 'I'll see you later.'

Chris went back next door and found that his mother and Pet were up, both sitting at the table with a pot of tea and rack of toast already made.

'Where have you been?' Pet asked.

'I had a word with Danny about the arrangements for today.'

'Is that *all*, or did you discuss something else?'

'Just work,' Chris said before he sat down at the table, his eyes going to his mother. 'Are you all right, Mum?'

'Of course I am.'

'I expect you're looking forward to Dad coming home.'

'Yes, I am, but when he does there'll be some changes. I don't want your father to be worried about anything. If he has peace and quiet, he might get better. Petula, there's to be no more loud music, and you, Chris, I don't want to hear any business talk. Is that clear?'

'Yes.'

'Good. In fact, the more the pair of you stay out of his way, the better.'

Chris saw Pet's look of dismay, and felt the same. Now that his father had been cut down, felled, his mother had become strong. She was shutting him out as always, and from his father too. Well, he wasn't going to stand for that.

Pet was fuming. She had been to see Danny before leaving for school and he had told her in no uncertain terms to keep her nose out of the family business. Danny had never spoken to her like that before, his eyes hard and manner implacable. It was as if, as with George and her father, she was seeing him in a new light.

Since the day that George attacked their father, Pet felt as though everything had changed – that her life would never be the same again. She still didn't know what her family was mixed up in, but from what Chris had said, it was obviously something illegal and dangerous. He'd lost his temper, saying she'd be better off not knowing. Yet that had only made her more determined to discover the truth, and now Pet's jaw jutted with determination.

Yet only moments later, she faltered. Did she really

want to know? If it was something really bad, how would she feel? Her father must be the leader, yet how could the man who loved and protected her be a criminal? Maybe it was better to remain in ignorance, to shut her eyes to what went on around her. For the first time in her life, Pet felt truly alone, and with this feeling the last vestige of childhood left her.

Pet reached the school gates, walking in to see first- and second-year kids running around as though they didn't have a care in the world. She felt remote from them, so much older now, and seeing two of her friends lounging against the wall, she traversed the playground to reach them.

Jane's expression lit up, her face animated. 'Pet, have you heard the news?'

'What news?'

'It's Wendy,' said Susan. 'She's pregnant.'

Pet gawked, and instantly a face sprang to her mind. 'Pregnant? Oh, my God. Who's the father? Was it that chap she danced with at the club?'

'If you mean Tony Thorn, no, it isn't his.'

'It was some bloke she was seeing on the sly, and her parents are going mad,' Susan said.

'Oh, poor Wendy. What is she going to do?' asked Pet.

'I think her parents want it adopted, but in the meantime, she isn't coming back to school,' said Jane. 'I don't blame her. If I was in her shoes I wouldn't be able to show my face.'

'But what if she doesn't want it adopted?'

'Well, Pet, I don't think she's got much choice,' said Susan. 'Oh, there's the bell. Come on, we'd better go in. We've got Miss Jones for history and you know what she's like if we're late.'

The three girls walked into the building, Pet's mind still on Wendy. Fourteen and pregnant – how awful. And then to have to have the baby adopted . . . She would be the talk of the school, the area, her life ruined. Pet knew what it was like to be talked about. All her life she had been shunned because she was a Draper, and her heart went out to poor Wendy Baker.

Danny looked at his watch. It was one o'clock and the film they were making was well underway. He moved over to Chris, saying quietly, 'I'm going to sort out the girls for our first hard-core film. You and Bob can finish up here.'

Danny left the building. In truth, he was going to the hospital and wanted to get there well ahead of his mother. He was tense as he drove off, gripping the steering wheel tightly. He cared about the old man, but didn't want him back in action. His father had always been the one in control, the one who made all the decisions, and Danny had lost count of the times he had suggested changes, only for his father to veto his ideas. The old man pretended to put them to the vote, but made it clear from the start whether he liked them or not. He was a wily old sod and knew that none of his sons would go against him. The last meeting had proved that.

Things had changed now, Danny thought. He was the one in control and didn't want to give it up. He loved it, but there was always the risk that his father would recover his speech, and if he did, there was no guarantee that he'd leave him in charge. Danny was determined to get through to his father, to make him understand that if he didn't want all his hard work over the years wasted he should leave him in control. Bob and Maurice were too weak, and Chris too young. Things would go to pot if the firm was taken out of his hands, and Danny was determined to tell the old man just that.

When he arrived at the hospital, Danny went to the ward, but as he walked in a nurse held up her hand. 'It isn't visiting time for another fifteen minutes.'

Danny used his charms, smiling ruefully at the nurse. 'I'm sorry, love, I must have got the visiting hours wrong. Look, I've had a long drive and I'm anxious to see my father. Surely it won't hurt if you let me in.'

'All right, but you're lucky. Matron just left and our ward sister is having her lunch.'

'Thanks, darling,' Danny said as he moved past the nurse.

His father was at the end of the ward, his bed the

last in the row, and as though his father was hard of hearing, Danny shouted, 'Hello, Dad.'

Dan's reaction was instantaneous. He tried to speak, his good arm waving as he spat out his odd gibberish.

'It's all right,' Danny placated. 'There's nothing to worry about. The business is fine and I'm looking after everything. I'm getting the other stuff we talked about up and running. We'll soon be making a mint and you'll be able to have that house in the country you've always wanted.'

He watched as his father struggled to sit up, the noise he was making now resembling that of a bellowing bull. Moments later something changed and, worried, Danny cried, 'Dad, Dad, are you all right? Nurse! Nurse!'

The nurse who had tried to bar his entry hurried down the ward. 'What happened?' she said as she reached the side of the bed.

Danny struggled to pull himself together. 'I . . . I don't know. He just sort of went funny, like he was having a fit.'

'I'll get the doctor.'

'Is he gonna be all right?'

'We'll know when the doctor has had a look at him. Now, please, wait outside,' the nurse said before closing the curtains around the bed.

Danny didn't need telling twice and almost ran out of the ward. He hovered outside, saw the doctor arrive and then he began to pace. He shouldn't have come. One look at him and his father became apoplectic. Bloody hell, all he'd tried to do was to reassure the old man, but instead he'd made things worse. He'd told him that the business was doing fine, said they'd make a mint producing hard porn . . . Danny paused, the blood draining from his face. Shit! Had his father thought he was talking about using kids? Oh God, what had he done? What if his father died? He'd have caused it!

Joan smiled when she saw Danny in the corridor, pleased that he had come to visit his father at last.

'Hello, Danny,' Yvonne said. 'I'm surprised to see you here during the day.'

'Me too,' Maurice said, obviously puzzled.

'I had a bit of time to kill, and as I was in the area I thought I'd pop in to see Dad.'

'Come on, let's go in,' Joan urged.

'We can't, Mum.'

'Why?' Joan asked, but something in Danny's expression caused her heart to thump with fear. 'What's wrong?'

'Dad was taken bad and the doctor's with him.'

'Bad! When?'

'It was only a little while ago. I had only been in there for a few minutes when he came over sort of funny.'

'Oh, Danny, don't tell me he's had another stroke!'

'I dunno, Mum. We'll have to wait and see what the doctor has to say.'

'But what brought it on?'

'Search me. I was just telling him that everything is fine with the business when he had some sort of fit.'

Joan felt her knees give way beneath her, grateful when Yvonne stepped forward to take her arm, saying gently, 'Come on, Mum, let's find you a seat. Danny will tell one of the nurses where we are.'

In a daze, Joan allowed herself to be led to a waiting room. She found herself silently praying. She knew the others were talking, but their voices washed over her as she begged for Dan's life.

At last the doctor appeared and Joan surged to her feet. 'How is my husband?'

'I'm afraid he's had another stroke.'

Joan managed to stay on her feet, but her voice was a croak. 'Is . . . is he going to be all right?'

The doctor's face was grave. 'We'll know more in twenty-four hours.'

'Can I see him?'

'For a few minutes and with only one other visitor.'

'Danny,' Joan said. She saw her son hesitate; saw the look of fear on his face. He looked so pale but she wasn't surprised. Like her, he was obviously worried sick about his father.

'No, it's all right. Maurice can go with you.'

'You're the eldest, Danny,' she said.

Danny appeared reluctant, but impatiently Joan urged him forward. When they walked into the ward the curtains were still around Dan's bed and for a moment Joan paused, fearful of what she'd find. She then drew in a huge gulp of air before moving forward to draw them back. With Danny just behind her she almost crept inside, her hand immediately going to her mouth in shock. Dan was unconscious, ashen, an oxygen mask covering his mouth.

'Oh, no. He looks awful.'

Joan turned panic-stricken eyes to her son, but saw a strange expression on his face, almost like one of relief, as he whispered, 'He's out for the count, Mum. Come on, we don't want to wake him up. You can come back later.'

'No, I can't leave him.'

Joan took Dan's hand. It felt cold, clammy, and after solicitously tucking it under the blanket, she bent to kiss his forehead.

'Come on, Mum,' Danny urged as he gripped her arm.

Joan's lips tightened in anger. Dan was her husband and she wanted to be there when he woke up. She glared at her son, annoyed that he was in such a hurry to go. 'We've only just got here.'

'The doctor said we can only stay for a few minutes.'

Joan was about to speak when the curtain was

pulled back. 'I'm sorry, Mrs Draper,' a nurse said, 'you really must leave now.'

'Can't I stay for five minutes?'

It wasn't the nurse who replied, it was Danny. 'No, Mum, you heard the nurse. We've got to go.'

'Why are you in such an all-fired hurry? You've hardly looked at your father.'

'I can't stand to see him like that.'

Joan could see the tension in her son's face and found her anger draining away. He loved his father and, yes, it was obviously breaking his heart to see him like this. She turned away to lean over Dan, her kiss soft above the oxygen mask.

'Don't leave me, Dan,' she whispered, her voice cracking. 'Come back to me.'

'You can see your husband again this evening,' the nurse said as she began to take Dan's blood pressure.

Her emotions in turmoil, Joan was only able to nod. Danny took her arm to lead her away from the ward.

'How is he?' Maurice asked when they joined the others.

'He wasn't conscious, so we don't know,' Danny told him. 'Now come on, let's get Mum home. She looks worn out and needs to rest before coming back this evening.'

As Danny took over, Joan felt a surge of grati-tude. He was a good boy, and as she had said, a chip

230

off the old block. He was taking care of her, just like his father. When Dan regained consciousness and she told him how good Danny had been, he'd be so proud of his eldest son.

It had been a fraught twenty-four hours, but at last Joan received the news she'd been waiting for. Dan would survive. His face looked dreadful, drooping on one side, with the right side of his paralysed body, further weakened. The doctor was doubtful now that Dan would ever make a full recovery. The second stroke had delayed his return home, but he was alive, and to Joan that was all that mattered.

With all her energies focused on her husband, Joan was hardly aware of what went on around her. She left everything to Danny, safe in the knowledge that he would continue to look after the family, and the business.

On Friday, Joan sat beside her husband, gripping his good hand. 'Hello, love.'

There was no response. None of his usual gibbering, no arm waving and sighing. Joan wiped the drool from the side of his mouth.

Loudly Maurice asked, 'How are you, Dad?'

'There's no need to shout,' Joan snapped. 'Your father isn't deaf.'

'I reckon it's a trait in your family,' the man from the next bed called. 'Your other son was just as bad, shouting at the poor bloke as though he's deaf.'

Joan was annoyed at the interruption, but puzzled too. 'What son? I don't know who you mean.'

'I'm talking about the one who came to see your husband just before he had another stroke.'

'Oh, you mean Danny. Why was he shouting?'

'Search me, but your hubby got really agitated when he saw him. Your son tried to calm him down. He told him that he was taking care of the business and there was nothing for him to worry about.'

'Yes, he's a good lad,' Joan said.

'If you ask me, these youngsters are all the same. They think that just because we're old, we've lost our marbles or we're hard of hearing. They forget that we fought for our country during the war. They should give us a bit more respect.'

Joan switched off as the man ranted on and on. Poor Danny, it must have been awful for him to see his father having another stroke.

She leaned forward, her voice soft. 'Oh, Dan, you'd be so proud of Danny. He makes sure I'm all right, taking care of me just like you did.'

There was a sound, a sort of groan and Joan felt a surge of hope. Dan had responded for the first time since his second stroke, and maybe there'd be other improvements soon.

Chapter Seventeen

It was now August and Danny was putting all his energies into the hard-core films. It was hot, and though the rafters were high, the barn felt stifling.

Danny's face was beaded with sweat, but his mind was set on the task in hand. He didn't want to think about his father – about what he'd done. The guilt swamped him, keeping him awake at night, until at last he decided there was only one thing he could do to assuage his guilt. His father hadn't got any better, and he'd been sent home last month, but from what Yvonne had told him, space was short now that he was in a wheelchair. He'd have to make sure they made lots of money, enough to ensure that his father had every comfort – even the house in the country that he'd dreamed of.

He looked through the camera, and as the two men and the girl got into position, he snapped his orders. 'Bob, check the lighting.'

'We could do with Maurice.'

'He's feeling rough today and anyway he's not a lot of help – so stop bloody carping and get on with it.'

Bob scowled but Danny ignored him. Chris came to stand behind the camera, having completed his work on the set, and at last they were ready to roll.

The girl had been told what to do, and when Danny said, 'Right, get on with it,' she went into action.

She was one of Lillie's girls and good – very good, Danny saw – but he'd watched some of Garston's films and it would have to be graphic to compete. As he'd instructed, one bloke was taking her from behind, but now it was time to up the action. Danny zoomed in, ready for a close-up of the oral sex. 'Right, Mary, take the other bloke in your mouth.'

Yes, it was graphic, but they needed more like this in the bag. The worry was getting to him, the responsibility, the need to make money, not for himself now, but for his father. He'd wanted to be in control, to run things, but now all his energies were focused on his old man, on his comfort. Danny knew that he'd caused his father's second stroke, knew it could have killed him, and once again the guilt overwhelmed him.

Late that night, Ivy was fidgeting nervously as she looked out of the window. The kids were tired, but she'd had to keep them up. Steve was chuffed, waiting for the off, as anxious as she was to leave Drapers Alley.

'I still can't believe we got this council exchange,' Steve said. 'It's bloody marvellous. I'd love to be around to see their faces when another family moves into this place.'

'Yeah, and Danny's when you ain't around to run the bloody yard,' said Ivy. She had waited until Auntie Joan's lights had gone out, and now regretted sneaking out to stick a note through her door. It would have been more satisfying to have just left without warning, but it was too late now. Mind, she hadn't told her the story about the exchange – just that they were leaving. Ivy smiled happily. There'd be little chance of them finding out where they had gone.

'I didn't even know that the council offered exchanges,' Steve said.

'Yeah, well, it's just as well that they do. Mind you, it wasn't easy. Most of the people on the list wanted the same area, but bigger places with more bedrooms. I was lucky to find a family in Kent who wanted to move to Battersea, *and* that they agreed to swap their place for Drapers Alley.'

'I still don't think that Dan will let them move in.'

Ivy shrugged. 'He ain't in a fit state to stop them. Anyway, he doesn't own this house, and as the council agreed the exchange nobody can stop them.'

'Danny might, and I wouldn't want to be in their shoes in the morning.'

235

'Look, the family used to live in this area, and if they haven't heard of the Drapers, it ain't our problem. The husband has been offered a good job in the brewery so they want to move back, and it's up to them to sort anyone out who wants to stop them.'

'Yeah, well, I wish them luck.'

Ivy risked a peek outside. The night was clear, the moon shining, yet she consoled herself with the thought that it wasn't far to the corner. If they went now they should make it unseen. 'I think we can risk it.'

'I hope you're right,' Steve said, 'but I still don't know why we're sneaking off like this.'

'For Gawd's sake, Steve, we talked about this. For one, you were too scared to tell Danny that you're leaving the yard, and secondly it's a way to pay him back for the way you've been treated. When we go without warning he'll be left in the shit with nobody to take your place.'

Steve scratched his head. 'Yeah, I suppose so, but it still seems a bit cloak and dagger.'

'What's cloak and dagger, Daddy?' Ernie asked.

It was Ivy who answered. 'It's an adventure. Now come on, kids, we're off. When we get outside I want you to scoot around the corner.'

Harry yawned and Ivy became impatient. 'Steve, you'll have to pick him up.'

'Leave it out. How am I supposed to do that *and* carry the suitcases?'

Ivy heaved a sigh. 'Ernie, I want you to hold Harry's hand, and make sure that he doesn't dawdle.'

'Why have we got to go? Why can't we stay here?'

'I've told you. We're moving to a new house, and when you see it, you'll love it. Now shut up about it, and as I said, hold Harry's hand.'

With that, Ivy picked up two suitcases, whilst Steve did the same. She took one last peek outside and then ushering the boys ahead of her, she urged them on as they all scooted out of the alley. Steve had been reluctant to use what little money they had saved to buy an old banger, but Ivy had told him that a car, even one that looked a bit of a wreck, was essential in the country. There'd be no buses to hop on, no underground trains, but despite the remoteness of the village, she couldn't wait to get there.

Steve found the old car hard to start and Ivy's nerves were jangling, but even so she was happy. After all this time everything she had hoped for had come to fruition. She had wanted to see her uncle brought low, and thanks to George he was suffering now, just as her mother had. Her Uncle Dan was finished, in a wheelchair, a gibbering wreck. Yes, it was time to leave Drapers Alley – time for her new life to begin.

When Joan got up the following morning, she saw the note that had been shoved through her letter box and ran to pick it up. It was from Ivy, to tell her that they had left the alley. Joan threw it down. It was a bit sudden, but in truth she didn't care. When she had first seen the note her heart had skipped, hoping it was from George, because despite what he had done he was still her son, and she couldn't help wondering where he was. It had been over three months now – three long months without news.

As though reading her mind, Pet asked, 'Mum, is that letter from George?'

Joan looked up, her eyes clouded for a moment. 'No, it's from Ivy to tell me that they've moved out.'

'What? But why would she leave without saying goodbye?'

'I don't know,' Joan said impatiently. She didn't care that Ivy had left the alley. She was just pleased to see the back of Dan's niece.

Hearing a soft groan, Joan went over to the day bed, smiling softly. 'Morning, love.'

There was no reply from Dan, just a wave of his good arm, and knowing what he wanted Joan said, 'Come on, Petula, give me a hand. Your dad wants to go to the bathroom.'

The morning routine began then, and Joan was glad of her daughter's help. She was at home from school during the summer holidays, which had been a godsend, but things would become difficult when she returned for her last term. Still, Joan thought, Yvonne was marvellous, always on hand to lend a hand, but it was a shame that she couldn't allow Danny in to see his father. One look at his eldest son and Dan went mad, so much so that she had been forced to tell Danny to stay away. She still didn't understand what caused it, but felt the only explanation could be that Dan resented that he was so helpless – that he was forced to let Danny take over running the business.

When Chris came downstairs half an hour later, Joan handed him Ivy's note, watching as his eyes widened.

'This doesn't make sense. Why has Ivy buggered off without saying anything?'

'Search me,' Joan said, 'but if you ask me it's good riddance to bad rubbish.'

Dan began to gibber and Joan wondered if he was upset that Ivy had left, but was distracted when Chris threw down the note.

'I'd better warn Danny that Steve won't be opening the yard,' he said.

'What about your breakfast?'

'I'll have it later.'

'Come on, Dan, calm down,' Joan urged as Chris hurried out. 'There's no need to take on just because Ivy's gone. She's a grown woman and not your responsibility. If you ask me you've done enough for her, and I ain't pleased that she didn't even bother to come to see you to say goodbye.'

'Dad, don't,' Petula said, taking her father's hand, and as usual, Dan responded immediately to his daughter, slumping ungainly in his chair.

'Petula, get the breakfast on and after that you can go upstairs to make our beds. Go on now, I can see to your father,' Joan snapped.

Petula did as she was told whilst Joan frowned, wondering why Dan always responded well to his daughter, but took no notice of her.

The brothers were at the yard. Danny, fuming, was unaware that a car was parked outside, the three men inside closely watching the entrance.

'I can't fucking believe this,' Danny said, his eyes sweeping over his brothers as he sat behind his dad's old desk. 'With Steve gone we're another man short – who's gonna do the bloody deliveries?'

'I know what dives in Soho have placed orders, so I can take the films out,' Chris offered. 'Are they already in the van?'

'Yeah, they're in the hidden compartment,' said Bob.

'All right. Chris, you take on the driving, and Bob, you'll have to handle the yard,' said Danny, shaking his head with annoyance. 'That just leaves me and Maurice in Wimbledon to handle the filming, but as soon as you've finished the deliveries, Chris, you can meet us there.'

'Why can't Maurice stay in the yard? I'd be more use at Wimbledon,' Bob complained.

'Oh, for fuck's sake, Bob, why do you have to question every decision I make? If we get a big order for building gear, Maurice ain't up to loading it on his own.'

'Yeah, yeah, all right.'

'Sorry, Bob,' said Maurice, his expression sheepish.

'Don't worry about it,' Bob said.

'Right, before we go, let's take a look at the books. How are we doing, Maurice?'

'We're doing all right, and profits are up on last month.'

Danny looked at Maurice's neat entries, somewhat mollified to see that he was right. Yes, things were looking up, but they still had to push harder. It wasn't going to be easy without Steve, and Danny was still annoyed that the git had buggered off without a word. He had no idea where he and Ivy had gone, but if he got his hands on Steve he'd wring his bloody neck.

The three men continued to watch the entrance. So far they had found out little and Jack Garston was growing impatient.

'If you ask me, this is a waste of time,' said one. 'We followed them here, and so far they ain't moved.'

'Are you gonna tell Garston that?' asked another, his wide-set shoulders straining the seams of his suit as he turned towards the back seat.

'Leave it out, of course not.'

The third man sniffed through a nose that had been broken, giving him a pug-faced look. He flexed his large muscular arms before speaking. 'Look, Garston wants us to teach them a lesson, but we need to get one of the Draper boys on his own. Now shut up and just keep watching.'

The sun was rising higher in the sky, all three sweltering and growing more impatient, but at last they saw movement. Two of the Draper boys were heading for a car, whilst another went to a van.

'He's on his own so we'll take him,' the pug-faced one said.

They waited until the van drove off and then followed, keeping a safe distance.

'The Drapers are mad to take on Garston,' the driver said. 'That's something they're soon gonna find out.'

'Yeah. Are we gonna take out his kneecaps like the last bloke?'

'No,' said the pug-faced one, 'it's gonna be in daylight and Garston said to just give him a warning. There'll be no shooters this time.'

They drove over the Thames, still keeping the van in sight, grinning when it eventually reached Soho. This was Garston's territory. He ruled this area and even if there were witnesses, not one of them would dare to say a word. On the rare occasions that anyone dared to cross Jack Garston, his revenge was swift, and so his reputation had grown. There was little he didn't have a hand in. He ran clubs, prostitutes, made hard-porn films, and had a protection racket that lined his coffers with even more money. He ran his empire on fear, his men knowing that they'd be taken out if they didn't obey his orders.

The van now turned into a side street, pulling up outside a sex shop, and the order was given to park behind it.

'Come on,' the pug-faced one said, slipping a knife out of his pocket. 'Grab him and hold him steady, while I mess up his pretty face.' Unaware that he'd been followed, Chris didn't stand a chance. He tried to fight off the men who held him, but two of them had him in a vicelike grip.

The pug-faced one leered, his face close to Chris's as he spat, 'This is a message from Jack Garston. He knows what you Drapers are up to, and wants you out.'

With that he moved back, a sickly grin on his face as he raised his hand, the knife slicing through Chris's cheek like butter. He ignored the scream, saying, 'Count yourself lucky that you're still alive. If you and your brothers don't stay out of Garston's territory, you won't be so lucky next time.'

They shoved Chris then, watching as he landed in the gutter, his face pouring blood. Laughing, they went back to their car and screeched away.

Chapter Eighteen

Danny and Maurice jumped into action as soon as they got the phone call, Danny breaking every speed limit as they drove to the hospital. Chris was already in the treatment room when they got there so Danny paced as he waited outside, whilst Maurice was slumped in a chair beside Bob.

The emergency department was packed, and Danny grimaced when he saw a couple of drunken tramps staggering in. He swiftly changed direction to avoid going near them, yet still their stench reached his nostrils, making them twitch with distaste. Since setting up the hard-porn side of the business in June, there'd been no sign of trouble and he cursed himself for not taking more precautions. From what Bob had told him, Chris's injury wasn't serious, but from now on they would have to raise their guard.

As Chris came out of the treatment room, his cheek covered in a wad of gauze, Maurice rose to his feet. 'Bloody hell, Mum's gonna have a fit when she sees him.'

Danny raised a hand to stroke his scar. 'It never did my reputation any harm.'

'Who did it, Chris? Was it Garston?' Maurice asked.

'Not personally, but a few of his mob.'

'So it's started, and this is probably just a warning. I reckon we should pack it in – get out now before Garston ups the stakes.'

'Leave it out, Maurice,' said Bob. 'We're just starting to rake in the money.'

'Yeah, and we can handle Garston,' said Danny.

Bob touched Chris's arm. 'How do you feel? Is it giving you gyp?'

'Nah, I'll survive. Now come on, let's get out of here.'

The four brothers left casualty, but as they climbed into Danny's car, Maurice continued to complain. 'I still think we should pack it in. What about you, Chris? What do you think? You're the one that got a kicking.'

'I'd hardly call it that. If I'd had a bit of backup, I'd have taken the bastards out.'

'It's my fault,' Danny admitted. 'Garston hasn't done a thing since we started up so I let myself become complacent. It was wrong to underestimate him and I should have seen it coming.'

'You haven't answered my question, Chris,'

Maurice persisted. 'Do you think we should pack it in?'

'No I don't. Stop acting like an old woman, Maurice. This is nothing – if we get a bit more muscle, we can handle Garston.'

'That'll cost an arm and a leg.'

'We'll find the money, so just shut up about it,' Danny said, shoving his foot onto the accelerator and screeching out of the car park.

Though Danny was watching the road, his mind was elsewhere, his thoughts on Garston and just how far the man would go to put them out of business. Well, sod him, because despite Maurice's carping, he wasn't about to give up. To make things right for his father, he needed money, lots of it, but so far almost everything they made went back into the business.

'It's not worth opening up the yard now, or going back to Wimbledon, so we might as well pack in for the day,' Danny said.

When they arrived home, Maurice was still acting like an old woman, looking nervously over his shoulder, and Danny shook his head in disgust. The alley was safe, but Maurice had always been a weakling, useless if there was any sign of trouble, all brains and no brawn.

As Bob and Maurice went into their houses, Chris said, 'Right, I'm going in to face the music. See you later, Danny.'

Danny knew there was no way he could go into his mother's house and just gave Chris a small wave. He had tried to see his father as soon as he came home from hospital, wanting to assure him that he wasn't going to use kids in the films. He hadn't been able to get a word in. When his father saw him he'd gone mad, bellowing like a maniac. His mother had rushed into the room, ordering him out, and telling him that he would have to stay away. Since then she had become like a sentinel, barring his entry. It cracked him up when Yvonne told him that his father wasn't getting any better and Danny knew that the conditions the old man lived in didn't help. He spent all of his time in the cramped living room, his outlook just a factory wall.

Danny felt swamped by depression. He wanted more for his father – decent accommodation and fresh country air – but they needed money to do that. It was getting so that every day was a fight, a fight to hold himself together, but he had to keep going, had to keep the business profitable. He owed his father – and big time.

'What happened to you?' Joan asked as soon as Chris walked in the door.

'I had a bit of an accident at the yard, that's all.'

Joan lifted the gauze to one side, seeing the cut and history repeating itself. Danny had once come home with a similar gash down his cheek. 'You've had stitches and that wound looks like it was caused by a knife.'

'It wasn't, Mum.'

Joan could see she wasn't going to get anything out of her son. Like the rest of the boys, he was secretive, but she was sure he'd been in a fight. Though she didn't want to admit it, Ivy leaving so suddenly had unsettled her. Like George she had just upped and gone. Though she would never be able to forgive her son for what he had done to his father, she couldn't help thinking about him. Had Chris attacked George? And if so, how badly? At times she wondered if she should talk to Danny about her fears, but then always decided against it. There had been enough trouble, enough violence, and anyway, maybe as Chris said, it hadn't been blood on the bathroom floor.

Joan pushed her fears to one side as usual, instead thinking about George's empty house. They had kept up the rent, and would continue to do so, making sure that another family didn't move into the alley, but there was still Ivy's house. She said in her note that she'd got an exchange, but so far nobody had moved into her house. It was bound to happen soon, though, but if strangers moved into the alley, they'd have to keep it away from Dan until they could be chased out. She was about to voice these thoughts to Chris, but then Dan began to grunt, his arm waving.

'What is it, love? Do you need the bathroom?'

When he made a bellowing sound, Chris said, 'I'll give you a hand, Mum.'

'Are you up to it?'

'Of course I am. It's only a cut.'

Joan was glad of the help. She still worried about Chris, the haunted look that was in his eyes, but Dan was her main concern. She could wheel him to the bathroom, but the effort of lifting him onto the toilet without help nearly broke her back. She had tried to get him to use a commode, but he had made his feelings plain even though he couldn't speak, becoming so agitated that she had feared he'd have another stroke. Joan closed her eyes at the thoughts that invaded her mind. She had prayed for Dan's survival and her prayers had been answered, but this wasn't Dan, not any more. He was now like a child, needing almost everything done for him. His days were spent just sitting in his wheelchair, his nights asleep on the day bed.

'Where's Pet?' Chris asked.

'She's in the kitchen making the dinner. I don't know what I'll do without her when she goes back to school in September.'

'You'll still have Yvonne to give you a hand, and what's the matter with Norma and Sue? They've offered to help out too.'

'I've told you before, I don't want those two in

here. Your dad is fond of Yvonne and doesn't mind her helping out, but he ain't so keen on the others.'

'Chris, what's wrong with your face?' Pet cried as she came into the room.

'I tripped over in the yard and caught my face on the edge of a pile of bricks.'

Pet's face paled. 'Oh, Chris . . .'

'Look, it's nothing. I don't know what all the fuss is about.'

There was a grunt, hand waving, and Joan berated herself. 'Come on, darling,' she said, 'let's get you to the bathroom.'

Dan closed his eyes in frustration. He hated being helpless, hated being trapped in a body that wouldn't respond. The worst thing was being taken to the bathroom, his wife having to help him onto the toilet and afterwards wiping his arse like a bloody baby. It wasn't dignified, and though Pet or Yvonne left the room as soon as he was lowered onto the toilet, he still felt that he was no longer a man, ashamed that either Yvonne, or worse Pet, would see his willie, or what was left of it.

He was useless now, incapable of speech, incapable of telling his wife that it wasn't the bathroom he wanted, it was to know what the bloody hell was going on. Chris had come in with his face cut, but Dan doubted it was an accident – more like the boys treading on Garston's toes. But what sort of films were they making? Now that he couldn't stop him, had Danny persuaded the others to use children?

There were times like this when his mind was clear, but others when he felt woolly, as though his brain wasn't functioning along with his body. Lately it was these woolly times that he sought, preferring it when he couldn't think clearly – couldn't worry about Danny and what he was doing with the business.

Dan groaned, unable to protest as he was wheeled to the bathroom. At least this time it was Chris who was helping and not his daughter. Pet was his pride and joy and he only felt calm when she was around him. Joan drove him mad, talking to him as if he was an imbecile, or talking over him as if he couldn't hear her every word.

He wasn't a bloody idiot, he still had a brain, but only Pet seemed capable of seeing this. Despite Joan telling the girl not to bother him, Pet would read him the morning paper, picking out articles that she knew he'd enjoy. His daughter was his one solace, but she'd be going back to school soon. Without her Dan knew that the house would close in around him, that he'd have to listen to his wife's inane chatter until she came home again.

'Here we go, Dan,' Joan said as she and Chris heaved him onto the toilet.

Dan bellowed in frustration, but as usual, he was ignored.

Chapter Nineteen

Summer passed, then came the autumn. One day at the beginning of November Pet was on Lavender Hill, shopping for her mother. She had little free time now, her days spent at school, evenings and weekends helping at home. She had given up trying to find out what her brothers were up to, preferring to believe that they were just running the family business. It was easier that way – easier than thinking about the alternative.

With her bags full of groceries she lugged them into the butcher's to join the queue, and her ears pricked when she heard two women gossiping ahead of her. They both reddened when they saw her, but Pet couldn't wait to get home, staggering indoors with her load to say excitedly, 'Mum, I've heard that Linda's had her baby.'

'Has she now?'

'Yes, and can I go to see her? Please, Mum.'

'You might not be welcome, and if you ask me,

if Linda wanted us to know, she'd have told us herself.'

'Oh, Mum, she's too frightened of George to come here.'

'Leave it out. She must know that he's missing.'

'You can't be sure of that. Please, can I go to see her?'

Pet watched her mother's lips purse, holding her breath, but at last she said, 'All right, I don't suppose it would hurt, but you'll have to ask Yvonne to call round to give me a hand with your dad.'

Pet ran to get her coat. She gave her father a swift kiss on the cheek and was about to hurry out when her mother called, 'Don't be long. We've got a lot to do today.'

'All right,' she said, swiftly closing the door behind her. After passing on her mother's message to Yvonne, she left the alley. It was cold and Pet stuffed her hands into her pockets, but she was also smiling. It was nice to have a bit of freedom. Oh, she didn't mind helping her mother, but it was all she did nowadays. She helped in the morning, after school and every weekend. In fact, this was the first time she'd been out on a Saturday for ages.

It was a long walk to Linda's house, and by the time she approached it, Pet was a little nervous. She was unsure of her welcome, and tentatively rang the doorbell.

Enid Simpson looked puzzled when she opened the door, her head cocked to one side.

'Mrs Simpson, it's me, Petula Draper. I've come to see the baby.'

'Petula. My goodness, I didn't recognise you – but then again, I've only seen you a couple of times.' She poked her head outside. 'You've come on your own?'

'My mother couldn't come. She can't leave my father.'

'Yes, well, I heard what happened to your dad. How is he?' Without waiting for a reply, Enid Simpson stood back. 'Oh look, you'd better come in.'

Pet followed the limping woman into the living room, but as soon as Linda saw her she jumped to her feet, the colour draining from her face.

'It's all right, Linda, she's on her own,' Enid said. 'She's come to see the baby,' and then turning to Pet, she added, 'As you can see, Linda is still a nervous wreck.'

'I heard that George was missing . . . but he hasn't turned up again, has he?' Linda gasped.

'No, no, we haven't seen him, and after what he did to my father, I doubt we ever will. My brothers have been searching for him, but he's nowhere to be found.'

'Are you telling the truth?' Enid snapped. 'Linda has filed for divorce, but without knowing where he is, it isn't going to be easy. Are you sure you haven't got his address?'

Pet shifted uncomfortably, wishing now that she hadn't come. 'I'm telling the truth, Mrs Simpson. We really don't know where George is.'

'You can't be sure that he won't come back. Please, Pet, make sure he stays away from me. I don't want him near my baby!'

'Linda, you've got to calm down. It's no wonder that you can't breast-feed. Now isn't it time for Louisa's bottle?'

Her mother's words seemed to have some effect. Linda looked to a crib that was placed near the fire. 'Yes, she's just waking up.'

'All right, I'll make her bottle.'

'I'll do it, Mum. I can see that your hip's playing up.'

'I can manage. What about you, Petula, can I get you anything?'

'No, thank you, Mrs Simpson.' As the woman left, Linda moved to take the baby from the crib.

'Louisa,' said Pet. 'It's a lovely name.'

Holding the baby, Linda seemed calm, and sitting down, she moved the shawl aside to reveal the baby's face. 'It was my grandmother's name.'

'She's beautiful,' Pet whispered. 'Can . . . can I hold her?'

Linda swiftly held the baby close to her chest. 'No, no, you can't, and anyway, I think she needs changing.'

'I won't hurt her.'

'You're a Draper, aren't you? Oh, I'm sorry, please don't look at me like that. It . . . it's just that since having the baby my emotions seem to be all over the place. One minute I'm fine, then the next I find myself down in the dumps. Look, come and sit down and once I've changed Louisa you can hold her.'

Pet perched on the edge of the sofa, watching as Linda changed the baby's nappy. When the pin was in place, she held her out. 'Here, you can have her now, but make sure that you support her head.'

With the baby in her arms, Pet smiled. Louisa was so pretty, and after all her nephews, this was her first niece.

'I wrote to tell Ivy that I've had the baby and she replied this morning,' Linda said, nodding towards a letter on the table. 'She certainly seems to have taken to life in the country.'

'Ivy! You're in touch with Ivy?'

'Well, yes, of course I am. We saw a lot of each other when I lived in the alley, and we're still friends, even if distant ones.'

'We haven't heard a word from her since she left.'

'I know, she told me, but she always speaks well of you, Pet.'

Ivy had left without saying goodbye, and it had always puzzled Pet. Her mother refused to talk about it and her brothers were the same. It was obvious that they didn't have any time for Ivy, but she didn't know why. Ivy had always been nice to her, as had

Steve, and she missed Ernie and Harry, even though they were a pair of scallywags.

'I'd like to write to Ivy. Can I have her address?'

Linda shook her head. 'I'm sorry, but Ivy has asked me not to pass it on.'

'But why?'

Linda was quiet for a moment, small teeth chewing on her lower lip, then said, 'Look, all I know is that she doesn't want anything to do with you Drapers.' The baby began to whimper, then cry, so Linda took her from Pet's arms. 'She's hungry and I don't know why it's taking my mother so long to make her bottle. I'll be back in a tick.'

When Linda left the room, Pet's eyes were drawn to the envelope on the table. She leaned forward, picking it up, and after just a moment's hesitation, she drew out the letter. Her eyes had only scanned the address when the door opened again, and guiltily she looked at Linda.

'Oh, how could you? Ivy will go mad if she finds out.'

'I . . . I'm sorry.'

'Did you see the address?'

'Yes, but that's all.'

'You mustn't tell Ivy. Don't write to her, and for God's sake don't tell anyone else that you know where she is.'

'But why?'

'What's going on?' Enid asked as she walked into the room.

'It's Pet, she read my letter.'

Enid's lips curled. 'What do you expect? She's a Draper, ain't she, and they're all the same.'

'But . . . but I didn't mean any harm.'

'Look at the state of my daughter! If you ask me, you've done enough harm just by coming here. I shouldn't have let you in and now I want you to leave. Tell your mother and the rest of your family that they're not welcome here, and you, miss, don't show your face at my door again.'

Pet fled the room, wrenched open the front door, ran outside, and kept on running until she was out of breath. Oh, it had been awful, dreadful. All right, she shouldn't have looked at Linda's letter, but surely they had overreacted?

By the time Pet arrived home, she had calmed down and looked composed as she walked inside.

'Oh, Pet, I'm glad you're back,' Yvonne said, her upper lip beaded with perspiration. 'I'm not feeling too well and think I've caught a chill, but I didn't want to leave your mum to manage on her own. How was Linda? Did you see the baby?'

'Yes, I saw her, and Linda has called her Louisa.'

'That's nice. Anyway, I'm off.'

Her mother waited until the door had closed behind Yvonne, and then said, 'Babies are always a touchy subject with Yvonne, and if you ask me, she's got more than a chill. I thought the poor girl was gonna pass out. Now then, tell me what happened at Linda's.'

Pet hesitated. If she told her mother the truth, it would only cause more bad feelings, so instead just said, 'There's not much to tell. Linda was fine and I saw the baby, but I didn't stay long.'

'Did she know that George is missing?'

'Yes, but she's still frightened that he'll turn up so I doubt she'll come here.'

'Well, with your father ill I can't leave him to go there, so I don't suppose I'll see the baby. Now then, come on, Pet, the bedrooms need turning out so you'd better make a start.'

Pet said nothing. She knew her mother had little time for her brothers' children, so wasn't surprised that she was showing little interest in the new baby.

She went over to her father, saying, 'I'll just get the bedrooms sorted and then I'll read you the paper.'

He managed a lopsided smile, but then hearing her mother's huff of impatience, Pet hurried upstairs. As she stripped her mother's bed, Pet's mood was low. She couldn't help thinking about Linda and the baby. Louisa was her niece, but it was unlikely that she'd ever see her again. Unexpectedly her eyes filled with tears.

* * *

As Pet went upstairs, Joan was glad to leave the bedrooms to her daughter. Pet was still turning out to be a godsend, helping her after school and at weekends. She'd be leaving school soon and, instead of her getting a job, Joan had decided that she could stay at home, helping out full time. In the meantime, Yvonne was good, coming round every day to give her a hand, but with Danny and her own house to look after, it didn't seem fair. When Pet was at home all day, it would no longer be necessary, and it would be nice not to feel beholden to her daughter-in-law. Norma and Sue still offered to muck in too, but she didn't want those two floozies in her house, chatting all the time and upsetting Dan. She hardly saw them these days and that suited her fine. She didn't want Dan disturbed any more than necessary, and that meant keeping her grandchildren out too, but with Paul's birthday coming up later this month, she'd better think about getting him a present.

She didn't want to think about Linda, or the baby, but was unable to push them from her mind. George was a father now, with a daughter, but unless he turned up again the child would grow up without ever knowing him. It didn't seem right somehow, and surely one day, he'd show his face.

Chapter Twenty

Steve Rawlings thanked his lucky stars that they'd left Drapers Alley. He hadn't gone back to totting, but didn't mind. Almost as soon as they'd moved in, their nearest neighbour told him about a job going on a local farm. He'd been doubtful at first, but had taken it on, and he'd found that he loved it. Though it was early in November, there had been a dusting of snow and the farmer had shaken his head, forecasting a hard winter with worse to come.

Steve trudged home, glad to arrive. In the porch he kicked off his boots before going into the living room to find Ivy sitting by the fire. The room was a mess, the housework untouched.

'What's the matter, love?' he asked, sinking onto a chair opposite her.

'Nothing's the matter.'

'Come on, Ivy. I know you ain't yourself.'

'It's nothing, just a bit of a tummy ache, that's all. I think it was that pie I ate last night.'

'You've been down in the dumps lately. If you're not ill, what is it? Did that letter from Linda to say that she's had her baby unsettle you?'

'No, but we got on well and there's times when I miss her.'

Steve frowned, sure there was more to Ivy's funny moods than that. 'Do you regret leaving Drapers Alley?'

'Leave it out, of course I don't.'

'I wonder how the family that swapped with us are getting on.'

'They didn't move into the alley.'

'What? How come we still got the swap?'

Ivy looked into the fire, then said, 'If you remember, they had already moved back to Battersea, living with the woman's mother until the exchange was agreed. It had just gone through when the mother was taken seriously ill. She needed constant care so they decided to stay with her instead of moving into our place.'

'Oh, yeah, and how do you know all this?'

'I got it from the old biddy in the village post office. She was a friend of the family and said that they're still in touch.'

'So our old place could still be empty.'

'I've no idea, but with a shortage of housing, I doubt it.'

'I wonder if they've found George.'

'Bad pennies always turn up. Anyway, why are you so interested?'

Steve shrugged. 'I'm not, but they're still your family.'

'You and the boys are my family. As far as I'm concerned, I don't care if I never set eyes on the Drapers again.'

'You've never told me why you hate them so much.'

Ivy looked into Steve's eyes, her expression thoughtful for a moment, but then she said, 'I don't suppose it would hurt to tell you now. When my father died, I was just a kid, but Uncle Dan took me and my mother under his wing. He would turn up in his posh car, flashing his money by topping up my mother's war widow's pension. I grew up hearing the gossip about the Drapers – that they were thieves, my father and Uncle Dan both good at cracking safes. It was when he bought the builders' merchants that I became suspicious of my Uncle Dan's so-called generosity, even more so when I became an adult and he continued to help me.'

'Suspicious of what?' Steve asked.

'Where do you think he got the money to start up the business?'

'I have no idea, but what's that got to do with anything?'

'It's got everything to do with it. You see, I think he got the money from the last job he did with my father, but instead of coming back from the war to his share, my father was killed in action. Uncle Dan should have given the money to my mother – money that would have ensured that she died in comfort instead of poverty. But no, he didn't do that. Instead he must have kept the lot.'

Steve shook his head. 'I think you're wrong. Dan might have done some dodgy things, but to him family is everything. He's got a code, a strict one, and though he might rob others, he would never rob his own.'

'OK, so what happened to the money from the last job he did with my father?'

Steve was quiet as he ruminated on Ivy's words. Then he said, 'Ivy, you were a child when your father was called up. How do you know they did a job?'

'When my dad was killed in action, Uncle Dan came round to see us. I was supposed to be in bed, but I sneaked downstairs and heard them talking. My mother was in a terrible state, crying, but then mentioned that at least she wouldn't have to struggle financially to bring me up. My Uncle Dan told her that the job hadn't been successful – that there wasn't any money.'

'Well, there's your answer then. It sounds to me like they didn't manage to pull it off.'

'If they didn't pull it off, where did he get all that money from?'

'Ivy, he didn't start up the yard for years, and I doubt it was the only job he did. No doubt he had a good few bob stashed away.'

'Exactly! I'm sure they pulled off other jobs before my father was called up. If my Uncle Dan had money stashed away, why didn't my father?'

Steve scratched his head. 'Yeah, well, you've got me there.'

'I'll tell you why. My uncle always handled the finances, so I think he kept my father's stash. Even if the last job was a washout, there still should have been cash for my mother, but we never saw a penny. When she died, Uncle Dan played the kind uncle, and when we got married he got us our house in Drapers Alley. Why do you think he did all that?'

'Well, you're his niece and he's big on looking after his family.'

'If you ask me, it was more like guilt.'

Steve stared into the fire. He still couldn't believe that Dan Draper would rob his own brother, but had to admit that it all sounded suspicious. He turned back to Ivy. 'If you're so sure about this, why didn't you confront your Uncle Dan?'

'Because I didn't have any proof, but when I used to bait him – to hint – I could tell that I had him rattled. I wanted to pay him back, to make him suffer, but then lo and behold, George did it for me.'

'Yeah, well, Dan certainly suffered. George nearly killed him.'

'When it happened, when I knew the state Uncle Dan was in, all my anger sort of left me. I hated the alley then, and everyone in it. I just wanted out, and thank God we got the exchange.'

'I'm with you there. I didn't like working for them, Ivy. I used to shit myself every time I went out on a delivery.'

Ivy's eyes narrowed. 'If you were only delivering building materials, I don't see why. Come on, Steve, we're never going to see the Drapers again so you can tell me what they were really up to.'

Steve looked into the fire, ruminating again. Surely there'd be no harm in telling her now. 'All right, Ivy, I suppose you deserve the truth. You thought they were doing jobs, robberies, but in fact they made money from porn. It was my job to deliver it.'

'Porn! My God, I can't believe it.'

'It's the truth, Ivy. They've got a place in Wimbledon where they make the films.'

'What sort of place?'

Steve told her where it was and about the setup, but then she suddenly slumped forward, clutching her tummy.

'What is it, love? Are you all right?'

The boys came running through the door, their cheeks rosy from the cold air. They loved playing outside and it was impossible to keep them in. Steve saw the effort Ivy made to straighten herself up, her face the colour of dough. 'I reckon you should see the doctor.'

'What's the matter, Mum?' Ernie asked.

'Nothing, love, it's just a bit of indigestion, that's all. Now, let's get you cleaned up before dinner.'

Steve could see what an effort it was for Ivy to stand up, and placed a staying hand on her arm. 'Let me get the stink of the farmyard off and then I'll see to them.'

'No, I can manage.'

She ushered the boys from the room, leaving Steve frowning. He wasn't convinced that Ivy had indigestion, sure there was more to it than that. She could be so stubborn at times and it drove him mad, but like it or not, he was going to make sure that she saw a doctor.

Chapter Twenty-one

The weekend passed and, in Drapers Alley, Yvonne still felt ill. She did her best to hide it as she placed Danny's dinner on the table, then sat opposite him. He had changed so much since taking over from his father. He had lost weight, his cheeks gaunt, and she knew he wasn't sleeping well. He often turned to her for sex, but that was different too, almost as if he was using it for comfort. Yet why? He had the responsibility of running the yard, but with three brothers to help him, surely there wasn't that much to worry about. Yvonne knew that business had been slow for a while and money tight, but with talk of some sort of expansion, things were sure to improve. She had tried talking to him about it, but he snapped her head off if she made any mention of business.

'Are you still feeling rough?' Danny asked.

'No, I'm fine now,' she lied, changing the subject. 'Danny, are you going round to see Linda's baby?'

'No, why should I?'

'She's your niece.'

'So what?' he said, his voice lacking interest as he pushed his plate to one side, his meal hardly touched. 'I've got to go out again for a couple of hours.'

'Oh, Danny, not again. It's already eight o'clock and you're hardly in these days.'

'Don't start, Yvonne. I've got a business to run, orders to get. I might be late, so don't wait up.'

Yvonne wanted to protest, to tell him to stop taking her for a mug. The yard was closed now, as were most businesses, so how could he be chasing orders?

When a scream pierced the air, Yvonne's eyes widened, then both she and Danny rushed outside, just in time to see Bob's younger son fleeing down the alley like a scalded cat.

Sue and Bob must have heard the scream too, Bob yelling, 'Paul! Paul, wait! Come here!'

As Paul disappeared past the bollards, Bob set out in pursuit.

'What happened? Did you see anything?' Sue gasped.

'We just heard a scream,' Yvonne told her.

'Where's Robby?' Sue cried, her eyes scanning the alley, but it was Bob who appeared, holding Paul's hand as he walked towards them.

'He's all right. He's just got a bit of a burn, that's all. A banger went off while he was holding it.'

'It was Robby,' wailed Paul. 'He lit the banger then he gave it to me, but I didn't have time to throw it before it went off.'

'Where is he?' Bob asked.

'I dunno. Oooh, Mum, my hand hurts.'

'Come on, let's get you sorted,' Sue said. 'And as for you, Bob, I ain't happy that you bought the kids those bangers. If you ask me, they're dangerous.'

'Leave it out, it's fireworks night and all the kids play with them.'

'I think I agree with Sue,' said Yvonne. 'They're far too young to be playing with fireworks. Oh, look, there's Robby.'

'I'll leave you to sort him out,' Sue said to Bob, before taking Paul inside.

The boy had come into the alley and ran towards them. 'Is Paul all right?'

'No he isn't, and well you know it, you little sod. Now get inside,' Bob snapped.

'I didn't do nuffin',' Robby protested, crying out as Bob grabbed him by the ear to drag him indoors.

'They shouldn't have matches, let alone fireworks,' Yvonne said as she and Danny went back to their own house.

'Half the kids in the area have penny bangers,' Danny said as he picked up his coat. 'Right, I'm off, and as I said, don't wait up.'

Yvonne nodded, unhappy but knowing better than to complain again. She still didn't feel right, and hadn't for some time, despite telling Danny that she felt fine. Maybe she should see the doctor, but what could she tell him? She wasn't in pain. It was just that she felt so drained. But knowing old Doc Addison, she thought he'd just prescribe a tonic.

Danny headed for his car. When Chris had been knifed in August, he knew it could be the start of a turf war, and had wanted to retaliate, to show Garston that the Drapers couldn't be messed with. He'd tried to be prepared, to find out all he could about Garston, his operation and the muscle behind him, but despite putting out feelers for months, it was still proving impossible. Time and time again he came up against a wall of silence and it was driving him mad. In the meantime he had put precautions in place, making films but only delivering them once a month, sending Chris out with a bit of hired muscle.

So far there hadn't been any more trouble, but Danny doubted it could last. He climbed into his car. All he had found out so far was that Garston was rarely seen, but he wasn't ready to give up yet, and at last Danny had got a whisper of a contact. The bloke was someone he knew from years ago, one he was told had worked for Garston recently. Whether Bert Mills was willing to talk remained to be seen, but Danny was prepared to pay for information.

There was thick smoke in the air from many bonfires, and the occasional rocket shot up into the sky before bursting into a shower of sparks as Danny drove to Tooting. When he walked into the pub he saw it was nearly empty, but the man he was looking for was propping up the bar.

'Hello, Bert. What are you drinking?'

'Danny! Blimey, long time no see. What are you doing in this neck of the woods?'

'I was hoping for a little chat.'

'Oh, yeah, what about?'

'Tell me what you're drinking first.'

'Bitter, mate. I'll have a pint of bitter.'

Danny waited until the landlord had pulled two pints, but after paying, the publican still hovered within hearing distance.

'Come and sit down, Bert,' Danny said, indicating a table.

Once seated, Danny leaned forward, saying softly, 'What can you tell me about Garston?'

'I can't tell you anything, Danny.'

'I'll make it worth your while.'

'If I open my mouth I wouldn't live long enough to spend it.'

'He wouldn't know the info came from you.'

'Huh, you don't know Jack Garston. He's got eyes and ears everywhere and, believe me, he'd find out.'

'Look, all I need to know is where he's based, and how much backup he's got.'

'Danny, I don't know what you're up to, but you don't want to cross Garston.'

'One of his mob knifed my brother and I ain't standing for that.'

'Yeah, well, I'm sorry to hear that, but I still can't tell you anything.'

'Yes you can, Bert, and before you say no again, remember – I can be just as nasty as Garston.'

Bert paled, but shook his head. 'Yeah, you frighten me, Danny, but not as much as Garston.' He then rose to his feet, his pint of beer untouched as he walked back to the bar where he leaned forward, saying something to the landlord.

The landlord's eyes shot towards Danny, and when Danny saw him walk to the back of the bar to make a phone call, he knew it was time to leave. Bert had obviously opened his mouth and now Garston would know he'd been trying to suss him out. Danny walked out of the bar, determined that one day, when Bert was least expecting it, he'd make him pay for dobbing him in.

Bert Mills had been ordered to the club. He'd been nervous around Danny Draper, but that was nothing compared to how he felt now.

Jack Garston sat behind his desk in the back room, his eyes rock hard. 'What did Draper want?'

'He was trying to find out about your operation.'

'What did you tell him?'

'Nothing, Jack.'

'Are you sure about that? I hear that you and Draper go back a while.'

As Jack's cold eyes bored into his, Bert felt like

prey. He had to convince the man or he'd be dead meat. 'Yeah, I know him, but I ain't seen him for years. I didn't say a word, Jack. I swear. I warned him off, that was all.'

Garston's smile was thin. 'All right, Bert, relax. Sit yourself down and we'll have a little chat. Rick here will get you a drink. Whisky, is it?'

'Yeah, thanks,' Bert said, still tense as he sat down. Rick was one of Garston's henchmen, known for his love of pulling out his victims' fingernails. Bert moved his hands to his lap as though this small act could protect them, but Rick went to the bar, pouring the drinks. Garston seemed satisfied, but Bert knew better than to let down his guard. The man didn't look like a villain. Short and overweight, he could appear benign, fooling anyone who wasn't aware of his reputation, but if crossed the change was instantaneous. He became a vicious monster, and there were those who had found this out to their cost.

Garston lit a fat cigar, his cheeks puffing like bellows, then ordered Bert, 'Tell me what you know about the Drapers.'

As Rick put a shot of whisky in front of him, Bert instantly picked the glass up, swallowing the lot in one gulp. 'As I said, I ain't seen them in years so I can't tell you what they get up to nowadays. They've been rumoured to have done a few jobs, but then Dan Draper bought a yard, becoming respectable.

Mind you, knowing the Drapers the business could be a front, but I don't know what for.'

'I do, and you ain't telling me anything that I don't know already. The Drapers need another lesson, a hard one. Tell me about the family, what makes them tick.'

'There ain't much I can tell you, except that they look after their own. The alley where they live is a bit like a fortress and nobody goes in there without invitation.'

'More stuff I already know, and it's not what I'm looking for. I want a weakness. For instance, what matters most to Dan Draper?'

Bert frowned, wondering what he could give Garston to get the man off his back. 'There's been talk that he ain't what he used to be, but in my time I know his daughter was his pride and joy.'

'His daughter,' Garston drawled, gimlet-eyed as he sucked deeply on his cigar. Then he smiled. 'All right, Bert, you've told me what I need to know. You can go now.'

Bert didn't need telling twice and hastily rose to his feet. 'Thanks, Jack.'

Garston waved him away and Bert almost ran from the room. There was a stripper on stage but so anxious was he to leave he didn't pause to take in the act. He didn't know what the Drapers had done to make an enemy of Jack Garston, but it looked like the daughter was going to pay the price.

Chapter Twenty-two

At the end of the week, Danny faced his brothers. 'I can't get any information on Garston. I've been asking around and I've tried everything – threats, bribes – but nobody will talk.'

'Shouldn't that tell you something?'

'Like what, Maurice?'

'It's obvious. If they won't talk to you, despite your threats, they're more afraid of Garston than us. As I've said before, we should get out now before he pulls another stunt.'

Chris fingered his cheek, his scar a match with Danny's. 'I owe Garston for this and I'm looking forward to his next move.'

'Yeah, well, you might just get your chance,' Danny told him. 'I had a chat with a geezer on Monday, and I think the fact that I was asking questions has got back to Garston. It might stir things up, and with any luck it'll force him to show his hand. I'm coming with you on the next delivery. If his henchmen show their faces, it could lead us back to Garston, and that's just what I want.'

'I don't like it, Danny. We should stick to soft porn.'

'And make peanuts, Maurice?'

'I'd hardly call it peanuts. We were doing all right – in fact more than all right.'

'You were the one who said that our profits were unlikely to increase.'

'Yes, I know, but we were still making good money.'

'I can't believe I'm hearing this! Garston has only made one move against us and you're acting like a frightened tart. The man just needs a taste of his own medicine. Once he gets it, he'll back off.'

'And if he doesn't?'

'We'll cross that bridge when we come to it. In the meantime, Maurice, we've got films to make. I think you're up to running the yard, so you stay here.'

'I can't handle the heavy lifting on my own, you know that. And what if Garston makes a move on this place? Have you thought about that?'

Danny's brow furrowed. 'To be honest, no, but you've got a point. It's no secret we own this business, but I've been more concerned about him finding our base in Wimbledon. All right, we'll get someone who can handle themselves to work here. In the meantime, I'll leave Bob with you.'

Maurice looked mollified, and after sorting out a few more things, Danny and Chris left to go to Wimbledon. As he drove, Danny kept his eyes peeled, but there was no sign of a tail. If Garston wanted to go up against them again, he'd make sure the man suffered for it. Nobody messed with the Drapers and got away with it.

Later that day, Pet was walking home from school. She found herself thinking about Linda and the awful things her mother had said, and the fact that Ivy didn't want any of them to know her address. Before forgetting it, she had scribbled it down in her diary, and though Pet knew she couldn't write to her cousin, at least she knew where she was. Maybe one day she would get in touch with Ivy, try to bring about some sort of reconciliation, but for now she would have to be content with that.

Pet's thoughts shifted. She would be leaving school soon, and had wanted to work in a shop, but with her father ill, and George gone, maybe she could help in some way with the family business. She had never thought much about the work involved at the yard, but by the amount of time her brothers spent running the place, it must be doing all right. There must be lots of paperwork such as orders, invoices, and perhaps they'd let her take over the office work. It would be lovely if she could prove everyone wrong – to find that nowadays her brothers really were respectable, and running a thriving family business.

Pet shivered as she was blasted by the cold wind. A van pulled up just ahead of her but, deep in thought, she hardly noticed. As she drew level the back doors flew open and two men jumped out. Startled out of her reveries, Pet saw them running towards her, but before she could react, they grabbed her, lifting her off her feet, and tossed her into the back of the van.

The doors slammed and then they were hurtling off down the road with Pet on the floor where they had thrown her. Dazed and bruised, she managed to turn her head, frightened out of her wits when she saw one of the men edging towards her.

'No . . . no,' she whimpered, 'please . . . don't—' Her words were cut off as sticky tape was stuck roughly across her mouth.

She was then hauled onto one of the long seats, one man next to her, and the other opposite. All she could see was his flint-like grey eyes, boring into hers. She looked away, petrified, but then the man next to her reached out to grip her thigh with his rough hand. Pet had never known such gut-wrenching terror – terror that caused her bladder to release.

'Fuck me, she's wet herself.'

'What do you expect, she's just a kid.'

'Yeah, but I can see why he wants her – she's a bit tasty. When she's cleaned up, I wouldn't mind a sample myself.'

'He'd kill you.'

Pet felt strange, giddy, her head buzzing. Her vision dimmed, pinpricks of lights floating before her eyes – and then she knew no more.

'She's passed out.'

'We're nearly there. He wants her in the basement.'

'Then what's he gonna do with her? Is he going to put her on the game?'

'She's been snatched as a warning to the Drapers. After that, I've got no idea, but I guess we'll find out soon enough.'

Yvonne had just taken off her coat when there was a knock on her door. She had been to the doctor's and was still in shock. But she was also surprised by her mother-in-law walking in. Joan rarely left the house now, leaving Pet to do all the shopping whilst she took care of Dan.

'Pet's late home from school. It isn't like her and I'm getting worried.'

'Perhaps she went to a friend's house,' Yvonne suggested.

'No, she wouldn't do that. She always comes straight home. Look, I've got to get back to Dan. Can you let the boys know and maybe they'll have a scout around to see if they can find her?'

'All right, I'll ring the yard.'

'Thanks, love,' Joan said.

Bob answered Yvonne's call. 'Is Danny around, Bob?'

'Er, no.'

'Do you know where he is?'

'I think he's out doing a bit of business.'

'What about Chris?'

'He's with Danny, but what's wrong? It ain't like you to ring the yard. Is there a problem? Is my dad all right?'

'Yes, but your mum's worried about Pet. She hasn't arrived home from school.'

'What! But it's gone five. Hang on, it's Paul's birthday and Sue has laid on a bit of a spread. Perhaps Pet's at my place.'

'I'll pop down there, but I don't think it's likely.'

'Have a look anyway. If she's not there, give me another ring.'

Yvonne replaced the receiver and then ran along to Sue's house. She rapped on the letter box before going inside to find that the birthday tea was over. The boys were playing on the rug in front of the fire, but Paul jumped to his feet when he saw her.

'Look what I've got,' he cried, running over to show her a fire engine.

Sue came out of the kitchen, wiping her hands on a tea towel. 'Yes, and it was your auntie who gave it to you, so say thank you.'

'Fanks, Auntie.'

'It's from your Uncle Danny too, but I'm glad you like it. What else did you get for your birthday?'

Paul ran back to the rug, and bending down he picked up a car. 'I got this from Petula.'

'He's car mad and we got him that,' Sue said as she nodded towards a big yellow dumper truck on the rug. 'Norma and Maurice gave him a puzzle, and his gran, practical as ever, gave him a new woolly hat, scarf and gloves.'

'Have you seen Petula?'

'Not since she dropped Paul's present off before she went to school.' Sue's head cocked to one side. 'Why, is there a problem?'

'She hasn't come home yet and Joan's worried.'

'Flaming hell, it's only just after five. What's all the fuss about?'

'She should have been home by now.'

'Huh, so she's a bit late, and to be honest, I don't blame her. When she ain't at school she's stuck indoors cooking and cleaning. It's no life for a girl who's coming up fifteen. If you ask me it's about time she was let off the apron strings.'

'Sue, I couldn't agree more, but the fact is, Petula always comes straight home. This is unlike her and you can't blame Joan for being worried.'

'She's probably just rebelling a bit, and it's about time too. If Joan would let us all give her a hand, Pet could have a bit more freedom.'

'Mum, tell Robby, he's nicked my car.'

'Robby, give it back to him.'

Yvonne said hastily, 'I'd best get back.'

282

'Mum . . .'

Yvonne scooted out to the sound of Paul's wail, leaving Sue to sort out her sons. She rang the yard and then went to her mother-in-law's. 'Bob and Maurice are locking up. They'll be here soon.'

'What about Danny and Chris?'

'They weren't there.'

Dan's good arm was waving as he made strange sounds without forming any coherent words. 'I think he's worried about Petula too,' Joan said, walking across to stroke his hair. 'Don't fret, love.'

It was awful to see Dan's distress, and Yvonne was touched by Joan's tenderness. He may not be able to communicate, but this proved he knew exactly what was going on around him. Petula might be nearly fifteen, but she hadn't had the sense to warn her mother that she might be late home. Dan was so upset and Yvonne couldn't help feeling annoyed at the girl's thoughtlessness.

By eleven that night, there was still no sign of Petula. The boys had been out for hours, Danny and Chris looking in one direction, Maurice and Bob in the other.

When they returned to Drapers Alley, Yvonne came flying out of number one. 'Did you find her?'

'Does it look like it?' Danny said.

'Your dad's been in such a state that your mum had to call the doctor. He's been sedated now, but

283

if he wakes up to find that Petula is still missing, I dread to think what will happen.'

'Do you think I don't know that?'

'Where did you look?'

'Everywhere, and before you ask, yes, we tried all the hospitals.'

'Maybe we should tell the police.'

'Leave it out, Yvonne.'

'Danny, think about it. The police have got resources that we haven't.'

'Yvonne's got a point,' Maurice said, and though it was freezing, sweat beaded his brow.

Danny was struggling to hold himself together. He'd hoped his suspicions were unfounded, but the longer Pet was missing, the more his guts churned. When his mother appeared, he couldn't meet her eyes.

'Oh, Danny, where is she?'

'I don't know, but don't worry, we'll find her.'

'Mum, you look awful,' Chris said, 'and it's freezing out here.'

'Yes, come on, let's get you inside,' Yvonne urged.

'You won't stop looking?'

'Of course we won't,' Danny said, a hard knot of worry like a rock in his stomach. He had wanted to stir Garston up, to force his hand, but hadn't expected the bastard to strike out at his family.

He waited until Yvonne and his mother had returned inside before voicing his thoughts to his brothers. 'I think Garston's got her.'

'I've been thinking the same,' Chris said. 'But if that was the case, surely he'd have been in touch?'

'Maybe he wants to make us sweat for a while.'

'I told you we should pack it in but none of you would have it. Now look what's happened. If he's got Pet, fuck knows what he'll do to her.'

Danny glared at Maurice. 'I'm in charge so this is down to me, but if the bastard so much as lays a finger on her – he's dead.'

'Yeah, you're in charge, but you should have listened to me – made Chris and Bob listen to me. But no, Danny, you had to stir things up, had to act Mr Big and now look what's happened.'

'Look, this isn't achieving anything,' said Chris. 'We need to concentrate on finding Pet. Have you any idea where Garston might be holding her?'

Danny shook his head. 'Do you think I'd be standing here if I did?'

Maurice moved to lean against the wall, his breathing tortured, and it was Bob who said, 'You look awful, Maurice. Go home and leave this to us.'

Maurice nodded. 'All right, but if Pet hasn't turned up by morning, I'm coming out with you again.'

As Maurice went into his house, Bob said, 'What are we going to do now, Danny?'

'We'll just have to wait for Garston to get in touch.'

'Until we know for sure that he's got her, we should keep looking,' Chris urged.

'Yes, all right,' Danny agreed, but his guts were

telling him it would be a waste of time. Garston had his sister. Pet's innocent face swam before his eyes. The thought of Garston touching her sickened him. *I'll kill him*, his mind screamed, his anger the only thing that was holding him together.

Pet couldn't stop shaking. The tape had been ripped from her mouth and then she'd been shoved into a back room and onto a bare bed, the mattress filthy and stained. She had been so cold, but then seeing a dirty quilt on the floor she had snatched it up, sitting with it wrapped around her whilst the smell of her own urine assailed her nostrils. In despair she had frantically looked for a way to escape, but the only window was barred. Hours passed. She didn't know why she'd been snatched, but terrifying thoughts assailed her mind. Oh God, what were they going to do to her?

She swallowed, her throat parched. In the next room she could hear the occasional sound of muffled voices, but so far she had been left alone.

When the door opened, Pet stiffened in fear as a man walked towards her, menacing in his balaclava. She cowered, but his voice was surprisingly gentle.

'Here, I've brought you a drink.'

As he held out a mug, Pet snatched it, gulping down the water as though it were nectar.

'Why . . . why am I here?'

'You'll find out soon enough.'

'Please . . . please let me go.'

'Sorry, I can't do that.'

Pet frowned, sure that she had heard his voice before. 'Do . . . do I know you?'

He shook his head, glancing behind him as another man entered the room.

'What's this?' he snapped. 'Having a taster, are you?'

'No, I just gave her a drink, that's all.'

'Good, 'cos I'm first.'

'No, she ain't to be touched.'

'Unless you tell him, he ain't likely to find out. Come on, let's have a bit of fun.'

Pet screamed, trying to scramble away as the man grabbed her.

'He probably wants a virgin, have you thought of that?'

'Fuck, she stinks to high heaven.'

'If you touch her, he'll kill you.'

'Keep your hair on. With her stinking of piss I don't fancy her anyway. Shame, though; cleaned up she'd be a bit of all right.'

'Yes, she is rather nice,' a voice said.

Both men spun around, the man who had grabbed Pet holding up his hands as though in surrender. 'We didn't touch her, honest.'

'Yes, but from what I heard, it's thanks to Tony.'

Pet was still shaking as she looked at the third man to enter the room. He was short, tubby and

287

wearing a three-piece suit. Unlike the other two, his face wasn't covered, and, as he looked at her, his smile was kindly.

'Are you all right, my dear?'

'Please . . . I want to go home.'

'Well, that's up to your brothers.'

'My . . . my brothers?'

'Don't look so surprised. Surely you know what your brothers have been up to?'

'N-no.'

'Really? Well, maybe I should put you in the picture.' He laughed. 'Oh, pardon the pun, but then again, looking at you, perhaps I *should* feature you in one of my films.'

Pet stared at the man. He didn't look menacing and he was talking about films, but what did that have to do with her brothers? 'I . . . I don't understand. My family supply building materials. They don't make films.'

The man's demeanour changed, his voice a snarl. 'Bring her upstairs.'

Before Pet could react she was dragged off the bed, each man taking an arm and pulling her towards a narrow wooden staircase. She was so afraid that her legs could barely support her.

Oh God, help me.

She was hauled upstairs, barely taking in the opulent hall before she was dragged into another room.

'Sit her down,' the fat man said, 'and then set up the projector.'

Pet was forced onto a plush sofa, cowering as the fat man sat next to her. 'Now, my dear,' he said, his demeanour once again benign, 'the films that I'm going to show you were made by your brothers, and are the reason why you're here.'

'Ready, boss.'

'Good,' he said, his voice once again hardening as he snapped, 'Turn off the lights and roll it.'

The room was plunged into darkness and then almost immediately a film was showing on a screen in front of Pet. At first, confused, she couldn't understand what was happening, but then as it unfolded she watched it in horror. A woman was thrown onto a bed, her wrists tied to the posts. She struggled, screaming as a man began to do things to her that made the bile rise in Pet's throat. She didn't know much about the sex act, only what her friends had told her, but this – this was awful. He was raping her! Oh God, it was terrible! Unable to watch any more, she turned her head away.

The fat man tittered. 'Don't worry, my dear, I'm sure they're only acting.' His voice then changed as he snapped, 'Run the next one.'

'No . . . no . . .' Pet whimpered as the film unfolded. This time it was a child being raped, the little girl crying out for her mother in terror. No – no, she couldn't watch it. 'Oh, please, please, turn it off.'

'Yes, I think that's enough, and anyway, my dear, I can't stand the smell of you for much longer.'

'She pissed herself.'

'Yes, Gary, I think that's obvious. Now then, Miss Draper, as I said, the films were made by your brothers.'

'No . . . no, I don't believe you.'

'Oh, I can assure you it's true. I've known about their operation for some time – in fact since they started production. It was fine when they stuck to making nice little soft-porn films – something that holds no interest for me – but, you see, they became greedy.'

Pet shook her head against his words. It couldn't be true, it just couldn't.

His voice droned on. 'I tried to warn them off, but it seems that scarring your brother's cheek wasn't enough.'

'You! You did that to Chris.'

'Ah, I see I've got your attention at last. My, you are a pretty little thing,' he mused. 'It would be a shame if I had to hand you back, but then again, I don't really have to.'

Pet cringed in fear as his pudgy hand reached out to stroke her leg. He then snapped, 'Tony, get her cleaned up and then for now, take her back to the basement.'

'What do you want me to do, boss?' the other man asked.

'I haven't forgotten what I heard downstairs. Get out of my sight and I'll deal with you later.'

'Come on, on your feet,' she was ordered as the other man grabbed her arm.

'Leave me alone.'

'Ah, that's nice, Tony; she's got a bit of spunk. If the Drapers don't learn their lesson she'll make a nice little addition to my stars, and I've got just the film in mind.'

Pet was dragged out of the room and then upstairs to a bathroom.

'Go on, get cleaned up.'

He made no move to leave, and arms folded defensively, Pet stammered, 'Not . . . not till you go.'

'All right, but don't try anything. I'll be back with some clean togs.'

As he left, Pet looked frantically around, but there wasn't a window, no means of escape. She sank down onto the cold tiles, sobbing.

Only minutes later the door opened and clothes were thrown onto the floor beside her.

'Come on, get a move on, and then get those on.'

Pet was unable to stop the sobs that racked her body. She sank onto her side, curling into a ball.

The man crouched down beside her, his voice surprisingly soft. 'Come on, your brothers ain't daft. As long as they play ball, you'll be out of here.'

As he reached out to touch her, Pet scrambled away.

There was a soft laugh. 'Still the innocent, I see. Still just a kid.'

His words sparked a memory. Tony! It was Tony Thorn, the boy she had met at the youth club. With a spark of hope she sat up. 'I . . . I know who you are. Please, Tony, please let me go.'

'I can't. Garston would kill me.'

'Oh, please, Tony . . . pleeease.'

'Look, I've told you, as long as your brothers play ball, you'll be all right.'

'But they don't make those horrible films.'

'They do, and they were idiots to take on Garston. Now come on, have a quick wash and get dressed. If I don't get you back to the basement we could both be in trouble.'

Pet was unresisting as Tony hauled her up, but when he didn't leave she just stared at him.

He sighed with exasperation. 'It ain't me you've got to worry about, but all right, I'll wait outside.' As he went out of the door he hissed, 'Get a move on.'

Pet washed. Though she hated the low-cut, tight black dress she'd been given, at least it was preferable to the smelly clothes she discarded. Her mind was racing. Despite refusing at first, surely she could persuade Tony to help her?

When Pet tried the handle she found that the door wasn't locked, but Tony was waiting outside. He urged her forward, down one flight of stairs, and then through a door that led to the basement.

'Tony, please, you've got to help me.'

'I've told you, I can't,' Tony said as he pulled off his balaclava, adding ruefully, 'Now that you've clocked me, wearing this is a waste of time.'

'Tony, please, there's been some sort of awful mistake. That man must have got it wrong. My brothers wouldn't be mixed up in . . . in . . .'

'Porn,' Tony finished for her. 'Garston's got eyes and ears everywhere and he doesn't make mistakes. As soon as there's a snifter of something, he hears about it. Take your brother Danny, for instance. As soon as he asked about getting hold of kids, Garston heard about it. Oh shit, you ain't gonna faint on me, are you? Look, sit down, bend over and take deep breaths.'

Her head swimming, Pet staggered to a chair. She had wanted to know what her brothers were involved in, expecting some sort of crime, but she had never in her wildest imaginings thought it would be as horrendous as this. Children – they used children to make those terrible films. It couldn't be true, it just couldn't.

'Here, drink this,' Tony urged, holding out a mug of water.

Pet gulped it down, and then at the sound of a door opening, Tony snatched up his balaclava, hastily pulling it on.

'Is everything all right down here?' Jack Garston asked as he appeared at the foot of the stairs.

'Yes, Mr Garston. She's no trouble.'

'I'm glad to hear it,' he said, his smile soft as he turned to Pet. 'Unfortunately, I won't be able to savour your lovely delights tonight, my dear. There's a problem at one of my clubs I have to deal with.' He turned to Tony again, his manner instantly changing. 'She should be in the back room. Put her in there and keep your hands to yourself. Do I make myself clear?'

'Yes, Mr Garston.'

With a sickly leer, Garston focused on Pet again. 'Good night, my dear, sleep well.'

Tony took Pet's arm, urging her to her feet as the man left. When it was all clear, he ripped off his mask again. 'At least you're safe for tonight. You'd better try to get some sleep.'

'Safe! What . . . what do you mean?'

'It's best you don't know.'

Garston's words spun in her mind. He wanted to savour her delights. The images she had seen on the film flashed into her mind. Oh, no, surely he wasn't going to rape her! 'Tony, I'm begging you. Don't let him touch me. Please . . . let me go.'

'There's nothing I can do. Garston is a nasty piece of work, as nasty as they come. You cross him at your cost, as your brothers have found out. I can't let you go, Pet. I've told you. He'd kill me.'

'Why do you work for him?'

''Cos I was a mug and didn't know what I was getting into. I only started out as a bouncer at one of his clubs, but then he started giving me other work to do and you don't say no to Jack Garston. Take tonight, for instance. You could have knocked me down with a feather when I was ordered to snatch you.'

'Why did you do it then?'

'Oh, grow up, Pet. I've told you why. When he says jump, you do it, and quickly.'

'You could leave. You don't have to work for him. Please, Tony, if you can't let me go, at least tell my brothers where I am.'

'Oh, yeah, and how am I supposed to do that without Garston finding out?'

Pet shook her head in despair. 'I don't know, but please, you must do something. You can't leave me here for that man to . . . to rape me.'

'Look, this is down to your brothers – not me. They shouldn't have crossed into Garston's territory. They should have listened to his warning, but they didn't and now you're paying the price. Now shut up about it and get some sleep.'

On that note, Tony left the room and Pet heard the key turn in the lock. Despair washed over her as she sank back on the bed, sobbing with fear as she clutched the filthy quilt around her.

Chapter Twenty-three

The brothers trooped home in the early hours of the morning. A light still shone in number one, but the other houses were in darkness.

'Do you think knocking up that publican will work, Danny? Do you think he'll pass on our message?' Chris asked.

'When I talked to Bert Mills in the pub, the landlord was doing his best to earwig. I saw him making a phone call, so I reckon he's one of Garston's narks. Anyway, trying to get a message to Garston is better than sitting around sweating until he decides to contact us.'

Chris yawned, exhausted, but he doubted he'd be able to sleep.

Yvonne emerged from number one, her face drawn with anxiety.

'Any luck?' she asked.

'No, but come on, we'd better try to get some sleep,' Danny told her.

Chris looked at the street door, dreading going inside. He knew his mother would be awake and waiting for news, but there was nothing he could say to put her mind at rest. He took a deep breath and walked in.

The room was almost in darkness with just the glow from the fire, aided by the solitary flicker of a single candle on the mantelpiece. Chris saw his mother huddled in a chair with a blanket wrapped around her, and then looking at the day bed, he saw that his father was asleep.

'You haven't found her?' his mother whispered.

'No, but we'll look again in the morning. Why don't you go to bed?'

'How can I sleep when I don't know what's happened to Petula? Oh, Chris, what if a nutter has got hold of her?'

His father stirred and she looked anxiously towards him. Chris waited until he settled again, then whispered, 'Don't think the worst, Mum. We'll find her, you'll see.'

'I hope you're right, son, because if you don't, I think this will just about finish your dad off.'

There was a soft groan and once again she looked towards the day bed, hissing, 'We don't want to wake him. You'd best get some sleep too.'

Chris was relieved to creep upstairs. Yes, a nutter probably had Pet, a nutter called Jack Garston. Inwardly he cursed Danny, cursed himself for agreeing

297

to make hard porn. If anything happened to Pet, it would be their fault. Shivering, he undressed and then, flinging back the blankets, he dived into bed, the icy sheets momentarily taking his breath away.

Chris wished he had Phil's body to snuggle up to, but he had to keep it a secret. He was sick of sneaking around, of hiding the truth, and had planned to leave home. He had the money, but one thing after another seemed to stand in his way. His father was still too ill, his mother worn out looking after him, and now to top it all, Pet had been snatched.

Chris rolled onto his side, clutching a pillow. Who was he kidding? If they found out, he'd lose his family – something he just couldn't face. They'd think he was weird, perverted and would never accept it – never!

Danny couldn't sleep. He lay with his back to Yvonne, images of his sister and what might be happening to her haunting his mind. He had never expected Garston to hit out at his family. In doing that, the man had broken the unwritten rules.

Yet as he turned over, flinging an arm around Yvonne, he knew that with Garston's reputation, he should have been prepared. There were no excuses. He'd been the one who had stirred the man up. This was down to him – his pride, his ambition, and his greed.

'Can't you sleep, Danny?'

'No, I'm worried about Pet.'

'Yeah, me too. I still think you should tell the police that she's missing.'

With a huff of annoyance Danny rolled onto his back. 'There's no need to involve the police. We'll find her.'

'But you've already been searching for hours and she hasn't turned up. What if someone's got hold of her?'

'All right, don't go on about it. If we don't find her tomorrow, I'll tell the police,' Danny snapped. He knew it was a lie, but at least it would placate Yvonne for the time being. With any luck Garston would get his message and once he knew they'd agreed to stop production, he'd let Pet go.

'Do you want me to make you a hot drink? It might help you to sleep.'

Danny ignored the question, breathing heavily to feign sleep. He heard Yvonne's soft sigh and then she flung an arm around him, snuggling close. Danny lay unmoving. If anything happened to Pet, he knew he'd never be able to live with himself. For the first time in his life, Danny found he was taking a look at himself – and not liking what he saw.

Maurice wasn't faring any better. He'd stayed up until his brothers returned again, but on finding that they hadn't found Pet, he sneaked upstairs, careful not to wake Norma as he climbed into bed. He felt dreadful and fought to control his ragged breathing. What if Danny was right? What if Pet was in Garston's hands? His chest tightened until he was wheezing in pain, his mind plagued by fear. When they first ventured into Garston territory, he'd feared the future, feared for Oliver's safety. Pet had been snatched, but it could just as easily have been his son.

Mentally he assessed his financial situation. Things had been tight after George had nicked the money, and though at first they'd all had to take a pay cut, things had started to look up. Even during the lean time and Norma's nagging, he hadn't dipped into his savings. For years he'd been putting regular amounts in a bank, money for the house he hoped to buy one day, and if Oliver continued to do well at school, he was salting money away for the boy's university expenses. It might be a silly dream to think that the boy would ever attend university, but nevertheless he'd been determined to be prepared.

Maurice didn't want to leave the alley and his family, but he had to put his son's safety first. He had the finances, if necessary, but he just hoped it wouldn't come to that. First things first, though – they were going to look for Pet again in the morning and he had to get some sleep. Asthma attack or not, he was determined to join in the search.

* * *

Bob was scowling as he got into bed. Yvonne had waited up, so why couldn't Sue? She was supposed to be fond of Pet, but obviously not enough to keep her awake.

He closed his eyes, but couldn't stop thinking about Petula. He shouldn't have listened to Danny, shouldn't have agreed to upping the ante. If they had stayed out of Garston's territory none of this would have happened.

'Did you find her?'

'No,' he said, wrapping his arms around his wife. 'I thought you were asleep.'

'I dozed off for a while, but I can't settle. Do you think she's run away?'

'No, Pet wouldn't do that.'

'She's had a rotten life since your father came home, so I wouldn't be so sure. If your mother wasn't so stubborn and had let me help, Pet could have had a bit more freedom.'

'Don't start now, Sue. I'm knackered and I need some kip.'

'Yeah, but take tonight, for instance. I went along to see your mum, but as usual she wouldn't let me in. Honestly, Bob, she drives me mad. I only wanted to help . . . to see if there was anything I can do, but she more or less shut the door in my face. Of course, Yvonne was there, Miss Goody Two-Shoes allowed admittance.'

'For Gawd's sake, change the record,' Bob snapped

301

as he flung himself over onto his back. 'I ain't listening to any more of this. My sister's missing and I'm worried sick. We're going out looking again in the morning and I've got to get some sleep.'

Thankfully Sue didn't say anything else, just huffed with annoyance as she yanked the blankets over herself. Bob closed his eyes, but it was an hour later before he finally managed to doze into an uneasy sleep.

By five in the morning, only one person in Drapers Alley remained awake. Joan was uncomfortable in the chair, but she was too worried about Dan to go upstairs. He was restless, and occasionally he groaned in his sleep.

She stood up, her knees and hips stiff. She had kept the fire going, and now, as quietly as possible, she picked up the poker to stir the coals. God, she was parched, but she daren't make a cup of tea. With Dan so fidgety, the least bit of noise could wake him.

Joan went into the kitchen, knowing she'd have to be content with a cup of water. It was freezing and she shivered. Was Pet cold too? Was she lying somewhere, injured? Joan returned to the living room where she sat in her chair again, drawing the blanket around her legs. She dreaded the dawn, dreaded how Dan would react when he woke to find that Pet was still missing.

Chapter Twenty-four

'Now then, Tony, you aren't supposed to be asleep.'

Tony jumped to his feet, woozy. 'Sorry, Mr Garston, but I only dozed off for a couple of minutes.' He quickly glanced at his watch, amazed to see that it was eight in the morning. Bloody hell, he'd been asleep for hours!

'Get the girl.'

Still woozy but trying to hide it, Tony did as he was told. He flung open the door to see Pet asleep on the bed, the quilt tangled around her.

'Come on you, get up!'

She woke, and though at first she looked dazed, groggy, her eyes suddenly widened with fear. 'Wh . . . what?'

Jack Garston walked into the room. 'Good morning, my dear, I hope you slept well. My, your brothers must be worried about you. It seems that they've sent me a message. They've agreed to stop production in return for getting you back.'

Tony saw the relief that surged in her eyes. She shakily got off the bed. 'Does . . . does this mean I can go?'

'Of course, but all in good time. Your brothers have caused me considerable time, effort and expense, so I think I deserve a little compensation – don't you?' He then turned, snapping out, 'Tony, take her upstairs to my room.'

Tony saw the colour drain from Pet's face, the fear in her eyes. 'Come on,' he said, grabbing her arm.

'No . . . no!' she cried, resisting him.

Tony hated this but, with no choice, he dragged her out of the room and upstairs, feeling like he was taking an innocent lamb to slaughter.

Jack Garston went ahead and, reaching his bedroom, he opened the door. 'Put her inside and then go. Wait downstairs.'

Pet clung to him, her eyes wide in appeal. 'Oh, Tony, please help me, ohhh, please . . .' but unable to stand it, Tony shook her off, almost running from the room.

Garston closed the door, and before Tony was out of earshot, he heard Pet's terrified screams. He tensed, but knowing there was nothing he could do, he continued to the basement. He'd seen and done some rotten things in the past, followed orders, but nothing had ever affected him like this. He felt sickened. Jack Garston was exacting his revenge of the

304

Drapers, but Pet hadn't done anything wrong. It was her bloody brothers who deserved to suffer, not her. God, he'd had enough, he was getting out, but he'd have to find somewhere well out of Garston's reach.

Tony sat in the basement, trying not to think about what was happening to Pet. Over an hour passed, time in which he filled his mind by planning how he was going to get away from Jack Garston. The door opened, and he stood up, trying to hide his feelings when he saw Pet. She looked awful, like a broken doll.

'You can take her home now, Tony. Drop her off close to where she lives, and, as you worked all night, you can have the rest of the day off.'

Unable to look at the man, Tony could only just about grind out the words, 'Thanks, Mr Garston.'

'Goodbye, my dear,' Garston said, but it drew no response from Pet. She stood as still as a statue, her eyes distant, unfocused.

Tony knew he had to get out of there before he did something silly. He wanted to smash the man in the face, to wipe the supercilious smile from his lips. He grabbed the van keys, threw Pet's stinking coat around her shoulders, and then snapped, 'Come on, you.'

Pet didn't move, so he took her arm, pulling her forward. She moved woodenly but he managed to get her outside and up the basement steps. Tony then bundled her in the van, driving off with his foot down hard on the accelerator. Once around the corner, he flicked a glance at Pet. 'Are you all right?'

She didn't answer, and though Tony tried again, there was no response. He gave up, concentrating on the road as he drove her to Battersea.

When Tony pulled up near the alley, Pet didn't move, so, jumping out, he went round to the passenger side, opening the door.

'Come on, Pet, you're home now.'

Still no response, so he reached up, gently urging her out and onto the pavement. 'Look, you've only got to walk through there,' he said, turning her round and pointing at the alley.

Bloody hell, Tony thought, it was like talking to a plank of wood. He turned her back to face him, looking into her eyes. 'Pet, you've got to go home. Your parents must be worried sick.'

There wasn't a flicker of response and seeing the dead look in Pet's eyes, he felt swamped with guilt. He'd heard rumours about Garston's appetites, his strange fancies, but too scared to disobey the man, he'd led Pet to his bedroom. He should have flattened the slimy git, stopped him from laying his filthy hands on Pet, but he'd done nothing!

'Come on, you're safe now,' he said, giving her shoulders a small shake.

When she didn't react, Tony dropped his hands

to his sides, his mind racing. He couldn't take her into the alley – the Drapers would kill him – yet his guilt made him feel that he couldn't just leave her standing like a zombie on the pavement. It was no good, he couldn't look into those dead eyes any longer. Tony turned her round again, giving her a gentle shove forward. 'Go home!'

Pet took a few steps and, his fingers crossed that she'd keep on walking, Tony jumped into the van, his foot like a diver's boot on the accelerator as he screeched away.

They were going out to search again, but Maurice wasn't ready and was holding them up. Whilst waiting, Chris decided to pop to the local shop for some cigarettes. He hurried out of the alley, saw a van speeding off, and then paused.

No, it couldn't be! His heart missed a beat. 'Pet! Pet!' he cried, running up to her. 'My God, are you all right?'

Pet was walking woodenly, her face expression-less.

'Oh, Pet, what has he done to you?'

She still didn't react, her eyes fixed ahead as she took one slow step after another.

Chris took her arm. 'Come on, Pet, let's get you home. We've been going out of our minds and we were out half the night looking for you.'

There was still no response, but thankfully she

kept moving, until at last Chris was able to urge her inside.

'Mum,' he called. 'Look.'

'Pet. Oh my God, Pet!'

Chris watched as his mother hurried forward, her face alight, only to pause when she saw her daughter's face. 'What is it, love? What's wrong?'

'Come on, talk to us,' Chris urged.

She stood like a statue and for the first time Chris noticed her clothes. Her coat was over her shoulders, but beneath it she was wearing a black dress, which thankfully his mother hadn't noticed. The smell reached him then, his nostrils twitching.

'Chris, her coat stinks,' his mother cried. 'I think she must have wet herself.'

Pet remained unmoving, her face pale, frozen, like alabaster.

'What's the matter with her, Chris?' but then as Dan began to wave his arm as he tried to speak, she hurried to his side. 'Look, love, I told you not to worry. Petula's here. She's come home.'

'Pet, come and sit by the fire,' Chris urged. 'You look frozen.'

Gently he led her forward, pushing her gently onto a chair. 'I think she's in some sort of shock, Mum. Maybe we should get the doc to have a look at her.'

He watched as his mother pursed her lips. She then shook her head saying, 'No, not yet. Let's see if she snaps out of it first. Pop next door and ask

Yvonne to come round. She can look after Pet, whilst I see to your dad.'

Chris nodded, taking a last look at his sister before he left. She was sitting stiffly, her eyes fixed, distant. His jaws worked in anger. What had Garston done to her?

He hurried next door to find that Danny and Bob were still waiting for Maurice. 'We can call off the search. When I went to buy some fags, I found Pet just outside the alley.'

'What? Is she all right?'

'I don't know, Danny. Physically she looks all right, but she seems a bit weird.'

'I'm going to see her,' Bob said, almost running out of the door.

'Yeah, me too,' said Danny.

'Hold on, Danny, you know how Dad reacts when he sees you.'

'I don't give a shit. I'm going to see Pet.'

'Mum asked me to fetch Yvonne. She needs a bit of help.'

'Yvonne!' Danny yelled, and as she came hurrying downstairs he said, 'Pet's turned up and Mum wants you to give her a hand.'

Danny didn't wait for his wife as he hurried out, but Yvonne was quick too, not far behind him as he went into number one. Chris took up the rear, but as soon as his father saw Danny, he went wild.

'You'll have to go, Danny,' cried Yvonne.

'Not till I've seen Pet,' he argued, ignoring the ranting sounds his father was making.

Chris saw that Pet was unmoved by what was going on around her, her face expressionless.

'Danny, go,' he heard his mother shout. 'Do you want your father to have another stroke!'

With a shake of his head, Danny pushed Bob to one side to kneel in front of Pet, his voice frantic. 'Where have you been, Pet? What happened?'

Pet didn't answer, and as Dan's noises increased in volume, Yvonne cried, 'Danny, please, you must go.'

As Danny straightened, Chris saw an expression on his brother's face that he had never seen before. Danny looked utterly dejected, broken. Without a word he walked across the room and out of the house, his shoulders bent like an old man's.

Yvonne had seen Danny's reactions too, and frowned, but with Dan playing up, she had to concentrate on helping her mother-in-law.

'Come on, love,' Joan urged. 'If you don't calm down I'll have to get the doctor to give you a sedative again.'

Dan moaned, his good arm waving to indicate his wheelchair.

'All right, we'll get you up,' Joan told him. 'Bob, there are too many people around your father so you'd best go, but you can come back later. Chris, you can give me a hand.'

'What about Pet?'

'Yvonne will see to her.'

Bob gently stroked Pet's hair, his face white with anxiety. 'Mum, can't I stay with her?'

'She needs cleaning up, so leave her to Yvonne.'

Bob bit on his bottom lip and for a moment Yvonne thought he was going to argue, but thankfully he gave Pet's hair a final stroke, saying as he left, 'If she's still like this in an hour or two, you should call the doctor.'

Chris and Joan hauled Dan up and into his wheelchair. He was still jabbering, whilst Joan answered as if she could understand his every word. 'Yes, I'll wheel you over to Pet, but not until you calm down.'

Dan became quiet at last, and as Joan pushed him across the room until his chair was close to his daughter, Yvonne saw that one side of his face twisted into the parody of a smile. His good arm shook as he reached out, his hand finally resting on Pet's arm. She didn't respond to his touch, didn't turn her head to look at her father, and once again Dan began to jabber, but softly, as though consoling his beloved child.

Yvonne's eyes filled with tears. Pet looked dreadful. Where had she been? What had happened to her?

'Look at her, Mum. I still think the doc should take a look at her,' Chris urged.

'She was frozen when you brought her in, and if

311

she was out all night in this weather, no wonder she's in such a state. A nice hot bath might bring her round. If that doesn't work, we'll call the surgery.' Joan became brusque. 'Right, Dan, let's get you to the bathroom first.'

Chris helped his mother, whilst Yvonne kneeled down in front of Pet. 'Oh, love, what's the matter? Were you in an accident? Are you hurt?'

Pet didn't respond, and Yvonne's nose wrinkled. The child stank, her coat filthy and creased. Maybe she'd been run over, left lying somewhere, but surely if that was the case, someone would have seen her?

'Come on, darling, let's get you out of that coat,' Yvonne urged, gently unravelling it from Pet's shoulders. There was no resistance and Yvonne fought tears. Pet looked traumatised, as though she had faced something so dreadful that she had died inside. Oh God, please – not that! Underneath the coat, Pet was wearing a dress that Yvonne hadn't seen before. She frowned, but was then distracted as Joan wheeled Dan back into the room.

'Right, the bathroom's free for Pet.'

'Come on, love,' Yvonne urged, but Pet didn't move.

Chris took her arm, gently pulling her up, and as though a puppet on strings, she rose to her feet. Yvonne took over then, finding as she took Pet's arm that the girl moved forward without resistance.

'Mum, I need a word with Danny,' Chris said. 'Can you manage without me now?'

'Yes, I'll be fine.'

When they reached the bathroom, Yvonne found that Pet just stood there as she ran a hot bath. She threw in some bath salts, then said, 'It's ready.'

Pet didn't move and Yvonne floundered. She would have to undress her, but it didn't feel right, an intrusion. Softly urging, Yvonne managed to peel down the dress, her eyes widening. Pet's small breasts were bruised and covered in bite marks. Oh God! Oh, no! As gently as possible she continued to pull the dress down, finding to her horror that Pet was naked underneath. There were more bruises around her thighs, but worse, traces of blood on the insides of her legs. Tears overspilled now, running down Yvonne's cheeks. Pet had been raped, and by the looks of it, violently. Who had done this to her? It must have been a maniac, a monster!

Chapter Twenty-five

'You saw the state Pet was in,' Bob said. 'I told Sue that she's been in some sort of accident, but I can't see her swallowing that for long. What do you think Garston did to her, Danny?'

'Ain't it bleeding obvious?'

Yes, it *was* obvious, Chris thought, his temper flaring. 'When I get my hands on Garston I'll slit his fucking throat.'

'You'll do nothing,' Danny said quietly, but his manner was subdued, as though just talking was an effort. 'This is down to me to sort out.'

Chris had expected Danny to go off on one, to rant and rave at Garston. Instead he appeared deflated, his voice lacking conviction. 'No, Danny, I'm not having that. When you find Garston, I want to be there. You saw Pet, and I want to make sure he suffers for what he did to her.'

'Yeah, I'm with Chris,' Bob said. 'Pet may be able to tell us where she was held, and then we'll have Garston.'

'You're both forgetting something,' said Danny. 'What do you think will happen when Pet starts to talk?'

'Well, as I said, hopefully she'll be able to lead us to Garston.'

'That's not what I'm getting at, Bob. When Pet does open her mouth, who do you think she'll talk to?'

'Oh, shit!' Chris exclaimed, suddenly understanding what Danny was getting at. 'Mum, or maybe Yvonne.'

'Yeah, that's right.'

Bob cottoned on too, his voice high with anxiety. 'Do you think Garston told her about us?'

'Yeah, probably.'

'That . . . that means Pet knows, and if she talks . . .' Bob's voice trailed off before it rose again. 'It's our fault that Garston snatched Pet, but we've got to keep her quiet, Danny.'

'And how are we supposed to do that?'

'We could get to her first. Have a word with her.'

'I could give it a go,' Chris suggested.

Danny shrugged. 'I suppose you could give it a try, but you'll have to do it out of Mum, Dad and Yvonne's hearing.'

'She didn't seem to take in a word of what was said to her. What if she doesn't listen?' Bob asked.

'If she doesn't, then our wives will probably find out about our little sideline.'

315

Bob ran a hand through his hair in agitation. 'I'd better warn Maurice.'

'He's still rough so it might be best to leave it for now,' Chris suggested. 'What about the yard, Danny? We usually open until one o'clock on a Saturday.'

Danny said nothing, his gaze once again distant.

'Danny, did you hear what I said?'

'Yeah, but don't bother to open up. We'll all meet up there after Chris has had a chat with Pet.'

Chris met Bob's eyes, but his brother just shrugged before saying, 'I'd best get back to Sue,' and on that note he gave one last glance at Danny before walking out.

'I'll go and have a talk to Pet and let's hope I can convince her to keep her mouth shut,' Chris said. There was no response from Danny, leaving Chris seriously worried about his brother. 'Danny, I'm off,' he said, yet as he walked to number one, he knew that Danny's state of mind was the least of his concerns at the moment. If he couldn't get through to Pet and she opened her mouth, the shit really was going to hit the fan.

Yvonne found a dressing gown on the back of the door, and after helping Pet to put it on, she led her out of the bathroom. Her mother-in-law's eyes were wide in appeal, and Dan was quiet, both looking at her expectantly.

316

'She's all right, ain't she, Yvonne? Tell me she's all right. She . . . she ain't been touched?'

Joan had been through so much and it showed. Since Dan had come home, the weight had fallen off her from the heavy burden of his care. The fact that her own son had beaten his father half to death could have destroyed her, but instead she had surprised them all with her strength. Yet Yvonne felt it was a tenuous strength, one that could crack under the strain.

Fearing both their reactions, Yvonne blurted out, 'She's fine, well, other than a few bruises. I think she's been in some sort of accident and maybe that's why she's in shock. She could have been laying somewhere, injured.'

'But you said she's only got a few bruises. What about her head? Did you check her head?'

'Yes, and don't worry, it's fine. There's not even a sign of a bump.'

When Yvonne saw her mother-in-law sag with relief, she felt a little less guilty about her lies. 'Do you want me to take her up to bed?'

'Yes, good idea, a bit of kip might be just what she needs.'

Pet was still in a trance as Yvonne led her upstairs, where she tucked her into bed like a child. As Yvonne sat down beside Pet, she realised that she shouldn't have lied to her in-laws. All it had done was to put off the inevitable. When Pet came out of this shock, they would find out the truth and it could destroy Dan. He adored his daughter and had always kept her protected, innocent, but now . . .

'Oh, Pet, if you can hear me, please, don't tell your parents what happened to you. It would break their hearts.'

Pet didn't respond, but her eyes closed and her breathing became regular as she fell asleep. Yvonne crept out of the room, going downstairs to see that Chris had returned.

'How is she?' he asked.

'She's asleep,' Yvonne told him, then saying, 'Mum, if you can manage without me, I'll pop home for a while.'

'Yeah, that's fine, love, and thanks for your help.'

Yvonne called goodbye and then hurried out, worried about Danny and anxious to see if he was all right.

She was relieved to find Danny alone. He was sitting on the sofa, his eyes closed. Drained, exhausted, her usual stamina gone, Yvonne felt like sinking down beside him. She'd had a good night's sleep, but lately that didn't seem to make any difference. Now she fretted, wondering what to do. Should she tell Danny the truth, tell him that Pet had been raped? Maybe it would be better to leave it for now, to wait until Danny was more like himself.

His eyes opened. 'How is she?' His tone was listless.

'She's in bed – asleep,' and worried about Danny's reaction if she told him that Pet had been raped, she added, 'I . . . I think she must have been in some sort of accident.'

'Yeah, one called Jack Garston.'

'What? Who's he?'

Danny rose abruptly to his feet. 'I'm going to the yard. I'll see you later.'

'Wait . . .' The door slammed and Yvonne was left, her question unanswered.

Danny knocked on Maurice's door. Norma opened it, her face showing her annoyance as she stood back to let him in.

'I need a word with Maurice.'

'He's still having trouble with his breathing.'

Danny stepped inside to find Maurice slumped in a chair, his face beaded with perspiration. 'We're all meeting up at the yard. Do you think you're up to it?'

'I doubt it,' Norma snapped. 'When Bob told us about Pet's accident, this is what happened. And let me tell you, it hasn't helped that your mother turned him away. He's got just as much right as the rest of you to see his sister.'

'It's all right, Norma, just leave it, will you?' Maurice gasped. 'How is she, Danny?'

'From what I saw, she's in a bad way.'

'What are we planning to do?'

'Nothing. *We're* doing nothing. This is all down to me – my fault.'

'What are you saying?' Norma cried. 'How can Pet's accident be your fault?'

With his head all over the place, Danny realised that he'd said too much in front of Norma. Yet what did it matter? What did any of it matter now? When Pet opened her mouth, they'd all find out. 'As I said, Maurice, we're meeting up at the yard. If you can make it, we'll talk then.' He walked abruptly out, closing the door behind him.

With his head down, Danny strode out of Drapers Alley. One look at Pet and he knew what had been done to her – knew that Garston had sent one last message before releasing her. Instead of rage, instead of wanting to find Garston to ring his bloody neck, Danny had felt only self-loathing. Pet was only fourteen – a child – and the realisation hit him like a blow to the solar plexus. He had wanted to use kids in porn. Kids even younger than Pet. He was a sick bastard – as sick as Garston.

Chris came downstairs, shaking his head. 'It's no good, Mum, she's still sort of out of it. I've got to go to the yard. Can you manage without me?'

'I expect Yvonne will come round again to give me a hand. You go, I'll be fine.'

When Chris left, Joan flopped onto a chair, but soon after when Dan drifted off to sleep she went upstairs, quietly walking into Pet's bedroom. She found her daughter awake, laying flat on her back, her eyes fixed on the ceiling.

'Are you all right, love?'

Pet didn't answer and, frowning, Joan sat on the side of the bed. She reached out, running her hands over Pet's head, parting her hair, but as Yvonne had said, there was no sign of any injury. Yet something had to be wrong for Pet to be in this peculiar state. Maybe if she talked to her she'd elicit some response.

'I can't tell you how pleased we are that you've come home. When you went missing, your poor dad got in a right old state. I had to get the doctor out to give him a sedative. He's having a bit of a kip now, but did you see how pleased he was to see you? You're the apple of his eye, so thank God you've come home safe and sound.'

Joan paused, but Pet didn't even blink. She reached out again to stroke her daughter's hair, finding that the action felt alien. Like the boys, she hadn't shown Petula any affection, and didn't really know how to start now. Yvonne said that Petula hadn't been touched, and it had been such a relief. If Dan thought anyone had laid a hand on his daughter, he'd go mad.

When there was still no response, Joan frowned. There may not be any sign of a head injury, but despite a nice hot bath and a bit of kip, Pet was still in this strange state.

'I'm going to ring the surgery, Petula. I think you need to see a doctor,' she said, hurrying out of the room.

Chris shook his head as he looked at his brothers. 'I tried, but talking to Pet is like talking to a stone wall. She seems to be sort of comatose.'

'The longer she stays like that the better,' Bob said.

Maurice knew he had to stay calm. He too feared what would happen when Pet began to talk, but he was sickened by Bob's remark. 'I don't know how you can say that. Surely you don't want her to stay in that state?'

'I didn't mean it, I'm just spouting, but we've told you what might happen when she opens her mouth and I'm worried sick.'

'Don't you think I am too?'

'Look, this isn't getting us anywhere,' Chris said.

Maurice looked at Danny. 'Any ideas?' Danny just shook his head and Maurice frowned. There was something wrong. Danny hadn't spoken since the meeting began. He was slumped behind the desk, his face downcast. 'What's up, Danny?'

'I'm finished – we're finished.'

'Come on, don't talk like that,' Maurice cajoled. 'We can't be sure that Garston said anything to Pet. We may be in the clear.'

There was a defeatist tone to Danny's voice. 'I doubt that.'

322

'I think we've got to consider the worst-case scenario,' said Chris. 'Either we wait to see what Pet has to say, or you prepare your wives and Mum for what she might tell them.'

'Leave it out!' Bob protested. 'Oh, yeah, I can see it now. By the way, Sue, I think you should know that we make porn films. One of our rivals wanted us to stop production, so he kidnapped and raped Pet as a warning.'

'All right, there's no need for sarcasm. If you've got a better idea, let's hear it.'

'I haven't got any ideas.'

'Right then, if you don't want to prepare them, I don't think we've got much choice,' Chris said. 'We'll just have to wait and see what happens when Pet comes out of shock. In the meantime I want to find Garston. He can't get away with what he did to our sister.'

'I've told you, leave Garston to me.'

Maurice stared at Danny worriedly. 'Wouldn't it be better to back off? If you go after Garston, he's going to retaliate and you've seen what he's done to Pet. If you stir things up again he could snatch one of our kids.'

'Bloody hell,' said Bob, 'I hadn't thought of that.'

'We should stop making films, close down the Wimbledon operation,' Maurice urged. 'It'll show Garston that we're no longer a threat.'

'No,' snapped Chris. 'We should go after Garston

– take him out, finish him and then there'll be no need to stop production.'

'I told you, Garston's mine,' Danny murmured.

Maurice knew that he wouldn't be able to talk them out of it. They wanted revenge and so it would go on, the violence, the turf war. He gulped in air, his mind racing. He knew what he had to do – that he had no choice. Not only did he fear for Oliver's safety, he feared for his marriage too. He had never taken Norma's threats about leaving him seriously, but if she found out about the porn business it would finish their marriage. Yvonne and Sue might cope, both aware that the Drapers were no angels, but Norma was different. She came from a different background, had different standards. She'd be horrified, disgusted.

It would be hard to leave his family, but Maurice knew now he had to act quickly, before Danny and Chris went after Garston. He began to breathe heavily, feigning illness. 'Sorry, but I feel a bit rough. I think I'd best go home.'

Danny said nothing, his head still down, and it was Chris who answered, 'Yeah, all right, but we'll need to talk again.'

Maurice continued to gasp for breath as he left. If possible he'd tell his parents and his brothers that he was leaving, but he wanted to be packed and ready first. Then they would just go, before anyone could persuade him to stay.

*　　*　　*

Another hour passed, but nothing was resolved.

Fed up with going round and round in circles, Bob said, 'Look, this is just a waste of time.'

'Yeah, you're right,' Chris said. 'Come on, we might as well go home.'

Danny didn't argue, his face set as he rose to his feet. They locked the yard, all climbing into Danny's car and heading back to Drapers Alley, each preoccupied with his own thoughts.

When they arrived, Bob had no sooner put his foot inside his house when Sue started.

'Your mother drives me mad, Bob. I only wanted to find out how Pet is, but she wouldn't let me in.'

'When I saw Pet earlier she was in a terrible state. No doubt Mum and Yvonne think she needs a bit of peace and quiet.'

'Bob, for God's sake, I care about your sister and I want to see her. I'm your wife, part of the family, but I'm treated like an outcast. Norma is too, and she's just as fed up with it. We're kept out of your mother's house as though we're contagious.'

'Don't be daft, it ain't like that. Dad's upset about Pet, and Mum's just doing her best to keep him calm, that's all. She looks worn out these days, and now this has happened. You should cut her a bit of slack.'

'If she's worn out, she should accept me and Norma's offer to help. We'd muck in, but she'll only allow Yvonne to give her a hand.'

'For Gawd's sake, I've only just got in the door. Do you have to keep going on and on about it?'

'I don't keep on about it, but what about the boys? When was the last time they saw their grandfather?'

'Where are the kids?'

'Playing in the yard, but don't try to change the subject.'

'Look, with half his face paralysed, my dad looks funny. As Mum said, it might scare them if they saw him, and that would upset Dad.'

'Is that why he's kept a virtual prisoner?'

'Prisoner! What are you on about now?'

'Your dad hasn't been outside the door since he came home. He's got a wheelchair, so there's no need for it.'

'Sue, I know my dad, and believe me, he wouldn't want anyone to see him the way he is now. If he wants to go out, he'll let Mum know.'

'How's he supposed to do that?'

'He'd point to the fucking door, you silly cow!'

Sue gasped, her neck stretching. 'Don't swear at me, and I ain't a silly cow.'

Bob had to smile at the indignant expression on Sue's face. He hated arguments, his voice now placatory. 'All right, don't get your knickers in a twist. I'm sorry. It's just that I'm tired and worried about Pet. I was going to grab a bite to eat and then go to see how she is.'

326

'Oh, yes, and unlike me you'll have no trouble getting past your mother.'

'Sue, my sister is in a bad way, but all you're going on about is my mother. Sod it, I'm going to see how Pet's doing.'

Bob marched out of the house, but when he got to his mother's she opened the door, her face white with anxiety. 'What's up, Mum?'

'I've rung the surgery, asked for a doctor to come out to see Pet, but as it's Saturday, it may be a while before one turns up. Your dad's been playing up too, but he's dozed off at last so I won't invite you in in case it wakes him up.'

'All right, Mum,' Bob said. 'I'll come back later,' and as the door closed he turned to make his way back home, fed up and knowing that when he got there, Sue would start nagging again. His stomach churned. Yes, she might be in a mood now, but if she found out about the porn all hell would be let loose.

Chapter Twenty-six

Sue finally calmed down, and later that day, with the kids playing in the yard, Bob was dozing in his chair when there was a knock on his door. He opened his eyes, blinking away sleep as Maurice walked in.

'Bob,' he said, face wan, 'I've got something to tell you.'

Instantly awake now, Bob's stomach jolted. 'What is it? Have you been to see Pet? Has she said anything?'

'No, I haven't seen her yet. I . . . I've come to tell you that I'm leaving.'

'What . . . ?'

'I'm out, Bob. We're all packed and once I've said goodbye to everyone, we're going.'

Bob stared at Maurice, unable to think coherently, able only to splutter, 'But . . . but why?'

Maurice flicked a glance at Sue before asking, 'Can we talk outside?'

She reared up. 'That's it – shut me out as if I'm not a part of this family.'

'Sue, please, not now,' Bob said before walking outside with Maurice, closing the door behind him. 'Now what's this all about? Why are you leaving?'

'I should think it's obvious. Danny and Chris ain't gonna let Garston get away with what he did to Pet, and as I said at the meeting, I'm worried about Oliver. I've had it, Bob. I'm sick of living like this. I'm sick of the violence, and I'm shit scared of Jack Garston.'

Bob's temper flared. 'You can't do this, Maurice. You can't just leave like this. Dad's still in a state, and it's obvious that Pet's been raped, but all you seem to care about is yourself.'

'There's nothing I can do to help Dad, or Pet. If there's trouble with Garston, you know I'd be useless. All I'm fit for is looking after the books, and it's not just myself I'm thinking about – it's my son!'

'We could talk to Danny and Chris – persuade them to leave Garston alone.'

Maurice shook his head. 'They'll never agree, but it's not only that, Bob. If Pet opens her mouth, Norma will find out what we've been up to. She'll leave me, Bob, and she'll take Oliver with her.'

'But where will you go? And what about Mum? She ain't gonna like it.'

'Dad's the most important person in Mum's life and he always has been. She has no time for Norma,

329

or Oliver, so I doubt she'll miss us. As for where we're going, well, until I can sort something out, we'll find digs.'

With a sigh of exasperation, Bob said, 'I can't believe this. Since George put Dad in hospital, it feels like this family is falling apart.'

'I may be leaving Drapers Alley, but you're all still my family and I'll keep in touch.'

Bob could see the sadness in his brother's eyes, could hear that his chest was staring to wheeze, and his anger seeped away. 'What about the yard – the books?'

'You, Chris and Danny will manage. Keeping the books for the yard is a doddle and as for the other books – I'll leave them with Danny.'

'Look, I can understand why you want to go, but isn't there anything I can do to persuade you to stay?'

'No, Bob. I'm sorry, but I can't risk staying and . . . and if you don't mind, I'd rather you kept out of the way when I tell the others.'

'Danny's gonna do his nut,' Bob warned.

'Yeah, I know.'

Bob impulsively wrapped his arms around his brother and, obviously unused to displays of brotherly affection, Maurice momentarily stiffened, but then Bob felt his embrace returned. 'Promise me you'll stay in touch, Maurice.'

'Of course I will,' he said, his voice gruff with emotion. Then with a forced smile, he walked to Danny's house.

Bob went back inside to find Sue waiting, her arms folded across her chest.

'What's going on? Why are they leaving?'

'I dunno, love.'

'Don't give me that. I ain't that stupid. It's obvious that Maurice is doing a runner. Are the police after him? Will they be after you?'

'No, of course not.'

'Then why are they leaving?'

'I've told you! I don't know.'

'Sod you then. I'm going round to see Norma.' And with that Sue marched out of the house.

Bob flopped onto a chair. It had happened so quickly that he couldn't take it in. Maurice was leaving, running off, and though he was upset, he couldn't really blame him. Pet was bound to open her mouth and when she did they'd all be in deep, deep mire.

When Maurice told Danny, he waited for the explosion, amazed when it didn't come.

Danny just shrugged. 'I'm surprised, but I can see why.'

Maurice frowned. He'd expected Danny to do his nut, but instead he remained slumped on the sofa. 'What's wrong, Danny?'

'Nothing's wrong,' he replied, at last rising to his feet. 'I don't suppose I can persuade you to stay?'

'No, sorry. Even if you and Chris agree to leave

331

Garston alone, I can't risk Norma finding out about the other stuff.'

'I've already decided to close down Wimbledon.'

'Do the others know?'

'Not yet.'

'I feel rotten for buggering off, but you don't need me, Danny. As I told Bob, I only look after the books and you can handle them,' Maurice said as he pulled them out of his pocket. 'This one is for the yard, but keep the other one out of sight.'

'What will you do for money?'

'I've got a few bob stashed away, and I can always look for a job.'

'Are you staying in the area?'

'I don't know, Danny. I haven't thought that far ahead.'

'You'll keep in touch?'

'Yes, of course I will.'

Yvonne walked in from the kitchen, frowning. 'I couldn't help overhearing some of what's been said. It sounds like you're running away, Maurice, but why?'

'Keep out of this, Yvonne,' Danny said.

'But—'

Maurice swiftly broke in, 'Look, I've got to go. Bye, Danny. Bye, Yvonne.'

Danny nodded, his voice hoarse as he said, 'Let me know where you are.'

Maurice gulped, finding saying goodbye to his

family agonising. Memories of his childhood flashed into his mind; the way his brothers had always looked after him, stood up for him, but now he felt like a rat deserting a sinking ship. 'I'm sorry, Danny,' he gasped.

'There's no need, mate. You warned against Garston in the first place, but I wouldn't listen. This is all down to me – my fault that you've been forced to do this.'

Maurice could feel his chest tightening. A full-blown asthma attack could delay his departure and that was the last thing he wanted. He shook his brother's hand, said goodbye and then quickly left.

Now outside, Maurice drew air into his lungs, trying to prepare himself as he knocked on his mother's door. She opened it, her expression harassed.

'Not now, Maurice. The doctor has just arrived to take a look at Pet, and your father's playing up a bit.'

'But, Mum—'

'Come back later.'

Maurice opened his mouth to protest again, but found the door shut in his face. He paled. The doctor was there. Would he be able to get Pet to talk? Yet how could he leave without saying goodbye to his parents, and Chris? For a moment he remained outside his mother's door, but then he turned swiftly, heading for Bob's house. He had to get Norma away from the alley before Pet opened her mouth, but once they had settled, he could come back to visit them without her.

When Bob opened the door his face lit up. 'Maurice! Have you changed your mind?'

'No, but the doctor's with Pet and Mum wouldn't let me in. I can't hang around, Bob. Will you tell her – and Chris?'

'Yeah, all right, but what excuse am I supposed to make?'

'If the doc gets through to Pet, I doubt you'll need one.'

'Oh shit, I hadn't thought of that.'

'If she still isn't talking, I suppose you can blame Norma. Tell Mum that she wanted to leave the alley.'

'All right, but she's still going to think it's odd that you left without saying goodbye.'

'I know and I'm sorry to lay this on you.'

'What did Danny say?'

'Not much. Only that he's going to close Wimbledon down, and then he said he doesn't blame me for leaving.'

'Close down? But why? I don't know what's up with Danny. We can still make soft porn.'

'He ain't himself, that's for sure.' Maurice looked at his mother's door, his heartbeat increasing. What if Pet was talking? 'Look, I've got to go, Bob.'

'I couldn't tell Sue why you're leaving, so she went round to see Norma. What excuse did you give her?'

'None. She's been nagging me for years to leave the alley, so I just told her that if she didn't stop asking questions, we'd stay. So far it's done the trick, but I'll have to come up with something to shut her up.'

'Sue thinks the police are after us.'

'I must go, Bob.'

'You'll let me know where you are?'

'Of course I will.'

Maurice found himself wrapped in an embrace again. He returned the pressure, almost cracking up as he gently pushed his brother away. 'Bye, mate,' and before Bob could answer, he hurried off.

When he walked inside his own house, Maurice found Sue and Norma facing each other like combatants.

'Maurice, will you please tell Sue that I don't know why we're leaving.'

'That's right.'

'She seems to think that we're running from the police. Is that why?'

'Look, Norma, you've been nagging me for years to get out of Drapers Alley and now you've got your wish. I have my reasons for leaving and you'll just have to trust me on this.'

'Sue's right, isn't she? It's the police – they're after you.'

'No, Norma, the police aren't after me. Now either we leave right away or we stay, and for good.' Maurice hoped this continued threat would be enough to silence his wife. It had been the one he used throughout the afternoon whenever she began to ask questions. She'd initially been thrilled when he told her they were leaving, happy at first to begin packing, but it hadn't lasted long. She wanted to know why they had to go in such a hurry without the chance to arrange a van for the furniture. He told her that once they'd settled he'd get the removals sorted out, and thankfully that had been enough to mollify her, but now Sue was stirring things up again.

'Leave it out, Maurice,' Sue snapped. 'You can't expect Norma to just leave without knowing why. And what about Oliver? How does he feel about it?'

'Sue, I don't want to fall out with you, but this is none of your business.' He turned to Norma. 'Well, what's it to be? Are we going, or are we staying?'

For a moment there was only silence, but then with a small nod, Norma said, 'We're going.'

'Where's Oliver?'

'He's upstairs, sulking. He doesn't want to go.'

Maurice shook his head in exasperation. When he told Oliver that they were moving, he'd been more upset about leaving his rabbit than his cousins. He was an only child, used to playing alone when the other boys weren't around. Maurice had found a box, stuffed Shaker inside, and just hoped that they could sneak the animal into digs. It had been worth it to see the smile on his son's face.

'Oliver,' Maurice called.

When the boy came reluctantly downstairs, Maurice kneeled in front of him. 'Look, son, we've got to go now. Do you want to pop round to say goodbye to your cousins?'

Oliver shook his head, only saying sulkily, 'No.'

Sue sniffed, and then tears began to roll down her cheeks. 'Oh, I can't believe this is happening. Paul's gonna miss him something rotten.'

'We'll stay in touch,' Maurice consoled and, knowing that he couldn't stand much more of this, he picked up two of their cases. 'Right, let's go. Oliver, you carry Shaker, and, Norma, can you manage a couple of cases? We've only got to hump them around to the car.'

'Yes, all right,' she said, her voice subdued as she added, 'Good . . . goodbye, Sue. I'll ring you. I promise.'

Maurice took one last look around the living room, finding his feet leaden as they left the house. There was no sign of Danny, but Bob was on his doorstep. Sue ran into his arms, sobbing, but after giving her a swift hug he gently disengaged himself.

'Go inside, love. See to the boys,' he urged.

With a strangled gasp she nodded, whilst Bob moved to take the cases out of Norma's hands. 'I'll carry these,' he said.

They walked silently to the garages, passing the two empty houses, one that had been George's, the other Ivy's. There would be three empty now. When they came to the end of the alley, Maurice found that he couldn't look back, his emotions barely under control.

He loaded the luggage into the car, knowing that if he looked at Bob it would be his downfall. Somehow he had to build a new life, but the thought of doing it without the support of his family was overwhelming. Norma climbed into the passenger seat, Oliver in the back, and almost choking, Maurice got behind the wheel. He started the engine, gasped, 'See you, Bob,' and then drove away, before his brother had a chance to answer.

Chapter Twenty-seven

When the doctor arrived, Chris hurriedly said that he was going out, and bolted, shutting the door behind him.

Dr Addison could see that Joan Draper was worried about leaving her husband on his own, but nevertheless she showed him upstairs.

When he saw the young girl lying on the bed, he cleared his throat. 'Would you stay whilst I examine your daughter?'

'But my husband . . .'

'I'm sure he'll be fine for a few minutes,' he said dismissively, going on to examine Petula.

He was appalled by the girl's injuries and examined her as gently as possible, but it wasn't only her physical injuries that concerned him, there was her mental state too.

'Do you know who did this to your daughter?' he asked, replacing the blankets.

There was no reply and he turned to see that Joan

Draper was white-faced, clinging to the end of the bed as she gasped, 'No! Oh, Doctor, I didn't realise that she's been . . . been touched. Petula arrived home this morning after being missing all night. My . . . my daughter-in-law said that she must have been in some sort of minor accident, that's all.'

'Yes, well, as you've now seen, your daughter has been touched, and violently.'

'Is . . . is that why she won't talk?'

'She's suffered an horrendous ordeal, so dreadful that her mind has closed down. I've seen this reaction before and if there's no response in forty-eight hours, she'll need to be admitted to hospital. I'll call again on Monday to see if there's any improvement. If you think she needs to see a doctor before then, call the surgery and you'll be put through to the locum service.'

'Please, my husband mustn't know that she's been . . . been . . .' Joan Draper floundered, unable to say the word. 'I don't think he could stand it, Doctor. He'd go mad.'

'Yes, I can understand that, but there may be consequences.'

'What do you mean?'

Dr Addison cleared his throat. This was difficult, but the signs would have to be looked for. 'What I'm trying to say is that you will need to keep an eye on your daughter's menstrual cycle.'

Joan Draper stared at him, ashen-faced. 'You . . . you don't mean that she could be pre . . . pregnant.'

'It's too soon to say, but there is always the possibility.'

'Oh, God,' she gasped. 'No, please, not that.'

'My advice is just a precaution.'

As they left the room he could see that Joan Draper was making a supreme effort to bring herself under control. Dan Draper was awake when they went back downstairs, and she even managed a parody of a smile.

'Petula's going to be fine, Dan. Ain't that right, Doctor?'

'Yes, well, I'll have another look at her on Monday.'

'See, Dan, I told you not to worry.'

Dr Addison saw the look of relief on the man's twisted face. He said goodbye, his expression grim as he left. The girl's injuries had been dreadful and he wondered if the police had been informed.

Chris strode quickly down Lavender Hill, anxious to get to Phil – anxious for comfort. He felt as though everything was falling apart. Danny had lost it, and not only that, none of his brothers had been concerned about their mother, about how she'd be affected if Pet opened her mouth. All they'd been concerned about was their wives. They'd forgotten that the old man had been involved with the porn from the start – all right, not the hard stuff – but even so, how would his mother take it if she found out? She had always been a bit of a prude, narrow-minded, not slow to show her disgust when Maurice had got Norma in the family way. She disapproved of Sue too, calling her a tart, and though she had put up with the old man when he swore, she would never allow a smutty joke. Would she turn against the old man if she found out about the porn? Yes, of course she would, and she'd turn against him too, against all of them.

Since his father's beating and George's disappearance, Chris had already sensed that his mother had changed towards him. At first she had seemed edgy, nervous around him and unable to meet his eyes, but when he'd questioned her she had denied that anything was wrong. At first he'd been shit scared that she'd found out who he was seeing, but had soon realised that it couldn't be that. If his mother knew, if any of his family knew, they'd have confronted him. His fear of discovery had served to make him extra careful when he sneaked off.

Thankfully, nowadays his mother seemed to have relaxed a little bit, but if she discovered that they'd been making porn, how would she react? Would she throw him out? He dreaded facing it, seeing the disgust on her face. Maybe he should get out now, leave before the shit hit the fan. Even though he hated the idea, it was better than the alternative.

Feeling desolate at the thought of leaving his mother, when Chris reached Phil's house he banged on the door, relieved when it was opened almost immediately.

'Chris, what's the matter, love? Come here, come to Mummy.'

Gratefully Chris fell into arms that enfolded him – comforted him.

Yvonne was puzzled and concerned. When she had told Danny about Pet, he had mentioned Jack Garston, and now when Maurice called round to say he was leaving, the same name had come up again.

'Danny, who is Jack Garston? Is he a copper?'

Danny didn't look at her, only saying shortly, 'No.'

'I don't understand. If he isn't a copper, why has Maurice been forced to leave?'

'Yvonne, you don't want to know. Just keep out of it.'

'Danny, please, I do need to know what's going on. It's important. Are the police after you too? Will you be doing a runner? Will *we* be doing a runner?'

'We ain't going anywhere.'

Yvonne heaved a sigh of relief, but it was short-lived. If this man Garston wasn't a copper, then who was he? God, she was worried sick. Danny seemed depressed, morose. All right, he had good reason to be upset. He adored Pet and it must have been a shock to see her in that state, yet she was sure there was more to it than that.

Yvonne was still hugging her news to herself. She had been itching to tell Danny, hoping it would snap him out of his depression, but then Pet had gone missing, making it an impossible time. She reached out, touching his arm. 'Danny, please talk to me. Tell me what's going on.'

'Yvonne, just leave me alone. I ain't in the mood for this.' And Danny leaned forward, burying his face in his hands.

Yvonne wanted to comfort him, to hold him. She hadn't planned it this way, but now she blurted out, 'Danny, I've got some wonderful news. I'm pregnant.'

He sat bolt upright, his eyes wide as he turned to look at her. 'You're what?'

Yvonne smiled softly. 'I'm having a baby, Danny. We're having a baby. I've been feeling rough for some time now and finally went to see the doctor on the same day that Pet went missing. When he told me that I'm four months pregnant, you could have knocked me down with a feather. I mean, I had no idea, especially as I've been having my periods. The show was small, but it just didn't occur to me that I might be having a baby.'

She had anticipated this moment so many times, expecting to see joy on Danny's face, but instead he jumped to his feet, his face the colour of chalk.

'No . . . no, you can't be.'

Yvonne touched her stomach. It had hardly

increased in size so was it any wonder that Danny didn't believe her? 'I know it doesn't show, but I am, really I am. Oh, Danny, what's wrong? I thought you'd be pleased.'

'I ain't fit to be a father.'

'Don't be silly, of course you are. You'll make a wonderful father.'

'You must be joking. I'm a bastard, Yvonne – a sick bastard.'

'I . . . I don't understand.'

Danny raked both hands through his hair, his expression wild. 'All right, you wanted to know, so I'll tell you. When I've finished, I won't blame you if you walk out of that door for good.'

He sat down again, his voice hesitant at first, but as it grew in strength, Yvonne wanted to put her hands over her ears, to shut out his words. She felt sick, bile rising to her throat, but this time it was nothing to do with her pregnancy.

'Please, I don't want to hear any more.'

It didn't stop Danny; nothing did. On and on he went, spewing out all the disgusting things he had done until Yvonne couldn't stand it. She fled, running upstairs where she slammed the bedroom door behind her. Wildly she grabbed a suitcase from under the bed, throwing clothes haphazardly inside.

Yvonne had always known that Danny was a bit of a rogue, that the Drapers were involved in shady deals, but never in her wildest imaginings had she

345

expected to hear that they produced filthy, disgusting films.

She had lost count of Danny's affairs, of the times she had forgiven him, but just how many of his so-called porn stars had he slept with? Her stomach churning, Yvonne closed the suitcase before lifting it from the bed.

When she carried it downstairs Danny was on his feet, but he didn't say a word as she walked towards the door. It was the look on his face that stilled her. He stood unmoving, looking utterly crushed, broken, and in that moment Yvonne knew she couldn't do it. Despite every sickening thing he had told her, she couldn't leave him. She loved him – she always had and always would.

She turned round and, without a word, walked back upstairs, tears rolling down her cheeks.

Chapter Twenty-eight

Next door, Bob dreaded going to see his mother, but Sue's questions finally drove him out. He paused outside Danny's door. Maybe he could have a word with his brother first and between the two of them, they could come up with an excuse for Maurice's departure.

'Danny,' he said as he walked straight in, 'Maurice didn't get a chance to say goodbye to Mum or Chris. I've got to tell them that he's gone. Chris will guess why, but Mum's gonna do her nut. Any ideas?'

Danny's voice was lacklustre. 'No, sorry.'

'Come on, Danny, buck up. We need to sort this out.'

'Bob, just leave me alone, will you?'

'You're supposed to be in charge, the one who's running things.'

'Not any more.'

'But—'

'Since I took over the firm, all I've done is fuck things up. You're in charge now.'

'I don't want to be in charge, but if I was I'd make sure that we leave Jack Garston alone. Maurice left because he's shit scared of him and, to be honest, now that I've had time to think about it, I feel the same.'

'Fine, we'll leave him alone. I'm finished with porn, with the lot of it.'

'Danny, you can't just bale out. What about Wimbledon?'

'Close it down.'

'Chris won't like that.'

'You're in charge now. You sort him out.'

'Danny, come on – don't leave all this to me. What am I supposed to tell Mum? And not only that, the doctor has been to see Pet. What if she's opened her mouth?'

'I dunno, Bob. I've told Yvonne the truth and, as I said, you can sort the rest out.'

'You've what? But she might tell Sue.'

Danny just shrugged and Bob's temper flared. 'You could have bloody warned me.'

'Yeah, sorry, but I don't think she'll say anything to Sue.'

'How did she take it?'

'Badly, but at least she's still here.'

'What about Mum? Do you think she'll tell Mum?'

'I dunno. She might.'

'Shit, Danny, you'll have to stop her.'

'What's the point?'

'What's the matter with you? As you said, you're the one who fucked everything up and you've got to sort it out.'

At last Bob got some response. Danny rose to his feet, but instead of annoyance, his voice rang with despair. 'Don't you think I know that, Bob? But I can't do anything . . . it's too late. Pet's in that state because of me. The firm's had it because of me. I'm finished, we're finished, and there's nothing – nothing I can do about it.'

Bob had never seen Danny in this state. He'd always played the big man, issuing orders, so sure that they could play Garston at his own game and win. He glared at his brother. 'Right, well, sod you then, but I'll tell you this: when Mum finds out, I'm not taking the blame. As you said, it was your idea, and you can take the fall, not me.' Bob spun on his heels and marched out of Danny's house, slamming the door behind him.

Without a thought he strode to his mother's house, rapping the letter box, and when she opened the door he said quickly, 'Mum, Maurice and Norma have gone. They've moved out of the alley.'

'What? Don't be daft. Come on, come inside, but keep your voice down. Your father has just dozed off again. It's all he seems to do lately.'

Bob stepped inside to see his father in his wheelchair, head back and mouth hanging open. 'Is he all right?'

'Yes, but he's been in a state about Pet and it's worn him out,' she whispered, beckoning Bob through to the kitchen.

'Where's Chris?'

'Out as usual. That boy's hardly around these days.'

'How's Pet?'

'Oh, Bob, I don't know how to tell you this, but . . . but she's been raped.'

Although he and his brothers had guessed this, Bob feigned shock. 'What? Who did it, Mum? Has she said?'

'No, she hasn't opened her mouth, but it was bad, Bob, really bad. The bastard needs catching, castrating.'

'We'll sort it out, Mum.'

'Yes, I know you will, but come on, what's this about Maurice?'

'I told you. He's moved out.'

'Of course he hasn't. He came down to see me a little while ago, but with the doctor here I told him to come back later.'

'He couldn't wait, Mum. He asked me to say goodbye and to tell you that he'll be in touch once he's settled.'

'Maurice has never said anything about moving before. Now you're telling me he's just upped and gone without saying goodbye – without seeing his father?'

Bob nodded, dreading his mother's questions.

'Why has he left in such an all-fired hurry?'

'I dunno, but I think it was Norma. She's been nagging him for ages to get out of the alley.'

As his mother looked up at him, it was as if he could see the wheels turning in her mind, but then there was a cry from the living room.

'Your father's awake. Don't say anything in front of him. He's had enough for one day. It'll have to keep until tomorrow, and if he's up to it I'll break it to him then.'

Bob heaved a sigh of relief as he followed her into the living room. 'Hello, Dad.'

His father's good arm waved, and seeing his mother moving to wipe the spittle from his chin, Bob said, 'I'll leave you to it, Mum. I'll see you later.' Before she could respond, he shot out of the door.

Bob knew that Sue would start on him again as soon as he walked in the door, but with only spare change in his pocket, he couldn't disappear to the pub. So far Pet hadn't told anyone what had happened to her, but he knew it was just a matter of time. It was going to come out, either through Pet or Yvonne, and there was nothing he could do to stop it. With no choice, Bob knew he'd have to tell Sue. He'd wait until the kids were in bed, and that would give him time to rehearse what he was going to say.

* * *

At eight o'clock, Bob sat down next to Sue. 'Er . . . we need to talk.'

'You're telling me. I want to know what's going on, but so far talking to you has been like trying to get blood out of stone. I want to know why Maurice has left, and don't try to fob me off again.'

'All right, but this ain't gonna be easy so hear me out before you do your nut.'

Bob took a deep breath before starting at the beginning. As his tale progressed he saw Sue's eyes widen with shock. When he got to the part about making hard-core films, he placed the blame at Danny's door.

'It was Danny's idea. He said there was big money in it, and so we got sucked in. We knew that we'd be going into Garston's territory, but Danny was sure we could handle him.'

Sue leaned back, her head down, and then it was Bob's turn to widen his eyes as she spoke without anger. 'It sounds to me like Danny got too greedy – as though everything was fine until you got into the other stuff.'

'Yeah, that's right.'

'So what happened next?'

'To warn us off, Garston snatched Pet and bloody hell, Sue, you should see what he's done to her.'

'You told me that she was in an accident, now you're saying that this man took her. Oh God, what did he do to her?'

Bob gulped. 'She was raped and it was violent – so bad that she's been sort of struck dumb.'

The colour drained from Sue's face, her voice quivering. 'Oh, no, poor Pet. I wish I could go to see her but I know your mum won't let me in.'

'When things calm down, I'm sure she will.'

'I doubt it. Oh, poor Pet,' she cried again. 'That Garston must be a right bastard and I hope you're going to sort him out.'

'He's a nasty piece of work and he's got a lot of backup.'

'Sod his backup. He raped Pet and he needs a good kicking,' Sue said, her eyes filling with tears. She became quiet then, sniffing and shaking her head with distress.

Bob said nothing, his eyes downcast, and then dashing the tears from her cheeks, Sue said she was going to make them a drink. When she came back from the kitchen, clutching two glasses of whisky, she downed hers quickly, coughing as the liquid hit her throat.

'Do you feel better now?' Bob asked.

'Yeah, but it's been a bit of a shock. I'm upset about Pet, and I suppose I should be annoyed about the porn, but strangely enough, I'm not. Blimey, dirty films. I never would have guessed. You should have told me. I could have been in some of them.'

'I can't believe this! You're my wife, the mother

of my children and you expect me to let you appear in porn films?'

'Calm down, love, I didn't mean the really dirty ones.'

'Leave it out, Sue. I wouldn't have you flaunting your body for everyone to see.'

'Yeah, well, I was only kidding.'

He smiled, mollified, and in truth relieved that Sue had taken it so well. 'I'm glad to hear it.'

'Does Yvonne know about the porn – and what about your mother?'

'Yvonne does now, but only because Danny told her. My mother doesn't know, and if she finds out I dread to think how she'll take it.'

'I'd like to be around when she finds out. It'll knock Her Highness off of her throne, that's for sure.'

'Don't be like that, Sue.'

'What do you expect? You know your mother treats me like a bleedin' leper. Not only that, she hardly bothers with the boys.'

'With Dad in that state, she's got a lot on her plate.'

'You always make excuses for her and it gets right up my nose.'

'For Gawd's sake, Sue, I've just told you about Pet and Jack Garston, but you seem more interested in my mother.'

'Yeah, yeah, you're right and I'm sickened about

what Garston did to your sister. You said Maurice did a runner because he's scared of Garston, but there must be more to it than that.'

'If we take on Garston, anything could happen. Maurice was worried that next time he might snatch Oliver.'

'What! Bloody hell! If that's the case – what about our boys?'

'If we leave Garston alone and if we stay out of the game, I think we'll be all right. Danny's agreed, but I don't know about Chris.'

Sue lost it then, her voice rising in anger. 'You fucking idiot! How could you put our kids at risk?'

'But I've told you, it wasn't me. It was Danny's idea. He's the one that got us in this mess.'

'You'll have to talk to Chris. Make sure he doesn't go after Garston.'

'Yeah, don't worry, I will. Chris won't want the kids harmed so he'll see sense. Come on, love, calm down, everything is going to be all right.'

With a huff, Sue sat down again. Bob pulled her close, nuzzling her neck.

'Pack it in,' she said, but as he carried on, her voice became husky. 'Porn, blimey, and I bet you enjoyed making those films. Describe one.'

'What?'

'Go on. I need something to take my mind off Pet and what that bastard did to her. Tell me about one of the films you made. Did you join in the action?'

'No, of course not. There's only one woman who turns me on.'

'I bet it was a laugh, though. Come on, let's have an early night and you can tell me all about it.'

Bob had expected a rollicking – worse – but Sue had surprised him. She had got out of her pram only over the kids, but now that he'd assured her that they'd be fine, she was getting all frisky. Blimey, he thought as he followed her upstairs, what a woman.

Chapter Twenty-nine

On Sunday, Pet came out of her stupor at four in the morning, her body bathed in sweat. She'd been having a nightmare and tried to fight it off, but as her mind cleared it was worse, the memory of what had happened hitting her with force. She curled into a ball, reliving it, sobbing. Jack Garston had been a monster, doing unspeakable things, the pain more than she could bear. He had laughed at her screams, relished it when she fought, slapping, pinching, forcing himself inside her even though she had cried out in agony. It didn't stop then, there was more to come, but when he had thrown her over onto her stomach, the pain as he entered had been so excruciating that something weird happened. She felt as though she was leaving her body, floating away, distant from all that followed. Until now! *No, I don't want to think about it!* But it was no good, the horror played over and over again in her mind. Her body felt filthy, dirty, degraded. *Oh God, oh please, I just want to die. Let me die.*

Sobbing, she flung back the blankets, uncaring of the cold as she ran downstairs and into the bathroom. With water gushing into the bath Pet climbed in. Then, taking a scrubbing brush, she attacked her body, on and on, scrubbing, hardly feeling the hard bristles or the pain. Only when she was red raw did her hands finally become still. Tears ran down her cheeks. It was no good. She still felt filthy, defiled, and she doubted that she'd ever feel clean again.

In despair she climbed out of the lukewarm water, dried herself and got back in her nightdress, walking with leaden feet to the living room. In the dim light she saw her father, his arm waving, and with a sob of anguish she ran across the room, throwing herself down beside him on the narrow day bed. 'Oh, Dad, Dad . . .' she wailed.

As his sweaty arm wrapped around her, Pet stiffened, but this was her father, a man who had always looked after her, protected her and one she didn't have to fear. She lay against him, and though he couldn't form words, she knew from the sounds he was making that he was trying to soothe her. The fire was still glowing in the hearth, banked up with nuggets of coke, the warmth and her father's murmurs finally lulling her to sleep.

Pet woke again three hours later, and the first face she saw was her brother's. He was leaning over her, gently shaking her shoulder. It all came flooding back, the films she'd been shown, the awful things she had seen. 'Get away from me!'

'Pet, it's all right. It's me, Chris.'

Unable to bear his touch, she shrugged off his hand, remembering almost word for word the things that Jack Garston and Tony Thorn had said about her brothers. She looked at Chris, saw the scar on his cheek, evidence of Garston's warning, but they hadn't listened. She'd been raped because of them, made to pay the price for their refusal to stop making those awful films.

Pet saw her mother walking into the room, a frown on her face as she took in the scene. 'What's going on? Pet, what are you doing on your father's bed?'

Pet rose to her feet, shivering. She couldn't speak, couldn't tell her mother about the terrible films she'd seen, one in which a child had been raped, or what Jack Garston had done to her. Pet was swamped with shame. She should have fought harder, found something, anything, to smash over his head. With a small sob she fled the room, running upstairs to the sanctuary of her bedroom where, almost leaping into bed, she drew the blankets over her head. She wanted to shut out the world – an evil world she no longer wanted to live in.

'Did she speak to you, Chris? Did she say anything?'

Chris stared at his mother, heart pounding in his

chest. Pet had come out of that strange stupor and now it was only a matter of time before it all came pouring out. 'Er . . . yeah, but I didn't catch what she said. I'll go and see if she's all right.'

'Come through to the kitchen first,' she hissed.

Chris frowned, but did as his mother asked, his face stretching when she spoke again.

'You didn't come in until after I was in bed last night, so I couldn't tell you what happened when the doctor examined Pet. Oh, Chris, I don't know how to tell you this, but she . . . she was raped. I can see you're shocked, but listen, we've got to keep this from your father. You know how he feels about Pet, and if he found out, well, I dread to think what will happen.'

'Did she say who did it?'

'No, she still wouldn't say a word, but if she's talking now, somehow we've got to make sure that she doesn't say anything in front of your father.'

'All right, Mum, I'll do my best,' Chris said.

'There's one more thing. Maybe *you* can tell me why Maurice and Norma buggered off without even saying goodbye.'

'What! Bloody hell, this is news to me. When did they leave?'

'It must have been when the doctor was here, and if you ask me, it's a bit funny. Bob said that Norma's been nagging him for ages to go, but why now and in such an all-fired hurry? Doesn't he care about his sister? Doesn't he care about his family? If you ask me, there's something going on – something that Bob didn't want to tell me. Now come on, you must know.'

'I don't. Maurice didn't say anything to me and I'm as surprised as you.'

He saw his mother's eyes narrowing suspiciously. Saying that he wouldn't be long, Chris hurried upstairs. He was shocked to hear that Maurice had left so suddenly, and was angry too. How could he go now – just when they all needed to pull together? He'd have a word with Danny and Bob later, but first he had to sort Pet out.

Chris found her buried under a mound of blankets. 'Pet, it's me, Chris, are you OK?'

The mound moved, but there was no reply. 'Pet, please, love, we need to talk.'

Once again there was only silence, but Chris knew she could hear him. 'Listen, when I get hold of Jack Garston, I'll slit his bloody throat.'

Still silence, but Chris continued, hoping that his words would get through. 'Mum knows that you were raped, but you can't tell her who did it, or why. She won't be able to take it. She'd crack up. There's Dad too – he'll go mad if he finds out that you've been touched. It might cause him to have another stroke. Mum's worried sick and she doesn't want him to find out.'

He heard a small sob and tried to move the

blankets aside but she fought him, keeping them tight over her head. 'Pet, come on, don't be like this.'

At last her head popped out, but the look on her face made Chris reel backward. Her eyes blazed with hate, spittle flying out of her mouth as she yelled venomously, 'Get away from me! Yes, he raped me, hurt me, and it's all your fault, but you don't seem to care about me. You're just scared that Mum might find out what her precious sons have been up to!'

'No, Pet, it isn't like that. Of course we care, and I've told you, the bastard will be made to pay for what he did to you. Come on, surely you know that we didn't want this to happen. We had no idea that Jack Garston would go this far.'

'He warned you, he told me, and your cheek is proof of that.'

'Yes, I admit he warned us off and we should have listened.'

As though she hadn't heard him, Pet's voice rose again. 'He made me watch your films. There was one with a little girl in it and she was only about ten years old. It was awful – she was terrified. How could you do that to her? My God, you're animals. You're monsters. You're as bad as him! I hate you, I hate all of you.'

'I don't know what you're talking about. What little girl?'

'The one in the film. A film you made!'

'Leave it out, Pet. It wasn't one of ours. We don't use kids. We'd never do that.'

'I don't believe you.'

'Listen to me. All right, I admit we make porn films, but we would never use children. I swear on my life, Pet, I promise you. I don't know what Garston showed you, but it wasn't one of ours.'

The anger seemed to drain from Pet, replaced by heart-rending sobs. She began to rock backwards and forwards as tears streamed down her face. Chris could hardly stand to see her pain and impulsively he leaned forward to drag her into his arms.

'No, no, don't touch me,' she cried, fighting off his hands. 'Go away. Leave me alone!'

'I can't, Pet, not until you promise me that you won't tell Mum, or speak about being raped in front of Dad. He couldn't take it, Pet, and you know that.'

'All right – all right!' she screamed. 'I won't say anything. Now get out. Get out of my room.'

Chris rose to his feet, relieved that she was going to keep her mouth shut, but hating himself for what they had done to their sister. Yet he hated Jack Garston more. Somehow he'd find the man – and when he did . . .

'Chris – Chris, can you come down? I need a hand with your father.'

'I'm coming,' he called back.

Pet was still crying and he didn't want to leave

her, but she refused to look at him, instead lying down whilst pulling the blankets back over her head.

He found his mother in the kitchen, her face anxious. 'Close the door,' she said, and when Chris had done so she asked, 'Petula was shouting. What did she say?'

'She's upset, but don't worry, she won't say anything in front of Dad.'

'Oh, thank goodness, but as I said, Chris, whoever did that to Petula was a monster, a maniac. He needs catching, locking up and the key thrown away.'

'Don't worry, Mum. I'll have a word with Danny and we'll sort it out.'

'Yes, I know you will. Now come on, we'd best get your father to the bathroom.'

Chris glanced at the clock. It was still early, but after giving his mum a hand he wanted a word with Danny and Bob. They had a lot to sort out – starting with Jack Garston.

Pet remained buried under the blankets until she heard Chris leave. As soon as he had touched her, images of Jack Garston rose in her mind, the things she'd been forced to watch, the things he had done to her. It had been awful, dreadful, but oh . . . that poor little girl.

Pet's stomach lurched. Oh God, her mother knew that she'd been raped! She would ask questions. She'd want to know how it happened and who did it. Chris had asked her not to say anything, but there had been no need. She couldn't tell her mother – couldn't speak about the disgusting things that Garston had done to her body.

She shifted, sore, bruised, unable to forget the things that Garston had said about her brothers. At first she refused to believe him, but had finally accepted the truth. Like Garston, like that monster, they made those films, peddled porn. Chris had said they didn't use children and she prayed it was true. The other film had been bad enough and now she shivered. Would Garston add his final warning? A warning that made her stomach chum. After he had raped her he had laughed, taking great delight in telling her that the whole act had been filmed.

Pet licked her lips, her mouth dry and throat parched. Her stomach was empty, hollow, and she couldn't remember the last time she had eaten. She wanted to go downstairs for a drink, but feared facing her mother, knowing that out of her father's hearing, the questions would start.

At last, unable to stand her thirst any longer, Pet threw back the blankets and rose to her feet. There was only one thing she could do. She'd go down-stairs and if her mother asked questions, she'd pretend she had no memory of what had happened. But, oh, if only that were true!

*　　*　　*

Danny was up, but was still in his dressing gown when Chris walked in.

Danny saw his brother's eyes flick to Yvonne before he said, 'Danny, we need to talk.'

The older brother ran a hand over his face, saying tiredly, 'Bob's in charge now. Speak to him.'

'Leave it out, Danny, we've got things to sort out,' Chris protested, his eyes once again flicking to Yvonne.

'It's all right. Yvonne knows everything – about Garston, about the porn. I told her last night.'

'Why did you do that? Why jump the gun? I've sorted Pet out and she's agreed to keep her mouth shut, but now you've gone and told Yvonne. What if she tells Mum?'

'She won't,' Danny said. 'Ain't that right, Yvonne?'

'Yes, that's right,' Yvonne snapped, her back stiff as she walked out of the room.

They had barely spoken last night, Yvonne saying only that she didn't want anyone to know about the baby yet. Baby! He didn't want to be a father – he wasn't fit to be a father. A wave of despair washed over him. He didn't want to think. All he wanted to do was sleep.

'Garston showed Pet a film using kids and told her it was one of ours.'

It didn't surprise Danny. Nothing Garston did could surprise him now. He shrugged, saying nothing.

'Come on, Danny, this had gone far enough. Snap out of it. You can't leave everything to me and Bob. We've got Garston to sort out.'

Danny just wanted Chris to leave. He said tiredly, 'Bob wants us to back off, and I think he's right. I'm finished with it, Chris, finished with Garston and porn.'

'You don't mean that, and what's all this about Maurice leaving?'

'Ask Bob.'

'For God's sake, Danny, what's the matter with you?'

Danny felt tears stinging his eyes, and he rose to his feet, ashamed, just shaking his head as he went upstairs.

Chris was dismayed, unable to believe that this was Danny. Big Danny, tough Danny, the one who took over, who ran things.

He turned, walked out and went to Bob's house, saying without preamble as he went in, 'Bob, what's going on? Danny said you're in charge.'

'Yeah, I know. I think he's lost it, Chris.'

'You're telling me. Where's Sue? We need to talk.'

'She's giving the kids a bath.'

'What's this about Maurice leaving?'

'You can't blame him, Chris. He was shit scared.'

'There was no need for him to do a runner. I've had a word with Pet and she's agreed to keep her mouth shut.'

'Bloody hell, that's good, but Maurice was just as freaked about Garston. Listen, Chris, if we go after him things will only get worse. Maurice was worried about him going for Oliver next, and to be honest I feel the same. It ain't worth it, Chris. It ain't worth putting my boys at risk.'

Chris closed his eyes for a moment, gathering his thoughts. He knew that Bob was right, but it stuck in his craw to let Garston get away with it. 'All right, Bob, we'll leave him alone for now, but I ain't happy about it.'

'Thanks, mate. I'll tell Sue and it will put her mind at rest.'

'She knows about Garston?'

'Yeah, I told her everything, and other than worrying about the boys, she took it really well.'

'She'd better keep her mouth shut around Mum.'

'Of course she will – she ain't daft.'

'We need to tell Maurice that's he's in the clear. Did he leave an address?'

'No, but he said that he'd be in touch as soon as they're settled.'

'That's good,' Chris said. 'In the meantime we're still got the business to run. Danny said he wants out of porn, but he's sure to come round.'

'I want out too.'

'But why? We can still make the soft stuff.'

Bob shook his head. 'I don't want to risk it. Too much has happened, Chris – too much has changed.

The old codes have gone, and Garston has proved that. If we go on making porn, we might step on another bastard's toes, one as bad as him.'

'We can handle them. We've done it before.'

'I told you, things are changing and there's too many wanting in on the game now. These new crews will do anything to put us out of business and I ain't risking my boys.'

Chris moved a few magazines from a chair before sitting down. He couldn't carry on without his brothers, and anyway, maybe Bob was right, maybe it was time to pack it all in. All they'd have left was the yard, but that didn't make enough to support them all. For years it had just been a front, with them selling just enough building materials to keep it ticking over, but surely it could be made profitable.

'All right, Bob, with the rest of you wanting out, I don't think I've got any choice. That leaves just the yard. We need to make it work, need to increase profits. Any ideas?'

'Leave it out, Chris. I ain't got a clue.'

'Do you know how much money we've got in the kitty?'

'Maurice looked after the books, but after ploughing everything back in to buy equipment, I don't think there's much.'

'What about the premises in Wimbledon? Could we sell the place?'

'No, it's in Dad's name so we couldn't do that without his agreement.'

'With Dad in that state, we won't be able to get it.' Chris was quiet for a while, his thoughts turning, finally coming up with an idea. 'If we get more stock, add more lines, it'll increase profits.'

'Yeah, good idea, but with sod all in the kitty, how are we supposed to pay for it?'

If they wanted to build up the business, Chris knew he'd have to do something. He heaved a sigh. 'I've got a few bob stashed away. I suppose we'll have to use that.'

'Blimey, how did you manage that?'

'Unlike you, I haven't got a wife and kids to support so I've managed to save a fair bit.'

'If it wasn't for George,' Bob complained, 'none of this would have happened. We had plenty in the kitty before he nicked the lot.'

'Yeah, well, we'll need to think about what sort of lines to add, and then source the best prices.'

'All right, Chris, we'll get on to it first thing tomorrow.'

Chris nodded, feeling he was more in charge than Bob as he walked out. Until Danny pulled himself together, they'd have to manage without him. He still wasn't happy that Maurice had left, but until he came back, there was one family fewer to support.

Chapter Thirty

Ten days passed, and Pet had withdrawn into herself. Unable to stand the memories, her body was mending, but not her mind. She ate, she drank, tried to help her mother, but she hardly spoke.

'Petula, I need some shopping. Here's a list.'

She stared at her mother in horror. Out? She didn't want to go out. What if Garston was out there? What if he was lying in wait to snatch her again?

'Don't gawk at me like that. It's about time you stirred yourself, and a bit of fresh air will do you good.'

Pet shook her head, her voice a hoarse whisper. 'I . . . I can't.'

'Don't be silly. I'm only asking you to go to the local shops. You can't spend the rest of your life stuck indoors.'

'But—'

'No buts, Petula. Now get your coat on and make sure the butcher doesn't fob you off with all fat on the belly of pork.'

Pet looked to her father, but he had dozed off, something he did more and more frequently. When awake he always seemed to want her close, something she knew annoyed her mother. Yet she drew comfort from him – from his lopsided smile and the love she saw in his eyes.

'Yes, that's right, take a good look at your father. The way you're carrying on is worrying the life out of him and it's got to stop. All right, I know you've had a rough time of it, but for your dad's sake you've got to pull yourself together. Now come on, it can start with a walk to the shops.'

Pet found her coat thrust into her arms, and reluctantly putting it on, she took the list. Her teeth bit into her lower lip as she looked at the door, but then her mother opened it, gesturing her outside. Hesitantly she stepped into the alley, the door closing immediately behind her. There was no one in sight, the alley empty, but still she shivered with fear. Slowly Pet walked to the end, skirting the bollards. When turning the corner she almost clung to the walls as she scuttled to the shops. Once she had felt safe, protected, but not any more. Now she only felt exposed and vulnerable.

The butcher's was her first stop – Mr Pearson, a rotund, red-faced man who was always cheery. 'Hello, Petula, what can I get you?'

'M-Mum wants a belly of pork.'

He nodded, his gaze keen. Why was he looking

at her like that? Did she look different? Did he know? Feeling a wave of self-disgust, she lowered her face. He unhooked the meat, wrapped it and, fumbling for the money, Pet grabbed the parcel and ran out of the shop.

Petula hadn't been gone long when Yvonne called round. Joan found it hard to forget that her daughter-in-law had lied to her about Petula being raped, but there were times when she still needed help with Dan and he had to come first.

'I saw out of the window that you've managed to get Petula to go out,' Yvonne said.

Joan placed the kettle onto the stove, then shook her head, her expression when she turned one of worry. 'She hardly opens her mouth, Yvonne. I've tried talking to her, but she clams up. She still insists that she can't remember what happened, but I find that hard to believe.'

'Maybe it's for the best. It would be a terrible memory, so it might be better to stop pushing her.'

'Yes, you could be right, and at least this way I haven't got to worry about her saying anything in front of Dan. Mind you, she's still funny with Chris, and when Bob makes a rare visit, she ignores him too. I don't get it, Yvonne. I mean, why be funny with them?'

Unable to admit that she knew why, Yvonne lowered her eyes. Poor Pet, she had been through hell because of her brothers and it was no wonder she hated them. She fumbled for an answer, only able to murmur, 'I don't know why, but I'm sure she'll come round. It's her birthday in a couple of weeks, but I'm not sure what to get her.'

'I'll give Chris the money to buy her something nice, and I hope it cheers her up because the way she's carrying on is worrying the life out of Dan. Come to that, you're looking a bit peaky too. Are you all right?'

'Yes, I'm fine,' Yvonne lied, but in truth, since Danny had told her about being involved in porn, she had hardly slept. Just the thought of it made her feel ill – the films, the easy women, and knowing Danny, he had sampled them all. They were finished with it now, yet it still had the power to turn her stomach. If she hadn't been pregnant, would she have left him? No, she admitted, she loved him too much and the thought of life without him was unbearable. There was also the increasing worry about his mental state. Danny needed her now. He didn't go out, didn't wash, shave or dress. Instead he spent most of the day flopped on the sofa. So far she'd been able to hide this behaviour from her mother-in-law, yet she was desperate to confide in someone. Bob and Chris knew, but they were so busy trying to make a go of the yard that they hardly came round. When they did call they tried to make Danny snap out of it – tried to get him to take an interest in the business – but he just didn't want to know.

'At least I've got one less thing to worry about,' Joan said. 'Petula had a show yesterday.'

'Did she? Oh, that's good.'

Once again, Yvonne lowered her eyes. Until Danny showed some interest in the baby, she didn't feel she could tell anyone that she was pregnant. She had waited so long for the moment, pictured it, telling everyone the joyous news with Danny playing his role as the proud father to be. If he would just snap out of this depression, it could still be that way. She was still hardly showing, but Christmas was only a few weeks away and it would be a wonderful time to break the news. After all the dreadful things that had happened lately, it was sure to lift everyone's spirits.

Chris and Bob were at the yard, discussing the new stock they had ordered. Without much competition in the area, they had decided to give a section of the building over to decorating supplies, with a range of wallpapers, paints and all the accoutrements needed by anyone in that trade. Stock had also been low on building materials, and now Bob smiled as he spoke to his brother.

'I don't know how you managed to save that much money, but we'd have been stumped without it. I just hope we make a go of this or you'll have no chance of getting it back.'

'The advertising should do the trick, and I've got an appointment with that developer on Monday. If we can offer him a good deal, he may buy all his materials from us.'

'Fingers crossed you can manage to strike a deal. It might just make Danny sit up and take notice. We've got all this shelving to erect for the new shop, and with the stock coming in, we could do with a hand.'

'It's about time we heard from Maurice.'

'Yes, I know, but let's face it – he wouldn't be much use with the hard graft.'

'He still should have been in touch.'

'Is Mum going on about it again?'

'A bit, but she's more worried about Pet. To tell you the truth, I dread going home nowadays. As soon as I walk in you can cut the atmosphere with a knife, and Mum can't understand why Pet is giving me the cold shoulder.'

'Pet's the same with me, and though I want to see Dad, I avoid popping in as much as possible. Still, you can't blame Pet for not wanting to talk to us.'

'I know. And change the subject because it still gets to me that Garston got away with it.'

'To be honest, I'm just glad that we're out of the game. We may not make a fortune, but at least we haven't got to worry about him, his kind, or the Vice Squad. Mind you,' Bob continued, shaking his head in bewilderment, 'my Sue never ceases to amaze me. With Christmas just over a month away I told her not to spend too much on presents, and instead of getting the hump she just said that we're mad to stop making the soft porn.'

'Yeah, well, she may be right. We made good money out of it.'

'If you're thinking of starting up again, you can count me out.'

'Keep your hair on. It was just a passing thought, that's all.'

Bob nodded, his voice clipped as he said, 'Good. Now come on, let's get on with this shelving or we'll have nowhere to put the new stock when it arrives.'

'It's being delivered on Monday, so let's hope I'm not too long with that developer. If I'm not back in time you'll be handling it on your own.'

'This is bloody ridiculous. We need an extra hand and I reckon we should have another go at Danny. We should tell him that if he wants to keep taking a cut, he'll have to do his share of the work.'

'Yeah, good idea. I just hope he listens this time.'

'He'd better,' Bob growled. 'I'm sick of doing all the work while he sits at home all day, doing sod all.'

Joan jumped as the door was thrown open, Petula darting into the room.

'What on earth's the matter?'

Obviously out of breath, Petula's chest heaved as she dumped the shopping bags onto the table. She then fled upstairs, but with Dan looking bewildered, Joan was unable to follow her daughter.

'Don't worry, Dan. I'm sure she's all right.'

He shook his head, babbling, good hand pointing to the stairs. 'All right, I'll go after her,' Joan placated, and though reluctant to leave Dan on his own, she knew it would be the only way to calm him down.

Joan's tread was heavy as she climbed the stairs. With all that had happened, she sometimes felt over-whelmed, her nerves almost at breaking point. It had been an awful year, one dreadful event after another. In May, George had almost beaten his father to death, and this had been followed by Dan having two strokes. She had no idea where George was, and try as she might, fearing it was his, she couldn't put out of her mind the blood on the bathroom floor. Following that, Ivy had left, but that was no loss, and then there was Chris. The boy wasn't the same, obviously hiding something, and then there had been that dreadful cut on his cheek.

Joan drew a breath. Her daughter had then been raped, and the strain of trying to keep it from Dan was wearing her down. He was suspicious; she was sure of it, his eyes always anxious when he looked at Petula.

Joan paused at the top of the stairs. Maurice had been next, leaving the alley without even saying goodbye. She knew that Norma had had a hand in it, but the speed of their departure still worried her. But first and foremost was Dan. She had to keep him calm, free from worry, and now as she opened her daughter's bedroom door, Joan was so worried about Dan that she didn't realise how hard her voice sounded.

'Petula, I don't know what's going on, but you've upset your father again. Did something happen when you were out? Is that it?'

Petula's face was hidden as she shook her head.

'Something must have upset you or you wouldn't have come home in that state.'

'They . . . they were all looking at me. They . . . they must know.'

'I don't know who you're talking about, but other than this family, nobody knows what happened to you.'

Joan saw tears on her daughter's cheeks and, despite Yvonne's advice, she said, 'Look, love, I know it must have been terrible, but you've got to stop bottling it up. If you'd only talk about it, tell me what happened, I'm sure it would help.'

'I . . . I can't. I don't remember.'

Worried about leaving Dan on his own any longer, Joan sighed in exasperation. 'Well, one way or another, as I said earlier, you've got to pull yourself together. It's upsetting your dad and it's got to stop. He needs to see that you're all right, so come on,

379

come downstairs, and for God's sake, try to put a smile on your face.'

With obvious reluctance, Petula stood up and wiped the tears from her face. Joan was relieved when she followed her downstairs. 'See, Dan, I told you that Petula's all right. Old Pearson tried to fob her off with a bit of dodgy meat and they had a bit of a falling-out. Ain't that right, Petula?'

Joan held her breath, her eyes on her daughter. Petula's smile was thin, but at least it was visible as she nodded in agreement.

Dan beckoned Petula to his side, and still with the thin smile on her face, Pet pulled a chair close to the fire before sitting next to him. Joan heaved a sigh of relief. He looked calm now, at peace, but nowadays he was only really content when he had Petula close by.

Bob and Chris closed the yard and, though worn out after a hard day's graft, they went straight to see Danny.

As usual he was slumped on the sofa and, as Yvonne went to make them a cup of tea, Bob said, 'Look, Danny, me and Chris have had enough. Chris has sunk all his savings into the yard and we've got a lot of stock coming in. We can't manage on our own and need a hand.'

When Danny didn't respond, Chris took over. 'You've got to do your share. You can't just sit there while me and Bob do all the work.'

Danny still said nothing, and now Bob exploded. 'We've been working our guts out all day and we're knackered, but look at you, sitting there like a lump of bloody lard with Yvonne waiting on you hand and foot. Well I've had it, Danny. Either you do your share, or you can forget taking a cut of the profits.'

With a small shrug, Danny said, 'Fair enough.'

Yvonne came into the room and, judging by the worried look on her face, Chris guessed that she had heard everything. His temper also snapped. 'You're a selfish bastard, Danny. You're so wrapped up in your own misery that you haven't given a thought to Yvonne. She's stuck by you, but you don't deserve her. With no money coming in, what's next? Will you send her out to work to keep you?'

At last it seemed that something had got through to Danny. Both brothers stared at him in shock as his chest began to heave and a strangled sob escaped his throat. They had never seen Danny cry and were shocked, but Yvonne ran forward to throw herself beside him on the sofa.

She pulled him into her arms. 'Don't, Danny, don't. It's all right. We'll be all right.'

'Oh, Yvonne, Yvonne . . .'

For a while there were only the sounds of Danny's heaving sobs and Yvonne's soft murmurings.

Maybe it was the catalyst their brother needed, but

381

Bob felt awful. He hadn't expected Danny to break down like this. 'Sorry, Danny,' he said sheepishly. 'We shouldn't have gone off on one, but, well, it's just that we're at the end of our tether.'

Yvonne looked up, saying softly, 'Would you mind leaving now?'

'Yeah, all right,' Chris said. 'Come on, Bob, let's go.'

They walked out, Danny still sobbing in Yvonne's arms.

'I didn't expect Danny to react like that,' Chris said.

'Nor me, but he needed something to snap him out of that bloody depression.'

'Yeah, and who knows, he might soon be back to throwing his weight around as usual.'

Bob frowned. 'He needn't think he can start playing the big boss again. It's us that came up with the ideas for the yard, and from now on we should have an equal say in running it.'

'We will, and as it'll be a new year soon, maybe we can make it a year that's a fresh start for all of us.'

'I'll drink to that,' Bob said, 'but I'd best go in for my dinner first or Sue will have my guts for garters.'

'I don't doubt it. I'll have some grub too, and then if you're up for a drink, I'll meet you in the Nag's Head.'

A new year, 1963, Chris thought as he waved to

Bob before going indoors. Mind you, there was still Christmas to face. Danny might be on the mend now, but it was still going to be difficult. There'd be no big family get-together this year, no parties, and unless Maurice got in touch, it would be another dampener on the proceedings. Come on, Maurice, he silently urged. Surely you're not too busy to pick up a phone.

Maurice wasn't too busy to get in touch with his family, he was just too ill. The first digs they had found had been awful, the room damp and heating scarce. Norma had been murder, constantly nagging, constantly questioning why they had left Drapers Alley, and only his attacks of asthma had made her shut up. Shortly after, they found this flat in Balham, but once again he had been struck down, this time with the flu. The flat was quite spacious, with the added bonus of being furnished, though of course Norma carped about wanting her own things. The landlord had agreed to let them have their own furniture, but until he was on his feet again, Maurice couldn't make arrangements to pick it up.

Norma was trying to get him to eat, but he shook his head, turning his mouth away.

'Come on, Maurice, just a little more.'

He ached, his whole body ached, and with his temperature fluctuating, he was one minute hot, the next cold. 'No, I don't want it.'

The bedroom door flew open, Oliver running into the room. 'Dad, I can't work out how to do this sum. Will you help me?'

'Oliver, not now. Your father isn't up to it.'

'It's all right,' Maurice protested, struggling to sit straighter in the bed.

'Don't get too close to your father. I don't want you going down with the flu too,' Norma warned, walking over to her son to take the exercise book from his hand.

When she handed it to him, Maurice frowned as he looked at the sum. It was long division and he could see where Oliver had gone wrong. 'Do you like your new school?'

'It's all right.' Then, adding on a rush: 'Dad, can I have a bike for Christmas?'

'If you can work out where you've gone wrong with this sum, without my help, then yes, you can.'

'Cor, thanks, Dad,' Oliver cried with a hop of excitement.

Norma returned the book and when Oliver ran from the room she asked, 'Can we afford a bike, Maurice?'

'Yes, don't worry, we're not short of money yet. Mind you, I'll have to look for a job as soon as I'm on my feet again.'

'What have you got in mind?'

'I don't know, but there's sure to be something I can do,' Maurice said, trying to sound optimistic, though he doubted he'd find much that paid more than twelve quid a week. He was tired, his head aching. For years he'd kept the family books, earned good money too, but now he feared the future.

Chapter Thirty-one

Yvonne was happy, happier than she'd been in a long time. A month had passed and Danny was more like his old self, though there was still a change in his personality. Where he had always been self-assured, dominant, he was now softer and she rather liked him this way. He now pulled his weight at the yard, going in every day, and even his relationship with his brothers had changed. There was a camaraderie now that had been lacking before, and from what Danny had told her, things were going well with the business.

She hurried into the alley, clutching her shopping bags, glad to get inside out of the cold. She'd have a hot drink before popping next door to help Joan, but had only just taken her coat off when the door opened again.

Sue walked in with the children trailing behind. 'Watcha, Yvonne. It's bleedin' freezing out there and too cold for the kids to play outside. Now they've broken up from school they're under my feet all day and it's driving me mad. I thought those pea-soup smogs we had in early December were bad enough, but I think this snow is worse.'

Yvonne smiled at the boys, and though Paul smiled back, Robby just scowled as she asked, 'What do you want Father Christmas to bring you?'

'There's no such thing as Father Christmas.'

'Yes there is,' Paul protested.

'Only babies believe in Father Christmas.'

'I'm not a baby.'

'Yes you are.'

'Please, boys, don't start,' Sue begged. 'You've been bickering since you got out of bed and you're giving me a headache.'

Yvonne walked over to the sideboard where she pulled out some paper and a couple of pencils. 'Come on, sit at the table and if you can draw me a nice picture, I might just find some chocolate for you.'

Sue smiled gratefully as the boys did Yvonne's bidding, then said, 'Have you got Pet's Christmas present?'

'Yes, I found her a nice cardigan.'

'What about your Christmas shopping? Have you finished?'

'Almost,' Yvonne said, indicating her shopping bags. 'There's still the chicken, but I've got it on order and I'll pick it up on Christmas Eve along with my vegetables.'

'Things are still a bit tight, and I only gave Pet some bath salts for her birthday, not that I was allowed in to number one to see her. I had to rely on Bob to pass them on. Pet never pops in to see me now either, and I haven't got a clue what to get her for Christmas. How is she? Is she any better?'

'No, not really. She hardly talks and I know it's getting Joan down.'

'Have you been invited for Christmas dinner?'

'Of course we haven't. With the way Dan reacts, it's impossible.'

'Yeah, it's funny the way he's taken against Danny. We haven't been invited either, but I can't say I'm surprised. How do you feel about us coming here?'

Yvonne's mind raced. Sue never cooked a Christmas dinner if she could get out of it, but maybe it wouldn't be so bad having them here. She was itching to break the news that she was pregnant and it would be nice to have them to join in the celebration. 'Yes, all right.'

'Mind you, it might get up old face-ache's nose,' Sue said, smiling widely.

'Oh, Sue, don't be cruel,' Yvonne cried, annoyed that the thought of upsetting Joan seemed to be giving Sue pleasure. 'With all that's happened she's got little to be happy about these days.'

'Look, Auntie Yvonne,' Paul cried, waving his picture as he ran to her side.

Yvonne smiled at his drawing of a Christmas tree,

complete with an angel on the top. 'It's lovely, darling.'

'What about mine?' Robby said as he too proffered a picture, but his angel looked as though it was hanging by its neck instead of perched on top.

Yvonne hid her distaste, saying only, 'Yours is lovely too.'

'Can we have our chocolate now?'

Yvonne went into the kitchen, returning with a bar of chocolate, which she broke in half, handing it to the boys.

Only Paul said thank you, but Sue didn't admonish Robby as the boy stuffed it into his mouth. She then cocked her head to one side, musing, 'I could get Pet some make-up. She once got me to show her how to put it on.'

'I don't know,' Yvonne said, shaking her head doubtfully. 'Pet doesn't seem to care about her appearance now. The poor girl went through hell and there's no sign of her getting over it.'

'Why did Auntie Pet go to hell, Mummy? What's hell?'

'Gawd, little pigs with big ears,' Sue said. 'Come on, time to go. I still think I'll get Pet some make-up. You never know, it might cheer her up. There's nothing like a bit of powder and paint to make a woman feel better.'

Yvonne made no comment, just saying goodbye as she closed the door. It would take more than powder and paint to put the smile back on Pet's face, and though it saddened her to see the girl in such a state, she was at a loss to know how to help her.

In the yard, Danny was arranging stock whilst Bob served a customer. Chris was outside with the fork-lift, loading the order onto the customer's van. He'd also come up trumps, securing them a deal with a large, local builder, but things were slowing down on the run-up to Christmas. Still, their profits were good, but without Chris putting cash into the business none of this would have been possible. They had come to an agreement, with Chris taking a bit extra each month until the money he'd put in was repaid.

Danny felt as though he had come out of a dark tunnel, his brother's words last month finally breaking through the mire of guilt and self-loathing that had swamped him. Chris was right, Yvonne had stood by him and it *was* more than he deserved. He'd been a bastard, a sick bastard, and would never forgive himself for what happened to Pet, but he knew now that he had to pull himself together for Yvonne's sake. He hadn't wanted to be a father, felt he didn't deserve to be a father, but when his brothers had gone, leaving him and Yvonne to have a good talk, he couldn't fail to see how much having a baby meant to her.

Reaching up, Danny placed rolls of wallpaper onto the rack. He had always wanted to be the boss, the big man, but now found himself happy just to work at the yard. He was also enjoying a burgeoning, easy relationship with his brothers. Along with that he felt more optimistic about the future. In the past, they had only just kept the yard ticking over, but now they could make a real go of it. Of course, they would never be rich, but they'd still enjoy a good living standard. It saddened him that the old man's dream of living in the country would never happen, but if they gave Mum an extra cut each month, he could have every comfort. Anyway, Danny consoled himself, his mother wouldn't want to live in a big house. She'd work herself to death keeping it clean, and with the old man to look after, she'd be happier in Drapers Alley.

'Danny, have you got a minute?' asked Bob.

'Yeah, I'm coming,' he called back, placing the last roll of wallpaper on the rack.

'We've just had a call from Mr Larson. He's starting another project in the new year and wants to place an advance order. It's huge, Danny, and I'm not sure if we can fill it.'

Chris came in, rubbing his hands. 'It's bloody freezing out there.'

'Chris, as I've just told Danny, we've got a bit of a problem. Larson wants to place a huge order.'

'How's that a problem?'

391

'I'm not sure if we can afford to fill it. Look,' he said, pushing the scribbled order towards Chris.

Chris whistled, his brows shooting up. 'Blimey. But if we don't fill it he'll go elsewhere and I doubt we'd get another customer like him. He's the biggest builder in the area. All our other customers are small fry in comparison.'

'Maybe we could try the bank – get a loan,' Danny offered.

'Yeah, good idea,' Bob said.

'You said he wants this order for the new year. We'd never get a loan through in time,' Chris said. He chewed on his lower lip, eyes downcast, before saying, 'There's only one thing for it. I'll just have to dib up the last of my savings.'

'You've got more?' Bob asked, voice high with surprise.

'It'll clean me out, but yes.'

Danny stared at Chris, hating the way his mind was working, but unable to quell his suspicions. Chris had already sunk a fair amount of money into the business, but was now offering more. Yes, he was a single man, but it was still going some to have that amount in savings. His mind went back to the morning they had found the empty cash box in the bathroom. He had blamed George, was sure it was George, but could remember how touchy Chris had been. No, no, it couldn't have been Chris. He was mad even to think it, yet was unable to stop himself from blurting out, 'How did you manage to save so much money?'

'It wasn't hard. Mum only takes my keep and, unlike you, I didn't keep my money in the cash box. Like Maurice, I put mine in the bank, earning a bit of interest.'

'I didn't know that. You never said, nor did Dad, so I assumed you kept your savings in with ours.'

'Yeah, well, it's just as well I didn't.'

'When we were struggling to raise money for the Wimbledon operation, you didn't offer to put money in. Why do it now?'

'Because this is legit – safe – and anyway, the yard is all we've got left. Why all the questions, Danny?'

'I was just wondering, that's all.'

It was Bob who broke the tension. 'Well, all I can say is thanks, Chris. This order will well and truly put us on our feet, and I might just celebrate by buying Sue a bottle of her favourite perfume for Christmas. Now come on, let's grab ourselves a cup of tea while we've got the chance.'

'Yeah, I'm all for that,' Danny said, and, knowing now that his suspicions had been unfounded, he threw a placatory arm around Chris's shoulder. He'd been daft to think that Chris had stolen the money – it was George, it had to be. 'Whose turn is it to make the brew?'

'Yours,' Chris said, walking through with him to the office.

'Here, I've got a good one,' Bob said whilst Danny filled the kettle.

'Go on then, let's hear it,' Chris said.

'What do you call a camel with three humps?'

'I dunno,' Chris said, 'but no doubt you'll tell us.'

'Humphrey.'

Danny couldn't help laughing. 'You silly sod,' he spluttered, 'but at least it was clean for a change.'

Chris laughed too, then said, 'Here, Bob, I've got one for Sue, but don't worry, it's another clean one.'

'Oh, yeah, go on then.'

'How did the blonde burn her ear?'

'I dunno.'

'The phone rang while she was ironing.'

Laughter rang out in the office and Danny felt a surge of relief. Because of his stupid suspicions he had almost blown the good relationship he now enjoyed with his brothers. He wouldn't make the same mistake again.

Pet sat close to the fire. Her father was opposite, dozing again, yet she drew comfort from his presence. She knew her state of mind upset him, and tried her best to hide her feelings, but it was so hard.

The front door opened, Yvonne bright-eyed as she walked in. 'God, it's bitter out there. Christmas will be here in less than a week and I reckon it could be a white one.'

Pet said nothing but listened to the conversation.

394

'Don't talk to me about Christmas,' her mother was saying. 'It won't be the same, and with just the four of us for dinner it hardly seems worth the effort. Not only that, we still haven't heard from Maurice.'

'I'm sure he'll be in touch soon,' Yvonne consoled.

'I hope you're right. Oh, Yvonne, Christmas was once such a happy time, but now there's nothing to celebrate.'

'Don't cry,' Yvonne pleaded. 'We have got something to celebrate. I wasn't going to say anything until Christmas Day, but I can't keep it to myself any longer. Me and Danny, well, we're going to have a baby. We're so happy, Mum.'

Pet felt as though all the blood had rushed to her face. She had kept her mouth shut, said nothing, bottling all the horror inside, but now images of the film she had been shown flashed in her mind. The little girl, the terror she had seen on her face. Chris had denied that they used children . . . but what if it was true?

Pet felt bile rise in her throat. Danny was happy – how dare he be happy! Something snapped inside her mind, all the horror, all the hate rushing forward as she jumped to her feet. 'No! No, you can't be having a baby. Danny isn't fit to be a father!'

'What are you talking about?' Joan cried. 'Don't be silly, Petula.'

'Him – them – my brothers. They make porn films using children! They're sick. They're monsters.'

'What? Yvonne, I think she's gone mad. I think she's lost her mind!'

Pet was unaware that her father had awoken, finding that now she had started, she couldn't stop, the words pouring from her mouth. 'They tried to take over Jack Garston's territory. He warned them but they wouldn't stop, so he took me and he made me watch their films and . . . and then he raped me.'

The bellow stopped Pet's outburst. Her father was making unholy sounds and she spun around, horrified that he had heard.

'Dan, Dan, it's all right,' Joan cried, rushing towards him, but then he flopped and her voice rose to a screech: 'Get an ambulance! Yvonne, get help. I think he's had another stroke.'

Pet stood frozen, but as Yvonne ran to the telephone, her mother turned, her eyes blazing as she spat, 'Get out of my sight. You've caused this, you and your lies.'

With a hand held over her mouth, Pet fled the room, running upstairs to throw herself onto the bed. Because of her big mouth – because she'd blurted it all out – her father was having another stroke. *Oh, Dad, Dad, please be all right.*

Pet had no idea how long she lay there, her mind in torment, before she heard the ambulance men arriving. Terrified for her father, she ran back downstairs. They were working on him, but from the look on their faces, she feared it was too late. One shook his head, and Pet stood helpless as her mother fell to pieces, wailing, her hands tearing at her hair.

She ran forward, trying to stay her hands. 'Mum, Mum, don't.'

She was pushed away as her mother turned to Yvonne, throwing herself into her arms. 'He's gone, Yvonne. My Dan's dead.'

The words hit Pet then like a blow to her stomach and, unable to bear it, she fled the room again. No! No, her father couldn't be dead! He just couldn't.

'What are you doing?' Joan cried as the ambulance men began to heave Dan onto a stretcher.

'We're taking him to hospital.'

Joan's face lit up. 'He's alive! Oh God, I thought he was dead.'

'I'm sorry, missus, he is, but he still needs to be seen by a doctor to ascertain the cause of death.'

'But can't he stay here? I can get our own doctor.'

'I'm afraid not. You see we were called out, so we have to follow through. You'll need to come with us because they'll want to talk to you about his medical history.'

Joan became aware of Yvonne urging her into a coat, and as they walked outside she said something, but Joan found she couldn't reply. Her stomach was so twisted with grief that she could barely put one foot in front of the other. Along with the grief came guilt. There had been times when she'd be so overwhelmed with exhaustion that she had wished Dan hadn't survived the second stroke. Yet now that he was gone, she just wanted him back, her life empty and meaningless without him.

Hardly aware of Yvonne beside her, Joan climbed into the ambulance, moving straight to Dan's side. His face looked different, at peace, and as she reached out to touch his cold cheek, she felt tears pouring from her eyes. *Oh, Dan – Dan, come back to me. I can't go on without you, I just can't.*

Chapter Thirty-two

Yvonne had made a frantic call to the yard, so when the three brothers ran into the hospital room soon afterwards, she knew that they must have broken all speed limits to get there.

'What happened?' Danny asked.

Yvonne drew them to one side, her voice a whisper. 'Pet finally snapped. She spilled it all out – about you, the porn, saying that you used children in the films.'

'But I spoke to her, told her it isn't true,' Chris hissed.

'She still spat it out, including that she'd been raped. Your dad, well, he went mad.'

Danny shook his head, his voice betraying his pain. 'I can't believe he's dead.'

'I know, Danny,' Yvonne consoled. 'It was so quick, so sudden.'

'I warned Pet that this might happen and I was right,' Chris said, his face ashen. 'Where is she?'

'She's still at home. Your mother turned on her, blamed her.'

'So Mum knows everything?' Bob said.

Yvonne nodded, her voice still low. 'Yes, but I'm not sure that she believed her.'

'Yeah, well, Pet should have kept her mouth shut.'

'Oh, Bob, how can you say that?' Yvonne protested. 'Pet's just a kid, and none of what happened was her fault.'

'Yvonne's right,' said Danny, 'it's all down to us, but come on, we can work this out later. For now, we had better see to Mum.'

'The doctors have spoken to her and confirmed your dad's death. If you can get her on her feet, we can leave.'

'I'd like to see Dad first,' Chris said.

Bob nodded. 'Yeah, me too.'

Danny walked across to his mother and, taking a seat beside her, took her hand. 'Mum, we're going to see Dad. Do you want to come with us?'

'He's dead, Danny.'

'I know, Mum, I know.'

'Yvonne, can you ask one of the nurses where my father is?' Danny urged.

She went across to one of the nurses to be told that Dan hadn't been moved yet. Bidding them all to follow her, the nurse led them into a side room.

All three brothers broke down when they saw their father, as though until now they hadn't accepted his death. It was painful to see them trying to be manly, trying to fight tears, with only Danny succeeding. Chris was the most badly affected, openly sobbing as he looked at his father, and Yvonne could see that her mother-in-law was close to collapse.

'Danny, I think we should get your mum home,' she urged.

He nodded, gently leading her away, and in a solemn procession they exited the room. Danny left his mother in the care of Bob and Chris whilst he went to speak to a nurse. Yvonne followed him, surprised by Danny's strength and presence of mind as he asked about the arrangements. Somehow she had expected Danny to fall apart again, that the depression he had suffered would make him mentally weak, but instead he had rallied, taking control.

'Yes, if you contact an undertaker,' the nurse told him, 'he can make all the necessary arrangements to have your father moved to a funeral parlour.'

Danny thanked her, and when he and Yvonne joined the others, Danny took his mother's arm to lead her gently out of the building to his car. Bob, the largest of them, sat in the front, and the rest of them in the back.

Yvonne reached out to clasp her mother-in-law's hand, finding it freezing. There was no returning pressure, Joan sitting as still as a statue during the journey home.

They parked and walked into Drapers Alley, Danny and Chris on each side of their mother. She still said nothing, and this continued as they entered number one. Joan went across the room to sit by the hearth, her face like chalk.

Danny poked the fire into life before adding a shovelful of coal. 'Are you all right, Mum?' he asked.

There was no reply, but when Joan looked at Dan's empty wheelchair she broke, placing both hands over her face as her body shook with sobs. 'Oh, Dan . . . Dan.'

It was obviously too much for Bob. With tears in his eyes he said, 'I'd best go and tell Sue.' With that he hurried out the door, closing it behind him.

Chris now stood next to his mother, his hand on her shoulder, obviously fighting tears too. Unable to watch the scene any longer, Yvonne went through to the kitchen. She felt helpless to comfort them and so did the only thing she could think of: she filled the kettle to make a cup of tea.

When Yvonne returned, she saw Danny sitting at the table, and Chris still close to his mother. Pet was nowhere in sight and Yvonne's heart went out to her. She was just a kid, and after what happened to her was it any wonder that she was unable to keep it bottled up inside?

Danny had his head in his hands, hardly aware of her when she placed a cup of tea beside him, and after giving one to Chris and her mother-in-law, Yvonne went upstairs.

Pet heard voices but, too afraid to face her mother, she remained in her room, huddled under the blankets for warmth.

Her door opened and Yvonne crossed the room to perch on the edge of the bed. 'How are you doing, love?' she asked.

The sympathy in Yvonne's voice was too much for Pet, and with tears flooding her eyes she cried, 'Mum said it's my fault, and she's right. Chris warned me and I should have kept my mouth shut, but I didn't and now . . . now . . . Oh, Yvonne, my dad's dead.'

'No, Pet, no. It's not your fault. After what you went through it was unfair to expect you to keep it locked inside. No wonder you broke down, love, and nobody blames you.'

'My mother does.'

'She's in a state, Pet. I'm sure she'll come round when she has had time to think about it.'

'I told her about my brothers too, about the . . . the porn. Did . . . did you know about it, Yvonne?'

'Not until recently, and when Danny told me I was shocked to the core. At first, I was going to leave him, but then I found that I couldn't. All right, I know that making porn films is awful, but when you think about it, there are worse things. They didn't hurt anyone, kill anyone, and—'

The image flashed into Pet's mind again, one that she found it impossible to forget. 'That man Garston, he made me watch a film,' Pet broke in. 'He said that my brothers made it . . .' She stopped, unable to go on.

'That must have been dreadful. For the life of me I'll never understand why men want to watch them, but honestly, nobody gets hurt in the making of them. It's just acting, Pet.'

'I was hurt, and the little girl I saw wasn't acting. She was screaming, terrified.'

'Oh God, the poor child,' Yvonne cried. 'But, Pet, I swear, your brothers didn't use children. Surely you know them better than that?'

No, Pet thought, she didn't know her brothers. The view she'd once had of them was an illusion. As tears continued to fall, she wanted the one man she felt safe with, one who looked at her with love in his eyes and who managed a lopsided smile every time he saw her. 'Oh, Yvonne, I want my dad. He can't be dead . . . he can't . . .' And as Yvonne's arms wrapped around her, Pet clung on as though she were drowning.

'Bloody hell, Bob, it must have been a bit sudden,' Sue said. 'I didn't hear or see anything, but the kids have been playing up, making a racket all morning, so it ain't surprising. What happened? Did he have another stroke?'

404

'Yeah,' Bob croaked, going on to tell her what Yvonne had said.

'Well, I can't say I'm surprised. From what you've told me, Pet must have been like a time bomb waiting to go off. But saying you used kids – that was terrible. What about your mum? Has she said anything? Has she mentioned it?'

'No, not yet, and I don't know what we're going to say when she does.'

'You wouldn't use children. I know you better than that, and your mother does too. As for the other stuff, if you ask me there was no harm in it, and she might see it that way too.'

'Leave it out, Sue. You know what a prude my mother is, and not only that, we've got to keep it from her that my dad was involved. It'd be too much. With what she's had to put up with lately it'd be the last straw. She'd go bloody mad.'

Sue hid her thoughts. Yes, the old cow was a prude, acting all high and mighty. It would bring her down a peg or two to know that her precious husband had been involved. Blimey, she'd love to see the expression on the old girl's face if it came out. They might try to hide it from her, but Sue knew she could put a spanner in the works.

There was no love between Sue and her sanctimonious mother-in-law, but Sue knew it wasn't her fault. She had tried, but from the start Joan had looked down on her, treated her like a tart, an outcast in the family. It was payback time, and nice to have something over on her mother-in-law at last. She'd leave it for a month or two, maybe wait until the old girl got over her grief, but as soon as she got on her high horse again, she'd let it slip.

'Oh, Sue, I can't believe he's dead,' Bob cried as his eyes filled with tears again.

Sue made the effort, wrapping her arms around her husband whilst she murmured, 'Oh, love, don't cry.'

Both boys came running in, their eyes widening. 'Why is Dad crying, Mum?' Robby asked.

Deciding it was better to tell them, she moved away from Bob, saying softly, 'He's upset because . . . well, because Granddad has passed away.'

The boys looked puzzled, but as they hadn't seen their grandfather for so long, it wasn't surprising. She tried again. 'He's dead. Dan, your granddad, is dead.'

Bob began to sob now and Paul ran to his side, grabbing his hand. 'It's all right, Dad. Oliver's rabbit was dead but then he woke up again.'

'Don't be daft,' Robby sneered. 'Shaker wasn't dead, he was just knocked out.'

'Shut up, Robby,' Sue snapped.

'Can I have a rabbit for Christmas?'

Unable to believe her ears, Sue glared at Robby. 'I can't believe you. I've just told you that your granddad's dead and you're asking me for a bleedin' rabbit.'

She heard a gasp and spun round to see Bob running upstairs. It was no surprise that he was taking his dad's death so badly, but Christmas wasn't far off and it would certainly put the kibosh on any celebrations. There was little chance of having Christmas dinner with Yvonne and Danny now. Bugger it, she'd have to make some sort of effort for the kids' sake, but would Bob be able to do the same?

Danny and Yvonne went home in the early evening, glad that Chris was there to keep an eye on Joan. She had finally stopped crying, but her face was still etched with pain. Yvonne had been unable to persuade Pet to come downstairs, the girl too frightened to face her mother. It broke Yvonne's heart to see Pet so lost, so alone, but finally she had left her, determined to do something about it, no matter what the consequences.

The house was cold when they went inside but Danny quickly lit a fire. He then sat down, deep in thought, but after a while, to Yvonne's surprise, he brought up the very subject.

'What do you think I should do?' he asked. 'I know you said Mum didn't believe Pet when she told her about the porn, but that was in the heat of the moment. Once she's over the shock and it begins to sink in, she's bound to start asking questions.'

'I think it's time to tell your mother the truth.

Pet's been through enough and she's so alone, Danny. Your mother blames her for your dad's death, but if she knew why Pet snapped and blurted it all out – if she knew what the poor kid has been through – I'm sure she'd forgive her.'

'Blimey, Yvonne, I can't tell my mother the truth now. You saw how fragile she is. I don't think she could take it.'

'So Pet's got to suffer. Don't you think she's suffered enough, Danny? Come on, you said it yourself, sooner or later your mother is bound to start asking questions. What if she aims them at Pet?'

'I hadn't thought of that. With Dad gone, Pet has no reason to keep her mouth shut and she might tell Mum that we use kids again.'

'I told her you didn't and I think she believed me. Even so, it would be fairer if the rest of it came from you.'

'Yeah, you're right, but I dread to think how Mum will take it. Maybe it can wait until after the funeral . . . And talking of the funeral, it's still got to be arranged. Mum isn't up to it, so I suppose it's down to me.'

'I doubt it can be held until after Christmas.'

As Danny looked at her Yvonne could see the pain in his eyes. She feared that he'd break down again, sink back into depression so, feeling the baby moving, she took his hand to lay it on her stomach. 'Can you feel it, love? The baby's kicking and it's so strong I reckon we've got a footballer in there.'

'You think it's a boy?'

'I don't know, love. We'll just have to wait and see.'

'My son,' he mused, 'or maybe my daughter.'

Yvonne heard the note of awe in his voice, but then his arms went around her as finally he broke, crying for his father, for the man he had been apart from for so long and who he would never see again.

Joan was glad when Yvonne and Danny left, relieved too when Chris finally went upstairs. She moved across the room to lie on Dan's day bed, feeling the indent of his body. With a sob she picked up his pillow, sniffing it to find his special smell. She felt lost, bereft. Dan had been her life – she was bound to him – and when he became helpless she had given herself to looking after him. She buried her face in the pillow, trying to muffle her sobs. If Chris heard her crying he would come downstairs again. He would try to comfort her, but there was no comfort.

She heard footfalls on the stairs and in the dim light saw Petula coming into the room. Joan held her breath, but thankfully her daughter didn't see her lying there as she went through the kitchen to the bathroom. Seeing Petula brought it all back: the look on Dan's face when Petula shouted that she'd been raped, the other things she had said about the boys that Joan couldn't bear to think about. It couldn't be true, it just couldn't. Petula must have gone mad, her sick mind conjuring up this fantasy because she couldn't remember what had really happened.

Petula was coming back, passing like a ghost through the room, and once again Joan held her breath, thankful that her daughter didn't see her. The house became silent again, Joan clutching the pillow as though it was a lifeline.

She cried on and off for what felt like hours, until finally, with a hiccuping sob, she stopped. She felt drained, empty, as if a part of her had died with Dan – that he had taken her heart with him, the two of them inseparable, even in death.

Finally, exhausted, she drifted off to sleep.

Chapter Thirty-three

When Pet woke up on Saturday morning, her first thought was for her father. She had spent most of the past three days alone in her room, unable to face the hate she could see in her mother's eyes. She huddled in her bed against the cold, haunted every night by nightmares. Oh, she was so thirsty, parched, so she quickly dressed, shivering as she tried to pluck up the courage to go downstairs.

Pet paused at the top of the stairs, but her thirst drove her down and she had just reached the living room when the front door was flung open.

Bob dashed in. 'Where's Mum?' he asked as his eyes scanned the room.

'In the bathroom,' Chris told him.

'How is she?'

'About the same. She gets up, washes, dresses, but it's as if she's on automatic. If you speak to her, she hardly listens, and her eyes have still got that vacant look about them.'

411

'What about you, Pet? How are you doing?'

Pet said nothing. She felt sickened, betrayed by her brothers, and ignored them as she went through to the kitchen. She filled the teapot and poured herself a cup of tea, quickly gulping it down. Then, hearing the bathroom door opening, she hurried out, about to return upstairs, when Bob's voice stilled her.

'Mum, there you are,' he said. 'I've just had a call from Maurice. I . . . I told him about Dad and he's on his way to see you. I had to get dressed before I came to tell you, so he should be here any minute now.'

She didn't respond, her gaze now fixed on the flames as they licked up the chimney.

'Did you hear what I said, Mum?'

'Yes, I heard you.'

'Maurice is living in Balham now and he hasn't been in touch because he's been ill. He had the flu, a really bad bout and ended up in hospital with pneumonia. Don't worry, he's on his feet again now. I'll just tell Danny that Maurice is on his way, and then I'll be back.'

As he hurried out, Chris accompanying him, Pet slumped onto a chair, the room silent. Her mother suddenly turned, their eyes locking. Her mother's gaze was long, hard, unfathomable and, unable to look away, Pet found her own eyes filling with tears.

'Petula—' Joan began, but then the door opened

to let in a blast of cold air as Danny, Yvonne and Bob trooped into the room.

'Bob just told us that Maurice is on his way,' Danny said.

Pet stood up, hurrying upstairs. Her stomach had lurched at the look in her mother's eyes, the accusation, the loathing. Yvonne had said that her brothers didn't blame her, but her mother still did. Oh, if only she had kept her mouth shut, hadn't blurted it all out. No wonder her mother hated her.

She felt so alone, an outcast with nobody she could turn to for comfort. At one time she would have gone to her brothers or their wives, but now she didn't want to be near them. It was their involvement in porn that had led to Garston taking his revenge on her – and every time she looked at them it all came flooding back. She longed to get away, far away, never to have to see them again. It was fear of the outside world that held her back, yet even if she found the courage to leave, she had nowhere to go, no family outside Drapers Alley.

Pet pulled the blankets around her, longing for the warmth of the fire. She couldn't go downstairs, her mother didn't want her around, and her brothers would be there. She burrowed further under the blankets, yearning for her father. She knew that Danny had arranged the funeral, but her mother didn't want her there. She'd be forced to stay at home, a home where she was no longer welcome. *Oh, Dad, Dad, I won't even get the chance to say goodbye.*

Minutes passed, but then Pet heard voices and guessed that Maurice had arrived. She didn't want to see him and hoped he didn't venture up to her room. He'd been involved too; they had all been involved. Like Ivy, he had left without saying goodbye . . . Pet's thoughts came to a standstill, her eyes suddenly widening. She *did* have somewhere to go, but would they take her in?

Pet looked around her tiny room. She knew that her mother would never forgive her, that unless she found the courage to leave Drapers Alley, this room would become her prison. Oh, but surely anything would be better than this. Finally, her mind made up, she began to stuff clothes into a bag.

Danny watched his mother's face as Maurice walked to her side, but she hardly reacted.

'Hello, Mum.'

She said nothing, and to break the tension Danny said, 'Blimey, Maurice, you look as thin as a rake.'

'Yeah, you look terrible,' Bob agreed.

Still his mother didn't move and Danny regarded her worriedly. She looked so old now, no longer plump, her face lined with wrinkles.

414

'You look frozen, Maurice. I'll make you a hot drink,' said Yvonne.

As his wife walked through to the kitchen, Danny said, 'I'm glad you're here, Maurice. I've made all the arrangements but the funeral can't be held until after Christmas.'

Maurice's voice was abrupt. 'When and where is it?'

'On the fourth of January at eleven in the morning, and we're using St Jude's.'

Maurice nodded before sitting opposite his mother, his hands held out to the fire as he said, 'Are you all right, Mum?'

Slowly she turned to look at him, her eyes suddenly clear, but when she spoke her tone was bitter. 'So, you've decided to show your face at last.'

'I'd have come sooner, but I've been ill, Mum, in hospital.'

'I'd still like to know why you went off without saying a word.'

'I came to say goodbye, but you wouldn't let me in and I couldn't hang around. Norma's been nagging for years, and if I didn't go with her, she'd have gone without me.'

'Yes, that's what Bob said, but I think there's more to it than that.' Her eyes suddenly flicked around the room, briefly settling on Danny, Chris and Bob, before they returned to the fire.

Danny found that he was holding his breath.

415

There had been suspicion in his mother's eyes when she had looked at them, but thankfully the moment seemed to have passed. He knew he would have to tell her, but not now – he couldn't face it now.

Yvonne came back into the room carrying a tray, and about to set it down when someone thumped loudly on the front door. Danny shot his brothers a look before opening it, but before he could react, two men pushed their way in, followed by several uniformed police.

'What the hell . . . ?'

The men flicked out identity cards, and though one spoke, both were smiling triumphantly. 'We have a warrant for the arrest of Mr Daniel Edward Draper.'

'What the fuck are you talking about?' Danny yelled. 'My father's dead.'

The smile dropped, but the man's eyes narrowed shrewdly. 'Dead, you say? Have you a copy of the death certificate?'

'Danny, what's going on?'

He turned to see his mother on her feet, her face white with shock. 'It's all right, Mum. There's been some sort of mistake, but don't worry, I'll sort it out.' He then grabbed the document from the mantel-piece, shoving it under the officer's nose. 'Read it, and when you've finished – *get out!*'

'Hold your horses,' the officer said. 'We'd still like

you and your brothers to accompany us to the station.'

'What for?' Danny snapped.

'Acting on information received, we obtained a search warrant for premises in Wimbledon where evidence of pornographic material was found.'

'For fuck's sake, Danny, I thought you closed the place down,' Chris yelled.

All of Danny's old nature rose to the surface as he yelled, 'Shut up!' He glared at his brother, but then saw Pet, hovering on the threshold of the room. She had her coat on, was holding a bag, obviously ready for flight. The copper's words sank in. *Acting on information received.* Spittle flew out of his mouth. 'You! You did this. I'll fucking kill you . . .'

Pet made a run for it, but as Danny reached out, his arms were grabbed, forced behind his back. 'Get off me,' he yelled, but it was too late, she was nearly out of the door. 'Come back, you bitch,' he screamed but, forcibly held, he could do nothing to stop her.

Pet fled the house and kept on running, her chest heaving until finally she was forced to stop. She walked then, rapidly, heading for Clapham Junction train station. Her mind was in turmoil, her heart thumping wildly in her chest. Danny thought she had been to the police. He said he would kill her and the look on his face had been manic. Oh, but she hadn't told the police, even though at times she

417

had been so haunted by the little girl in the film that she had wanted to do something, anything to bring about her rescue. Yet she had done nothing, a coward, afraid that if she reported Jack Garston he'd come after her again.

The wind was bitter, stinging her cheeks, her fingers numb as she gripped the bag. A part of her wanted to go back, to run home again, but even as the thought crossed her mind, Pet knew it was impossible. Even if she could convince them that she hadn't been to the police, her mother's hate remained and it was no more than she deserved.

Frozen to the core now, Pet went into the post office, taking out money from her savings account. From there, it wasn't far to the station, but with a change of trains she knew it would be a long time before she reached her destination.

When a train arrived, Pet climbed aboard, barely thawing out before she had to get off again. On the second train she settled down for a longer journey, hardly noticing the passing scenery as her mind twisted and turned.

Finally, as the train pulled into her station, Pet stood up, her mind at last still. She had left, doubted she'd go back, but with no idea of what the future held, it was with trepidation that she began the last leg of her journey.

After asking directions, Pet started to walk, footsore

and weary by the time she turned into a lane, thick with snow. It was lined with trees, their branches skeletal, the sky a blanket of grey, heavy with more snow. Pet trudged along, both mentally and physically exhausted as she finally approached the house. When she opened the little wooden gate, the path lay clear ahead, and reaching the front door, she knocked, standing back a little as the door opened.

A face peered out at her, one that at first frowned, but then looked worried. 'Pet, oh my God, what on earth are you doing here?'

'Oh, Ivy, please, can I stay with you? I haven't got anywhere else to go.'

Pet was drawn inside, the fire acting like a magnet as she staggered, frozen, towards it. When Ivy spoke, she turned, but instead of a welcome on her cousin's face, she saw what looked like apprehension.

'Pet, how did you find me? Does anyone else know that you're here?'

'I took the address from Linda, but I didn't give it to anyone else.' Her voice cracked when she said, 'Oh, Ivy, my dad's dead.'

'What? When? Oh Gawd, I'm all of a dither. Look, sit down and I'll make us both a drink.'

As Ivy left the room, Pet sat by the hearth, taking in her surroundings. It was a nice room, chintzy and cosy, with brass ornaments reflecting the glow from the fire. A Christmas tree stood in one corner, sparkling with tinsel and baubles. Paper chains festooned the ceiling, each corner holding a bunch of coloured balloons. She leaned her head back, closing her eyes until her cousin returned.

'Right,' Ivy said, handing Pet a cup and saucer before taking a seat on the opposite side of the hearth. 'I think you had better start at the beginning.'

And Pet did, spilling it all out, her voice quivering with emotion until at last she was spent, ending with, 'I was ready to leave, but when the police turned up Danny must have thought I'd called them. He said he'd kill me. I had to run, Ivy, I had to get away.'

'Oh, you poor kid,' Ivy said. She was quiet for a moment, her head low, but then she looked up. 'All right, love, you can stay here, but only if you promise not to tell anyone where you are. I don't want any of that lot turning up here.'

'Oh, Ivy, I won't, I promise, and thank you . . . thank you so much for taking me in.'

Ivy suddenly grimaced, doubling over to clutch her stomach.

'What's wrong? Are you all right?'

'Yeah, yeah, it's just a bit of cramp, that's all,' she said through clenched teeth.

'Can I get you anything?'

Ivy sat up again, shaking her head. 'No, I'm fine now. Come on, let's get you sorted out,' and pushing herself to her feet, she beckoned Pet to follow her.

They went upstairs where, throwing open a

bedroom door, Ivy said, 'I'll double the boys up and then you can have this room. We'll just have to move Harry's clothes and toys.'

'Oh, Ivy, he won't like that.'

'He won't mind. The boys used to share a room in Drapers Alley and, to be honest, I think they miss it. Nine times out of ten when I come to wake Harry up, I find him in Ernie's room, asleep on the bottom bunk . . .' Ivy groaned, doubling over again as she sank onto the single bed.

'Ivy!' Pet cried.

'It's all right, it's just cramp again. It's my time of the month.'

Pet knew what it was like to suffer painful cramps, but she had never been as bad as this. 'Look, if you show me what things to move, I can manage on my own.'

'All right, love, I won't say no. You'll find clean sheets in the airing cupboard on the landing, but you look a bit bushed too, so just change the bed for now and we'll sort the rest tomorrow. While you're doing that, I'll get the spuds on the boil for dinner.'

'Is Steve at work?'

'He had to go in this morning, but now he's taken the boys into town to get some last-minute Christmas shopping.'

'Where does he work?'

'On a farm. I never thought he'd take to it, but he loves it.'

'Ivy, I know you said I can stay, but what about Steve?'

'He won't mind and the boys will be dead chuffed to see you. Right, I'm off and I'll see you downstairs.'

As Ivy left, Pet looked around the room. It was nice, under the eaves with a sloping ceiling and a little leaded window. She was so relieved that Ivy was letting her stay, but it was so quiet, so strange here that for a moment she felt a wave of desolation. She had a little money left in her Post Office book, but she couldn't expect Ivy to keep her indefinitely. If she could find a job, anything to pay her way, she wouldn't be a burden.

After changing the bed, Pet went downstairs to find Ivy sitting in front of the fire.

'The spuds are cooking,' she said, 'and I've lit the oven to heat up the casserole.'

'Is there anything I can do?' Pet asked, but then the front door opened, and with a flurry of cold air Steve and the boys rushed in.

Steve drew to a halt, his face registering his surprise. 'Blimey, Pet. What are you doing here?'

'She's come to stay for a while. I'll tell you about it later, but it can wait for now.'

'Look, Ernie, it's Auntie Pet,' Harry cried, the five-year-old hopping with excitement.

Pet gave them a hug, but then Ivy said, 'All right, boys, no doubt you're hungry, so go and wash your hands while I dish up dinner.'

Ernie grinned widely, green eyes just like his father's, twinkling. Pet smiled back at him, feeling a little happier. They were pleased to see her, welcomed her, and at last she felt like she was part of a family again.

Chapter Thirty-four

In Drapers Alley, Yvonne was unable to sit still. She paced the floor, wringing her hands whilst her mother-in-law sat staring into the fire. It was eight in the evening when the door opened and Sue walked in.

'The boys are asleep, but I can't leave them on their own for long. Is there any news?'

'No, nothing,' Yvonne told her. 'I went down to the station, but they wouldn't let me see Danny. All I was told was that he was still being questioned.'

Yvonne was startled when her mother-in-law suddenly rose to her feet. 'I didn't want to believe Petula – I thought she'd lost her mind – but now I know that she was telling the truth. I've got to find her. Where do you think she's gone?'

'I don't know, Mum, she could be anywhere. She was ready to go when the police came so she must have had something planned.'

'As far as I'm concerned, she'd better stay away,' Sue

snapped. 'I used to think a lot of Pet, but she's a grass and if I get my hands on her I'll bloody kill her.'

'Oh no you won't,' Joan snapped. 'Since the boys were taken for questioning I've been sitting here, turning it all over in my mind, and I'm sickened by the lot of you. When Dan died, I went into a sort of stupor and like a fool I blamed Petula. My God, what I've put that poor girl through doesn't bear thinking about. Porn – my sons making porn! It's disgusting, and you two must have known about it. Get out of my house, go on, get out, and don't show your faces in here again.'

'Don't come the high and mighty with us,' Sue yelled. 'From what Yvonne told me, the police had an arrest warrant for Dan.'

'That was a mistake. My Dan would never be mixed up in porn.'

'Don't kid yourself,' Sue snapped. 'He was up to his eyeballs in it from the beginning and don't tell me that you haven't worked that out for yourself, and let me tell you—'

'Come on, Sue, leave it. Can't you see she's had enough?' Yvonne urged, taking Sue's arm.

Joan looked awful, her skin the colour of putty.

'I've hardly started, but don't worry, I'm going. I can't risk leaving the kids for much longer.' Sue's eyes snapped to Joan again. 'Oh, yes, and talking about my boys, they're your grandsons but you hardly know they exist.'

'Get out!'

Sue threw Joan a look of disgust before leaving, but Yvonne remained, only for Joan to say, 'And you can get out too.'

'Oh, Mum, don't say that. I can't leave you like this. Look, I'll make us both a cup of tea.'

Yvonne hurried through to the kitchen, stiff with tension as she made a brew. She moved slowly, hoping that by the time it was made, her mother-in-law would have calmed down. When it was ready she tentatively carried it through to the living room, only to find that Joan still glared at her angrily.

'You knew, didn't you – knew that the boys were mixed up in porn, and worse, from what Petula said, they use kids?'

'No, Mum, no, they would never do that. Pet got it wrong and she knows that now.'

'Huh, and I'm supposed to believe you?' Joan snapped. 'Well, I don't. You lied to me about Petula. You said she hadn't been raped, or are you going to say she got that wrong too? No, of course you can't. When the doctor examined her, I saw the state of her with my own eyes.'

'I was just trying to protect you – to protect Dan.'

'Sue said that Dan was mixed up in making mucky films too. Is that true?'

Yvonne was saved from answering when the front door opened again, Danny and Chris walking in.

426

With a gasp Yvonne ran into her husband's arms. 'Oh, Danny, Danny.'

'It's all right, we're in the clear. The premises are in Dad's name so they don't have any proof that we were involved.'

'But Chris said that you hadn't closed down.'

With a rueful smile Chris said, 'Yeah, me and my big mouth, but at the end of the day it didn't matter. All they found was the equipment and a few reels of films that hadn't been distributed. As Danny said, the place is in Dad's name so there was nothing to tie it directly to us.'

Danny frowned as he looked at his mother. 'You look awful, Mum, but don't worry. It's all over now.'

'All over?' she snapped. 'How can it be over when my daughter has run off and I don't know where she is? Sue tells me that your father was wrapped up in porn too. I want the truth, Danny, and from the beginning.'

Danny ran both hands over his face. 'Mum, it's been a long day and we're bushed. Can't this wait until tomorrow?'

'No, it can't. I want the truth – and now!'

'All right, calm down. I'll tell you, but sit down first.'

She glared at him, but nevertheless sat down. 'Right, let's hear it.'

'Danny, no . . .' Chris warned.

Danny ignored him. 'Dad was past cracking safes,

Mum, and it was my idea to make porn films. He wasn't interested at first, but I talked him round.' Danny paused to take a breath, then went on to tell his mother everything, finally saying, 'So you see, Pet was snatched because we went into Jack Garston's territory.'

Joan looked stunned. Then she suddenly reared to her feet, screeching, 'Get out! Get out of my house!'

'What?'

'You heard me!' And turning to Chris she shrieked, 'And that goes for you too.'

'Mum, calm down.'

'Calm down? You expect me to calm down? Your father was sick, you're sick, the lot of you. Now go, get out of my house!'

Yvonne could see that her mother-in-law was near breaking point, her chest heaving as she glared at them. 'Come on, Danny,' she urged. 'Your mother's had enough for one day.'

For a moment she thought he was going to argue, but then he nodded. 'Yeah, come on, Chris. Yvonne's right.'

Yvonne shivered as they walked outside, pulling her cardigan around her chest.

'You should have kept your mouth shut, Danny,' Chris spat.

'She had to know sometime.'

'She took it badly,' said Chris, 'and I'm not surprised.'

'She'll come round,' Yvonne placated, 'and in the meantime, Chris, you're welcome to stay with us.'

'No thanks.'

'But where will you sleep?'

'Don't worry about me. I'll sort something out.'

'What happened to Maurice?'

'He went straight home, and Gawd knows what he's gonna tell Norma. Anyway, I'm off,' he said, stuffing his hands into his pockets as he walked out of the alley.

When they went indoors, Danny lit the fire. Then, sighing heavily, he said, 'I made a right mess of that. Maybe I should go back. I don't like leaving Mum in that state.'

'No, not yet. She's been through enough and needs time to calm down. Leave her to sleep on it, love.'

As the fire took hold, Danny slumped onto the sofa. Yvonne sat beside him, taking a deep breath before voicing her thoughts. 'Danny, I've been thinking about Pet.'

'Grassing on us didn't do her any good. As I said, the place is in Dad's name so they've got nothing on us.'

'That's just it. Didn't the police say that acting on information received, they searched the premises?'

'Yeah, that's right.'

'Danny, think about it. Jack Garston showed Pet some films, told her they were yours, but not where you made them. She knew nothing about the premises so how could she have dobbed you in?'

Danny frowned, but as the penny dropped, he jumped to his feet. 'Bloody hell, you're right. It couldn't have been Pet.' He rubbed a hand across his forehead. 'But if it wasn't her – who was it?'

Yvonne shook her head, unable to give him an answer, whilst Danny began to pace the room.

'Jack Garston!' he suddenly yelled. 'It must have been him. Wait till I get my hands on that bastard.'

Yvonne's stomach clenched. 'No, Danny, no. Think, you've got to think. If you go after Garston he'll retaliate. Last time he took Pet, and you know what he did to her. What if this time he takes me, or one of the kids?'

'He wouldn't fucking dare.'

Yvonne jumped to her feet, but feeling a surge of dizziness she sank back onto the sofa. It had been a dreadful day, and now this. She felt sick, nauseous, her nerves at breaking point.

'Yvonne, what is it? What's wrong?'

Though she hated herself for doing it – hated using it as a weapon – Yvonne knew she had no choice. She had to stop Danny from going after Garston. 'It . . . it's my blood pressure. The doctor warned me that it's high. He . . . he said it can be dangerous, both for me and the baby. I'm supposed to rest and avoid stress.'

'Right, come on then,' Danny said, leaning over to heave her into his arms. 'Let's get you up to bed.'

'Please, Danny,' Yvonne begged as she leaned her

head on his shoulder. 'Please don't go after Garston. I'm frightened – scared of what he'll do.'

She felt his arms tighten around her and tensed, but then he said, 'All right, don't get upset. I'll leave him alone for now.'

Yvonne raised her head to look at Danny's face. 'For now', he had said. She sighed, knowing from his expression that for the time being, she'd have to be content with that.

Sue snuggled up to Bob, relieved that he was home and in the clear. 'They kept you at the station for bloody hours,' she complained. 'I went to your mum's to see if there was any news, but the old cow chucked me out.'

'Why did she do that?'

'Ain't it obvious? She knows about the porn now and said she's disgusted with the lot of us.'

'She's upset, love, but I'm sure she doesn't blame you.'

'Huh, knowing your mother she probably thinks I put you up to it,' Sue said as her eyes flicked round the room. She had made a bit of an effort for the kids' sake, putting up a few decorations, but even so, it was going to be a lousy Christmas. Mind you, she consoled herself, they'd be all right next year. When Dan's will was read, Bob was sure to get a chunk of the business and it must be worth a pretty penny.

'Have you seen your dad's will?'

'Leave it out. Mum's been in too much of a state to think about the will – we all have. I think she's got it, but it can wait until after the funeral.'

Sue hid her disappointment, but it wasn't the only thing that was disappointing her lately. She ran her hand along Bob's leg, but there was no response. He wasn't interested and hadn't been since his father died, but maybe she could try something else to tickle his fancy. 'Bob,' she said, leading up to it, 'it'll be Christmas Eve in a couple of days and we'll have to make a bit of an effort for the kids.'

'It doesn't seem right.'

'It isn't fair to ruin their Christmas. I'm not asking for much, just that we let them put out a mince pie for Father Christmas and some milk for the reindeers as usual.'

'Yeah, all right.'

'I don't expect you to dress up as Santa this year, but what about your Christmas treat? Instead of waiting, you can have it now if you like.'

'You've still got the outfit?'

'Of course I have. I'll go and put it on.'

'Not tonight, love. I'm bushed and I ain't in the mood.'

'You don't want Santa's little helper?' she asked as she ran her hand along the inside of Bob's leg.

'Leave off, love,' he said, moving her hand away

432

as he stood up. 'I'm knackered and I think I'll have an early night. Are you coming?'

'There ain't much chance of that these days,' she snapped.

'Trust you to take it the wrong way. I meant are you coming to bed?' but then seeing the funny side, he began to laugh.

Sue found it infectious, the pair of them soon doubled up with mirth. Sue didn't know what caused it, but as though the laughter had released something in Bob, the tension that had lined his face dissipated. He held out his hand, and with a wink said, 'Come on then, let's see you in that outfit.'

Sue didn't need telling twice. Giggling, she ran upstairs, but she didn't have time to put the pixie costume on before Bob grabbed her, pulling her onto the bed.

Joan sat alone in a silent house. Now, instead of grief, she felt only anger. Dan had been mixed up in porn and her stomach churned. He had ruled the boys and the business, one that she now knew was just a front. Oh, she had known that Dan was a bit of a rogue when she married him, but despite that she had admired his morals, the code that he lived by. Women, he always said, were to be respected, protected, looked after, and it was something he had instilled in his sons. Or so she had thought. Her teeth ground together. How could using women to make disgusting pornographic films be respecting them? And children – Pet said they used children. It was awful, dreadful. Oh God, what an idiot she'd been, a blind fool. The man she had loved, looked up to, had turned out to be a sick monster.

She glanced at the clock, worried about her daughter and hating herself for what she had put her through. Petula had been raped, violently, but she had hardly shown her an ounce of sympathy, her concern only for Dan and that he didn't find out.

The poor girl had held it all inside, eating away at her, and was it any wonder that it had all burst out? She had blamed her daughter for Dan's death, and maybe him hearing about the rape had been the catalyst, but in truth she knew that Dan had been going downhill for a while.

Joan sat wringing her hands. Danny had threatened to kill Petula. The poor girl must be so frightened, hiding, but Joan didn't blame her for going to the police. If she had known what they were up to, she'd have done the same. They were sick, disgusting, using poor children to make those awful films.

There was only one thing Joan wanted now and that was to have her daughter safely home again. She'd never been much of a mother, had treated her daughter badly, but now she just wanted the chance to make it up to her.

Oh, Pet, where are you? her mind cried out. You're all I have left now. Please come home. Don't be frightened. I'll make sure that Danny doesn't lay a hand on you, that nobody ever lays a hand on you again. It'll be just you and me, Pet, and as far as I'm concerned, the rest of them can rot in hell.

Joan's mind twisted and turned, wondering how she could find her daughter, until, exhausted, she fell asleep where she was sitting, the fire slowly dying until at last it went out.

Chapter Thirty-five

When Pet awoke in a strange room the following morning, for a moment she was disorientated, but then it all came flooding back: her father's death, her mother's hate, the police turning up, and Danny – Danny blaming her, threatening to kill her. Tears stung her eyes, but then, hearing the sound of giggling, she forced them away as her door was thrown open.

Harry and Ernie tumbled into the room. 'Auntie Pet, Auntie Pet, are you getting up?' Ernie urged.

'It looks like it,' she said, throwing back the covers. It was still dark outside and she had no idea of the time, but if the boys were awake, it must mean that Ivy and Steve were up too. 'Let me get dressed and then I'll come downstairs.'

'Yeah, all right, but don't be long,' Ernie cried, his eyes alight with excitement. 'It's snowing again, Auntie Pet, and Mum said that as soon as it's light we can build a snowman. Will you help us?'

'Of course I will.'

'Yippee,' Harry shouted, the two boys scampered out.

Pet went to the bathroom and after a quick wash she threw on some clothes before running downstairs to find the boys and Ivy in the kitchen. It was a nice room, far bigger than the kitchens in Drapers Alley, with an oak table and chairs in the centre and a large dresser against one wall, lined with blue willow-pattern china.

'Morning, love,' Ivy said. 'Help yourself to a cup of tea, and what would you like for breakfast?'

'I don't mind. Anything will do,' Pet said, reaching out for the teapot as she sat at the table.

'The boys usually have something hot and they want beans on toast this morning. Will that do?'

'Yes, and thanks. Where's Steve?'

'He's gone to work. I know it's Sunday, but the livestock still need sorting out. He's got Christmas Day off, but that's all.'

Pet paused in the act of pouring a cup of tea. She could see that Ivy was in pain, but obviously making a supreme effort to hide it. Pet frowned, sure that this was more than cramp. Ivy looked ill, really ill, and now putting the teapot down, she rose to her feet.

'Ivy, sit down. I want to make myself useful so I'll cook the breakfast.'

'There's no need.'

'Please, you took me in and it will make me feel better if you let me help.'

For a moment Ivy hesitated, but then she sat at the table, her hands clutching her stomach. 'All right, I won't say no. You'll find bread in the bin and beans in that cupboard over there.'

Pet opened the cupboard and frowned. It was dirty inside, very dirty. She took out the beans before turning to Ivy. 'Where's the tin opener?'

'In that drawer,' she indicated.

The cutlery drawer was dirty too, some knives and forks still showing remnants of food. She found the tin opener, her eyes involuntarily meeting Ivy's as she turned.

'I know, Pet, I know,' she murmured. 'The house-work is getting on top of me, and I'll be glad of your help. If you ask me, your turning up will prove to be a godsend.'

Pet frowned, wondering what Ivy meant, but saw that Harry and Ernie were still, listening to the conversation. 'Right, boys, one piece of toast or two?'

'Two, please,' they chorused.

Pet found a saucepan, unable to help noticing that though the kitchen appeared clean on the surface, inside every cupboard it was a different story. Something was very wrong with Ivy, she was sure of it, and if her cousin wouldn't tell her what the problem was, she'd ask Steve. In the mean-time she would do all she could to help Ivy, starting with the breakfast.

Chris left Phil's house and as he passed Arding and Hobbs, he glanced in the windows at their Christmas displays. Chris sniffed, fighting his emotions. It was going to be awful, the first Christmas without his father, and unless his mother let him back in, he'd be without her too. He could have stayed where he was, but Phil was constantly nagging about bringing their relationship into the open and it was driving him mad. He couldn't do it – couldn't face his family's reaction. If they found out they would never understand, and not only that, locally he'd be a laughing stock.

At last, his feet feeling like blocks of ice, Chris turned into Drapers Alley, fumbling for his key, but as he tried to turn it in the lock, it wouldn't move. His mother must have put the catch down, but as she was alone in the house he wasn't surprised, so lifting the door knocker, he rapped several times.

When she didn't come to the door he lifted the letter box, calling, 'Mum, come on, open up. It's bloody freezing out here.'

Through the narrow gap he could see that she was sitting by the fire, but she didn't move. 'Mum. Come on. Open the door!'

'What's going on?' Danny called from next door, his head poking out of an upstairs window.

'It's Mum. I can see her through the letter box, but she won't let me in.'

'Is she all right?'

'I dunno,' Chris called, bending down to peer through the letter box again. He frowned, standing up to call out, 'She ain't moving.'

'Hold on, I'm coming down.'

In what felt like moments, Danny was beside him, thumping loudly on the door. 'Come on, Mum, open this door.'

With a tut of impatience he too peered through the letter box. 'Yeah, I can see her, but you're right, she ain't moving.' His brow creased with anxiety and then, lifting the letter box again, he shouted, 'Mum, if you don't open this door I'm gonna kick it in.'

The door opened, their mother glaring at them as she spat, 'Don't you dare kick my door.' She stood in front of them, arms folded across her chest to bar their entry.

'Come on, Mum, let me in,' Chris urged.

'I don't want you in my house, any of you. My daughter is the only decent child I've got, but you threatened her, Danny, and now she'll never come home.'

'We'll find her, Mum, we'll put it right. She didn't grass on us, I know that now.'

'She didn't? What makes you think that?' Chris asked.

'I'll explain later,' Danny told him.

'Mum, what about my stuff?' Chris urged. 'I need clean clothes.'

'All right, you can come in to pack, but then, until you find Petula, I don't want to see your face again.'

Chris stepped inside and when his mother slammed the door in Danny's face, he said, 'Mum, come on, there's no need for that.'

'Just get your stuff and then get out.'

'Can't we at least talk about it?'

'I don't want to talk. I just want to see the back of you. Now either you go upstairs to pack, or you get out now.'

With a sigh Chris went up to his room. With his mother in this mood there was no point in arguing with her, but surely in another twenty-four hours she'd come round. He packed a case, and with his dark suit over his arm he returned downstairs. 'I'm going now, Mum.'

'Good.'

'I don't like leaving you on your own.'

'Find my daughter and I won't be. Now go on, bugger off.'

His head low, Chris left and went straight to Danny's house, saying as he went in, 'There's no talking to her.'

'We'll just have to find Pet.'

'She could be anywhere, Danny, and with your threat hanging over her head, she'll be keeping her head down. But what's this about her not grassing on us?'

'As Yvonne pointed out, Pet didn't know about our place in Wimbledon so it couldn't have been her.'

'Bloody hell, but if she didn't, who did?'

'I don't know, but my first guess is Jack Garston.'

Chris knew he'd have to kip down in Danny's for now, but uppermost in his mind was Jack Garston. He'd find the bastard, and when he did . . .

Maurice arrived at nine thirty and got the same reception. His mother opened the door, told him to bugger off and then slammed it in his face. He didn't really want to see Danny, but there were things to be sorted that couldn't wait. He went next door to find that Bob and Chris were there, the pair of them sitting on Danny's sofa.

'Mum wouldn't let me in,' Maurice said as he took a seat by the fire.

'She won't let any of us in, and she chucked Chris out,' Danny told him, going on to relate all that had happened when they returned from the police station.

Maurice's breath wheezed in his chest. 'So, it's all out in the open. No wonder she wouldn't let me in.'

'What about Norma? Did you tell her that we were taken in for questioning?' Bob asked.

'No, I just said that I spent the day with Mum.'

'What excuse did you come up with for leaving the alley?'

'None, and I don't intend to. Just the threat of us coming back is enough to shut her up.'

'My Sue knows all about it and instead of doing her nut, she took it well. Yvonne knows too, ain't that right, Danny?'

'Yes, she does. Maybe you should tell your wife, Maurice. It's bound to come out sooner or later and it'll be better coming from you.'

Maurice wanted to spit in Danny's face, but hid his feelings. 'No, Danny. I know Norma, and if she finds out it'll be the end of my marriage. We're in the clear; we're not involved in making films any more, so as long as I keep her away from the alley, there's no need to tell her.'

'What about Dad's funeral? We can tell Sue and Yvonne to keep their mouths shut around Norma, but we can't say the same for Mum.'

'I'll come alone.'

'How will you manage that?'

'I doubt Norma will want to come, so it won't be hard.'

'How are you managing for money?' Danny asked.

'I've still got a fair bit saved, and I'll get a job after Christmas.'

'What about the yard?' Bob asked. 'Dad has probably split it between us, so even if you don't want to join us in running it, you'll still be entitled to a share of the profits.'

'I haven't given Dad's will a thought,' Maurice lied, 'and anyway, until it's read, we won't know how we stand.'

'Yeah, well, none of us have mentioned it to Mum yet. She's been in such a state that we decided to leave it until after the funeral.'

'Look, forget about the will,' Chris said impatiently. 'You seem to have forgotten that we've got to find Pet.'

Danny nodded. 'Yes, Chris is right, and as I told Bob earlier, it wasn't Pet who grassed on us. I reckon it was Jack Garston, but now Pet thinks I'm after her and I feel like shit.'

Maurice frowned. 'I doubt it was Garston. If word got out that he's a grass, he'd be finished. Not only that, Garston had no reason to dob us in. We're out of the game now and he knows it.'

'Yeah,' Bob said, 'Maurice is right.'

'All right, so it wasn't Garston,' said Danny. 'We'll just have to find out who it was, and then sort him out, but for now we need to put our heads together to find Pet.'

'What about her friends? She could be with one of them,' Bob suggested.

'I know where one lives, a girl called Jane, but that's all,' Chris said.

444

Danny rose to his feet. 'Right, let's start there.'

'Do you mind if I leave you to it?' Maurice asked. 'I'm still a bit rough and the cold weather really gets to my chest.'

'Yeah, go on home. We can manage,' Danny told him. 'I'll just pop upstairs to tell Yvonne what we're up to, and then we can leave.'

'I'll tell Sue,' Bob said, saying goodbye to Maurice before he hurried out.

Maurice turned to Chris. 'If Mum doesn't change her mind, you could move into George's place.'

'No, I don't fancy that. Too many memories,' Chris said.

Maurice frowned at his cryptic reply, but then Danny came downstairs, wrapped up against the cold in his camel coat and carrying brown leather gloves.

'Right, let's go,' he said.

As they walked outside snow was falling and Maurice shivered. He said a hasty goodbye, calling to his brothers that he'd see them the next day before hurrying out of the alley to his car.

Maurice drove off, his mood low. He'd told his brothers that he hadn't given his father's will a thought, but it wasn't true. In fact he was disappointed that they were waiting until after the funeral to read it.

On Lavender Hill, the traffic lights turned to red. Maurice pulled up automatically, his mind hardly on the road. Since leaving the alley he'd been constantly worried about the future, but on hearing of his father's death the burden had lifted. He would receive an inheritance, and had mentally calculated the business assets. There was the yard and the small-holding in Wimbledon, both worth a lot of money. They could be sold, the money shared, and his worries would be over.

Maurice gripped the steering wheel, fighting off feelings of guilt. Yes, he was sad when his father died, but since having two strokes and coming home from hospital, his mother had guarded him so well that Maurice had hardly seen him. It had saddened him that his father had been left helpless, half alive, a shadow of the man he used to be. When he had stopped holding the reins of the family business, it had gone to pieces, and most of that had been down to Danny. The distance from his family had given Maurice time to think, for his resentment to build. It had been Danny's ambitions, his obsession with making money that had put Oliver at risk, forcing Maurice to leave the alley. He had managed to hide his feelings this morning, but just looking at Danny sickened him.

Once he had his inheritance, Maurice was determined to start a new life, somewhere where there was no chance of Norma ever finding out about his past. If it wasn't for his health, they could have emigrated, but they could still move to the other end of the country, maybe Devon or Cornwall, where they could buy some sort of small business, a tea shop or one selling souvenirs. They might never be rich, but he would be his own boss without the worry of finding employment. He wouldn't miss Danny, though he'd miss the rest of the family, but once away from London he would never have to worry about losing his wife and son again.

Danny, Chris and Bob were propping up the bar in a local pub, all drinking shorts. They had been to see Jane, but the girl said she hadn't seen Pet and didn't know where she was. She had given them a couple of other addresses to try, but again they drew blanks.

'That's it then,' Bob said. 'We've been everywhere, and put out the word, but nobody's seen her.'

Danny downed his third whisky. 'She can't be walking the streets in this weather. Somebody must have taken her in.'

'I still can't get over the reception we got when we tried Linda's parents' place. I thought the old boy was going to have a fit when he saw us,' said Chris.

'Yeah, and I thought Linda was going to pass out,' Bob said as he waved his glass at the barman to indicate another round.

Danny shrugged. 'It was worth a try, and once

Linda knew that we weren't interested in her baby, she calmed down, especially when we told her that there's still no sign of George.'

As another drink was put in front of Chris he threw it down his throat, then said, 'Shit, I dread telling Mum that we ain't found Pet.'

'You and me both,' Danny said, waving his glass and adding, 'but a few more of these might help.'

By closing time, all three were drunk, none bothering that Danny was in no fit state to drive as they got into his car. After a few fumbled attempts Danny managed to find the ignition, and though mounting the pavement at every corner, he somehow managed to drive home.

They staggered into the alley, propping each other up, and stopped outside their mother's door.

Chris was swaying on his feet but managed to rattle the letter box. He shook his head, trying to focus, and when the door was flung open he slurred, 'We've tried, Mum, but we couldn't find her. Can I come in now?'

'No you bloody well can't. I've told you, find my daughter, and until you do, you can bugger off,' she shouted, slamming the door shut.

'Blimey, I never thought I'd see the day,' Bob chuckled. 'Mum's starting to swear like a trooper.'

'Ish not funny,' Chris slurred.

'Sod you then, I'm going home,' Bob said, taking his arm from around Danny to stumble to his own front door.

Danny held Chris up as they went into his house, where he heaved his brother onto the sofa, almost falling as he sank down beside him. He was drunk, but seeing his mother had sobered him a little. Yvonne came into the room from the kitchen, her face anxious.

'Did you find Pet?'

He shook his head. 'No, but we'll keep looking.'

Her eyes flicked to Chris and he grinned inanely. 'Watcha, Yvonne.'

'Have you been drinking?'

'We only had a few, love,' Danny told her, his eyes drooping until, unable to keep them open any longer, he sank back and in moments was asleep.

When Chris did the same, Yvonne shook her head before returning to the kitchen. They were supposed to be looking for Petula, but instead they had been in the pub, and judging by the look of them they'd been drinking since opening time. She wanted to talk to Danny about Christmas, but now it would have to wait until he sobered up.

It was Christmas Eve tomorrow, her order waiting to be picked up, but how could she cook a Christmas dinner knowing that her mother-in-law was alone next door? Then there was the funeral to face. Two cars had been ordered, but with Joan feeling the way she did, would she refuse to travel to the cemetery with her sons? It was a mess, everything was a mess and the last thing she needed was her husband coming home drunk. Her head began to thump, and tiredly she rubbed her forehead. It was no good, she'd have to lie down. So, having poured a glass of water, Yvonne carried it upstairs. Drunk or sober, Danny would have to sort it out. She'd had enough.

Chapter Thirty-six

Pet was dusting the living room, but paused to look out of the window. The landscape was white, a blanket of snow thick on the ground. It had been snowing heavily since Christmas, and according to the weather forecast, there was no sign of a let-up.

Today was her father's funeral, the thought of it almost more than she could bear. When the door opened, Pet spun round to see Ivy coming into the room, her cousin frowning when she looked at her.

'Are you all right, Pet?'

'It's today – my father's funeral.'

'Blimey, no wonder you look upset. Come on, leave the housework and I'll make us both a nice cup of hot chocolate. Honestly, you're just like your mother, always on the go, but for once, give it a rest.'

'I'd rather keep busy.'

Ivy grimaced, her hands involuntarily rubbing her tummy. 'Bloody ulcer,' she complained, 'and that jollop the doctor gave me is a waste of time.'

Pet frowned as she looked at Ivy. 'I think you've lost more weight.'

'There isn't much I can eat that doesn't give me gyp so is it any wonder?'

'No, I suppose not,' said Pet, 'but if the medicine isn't helping, maybe you should go back to see the doctor.'

'It'd be a waste of time. The old quack is well past it, and if you ask me, he should retire. I reckon his eyesight is going and when I told him about the pains in my tummy he asked a few questions, but didn't examine me before saying it's an ulcer.'

Pet hadn't been close to Ivy when they had lived in Drapers Alley, but living with her now had proved a revelation. Ivy was kind, a good mother, her marriage a happy one.

When Pet had asked Steve about Ivy's constant pain he'd told her it was an ulcer, but Pet knew nothing about them, only seeing how debilitating the pain could be. She did all she could to help Ivy, taking on the housework and sometimes the cooking, pleased to be useful. It helped to keep busy, helped to keep thoughts of her family at bay, but at night, alone in her room, it was impossible.

Ivy's clock struck the hour, and seeing the time, Pet's eyes filled with tears. It was happening now, her father was being buried. She felt a touch on her arm, the duster pulled from her hand.

'Come on, Pet,' Ivy said, her voice unusually gentle. 'I said leave the housework.'

'Oh, Ivy, I should be there. I should be at his funeral.'

'I know, love, I know,' Ivy murmured, pulling Pet into her arms and holding her whilst she cried.

Danny's face was grim as he listened to Yvonne. It had been a lousy Christmas and New Year, culminating in this, his father's funeral. His mother still wouldn't have anything to do with them, stubbornly spending Christmas Day alone, and only that morning had she conceded to let Yvonne in the door.

'She doesn't want you or anyone else in the car with her,' Yvonne said when she returned, 'but she finally agreed that we can follow.'

'What about the service?'

'She wants to sit alone in the chapel.'

'This is bloody ridiculous.'

'I know, and I did the best I could, but it's like talking to a brick wall.' Tears suddenly filled Yvonne's eyes. 'We used to be so close, Danny, but now your mum hates me.'

'She'll come round, love, you'll see.'

'No, Danny, I don't think so. She's so bitter and I don't know what she meant, but she said something about the lot of us having a shock coming. Oh, look at the time. The cars will be here soon so I'd better get changed.'

Danny was already in his suit, with white shirt and black tie. Chris was upstairs putting his on, but he'd have to warn Bob that they would have to use the second car, one that had been booked to take the wives and children to the service. 'All right, and while you're getting ready, I'll pop round to tell Bob about the arrangements.'

When Danny went into his brother's, his overcoat flung around his shoulders, he saw that the kids were ready, both Robby and Paul dressed smartly and, like him, wearing black ties. Sue was wearing a black coat, but to him her hat looked frivolous, perched on the side of her head with a small veil covering her eyes.

'Any sign of Maurice?' she asked.

'No, not yet,' Danny told her as Bob came downstairs. 'Mum doesn't want any of us in the car with her so we've got to follow. Seven of us won't fit in the second car, so you go in that with Maurice, Sue and the boys. I'll take Yvonne in my car.'

'So, Mum finally let you in,' Bob said.

'No, not me, it was Yvonne.'

Sue's lips curled in derision. 'Huh, I might have guessed.'

The door opened, Maurice saying as he walked in, 'I saw the cars outside the alley and there's a bloke in a top hat knocking on Mum's door.'

'Right, I'll get Yvonne and Chris,' Danny said, hurrying next door.

Soon everyone was on the pavement, all eyes gaping as their mother walked outside. Instead of black, she was wearing a fawn-coloured coat with a wide-brimmed hat in the same shade, the outfit more suited to a wedding than a funeral.

'She said we had a shock coming and this must be it,' Yvonne whispered.

'What's her game? Look at her – it's bloody disgusting,' Sue snapped.

Without a backward glance Joan walked out of the alley, the rest of them following. Danny glanced at the hearse; saw the flowers surrounding his father's coffin before quickly looking away. He fought to pull himself together and, telling the others to get into the second car, he hustled Yvonne to the lockup to get his.

Danny needn't have hurried. With his top hat under his arm, and umbrella held out in front of him, the funeral director stepped in front of the hearse, slowly walking in front of it, the cars moving behind at a snail's pace. Danny waited until he could slot in behind the second car, and as he drove slowly along he saw that the pavement was lined with locals solemnly watching the small procession pass. He was pleased to see that they were showing their respects, and though they had held his father in fear, many had turned to him when they had a problem.

When the hearse turned onto Lavender Hill the funeral director hopped into the front, the car

455

picking up pace. At last they reached the chapel where they all stood silently as the coffin was carried in. Then their mother was beckoned forward, dry-eyed as she walked straight to the first pew. The others then followed, all shuffling into the row behind her, but before the service could start, Robby's voice echoed as he piped, 'Nanny, is Granddad in that box?'

His mother didn't turn, but Danny saw that her shoulders had begun to shake. He wanted to run to her, to offer comfort, but then to his horror he heard a titter of laughter. His mother wasn't crying, she was laughing. My God, she was actually laughing!

When the chapel service was over Joan walked to the cemetery, aware that the rest of them were close behind, but ignoring them. It was freezing, snow laying on the ground, the path slippery underfoot. When they reached the graveside, Joan saw the way the vicar looked at her, his disapproval plain, his expression pompous. Who was he to judge her? What did he know of her life, her disillusion? All right, she wasn't wearing black, the mark of respect, but Dan didn't deserve respect, only contempt.

Robby began to run around and, bending down, he scooped up a handful of snow to throw at his brother. Bob restrained the boy, shaking his shoulders before pulling him to stand beside them at the graveside.

Joan wasn't listening as the vicar began his intonation, her mind on her plans. As she had told Yvonne, they were in for a shock. When this was over she'd allow them in her house for one last time and then, if her plan worked, she would never have to see the lot of them again.

Joan was brought back to the present as Danny threw a flower into the grave where it landed on top of Dan's coffin. As the others did the same, Joan saw the vicar moving towards her. She didn't want to hear his platitudes, his talk of Dan being in a better place. Huh, she just hoped it wasn't true because as far as she was concerned her husband should rot in hell.

Joan ignored the vicar's outstretched hand, turning instead to head for the car that was to take her home. She was ready now, ready for the confrontation, her mouth set in a grim line as she settled back in her seat.

It wasn't a long drive, hardly time for her feet to thaw before Joan got out of the car, only pausing long enough to thank the man who had held the door open. In a few minutes she was indoors, and though she had banked up the fire, it had burned low. She hurried to add more coal. Taking off her coat, she stuffed her feet into slippers whilst her eyes flew to the document tucked behind the clock on the mantelpiece. She waited then, looking out of the window, until shortly after they all walked into the alley.

Joan flung the front door open. 'Danny, Bob, Maurice, Chris,' she snapped, 'I want to talk to you. Not you, Sue,' she ordered as the woman moved forward, dragging the boys. 'Nor you, Yvonne.'

Sue shot daggers, but Joan didn't care. Yvonne looked sad and for a moment Joan almost wavered. She was fond of Danny's wife, more than fond, and if just one of them could remain, she would want it to be Yvonne.

Joan walked back inside, the boys following her, with Chris, the last in, closing the door.

'Right, this is your father's will,' she said as she took the document from behind the clock, 'and I suggest you sit down before I read it.'

They each took a seat, all looking at her expectantly, so taking a deep breath, she began. 'Before I read the will, I'd like to know how I stand financially. How is the yard doing?'

'Mum, I know that Dad wouldn't want you to worry about the business,' Danny said. 'You can leave all that to us. The yard's doing all right and we'll see that you're taken care of as usual.'

Joan smiled thinly, her eyes sweeping over her sons as she opened the document. 'I was with your father when this was drawn up. It's been in my possession ever since, and before you ask, it's the only will he made. Now I won't go into all the legal jargon, or read it word for word, as the sooner you get out of here the better. All you need to know is that everything, your father's entire estate, has been left to me.'

'What?' Maurice cried. 'But he can't do that. What about us?'

'You are mentioned, all of you. Your father says that he'd like you to run the business, continuing to take a cut of the profits each month as wages.'

'But we thought he'd share it between us,' Maurice protested.

Joan's eyes swept over her sons again. Maurice was the only one who had spoken; the others looked at her in stunned silence. 'If I had predeceased your father, then yes, the estate would have been shared equally between you, but I didn't die first, *he did.*' Joan smiled thinly again. 'Mind you, your father still thought he had it covered – that one day his precious sons would get their inheritance.'

Danny spoke at last, to ask, 'What do you mean, Mum?'

'At your father's insistence, my will was drawn up at the same time as his, and he made sure that I named you all as my beneficiaries.'

Joan now stood up. Drawing another document from behind the clock, she held it up, speaking to her husband as though he was there, in the room. 'See this, Dan? It's my will. You thought you were infallible, that you'd always be able to control me, the meek, biddable little wife. Well, let's see you control this,' she shouted as she threw her will onto the fire, watching with satisfaction as it was taken by the flames and devoured. 'They'll get nothing from me – *nothing*.'

'Mum, what are you doing? Have you lost your mind?' Danny shouted.

'No,' Joan spat, 'I haven't lost my mind. In fact, for the first time in my life, I'm seeing things clearly, thinking for myself.'

'Mum, come on, calm down,' Chris urged. 'If you carry on like this you'll make yourself ill.'

'Looking at you lot is enough to make me ill, but I ain't finished yet so you'd better sit down again.'

'Look, Mum, let's talk calmly,' Chris said as he took a seat. 'I don't care about Dad's will, or yours, but he did say that he wants us to look after you, to run the business, and that suits me fine.'

'I own the yard now and there's no way on earth I'd let you lot run it,' Joan snapped. 'In fact there'll be no business to run. I'm going to sell it.'

'You're going to do what? But you can't,' Danny cried.

'Oh yes I can, Danny. I can do what I like.'

'Look, is this about Pet? Because if it is, give us a chance to find her.'

'I gave you a chance.'

'She could be anywhere. We need more time.'

'No, Danny, with your threat hanging over her head, like George, she's gone. She'll never come back unless you lot are out of the way, and with this in mind, I've got a proposition for you.'

'What sort of proposition?' Maurice asked.

'As I said, I'm selling the yard, but there's still that other place, the one in Wimbledon. I want nothing to do with it. In fact, the thought of it makes me sick to my stomach. Now I'm going to make you an offer, and you'd better take it because it's the only one you're going to get.' Joan paused, but saw that Maurice had leaned forward, his face eager with anticipation.

'Go on, Mum,' he urged.

'All right, let's get down to business,' she said curtly. 'I want you all out of Drapers Alley and, once gone, I don't want to ever see your faces again. If you agree to go I'll give you that place in Wimbledon. You can sell it and split the profits between you.'

Maurice looked delighted. 'Blimey, thanks, Mum.'

'Hold on, Maurice,' said Bob. 'It's all right for you, you've got a flat, but where are we supposed to live?'

'Come on, it wouldn't be the end of the world. I found a place and you can do the same.'

'Mum, please, don't do this,' Chris begged. 'We're out of the porn game now and we'll never go back to it. I had to put all my savings into the yard to expand our stock and it's just starting to pay dividends.'

'You'll get your money back.'

'But I can't leave the alley, Mum. Who'll look after you?'

'Look after me? You? Don't make me laugh. I can look after myself and I don't need a sick disgusting animal that used children to make pornographic films living under my roof.'

'We didn't use kids. We'd never do that. Tell her, Danny.'

'He's telling the truth, Mum.'

'Even if I believed you, which I don't, it wouldn't make any difference. You still made other films and you can't deny that. Now are you going to accept my offer or not? Because if you don't, you'll end up with nothing.'

'We'll accept it,' Maurice hastily said.

Danny's temper spilled over. 'Maurice, are you out of your mind? Of course we're not accepting it.'

'If we don't, as Mum said, we'll end up without a penny.'

Joan watched as her eldest son ran a hand through his hair, obviously trying to calm down before he met her eyes. 'Mum, I know you're upset, but this is silly. Surely you don't really want us to leave the alley.'

'Yes I do, and my mind's made up. In fact, I don't want any of you to put a foot inside *my* yard again.'

'It won't run itself, Mum. If you close down you won't have any money coming in.'

'I told you, I'm selling it, and if you must know, the sale's already in hand.'

'I can't believe you're doing this,' Danny groaned. 'Mum, at least give us time to think about it.'

'Oh, I know your game, Danny. You're trying to stall me, hoping I'll change my mind, but I won't, you can be sure of that. Now you've got one hour, and after that you either accept my offer or you can forget it. Now bugger off, the lot of you.'

'Come on, Danny, you can see she means it,' Maurice urged.

As Danny looked at her, Joan kept her head high, her expression hard. At last, with a sigh of exasperation he turned to march out, his brothers behind him.

Joan was glad to see the back of them and slumped in her chair. Her plan *had* to work, it just had to, or Petula would never come home. She closed her eyes, praying silently as she waited for her sons to make their decision.

Bob said he'd talk to Sue and hurried into his own house, his face white as he broke the news.

'So your father left you nothing, not even a few bob?'

'That's right.'

'But your mum's offering to give you the premises in Wimbledon?'

'Yeah, but as I said, only if we move out of the alley.'

'That suits me fine.'

'Do you really mean that? It means finding somewhere else to live, but by the time the money is split between four of us, I don't know how much we'll get.'

'Of course I bloody mean it, now shut up and give me time to think.' Sue was quiet, her eyes narrowed. Then she said, 'I reckon you'd get a good few thousand, and if you pool it with your brothers, what's to stop you starting up your own business? With your contacts you could carry on supplying building materials. You'd only have to find premises and buy in stock.'

Bob's face lit up. 'Sue, you're a genius. I'll go and put it to the others.'

He hurried next door and without preamble said, 'Sue's had a great idea. If we take Mum's offer and sell Wimbledon, we could start up our own business.'

'Count me out,' said Maurice. 'I've got my own plans.'

'That still leaves three of us,' Bob said eagerly.

'None of you seems to be thinking about your mother,' Yvonne protested. 'If we leave the alley it'll be empty. She'll be all on her own.'

'It's what she wants – she made that clear,' Maurice said.

'We can't do it, we can't just leave,' Chris said.

'If you stay in the borough,' Maurice argued, 'you can keep an eye on her and, who knows, she might eventually come round.'

'Yeah, Maurice is right,' said Bob, 'and anyway,

I don't think we've got much choice. If we don't take the offer, we'll all be left with nothing.'

'I've just thought of something,' said Chris. 'Even if we agree to take up Mum's offer, we've still got to sell Wimbledon and that could take time, maybe months, and it would give us a chance to bring her round.'

'Bloody hell, I hadn't thought of that,' said Bob, 'but if it takes that long to sell, what will we do for money? Shit, I'll have to get a job, work for someone else, and I don't know about you lot, but I don't fancy that.'

So far Danny had just listened, but now he said, 'It's funny really, almost like fate, if you believe in all that rubbish. The last time I was at Wimbledon it was to tell Pete Saunders that we were closing down, but he didn't seem surprised. When I told him that he could stay on at the cottage for a while, he said he'd already been looking round for another place.'

'Hang on, Danny. How could Pete have known in advance that we were closing down?' asked Chris.

'With all that was going on at the time, I wasn't myself, and to be honest it sort of went over my head. He said something about a big developer sniffing around, looking to buy the land, and that he was looking for another place in case we took the bloke's offer.'

'What offer?' asked Maurice.

'Pete gave me a letter that had been delivered to

the cottage, but as I said, I was in a bit of a state and hardly looked at it.'

'Blimey, talk about luck,' Maurice said, then asked eagerly, 'Where's the letter, Danny?'

'I dunno.'

'Think, Danny. Did you leave it at the cottage or bring it home?'

'At the time it didn't seem important so I've no idea. I might have just stuffed it in my pocket.'

'Try the sideboard, Danny,' Yvonne suggested. 'You usually clear your pockets when you take off your jacket so you might have put it in the drawer, the one that you keep locked.'

'Yeah, all right,' Danny said, taking out a bunch of keys to find the small one that fitted the drawer. He walked over to the sideboard, saying as he unlocked it, 'I doubt it's here, though.'

They all watched as Danny pulled out papers. Then, finding a book, he said, 'Blimey, the hooky business accounts. I should have destroyed these. If the police had warrants to search this place, it would have left us in the shit.'

'Give it to me,' Maurice urged. 'I'll burn it now.'

Danny handed the book to Maurice, watching as his brother threw it onto the fire.

'It seems sort of symbolic,' he murmured, 'our old lives going up in flames.' He shrugged and returned to his search. 'Got it,' he said at last, pulling out an envelope.

'Give it here, Danny,' Maurice urged, and after scanning the contents he said, 'This is too good an offer to turn down, but we don't know if he's still interested. Give him a ring, Danny.'

'Are you all sure about this?' Danny asked. 'Do we really want to take Mum's offer?'

'I do,' said Maurice, 'and if you ask me, we'd be mad not to.'

'Yeah, and as my Sue said, it'll give us the chance to set up our own business.'

'What about you, Chris?'

'You seem to have made up your minds, so I don't suppose I've got much choice.'

'Right, the decision's made,' Danny said.

Moving to the telephone, he dialled the number. They all listened, hearing only one side of the conversation, but even from that it soon became clear that Danny had struck a deal.

He finally replaced the receiver, turning to say, 'We're on. There's only the legal stuff to be sorted now.'

'Blimey, you were right, Danny. Talk about fate,' Bob said.

Only Yvonne and Chris looked doubtful, Chris saying, 'That's it then. Once it's all finalised, we're all going, but it still doesn't seem right to leave Mum.'

'I feel the same,' said Yvonne.

'Bloody hell, Yvonne, do you think I'm happy

about it?' Danny snapped. 'But as Bob pointed out, if we don't take Mum's offer we're stuck with nothing. Like him, I'd have to get a job to pay the rent, but doing what? Without any skills I'd be down to labouring on a building site or something like that, and earning shit money. Is that what you want?'

'No, no, of course not, but—'

Before Yvonne had finished speaking, Danny interrupted, turning to look at Chris. 'What about you? Once the money is in place, do you want to come in with me and Bob, or do you want to go it alone?'

'I don't know. I'll need to think about it.'

'Please yourself, but don't take too long about it,' Danny said, obviously fired with enthusiasm as he continued, 'because after telling Mum that we'll accept her offer, me and Bob are going to start looking for some decent premises. Ain't that right, Bob?'

'Yeah, and somewhere else to live.'

Danny glanced at his watch. 'The hour is nearly up so let's get back to Mum's.'

Only Chris hesitated, but Maurice said quietly, 'Come on, Chris. It'll all work out, you'll see. This is a fresh start for all of us, a chance to make something of our lives. I want to start up a little business and if you don't go in with Danny and Bob, you could do the same. If you make it a success, make Mum proud, she's bound to come round.'

Chris still hesitated, but as though Maurice's words had touched his heart, he at last nodded. 'Yeah, you're right. Mum's disgusted with the lot of us and until I can give her something to be proud of, she's never going to forgive me. Not only that, if I can find a business that's close by, I can still keep an eye on her.'

Danny knocked on his mother's door, she opened it and they stepped inside. Chris's eyes flicked along the alley and settled on George's house. So much had happened in such a short time, but it had all started there. Chris shivered, looking swiftly away. He was the last to walk into his mother's house, wondering if it would be for the last time.

Chapter Thirty-seven

By March, everyone was sick of snow. It had been the worst winter that anyone could remember, with the River Thames freezing over in places, but at last a thaw was settling in.

Petula filled a hot-water bottle, firmly screwing on the top before taking it upstairs. She didn't care about the weather, was unaware that in Ivy's garden the tips of daffodils were poking through. Pet's only concern was for her cousin. They had watched her go downhill, until finally, that morning, Steve had put his foot down, insisting that she saw the doctor again. With Ivy in so much pain, Steve had demanded a house call.

Now, as Pet pushed open the bedroom door, she said, 'Here, I've brought you a hot-water bottle. The doctor should be here soon.'

'I bet the old quack wasn't happy about being called out,' Ivy said, but her voice was weak, the pain wearing her down.

Pet tucked the hot-water bottle under the blankets and then heard a knock on the front door. 'That must be him now.'

When she hurried back downstairs, Pet opened the front door to find a young man on the front step, his eyes crinkling at the corners when he smiled. 'Dr Finch is down with the flu. I'm Dr Davidson, his locum.'

'Oh, right, you'd better come in,' Pet said. She led him upstairs, saying, 'My cousin is in a lot of pain. Dr Finch said she has an ulcer, but she's getting worse and the medicine he prescribed doesn't help.'

As they walked into the bedroom, Ivy struggled unsuccessfully to sit up.

'Good morning, Mrs Rawlings,' the doctor said. 'I'm Dr Finch's locum. My name is Dr Davidson, and this young lady tells me that you have an ulcer.'

'Yeah, that's right, and it's bloody killing me.'

'Right, let's take a look at you.'

Pet remained whilst the doctor carried out his examination, and though he frowned, his voice remained impassive as he said, 'I'd like to send you for a few tests. If you have a telephone, I'll ring the hospital now.'

'Tests? What sort of tests?'

'An X-ray, bloods and maybe a barium meal.' He turned brusquely to Pet. 'Do you have a telephone?'

'Yes, it's downstairs.'

He followed Pet, saying as he picked up the

471

receiver, 'I'll arrange for an ambulance to take Mrs Rawlings to the local hospital. With any luck there'll be one available.'

'What? You want her to go now?'

'Yes, that's right,' he said, hastily dialling the number.

As she picked up on the doctor's urgency, Pet's stomach lurched. 'It . . . it isn't an ulcer?'

The call went through, Pet's question unanswered.

In Drapers Alley, Joan read the letter again before screwing it up and throwing it onto the fire. She didn't care what the council said, because when the time came, she wasn't budging from the alley. It explained why the rest of the houses remained empty, the alley now looking run down and desolate, but until her daughter came home, she was staying put.

Grim-faced, she put on her coat and after tying a headscarf around her head Joan stepped outside. The snow was thawing, the pavement mushy but, deep in thought, she hardly noticed. The sale had gone through on the yard, and after making sure that Chris was paid off, the rest was safely in the bank. Her new will was drawn up and the solicitor wanted her at his office to sign it. She had hated making a will the first time, feeling that it was like tempting fate, but in the end, with Dan going first, fate had been on her side.

It rankled that the boys had done all right from the deal she had struck with them, but she just wanted rid of them and had no choice. Petula was her only concern now – her need to make it up to her daughter. At least when anything happened to her, Joan thought, her daughter would do all right, her new will made out in Petula's favour.

Danny and Bob had started up on their own as builders' merchants, but she had no idea what Maurice was up to. To her annoyance, when old Bill Tweedy retired Chris had bought his shop, her son now living on the corner of Aspen Street to remain within spitting distance. He usually called round on a Wednesday afternoon and, sick of telling him to bugger off, she was glad that the solicitor's appointment coincided with his visit. Joan sighed. Though loath to admit it, she was lonely, sorely tempted at times to let Chris in, but she couldn't do that, not after what he had been involved in.

She had hoped that when her sons left, Petula would show her face, but so far there was no sign of her. Of course it didn't help that Chris's shop was just around the corner, but as it was Danny who had made the threats, she still hoped, still prayed, for her daughter to come home before it was too late.

Few people spoke to Joan, but she had kept herself to herself for years so it wasn't surprising. Yet now, as she turned into Aspen Street, she saw that Betty

Fuller was standing on her doorstep, deep in conversation with her neighbour. They went back years and at one time Betty had been after Dan. He hadn't been interested, and at the time Joan had been thrilled that, instead of Betty, he had chosen her. Thrilled – yes, she'd been thrilled, but now she had lived to regret it.

Betty broke off her conversation when she saw her, but Joan didn't miss the wink that she threw at her neighbour before she spoke. 'Watcha, Joan. We were just talking about Chris and we're wondering how you feel about his friend – you know, the one that works in his shop.'

'Sorry, can't stop,' Joan said.

'You should have a word with him. He's making himself a laughing stock.'

'I don't know what you're talking about,' Joan snapped as she hurried away, yet even so, her curiosity was piqued. Chris, a laughing stock? But why? Oh, what did it matter? She was finished with him, with all of them. All she wanted was her daughter, but it had been so long now, months since Petula had run away. Would she ever come back? Oh, please, God, she must.

Danny was bent over a battered desk, adding up columns in the account book, his tongue sticking out of the corner of his mouth in concentration. Maurice had always handled the accounts and this was new territory for him. At last they balanced and, leaning back, he smiled with satisfaction. They were doing all right, and though it had taken a bit of wrangling, they had managed to hold on to their biggest customer, his order now filled. Chris had told him that his mother had sold the yard as a going concern, and that would mean competition, but so far, with the promise of discounts, they had managed to bring all their old customers with them.

It was a shame that Chris had decided to go it alone, and now Danny's face straightened. In a million years he had never expected Chris to turn soft, buying a piddling little corner shop to be close to their mother. Not only that, he'd begun to hear rumours, ridiculous ones that needed to be snuffed out. Chris was a Draper, a name that still meant something in the borough, and he wasn't going to stand for the local gossip turning his brother, and by association them, into a pervert and a laughing stock.

Danny scowled. He might be out of the porn game and running a truly legit business, but he was still a Draper, still his father's son, and still wanted the respect that the name deserved.

Bob came into the office, grinning widely. 'Dick Larson's had me in stitches. He told me a couple of really good ones.'

'Go on then.'

'What do you call a donkey with three legs?'

'All right, tell me.'

'A wonkey.'

Danny just chuckled, before saying, 'Rubbish. He must have got that one out of a Christmas cracker.'

'All right then. What did the elephant say to the naked man?'

'I dunno.'

'How do you suck up water with that dangly little thing?'

Danny laughed. 'Better.'

'A snail goes into a pub, but it's against policy to serve snails so the barman kicks him out. A year later the snail comes in again, looks up at the barman and says, "What did you do that for?"'

This time Danny roared. 'Yeah, I like that one.'

Bob saw the account book lying open on the desk. 'How are we doing?'

'Considering that we've only been up and running for just over a month, we're doing fine, but I want to talk to you about Chris and the local gossip.'

'Danny, I've told you, it's rubbish.'

'I know it's rubbish, but someone is spreading this shit and I ain't standing for it. We may have left the alley but we're still Drapers and the locals need to remember that.'

'Yeah, well, once we've had a quiet word in a few people's ears, it's bound to stop.'

'It'd better,' Danny growled.

'Talking about the alley, I wonder how Mum's doing.'

'Chris said she still won't let him in, but he'll keep trying.'

'Maybe Yvonne could give it a go.'

'She had a rough time when the baby came early. She isn't ready for a run-in with Mum.'

'Sending Sue round would be a waste of time. Those two have never seen eye to eye. I suppose we'll just have to leave it to Chris to make a break-through. Still, at least Yvonne and Sue are getting on well, the pair of them as thick as thieves now.'

'Sue was brilliant when Yvonne came home with Danny junior, and with him being so tiny, Yvonne was a nervous wreck. It was good of Sue to help out, and anyway, with us living in the upstairs flat, and you down, it's just as well they get on.'

Bob grinned. 'It was a bit of luck finding that house, and with it already divided into two flats, it's ideal. Sue prefers it to Drapers Alley, and the kids love the garden.'

Danny yawned. 'He may have been early, but my boy was screaming his lungs out last night.'

'Yeah, I heard him and it's a wonder Maurice didn't hear him in Devon. Has he been in touch with you yet?'

'No, but at least I hear how he's getting on through you. I think he blames me for everything and, to be honest, he's right.'

'He'll come round. Last time he rang me he said

that Oliver has taken to country life like a duck to water.'

Despite the lack of sleep, Danny smiled. He knew how it felt to have a son now, his boy his pride and joy. He had never wanted kids, but that had changed the instant he saw Danny junior. The urge to find Garston, to take revenge, had left him, his one desire now to provide a secure future for his son. At one time he had let depression swamp him, and he was still ashamed of his weakness. He was back to his old self now, and he'd show his son what it meant to be a Draper. Legit or not, he would make sure the name still brought the respect it deserved.

'Customers,' Bob said.

Danny closed the account book and, Bob ahead of him, left the tiny office. Yes, he thought, they were doing all right, the proceeds from Wimbledon setting them all up, but there was still something unfinished. They still hadn't found Petula.

Chapter Thirty-eight

Pet's stomach churned as she listened to Steve. It couldn't be true. It just couldn't.

'Does . . . does Ivy know?'

'Yes, she knows.'

Pet had to ask, swallowing deeply before saying, 'How . . . how long?'

'From what the doctor said, there's no way of knowing. It could be weeks, months. If it had been found earlier, there may have been a chance, but it's too far advanced now and it . . . it's spread to her bones.'

'Can't they do something . . . anything?'

'No,' Steve replied, his eyes moist and, raising his arm, he cuffed at them with the sleeve of his jumper.

Pet was crying now too. Ivy had been in hospital for two weeks, undergoing test after test, but she had never expected this – never expected to hear that her cousin was dying. Since Ivy had taken her in, they had become close, a relationship forming that had been absent in Drapers Alley. She had seen Ivy battling with her pain, trying to pretend that she was fine in front of the boys, always trying to be cheerful. Oh God, the boys! They were going to lose their mother. The thought was unbearable and, sobbing now, Pet buried her face in her hands.

It was quiet for a while, but then Steve said, 'Pet, she wants to come home. I tried to talk her out of it, but she won't have it. The thing is, she's going to need looking after. I know you're only fifteen, and it's a lot to ask, but do you think you could take it on?'

'I'll try,' Pet said, rubbing the tears from her cheeks.

'You'll have a bit of help with the district nurse calling in every day.'

'What about Harry and Ernie?'

'They'll be at school most of the day, and . . . and maybe I can get one of the neighbours to give you a hand, perhaps take them on after school until I come home.'

'Yes, that could work.'

They were quiet again then, both with their own thoughts. Pet was still reeling with shock, fighting tears. Without hesitation she had agreed to look after Ivy, but had no idea what to do, what care her cousin would need. She owed it to Ivy, wanted to help her cousin to repay her kindness, but what if she made a mess of it? What if she couldn't cope? With a sob she prayed for strength – strength to be there for Ivy and the strength to watch her die.

Phil had just cuddled him again and Chris was red-faced as he served a customer. The two old biddies standing in the queue were looking at them with disgust, whispering, and Chris knew that he'd been a fool, an idiot, for agreeing to let Phil work with him in the shop.

No matter how many times he warned Phil he was ignored. But determined to have it out once and for all, Chris waited until the shop emptied. Then he said, 'Phil, you've got to stop cuddling me in front of the customers.'

'Not this again. Look, when you said I could work with you, I thought it meant we were bringing our relationship out into the open at last, but instead you're acting like you're ashamed of me.'

'Don't be silly, of course I'm not. It's just that we're running a business and cuddling me in front of the customers isn't . . . well, it doesn't look very professional.'

'Professional my arse. You're ashamed of me, I know you are. Go on, admit it.'

'I'm not ashamed of you.'

'Well, how come you haven't told your brothers about me, or your mother?'

'I will. I'm just waiting for the right time.'

'Yeah, that's what you always say, but that time never comes.'

The bell above the door tinkled, another customer coming into the shop. 'Twenty Woodbines, please,' the young man said.

'Coming up, darlin',' Phil said, smiling coquettishly. 'My, ain't you handsome.'

Chris knew that it was a tactic to make him jealous, but it didn't work. The young man obviously wasn't interested – few would be – his smile nervous as he paid for his cigarettes before almost fleeing the shop.

Chris shook head with exasperation. Since their relationship began, Phil had fiercely fought to keep him, looking after him, spoiling him, seeing to his every wish – except one. In front of the customers, Phil continued to touch him, to make it obvious that they were a couple. Chris knew that he was fighting a losing battle. From now on it would be impossible to hide it. His secret was out.

Two days after Pet promised to care for her cousin, Ivy came home, and at midday, as the ambulance drew up outside, Pet ran to the gate, watching as Ivy was lifted from the back. Steve had been up since the crack of dawn, clearing the path to make it safe before rushing off to work. He hadn't wanted to go in, but the animals still needed tending, the farmer saying kindly that he could finish early.

'Hello, Pet,' Ivy said. 'It's lovely to be home.'

Pet fought tears. She couldn't cry. For Ivy's sake she had to be strong, but oh, it was going to be so hard. Forcing a smile she said, 'It's about time you showed up. I made a pot of tea ages ago and it must be stone cold by now.'

'You'll just have to make another one,' Ivy quipped as Pet ran ahead to open the front door.

'Where do you want her?' one of the men asked as they carried Ivy over the threshold.

'Oi, I ain't an imbecile and I can talk for myself,' Ivy said. 'If you ain't a pair of weaklings, you can carry me up to my boudoir.'

'Oh, your boudoir is it? Right, Your Majesty,' and on that light note, they did indeed carry the chair upstairs.

Pet had hurried ahead, and in Ivy's bedroom she threw back the blankets, watching nervously as her cousin was lifted out of the chair and into the bed. Ivy seemed in good spirits, laughing with the ambulance men, and though she looked haggard, thin, she didn't seem to be in pain.

'Right, Pet, show these pair of clowns out and then you can make me a fresh pot of tea.'

'It sounds like you've got yourself a handful, miss,' said one as Pet led them downstairs.

'I heard that,' Ivy called, 'and the only handful I've got is for my hubby.'

The men laughed, but no sooner had Pet closed the door behind them than she had to open it again, finding the district nurse on the step. The woman was tubby, cheery-looking with round pink cheeks and a kind smile as she stepped inside.

'Hello, ducks,' she said. 'Now where's my patient?'

'This way,' said Pet, leading her upstairs. 'Ivy has only just arrived home.'

'Yes, I know, I passed the ambulance men on the path,' and as they walked into the bedroom Ivy received an equally cheery greeting. 'Hello, ducks. I'm Nurse Alwood, but you can call me Gloria.'

'Watcha,' said Ivy.

'I was just about to make a cup of tea – would you like one, er, Gloria?'

'Yes, please, and biscuits if you've got some. I've not stopped this morning and I could eat a scabby horse.'

Smiling, Pet left the room, her heart a little lighter. She liked Nurse Alwood, and with her help, maybe she really would be able to cope.

'All right, Charlie, I'm going,' Danny said, scowling as he walked out of the pub. He might not be going after Garston, but in his own borough he wanted the Drapers' reputation to remain intact.

When he'd first entered the pub, Danny had

thrown his weight about, but the landlord, Charlie Parkinson, had intervened. As an old friend of his father's, Danny allowed it. However, he'd been unprepared for what Charlie had told him.

He went back to the yard, saying as he went in, 'Bob, can you manage on your own for a bit longer?'

'I suppose so, but what did you find out?'

'From what Charlie told me, I don't think it's just rumours.'

'It can't be true, Danny. You know Chris, and as I've said before, it's got to be rubbish.'

'I'll soon find out. I'm going to see for myself.'

'Maybe you should leave it, Danny. If it's true, which I doubt, and Chris wanted us to know, he'd have told us.'

'You must be joking. Chris must be sick, a pervert, and I'm not standing for it, Bob. We're Drapers, but he's turning us into laughing stocks.'

'Why don't we lock up for an hour and I'll come with you? I can just stick a note on the gates to say that we're closed for lunch.'

'No, we can't afford to turn customers away. I'll be as quick as I can,' Danny said, turning to leave before Bob could argue.

Danny took his car and in ten minutes he was pulling up outside his brother's shop. He had never understood why Chris had wanted to go it alone, buying a poky corner shop that was unlikely to show much of a profit, but if the rumours were true, maybe this explained it. He and Bob had been so busy setting up the yard that they had seen little of Chris, this the first time he'd been to the premises.

He got out of his car, but before entering the shop Danny looked through the window. Chris was behind the counter, but he couldn't see anyone else, so moving to the door, he threw it open, hearing a bell tinkling above his head.

'Hello, Chris.'

'Danny, what are you doing here?'

'I've been hearing rumours, gossip, talk about you being a pervert. Where's this so-called assistant?'

Chris was red-faced, blustering as he said, 'I don't know what you're talking about.'

A curtain was pulled back, and as a woman walked through holding two cups of tea, Danny blanched. She was old, at least sixty, her face lined with wrinkles, and though he had thought himself prepared, Danny found his stomach lurching. Bile rose in his throat. No, no, this couldn't be right – Chris couldn't be sleeping with that!

'Here you are, love,' she said, holding a cup of tea out to Chris, 'and I've made us both a sandwich.'

'For fuck's sake, Chris, tell me it isn't her.'

She turned, looked at him, puzzled. 'Who are you? Chris, what's going on?'

Chris drew in a great gulp of air, then said, 'Danny, this is Phil, my girlfriend. Well, it's Philomena really,

486

but that's a bit of a mouthful. Phil, this is my brother Danny.'

'Oh, hello, ducks. Nice to meet you.'

Danny ignored her greeting, instead spitting out, 'You must be out of your mind, Chris. Get rid of her, and now. I ain't having you turning us into laughing stocks.'

Chris stared at him, their eyes locking, a range of emotions crossing his features, but then his eyes narrowed and, shaking his head, he said, 'No, Danny. I've been seeing Phil for years, hiding her, sneaking around to her place, but not any more.'

'Leave it out. Look at her. She's older than Mum.' Danny paused, frowning. 'I know Mum didn't show us any affection. Is that it? Have you got some sort of mother complex? Is that old hag some sort of replacement?'

'No, of course not and stop insulting her. I love Phil, and whether you like it or not, she's my choice. You can either accept her, or you can get out.'

'Right, if that's the way you want it, you're no brother of mine. I'll make sure that everyone knows it too – that as far as the rest of us are concerned, you are no longer a Draper.'

'That's fine with me.'

Danny spun on his heel, leaving the shop without a backward glance. He still felt sick to his stomach, and knew that Bob would feel the same. With George still missing, Maurice in Devon, and Chris out of the picture, it left just two of them – two of the Draper boys. Chris had made fools of them, but as he'd told his brother, he'd put it about that they were finished with him, and then, if anyone so much as looked at them the wrong way, they'd suffer for it. He and Bob were still Drapers, a name that still meant something, a name to be feared, and a name that he passed proudly on to his son.

Chapter Thirty-nine

Spring turned into early summer, and Ivy was still clinging to life. For most of the time she was barely lucid, the nurse warning Pet that when the medication had to be increased again, Ivy would probably slip into a coma. Pet had seen Ivy's agony and thought it would be a blessing. At least her cousin wouldn't be suffering any more.

Whilst Ivy slept, Pet spent a lot of time thinking, her mind often turning to Garston and that poor little girl in the film. She was still swamped with guilt that she had done nothing to help her, but doubted that she was the only child who had fallen into Garston's hands. As always, fear of the man held her back, but gradually an inkling of an idea began to form, one that grew more and more compelling.

Ivy turned her head, her voice a rasp as she struggled to speak. 'I deserve this, Pet. The guilt caused this. It's been eating me up.'

Pet shook her head. Of course Ivy didn't deserve

this, but she often said strange things, the drug sometimes making her hallucinate. She always made a supreme effort for Harry and Ernie, but even that was beyond her now, and lately, when Steve sat with her, she didn't always recognise him.

Ivy groaned and Pet glanced at the clock, hoping that Gloria would soon arrive. She was a wonderful nurse, offering so much support, and Pet knew she couldn't have coped without her.

'Pet, did you hear me? I said I deserve this.'

'Of course you don't. Rest, love, don't try to speak. Gloria will be here soon, and the doctor to give you your medication.'

'It'll knock me out again, you know it will. I've got to tell you now before it's too late.' Ivy gasped then, unable to help crying out in pain.

'It's all right, Ivy, it's all right.'

'I killed him, Pet.'

'You're dreaming, Ivy. It isn't real.'

'No, it isn't a dream. I . . . I killed George.'

Pet shook her head. Poor Ivy, these hallucinations were nightmarish.

'It was after he attacked your dad,' Ivy said, the pain causing her to clench her teeth in agony before she was able to continue. 'I guessed your dad had money stashed and as George ran off with nothing, I hoped he'd come back to get it. With this in mind I waited until you all came home from the hospital that night and spiked your chocolate drinks to make sure you slept soundly.'

'Stop it, Ivy, please. This can't be real – it can't.'

'It's the truth,' Ivy insisted, groaning before she began to speak again. 'I was right about George too. He did come back and . . . and I killed him. It was in your mother's bathroom and . . . and I took all the money.'

Pet frowned. Ivy was talking about the past, not the present, but it couldn't be true, it just couldn't. 'You're hallucinating, you've got to be.'

'No, no, it's real, it happened. He's in the factory.'

'Who's in the factory?'

'George . . . he . . . he's in one of the big vats and I covered him with coal.'

Pet slumped with relief. The factory had been closed for years. There wouldn't be any vats in there, let alone coal. 'There's nothing in the factory, Ivy. It's empty.'

'Pet, please, listen to me. It was a jam factory and the vats are still there. I found coal too, in a bunker. Oh God,' she cried, 'this pain, I can't stand it . . .'

As Ivy gripped her hand, Pet's mind was reeling. Ivy seemed lucid; her eyes, though filled with pain, were clear. 'No, Ivy, please, tell me it isn't true.'

'Th-this house. I didn't get a council exchange, Pet. I bought it with some of the money I stole from the box. The rest is in—'

There was a knock on the street door, Pet fleeing

the room to answer it. She pulled it open to see Gloria and the doctor. Their faces creased as they looked at her, both brushing past to hurry upstairs. In a daze, Pet walked into the sitting room, shaking her head in anguish at what she now believed was the truth.

'Goodness, Petula, when I saw your face I thought that Ivy had gone,' Gloria said as she bustled into the room. 'The doctor is giving her morphine now, increasing the dose. Oh, my dear, don't cry. I know how hard it is when the end is near, but you've been so brave, so strong.'

Pet's throat was so constricted that she couldn't speak. She'd been looking after Ivy, caring for her, a woman who had killed her brother. Oh God, she couldn't stand it, she had to get away. With a sob she fled the room, running upstairs to thrust a few things into a bag.

As Pet ran from her room and onto the landing she almost collided with Gloria, the woman calling as she thrust past her to run downstairs. 'Wait . . . where are you going?'

Pet didn't answer. She flung open the street door, and only stopped running to draw breath as she headed for the train station. It had been ages since Pet had been to the village post office, but Steve had refused to take anything for her keep, so the money she had drawn out had remained in her purse.

When Pet reached the station she found that there

was more than enough to buy her a ticket to London, but it was over half an hour before the train was due. Desolately she sat in the waiting room, her bag clutched to her chest.

Her mind churned and Pet was surprised to find that she was fighting guilt – guilt that she had abandoned Ivy. What would happen to her cousin now? No, no, she'd be all right. The nurse was there, and the doctor. They'd sort something out, and anyway, it was likely that Ivy was now in a coma so they could have her admitted to hospital.

Pet's eyes filled with tears. *Ivy, Ivy, why did you do it? Why did you kill George?* Money, she had mentioned money, his life snuffed out to buy Ivy a house. Oh, she knew that George was no angel – that he had attacked her father – but despite that he was still her brother and she loved him. *Oh God, he's dead, my brother's dead! Ivy murdered him!*

Pet was barely able to hold herself together, and when the train pulled in she climbed into an empty carriage, sobbing as she slumped onto a seat.

It was some time before Pet stopped crying, but as she drew in juddering breaths, her mind began to clear. Without thought she had purchased a ticket to London, yet how could she go back? She had been with Ivy for over six months, so intent on her cousin's care that she had tried to put the past behind her, to forget her family and what Jack Garston had done to her. Yet during the many hours she had sat by Ivy's side, her mind would wander and she was unable to hold back the memories – the sickening things she had seen and heard replaying again and again in her mind.

She had tried to focus on her future, on what she wanted to do with her life, and a tentative idea formed. Now, sickened by Ivy's confession, her determination strengthened and Pet knew what she wanted to do. It would take her a long time to reach her goal, and in the meantime she would have to find a job, along with somewhere to live.

Her eyes closed, fighting tears again. First there was George – poor George, thrown in a vat and covered with coal. She had to tell the police, had to tell her mother. If nothing else, George deserved a decent burial. Pet's mind churned. God, what would happen to Ivy? But Ivy was dying, might already be in a coma. Did Steve know? Did he have a hand in George's death?

Finally, unable to face the questions that plagued her mind, and mentally exhausted, she slept.

Pet woke with a start as the train pulled into the station, groggily climbing out of the carriage to stand lost, alone, on the platform. People rushed past her, barged against her, and at last her feet moved.

After handing in her ticket, Pet's eyes roamed the station, and though she wasn't yet in Battersea, her stomach clenched with fear. Danny was in London – Danny and his threat. She licked her lips, her throat dry, and seeing a café on the far side of the main concourse she headed towards it.

Pet ordered a Coke and then carried it to an empty table by the window where she sat, bleakly looking out of the window. After the stillness of Kent, Pet found the hustle and bustle of the station, the cacophony of sounds, intimidating. She knew she couldn't sit there for ever, but so great was her problem that her mind refused to function.

A voice spoke in her ear and as Pet spun round her arm shot out, knocking over the Coke, the liquid running across the Formica-topped table before spilling onto the floor. The colour drained from Pet's cheeks.

'Mrs Fuller, what are you doing here?'

'I could ask the same of you,' Betty Fuller said, moving forward with a cloth in her hand to wipe the table. 'I work here, love, have done for years. It's a short hop from Clapham Junction station and the hours ain't bad.' She eyed Pet's bag. 'On your way home, are you?'

Unable to think of an explanation Pet sputtered, 'Er, yes.'

'You'll find some changes,' Betty said, her eyes flicking behind her. 'I'd better get a move on or the boss will be after me.'

'Wait, Mrs Fuller. What do you mean by changes?'

'Well, to start with, your mum's the only one left in Drapers Alley.'

'But why? What happened to my brothers?'

'I ain't privy to how it came about, but from what I've heard, Danny and Bob have set up a builders' yard just off Northcote Road, and Chris, well, the least said about him the better. If you ask me, it's disgusting.'

Pet's stomach lurched. Did Mrs Fuller know about the pornographic films her brother had made? But no, that had involved more than just Chris. The woman's eyes flicked behind her again, but as she went to move away, Pet clutched her arm. 'Please, tell me what Chris has done.'

'He's got the corner shop now and has moved his woman friend in to work with him. She's at least sixty, old enough to be his grandmother, and from what I heard, your other brothers have disowned him. Now look, I've got to go.'

As Betty Fuller bustled off, Pet's head was spinning. They had gone, they had all gone. She could go home.

Nervously, Pet approached Drapers Alley. She had been told the houses, all but one, were empty, yet still her heart thudded with fear.

For a moment she hesitated outside the street door. What if Betty Fuller had lied – what if her mother wasn't alone? Come on, she told herself, show a bit of spunk. You've come this far and nobody would have dared to call it Rapers Alley if they were still around.

Her hand slowly lifted to the small lion's-head knocker, and after rapping three times she involuntarily stepped back a pace.

The door slowly opened. 'Is it really you?'

'Yes, Mum,' she said, and seeing the smile of welcome on her mother's face, her eyes filled with tears as she stepped inside. What she had to tell her mother would break her heart.

'Oh, Petula, I can't believe you've come home. I've been hoping, praying, but when the boys couldn't find you I began to think that, like George, I'd never see you again.'

'Mum, I've got something dreadful to tell you. You . . . you'd better sit down.'

'If it's to do with the stuff that your father and brothers got up to, I already know all about it.'

'Dad! Dad was mixed up in making those films?'

'Yes, and from the start. Now come on, put that bag down and I'll make you a nice cup of tea. Your room is waiting for you and I've done it up a bit. Oh, Petula, I still can't believe that you're here,' she cried, her eyes moist with emotion as she bustled into the kitchen.

Pet was still in shock as she slumped onto a chair. Her dad, her father, mixed up in pornography too. Her last illusion was shattered, her memories of the man she had adored, forever tainted. Pet rubbed both hands over her face, only looking up as her mother came back into the room.

'The kettle's on. Now come on, tell me where you've been and what you've been up to.'

'Oh, Mum, I don't know where to start.'

'Try the beginning.'

'I've been staying with Ivy in Kent. She took me in, but then she became ill – really ill – and when I left, she was dying. That's not all, Mum,' Pet said, dreading this. 'It's George, Mum. He . . . he's dead.'

'What? Oh, no, Pet. No . . .'

Chapter Forty

It had been a fraught seventy-two hours. The police had been told, George's body found, the questions endless, but at last Pet and her mother were alone.

'Pet, a long time ago, I found blood on the bathroom floor, and I . . . I thought that Chris had done something to George, that he had hurt him, but I never expected this. For over a year my George was lying in that factory. I should have known. I should have felt something. It proves what a useless mother I am.'

'No, Mum, that isn't true.'

'Yes it is, and not only that, I can't believe that that Ivy has got away with it. Sod's law, that's what it is. The rotten cow went and died just when the police went to question her.'

'I know, Mum, I know,' Pet said, yet in reality hating herself – hating her feelings. When the police told them that Ivy had died, she actually cried, was mourning her cousin and the closeness they had shared. Yet even as she mourned, Pet felt betrayed and knew that she would never be able to forgive Ivy for killing George. How could she feel like this about Ivy? Part sorrow, part anger, part love, part hate?

'Do you think Steve was telling the truth? Do you think he knew nothing about it?'

Pet chewed on her lower lip. She had asked herself the same question, but felt she knew the answer. 'I got to know him well, Mum, and he's a lovely man. I don't think he had a clue and I dread to think how he's taking it. He thought the world of Ivy, and it must be tearing him apart to know that he was married to a . . . a murderess.'

'Will you go back to see him?'

'No, I don't think so.'

'I treated you badly. All I cared about was your father and I didn't show you an ounce of sympathy, but you're all I've got left, Petula. You will stay, won't you?'

'Yes, of course I will.'

'There's something I haven't told you. It's coming down, Petula. Drapers Alley is coming down. Along with the factory it's going to be demolished and a housing estate is going to take its place.'

'When, Mum?'

'I dunno, but soon, I think. I'm just glad that you came home before I had to move out.'

Pet was pleased about the factory, knowing that

every time she looked at it she would remember that her brother's body had been dumped there. She knew that Linda had been informed, could guess her reaction, but it was still awful to know that George had died without ever seeing his daughter. Oh, why was it that when someone died you only remembered the good times, the good things? She could remember laughter, celebrations, every birthday, every Christmas a time when the family came together, but all that had changed when just over a year ago, her illusions had been shattered. 'Do the boys know about the alley?'

'I haven't told them. In fact, other than Chris pestering me, I hadn't seen them until the police told them about George.'

'They weren't too happy that you wouldn't let them in.'

'I told them that I didn't want to see their faces again, and I meant it.'

'What about . . . about the funeral?'

'There's to be a post mortem before George's body can be released. I can't do anything, make any arrangements, until then, and anyway, I don't want them there.'

Pet heard the bitterness in her mother's voice, saw the hardness in her eyes. It had been six months since she had seen her brothers, but the pain remained raw. She knew that she was safe now, that Danny wasn't after her, but like her mother, she still didn't want to see them. They would be at the funeral; there would be nothing her mother could do to keep them away. Her seeing them again was inevitable.

When there was a knock on the street door, Pet had been so deep in thought that she jumped.

'What now?' her mother moaned as she moved across the room to open it. Then she said, 'No, Chris, you can't come in, but you can answer me one question before you bugger off. When George went missing and I found blood on the bathroom floor, why did you lie about it? It must have been George's, I know that now.'

'Blimey, Mum, that was ages ago. Why bring it up now?'

'Because I thought you had hurt George, injured him, and that you were covering it up.'

'Me! You thought it was me? No, Mum, when you found that blood I just assumed that George had been injured in that fight with Dad. You were already upset, in an awful state, so I just said the first thing that came into my head.'

'George wasn't injured, he was already dead.'

'Don't, Mum. I know that now and the thought makes my guts churn. Please, can I come in? I'd like to see Pet.'

'No you can't. Like me, she doesn't want anything to do with you. Now bugger off back to your tart, or should I say your grandmother,' and with that, she slammed the door. 'Honestly, Pet, I never used to swear, but now I even swear in my thoughts. Everyone is talking about Chris and that old woman he's living with. They're laughing at him and because he's my son, at me. Oh, I'll be glad to move, Pet, glad to be away from here.'

'Where will we live?'

'I dunno, love. The council will have to offer us something, and to be honest, I can't wait to go. This place holds nothing but bad memories and the further away we're housed the better.'

An hour passed, Pet helping her mother with the housework that she refused to leave, insisting that even if the house was going to be demolished she had no intention of lowering her standards. As they worked, Pet found that her mother's fussy cleaning, every nook and cranny getting a thorough dusting, kept her mind occupied, and for the first time began to understand her mother. This must be why she always worked like a beaver, all her mind and energies on the housework, her fears and worries at bay as long as she continued to scrub, polish and dust.

Once again there was a knock on the door, her mother's face reddening with anger. 'That'll be Chris again and I'm sick of telling him to bugger off.' With that she marched to the door, flinging it open. 'I told you to— Steve, what are you doing here?'

'I had to come. Can I come in?'

'I suppose so.'

Pet rose to her feet as Steve walked in, horrified by how haggard he looked. She tensed, expecting him to have a go at her, but instead he broke down, sobbing as he said, 'When . . . when the police told me, I couldn't believe it. Oh God, I'm so sorry, Joan. I didn't know, honest I didn't.'

'Yeah, that's what Petula said.' As Steve continued to sob, Joan said, 'Sit down before you fall down.'

It took Steve some time to calm down, but when he finally did, he said, 'Ivy told me about her childhood, about Dan taking her father's money. I knew she was bitter, but why kill George?'

'What are you talking about?' Joan asked. 'What money?'

Steve drew in a gulp of air. 'Ivy said that Dan and her father had money stashed away, money that should have been her mother's.'

'This is news to me, Steve. If you'd told me before I found out what a bastard my husband was, I wouldn't have believed you. Now, though, I feel like I was married to a stranger, that the man I thought I knew didn't exist.'

'Yeah, that's how I feel about Ivy,' Steve said, his voice rising to a strangled cry, 'but she's dead, my Ivy's dead, and I don't know how I'm going to cope with the boys.'

'Oh, Steve,' Pet cried. 'I'm sorry that I ran off like

that, but . . . but when Ivy told me that she . . . that she had killed George, I was in a bit of a state.'

Steve fought to pull himself together, his voice calmer when he answered, 'Of course you were, and no wonder. I don't blame you, Pet, for running off or for telling the police.'

'Where are the boys, Steve? Who's looking after them?'

'They're with a neighbour. I know I shouldn't have left them, but at the moment I'm in no fit state to look after them. Pet, please, will you come back? They're fond of you, they . . . they need you.'

'She'll do no such thing. My daughter is staying with me.'

'It's all right, Mum,' Pet said. She then turned to Steve. 'I'm sorry, really I am, but living with you wouldn't be, well, appropriate, and not only that, I can't leave my mother, not now, and there's still the funeral.'

'I know, and I'm sorry, I shouldn't have asked. I'm not thinking straight and it was daft.'

'What about the rest of the money? Have you found it?' Joan snapped.

'What are you talking about?'

'Ivy killed George for money. She murdered my son to buy the house you live in. Tell him, Petula, tell him what Ivy confessed to you before she died.'

And so Pet did, Steve's eyes, red from crying,

widening. 'I didn't know. I thought we'd got an exchange – that our house is council property.'

'Don't give me that. If it belongs to the council, what about the rent?'

'I can answer that,' Pet said. Her mother was so bitter, so hard, taking her angst out on Steve. 'I lived with Ivy for over six months and I know that she handled all the finances.'

'That's true,' Steve said. 'I always left the running of the house to Ivy. I just stumped up my wages and she paid all the bills, which I assumed included the rent.' Steve then lowered his head, raising both hands to bury his face. For a while he was quiet, but then he looked up, saying, 'If the house was bought on money that Ivy stole from you, there's only one thing I can do. I'll have to sell it to pay you back.'

'No, Steve, no, you can't do that. It's the boys' home. If you sell it, you'll have nowhere to live,' Pet protested.

'Oh yes he can. Ivy stole that money and I want it back.'

It was too much for Pet and she surged to her feet, glaring at her mother. 'Hasn't there been enough pain? Enough death, enough hate and anger. You don't need the money, Mum. From what you've told me, you did well on the sale of the yard and have you forgotten that the money Ivy took was made from porn? I don't want anything to do with it. The thought of it makes me sick. So tell me, do you really want it back? Do you really want to take Harry and Ernie's home? Because if you do, if you're so bitter and twisted that you'd make two innocent children and their father homeless, I'm going, and this time I won't be coming back.'

Her mother was gawking whilst Pet's shoulders heaved with emotion. With a sob she ran from the room, dashing upstairs to fling herself across her bed. Oh God, when would it end?

Pet's door opened and her mother came into the room. She stiffened, expecting a tirade, but instead the bed dipped and she found herself in her mother's arms.

'Petula, I'm so sorry, really I am. I've been so wrapped up in anger, so disgusted at what your father and my sons did to make money, that my mind has become bitter and twisted. When you came home I was so happy to see you, but then you had to tell me about George and, well, it all started up again. I know he was a bad 'un, but he was still my son. She killed him, Pet, Ivy killed him, and I can't stand it that she got away with it.'

Pet clung to her mother. 'No, Mum, it's me who should be sorry. You've been through so much and no wonder it's made you bitter, but Ivy didn't get away with it. She told me that the guilt had eaten at her, sure that it had caused the cancer that took her life. She suffered, Mum, months of dreadful pain before she died.'

'It's no more than she deserved.'

'Mum, please . . .'

'Oh, Pet, take no notice of me. I've been so wrapped up in George that I've forgotten you've been through hell and back too. You didn't deserve it, and it must have been dreadful, but you're all I've got left now. Pet, please don't leave me. As you said, I've got money and I could even buy a little house. We could make a fresh start, just the two of us.'

'Mum, I'm not leaving you. When that . . . that man raped me, it almost destroyed me and, like you, I became bitter. I don't want to go on like this, Mum. I don't want what happened to ruin my life. If I do, he'll have won. Do you really think we can make a fresh start? Do you think we could put the past behind us?'

'I dunno, love, but we could give it a bloody good try. Look, I'll tell you what, after George's funeral we'll make a start. We'll have a look at some property, maybe somewhere out of London. How about the coast? I've always fancied living by the sea.'

'What about Steve? The house?'

'You were right, Pet, and I'm ashamed to say it took you doing your nut to bring me to my senses. I don't want anything to do with it. As you said, it was bought on money from porn and if Steve ever finds the rest of the money, as far as I'm concerned he can keep it. At least it will give the boys a start in life, so something good will come out of it.'

'Oh, Mum,' Pet said impulsively, 'I love you.'

'And I love you too.'

For the first time in her life, her mother had said she loved her, and Pet clung to her waist as tears spurted from her eyes. Yes, they could make a fresh start. They had each other, and as memories returned again of happier times, she wondered if she would ever be able to forgive her bothers – if her mother could ever forgive her sons. Even if they found it impossible, Pet knew that her brothers would be all right. Thanks to their mother they all had businesses. They had their wives, and Chris his woman, albeit in a strange relationship. Pet wondered if she'd ever marry, if she'd ever have children, yet even if she did, now that she knew her mother loved her, needed her, she would always remain central in her life.

Yet before any thoughts of marriage, Pet had an ambition to fulfil. She knew what she wanted to do with her life. She wanted to break the mould – to be a Draper who wasn't involved in crime. When she eventually had children Pet wanted them to be brought up without the stigma she had suffered – to see that they grew up knowing right from wrong, but there was more to it than that. The film that Jack Garston had forced her to watch, the terror she had seen on the little girl's face, would always haunt her. She wanted men like him stopped, but alone Pet knew she could do nothing – that alone she could never make a difference.

During the last few days, for the first time in her life, Pet had had dealings with the police and it had strengthened her ambition. That was what she wanted – to join the force – and as soon as she and her mother were settled she would work towards that goal.

She hugged her mother, feeling a hug in return. 'Come on, Mum, let's go and tell Steve that he can keep the house.'

Her mother smiled at last, nodding in agreement, both leaving the room, both now knowing that when the pain of George's funeral was over, their new life would begin.

Read on for an exclusive extract of Kitty Neale's
Desperate Measures

Prologue

The woman was sure her actions were justified, not just for her, but for the others she had managed to harvest into her small circle.

It was 1969 and women had come a long way since the war, gaining independence with the opportunity to take up careers that were once considered outside the norm. Yet to gain promotion they still had to fight every step of the way, to prove themselves as good as men and as capable.

She had been one of these women, her career her life and promotions hard fought. She knew she was considered a feminist by many of her male colleagues, but in truth she wasn't interested in emasculating men, only wanting the same opportunities they all took for granted. She worked equally hard, in truth harder, and by doing so she had increased sales by a far greater percentage than any other sales rep, male or female, that her company employed.

To achieve this she had travelled the country extensively, working long hours and often having to stay overnight in hotels, some grotty, but some comfortable.

She had given her life to her career, sacrificing any chance of marriage, a home, and children, only to be betrayed by a man who professed to love her.

The woman tugged on her small dog's lead as her thoughts raged. The anger consumed her, ate at her, becoming the whole focus of her life. She got up every morning, she went to work, she functioned, but as though on automatic. Since the day it had happened, since he ruined her life, she wanted only one thing. Revenge.

Chapter One

Battersea, South London, 1969

It happened on June 28th – a day that had changed everything. Four years had passed, but for Betty Grayson it was as though it were yesterday. She hadn't moved forward – couldn't move forward, her bitterness a living thing that gnawed away in her brain, the memory of Richard's gut-wrenching words forever fresh in her mind.

Early on Saturday morning there were already signs that it was going to be a hot day, the sunshine drawing Betty out of her poky flat to the park that was on the opposite side of the road. She watched a small, brown dog as it circled a large tree, sniffing the trunk, until finally satisfied, it lifted its leg.

'Treacle, come here,' a woman's voice called.

Betty saw the dog's ears twitch, but intent on fresh pastures the command was ignored. It trotted towards the bench she was sitting on, tail up, and obviously liking what it saw, reared up to place its paws on her lap.

'Oh, I'm so sorry. Get down, Treacle.'

Whilst stroking the dog's head, Betty looked up at his owner. She had seen the elegant, middle-aged woman before, had noticed her dark-brown hair, styled into a French pleat that emphasised her high cheekbones. 'It's all right, I like dogs,' she said.

'Not everyone feels the same and he's a holy terror. I shouldn't have let him off the lead, but I'm trying to get him to obey me,' she chuckled. 'As you can see, it isn't working.'

'He looks so sweet.'

'Don't let that fool you,' the woman said as she sat down. Treacle immediately jumped onto her lap, the woman laughing as he slobbered her face. 'Oh, what am I saying. He's a darling really, but as I said, he won't obey my commands.'

'What breed is he?'

'He's a Bitsa. You know, bits of this and bits of that.'

As Betty smiled, Treacle turned to look at her again, his head cocked and soft brown eyes intent on her face. He then left his owner, moving across to sit on Betty's lap, his tongue soft and wet on her cheek.

'He likes you,' the woman said. 'I'm Val by the way. Valerie Thorn.'

'I'm Betty. Betty Grayson.'

Treacle jumped down, heading for the nearest tree as Val said, 'It's nice to meet you at last. We live in the same block of flats and I've been meaning to introduce myself.'

'Yes, I've seen you. You're on the ground floor.'

'That's right,' Val said, but then seeing that her dog was running off she rose swiftly to her feet. 'Treacle! Treacle,' she called, and saying a quick goodbye she hurried after him.

After this brief interlude, Betty was alone again. Since moving into her flat she had seen Valerie Thorn a few times, but this was the first time they had spoken. It wasn't unusual. Betty had found that living in London was very different from her life in Surrey, the other tenants were usually distant. Ascot Court was a small, purpose-built block of flats and no worse than others she had rented, and at least it faced the park so the outlook was lovely.

Betty had found the pace of life faster in the capital than in the country, all rush, hustle and bustle, with everyone seemingly intent on their own business. She had judged Valerie Thorn on her appearance, her hard veneer, expecting her to be brittle and stand-offish. Instead she had found her warm with a lovely sense of humour and hoped she'd bump into her again.

The park began to fill and Betty surreptitiously eyed two young women as they walked by, guessing them to be around eighteen years old. She frowned, still unable to get used to the way youngsters dressed nowadays. They were both in A-line mini dresses, one blonde, one dark, their hair cut in the geometrical shapes made popular by the hairdresser Vidal Sassoon. Make-up was skilfully applied, and at least they weren't wearing the thick, black, false eyelashes that were at last going out of fashion.

Betty sighed as she stood up. She was fifty-one now, but when a young woman a bit of powder and lipstick were all she'd been allowed to wear, and her clothes had been respectable, in the same style as her mother's. And not only that – what about underwear? These young girls didn't wear vests, or corsets, and worse, sometimes they didn't even wear a brassiere. Betty heaved a sigh. Her daughter, Anne, accused her of being old-fashioned, saying that things were different now. Women were no longer beholden to men, Anne insisted, and were no longer shackled. They had freedom, equality, the means to make their own way in the world.

As Betty walked towards the gate, a young hippy couple came towards her. The girl was wearing a cotton, flowing, maxi dress with long strands of love beads around her neck; her hair was long, fair and with a flower tucked behind her ear. She looked carefree, happy, but when Betty looked at her young man she frowned. He was wearing a colourful kaftan, purple trousers and sandals, his hair almost as long as the girl's. Betty thought he looked disgraceful and if her son dressed like that she would die of shame.

The couple were intent on each other as they passed, their faces wreathed in smiles, and now Betty felt a surge of envy. They were in love. She had felt like that once – just once in her life, but oh, what a fool she had been – a blind, stupid fool.

Betty saw the red mini as soon as she left the park and as she approached it, her daughter climbed out of the car. It never ceased to amaze her that Anne had her own car – that she could drive – something she would never have dreamed of achieving as a young woman and something she still couldn't master. Of course when she was Anne's age few women drove, in fact, unless very well off, a car was a rarity. When she had Richard she'd been eighteen years old and had felt fortunate to have a bicycle, one that she rode to the local village, the basket on the front crammed with local produce when she cycled home. *Home*. Her stomach lurched. No, she couldn't think about it, not when Anne was standing there, a bright smile on her face.

'Hi, Mum. I can't stay long but I thought I'd pop round to see how you're doing.'

'I'd hardly call driving from Farnham, popping round,' Betty said as they walked into the flats where climbing two flights of stairs, she opened her front door.

Anne followed her in, her face dropping as she took in the small living room. 'Oh, Mum, this is almost as bad as your last place.'

'It has a nice outlook and after the pittance I got as a settlement, it's all I can afford.'

'Please, Mum, don't start. Every time I come to see you it's the same old thing.'

Betty clamped her lips together. Her daughter had always been a daddy's girl and despite everything, quick to Richard's defence. Betty knew that if she said any more Anne would leave and as she hadn't seen her since she moved into the flat, it was the last thing she wanted. She forced the parody of a smile, asking, 'What would you like to drink?'

'A bottle of Coke if you've got one.'

'Yes, of course I have,' Betty assured as she went through to her tiny kitchenette. Coca Cola was something Anne always asked for on her rare visits so she always kept a couple of bottles in the fridge for just such an occasion. She found the bottle opener, snapped off the top, and wondered as she returned to the living room if Anne had seen her brother. 'Have you heard from Mark?'

'Not for a while. He's too busy with his latest conquest.'

'Like father like son.'

'Mum,' warned Anne.

As soon as the words left her mouth, Betty had regretted them, but it was hard to stay silent in the face of her daughter's loyalty to Richard. She felt that like her, Anne should hate her father for what he had done – that she should be on *her* side, but instead Anne had refused to cut him out of her life. When it happened, Anne had been twenty-five, living away from home in a flat share with another young woman. Her son, Mark, had been twenty-eight, a surveyor and buying his own mews house, but unlike Anne he'd been sympathetic, severing all ties with his father. For that Betty was thankful, but with a busy career she rarely saw her son these days.

'How's Anthony?' Betty enquired, hoping that asking about Anne's boyfriend would mollify her daughter.

'He's still pushing to get married, but I'm happy to stay as we are. I mean, what's the point? It's only a ring and a piece of paper.'

Betty managed to hold her tongue this time. When she met Anne's boyfriend eighteen months ago they had moved in together. She had been shocked to the core, glad that she no longer lived in Farnham for her neighbours to witness her shame. It had also surprised her that according to Anne, her father didn't object, but as he had lived in sin until their divorce came through, he was hardly an example.

'What about children? You're twenty-nine now.'

'I'm up for promotion and a baby would ruin that. I'm happy to stay as we are.'

'You could still become pregnant. If that happens, surely you'll marry?'

'I'm on the pill so there's no chance of unwanted babies. Anyway, I'm not a hundred per cent sure that I want to spend the rest of my life with Tony. Living together is ideal. It's like a trial marriage and if things don't work out we can both walk away without regrets.'

Despite herself, Betty found that she envied her daughter. There had been no trial marriage for her – no chance to find out that her husband was a womaniser before he put a ring on her finger. Divorce had been frowned on too, so when she married Richard she'd expected it to be for life. Instead at forty-seven years old she'd been cruelly discarded as though Richard had thrown out an old, worn-out coat.

'Mum, I've got to go.'

'But you've only just got here.'

'I know, but Tony and I have booked a holiday to Spain and I need a couple of outfits. I couldn't find anything swish in Farnham, so I'm off to Selfridges.'

'Spain! You're going abroad?'

'Yes, but only for a week. We got a good price on a flight with Laker Airways.'

'You're . . . you're flying?'

'Don't look so shocked, Mum. I know your idea of a holiday is a caravan in Margate, but things are changing nowadays and more and more people are going abroad. I doubt I'll see you before we get back, but I'll send you a postcard.'

Anne then swallowed the last of her drink, picked up her bag, and left in a whirlwind before Betty got the chance to say a proper goodbye. With a small wave her daughter was gone, hurrying down the stairs while Betty managed to gather her wits in time to call, 'Have a good time.'

'Thanks, Mum. See you when I get back.'

With a sigh, Betty closed the door. Never in her wildest dreams had she expected to holiday abroad, but as Anne had a career as a Personnel Officer, and Tony an engineer, no doubt they could afford it. Once again Betty felt a frisson of envy, which was soon followed by bitterness. Unlike her daughter, she'd never had a career, her life spent intent on being the perfect wife and mother. She had married Richard in 1936 and Mark had followed a year later. They hadn't been well off and it was sometimes a struggle to make ends meet, but then war had been declared and Richard eventually got called up. Anne had been conceived when Richard had been on leave and when he returned to the fighting she'd been terrified of losing him.

When the war was over and Richard came home without a scratch, Betty had been overjoyed, but he was different, more assured, and full of ideas to start up his own business. He said cars were going to be the up and coming thing, available not just to the wealthy, but the middle classes too. To start up the business they had to make many sacrifices but she'd been one hundred per cent behind him. Her friends and neighbours were getting modern appliances, vacuum cleaners, the latest electric boilers with mangles, but every penny that Richard made had to be ploughed back into the business. She'd continued to make do with hand washing, brushes and brooms, with any spare time spent knitting or sewing to make clothes for both herself and the children.

Betty smiled grimly. Of course Richard had to make an impression, so he'd worn nice suits, shirts and ties. Her thoughts were interrupted when the telephone rang. She hurried to answer it, thrilled to hear her son's voice. 'Mark, how are you?'

Unaware that she had a huge grin on her face, Betty listened to her son, pleased to hear that he was doing well, though disappointed when he said that he was too busy to pay her a visit. 'But I haven't seen you for ages,' she protested.

Mark made his usual excuses, Betty now saying, 'Anne called round today and she's booked a holiday to Spain.'

Mark didn't sound all that interested and soon said he had to go. Betty replaced the receiver, her face now straight as she wandered over to the window. She looked across to the park, wishing that she still had a garden to fill her time. When married to Richard she had spent hours gardening, growing fruit and vegetables to save money on food bills, and though it had been hard work, she had grown to love it.

The sun was shining in a clear blue sky and now Betty knew that Mark wouldn't be paying her a visit, she was tempted to go out again. She could walk to the pond, feed the ducks and it would be better than sitting here alone. When she threw bread, the ducks would leave the pond to crowd around her – they'd be aware of her existence, and at least for a short time she wouldn't feel as she always did in London – invisible.

Betty made herself a quick snack, then stuffed a few slices of bread into a paper bag, her thoughts returning to her daughter. Unlike Anne, she couldn't remember the last time she'd had a holiday. If she'd been treated fairly, she too could have gone overseas, but thanks to Richard it was impossible. It wasn't fair, it just wasn't, but there was nothing she could do about it – Richard and his solicitor had seen to that.

Chapter Two

Valerie Thorn was standing at her window, her eyes following Betty Grayson as she left the flats. The woman had moved in upstairs about a month ago and since then Val had taken every opportunity to surreptitiously observe her. She had contrived to bump into the woman earlier and at least she now knew her name. Betty was short, stocky, her expression sad and manner browbeaten. Her clothes were old-fashioned, her light brown hair tightly permed, and Val had judged her to be in her mid fifties.

Was Betty a possible candidate? Val wondered. The woman certainly looked unhappy so that was a good start, and she had seen few visitors which boded well. It had already been a long haul to find her first two recruits and if this woman could be the third, her harvest would be complete.

She would have to contrive to bump into Betty again, to open another conversation and perhaps make tentative overtures of friendship. If she could discover a shared interest it would break the ice, give them common ground, and then, when the time was right, she'd make her move.

Softly, softly catchy monkey, Val thought as she turned away from the window. She had been too wound up to eat any breakfast and now went to her tiny kitchenette to make a sandwich, her eyes avoiding the empty mantelshelf. It was her birthday, but she didn't have one single card on show. Her mother had died when Val was forty-one, followed only three years later by her father. As an only child there had been no siblings to share her grief, just two distant aunts and a few cousins that she hardly saw. Heartbroken she had channelled all her energies into her career, rising to the top, hoping that if her parents were looking down on her, they'd be proud of what she had achieved. She'd been so busy, so intent that she'd lost touch with her scant relatives, yet on days like this, when the postman didn't deliver at least one card, she sometimes regretted it.

Val tried to push her unhappiness to one side but found it impossible. It was always the same on birthdays or Christmas, when, unbidden, memories of her happy childhood filled her mind. There had been parties, laughter, love, but she wasn't a child now, she was a mature woman and it was silly to let things like birthday cards upset her.

If her parents *were* watching over her, it upset Val

that they would have seen her promising career destroyed – seen her foolishness and therefore her failure. Val's unhappiness now festered in anger, the sandwich tasting like sawdust in her mouth. It was always harder for women to make it to the top, but through sheer hard work and dedication she had gained promotion, eventually becoming the Sales Manager. Yes, she'd been ambitious, yes she wanted to rise, but then like a fool she had trusted a man – one she had thought herself in love with – and he had betrayed her and ruined her career.

There were times when Val's anger almost consumed her, when impatience overwhelmed her. She wanted to get on with it, and with a grunt she pushed her sandwich to one side. It was no good, she had to get out, to breathe fresh air and as her possible candidate had gone to the park again it would be another opportunity to bump into her. At work during the week, there were only the week-ends to carry out her plans so she had to make the most of them. 'Treacle, walkies,' she called, the dog's ears pricking up as he immediately ran to her side.

As Val bent down to clip on the dog's lead, he eagerly pulled her towards the door. Treacle was her one consolation and she had never regretted getting him from Battersea Dogs Home. He might be a bit naughty, but he was loving, loyal, and on that thought Val's lips thinned again. She wanted to get on with her plan, to wreak her revenge, but without another recruit it would be almost impossible. She left the flat, crossed the road to the park, her eyes peeled for Betty Grayson.

It was still a glorious day, the park full of people intent on making the most of the brilliant summer weather. She unclipped Treacle's lead, the dog scampering off in front of her, but so far there was no sign of Betty. She walked the paths, her eyes constantly on the lookout, but it wasn't until Val neared the duck pond that she saw the woman.

Val drew in a deep gulp of air, forcing her shoulders to relax. Take it slowly – just be friendly, she told herself. She called Treacle and knowing that the dog couldn't resist trying to catch the wild fowl, she clipped on his lead.

'Hello, Betty isn't it?' Val said. 'Treacle wanted another walk but I didn't expect to bump into you again.'

'It was too nice to stay indoors,' the woman answered, 'and lovely to have the park so close by.'

'Yes, and with a dog but no garden, it's a Godsend. Do you mind if I sit down?'

'Please do,' Betty said, her smile one of pleasure. With Treacle around, the ducks had waddled quickly away, and after shoving a paper bag into her pocket, Betty bent to stroke the dog's head. 'I'd like a dog too, but as I work full-time it wouldn't be fair to leave it in my flat all day.'

'Oh, do you live alone?' Val asked, yet she already knew the answer.

'Yes, I do. I have two children but they're grown up now and living their own lives.'

'I live alone too, but fortunately my employer is a lovely man and lets me take Treacle to work. He even got him a basket to sit beside my desk.'

'That's nice,' Betty said, then raising a hand to wipe it across her forehead. 'Goodness, it's hot.'

'Yes, and look at poor Treacle, he's panting. If you're going home now I'll walk with you.'

'Yes, that would be lovely.'

They began to stroll along and Betty enthusiastically spoke about the summer planting in the flower beds that lined the path. 'Oh, look at those petunias. Don't they make a lovely display. I used to have a large garden and miss it.'

'I'm afraid I know nothing about gardening, but they're certainly colourful.'

Betty indicated another flower bed, saying, 'They've used geraniums in that one.'

They continued to chat, but when they arrived at the flats, Betty sort of hovered smiling tentatively and Val could sense the woman's loneliness. She spoke as though on impulse, 'Look, I tell you what. I live alone – you live alone, so if you've nothing planned, why don't you join me for tea?'

'Oh, I'd love that,' Betty said.

'I expect you want to freshen up, so give me half

an hour to make some sandwiches and then pop down.'

'Yes, all right,' Betty said and with a small wave she went upstairs.

Val went inside her own flat to make a plate of cucumber sandwiches, and then finding a packet of individual chocolate rolls she arranged them before going to the bathroom to refresh her make-up.

Shortly afterwards the doorbell rang and Val tucked a stray lock of hair back into her French pleat as she answered it, a smile of welcome on her face. 'Come on in.'

Betty stepped inside, her eyes scanning the room. 'Oh, this is lovely and I just love your décor. Youngsters nowadays go for all the modern stuff with bright, garish wallpaper, whereas this is so soothing, so sophisticated.'

'I prefer soft colours and as I can't tackle wall-papering, I just gave it all a coat of paint. Would you like tea or coffee?' she asked.

'Tea please,' Betty said.

'Sit yourself down and I won't be a tick,' Val said, before going back to her small kitchenette.

When the tea was made she carried the tray through. 'I hope you like cucumber sandwiches.'

'Yes, lovely,' Betty said, whilst eyeing the plate of cakes with appreciation.

Val sat opposite Betty, pouring the tea into small, delicate china cups and then offering cubes of sugar from a bowl, complete with little sliver tongs. Betty took two lumps, then said, 'My daughter was waiting for me when I came home from the park this morning. She couldn't stay long as she was off to buy new clothes for a holiday in Spain.'

'I once went to Barcelona and the architecture was stunning.'

'You're lucky. I've never been abroad.'

'Yes, well, nowadays I'm lucky if I can afford a day trip to Brighton.'

'Me too,' said Betty.

So, the woman was hard up, Val thought as she mentally stored this small piece of information before saying, 'There are some lovely places in England and I've always been fond of Dorset. Do help yourself to a sandwich.'

'Thanks,' Betty said.

Val fumbled for common ground. 'I suppose you heard that Judy Garland died on Monday?'

'Yes, I saw it in the newspaper. It said she died from an overdose of sleeping pills.'

'She was one of my favourite actresses and I was so sad to hear of her death. Do you go to the cinema much?'

'Not really, but I did go to see Maggie Smith in *The Prime of Miss Jean Brodie*.'

'Me too and it won a well-deserved Oscar.'

Betty just nodded, munching on her sandwich, and when it was finished, Val held out the cakes.

'Thanks,' Betty said, taking one and biting into it with obvious relish.

Maybe food could be a common interest, Val thought. 'I'm not much of a cook. What about you?'

'I used to be, but now that I just cook for myself I usually make something simple.'

'I love eating out, and I often go to a lovely little French restaurant in Chelsea.'

'I've never tried French food.'

'It's delicious, Betty, and if you aren't doing anything tomorrow, we could go there for lunch.'

Betty's eyes lit up for a moment, but then her face straightened as she said, 'I . . . I don't know. Is . . . is it expensive?'

'Not really, but don't worry, it's a family run business and I know the owner so he usually gives me a discount.'

'Oh, in that case, I'd love to.'

'Wonderful,' Val said as she stood up to move to the mantelshelf where she picked up a packet of cigarettes. She took one out, and then proffered the packet to Betty.

'No thanks, I don't smoke.'

'At six shillings a packet I know I should stop too, but I have managed to cut down.'

'Do you work locally?' Betty asked.

'I'm a receptionist for a solicitor on the Kings Road.'

'It must be nice to work in an office, especially in such an interesting profession.'

'It can be sometimes and Mr Warriner is a lovely man. What do you do, Betty?'

'I'm just a sort of cleaner cum housekeeper in Kensington. I used to live in Surrey, but when I heard about the job I moved to London. My employer is away at the moment so there's little to do, but when he's in town he keeps me busy with his incessant demands.'

'Oh dear, he sounds a bit of an ogre,' Val sympathised.

'He's all right, it's just that he's used to servants seeing to his every wish. His home is just amazing and such a shame that it remains empty for most of the year. He has wonderful antique furniture, paintings and bronzes which he has a passion for. He used to have a large staff, but when his wife died he started to spend most of his time in his country home. I was lucky to be kept on in the London house, but as I said, only as a sort of caretaker cum housekeeper.'

'If you're the only one there, don't you find it lonely?'

'Yes, sometimes, but I keep myself busy. It's a very large house with lots to do to keep it up to scratch. Just polishing the silver can take all day, but I keep dust covers over most of the furniture. I'd love to work in an office like you, but I was a stay at home wife and mother so I'm not trained for anything else.'

'There's nothing wrong with being a housewife and mother,' Val said. She had caught the trace of bitterness in Betty's voice and though tempted to ask questions, she held back. It wouldn't do to show her impatience, so instead she smiled softly, 'Would you like another cup of tea, Betty?'

'Yes, I'd love one.'

'I'll just top up the pot,' Val said, taking it through to the kitchenette. So far she had gleaned a little information, but her experience had found that if you shared a confidence it was likely to be returned. When she knew Betty a little more, she would start to open up, and with any luck Betty would do the same. Val crossed her fingers, hoping she wasn't wasting her time and that Betty would turn out to be a suitable candidate.